Dance

All Things ﾟ　　　.ﾚﾟﾒ

by

J. Ewins and L. Telfer

WordHive Limited

First published in Great Britain in 2022 by WordHive Ltd, 77 Victoria St, London, SW1H 0HW.

WordHive Limited Reg. No. 105153310

Forward

This novel is a work of fiction based on issues in policing in 1874. Various national and international events are recorded and blended into the story, as are influencers of the time.

Constable John William Sargent, known as Jack, was an ancestor of the authors. He joined the Metropolitan Police in 1872, worked south of the river and in Stepney, then Bow, and later Kensington as part of the Hammersmith division. He was soon given the rank of Second-Class Reserve, implying he was a Constable the Sergeant could trust.

Before joining the police, Jack had worked as a farm labourer near Battle, Sussex and originally came from a market gardening family in Bexhill. Like many other labouring young men from outside London in 1872 Jack answered the recruitment drive launched by the Metropolitan Police.

Professor Clive Emsley has mentioned that police constables in the nineteenth century would pursue their quarry overseas, quietly changing from their constable's uniform into plain clothes and equally quietly donning it again on their return. (The Great British Bobby: A History of British Policing from the 18th Century to the Present.)

We have followed this theme.

3

Many thanks to the Biblioteque, Departments of Law and Social Sciences, University of Geneva, for their help on the crime in that city in 1874. Research there was undertaken over many months in 2019 and the first few months of 2020.

Sources of research into events, and actual historical characters at that time, are referred to in the Acknowledgements at the end of the book.

We have also recorded phrases used in East, Mid and West Sussex at the time some of which are in use today, and the language Jerriais in Jersey.

J Ewins and L Telfer.

Dedication

For Jemma

Characters in Dancer's End

Metropolitan Police Personnel, London:
Leman Street, Division H.

Sergeant William Thick.
Constable Charlie Banks.
Constable, Second Class Reserve, Jack Sargent.

Camberwell New Road, Division P.
Inspector Tom Hunt.
Sergeant Morris.
Sergeant Ted Phillips.
Percival Green, civilian (Boot Boy).
Shadwell Police Station.
Detective Sergeant Harry Franks.
Sergeant Stan Green.

West and East India Docks
(see acknowledgements for details of these two policemen and civilians).
Constable John William Smith.
Constable Flynn.
Planterose Boyes.
Joseph Johnson.

Brighton Police
Constable Brook, Selmeston.

Inspector Field.

Sergeant Shaw Hockham.

Paris

Carnot of the Sûreté, Paris.

Characters in England:

Mrs Hunt senior.

Sam Curzon.

Mrs Curzon.

Grandma Curzon.

Luke Curzon.

Ann Black.

Dr Brown.

Rose Phillips.

Mrs Phillips.

Mary Cunliffe.

Reverend Peter Fisher.

Mrs Simcock.

Coastguard Edward Croft.

Lucy Croft.

Martha Croft.

Andrew Croft.

Mr Langton, solicitor.

Queen Victoria.

Prince Edward, Prince of Wales.

Princess Alexandra, Princess of Wales.

Duke of Edinburgh.

Duchess of Edinburgh.

Emperor of Russia.

Gladstone.

Disraeli.

Harriet Fildew.

Tim Crutchley.

Martin Crutchley.

Mr Robson.

Annie Quayle.

Emma Lewis.

Charles Burgess.

Alice Burgess.

Eleanor Davies.

Helena Ward.

Rev Timothy Ward.

Rev Berthon.

Rossiter.

Cook's agent at the office in Ludgate Circus

Cabbie.

Elizabeth Garrett Anderson.

Barmaid in the Mason's Arms.

Landlord.

Jersey

Private Adams.

Corporal Bruce.

Sergeant Samson.

Guesthouse keeper.

Characters in France and Switzerland:

Captains of the fishing boat and the Marie

Madame Guibon

Thomas Cook guides: Coombs and Allen.

Mr and Mrs Wheeler.

Lauren Wheeler.

Concierge.

Mr and Mrs Tully

Kari.

The Right Honourable William Gilbert

Helly

Torg.

All things are poison and nothing is without poison,

only the dose permits something not to be poisonous.

Paracelsus (1493–1541)

One

It was early May 1874, and an indifferent spring day in London. The man at the window was dressed in the well-worn uniform of a police inspector. And he acknowledged that he was tired as he stared out towards the Lambeth Law Court instead of continuing with his task of reviewing the arrangements for the next few weeks. Another royal visit, he thought … but his mind strayed. It was three months since that bitter day in February when last at Windsor. It would be true to say since then that his life had become more difficult and the investigation had almost ground to a halt.

Tired of waiting for a constable he was expecting, the Inspector opened the door, glanced up the corridor towards a duty sergeant and called: "Any sign?"

A look was exchanged between the two men.

"Not yet, sir, I'll send him down when he gets here," said the Sergeant before he returned to explaining the papers on the desk to a new constable. He had registered that the Inspector walked towards the occupants of the bench at the side of the front desk.

One young woman, about mid-twenties in age, spat towards him but her spittle just missed his boots. Some obscenity followed it before she lolled back into the next occupant on the bench. A constable was round to her immediately, remonstrating with her about her behaviour. But the inspector raised his eyebrows in an inquiry to the Sergeant.

"Out alone late last night, sir, drunk,' said the Sergeant.

"Charge?"

"Prostitution was reported, sir," said the Constable, straightening up to attention.

The Inspector gave the man a once-over and wondered what had drawn him into the police: probably a semi-skilled office worker, a local man by the sound of the accent, certainly not a labourer. Unsure he wanted him, the Inspector crooked a finger at the young man to come closer and as he bent forwards the Inspector said into his ear in a confidential manner: "But nothing seen otherwise she wouldn't still be sitting here, she'd be in a cell."

"But sir, she spat at you," the young man said, loudly.

"And missed," said the Inspector quietly. He continued to the desk-sergeant: "Get her out of here, Ted, and make some room on the bench. We don't have time, or the space, to charge every woman who was out after dark, probably alone and reeking of alcohol, with prostitution. Send Jack in when he finally arrives."

The Sergeant, Ted Phillips, nodded and glanced at the clock. The inspector followed the direction of his Sergeant's eyes and registered that the expected man was still not late. He retreated into his room and fumbled as he picked up the order. But his heart was not in it. Again, his memory held sway over the present.

Once the news had broken back in February the inspector had a fair understanding of the chaos in which he would find himself. Gladstone had lost decisively to Benjamin Disraeli's Conservatives after surprisingly calling an election. It had been

12

a moment of history as for the first time there had been a secret ballot and the Irish Nationalists, who had won sixty seats, formed the third party in Parliament.

At the time Gladstone had said: "We have been swept away in a torrent of gin and beer."

In Tom Hunt's reflection, for that was the name of the inspector, just as the liquor with which the voters had been plied swirled into the drain, so down with it had gone the support Gladstone had given him.

Or so he had thought.

The victor, Disraeli, had prepared to travel to Windsor Castle for an audience with Queen Victoria on the same day Hunt was there. Perhaps it was a coincidence that it was on that very day, but Tom Hunt rather doubted it. February eighteenth and Tom Hunt had taken young Jack Sargent with him to his mother's cottage on the estate, where they had tidied the garden, then both men had ridden up front on the Queen's carriage.

Now in May a glance at the clock told the inspector that his colleague had a matter of minutes before he would be cutting it fine. Suppressing the irritation that he always felt when his men did not arrive early, he sat opposite the portrait of his monarch and gave her a hard stare.

It was matched in return. Always let down by her men.

Gladstone had appeared to completely withdraw from politics, although with him one never really knew. Hunt had his own investigation into the top of the organised crime group. It was all he and Gladstone had in common. Apart from the

---

obvious loss of office for Gladstone the election outcome had directly affected the crime group investigation. The lives of a monarch, a former clerk living in Brighton and three others apart from Hunt in the Metropolitan Police, were all affected. a detective sergeant and his uniformed counterpart in Shadwell and a young constable at Leman Street in H Division would soon be going on a journey.

Hunt focused like an addict on that day in February: the eighteenth of February to be precise, he told himself lest he forget. It was unusual to be called to see the Queen. She generally knew he was in Windsor as she saw him from a window while tending his mother's garden at the tied cottage home of his childhood. Hunt had grown used to being summoned as a child too, expected as he had been to take over from his father as the Queen's coachman.

It had been early morning when Hunt had received an order to attend her Majesty at Windsor on her return from Osborne House. The fact that he was already due to go to visit his mother was a convenience. Hunt had arrived at Windsor early having suggested a trip out of London would do Jack from H division the world of good. Young Jack Sargent would walk through fire for Inspector Hunt and he had readily agreed to spend his rest day helping in a garden at Windsor.

It was the first time the Queen had interested herself in the failure to solve an embarrassing theft of diamonds the previous summer. They had been audaciously taken from the bridle of a horse during the Shah of Persia's visit in 1873. It had been an ostentatious way to dress a horse and the theft had been in

14

front of half the nobility and military at the Woolwich Review. And no-one, apparently, had noticed.

Inspector Hunt's liaison until then on the theft had been via a secretary and upwards to an equerry. The thief, or thieves, (who knew at that point) had vanished and the case had lain dormant. However, a cryptic remark in a recent letter from the Shah had irritated the Queen and given her an excuse, as Hunt was sure that was what it was, to profess embarrassment at the theft.

It had been at half-past one when Hunt had finished picking his way through the vegetable garden at the back of his mother's cottage. Hunt and his young colleague had been clearing stones ready for his next visit in a month's time when the hope was to do some spring planting. Jack had enthusiastically offered to return with the Inspector to help. But Hunt had only half heard his offer. Believing the equerry's advice to attend Her Majesty that afternoon after half-past two Hunt had continued with the gardening thinking he had time to change before he went up to the castle. Now a middle-aged man, of more than regulation height for his generation of policeman and strong, Hunt had straightened up from the digging. Some, his wife mainly, would say he was still attractive.

Hunt had been dressed in the set of clothes he always left at the cottage so that he could carry out a range of "jobs" for his mother. They were not the kind of clothes one wore to visit the castle. His intention was to wash and change before his appointment.

15

Jack was not quite the regulation height, but the broadness of his build disguised it and the recruiting officer had decided to ignore the issue after watching the recruit lift himself up and down on a doorframe more than ten times. He was not a local either and that had augured well for remaining independent of "influences." Like the inspector he was dressed for manual work and the young constable had travelled there in a set of clothes which harked back to his days as a Sussex farm labourer.

There had been a frost that morning and the ground was in an un-cooperative state. The younger man, brought up in a market gardening business in Sussex, had shaken his head at the idea of tending the garden this early in the year. Despite this the two men had laboured for half the morning clearing stones.

Hunt remembered glancing at Jack, whose fair head had been bent over the round sieve, as he shook the soil piled up in it and sieved out the lumps until it was like powder. Hunt reflected as he had many times that Jack was the sort that provided his superior officers with comfort to have him with them in a fight.

Young Jack still had the trace of a cough from the damage caused from smoke inhalation in the Alexandra Palace fire and that tendency to a cough had not done well in the damp winter of London. Hunt thought it was time they finished and took their places by his mother's fire. Mrs Hunt was of the same mind as she called from her kitchen window:

"Tom, you had better get yourself washed and ready."

"I think you might be too late, sir," Jack had said, focussing on the lane running past the cottage. Hunt had turned and followed Jack's direction of gaze while Mrs Hunt had come quickly out of the kitchen, wiping her hands on her apron.

"What is it, Mother?" asked the inspector.

"You had better both wash under the pump, quickly. Then come through to the lane. Her Majesty is coming to *you*, Tom," said Mrs Hunt, her brow furrowed. She added: "I hate it when she does this. None of us are ready."

The two men had put their heads under the pump and taken the shock of the freezing water, finally reaching for a piece of sacking to mop up the excess from their faces and forearms. The younger policeman had followed Hunt around the cottage to the front gate and out to where a carriage was drawing up.

"Hold the horses, Tom," ordered Queen Victoria, fixing Hunt with a hard stare that said she meant business. The royal steeds had stopped and while a look had passed between Hunt and the Queen's Coachman the liveried man climbed down to make way for Hunt.

"And who is this?" asked the Queen, having assessed the young man next to her former servant.

Tom Hunt had opened his mouth to respond but his young colleague was to attention, staring straight ahead.

"Constable Jack Sargent, ma'am, second class reserve, Leman Street, H Division," said Jack.

"Not an area I have visited," said the Queen. She took in the build, the youthful look and tendency still to blush.

17

The Queen continued but looked away as she spoke: "I doubt your mother christened you Jack."

To his horror Hunt had heard Jack respond: "I expact not, it would be John at a christening, Your Majesty."

The steel eyes had flicked back to the young constable. Jack had met a Queen's sharp look and the blush had deepened. He had tried a half smile, but the Queen had looked at Hunt who waited for the dismissal. However, the Queen countered with: "You'd better climb up next to Tom."

There had been a brief pause before the two men obeyed, Hunt beckoned to the shocked Jack to come forward. Jack climbed up and slithered across the seat too close to Hunt. Hunt advised in a low voice: "Keep silent and look ahead, if she speaks to you answer with, "Ma'am," and don't ask her questions." He urged the horses forward.

"Disraeli has just left Tom, as surprised as any of us that the election is won." Then the Queen had paused, removing a handkerchief from the muff.

"Ma'am," had been Hunt's only response.

"When Mr Gladstone's letters came to Osborne in January our heads were full of the wedding and Russia. I was very busy preparing for the messenger to St. Petersburg, by whom I was sending a sprig of myrtle for Marie's bouquet and two prayer books for her and Affie. The advice was that it was better to have the crisis of the election now as a crisis it was going to be. I gave permission for dissolution of Parliament then. I suppose that was right. It was such a foggy day. Mr Gladstone had said he wished to have the dissolution

---

18

immediately. He was anticipating great difficulties with the House of Commons. And then we had to get through lunch with the Lord Chancellor and keep it all quiet as he had no idea about Mr Gladstone's intentions."

Jack had fumbled in his pocket for a handkerchief, aware the cold water had made his nose run. He had glanced at Tom Hunt as he did so with a concerned look at what he was now privy to. Hunt had made a slight frown and given an almost imperceptible shake of the head, at the same time making a noise with his tongue to the horses to give them encouragement. Jack cautiously had replaced the item in his pocket and stared ahead.

The Queen had continued:

"And then I saw Mr Gladstone on the twenty-fifth. He discussed the dissolution, the cause of it, and my not disapproving as if anything I said would make any difference with that man. I told him I was surprised it was all so sudden. It was quite cold, and I had a return of the chill I'd had." A pause and she changed subject suddenly: "Have you read the descriptions of the wedding? I've had some wonderful letters. The Dean described the marriage beautifully."

"In the papers, yes, Ma'am," said Tom Hunt.

The Queen was back onto the subject of the election:

"I knew the elections were going against the government by February fourth. Then I heard a Conservative had come in for Windsor and it seemed to get worse and worse each day. Of course, at that point I couldn't help but think the fault was throwing out the proposal to remove the Income Tax, to catch the elections, and Mr Gladstone seriously failed."

There had been a brief pause. And then another change of subject: "Do you know it is thirty-four years since the Prince Consort arrived in England for our marriage?"

"It certainly is a time, Ma'am," Hunt had said.

"And you remember him, Tom? Although you were a small child?" The Queen had known the answer which was to come.

And Hunt had given her what she wanted: "Every time I have to look a man in the eyes with an order," Hunt had said. "We were all grateful for the Prince Consort's interest in us children."

"Ah yes, he was very strong on that, face up to it," her voice had hinted at a smile with the memory.

The Queen had been silent for a while after the last comment. Both men had become aware of the cold wind whipping around them. Then their attention had been pulled back to the subject of the wedding of the Duke of Edinburgh and the Russian Princess as the Queen had continued:

"The Emperor has said he hoped I would let him come over in May to see his daughter for a day or two and pay me a visit. I shall expect your help, both of you, of course."

"Ma'am," had been Hunt's only response. Jack missed the word, "both" but his eyes had widened at the thought of another royal visit after the impact of the Shah's visit the previous year.

Then the Queen had returned to the election.

—

"You've probably read that Mr Disraeli was returned with a majority of over 29,000. *Enormous.* After that I heard from Mr Gladstone on Saturday acknowledging the increasing majority but saying he didn't know whether to resign or wait. I'd already written on Friday urging resignation to Lord Granville and I repeated that to Mr Gladstone. Lord Granville responded that he thought Mr Gladstone, although disinclined at first, would resign now and all his colleagues thought so as well. "

The Queen had paused to study the backs of the two men riding up top. She noted young Tom Hunt was going grey but reminded herself that he was of a wiry breed. That type tended to last. But then his father had not. The young man next to him on the other hand, was dressed as a labourer and the clothes and build across the shoulders gave testimony to hard work in his young life. So fair-headed, noted the Queen as she had pulled the tartan rug closer around her and the coach had turned into the February wind.

"We left Osborne on Tuesday," The Queen had started again, "And I saw Mr Gladstone after luncheon. He said he came to a decision with his colleagues to tender the resignation to me at once. I talked with him of the causes of the defeat. Do you know, Tom, they didn't put candidates up in a hundred constituencies? Can you believe that? No Liberal there to even try and win. He thought it was also due to the Publican's attitude about the licensing as well as divisions in the party. Of course, we had to have the honours for various persons connected with the Government."

The Queen tutted at the memory: "So many of them and I did say that I didn't think it was necessary."

She paused and had looked around at the bareness of the gardens before continuing: "I also asked him what I could do for him but all he said was, "Nothing," and that it was his wish to retire. I tell you of this as I know you have been meeting with him once a month."

Hunt's face had set while he wondered what the fate of his enquiries would be if Gladstone disappeared from office. At the Queen's mention of his meetings with Gladstone he just managed to stop the shock showing on his face but knew his shoulders had tensed. Had Gladstone told her? Why would he have done that but how else would she know?

Hunt had realised that Jack was staring at him.

"Damn," Hunt had whispered only to himself. He had forgotten only Harry had known. Even that was one too many but a necessary evil in case the worst happened. Now Jack was caught up in it before he needed to be. Hunt whispered to Jack: "Look ahead," and he had almost spat out the words.

At that point Jack's head had spun round to face forwards.

And the Queen? Canny woman, thought Hunt, releasing photographs of herself as the grieving widow to manage her image. Every picture had included an image of Prince Albert in some form and that way she had managed to remain away from the duties otherwise expected of her but include the public in her grief. How long could she manage to delay the expectation of a monarch being more visible?

Hunt had started to wonder what else she knew. Was this her way of warning him? Despite the preamble she was a shrewd woman.

But the Queen had begun to speak again, and Hunt's musings had been brought to a stop.

"And, of course, this morning a frost but a fine walk with Beatrice to the kennels. At half past twelve Mr Disraeli came and told me he was greatly surprised at the result of the elections. You voted of course?"

"Yes Ma'am," Hunt had replied and thought, for Gladstone but only to cover my back and not for reasons I can tell you.

The Queen had carried on speaking and Hunt had missed her first words.

"...... He had thought a very small majority possible but not a majority of sixty-four. We talked about who he proposed for the Cabinet and he was straight into it. Parliament could be opened by the twentieth." Another silence and Hunt clicked his tongue at the horses. Perhaps he could speed this monologue along if they quickened their pace.

Another pause, then: "Mr Gladstone will return tomorrow I will urge him to lead the opposition, but he is a trying man. Now, take me back as I'm to drive with Beatrice. I must look at the Tapestry Rooms later which are being freshened up for Affie and Marie. Their cyphers are being put on the doors." The Queen had settled back into the shelter of the carriage and nothing more had been said.

They had taken a shorter way back and Hunt brought the horses to a stop outside his mother's cottage. Jack had clambered down without any prompting and stood to attention by the Queen's door. Her Head Coachman came out from Mrs Hunt's kitchen, still chewing a fresh biscuit, and resumed his position in Hunt's place. The Queen had waited for Jack to look at her. As he had the blush had again coloured his cheeks.

Stand to attention, Hunt had thought, unable to say anything to Jack but hoping the man's training would hold firm.

Jack had stared straight ahead, rigid but had wished he was not in his labourer's clothes in comparison to the finery of the monarch. Tom Hunt had moved to the carriage door waiting for the dismissal. Jack and he stared at each other, the inspector slightly the taller man. However, the Queen had not done yet and there was one last point she meant to make.

She said: "Disappointing that those diamonds haven't been found yet, Tom. I suppose you might have better news for me by May. We don't want something similar happening when the Emperor of all the Russia's arrives."

Hunt had momentarily forgotten himself with the surprise and looked into the royal eyes. It had not been his investigation, but the eyes were full of reproof. Years melted away and he was a small child in the school for the children of those serving on the Windsor Estate. Young Tom Hunt had had a good memory and had frequently recited poems he had been set to learn as a challenge under the tutelage of the Prince Consort.

"Look your audience in the eye, Tom," Prince Albert had directed the small boy. It had been good advice for court and in an arrest, but the Prince had not meant the Queen.

24

Hunt had quickly dropped his eyes as he realised the Queen had started speaking again to ensure she hammered home the point: "So embarrassing – how people let one down, don't they Tom? And that spectacular little man, the Shah, finds it amusing that the England he visited cannot catch a thief. Blow the diamonds, he'll hardly miss them. I'm told they're undoubtedly "fenced" by now. Is that the term? I expect you to catch the man though and get the diamonds back."

"Yes Ma'am," Hunt had said staring slightly to the right of Jack's shoulder.

There had been nothing further and the carriage had moved off. Hunt had remained at attention, watching it for a while in silence, more resolved than ever that it was time for his mother to leave Windsor. Jack had waited to take his lead from the inspector before he moved. Eventually the carriage was out of sight and only then had Hunt turned to look cautiously at Jack. "Alright, you can be at ease now, relax," Hunt had said.

"That was 'extrardinry. I'm sorry I answered her, sir," Jack had said.

"Well, nothing came of it."

"One thing, sir?" Jack had asked still staring in the direction that the carriage had gone.

"Yes?"

"The way she spoke to you, sir. It was like she trusts you."

"There's been a Hunt here as coachman for generations," Hunt had said by way of explanation. He added: "Sometimes I think she forgets I'm not my father. Other times she's as sharp as a knife, like today. I'm the first to break away, but with

mother still living here the tentacles continue to reach me."
Hunt had started to open the door into the kitchen but paused
on the door-step before he continued: "She's irritated not to be
able to tell the Shah we caught the thief. It wasn't for us at
Camberwell to investigate, but I had heard that the trail went
cold."

Hunt had paused while he slipped his boots off and put them
under the wooden bench. After a moment's thought he had
continued: "If you remember the thief, Jack, at the West India
Dock Offices that morning of the fire? You were the only one
who could identify him."

"Right, sir," said Jack.

"The description of the thief at the Woolwich review was a
match. I'll check how far the investigation went and look at the
case again. There was something else her Majesty said but
perhaps I misheard. Jack, did you hear that she expected *both*
of us to help with the visit of the Russian Emperor or did I
imagine that?"

"I'm not sure, sir, I was too mazed that she was talking to
us," Jack had answered.

"We should go in and get warm, Mother will have some tea
ready for us after that cold drive and it smells like her cheese
scones are ready."

"Wonderful," said Jack.

"Don't repeat any of this to anyone," Hunt said before he had
turned away.

Jack had followed Hunt's example and left his boots at the
door. Both men had warmed themselves by the range as Mrs

Hunt poured steaming tea into tin mugs. Once the hot tea was in front of them, she ensured the boots were before the fire so they would be warm on their owners' departure. Next, she had turned her attention to buttering the fresh scones. Jack had watched the butter melt into them while he spooned sugar into his tea. Satisfied with the way the two men had set about her baking, Mrs Hunt had taken a scone for herself.

Heat from the fire together with the food and drink had produced silence from both men. Jack had closed his eyes briefly but had woken himself as his head went back and his chin jerked up. He came to sharply and had briefly wondered where he was.

For his part Hunt had been torn between the implications of the changes that would follow the general election and the thought of the impending duties accompanying the arrival of another foreign royal in London. He did not dwell for long as his attention had been pulled back to his young colleague as Jack had started to ask Mrs Hunt a question. The sight of the red flecks in the scones had caught Jack's interest.

"Unusual cheese," Jack had commented.

"Red Leicester," Mrs Hunt had explained as she had taken her seat at the kitchen table again to lather butter onto more scones. She added: "It crumbles better than cheddar. Have you not come across it before?"

Jack had shaken his head and mumbled: "No."

Mrs Hunt had re-filled their plates and left the two men to eat quietly after that. Occasionally, she had glanced across at her son and tried to assess what was on his mind. She had

---

27

thought how hard he looked and that he had seen more things in his work than he told her about. Hunt had caught her look and seen the concern. He had tried to brighten his expression after that.

Mrs Hunt had asked: "Has she something for you to do, Tom?"

"Eventually, yes Mother, as always," Hunt had replied. "No doubt I shall get sucked into the visit of the Emperor of Russia but at least when her son and his new wife come to England it will be to Windsor. The Castle Guard will handle that outing for the Queen. There's another issue though, which the police didn't solve, and I shall have to revive the case."

Mother and son had met each other's eyes with a knowing look. Hunt decided to seize the opportunity and had asked:

"Have you thought any more of leaving, Mother?"

Jack had paused in his chewing.

"She won't like me going, Tom." Mrs Hunt had said.

"The Queen would cut up rough?" Jack had asked.

"Rough?" Hunt had repeated.

"Angry," Jack had explained. "I mean would it make her angry?"

Hunt had shrugged but did not give an answer. He had felt beyond caring that day but had turned to his mother: "I'll see the estate manager before I go. We'll fix up a date before I'm due to come back and your things can be collected, Mother."

"Perhaps I should ask to explain, try and see him myself," Mrs Hunt had suggested.

Tom Hunt had exhaled, weary of it all and had said: "You're not her servant any longer Mother, that ended with Father's death. You're free to come and go where you like. Let's have done with it finally and start a life where you're not watched because it gives an over-indulged woman comfort to see someone who knew the Prince in better days. We don't all have to be included in her grief."

"That sounds harsh, Tom. Aren't we all her servants?" Mrs Hunt had said.

"Not in that way," Hunt had said. "The Queen has enough people around her to remind her of her late husband without dragging you down with her any longer. You've said you don't want to stay. If that's true let's get on with moving you across the river to a new life, eh?" Hunt had sat back in his chair.

Jack had deliberately dropped his eyes to his mug of tea. Hunt had looked across at him and said: "I'm sorry to touch on private things and potentially embarrass you."

Jack had been quick to respond: "Not at all, sir, I understand. It's hard knowing your mother's alone." He had looked across to Mrs Hunt and continued: "Being on the Queen's estate isn't quite the same as exchanging the time of day with passer's by, is it, Mrs Hunt. Being closer to your grandchildren must be a pull for you?"

And that simple statement had clinched it. Hunt smiled as he watched the truth register on his mother's face. By four o'clock Hunt had slipped out of the cottage and spoken to the Deputy Ranger's factotum. Hunt had continued to resist the idea of his mother writing to the Queen.

—

It had been nearly six o'clock when Hunt and Jack had taken their leave of Mrs Hunt at her cottage door. They made their way to the Windsor and Eton Riverside Station for a train to Waterloo. Hunt had led the way and Jack had trailed behind him, at times looking back towards a misty North Terrace beyond the Home Park at Windsor Castle, while trucks loaded with coal passed the two men.

Little had been said between them on the journey. They had travelled third class and the company in the carriage meant it was not conducive to discuss the day. Many fellow passengers were asleep or wrapped up against the cold, their eyes closed. Others talked quietly in small groups. At Waterloo Hunt had hesitated but then to Jack's surprise had extended a hand. Jack had willingly offered his own in response.

"I shall send for you," Hunt had said. "Today has not been for sharing with anyone mind, not colleagues, friends, or lovers. Do you understand me?"

Jack had nodded.

Hunt had continued: "The Queen saw in you something today. She's not a fool. There will never be any thanks, just another summons. The work won't make you rich and it will be hard. Just occasionally she will acknowledge it in some way. If something happens to me, she will call on you at some point in your career. Not personally, of course, but you'll find you're given a commission to fulfil. As to those diamonds and the trail of our young thief, I shall have to think a little more creatively."

And that had been all. Hunt had made his goodbye, turned, and walked into the crowd.

———

All, that is, until the beginning of May.

Sergeant Thick, at Leman Street Police Station, read the order for Constable Jack Sargent to report to Inspector Hunt at Camberwell New Road, on May 5th at 10.00 hours.

Thick had resigned himself to the re-organisation of the patrol and the loss of Constable Sargent yet again. It would be for however long Hunt wanted him, that was always the pattern. True, constables did lay aside their uniform and follow a quarry across the world. Then they would equally quietly reappear, don their uniform again and resume their duties.

Thick re-read the order. There were insufficient details to work out what Inspector Hunt was up to again. He stared at the sheet in front of him and thought philosophically about losing Sargent. Then he shrugged as the man was a bit of a maverick, and at least Sargent would be someone else's problem. That is for a while. What the new Chief Inspector would make of it all was another issue.

Unaware of the deliberations of the desk sergeant and Inspector Hunt Jack stretched his legs out under the table at the West India Dock cottage where he lodged and yawned. After a late shift he had slept until seven. Half an hour more with the paper and then he must get going across the river to Camberwell New Road Police Station if he was to make ten o'clock for the meeting with Inspector Hunt. He stared at the crates around him and thought the kitchen had started to take on the appearance of a warehouse. It blended in with the area thought Jack.

Mrs Phillips and her daughter Rose had started packing in April in preparation to leave. Two destinations were chalked on the crates: Brighton was on the minority of them, as Mrs Phillips divested herself of her domestic belongings, giving many of the items to Rose for her new kitchen. What Rose did not want to take to her new home was to be given to the neighbours.

Mrs Phillips was to become the lodger with Sam Curzon's family, having struck up a great friendship with Sam's mother over the last year. She had visited her prospective new home several times since her first visit to Brighton last June, involving herself with the parish church of St Peter's when there, and taking out a subscription to the reading room at the end of the Chain Pier. Jack thought he could learn a thing or two from the way she was preparing for her new life.

Bow was the destination chalked on the rest of the boxes and crates and these would go to Rose's new home by June, the nineteenth. Rose would follow as a bride on Saturday, the twentieth of June. Her future husband, Sergeant Harry Frank's still suffered from the injuries which had been incurred last year at the naval review at Spithead. Doctor Brown and Ann Black had said that the injury was more complicated than had been anticipated and it was Harry who had therefore delayed the wedding from its original date in 1873. At one point, Jack had wondered if it would be cancelled altogether. Harry had taken the injury hard and lost a good deal of his bonhomie. Rose had remained patient and Jack thought Harry was lucky to have her. Time and Rose's beauty, both in looks and

---

character, had done the trick and in recent months Harry had started to be more like his old self. The hand would never be fully functional again though. Harry could no longer fire a gun with his right hand and had lost the flexibility between the thumb and the first finger. Although he had achieved some precision using his left hand it was not as good and he was wary of drawing arms when a situation called for it. His convalescence had taken months rather than weeks and the length of it had surprised Doctor Brown. Through it all Rose had not given up on Harry and a new date had been set and the bans had been called.

Each day now more packed boxes appeared around the cottage with Rose calling to Jack: "I've left more boxes in the hall, Jack, just to let you know."

The previous night, not having bothered to light his way, Jack had walked into two new crates which were on the landing.

His own departure would coincide with Rose's delayed wedding to Harry next month and Jack's packing would consist of filling a bag with his clothes and boxing up a small collection of books which he had acquired over the last eighteen months. At present it was assumed he would follow the couple to the new house in Bow, as their lodger, after a two-week honeymoon.

Jack was unsure how he felt about moving home again. He had pushed the issue of where he was to live to the back of his mind for months and today was no different. Instead, he focused on the forthcoming cricket season and turned the page of the Daily Telegraph and Courier to find the report of the annual meeting of the Surrey Club on 4th May. Seeing politics through the eyes of a cricket team had brought Jack to the conclusion that the men who had dominated Britain's ruling class thought they knew what was in and out of bounds. He thought that the former Prime Minister, Gladstone, had relied on the good faith of his party and now they were out of power.

Jack's interest in the article was really in James Southerton, considered by many to be the greatest right-arm slow bowler to date. A change in rules which Jack had poured over last year limited players being able to play for more than one county. Southerton would have to choose Surrey or Sussex and Jack assumed Southerton would prefer to play in Surrey's longer season. For Jack's home county of Sussex that was a real loss.

Jack also noted that W.G. Grace was due back from the Australia tour later in May and the man would quickly get back into play for Gloucestershire. Jack had seen the great towering figure once and noted the astonishing straight bat and strength. The tour, though, had not gone well. The Australians had found Grace stand-offish. Southerton seemed the only one to contain Grace's brilliant batting. Yes, Jack was looking forward to the coming season, weather permitting.

"Cricket again?" asked Rose with a smile as she passed behind him carrying an armful of freshly ironed linen. Placing the items into an open drawer she took two cups from the rack above her head and reached for the tea pot on the range. She poured the hot steaming liquid and handed one cup to Jack while reading the article over his shoulder.

"Yes," said Jack, "but there's also news that letter boxes will be painted red. People are having problems finding them because they're all colours. Look, I am a-going," replied Jack, glancing at the clock. "I'm due at New Road at ten." He noisily slurped his tea despite its heat with the knowledge that he was unlikely to get another for many hours.

"Oh, Inspector Hunt's sent for you? That must be for the opening of the Chelsea Embankment on the ninth. Harry's involved, of course," said Rose.

Assumptions, thought Jack, but he did not dissuade Rose.

"It well could be. I'm not sure. Be good to work with Harry awhile," was all Jack said in response.

She could be right, thought Jack but, until he saw Hunt, he had no idea what the duty would be. The Queen had said "both" of them that day in February when he and Hunt had listened to her. "Both" Hunt had thought had referred to the visit of the Russian Emperor. There was just under two weeks before that spectacle was due. True, Affie as the Queen had called him, or Alfred, Duke of Edinburgh, was due to open the Chelsea Embankment on the ninth of May but somehow Jack did not think the Queen had been referring to looking after him.

The newspaper had a short article lower down on the page explaining that Affie and the Russian Marie were now Duke and Duchess of Edinburgh. Here was the rub for the policing of London as the Duchess was due to have a visit from her father and brother with all the pomp displayed last year for the visit of the Shah. it was as if that earlier visit in '73 had written a blueprint for state visits. Back in March, as the couple arrived from Russia there had been a sudden panic as the rumours of the Duchess's diamonds had been confirmed. As an Imperial Princess the Duchess saw no reason why she should not display her jewels. The Queen's displeasure at the sight of Marie's tiara in comparison to the jewellery of the royal princesses had produced an expression Inspector Hunt had learned to dread on his monarch's face. Jack grinned as he recalled Hunt's story.

Now the Emperor of Russia and his son were due to arrive probably by yacht. However, Jack was not aware of the details. All he knew, with some amusement, was that tickets had been issued for their arrival at Gravesend. After the visit of the Shah of Persia the previous year there seemed to be a real appetite for spectacle, with all the security issues that such occasions created. Jack found himself hoping he would not be involved.

"There's a letter for you. It came yesterday. I forgot to mention it last night with all the packing. I left it in the hall," said Rose.

Jack doubled back to the hall and looked at the handwriting. It was from Sussex and he knew it was the solicitor, Mr Langton, who had handled the reading of his parent's will on Jack's twenty-first birthday last September. As his parents had died when he was nine years old their wills had been in the form of a trust. Langton was no doubt chasing him for a decision. Well, he was finally resolved to take the solicitor's advice and buy the cottage in Turnham Green. It was within the value they had discussed last September.

His birthday had been a grand evening. All three trustees and Jack had gathered in the cottage at Selmeston, or Simpson, as Jack pronounced it. They had first toasted Jack's birthday as the Reverend Peter Fisher, known as "Parson," to Jack, had kept the promised bottle ready. Carefully pouring the wine into fine glasses while Jack had cut a cake, the Parson had made a speech. Embarrassed and quite moved by the references to the great friendships between the old vicar and Jack's parents Jack had concentrated on the cake especially made for the occasion by the housekeeper, Mrs Simcock. Jack had shovelled it onto china plates produced from a carved sideboard and there had been silence as he passed the plates to each person.

The Coastguard, Edward Croft, who was also Jack's godfather, was the second trustee present and he had travelled across from the Fairlight station near Hastings for the event. It had been in the diary for many months and with him he brought a prize-winning cheese from Mrs Crowhurst's farm, where Jack and the Brighton Policeman Shaw, had stayed the previous June. Jack had tried to make the cheese a gift to Mrs Simcock as thanks for her care of the Parson. She, however, would not hear of the idea and gave it pride of place next to her cake.

Lucy Croft had not been able to come with Edward because of travelling with the children but had sent two letters. One from herself and the other carefully written by the Croft children, Martha, and Andrew, for "Uncle Jack's birthday." Jack had placed them on a corner of the tall boy in his room and there they still sat.

The solicitor, Mr Langton, was the third trustee acting as such for the firm. After Jack's initial shock that his mother had had some money which she brought to the marriage the trustees had all encouraged him to consider acquiring a property. Langton advised him that it would increase the value of the trust over time and that night he and Langton had drawn up a will.

Jack had waited to undertake the task of finding a house since September. Another issue had been on his mind as he considered the future and Jack had sought Sergeant Stan Green's advice from Shadwell about when to try for promotion and to think about the division he worked in long-term. Jack had opted to look at property in an area out of central London. He focussed on areas which were growing but on a good rail link. There were green fields and small villages still in West London and the cottage he had selected was in an area still reminiscent of his country days.

All Jack had to do was get an answer from P.C. Charlie Banks before he could go back to Langton. Once he did, provided the Trustees felt it was in his best interests, the deal would be done by the trustees and capital released to purchase the property. Turnham Green would do nicely, Jack thought. The opening of the railway station in 1869 promised the area a future as did the opening of the furniture depository. The small streets overlooked the common and there was the promise of more shops and houses to follow. Jack had understood that middle class avenues were planned. The tall church helped make the common a dignified centre to the area and probably there would be a school soon.

Jack could almost hear his mother's voice saying: "Money turned into property." He thought, with a smile, back across the years as she and Jack had poured over the sums which she gave him to add up in the ledgers she had kept for the market garden business. He had learned as a small boy that receipts had to be more than payments to put food on the table.

Jack pocketed the letter and walked back through to the kitchen. He would wait for Charlie tonight even though it would mean he was at Leman Street again until ten o'clock.

"I'll be late," said Jack, patting his pocket.

"Because of the letter?" asked Rose.

Jack nodded.

"I'll leave a plated dinner for you. I hope it's good news," said Rose.

"It's from the solicitor. He wants my decision about making the money work well. I need to see Charlie and find out what he and Hannah have decided. If he's transferring to Hammersmith division, I feel I can go ahead with buying the cottage in Turnham Green and know I'll have someone who will look after the place. They'll take a lodger to pay the rent and Hannah will do a good job at keeping house. There's enough garden to keep Charlie busy with a vegetable plot."

"You could put in for a transfer yourself and live in it and do the same." suggested Rose.

———

39

"No …. not alone," said Jack.

Not without Harriet, interpreted Rose, to herself. Should she say something? The subject of Jack's lost love had created a hush in the cottage between them. Rose and Mrs Phillips had been cautious about the subject of relationships. It had meant that Rose had presented her own wedding in a very matter of fact way when she had spoken of it to Jack. Her deepest excitement had been locked away when in his presence and remained un-expressed. So much so Jack had started to make comparisons with other brides he had seen when he worked on the farm in Battle. Giddy and happy, laughing with their friends as they prepared the very little in the way of possessions that they had to take with them to their new life. Of course, Rose was older than those girls, but Jack had wondered at the sort of contract there would be between his two friends, Rose, and Harry. For Rose it had only been when he was out of the cottage that she had shown her full feelings to her mother and become the bride that Jack would have recognised.

"I'll be a-going. I expect it will be closer to eleven tonight when I get in so, don't worry," said Jack.

Rose walked back to the linen drawer and busied herself, smoothing the fabric of the napkins that made an appearance each week for Sunday lunch. If she didn't look at Jack, she could say it: "I hope Charlie and Hannah will take the cottage. It's a good plan for you. Protects the capital, Harry says, by putting it into a house. And one day, you never know, it might provide you with a home to live in yourself, Jack. I know it's still raw about Harriet, but it's surprising how suddenly you can meet someone. Look at Harry and me? How likely was that to happen?"

Now Rose looked up. The pain in Jack's eyes made her wish she had not mentioned Harriet. She had used the sacred name and hearing it spoken had been a shock for him. Harriet had been everything to him. In the inky black of a night sky pitted with light from the stars, she was there. Even now when a storm cut through the trees, in any room he entered filled with laughter or sadness it was all about Harriet.

Jack made something of an effort. He said: "I must go, or I'll not get this bout done. Inspector Hunt has no tolerance of tardiness. The day's work, I mean," said Jack, realising he had been slipping into his Sussex way of speaking. Then, he remembered Rose might need an escort for her own work through the crowds of men ending their shift at the dock, so he asked: "Are you at the café today?"

"No, I'll not go today. I've more packing," said Rose, making a face hoping to encourage a smile from Jack. "I think I've found a buyer for the business."

Jack raised his eyebrows: "That was fast, but well done. When do you think you'll stop altogether?"

"By the first week in June unless it looks like a buyer might be impatient to get in there. I don't want to lose the sale and it's a better deal for there to be a clientele than to have to build up again after a period of closure," explained Rose.

Jack grinned at the use of the word, "clientele."

The café near the ferry had regulars working in the docks. Rose had been her brother Ted's eyes and ears there.

Rose threw a napkin at him. She added as an explanation: "Ted is cultivating a barmaid at "The Nelson" to take over observations after I've gone."

Jack's eyes went wide, and he received another napkin for his humour. "I was thinking it was a very un-Ted thing to do and could get him into all sorts of problems."

"Well, she's no Mary, if that's what you're thinking," said Rose, with reference to the young barmaid from the Mason's Arms on the Commercial Road. Rose had met her at a hotel in Brighton last summer where Mary now worked and had worked out that Mary clearly had Jack in her sights. He, however, could not see it.

Rose returned to the subject of Ted and the barmaid from the Nelson: "This woman is in her late fifties, has had five children and her husband is employed at the Chain and Anchor Works so no jumping to conclusions about Ted."

"Point taken," said Jack. Changing the subject he asked: "How much more packing do you have to do?"

"We should have finished in a few more days and then Mother will make a decision about the rest of the things. We'll be living out of empty cupboards for a while," said Rose.

"More crates to fall over tonight, then," said Jack, scuttling out of the back door before another napkin came winging across the room and caught him.

*

———

42

Jack turned out of the cottage door towards the West India Dock Station to pick up a train on the Blackwall Railway. A myriad of masts faced him as he walked past a team of men whose faces told him they were from everywhere under the sun. They were engaged in re-filling tea chests after bulking: re-mixing the tea after journeys where the smaller leaves and dust worked to the bottom of the chests.

Jack watched as carcases bound in cloth were unloaded from a cart. He had heard meat was now being shipped from Australia in a frozen state and had meant to have a look at the operation at South West India Dock in Millwall, to see for himself. He could not believe it would work and harked back to his labouring past at Battle where his meat came from an animal on the farm which he had seen alive.

Looking over to his right was the direction of the City of London but he had to trust it was there as the City could no longer be seen for buildings. On his left he looked towards the Poplar Workhouse, the Town Hall, a Savings Bank, and a National School.

He was quickly at the station and Jack's intention was to eventually change and pick up the London, Chatham, and Dover Railway to get to Camberwell New Road. Today he would ride past Leman Street instead of going into the Police Station. Some days he had gone as far as Shadwell to see Harry Franks or Sergeant Stan Green. But not today as his objective was to get across the river and make the meeting with Inspector Tom Hunt and to arrive sufficiently early before ten o'clock. Respect for Inspector Hunt was a double reason to be early, but Jack also had no intention of getting into Sergeant Ted Phillips's bad books. But as he arrived for the train at the West India Dock Station Jack heard shouting off to his right.

On the West India Dock Road, by the junction of King Street and Garford Street, Jack could see a black man down on the floor. He was being beaten about the head by a woman using a bag, while another screamed at him to be still as she attempted to rifle his pockets.

The man had covered his head with his hands and rolled himself into a ball. He twisted right and left and was largely successful at avoiding kicks to his head.

Jack pulled out his rattle, creating as much noise as he could while he ran toward the group on the floor, shouting: "Police, stop, stop, get off him, *now.*"

He hoped the noise his rattle made would be heard by other constables in the vicinity and any Port Police around. Too late he realised that the women were not working alone. Stupid, he told himself, they rarely did.

Two men were "working" the women and they were on Jack before he could turn to face them. Like the man he had gone to rescue Jack was down and he too rolled himself into a ball and covered his head before the first kick came into his side. The pain was sharp and like a knife and Jack briefly thought of bone cutting into flesh as another boot caught him in the same place. The noise he produced through the pain would have summoned help if there was any chance it was available.

44

Two

Jack was aware of a powerfully built man coming to his rescue, and he could hear the impact of blows from large fists as his saviour knocked the first assailant away. Jack allowed himself a look and saw a black face he recognised as a man he had seen on the West India Dock Road. The man caught the foot of the second assailant as it went in to kick Jack again in the ribs. His rescuer used the man's own weight to unbalance him and Jack saw the two men who had attacked him dazed as they fell against bales by the side of the road. Neither assailant moved, and Jack concluded they were unlikely to for a while. The women had run at the first sign of Jack's powerfully built rescuer, taking their spoils with them and their victim was presently sitting up looking dazed.

"Thank-you," said Jack, as he accepted a hand from his rescuer. The man was a good third of Jack's height taller than him and the power in his grip was not lost on Jack as he registered that the man would be a good ally. He stopped musing as there was a sharp pain on his left side as Jack got up and he wondered if a rib had gone. Unable to straighten up he accepted the arm around his torso to get him across to a crate where he could sit.

Other rattles were now sounding in response to his own call for help and two men from the East and West India Docks Police were running in the distance. Because of the layout of the dock, it would be a couple of minutes before they would arrive, thought Jack. He managed a smile at his rescuer.

—

45

"I thought I was done for," said Jack, with a grin. He held out his hand to the black man before him who grasped it and smiled in return.

"P.C. Jack Sargent, Leman Street," said Jack. "What do you do?" he asked, again eyeing the size and build of the man.

"Planterose Boyes, Artist but I feed myself using these in fights," said the man with a grin, as he held up his fists. "You're away from your area here, aren't you?"

"Just about to go on duty, I lodge in the cottages over there." Jack nodded towards Mrs Phillips's home. "That's quite a name you've got," Jack continued.

Standing tentatively to check the pain level Jack slowly moved to the man still on the floor.

"A mother aspiring to noble virtues," said Boyes, smiling in return.

Jack nodded: "Tell her she succeeded," he said. "My thanks to you."

Jack spoke to the dazed man on the floor and said: "Let's help you up, sir."

"It's Mr Joseph, lives near me," Boyes explained.

Jack and Boyes started to assist Joseph to stand but Jack winced, and Boyes took the strain of the man's weight as Jack pulled back a little, hoping to avoid the sharp pain again.

"I'm sorry. I think I may have cracked a rib," said Jack.

"You should sit," said Boyes. and Jack nodded. He looked around and decided on the crates at the side again. He perched on one of them, leaning slightly to the side to ease the discomfort.

—

Pulling out his notebook and pencil Jack asked: "is it Mr Joseph?"

Boyes got the man seated.

"Joseph Johnson, I live up the road," replied Johnson.

"Are you in work?" asked Jack.

"I'm a ship's steward and on my way home. I've seen those women often before. Always hanging around, they are." He put his hand into his pocket and drew out some coins. He felt again and said: "I think they've stolen one pound from my pocket."

"What happened here, constable?" called the first of the Dock Police to arrive.

Jack stood slowly and quickly explained. He agreed to wait with the victim while the two constables, who introduced themselves as Sergeant Flynn and P.C. Smith, would go along the West India Dock Road after the women. The constable handcuffed Jack's unconscious assailants and the men were left by the bales to continue their involuntary slumber. Satisfied they were secure and unlikely to wake Sergeant Flynn started after the women.

P.C. Smith said: "If it's the two women I think it is we know where to find them. It sounds like Annie Quayle and Emma Lewis to me. Quayle took a ship to Liverpool from the Isle of Man and unfortunately made her way to London. Just a matter of time 'til we pick them up. If you don't mind me saying your sleeve is torn and the back of your tunic is marked. Would you take the details from the man who was attacked while I keep an eye on your two attackers sleeping peacefully?"

Jack nodded over to the side of the dock. He said: "Here's two more constables coming now."

"Right, I'll get off to help the Sergeant. If you could give them your account, there's no need for you to wait for me to come back. I've got your police number and just need your name and where to find you." Smith turned and moved off into a trot after Sergeant Flynn.

Jack watched him go aware that he would be late arriving at his meeting with Hunt. The older of the constables who had just arrived directed his younger colleague to stand by the unconscious men, while he pulled his notebook out to start taking Jack's story. Boyes also gave his details and Jack noted the road mentioned. That done, Boyes, Johnson and Jack gave the older of the two constables their addresses and some brief details and when he was satisfied that he had all the information he needed Jack and the two policemen watched as Boyes helped Johnson up the road towards home. Jack explained the sequence of events to the older policeman and after ten minutes as he prepared to leave he said: "If I was a betting man, I'd back Boyes in a fight every time."

One of the constables nodded. "Interesting life he's had too. You should see his paintings. Anyway, if you're alright we'll get off."

"I'll get across to Leman Street and see my Sergeant," Jack explained. The sharp pain in his side was like a knife. He could imagine Hunt's face when he did not arrive at New Road and decided that there was no point trying to get across to Camberwell now as so much time had gone by. He had been tossing up about what his best bet was now and decided that he should get to Leman Street, see the Police Surgeon who was due in by ten o'clock, or Ann Black, if she was there. Jack always described her as his "doctor," even though it would have been illegal for her to practice. The British Medical Association had taken a subsequent vote not to admit any more women to its membership following Elizabeth Garrett Anderson's election. Ann Black had a medical degree from the Sorbonne in Paris; however, she would not be recognised until there was a wind of change.

Opting for Leman Street was the better option. Wherever he decided to go he needed to send a message to Hunt quickly though, otherwise the balloon would go up.

Jack made his way first as far as the Poplar Post Office. A telegram was sent immediately to Inspector Hunt. All being well Hunt would have it before ten o'clock. Then Jack started the walk to the West India Dock railway station and boarded the Blackwall Railway to get as close to Leman Street as he could. In his pocket was some change and it would be enough for a cabbie to get him to the door of the Police Station from Stepney Railway Station. He could flag down a cab on the Commercial Road if he got bad. The theory was better than the practice as each movement made him react to the sharp pains. He coped on the train aware his expression must look angry as he was consumed by pain. Being in a torn uniform, audibly exclaiming with each movement, it did not take long for two workmen to come across.

"Do you need help, officer?"

49

"Thank-you, I'm trying to get back to Leman Street Police Station, but I've taken a kicking and every movement is getting more difficult."

One of the men walked to the exit to hail a cab for Jack while the other man gave him support. Trying to be cheerful, the workman said to Jack: "Not often I puts my arm round a policeman. It's usually the other way and I gets his arm around me."

Jack appreciated the attempt at humour, but the pain was getting worse and he could do little more than grunt as he and the man walked slowly to the cab.

"Many thanks," Jack said as he slowly climbed in.

Once seated Jack braced himself for the impact on his side as it rolled and bumped across the road surface to the Police Station at Leman Street. It was a dusty route and busy with traffic the cabbie was inclined to stop suddenly. Jack hated this route anyway and deliberately turned his face to the left as they passed the entrance into Arbour Street East. Memories from the ill-fated case of the Faceless Woman still seemed far too real to return to the once loved house and square. Jack thought of the impact of that case not only on his mind but on what continued to unfold from it.

Perhaps Rose was right. A transfer to another division might be sensible and would help the memories heal. But today, in this state, he realised he was not being too rational.

The cabbie stopped outside Leman Street Police Station and Jack over-paid him for his trouble. It was not generosity but pain as he searched for coins. The man helped him out and into the station. Then it was a pushing through a mix of constables and their quarry to Sergeant Thick's desk.

There was a spontaneous oath at Jack's appearance as Thick peered at him through the group of men in front of him.

"By God, what's happened to you? More scrapes I see."

Jack leant against the wall and gave the Sergeant a quick account for his presence at Leman Street. The cabbie was still hovering behind the Sergeant.

"Thank you for your help," said Jack.

"Remember I might need yer 'elp one day," said the man.

"Get yourself into the back," barked Thick at Jack, and turning to another constable said: "Thompson, get down immediately to Doctor Brown and tell him he's needed urgently up here and to leave those reprobates that he's tending. We need to get word to the Inspector that you're injured."

"I've done it from Poplar," said Jack. "The pain's got worse though on the way here."

"Right," said Thick, moving to help support Jack, "Let's get you get out of here. By the time the doctor's finished with you I should know what we're to do with you."

*

Jack took a sip of the scalding tea. The pain in his mouth distracted him from the pain in his side but even for him the number of sugars Sergeant Thick had spooned into it was too many.

51

From his chair he could clearly hear the evidence of police officers dealing with their lively quarry as the noise invaded the room through the partially open door. Jack caught a glimpse of Doctor Brown on several occasions during his wait as the man moved quickly past to attend to the results of a fight or resisting arrest. Doctor's always had priorities Jack had learnt.

A man was carried past, his clothes in disarray and Brown was at his side in moments listening for signs of life. Sergeant Thick had two constables in a corner ticking them off for bringing the man into the police station. Jack gave the door a push with his foot and it swung to so that the noise died with its closure. He lifted the mug of steaming liquid to his lips, closed his eyes and sipped. He could feel the warmth of the steam on his nose and top lip and found comfort in it.

The sharp pains pulled him back to the hope that the doctor would not be too long. Jack had asked for Mrs Ann Black, as the doctor was so busy, in the hope that she had come today. It was now a week since Jack had seen her and the constable he had asked to go and find her had told Jack there was some talk of her being unwell.

Jack waited, closing his eyes to lose himself, hoping the mêlée outside would die down. He had no stomach to get through his colleagues to Doctor Brown. Preparing his mind for delay Jack tried to drown the gnawing pain that had registered as shouting into his brain by focussing on the expenses that would come with buying the cottage in Turnham Green. If he could just concentrate hard enough….

He dozed briefly but came to suddenly as a noise disturbed him. Jack instinctively tried to scramble to his feet before a sharp stab consumed him. He collapsed back onto the chair with a jolt which made him feel sick. Constable Charlie Banks leaned over him as Jack grimaced.

Charlie had come in to cover Jack's beat and had been surprised to hear from the Sergeant that Jack was in the back room. He had sat opposite the slumbering Jack, placed his police helmet on his knee, and waited.

Charlie had earned the reputation of being the "quiet" one of the three recruits in 1872. Captain Harris had sworn three men in on that day, the fourteenth of October. Since then, Sam Curzon had gone into civilian work after a long convalescence following the dreadful effects on him from the poison administered by Emily Doyle. Jack had remained in Leman Street, H Division, having been assigned there, been injured in the Alexandra Palace Fire in '73. Sergeant Thick accepted Jack but there was this irritating issue about him that when an order from Inspector Tom Hunt arrived Jack would disappear. Thick had resigned himself that the constable was really the property of that Inspector, despite only once since that Faceless Woman case having gone into plain clothes.

And then there had been Charlie Banks. The quiet one he was. Charlie had arrived from Macclesfield in 1872 and like Jack answered the advert to join the Met. Both were encouraged by the Desk Sergeant to work on dropping their local dialects, particularly in writing reports. Jack had a good hand, but Charlie's writing was sometimes illegible. However,

Charlie's main talent was that he had the stamina of a snake and could watch and wait for his prey for days, half starving himself until he struck. Charlie could do his own beat, and pick-up Jack's on top, still turn in the next day and quietly resume his own duties with little rest.

Charlie was the only one of the three of them that had already married and Mrs Banks … Hannah as she had been to Jack and Sam in Arbour Square … was expected to contribute a wage but had found the opportunities limited because of Charlie's job. She had been a maid of all work but now she and Charlie had taken policemen as lodgers and become boarding house keepers. Charlie was also the one who was likely to progress faster up the ranks because he was ready to transfer at the drop of a hat to get out of central London.

Charlie caught Jack's elbow to steady him.

"I'll sit on the arm of the chair," said Jack. "The armchair is too low, and I need to be straighter."

"I was just off to pick up your patrol, not expectin' to see you 'ere. Sergeant Thick told me you were injured from a brawl and waitin' for Doctor Brown. What do you think is wrong?" asked Charlie.

"Ribs I expact. I took a kicking," Jack explained.

"I'll go and get the doctor for you, now," said Charlie.

"That would be good excapt he's busy with the last bunch who came in. Charlie, I have to see you, but it can wait for tonight if you're on your way now," said Jack.

"You shouldn't be back 'ere tonight. Is it about the 'ouse?" asked Charlie, raising his eyebrows.

—

Jack nodded. "More a cottage, in Turnham Green."

"I'll get out on patrol and when I've done, I'll come to West India Dock if you're 'appy to talk. My girl will be pleased it's going to 'appen." Charlie glanced at the clock aware he would bear Sergeant Thick's wrath if he was much later leaving.

Jack sighed as the pain settled into an ache. "I'm keeping you," he said. "You've enough on covering my patrol as well."

"It's alright, Thick sent me in here to 'ave a look at you. I'll get the doctor first and then go. I'll be along to the dock cottage by eight." Charlie paused.

Jack said: "What is it?"

"I was just thinkin' this is the second time for you," said Charlie. "Bein' injured I mean. You'll not be doin' the runnin' for the division this summer. I'll go an' find the doctor."

*

"You're in luck," declared Doctor Brown, entering the room moments later. "I hear you've had a beating and are in pain around the ribs. Due to a whole rash of broken rib cases and publicity of maltreatment in Asylums there's been such a penchant by the press for doctors to spot a broken rib or two that I'm quite the expert."

"Is it that bad in the Asylums?" asked Jack, trying to sit up.

"Yes, it appears so. Stay still will you. I'm going to pull your shirt out. Factories are also my forte with people falling and no railings up to stop them. How did this happen?" asked Brown.

"Trying to stop a man being beaten by pickpockets. I forgot they were likely to be part of a larger gang and got a beating myself. I was knocked down and then kicked." Jack drew a sharp breath as Brown examined him.

"Well you're young and strong, which is in your favour. Does it hurt when you breathe?"

"If I breathe deeply, yes," said Jack.

"Just do that, will you." Doctor Brown stepped back after touching the painful area. He watched Jack and saw the frown come while the deep breathing was underway. He stepped forward and felt the area as Jack took another breath.

"I thought Ann Black might have been here," said Jack.

"Well, she wouldn't have examined you so you're lucky it's me. No, no, it's all systems go with the move to Marylebone for the women's hospital. She's not too well either and I've told her not to come. I suspect you've two cracked ribs which is going to take some time to heal. No running, and no cricket for you, young man for some months. Rest up for the next few days. Cold sheets wrapped around the area might give you some relief. I'll let the Sergeant know it will be weeks rather than days before you can resume normal duties. Seriously, there should be time given for this to heal. Look after it now and you'll be back to normal faster. Nothing will change my position on that," said Doctor Brown.

"I was due to see Inspector Hunt this morning," Jack explained.

"Were you?" Doctor Brown stepped back and crossed his arms as he looked at Jack. "What's the game this time? Well whatever that was about will not be going ahead. You're to go home and rest. Hunt can come to you if its urgent but the only place you're going as far as I'm concerned is back to the West India Docks. Hunt has other reserves on his list that he can use. I can't see why anything should ride on you being assigned to him. Can you?" Doctor Brown looked at Jack and paused in the act of rolling down his shirt sleeves. Brown had seen that earnest look before. The doctor turned looking round for his bag and said: "I see from that look on your face that something's afoot again."

Jack did not answer, thinking about the prospective visit of the Russian Emperor and a Queen's command. To ease his conscience, he said: "I expact its special duties with the visit of the Russian Emperor. It's soon Doctor. That's the only thing I can think it was about. Most Reserves will be on duty for that."

Brown reached into his bag and pulled white cloth from it. He sat down in the same chair Charlie had occupied and leant forward looking Jack in the eyes. He said: "I have no idea what state of disorder your presence may help avoid, Jack. However, frankly, you're of little use in this condition, Desk duty I can foresee in a while but nothing like a patrol for a couple of months."

"That's worse than the cough!" said Jack, horrified.

"It's a different injury." Doctor Brown frowned. "And you'd get no sympathy from Ann either if she was here. You've recovered from a lot of the smoke inhalation, although the winter hasn't helped it. You're lucky the kicks didn't break a rib completely given the organs around the area. You'll be back on patrol eventually but it's desk work for you after a rest of forty-eight hours. I shan't move on that. I suspect Hunt will be on to me for this decision. as you're becoming quite a personality, you know."

"I can't see that Doctor," said Jack, surprised.

"Well, judging from discussions I hear, your name comes up quite often." Brown tore the muslin at one end to create a decent sized strip and indicated to Jack to take off his shirt. Once done the doctor started to wrap the fabric around Jack's torso.

He stood back and looked at his handiwork.

Brown said: "There, that will give you some support on the way home. You get off in a cab and I'll see the Desk Sergeant. He'll get a message across the river to the Inspector that I've interfered and you're going home. Go on get off with you now before the pain and the stiffness worsens."

*

Packing was still underway at the West India Dock Cottage as Jack entered the scene. His brow furrowed with discomfort as he twisted past a crate to find the slim and compact figure of Rose bent double over another. She was about to pack her mother's silver forks and came up quickly at the sound of someone in the room. Rose was round the chair at the sight of Jack flinching with pain and grasped his arm. She waited for the pained expression to relax on Jack's face before she spoke.

"Why, Jack! What's happened?" Rose asked, dropping the forks onto the table.

Hesitantly, Jack lowered himself onto a kitchen chair. He looked up at Rose and managed a grimace rather than a smile.

"I took a kicking stopping two pickpockets. My own fault as I forgot they generally move in groups."

"Ted always says never go in on your own. You should rest on your bed, Jack. You've seen the Police Surgeon?" asked Rose.

Jack nodded, weighed down with summoning the energy to climb stairs. He stared at the clock for some seconds registering the time and wondering about Hunt's reaction to his telegram. As if he was an elderly person and not a man of twenty-one, he pushed himself up from the chair, his jaw jutting out with the determination to deal with the discomfort of a body that did not cooperate.

"I'll bring you up a drink and some food," called Rose from the door as Jack started up the stairs. From the kitchen she could hear him grunt and puff with the effort of each step. Rose shook her head as she went into the pantry.

Once in his room there was nothing to do except rest. Getting onto his bed was an interesting experience as he could neither lower himself down or just flop onto it. He let out a yell more to summon the determination to get onto the bed than anything else and another as the pain overcame him. Then he lay still until Mrs Phillips appeared in the doorway looking alarmed at the two shouts she had heard.

"What on earth happened?" she asked.

"Sorry about that, I've taken a kicking in me ribs and Doctor Brown has sent me home. The only way I could get down onto the bed was to do it quickly."

"You should have called us, we'd have helped you," said Mrs Phillips.

Rose came up the stairs with a tray on which was a bowl of broth and chunks of fresh bread covered with butter. The two women exchanged a look. "He's had a kicking in an arrest, Mother," explained Rose.

"He was just telling me," said Mrs Phillips. "What's to be done for you, Jack?"

"Rest for a few days and then probably desk duty for a few weeks," said Jack.

"You'd better be right for the wedding," said Rose, giving Jack a look. "I'm not having any more delays with you men getting injured."

*

Jack set the empty bowl and plate down and reached for his book, but his eyes were heavy as he started to read, and he fell into a grey sleep pitted with shadows. Waking almost an hour later at some movement that he took to be Rose he found Inspector Hunt looking down at him. Jack was disorientated and unsure of the time of day and stared at Hunt as if still in a dream.

"You didn't pay me a visit," Hunt said; "so I must come to you. No, don't try and get up, I can see you're hurt." Hunt bent and picked up the book which had slipped from Jack's hand while he slept. 'Trollope's 'The Eustace Diamonds.'

"A fine taste in your reading matter. It's new is it?" Hunt placed the book back on the bed.

"Yes," replied Jack. "I'm sorry sir, the doctor insisted I came home," Jack explained.

"Yes, so I heard from Sergeant Thick," said Hunt, noting how white Jack looked. "It doesn't look like this will be home for much longer from the state of things downstairs. Remind me when the wedding is?"

"Next month," said Jack.

"Ah, yes, for some reason I thought it was September." Hunt looked thoughtful.

"Probably you're remembering it was supposed to be September last year, but Harry's injuries from Spithead delayed things." Jack smiled, "I recall Harry had said that he didn't want to go to the altar in a bath chair."

Hunt smiled at the image knowing that Harry Franks was not to be kept down and no doubt, having waited, would stagger up the aisle this year regardless of the state he was in.

The door opened and Rose appeared behind a tray on which was a pot of tea and a plate covered with a neat embroidered cloth.

"Ah, you're awake, I had a look at you about half-an-hour ago Jack and you were still soundly out, so I didn't disturb you.

I've brought the rest of the food I put ready for you." Rose removed the cloth to reveal two pork pies.

"You'll not get rid of your lodger feeding him like this," said Hunt with a smile.

Rose poured tea for the two men and half smiled at the compliment. She glanced at Jack and said: "We don't want to. It's strange enough with Mother moving to Brighton. I put a pie for you, Inspector, in case you won't get back to the station in time. There's also a note for Ted about the dates for the crates to go to Harry's. Would you mind very much passing it to him?" asked Rose, holding out the envelope to Hunt.

"Not at all," said Hunt, taking the letter and pocketing it. He said: "Ted's not due in until this evening but I'll leave it with Sergeant Morris for when they do the handover. Remind me of the date of your wedding?" asked Hunt.

"Saturday, June twentieth," said Rose. "Harry gets the house on the nineteenth. We hope you and Mrs Hunt might come?"

Hunt looked distracted; "Thank-you. The twentieth of June, did you say. That gives more than five weeks, doesn't it?" Recovering his manners, he forced a smile and added: "And Ted will give you away no doubt. There must be so much to do, especially with your mother leaving."

"Just the furniture to see to after Mother's special few pieces go to Brighton this week," explained Rose. "She's decided to have some new things so our neighbours will come and choose what they'd like before we go, and they can collect it all after the wedding. Harry's ordered new furniture for the house in Bow, so I go to a completely new home. There's linen and china from mother and father's wedding and the cutlery they were given that she wants me to have and I'll take my kitchen pans."

Hunt looked around at Jack's few possessions. "At least your lodger is quick to get rid of."

"Staying fleet-footed, sir," said Jack, with a grin.

"Yes …. but not very fleet-footed now. I suspect it will take Jack five minutes to pack. But I must leave you to your work," said Rose.

"Many thanks for your kindness, the pie is much appreciated," said Hunt as he got up to open the door for Rose. Before he sat down again, he offered the plate to Jack who took one of the pies. The next few minutes were involved in both men savouring the flavours as they ate.

"This has been a good lodging for you," said Hunt, as he finished.

"Yes, for the comfort, the company, and the food, but the area was difficult this winter on my breathing. I shan't do another around here," said Jack.

"Will Bow suit you better?" Hunt asked.

"I'm not sure," said Jack, with a slight frown. "I haven't been to the house yet. It's better to go and try it as Rose and I are comfortable as lodger and landlady and Harry and I work well together. It looks easy enough to move around from Bow station to Leman Street on the Blackwall railway as I can get off at Stepney. It's nothing other than the air, sir, that makes me doubt about staying around here. At times last winter I felt I was going to choke. Harry and Rose will be near Victoria Park and I'm willing to try it. The park has a boating lake and there's bathing up there. In the summer I thought I could join the cricket team that practices in the park. I'll know by the autumn as the smoke worsens and at that point I can move if it's a problem with my chest. But you didn't come here to talk about that, sir. There's more serious issues I know."

Hunt was quiet, taking in the state Jack was in as he could barely move without wincing. This constable had had two injuries now since he had joined the Metropolitan Police. Both or either, might shorten his career. Hunt had a liking for Jack but there was more to it than that. There were few the inspector could trust, and this man reflected many of his own attitudes. Like Hunt, Jack had taken the difficult decision to leave his home area, join the Metropolitan Police and begin a climb to better himself. In Jack's case it was from farm labourer but both men had been servants in one way or another and that role did not suit either of them.

"We should drink our tea," Hunt said, moving to pass Jack a cup. "How many sugars?"

"Two, please, sir. I've wasted time for you," said Jack, taking the cup Hunt offered him.

"As it happens the delay was beneficial. My orders for you changed through the morning. Had you arrived by ten as arranged I would have been left with a problem now." Hunt paused and then asked: "Just before I explain what role have you in the wedding?"

"Harry and Rose's?" Jack asked, rather surprised.

"The only wedding I know of," said Hunt.

"Only seating people in church. Ted's the man as he plays the Old Father and will give Rose away. Why do you ask?"

"No matter at this point," said Hunt. There may be enough time, he thought. Hunt hesitated before he carried on: "I had a message from the enquiries I made about the theft of those diamonds last year. You may recall there were two issues the Queen charged me with that day in February when we were both at Windsor."

"Yes, sir, one was duty for the Emperor of Russia's visit, and you thought she meant for me to help."

"That's right, you were included in that first charge. However active duty in that way is out of the question through your injuries this morning. On that basis I think Her Majesty will accept me using you in the second charge she laid at my door. It's in your interest for me to use you in tracking the thief of the Shah's diamonds."

Jack looked confused. "I don't understand, sir," he said.

Hunt paused about how to explain. Better to be honest, he thought. He said: "The Queen never forgets a face. I'm afraid as you were with me that day in Windsor, she will have taken it that I brought you there deliberately.

"Why, sir?" asked Jack.

"She would take it that I was introducing another policeman to her, one I trust, or I wouldn't have invited you. If something happened to me, she would take it that you would pick things up. The part about being someone I trust is true by the way. But I did not think to place you in the royal gaze." Hunt said.

He chuckled and continued: "Still I have no intention of succumbing to death just yet, so you are safe from the Widow of Windsor at present. But let me recap for you. The man seen near the Shah's horse that day in Woolwich fitted the description you gave of the thief at Alexandra Palace on the day of the fire and the earlier theft at the West India Dock Offices. You are the only one who has seen him. That alone should justify me sending you." Hunt waited for Jack's response. but as Jack sat up the movement made him flinch with pain. Hunt waited until Jack's face relaxed and the eyes cleared.

"Try and remain still for a while," suggested Hunt.

Eventually Jack's face started to relax, and Hunt smiled at the young constable.

Jack asked: "Did you turn anything up sir, in your enquiries about the man?"

"We may have found a warm trail. On a casual impulse we widened the routes the man might have taken back to the continent. You remember the assumption that he was not local? The trail, we thought, may have gone cold as its months ago. At first, you see, those investigating only looked at crossings to areas dealing with the diamond trade. Those were cold. It dawned on me that, if my instinct was right the thief was not working for himself and he was obtaining items to order from someone who has no intention of disposing of those diamonds. Motive, Jack, that's where the investigation went wrong."

"At least thanks to you the police have come to it now though," said Jack.

"Yes," said Hunt. He took a sip of his tea before he continued: "If our thief is working for the quarry I seek, and I believe he is, the fact the diamonds had belonged to the Shah would be reason enough to hold onto them. The thefts you witnessed of the watch from the dock office and the pieces of artwork taken at Alexandra Palace indicate an art collector to me. They may form part of a cache of precious items. Trophies, if you like. That was one thought."

'And you have another idea, sir?" asked Jack.

"Yes. The other thought at the back of my mind was that the theft was an action of spite. A power play, perhaps a sense of revenge. The man I think is behind the theft does not need to sell diamonds. He has no *reason* to, such is his wealth from crime. Yes, he may want them because of who owned them, but he doesn't need them."

"The diamonds were worth about three hundred and fifty pounds, weren't they?" asked Jack.

"That's right. Less if they were to be fenced. I don't believe money is what is motivating him. Perhaps the risk involved provides excitement, but even that I doubt. More and more I'm coming down on the side of the conclusion that he just decided to cause the establishment embarrassment by ordering a theft that was audacious. With the watch and the piece of art? Well, my suspicion is that's because he wants them as prize pieces. But with the diamonds? No, there's a different motive, I think. Look at where it was done, Jack. It was at the Woolwich

---

Review, from the bridle of the Shah's horse. It was done in full view of the army, the Lords and half the royalty."

"Then that gives us an idea or two about him, sir."

"And what do you conclude?" asked Hunt.

"He's a radical. On the farm, when a worker went bad, we'd say he was radical, which meant tiresome and that he took risks. It would be no use no matter how many times you told him or what you said to him, because he wouldn't believe he could come a cropper. He would just rap and run we would say. Run headlong into trouble and take others down with him. A man like that was dangerous to be with," said Jack.

Hunt had paused, struck by Jack's explanation of a dangerous man.

But Jack added: "Of course, the second idea I've been wonderin' about."

"And what is that?" asked Hunt.

"That he wanted to be caught. It's the skills he had that make me think," said Jack. "It was such a highly decorated horse that so many eyes would have been fixed on it. But if he was a radical perhaps he didn't care if he was caught. Maybe it was a deliberate attempt to be noticed and detained."

"We'd say it was audacious I think. Cocky even," said Hunt.

"Stands to reason in front of that lot at Woolwich that someone should have caught him. The fact they didn't shows how good the thief must be doesn't it?" asked Jack.

"Not necessarily, put yourself in the position of the people present. Anyway, it's the man behind all this we want not some petty thief," said Hunt.

—

Three

Hunt fought back the desire to laugh. From a layman's point of view he would have agreed with Jack, but he knew the types that would have been at the review and none of them would have seen it as their responsibility. He contemplated if he should disclose anything further such as his own link to Gladstone. Hunt decided against the idea of giving Jack a name, but he might feed some information implying high-level support. After all Harry Franks was the fall-back position and if anything happened to Hunt, Harry could ensure someone else would pick up the baton and carry on the race.

Hunt watched Jack and remembered the exchange about his name with the Queen. She was unlikely to forget the fresh-faced young constable that had been to Windsor, or his name and rank. Hunt knew Jack could find himself summoned there if Hunt died.

"Until recently I had some support from a man in a high position," said Hunt. "I am sure he and I suspected the same person. as being behind various crimes. I no longer have that support, but that contact did help move my thinking on."

Hunt hesitated to say more. After all Gladstone had not contacted Hunt after losing the election apart from sending a brief note that he was resigning and for all Hunt knew he now never would hear from the "Grand Old Man," again. The nick-name Gladstone had been known by would probably fade from people's minds. After all the man was had been known, was sixty-five. Gladstone's, "Great Romance with the people of

---

England," seemed to be over forever. One person that was unlikely to care was the Queen.

Jack had looked energised as Hunt explained his reasoning but now his expression changed to deflation at the mention of the loss of support. Hunt came out of his reverie. Better to forget any further idea of disclosure.

Carefully, Jack said: "I thank you for thinking of me, sir, but how can I be involved now?"

"I think a short spell with your old Parson in Selmeston would put you right," said Hunt. "Doctor Brown said you should rest here for forty-eight hours and then desk duty. Well, you're assigned to me until further notice. No-one will ask any questions about you, not for a few weeks anyway. Thick will assume you're either grounded on doctor's orders or at Camberwell behind a desk. A convalescence in the Sussex air for a week could be just the cover we need for you to make a sea journey."

"Sea journey, sir?" Jack asked. "Where would I be going? I thought you said the man hadn't gone abroad. Have you traced him then, Inspector?"

"I said he hadn't used the routes we checked." Hunt paused, choosing his words carefully. "I think we've got a trail now and certainly a man answering his description has crossed to Jersey some months ago. The hair colour, Jack, as you may be aware yourself tends to get a man remembered. A short trip from Southampton will get you to Jersey and you can pick up the trail from there. I'll arrange for Harry to join you at the port."

"Back into plain clothes," said Jack with a grin. "Should I check with the doctor what I can do?"

Hunt suppressed the mild annoyance he felt. After all Jack was not completely in full possession of the facts about their quarry. Hunt had decided it was better that he remained partially in the dark and he relaxed his expression, shook his head, and said: "No, don't forget the surgeon is a civilian."

Jack looked confused. Irritated Hunt thought Jack was still too open, but then he had had a close working relationship with Ann Black over the last year.

Hunt added: "Look Jack, only tell a doctor what they need to know, and this case doesn't fit that category. There's always the danger for the person that you take into your confidence that you put them at risk. Ann Black, for example, I know has been helpful in the past, but she and Doctor Brown belong in their surgeries and laboratories. That's where they can give the most help. Our lead that the thief has gone overseas needs checking out. At this point that's all there is to it. There would be some coming and going, asking of questions, and pursuing gentle enquiries. You don't need a doctor for that, and you wouldn't be going on your own."

"Well, if I can tie in a personal visit to the Parson, sir and breath some sea air, that will suit me fine. There's some other business I should take care of as well," said Jack.

"Oh, yes?" Hunt cocked his head on one side.

"I'm being told I should make a will, put some money into a cottage in London as part of the will trust my parents left. I thought to let it to Charlie Banks and his wife as he's moving to Hammersmith," Jack explained.

Hunt said: "Good, that sounds wise for your life. I can let the right channels know that I've a man on the thief's trail, which should satisfy Her Majesty for now. No name needs to be given but she may assume it's the constable I brought with me on her carriage ride. The fact that we're in pursuit of the thief potentially internationally will look impressive and she'll enjoy dictating that to her equerry to drop out in a diplomatic communiqué to the Shah," said Hunt.

"There shouldn't be any more vigorous action than observation then sir?" asked Jack.

"No, no," said Hunt, more firmly than he felt was the reality. "The main reason for this duty is to get evidence on our quarry at the top. We're not interested in our thief as I believe he isn't English. No action is to be taken against him regardless of what you witness or find out. I can make the information on him known in his own domicile eventually," Hunt reflected and added: "Wherever that is. I think his reason to go to Jersey may have been to lie low or he may have crossed from there to the continent. There's been nothing of any consequence reported in Jersey that we could tie him to. You may get there and find he's crossed back to England or simply vanished through France. Given his skills I suspect there's probably already interest in him in his home country. But as I say we have no idea where that may be. if things do develop Harry will be with you and he can make the decision if you both need help."

"So, I expact we may be back home within a few days?" asked Jack.

"Yes, possibly," said Hunt. He hoped that his face did not reveal that he was being economical with the truth.

Hunt turned the subject to the time scale of Harry's forthcoming wedding and continued: "Although I'm not sure how the lady downstairs will feel about her groom disappearing at this point. Still, we have five weeks before the date that Harry ties the knot. That should be more than enough time. I'll get word to you via Sam while you're at Selmeston of the next steps. I'm assuming your Parson won't object to a visit from you?"

"If he's there. Parson mentioned visiting a younger sister in Hampshire at some point this summer. I'll need to contact him," said Jack. He shifted his position to stand thinking it would help and winced at the pain as he did so.

Hunt noted it. He offered a hand to help Jack up and added: "If your Parson is leaving for Hampshire, assuming you're in time to go with him it's ideal for you to sail to Jersey from Southampton. But we've talked enough for today. Give me a brief note for the Parson and I'll send a telegram for you. Rest up now and in two days, if you're able, and unless you hear to the contrary, leave for Sussex. If the Parson has already gone away go to Sam's in Brighton. I'll brief Sam and he may well travel with you if you're alone in case you need help. He and I have a well-established method of communicating now so he can play go between for you and I."

Jack nodded and reached for some paper, noting that Sam Curzon's work for Hunt had continued. That arrangement had been established during the Shah of Persia's intended visit to Brighton in June 1873. It had been after Sam's injuries had meant his discharge from the police. As Sam's father had died leaving a widowed other and Sam's four younger brothers, Hunt had given Sam work. Jack was glad for Sam as his source of income was secure thanks to Hunt.

Jack scribbled a few short sentences giving the reason for an unexpected visit. He added the need to see the solicitor about his will and the purchase of the Turnham Green cottage. He could kill two birds with one stone if the Parson would arrange for Mr Langton to pay a visit to Selmeston. He handed the paper to Hunt and hesitated, a question in his mind.

"Sir, I can see a man might lay low for a while in a place like Jersey, but expact you're in doubt it would be for long. If I find our quarry has left what then?"

"Then you follow," said Hunt.

"Only back to England?" Jack asked the question wanting to make sure he understood. He wanted confirmation they would only operate within their jurisdiction, but he was not expecting Hunt's answer.

"I doubt it," said Hunt, quietly.

Jack stared at the inspector. Hunt's look was enough.

Journeys had taken Jack between Sussex and London and Charlie Banks's wedding west of Portsmouth, but he had not travelled anywhere else. Jack's side ached but the sense of the unknown was calling, and his head throbbed with the rush

---

of excitement that he felt. Jack reduced the pain by again moving position, this time straightening his back and leaning against the wall. His face registered the discomfort and Hunt saw it. Would Jack be fit enough for what Hunt had in mind?

"To be fit for duty is one thing but with such a commission and in this state, sir? Perhaps in a week I'll feel differently as the healing takes hold but now, I can barely move without pain," said Jack. "I'm not certain what use I can be."

"Well, let's face that if we need to. Rest up for the next two days as Doctor Brown said and see how you get on. The train journey down to Sussex will be a good test," said Hunt.

Jack made a mental note to try and contact Ann Black before he left. Despite not being recognised as a doctor in England her medical degree from Paris might mean she could give him advice other than simply to rest. He had no intention of letting Hunt know he was doing that.

The time had gone as far as Hunt was concerned. He pulled out his watch and checked. He said: "I must go. It will take time to judge the situation and the decisions are not to be all yours. You'll report to Harry while he's with you. Let me know when you get a response from your Parson and I'll make sure you have what you need." Hunt hesitated as a thought occurred to him. "Look, do you remember what I said in February? That you should not share any of this with lovers, colleagues, or friends?"

"I do. Let me reassure you, sir, that there is no one at present that fits the term, "lover.""

Hunt noted the hard tone and looked away.

———

Jack frowned at the memory of Harriet's letter ending the relationship nearly a year ago. He had written to her after that, twice, as per the Parson's suggestion. Kind letters, devoid of the need that he felt, no mention in them of his repeated proposals. There had been no response from Harriet. Again, on the Parson's advice, Jack had let any further correspondence go by the board.

There was a silence between the two men and seconds went by while Hunt took on board that Jack's relationship with Harriet had not resumed. Well, more the better for such a commission as this, thought Hunt. Better there was no wife or children at this stage. His attention was drawn back as Jack was asking him a question.

"Sir, isn't this a lot of trouble to go to for a handful of diamonds that the owner will not miss? I understand the Queen's irritation and embarrassment that we didn't catch the thief but surely there's more important cases which we should spend our time on?"

"Yes, you have a point," Hunt said. "However, it's not the diamond theft that matters, it's what our ultimate quarry is involved with. This investigation is a means to an end, Jack. On that basis it's worth pursuing. We have three thefts for which we believe the thief is responsible. You witnessed two of them and you can identify the thief as I said from both the Docks theft and from the Alexandra Palace."

Hunt opened the door and said finally: "If it wasn't for that and my suspicion that the ultimate quarry we seek moves in the highest levels of society, even perhaps the Queen's company, I wouldn't commit the team this way. But I can't ignore how this man's lines have become blurred so that he wields so much power. We have both lost people from the force that we cared about in less than two years, due to one man's activities." Hunt paused as he recalled the facts.

At least three people had died, several had been injured irrevocably and those affected included two men who were good friends: a former inspector, Matthew Doyle and an ex-detective, Burgess. Both careers had been destroyed. Hunt had one more thing to say and he was still unsure whether he should let Jack in on his ultimate worry as someone Hunt worked with was leaking information to the crime group. But Hunt decided against disclosing his fear and chose to focus on a strategy for the future rather than dwelling on the trail of destruction wrought by one person. It was the healthier option.

Jack had nodded and remained silent while Hunt had retreated into introspection. Treating Hunt with deference he could hear the emotion in the inspector's voice. Jack reflected on his own situation as he had not gone untouched himself from that first murder case. The physical scars from a fight or exposure to the smoke in the fire were one thing. The psychological impact of the Faceless Woman case had remained a scar but was hidden in his own case in the last eighteen months. Neither he, nor Hunt, could remain on the side lines for those reasons alone.

And then there was a Queen's command, which could not be ignored.

*

―

It was eight o'clock that evening when Charlie Banks arrived at the West India Dock Cottage.

Jack had dozed in a chair after the evening meal and Rose and Mrs Phillips had sat talking quietly about the future. The knock came as Rose stifled a yawn. Jack had forgotten to mention that Charlie would call on his way home.

"Who could that be now?" asked Mrs Phillips, starting to get up, "I was about to make a hot drink."

"I'll go, Mother," said Rose. She opened the back door to a young constable in the process of removing his helmet. Habit made her note the police number.

"Are you in trouble, Constable?" Rose asked, opening the door wider as the uniform showed signs of the man having been in a struggle.

"Not now, Miss, but thank-you. I know I pretty much need cleanin' up but I came off better than the other man. I'm on my way 'ome and arranged to call in 'ere and see Jack about the cottage. It's Charlie Banks, Miss."

Although Jack spoke often of Charlie and Hannah Banks Rose had not met either of them. She swung the door wide and said: "Of course, come in, Jack's dozing."

Rose stepped back to let Charlie in, and he shyly walked to the kitchen.

"Mother, you've heard Jack speak of a colleague, Charlie Banks?" Rose called. "He's here to have a word with Jack. Do go through and have a seat, Charlie. I'll just wake Jack." Rose followed Charlie in and gently patted Jack's arm a few times until the eyes opened.

———

78

"Charlie's here," Rose said softly.

"We were about to make a hot drink, Charlie. Will you have a cup? You know my son, Ted, of course?" Mrs Phillips lifted the kettle off the range and poured the scalding water into the tea pot.

Charlie answered: "Sergeant Phillips to me, ma'am. I do indeed. Evenin' Jack, how are ya?"

Mrs Phillips swirled the hot water around three times inside the pot and then tipped it out into the sink. Four scoops of tea were shovelled into the teapot and through all this Jack tried to pull himself round, watching her actions and repeating in his mind: one spoonful per person and one for the pot.

"Charlie. How was the day?" asked Jack.

"Fair. And yourself?" asked Charlie.

"I'm brave, thank-you. A liddle tired but well looked after as always here," said Jack.

Rose noted the slip with the word little.

"Miss Cohen at the orphanage asked me to say she 'oped you would soon be on the mend," said Charlie. "She knew somat was wrong as soon as she saw me on patrol instead of you and said it took her back to last year after the fire. Oh, and she asked to be remembered to you. Apart from that I 'ad quite an interestin' case this evening."

Jack took a cup of tea from Rose. "Oh yes, what was that?"

"Ex-groom mutilated a 'orse. Said 'e 'adn't but the scullery maid said she'd seen 'im and 'e'd been laid off sick and needed lighter work and there wasn't any. So, the owner 'ad given 'im a testimonial and let 'im go."

———

79

"Sounds harsh," said Jack.

"Long term illness, not much the owner could do if there's no other work. Anyway 'e's in custody now." Charlie accepted the cup of tea from Mrs Phillips. She placed the sugar at his elbow, and he spooned it in like shovelfuls of snow.

"What is it he's supposed to have done to the poor animal?" asked Mrs Phillips.

"Cut the mane and tail off. Scullery maid said 'e 'ad a certain noise 'e made with 'is tongue when 'e went into the 'orses. Says she 'eard it when she was by the stables." Charlie took a mouthful of the tea. "That's right good."

"Bit of a weak story, Charlie," said Jack.

"I was thinking that. She didn't see him do anything to the horse?" asked Rose.

"We'll have the magistrate snickering at us," said Jack.

"Well, I know. But I 'ad the owner at me. The groom can cool 'is 'eels in a cell tonight and Sergeant Thick no doubt will probably let 'im go in the morning for lack of evidence. Put up a bit of a struggle, and I 'it a wall that had been white-washed." Charlie showed the underside of his sleeve.

Rose thought Charlie was older than Jack but not yet thirty. An interesting accent that she had not heard before and she did not know what to think of it. Further north than London, but where from exactly, she would not know. He had a scrawniness that smacked of lack of feeding as a child and she made up her mind to ask Ted what it was that had made the recruiter take Charlie Banks.

"I could sponge that tunic arm for you," Mrs Phillips offered.

"Thank-you Mrs Phillips, but my girl will do it fine once I'm 'ome."

Jack grinned at Charlie. "When did you start calling Hannah, "my girl?" It sounds like the Cockney, "Trouble and Strife," for wife."

"Trouble she'll never be, but my girl she always will be," Charlie said, proudly.

"That's lovely. I hope Harry will think like that about me after a few months of marriage," said Rose.

"No doubt of that," said Charlie, smiling.

"Oh, I don't know," Jack said, grinning. "I think he'll realise what a problem he's married and want to send you back."

"Someone's feeling better," said Mrs Phillips. "Oh …. As for taking Rose back …. What can I say?"

"Mother, you're as bad as Jack!" said Rose.

Mrs Phillips laughed. She said: "There you are, Rose. Harry's old enough to have studied a large sample and know a good thing when he sees it. He has eyes for no other, I'm sure. Now, Jack should tell Charlie about the house he wants to buy so that Mrs Banks isn't up all night, getting whitewash off that tunic. You and I have that cupboard to go through before we sleep tonight so why don't we start now."

Rose nodded.

"Well, Jack. This is a grand thing you're about to do," said Charlie as Rose and Mrs Phillips took their tea and went into the hall.

"If you are both sure about taking the cottage then it makes sense for me," said Jack. "Mother put it into my head to put money into bricks and mortar as she would say, and the trustees think it's a good idea for the future. It helps the trust grow in value according to the lawyer. But what about some food, Charlie? You're covering my beat as well as your own and it's been a long day. There's always bread and a good cheese here in the pantry. Rose would be the first to offer if she realised how long you'd worked," Jack nodded towards a door off the kitchen.

"If you're sure, then I will. My girl will 'ave a plate ready for me but I'm fair famished," said Charlie, getting up.

Talk paused while Charlie cut and buttered bread, putting thin slices of a crumbly cheese between two pieces. Jack waited for him to bring his sandwich in and sit down again before he described the cottage. Once Charlie had got through half of the sandwich Jack resumed: "The cottage needs a bit of work but there's two good bedrooms, Charlie."

"That sounds grand," said Charlie.

Jack nodded and explained: "There's two rooms, including the kitchen, downstairs. It's not a big place and, if you had a family, you'd probably want to go somewhere bigger. The cellars in a mess but we can fix that. It's only been used as a coal hole but we can put a window in where the coal shoot is and re-pave the floor so it could be used as a washroom, and storeroom for you. There's enough room out the back to build a small coal store with access from the alley. There are stairs down to the cellar from the garden. It's a nice bit of garden and I reckon with some planning you could make it work for your table. When would you transfer?"

"To 'ammersmith? I can go in a month. The order's got to be done. You know there's a purpose-built station now since 1872 on the Chiswick 'igh Road? Well, there's sixty constables and one wanting, so it might as well be me. There's a station at Bedford Park and Chiswick out of Waterloo on the London and South Western line, which says to me, the place will grow. Which side of the 'igh road is the Terrace?"

"South of Christchurch and the Green. You'd be about ten minutes walking from your front door to the Police Station," said Jack. "Good for a lodger working in the city with that railway into Waterloo."

"Sounds a good position. Do you mind me asking how much you'll 'ave to pay? "asked Charlie.

"The asking price is £450. There's a good long lease of years and an annual ground rent of £8. If you'll take it, Charlie I'll let Mr Langton know in a couple of days and he can get on with the buying side. You and Hannah can get things organised in the way you want them, but I doubt it would be ready in a month," said Jack.

"You forget what we come from Jack. If there's one room ready that will do for us. We'll work on the rest together. I'm one of many children and we all slept in one room. My girl and me, we'll do bravely together in our own place. There's just the matter of rent, Jack," said Charlie.

"Well, whatever you'd pay in lodgings. Once the place is ready for you to take a lodger, we can work out something different but it's putting the trust money in something that will increase it that's the idea, not to earn a lot from someone in rent. I'll rest easier knowing you're in it rather than someone who's a stranger. Do you understand?" Jack's brow furrowed as he tried to make it clear to Charlie that his intention was not to make money out of them.

"And per'aps one day it'd be a 'ome for yourself?" suggested Charlie, with a grin.

"Time will tell," said Jack. Alone, as he felt he was now, he needed to distance himself from the very idea. Jack shifted his position to ease the discomfort in his side.

"I should just say, Charlie," Jack continued, "that anything that needs spending to bring the place up to standard should be billed to the Trust. If you'll get records of what's to be done and let me have them, or I expact I can set up an arrangement with Mr Langton, the solicitor, to take them from you direct if you like. That might be quicker."

"It's the right time of the year to repair it," said Charlie. He noticed Jack was looking a little white around the gills. "You look weary an' I must go. My journey's easier in the light of a May night. I shan't be sorry to move to a gentler place. Let me know when and then we can give notice. I'll get off to the West India Dock station and take the train to cut my walkin' down back to York Street. At least from Stepney it's only a matter o' minutes."

"One more thing, Charlie," said Jack. "It may be a while before I'm back in Stepney so don't you go covering two beats for too long."

Charlie looked long at Jack. He said: "You off again?"

"Got to let the ribs heal," replied Jack.

—

84

"I see. No, tomorrow's the last time. Sergeant Thick's got a new man out with me in the mornin' and will see to 'im from then on. 'Ave a good night, Jack. whatever you're up to." Charlie turned to go.

"Are you off?" asked Mrs Phillips, as she came from the hall. She did not want to seem to be waiting for him to go so she resumed some packing she had left from the afternoon. Charlie's stringy build would worry her if he had been her son she decided.

"I 'ad some bread and cheese at Jack's invitation." Charlie explained to Mrs Phillips in his serious way. "Wouldn't want you to think I'd just 'elped myself. The bread took some cutting, it was so fresh. You'll notice it's not been cut well. I'll be off then."

"I'm glad you did," called Mrs Phillips as she went towards him, however her common sense then told her he would not shake hands.

"Well Jack," said Mrs Phillips, after Charlie had closed the door behind him. "I believe it's a miracle he survived to adulthood."

"Really? He's put-on weight since he and Hannah married. He eats well enough; you should have seen him tuck into that bread and cheese. Hannah's a good cook too."

"I would not have liked to see how thin he was before then. Now do you need help getting up the stairs?" Mrs Phillips asked. "I could do with some help wrapping china."

"I think I may have a relapse coming on," said Jack.

Four

A week before his annual holiday into Hampshire the Reverend Peter Fisher left his tile-hung cottage near the church and walked towards the Selmeston railway halt. It had been cold overnight, but a bright sun now shone on the "Parson," as he was locally known. Although no longer the incumbent of Selmeston he believed he would die with his boots on and that God's calling did not end at a certain age. Despite being well into his eighties he still patrolled the parish daily, having a word here and there, generally being the stalwart helper to the current vicar.

His thoughts were on the forthcoming visit of his young friend, Jack Sargent, when his housekeeper, Mrs Simcock, broke into his reverie.

"Good fortune means you don't have far to walk, Parson."

Peter Fisher grunted: "Not that we believe in fortune, do we Mrs Simcock. More the kindness of a gracious vicar at giving me a well-positioned cottage in my retirement, and God's blessing."

"That's right, Parson," said Mrs Simcock with a nod.

Peter Fisher waved an arm in farewell as he let himself out of the cottage and walked to the gate at the bottom of his garden path. Once through it into the lane he kept to the left of the stream, which meandered close to the path. There had been a good deal of rain that spring and he thought that the low bank was in danger of being washed away. The porous chalk Downs had fed the local springs to overflowing that

—

winter. However, as he looked up at the sky, Peter Fisher thought the weather had turned a corner and there would be no more rain that day. It was a lovely sight with all the trees and blossoms and the meadow flowers coming out. By midday it was likely to be a clear view and the few clouds that were left rolling up the sides of the hills towards Firle Beacon would have been burnt off by the sun.

Peter Fisher had formed a close relationship with Jack since his first visit last summer. He had been very keen to ensure his own role of trustee of the will left by Jack's parents and had liaised with his fellow trustees, the solicitor Langton, and the Coastguard Edward Croft. As far as Peter Fisher was concerned, he had assumed personal responsibility for what had happened to Jack as a child after his parent's funeral. It was an unreasonable assumption but nonetheless one the old Parson bore heavily.

In honour of Jack's pending visit Mrs Simcock had come in early that morning and Peter Fisher had left her with her hands covered with flour as she rolled out pastry and put ready batches of biscuits and scones. Bread had proved overnight in the kitchen and Peter Fisher had woken to the smell of fresh loaves in the final stages of cooking. He kept a good table generally, but today he was aware that Mrs Simcock as a cook was like a glorious steam ship in full power before one of Jack's visits.

By the Poor House, the Parson had caught up with the local sheep farmer, Tim Crutchley and his son, Martin, who were herding sheep towards the halt.

"Marnin' Parson," called Tim Crutchley, touching his cap. His son, Martin, did the same and then turned his attention back to the ewe he had been struggling to release from the hedge.

"A good morning to you, Mr Crutchley, Martin. Are you loading at the halt today?" asked Peter Fisher.

"We are, sir, for London. If you'll forgive us, we've to get on as the up train is due. Are you travelling today, Parson?" Crutchley asked.

"No, meeting my young friend, Jack Sargent. He's staying with me for a few days before I take my holiday," answered Peter Fisher.

"Will you be away awhile?" asked Crutchley.

"A week or so, it's my annual visit to my sister," replied Peter Fisher.

Any more conversation was stopped as Crutchley shouted to his son:

"What the Rabbits, Martin! Why it's never ye letting the yoe get past ye, surelye!"

Peter Fisher walked on towards the halt, leaving the two men struggling with the ewe. He took his watch out and checked the time. Slowly the two Crutchley men released the animal from the brier. The agent Robson, who held responsibility to the local landowner to develop the farm which the Crutchley's worked, was already by the line and he acknowledged the old vicar as he approached.

"Not as many as last year from the Crutchley's by the looks of things, Mr Robson, or is my memory faulty?" asked Peter Fisher.

"I'd not be the man to say you were wrong on anything, Parson. No, you're right about the number being light but there's good reason for that as they've had bad fortune this spring." Robson shifted his weight off his left leg and looked around for a crate to sit on. Lowering himself down Robson continued: "And now old Crutchley is down to just Martin as the men are leaving for London. It was last winter that did it. He could only pay them 10 shillings and they can get more in the city. I tell you, sir, they're barely above existing. Martin tells me he feels there's no future in it, despite the animals being finest Southdown Sheep. A great shame as it should be a good business, what with access to London for fat stock."

"Yes, indeed," said Peter Fisher. "Hard for Mr Crutchley if his son goes. Hard for the area as we're losing our workforce. A good many daughters have already gone, and I see the young men coming and going to work the building sites up in London to help pay rents."

Robson nodded. "Crutchley's land's in a good position and the Southdown breed has flourished since Ellman's day, but now with the loss of labour, the thefts, and the changes in farming operations and the need for more capital, I can't see them lasting. I've asked his Lordship for rent reductions so they can carry on. That's not likely, though, as the estate has had a lot of expenditure on the farms and he's not too certain of things in the future. Cost of capital is more per year than the rents bring in, you see."

"Difficult. And there you have the problem Mr Robson," said Peter Fisher. "The landowners naturally want to increase their return on an investment. But Crutchley is concerned about his family's interest. I believe a lot of the local farmers have been lending each other labour at busy times of the year, paying them in kind." Peter Fisher looked back at the sheep farmer and his son. Another year he thought, and Martin will not be here. Turning back to Robson Peter Fisher asked: "Did I hear right, you said thefts?"

"That's right. Crutchley lost a significant number of pregnant ewes in the spring, many of them taken from the fields near the drove road. He was hit twice over so to speak. Very distressed he was," explained Robson.

"Understandably. I suppose the constable hasn't found anything?" asked Peter Fisher.

"He's got his work cut out patrolling the area on foot. There's only got to be a fight at the Barley Mow and he's enough to deal with," Robson said. He thought for a moment and added:

"Funnily enough on both the nights of the fights there were strangers in. They started arguments and once fighting started they cut and ran according to the story. The constable was nicely occupied pursuing the perpetrators but of course, found no one and by the time he was back, singularly exhausted I should say, the sheep had probably already been moved. The rustlers must have dispersed them somehow into smaller groups. Crutchley didn't discover anything was amiss until the following morning. I wondered if the old smuggling tunnels were being used to move them."

"That's the problem with keeping an eye on the sheep, it's impossible as they're everywhere," said Peter Fisher, glancing to the lower levels of the Downs.

"And too good a market in London. It makes the rustling worthwhile. I suspect the animals are moved to a location and then butchered. That way the brand is never of any use in finding them. Ah, here's the train coming now." Robson nodded and the sound of the engine grew giving the two men notice of the train's imminent arrival.

"Are you travelling today, Parson?" asked Robson.

"No, I have a visitor for a few days. The young constable from London whom you met last summer," answered Peter Fisher.

"Perhaps he could give Constable Brook some help?" suggested Robson.

"Unlikely this time. The reason for Jack's visit is to recover from an injury." Peter Fisher patted his side and said, "Ribs, after a fight. He's not here for long."

The train slowed to the halt and Jack's head appeared through the open carriage window.

"*Parson,*" called Jack, waving. He opened the carriage door before the train stopped but this time did not follow through with a jump down as was his usual way. He looked at the man standing next to Peter Fisher, remembering the face but not the name.

"Good to see you but carefully does it, Jack," Peter Fisher responded. Robson caught the leather bag as Jack dropped it.

"You remember Mr Robson, his Lordship's agent?" asked the Parson.

"I do," said Jack, climbing down. Ah, that was it, he thought, recalling the brief meeting during a stay at the Parson's cottage. He extended a hand to Robson. "You called at the cottage last summer." The two men shook hands warmly.

"Mr Sargent, isn't it? Let me carry your bag for you. I hear you've had an injury?"

"I have, Mr Robson," Jack answered. "That's kind of you but I deliberately kept the contents light. It's just some positions I get myself into more than others that cause the pain. The end of the day it starts to pain."

"Crutchley, load the sheep, will you? I'll be back shortly," called Robson. Crutchley senior responded sharply but Robson turned away.

"I'll walk back with you both to the Parson's cottage to lend a hand with the bag anyway. Don't mind Crutchley, he's out of sorts. Can't say I blame him really, sheep rustling here and now he's losing his men to work in London. He's sour at life. How is London?"

"Not as fresh as here," answered Jack. His eyes went back to the two men struggling with the sheep as he followed Robson away from the track. "You have a constable here now, don't you?"

"We do, Jack, but there's quite some ground that the man has to cover," answered Peter Fisher.

Robson edged his way around the old Parson to give himself more space in the lane with the bag. Jack nodded his thanks.

—

As they walked Robson said: "At one time Crutchley would have posted his own men on watch but so many have left."

"Not much one constable can do against a gang," said Jack.

"Well, with all Crutchley's men leaving for better paid work I don't see what he can do, either. Who knows a few of them might end up working in the police like you have? I recall the Parson mentioned you were over at Battle on a farm before you went to London."

"That's right," said Jack, he stared into the distance, registering a change. "Am I right? Has the Long Man of Wilmington turned yellow?"

"You aren't imagining things," said Peter Fisher, chuckling, "Reverend William de St. Croix has outlined it in yellow brick, but I gather the Duke of Devonshire disputes he's got the outline right. The Eastbourne Gazette said there were Roman bricks found nearby while the restoration of the giant was underway. The place has been crawling with archaeologists ever since."

"Where are they all staying?" asked Jack, wondering if the man he had met at Pett Level the previous year was among them.

"Lewes mainly," said Peter Fisher. "Summer has been a profitable time for the town each year since workmen found a large crock full of Celtic axe heads, just south of the Wilmington Railway Gate, back in '61. This year's Roman finds will guarantee the historical interest carries on, and the landlords and ladies of Lewes will benefit."

"It's good someone's turning a profit," said Robson.

—

The three men walked at a casual pace until they reached Peter Fisher's gate. Robson had noted Jack's respectable clothes and wondered at a constable dressed so well. For his own part Jack had donned the clothes Hunt had sent him a year ago for the Brighton surveillance.

Jack buttoned up his jacket as the early May wind off the Downs was searching. However, Peter Fisher shrugged the cold off, so used was he to the area's weather. Turning to Robson the Parson took it as a natural possibility that he should invite the agent in for refreshment, but Robson declined the invitation and turned to go.

"I wondered if you would mind my suggesting to the constable that he comes and has a chat while you're here?" Robson asked Jack.

"Of course, but I can't see what good it would do? I've no experience of rural policing," said Jack.

"But you do of rural matters and it may be helpful. His colleagues are mainly in the towns. Some go as far as laughing at the problem of sheep rustling," said Robson.

"I suppose it would be useless of me to say that you are supposed to be having a rest?" chipped in Peter Fisher. "It's only five days since your injury."

Jack smiled at the concern and said: "Not at all. And after I've explained you'll realise that resting isn't the whole reason that I'm here, Parson. Although I'll ache waiting so long to sit in a comfortable chair such as the one in your parlour. If it's just a chat and no action, then what's the harm?"

Jack turned to the agent and explained: "The Police Surgeon found I'd two cracked ribs from a kicking, you see Mr Robson, so resting a few more days after the travelling is the order."

"You're a strong young man and no doubt you'll be moving around normally soon. I'll mention you're here to Constable Brook but will suggest he leaves coming for a few days. A good-day to you, Parson, Mr Sargent." Robson turned to walk back towards the Halt.

"We'll be quiet here except for when Mr Langton is to come on the twelfth. I got a message to him about you making a will," said Peter Fisher. They had reached the gate into the garden. The Parson continued: "Perhaps after that we can give Constable Brook a bite of supper and the two of you can chew the cud? I leave for Hampshire on Wednesday next week. What are your movements when I go?" asked Peter Fisher, lifting the latch of the kitchen door.

Jack's answer was delayed by the greeting from Mrs Simcock and within minutes he was told he looked in need of a good meal. Jack laughed, imagining what Rose would make of that. Mrs Simcock was ready to seat him and put a plate beside him of newly baked biscuits, but Jack remained at the door as he had not removed his boots. He looked around for something to sit on and dragged over a stool with his foot which had been placed for such a purpose.

"Thank-you, Mrs Simcock. I'm fair chokly. How is your family?" asked Jack.

Mrs Simcock poured tea as she answered: "My youngest lad is finally shooting up and is nearly your size. Here, Parson, the shortbread is ready." She proceeded to place tea and the freshly baked biscuits next to where the Parson had sat to remove his own boots.

"It's a good job you only come on high days and holidays, and when you're injured. I would grow rather fat from all the industry in this kitchen when there's a visit of yours pending," said Peter Fisher.

"I expact you live like a king every day, Parson," said Jack, picking a shortbread off the plate. Satisfied, Mrs Simcock moved back to her preparations for the midday meal while Jack worked his left boot off by digging the toe of his right foot into the back of the boot. Peter Fisher noticed that neither of the boots were fully done up. A sign Jack could not bend.

"You'll be a few weeks resting, young Jack. We should get a doctor to have a look at you in a week and see how you are doing. I can always delay my visit to my sister's, you know," said Peter Fisher. "We can have a quiet time of it, a gentle stroll, no climbing, no digging over the garden, just some gentle maintenance of the blooms as they start."

"It's about your visit to your sister's I wanted to talk to you, Parson. It would suit my Inspector Hunt if I travelled with you next week, as I need to get to Southampton," said Jack.

Peter Fisher's expression did not change, but his gaze made Jack feel the Parson's eyes could see into his soul. Years of being taken into many confidences had developed skills of listening with a completely set face. Aware his housekeeper was listening Peter Fisher picked up his cup and plate and led the way into the sitting room.

———

"We'll have a sit for a while Mrs Simcock," Peter Fisher called over his shoulder.

"Very good, Parson," his housekeeper answered, being used to the exodus from her kitchen when confidential information was to be passed.

Jack followed, gathering up several shortbread biscuits with a grin at their creator. It was better to get things on the table now, he thought, despite Inspector Hunt's warning not to put the old man into the picture completely. That was not the relationship Jack and the Parson had and Jack had already decided to explain his visit.

"So, another mission?" asked Peter Fisher, not looking at Jack, while he tidied some books he had left on the table. "How adventurous is this one going to be in your current state?"

"I know I'm to rest or I'll be solly," said Jack.

"A tottering state is that? Some would say you're in such a way now. I noticed your boots; you can't even bend to do them up. Were you going to eat all that shortbread, or could you pass a piece over here?" Peter Fisher held his hand out for a biscuit.

Jack smiled, both at the Parson's understanding of the dialect and the sense of concern in the old man's tone. Jack knew his work could become dangerous, but that sense suited him. However, he also realised that in his current state he would not be that useful if the situation demanded something more than being a shadow.

Peter Fisher said: "I tell you, Jack, when we are young, we are careless of our health." The old man glanced out of the window as if searching for something he had lost.

Continuing he said: "I remember never believing that anything would stop me. I am not of the same opinion now. You need time to let the ribs heal. I'm sure you've already been told that. What does your good friend Doctor Ann say on the subject?"

"I haven't seen her, I heard she was unwell which does worry me. Doctor Brown said Ann was busy helping with the move of the hospital, but I'd thought to write to her later and get an opinion about my ribs and to let her know she's thought of. May I mention your good wishes?" Jack asked.

"Of course, send my best regards. Tell her to come and see me with that husband of hers. Was it Doctor Brown that tended to you?"

"Yes, the Police Surgeon, and he knows what he's about. He did say it would be weeks. I was to be on desk duty at the station. But I've been given a special duty, Parson, and I'm afraid I can't give you all the details. I'm not supposed to tell you anything, but I can't live like that with you. There's a thief and I'm the only one who has seen him. I've been involved in witnessing two thefts by the same man and there's a third his description fits, only that one has international connections." Jack paused and sipped his tea.

"As grand as that sounds Jack, surely there's someone else that could go?" asked Peter Fisher.

98

"That's where the complications come, Parson. There's also an order from a high source and I'm afraid they involve me on a special duty. I don't think I can tell you all the details, but I want to come clean and explain that rest here is not the full reason I've come."

"A high source? Moving in exalted circles now? How did you get yourself into that situation?" asked Peter Fisher as he sat back in his armchair. He pictured the small boy he had known, seeing him playing on the rug in the front room of his parent's home in Bexhill. Jack's mother took time away from the business accounts she kept, to entertain their vicar on his unexpected calls. His mind then strayed to the scene of the same nine-year old standing by his parent's grave, holding the hand of an aunt who afterwards abandoned him to an orphanage. Lost years and his own failure, as the Parson saw it, but really it was due to the circumstances. For whatever good reason he had not discharged the duty entrusted to him by the parents he believed God had given him a further opportunity to help Jack. Jack's mother and father had stated three trustees would keep a watching brief for their child's welfare. As their former vicar and their friend Peter Fisher felt the failure keenly. He shook the memories off. Sometimes in the early hours of the morning he felt the distress. Lost years for Jack when it could all have been so different. Well, the child had become a man, and the old vicar had tried in the last year to put it right. As a result, he had formed a growing friendship with the young constable, which had personally brought the old vicar great pleasure. But Jack was in the middle of answering his question and Peter Fisher must pay attention.

"It was an accident really," said Jack. "I was at Windsor one day with an inspector, just to help him with his mother's garden. He thought it would help my chest to get out of London." Jack had the Parson's attention on the mention of the location.

"On duty?" Peter Fisher asked.

"No, it was on a rest day, helping with his mother's garden," Jack said, meeting the Pastor's all-seeing gaze. "It's Inspector Hunt. He goes over once a month. She lives in a tied cottage on the Windsor estate and probably should have gone years ago after her husband died but the Queen gave permission for her to stay. A kindness but one which has become a burden to the inspector because of the distance." Jack paused. How much more should he tell? Jack saw the clear gaze of the man before him and smiled.

"Inspector Hunt thought I would benefit from getting out of London for fresher air and we spent some time together in the spring cold. He was to see the Queen that afternoon, but she came early in her carriage as Mr Disraeli was coming."

"So, it was February," said Peter Fisher recalling the election date and the change of government.

"Yes, and bitter weather, too early for any tilling of the soil. We were commissioned to catch a thief. I expact I've probably said more than I should and it's a bit more involved than that but I'm telling you so that you realise it's not something I can pass over. It's a Queen's command. Do you see?"

The pause was heavy.

"What was stolen?" asked Peter Fisher finally.

"I think I would prefer not to go into it any deeper. It was something belonging to a foreign dignitary, causing embarrassment to our monarch. The trail had gone cold but in the past few months the inspector managed to find there'd been a sighting of the thief at a port." Jack looked to block the subject further by reaching for the paper on the table in front of him.

Peter Fisher thought it was a strange action of the inspector's, to take a young constable to his mother's home. Could it have been deliberate?

Peter Fisher instinctively followed Jack's action with his eyes and looked at the headlines. Then his eyes swivelled to his bookshelves behind Jack.

"And your trip to Hampshire could involve you leaving from a port to follow.... where did you say when you were in the kitchen? Portsmouth, or Southampton? Ah yes, you said it would suit your inspector for you to go to Southampton. Because.... you're to travel somewhere else. France? And because you're injured you can maintain the façade of having time to rest here and accompanying me into Hampshire, from where you will slip away. How convenient for your inspector. Now, let me see, where did I put that Bradshaw's guide?" Peter Fisher got up from his chair and pulled the guide off the shelf.

"Ah, here we are," he continued, "And I believe I had a flyer from Thomas Cook & Son when I was up in St. Paul's last week. Cook's headquarters are in Ludgate Circus now, you know."

Jack shook his head and smiled. Peter Fisher had said this as if it would mean something to his listener. Jack watched as the old vicar found Cook's tours on a second shelf and placed them both on the table next to Jack. Sitting back in his chair again Peter Fisher looked back into his own past.

"I met her myself, you know," said Peter Fisher.

"The Queen?" asked Jack, surprised.

"Not as Queen but as the Princess Victoria, in the 1830's."

Jack sat forward with interest and Peter Fisher carried on. He said: "So that she wouldn't get bored with her studies and also so we, the people could see her, she used to come with her mother, the Duchess of Kent," Peter Fisher smiled at the memory of another time. Continuing he said: "They stayed at the Earl of Liverpool's place at Buxted. I believe she was great friends with his daughters. She came over several years, often riding through Lewes on a pony, even presenting a cup at the Lewes races. In those days they went to Brighton as well."

Jack's common sense told him he could be open: "How did you find her then?" Jack asked.

"Nervous, frankly," answered Peter Fisher. "She was young, Jack. And you? What did you think of our Queen?"

"At times, sharp and very much in control. At other's full of grief and a bit rambling, frankly," said Jack. "The eyes can look sorrowful one minute and sharp the next. I was surprised at how much she said to the inspector, but she clearly trusted him. She knew him on the estate as a child, you see, and he was supposed to have his father's job. But I was there, and she didn't know me, so it surprised me things were discussed."

"But you were with him, your inspector, and presumably she took it that you were under his direction. A man she trusts brings with him another policeman and that tells her your ilk," said Peter Fisher. He turned a prolonged and intense look on Jack and asked: "Do you think it was deliberate?"

"What? That he took me there? Yes, I told you it was for my health," Jack explained again.

"So that a successor is seen to be trusted by someone who has confided in the inspector for some time? Tell me, for whom was he giving that sign to, your inspector?"

"I'm just a constable. I doubt there's anything to it, Parson," Jack brushed the idea off.

"Perhaps you're right, time will tell," said Peter Fisher. "Whatever the motive behind the Inspector's invitation that day the outcome is that you're involved." Peter Fisher changed his mood, managing himself despite the foreboding that he felt. "So, where are you sailing to?"

"There's been a sighting of the thief in Jersey," said Jack.

"That's why its Southampton then," said the Parson, nodding.

"Yes. I had thought of seeing some friends in Brighton before we go," said Jack.

"That was Sam, as I remember, and the hotelier?" asked Peter Fisher.

Jack nodded: "There's a few people I'd like to see. It's been almost a year and I don't like the idea of time going on too long." Jack paused. Had he said too much? Jack thought that the Parson had some fanciful ideas but continued: "Do you remember Sam was working for Inspector Hunt? And Burgess and his wife were very good to me last year at the Old Ship Hotel. I wouldn't like to lose that contact. There were also a couple of policemen I wanted to take the opportunity to see and a friend working at a hotel."

"The same young lady to whom you gave a rose? So, there still is no contact from Harriet?" asked Peter Fisher.

Jack was taken aback at how the Parson had remembered the detail in Harriet's last letter. He shrugged but explained: "No, I've not heard from Harriet at all, and I gave up writing after my second letter. It was what you suggested but that's not the reason I want to see Mary. I would try and see her anyway."

Jack paused again. Peter Fisher waited. Then Jack laughed: "No match-making, Parson," he said.

"Which I never have done, but for what it's worth my opinion of Mary is that you would be very fortunate," said Peter Fisher. After a small hesitation he added, "I was in Brighton for a meeting last month. I took tea at the Royal and was served by a young waitress called Mary. I assumed she was the same young lady to whom you had given the rose."

Jack looked at Peter Fisher warily. "You mean you went deliberately to weigh her up, make sure about her?"

"No, but as a trustee, and I hope, a friend, I formed an opinion. I needed tea somewhere. I naturally don't want to see you alone in your life, Jack. She blushed when I mentioned your name, by the way." Peter Fisher looked out of the window, a small smile tweaking the corners of his mouth.

Jack screwed a piece of the shortbread between his fingers until the crumbs fell onto the floor. Remembering himself he bent down and picked them up, looking across at the Parson as he deposited the crumbs onto a plate. He had no reason to be angry, but he had to admit that the old vicar's suspicions of Inspector Hunt had unsettled Jack. It was also the thought that something may happen to the Inspector and how that would leave himself if called on by the Queen. Hunt had, after all, hinted at the same thing. And this business of seeing Mary in Brighton. What was the harm? Jack asked himself. He shook the mood off, and his natural humour got the better of him. Jack subsided into a chuckle and said: "Poor girl, no doubt you get away with murder because of your collar. But there is nothing there, Parson, except friendship. Can't a young constable and a waitress be friends?" asked Jack.

"Friendship is an excellent way to start. And yes, I do take advantage because of my calling, but only out of concern for your well-being and happiness. A year is a long time not to hear from someone you were fond of. No-one would think badly of you for finding a fresh romance now. It's your decision after all."

"I would have gone through fire for Harriet," said Jack, staring at the bookcase. His eyes saw other things than the beautiful editions. He made the effort to look at Peter Fisher, but his eyes flicked back to the leather-bound books.

"I know," said Peter Fisher.

Jack said: "But as she wants it so it will be. Sometimes I dream of her and she's somewhere a little ahead of me and I can't get to her. I'm trying to but she always eludes me. Other times I'm searching for her and I can't find her. Not contacting her is the hardest thing and I've accepted that must be the way, but I can't do the impossible and forget her."

There was a movement in the doorway and Jack came out of his reverie. Mrs Simcock stood with a jug of hot water for the teapot. She looked embarrassed but Peter Fisher nodded for her to come in. While his housekeeper was in the room, he changed the subject. He said: "Anyway, to go back to your health an idea occurs to me. If I delayed my visit to my sister a couple of days and we travelled to Hampshire on Saturday May sixteenth what say you to the idea of us boarding and lodging with Sam and his mother for a few nights before that? Assuming of course that they have room?" suggested Peter Fisher.

"A good idea as it serves to kill two birds with one stone," said Jack. "How quickly can I get word to Sam?"

"Write a brief note for a telegram and perhaps, when Mrs Simcock leaves, she will take it with the money down to the halt to give to the guard on the next London train," suggested Peter Fisher, glancing at the lady.

Mrs Simcock dropped a little curtsey and smiled at her employer. She said: "I'll happily do it, sir and if you include a tip for him the guard will see it home to the very door for you, The next train is at half past the hour."

*

106

It was the thirteenth of May and as a prospective property owner Jack began the journey from Lewes for his second visit to Brighton in a year. With him went the elderly Peter Fisher whose trunk had been collected by cart for the railway the previous day. Jack's will had been dealt with by the solicitor, Mr Langton, who had been briefed over a good dinner on Monday evening on the purchase of the terraced cottage in Turnham Green. The man had his instructions to go ahead with the purchase and Jack had named the Croft children, Martha, and Andrew, as his beneficiaries with Langton and Peter Fisher as trustees.

"Of course, they're no relation to you," Langton had said, pointing out the obvious.

"But if something happens to me, they'll benefit, and it would be a happiness to their parents. I've none other to leave it to," Jack said.

Langton had turned his attention to the other issue that gave him disquiet. He said: "Forgive me, Reverend, at pointing this out but we should also have another Trustee who is a little younger than yourself," Langton said.

"I agree, Langton, but it's a question of who? And what happens when Jack marries and produces progeny of his own?" asked Peter Fisher.

"That's not likely," said Jack.

"Time will tell," said Peter Fisher.

"I can take care of that in the drafting," Langton said in his most assuring tone. He waved away the difficulties with a hand and said: "And you never know what will develop in years to come. You presumably would like the Croft children to have a gift in the likely event of you marrying and having children of your own?" asked Langton

"If that ever happened, of course," said Jack. "A good one, perhaps for their education so they see some benefit."

"I'll have that ready for you on your return from Southampton," said Langton.

Jack looked sharply at Peter Fisher, who gave an almost imperceptible shake of his head.

"Perhaps have the draft sent to my sister's in Hampshire," suggested Peter Fisher. "One never knows with policemen and we can get it witnessed and back to you quickly."

"Excellent," said Langton. "As we have that business out of the way I'll get on my way home. Thank Mrs Simcock for yet another good meal and my best wishes for your journey, gentlemen on the thirteenth."

*

Sam Curzon had received the telegram from Jack enquiring if there were two rooms for paying guests from the thirteenth of May for three nights. Delighted at the prospective visit of Jack and his old Parson Sam made the announcement to the family.

"About time, it's too long since we saw him," said Sam's grandmother.

"He was going to take us fishing," said Luke, a younger Curzon brother, recalling a promise from the previous June.

"Well, he may not be able to do that this time," said Sam. "He's injured, two cracked ribs, so a boat trip will be out. But we can go anyway, I'll get the name of the fisherman from Jack and we can all go."

Sam sent a firm response back to the small cottage in Selmeston that the rooms were reserved for the Parson and Jack. He also sent word to Inspector Hunt that Jack had made contact as anticipated and would visit Brighton and stay with the Curzon's for a few nights before travelling into Hampshire.

Inspector Hunt had decided that Sam could wait to brief Jack until the thirteenth of May. Until then Jack and the Parson continued a gentle existence, trimming the early roses and tying back the Canterbury bells which had not yet flowered in the Parson's west facing garden. Jack was soon moving about the village as if nothing was wrong.

By midday on the thirteenth of May Jack and the Parson arrived in Brighton. They had made an early start as the Parson kept regular habits, rising at five o'clock to accompany the milk round and have a word with those in the parish who were up.

Mrs Curzon and Sam had prepared the two guest rooms during the morning and the younger boys went off to school with the expectation that Jack would be there with his tall stories on their return.

However, not everyone was as satisfied with travel arrangements on the thirteenth of May and a prospective hostess in Windsor was irritated by a delay.

The expected arrival of the Emperor of Russia and his entourage was delayed as his yacht went aground. The Queen was informed that instead of arriving at Dover at half past eleven that morning the Emperor's new time of seven in the evening was more likely.

Queen Victoria issued an instruction that everyone should be put off until later and afterwards promptly went for a drive around Windsor. A nightmare ensued as all the people were crowding into the town not knowing that the Emperor had been delayed.

Seeing the funny side of this, the Queen returned to the Great Park and as Mrs Hunt's cottage was on the way she ordered her coachman to stop so that she could share the joke that "Tom," as she called Inspector Hunt, would be glad he was out of it, and she sorely wished that she was too.

As the Queen's carriage pulled away, she called back to Mrs Hunt: "What a lovely day, so warm. You'll miss that here. Well, I must go and rest as they'll now be so late. Alix will be arriving shortly."

So, she does know I'm going eventually, thought Mrs Hunt.

Lord Paget, the Queen's Chief Equerry, served as her personal assistant. He met the Queen on her return to explain that the Emperor would not arrive until nine o'clock that evening, or possibly even ten. She was quite fond of her Equerry, as he had worn her portrait around his neck when appointed as a young man, even placing a copy around the neck of his Golden Retriever, known as Mr Bumps.

Elsewhere in the Queen's kingdom a young constable was enjoying a game of draughts by half-past eight that evening. In Brighton Jack was well fed and over their game, which Sam was winning, felt lighter in spirits than he had for some while. Peter Fisher had taken up a position in the Curzon garden with a rug over his knees and his latest novel was ready at his side.

The Royals at Windsor, however, had not dined and only taken some small refreshment when a telegram arrived explaining that the Emperor's party would not arrive at Windsor until almost ten o'clock. The Queen decided to dress and by nine-thirty the royal party went across to the State Rooms.

"Alix," the Princess of Wales, had a cold and could be heard sneezing. Even the Queen's stare would not deter the poor woman. Eventually the Queen gave her attention to the flowers and the Yeoman of the Guard who were lining the grand staircase.

By a quarter past ten word was brought that the train carrying the Emperor's party had arrived in Windsor. The royal party went down to meet the Emperor's carriage as it arrived and at half past ten the Escort came into view followed by the Emperor's party.

But in Brighton Jack and Sam decided by a quarter to eleven that they had talked enough, and it was time to retire for the night. The Queen, however, in Windsor was about to sit down to supper.

Mrs Curzon had no such grand ending to her day, kneading bread and completing the blacking of the range

Sam poked his head into the kitchen and asked: "Can't it wait until morning, Mother? It's eleven o'clock."

"I can't imagine when I will do it if not now," Mrs Curzon said. "Are you both finished for the night?"

"Yes, all done. Jack's gone up. It seems from my instructions that he is not to have a quiet life although I doubt he would want one if he had the option."

"As an injured man," Mrs Curzon said, "surely he's not expected to put himself in the way of harm?"

"That's what I'm told," said Sam. "He may not be able to help himself knowing him as I do. But he won't be going alone."

"That's good, you said there would be two other policemen with him. Is the Parson still up?" asked Mrs Curzon.

"No, he went to bed a good hour ago. We were able to get on with the arrangements as a result. I've saved some time tomorrow by covering the ground with Jack tonight. I can help you with those rooms in the morning."

Mrs Curzon wiped her hands and surveyed her hard work. It would do. She brushed an imaginary speck from her son's sleeve. He was putting on weight at last and looked better for it, although his hair would never grow back again. His colour was better though, the best she had seen since his poisoning, and he was getting his looks back. At least she hoped that a certain Welsh music teacher who was coming to tea on Sunday with her mother would think so.

"I'll be off to London on Friday, Mother."

"*What?* That's out of the blue, isn't it? All this back and forth suddenly," said Mrs Curzon.

"Well, we knew it could happen. Things to do with Jack's trip." Sam smiled as an idea occurred to him. "Why don't you come with me and do some shopping for yourself?"

"What and leave everything here?" said Mrs Curzon.

"Grandma can cope with getting the boys off to school and Jack and the Parson only need breakfast," suggested Sam. 'They'll be out visiting later. We could do a stew which Grandma only has to dish up for the boys and our guests. No-one needs the other rooms 'til next week. We'll be back before seven in the evening. Think on it."

"Alright, I will," said Mrs Curzon. "Any plans for tomorrow?"

"Morning refreshments with the Burgesses at the Ship, so that Jack sees some friends and introduces the Parson to them. I think a couple of local policemen may call in for breakfast by the way. I can get it ready and it will be after the boys have left for school. No need for you to worry about being here."

"That is a polite way of saying leave us to it, Mother, which I am happy to do." Mrs Curzon patted Sam's arm. "I'll get off to the market early that way. But I'll lay up now so there's less to do in the morning for you."

Looking at Sam as he lifted the homemade marmalade from last year from the cupboard and placed it in the middle of the table, Mrs Curzon asked: "When will you speak to Eleanor?"

"As soon as I see her," said Sam trying to keep a straight face. "It would be a little strange if I didn't say hello."

"You know what I mean," said Mrs Curzon. "*Propose.*"

Five

By the time breakfast came to an end the next morning Luke Curzon had become the spokesman for Sam's younger brothers:

"You did promise, you know," said Luke, giving Jack what Grandma termed the evil eye.

"Quite right, I did. Well, if your mother says it's alright, and Sam can take you, I'll see if the fisherman I know is at the shore today. If I can I'll set it up for you. I can't come this time but for the next sea trip I hope to. Once my ribs have healed." Jack smiled at the change in the expression on the boys' faces.

"Where are your manners, boys?" said Mrs Curzon.

"Thank-you, Jack," four boys said, with varying levels of enthusiasm.

"Come on, let's get you all off to school and then I'll be off to the market. What time do your friends come, Jack?" asked Mrs Curzon.

"Sam's set it up, I'm not sure," said Jack.

"They'll be here after half past eight, that's as close to a time they could give. Field tells me they've news for us, apparently," explained Sam.

"Good news, I hope," Jack said as he stood to pick up a tray covered with an embroidered cloth, under which was Peter Fisher's breakfast.

"I'll take the Parson's tray up now," said Jack, "Good he's decided to breakfast in his room. He's up at five o'clock each morning when he's at Simpson but said when on holiday he lays in."

"Jack, if you're going down to the sea front would you bring back some fish for dinner?" Mrs Curzon asked. "I had thought to use the stew that's in the slow oven but fish straight from the catch would make a nice change. The stew will do for tomorrow."

"Gladly," said Jack and he smiled across at Mrs Curzon, recalling how different she was now, a year on from her husband's death, to the bereft woman in black who had walked with him on that day he had found the fisherman. Sam had been right that the move to Brighton would be good for her. It had been good for them all.

Jack said: "I can see if there's any Sole. If there's enough, I can take a good sized one for Burgess as well. I was thinking the Parson and I could get off about ten from here. That gives us time enough to walk it and see the fisherman."

Shortly after half-past eight Jack opened the front door to the penetrating gaze of two detectives: Sergeant James Field and Constable Shaw Hockham. As on their first meeting Field gave Jack the once over. It was his way. Jack stifled a laugh as he pumped both men's hands up and down.

Field was another East Sussex man who had been a labourer before he joined the police and he still carried his heavy build with him. Although now in his forties he seldom got to use the strength across the shoulders. Behind him, the portly build of Constable Shaw Hockham filled Jack's view.

"My partner in crime," said Jack to Shaw, who patted Jack on the shoulder. Together they had searched the cliffs near Fairlight almost a year before and Shaw's jovial face brought out Jack's ready smile. Sam, who had remained by the kitchen door nodded to the two Brighton men. It had been a while even for him living in the town since he had seen them.

"Understand you have some disreputable guest on the premises, Mr Curzon?" said Field to Sam. That broke the ice.

"Nothing we can't handle," Sam said.

The four men laughed together. The greetings and brief news finally over Sam led the way into the kitchen and started to lay up the table. Despite his reassurances to his mother the previous night Mrs Curzon had still left fresh bread for them and hard boiled the eggs. All that was left for Sam to do was to slice the ham onto a serving plate and put it into the middle of the table. This he did, presenting it with a flourish to his guests. He followed it up with the loaf of bread and the bowl of eggs. Shaw made himself useful and started to slice the bread. It was a sight as it fell apart into chunks being still so warm. Hands still reached across to get it, regardless.

Helping himself to ham and eggs, Field said: "I hear you're seeing the Burgesses later. I was due to see him over an attempted theft. Mind if I walk down with you?"

"Of course, you can," said Jack, "If we can go via the sea front and try and find a fisherman that I used last year it would mean I can arrange a trip for Sam's brothers. It's a point of honour as I made a promise to them that I'd take them fishing when I was next here. I've promised Mrs Curzon to bring back a good-sized Sole, too and as it's a fish Burgess enjoys, I can get one for him."

"I remember that lunch," said Field, "It was the day we met wasn't it?"

Jack helped himself to ham and bread, spreading the butter thickly. He replied: "Yes, I'd forgotten."

"How's our doctor Mrs Black these days, or should I call her Doctor George as she was to us?" asked Shaw, mentioning the alias Ann had used at Pett Level.

"Not too well, I hear," said Jack. "I sent her a letter last week to get her advice on the cracked ribs. I'd not seen her for a few weeks and was concerned as I heard she was unwell. A letter came before we left Simpson and she says … she's a little delicate but well." Jack paused. Would it matter if he mentioned Anne's news? Why should it? It was a happy thing to tell: "The truth is, she and George are expecting their first child and we have to do without her for a while."

"That's grand news. Please give her our best wishes. She won't be helping you on your next jaunt then?" said Shaw.

"There's no next jaunt," Jack said, meeting Shaw's gaze, "I'm just getting over a couple of cracked ribs. I've a bit of time off and thought I'd spend it with the Parson over at Simpson. He's got a trip to make to his sister's in Hampshire so I'm going with him."

"That's your story is it? According to Constable Brook at Simpson you were there last week," Field grinned at Jack and picked a piece of ham out of a back tooth. "That's an awful lot of time off for a couple of cracked ribs. I'd have you behind the duty desk for a few weeks but on no account would a Sergeant give you so much time off. Come on Jack, come clean, what are you up to?"

Shaw chuckled as he started to take the shell off an egg. His eyes were on Sam, but he too gave nothing away.

Jack looked round the table with an open expression and avoided the question. Instead, he said: "Talking of Constable Brook, there's an issue with sheep rustling locally. Yes, I met him last week while I was at the Parson's. He's finding it hard to get any of his colleagues in the Brighton force to take it seriously. That wouldn't include you two, would it? That's quite an area to cover for one man and its starting to really affect the livelihood of some of the farms. Perhaps you could give him some help?"

Field glanced at Shaw and said: "As expected, we're not getting anything out of him."

Shaw nodded in his hearty way. "I'll go over and see Brook. Where do you go to in Hampshire?" he asked.

"To the Parson's sister at Lymington," said Jack.

"New Forest?" said Sam, acting surprised, "That's quite a way."

"That's why he only makes it once a year now. He goes each summer. I'm going down for a few days with him before I go back to London via Southampton," said Jack, focussing on his food. He could have kicked himself for mentioning Southampton.

Sam stared through the window at the kitchen garden. He was also aware Jack had been too open.

Sam attempted to change the subject and said: "I should do some cutting back later."

Shaw followed Sam's gaze. "That's a nice area for a kitchen garden you've got there," he said.

"Thanks to Jack, last year," said Sam, "He got it laid out. Grandma loves it."

Something Shaw had said didn't sit right with Jack. He asked: "Shouldn't it be Field that sees Brook?"

"You're right if you mean it's the Sergeant's prerogative," said Field, with a smile. "That's our good news. Thanks to our work with you last year we've both risen in the ranks. I'm now Inspector Field and Shaw is Sergeant Hockham,"

Peter Fisher entered the room to a scene of general handshaking and backslapping as the two Brighton policemen were congratulated by Jack and Sam. Seeing the Parson Jack called everyone's attention towards his friend.

"Let me introduce Reverend Peter Fisher, or Parson, as I call him. Parson, these two gentlemen are the policemen you provided all the information for last year, Inspector Field and Sergeant Hockham, as they now are," explained Jack.

'Ah yes, that sad case. Gentlemen, good to meet you, but don't let me interrupt your breakfast. I came in search of hot tea only," said Peter Fisher.

Sam went across to the range. He pulled one of his mother's fine china teacups off the shelf on the dresser and started to pour the well-brewed tea for Peter Fisher. Arranging the cup and matching saucer he placed a teaspoon ready by the sugar bowl.

"I'll be coming over your way, Parson, if you don't mind me stealing Jack's term of affection for you?" Shaw asked. "I need to see Constable Brook. According to Jack there's been some sheep rustling in your locality."

"No that's fine, it's the name I go by. Good, then let me know when you're coming, and you must have a meal with me. There's another man it would be helpful for you to meet on the issue, his lordship's agent, Robson. He's got quite an insight into what's going on. Give it a week to ten days will you so that I'm back?" said Peter Fisher.

"I'd be delighted to." Shaw took out his notebook and scribbled Robson's name down. "Never turn down a meal do I Jack? And I'll look forward to getting your insight into a few things, sir," said Shaw.

"Delighted to help if I can. What time are we off, Jack?" asked the Parson.

"In about ten minutes if that's alright with you?" said Jack. "I need to go via the sea front. Inspector Field is going to walk with us to see Burgess and we've also got a bit of fish buying to do."

"Right, that will be interesting," said Peter Fisher, downing his tea. "I'll get my hat and I'll be with you. I'll look forward to seeing you in Selmeston, Sergeant Hockham."

*

The sky over Brighton was heavy but there was a promise of better weather to come if the glimmer of brightness on the horizon could be relied upon. The three men walked past St Peter's Church into the more built-up areas of the town. Field was the faster walker of the three men but realised within a few steps that he had to slow his pace to match that of his two companions. Jack's pace was set at the level of not feeling the discomfort and Shaw adjusted his step to accommodate the Parson. The men steered their direction towards the area of the beach where the fishing fleet with the net shops and the rope makers would be found.

Once at the sea Jack edged his way through the boats which extended some way along the beach. He cast his eyes over the men and women resting and working there, some spreading nets out to dry over the railings of the esplanade, others eating whatever provisions they had brought with them that morning. Eventually, Jack found the fisherman he had paid to take him and Mrs Curzon out one morning last June. The man was sitting by his "hoggie," an ordinary offshore and decked fishing boat. On that sea trip Jack had surveyed the coastal access to the town while the recently widowed Mrs Curzon had sat trailing her fingers in the cold sea water. It seemed a lifetime away.

It had been the fisherman's understanding of the uses of a marlin spike that had helped with solving a case some days after that trip. Although the man's last contact with Jack had made him wary to renew the acquaintance the sight of the money Jack was offering him to take Sam and his brothers out encouraged his cooperation. Jack made the arrangements for Saturday morning and paid the man. That task completed Jack gave all his attention to finding a couple of good-sized fish which would feed nine that night. An extra fish for Burgess as well was bought and wrapped and Field put some business the fisherman's way as well. That task completed, Jack paid a boy to take one parcel of fish to the Curzon's house, while he tucked the other parcel under his arm. Jack and his two companions made their way along the sea front towards the Ship Hotel.

Ahead of them Jack could make out the portly silhouette of Charles Burgess on the front step. With all his joviality the former detective greeted them as they crossed the road towards him.

"A timely visit Jack! And you've met up with Inspector Field."

"Burgess, how *well* you look.' Jack said, as they arrived on the front steps. 'Let me introduce you to the Parson, Reverend Peter Fisher."

"It's good to meet you Mr Burgess," said Peter Fisher with a smile. "I heard a good deal about you last year. We don't bring you a crime to solve, I'm afraid."

Burgess's eyes twinkled and he glanced at Field. The two men exchanged a knowing look. Burgess laughed and said:

"We live in the expectation of it, Reverend. Jack is always involved in something. Come in, come in, all of you."

Jack held out the parcel to Burgess.

"My, my, what's this?" asked Burgess.

"I remembered how you enjoyed the "daddy of a Sole," last year as you called it," said Jack.

"That's kind of you … and we have hot chocolate waiting and arrow root biscuits laid up in our small garden at the back of the hotel. Ah, here's Alice to see you now. I'll get this beast into the kitchen and join you all in a moment."

Burgess as always exuded pride in the small, stout, woman with eyes that were full of life. She joined the group and as Burgess continued to excuse himself Alice greeted Jack and met Peter Fisher by holding out both hands to them. For Jack she had a motherly kiss and he beamed down at her.

"Jack, you look better than you did last time I saw you," said Alice. "It's too long and we must see you more often."

Turning to Peter Fisher who had patted the warm hand he had received into his own, Alice bobbed a small curtsey. She said: "Delighted to meet you, Reverend, but do come through. We're just down the corridor past the reception desk. Careful, or we'll be mown down in the exodus as so many guests are checking out this morning."

The three men followed Alice down a long corridor into the small, courtyard garden, which Alice and Charles Burgess retained for their own use. Burgess arrived with a silver pot and three small porcelain cups. He proceeded to fuss around them, pumping up a cushion for Peter Fisher, offering Field a pipe and a pouch of tobacco. Jack glanced around the room, remembering the previous time they had sat together. It had been to read the sailor's confession. There would be unfinished business on that case in a year's time when the man was due to return.

"I'll go and look after reception," Alice quietly said to Burgess, and she slipped out into the public area of the hotel.

"Well, that's delightful," said Peter Fisher after he had taken a sip of the chocolate. "So rich, yet I suppose it's a fashion here, is it?"

"As always Brighton leads the way," Burgess answered, as he offered Peter Fisher an arrow root biscuit. "Try one of these they help to take the richness away."

"Are you not joining us?" asked Peter Fisher.

"No, Alice has me taking the doctor's advice," Burgess replied, patting his stomach.

"I never thought I'd see the day," said Field.

Burgess smiled briefly but steadied his gaze onto Jack and said: "I heard from Tom Hunt that you were coming down on your way to Hampshire. Did he let you know he'd briefed me?"

Jack was unsure what to say. Burgess was close to Hunt, often enabling an injured policeman to rest in the hotel as he had done with Jack. He hoped he was hiding his confusion as he felt wrong-footed.

Jack said: "No reason for Inspector Hunt to tell me anything, if he needs your help that's between you and him."

Burgess nodded and continued: "He fully appreciates that the Parson will understand your movements by now so you can speak freely. When Tom gets in touch it usually means we stand in reserve, as you know from your time here last year. Call it: "just in case," Jack. I let you know this should you have need of reinforcements. Give my best to Harry and Stan when you see them."

Jack looked from Field to Burgess, at a loss what to do. It was true that Hunt had his own way of doing things. However, the mention of Stan and Harry confused Jack. Harry had been housed by Burgess after his injury at Spithead last year and Stan and a constable had tended the wounded detective. As far as he could remember Hunt had only spoken of Harry Franks travelling with him. Maybe he had missed Hunt mentioning Stan. It was, after all, on the day he had been injured that Hunt had briefed him and perhaps he had stopped concentrating when Hunt had explained he was due to meet up with Harry. Jack attempted to brush it off. Where Harry went Stan wasn't usually too far behind.

Field had started speaking again and Jack slowly switched his attention away from Burgess.

"Now, Burgess, you know you'll have problems getting anything out of him," laughed Field. "I tried earlier, but we have to accept that this time all we are is the reserve. He's assuming things, Jack. However, I have one question from the point of view of the Brighton force. We know you're after a man. Is there one distinguishing feature for me to hold in my mind when we welcome visitors to this town that should make me alert to the possibility that your quarry may come to Brighton?"

Jack was speechless. Peter Fisher could see the dilemma Jack was in from his eyes as Jack's mind raced. The old vicar fixed Jack with a hard stare. So, this is unexpected he thought. Had Jack's inspector apparently lined these men up? Watch your expression, Jack, he hoped he was communicating.

Jack for his part had Hunt's statement in his mind not to share anything with lovers, colleagues, or friends. What was it that he was not to share if Hunt had already disclosed information to Burgess? What would Sam make of this? Confused, he knew he had the tendency to be an open book if unprepared. What part of his briefing had Hunt meant Jack to keep it to himself? Was it that part about the Queen? But Burgess knew Hunt well. Jack looked at the old vicar, but his Parson's expression was vacuous. He knew he could rely on Peter Fisher not to disclose anything even under pain of death. However, Jack decided he must speak to the Parson later and make sure of his silence. Still, it couldn't hurt to give Field a basic description of the blonde thief as there was always the possibility the man would return to England.

Jack said: "He's much the same colouring of hair as myself. I'm told its unusual and certainly helps him, and me unfortunately, stand out in a crowd. It's possible he's foreign. I don't expact he'll be back in England."

"Foreign? What makes you think that?" Field asked.

"Overall appearance of the clothing he had on, his strength climbing. He was well-fed in a lean way. I saw him twice. Two separate thefts but both on the same day and an ability to blend into a crowd with a confident manner." Jack paused remembering the climb the man had done on the first theft to break into the West India Dock offices.

The other three men waited.

Jack looked at Burgess. He seemed satisfied as if this had been expected. Field sat forward waiting for further detail.

———

Only Peter Fisher was passive.

Jack said: "Seeing him climb … the speed reminded me of an acrobat, or a sailor shinning up a rope, but fitter and stronger. He was certainly familiar with heights, like someone shinning up a mast would be but somehow it was different, like he could see hand holds on the stone, even though there weren't any. I can't put my finger on it but I daresay it will come to me."

"You mean he had a skill you don't have. He could see where to put his hands as he went up?" asked Field.

"Circus background perhaps?" suggested Burgess.

"Not sure." Jack said. "No, I don't think so. He looked wrong for a circus. Who knows?" Jack shook his head but smiled at his friends. These men had helped him last year, looked after him.

Jack continued: "What he stole was precious both times. That said he either had a skill to identify valuable items, or he'd been well briefed by someone with such a skill and was good enough at his trade to be trusted. His trail has gone to Southampton. He's had months to lose himself somewhere. I'll leave the Parson at Lymington and double back to check the link." Jack paused, stopping short of confirming Harry and Stan were to join him at the port and that they would go to Jersey. He switched the subject to his injury. "As you've no doubt heard, I need a little longer for the ribs to heal so there will only be enquiries to make and then back on the train to London."

Peter Fisher's eyes flickered to Jack, registering the lie and his lack of trust in the policeman and hotelier, then he glanced away at the small rockery Burgess had built for them in their private garden.

"Beautiful stone you've used," said Peter Fisher.

"Thank you, I'm trying to follow Lady Broughton's rockery from Hoole House. Do you know it?" asked Burgess.

"Not in person but I've seen a photograph. Where do you obtain the rock plants?" asked Peter Fisher.

"Alice found a supplier. I …."

Peter Fisher interrupted Burgess before he could continue.

"Jack, we should build a rockery in my garden on one of your visits. I have quite a taking for one seeing how delightfully the stone catches the light. We could make it a project while you're recovering."

"Alright, Parson, we will," said Jack.

"I've lost my drift," said Burgess.

Field, however, had never taken his eyes off Jack.

"Seeing where he leads you. Let Sam know he can count on us if we're needed, will you?" said Field.

Burgess said: "You know my past, Jack, and I know Tom Hunt. If there's a link that I think there is it ties in with me having left the force. I'd quite like to be in at the kill when it comes."

"I don't know if there will be a kill, Mr Burgess," said Jack, smiling disarmingly, "At least not one that involves me. Just enquiries while I'm convalescing in the area."

A knock at the door announced Alice with sandwiches. The humour in the room lightened as she came in. Jack and Peter

Fisher declined any more food, but Alice insisted on wrapping a selection for them to take away.

Peter Fisher accepted her kind offer. He said: "I intend to sit on the beach this afternoon and these will do nicely."

'The air will do you good, Parson," Alice replied. While she was present nothing was likely to be discussed. Peter Fisher gambled on Alice taking a dim view of Burgess being driven to find the link with his own past in the Met.

"I would value the address of the supplier of the rockery stone you used," said Peter Fisher.

"I have it in the bureau there. Bear with me while I find it for you." Alice went to the Walnut Davenport in the corner and opened a drawer.

Field enquired after the Crofts at Fairlight and Jack recounted tall tales of his last expedition to find fossils with the children. Alice found the details a little faster than Peter Fisher had hoped but Burgess and Field had decided to each smoke a pipe as no further discussion was possible. It seemed a convenient time to end things. Readying himself to leave Jack started to stand and felt a sharp pain in his side. He steadied himself and held on to the back of the chair. Burgess started to rise to help but Jack waved his aid away with good humour. He put out his hand, first to Burgess, then to Field, hoping these were men he could still trust.

Jack said: "I'm alright, just certain positions make me a bit solly and it sometimes causes a problem. It's been good to see you again, even though briefly."

"And you Jack and good to finally meet Reverend Fisher," said Burgess.

"Delighted to come. It's some years since I was in Brighton, but I hope it won't be as long before I'm here again. Would you show me your public rooms?" Peter Fisher asked Burgess. "I'd love to see them."

The group made their way through the hotel with Burgess taking Peter Fisher into the dining room and the lounge. Jack waited by the front door with Field and Alice.

"Now, I must get back home," said Field, "I was on duty last night so sleep calls." He nodded as Burgess and Peter Fisher came into view. "Your Parson is on his way back now."

"Inspector, good of you to have come and seen us, I enjoyed meeting you," said Peter Fisher.

"A pleasure to have met you, Parson. Shaw will look in on you," Turning to Alice, Field said: "As always, Mrs Burgess, my thanks." He nodded to Burgess and left the hotel. They briefly watched him stride off into Ship Street.

"Take care of yourself, Jack," said Burgess.

"I will. The Parson will keep me in line," smiled Jack. "Thank-you Alice as always for your wonderful hospitality."

Peter Fisher made a small bow to Alice and added to Burgess, "I'll let you know those dates and numbers."

"I'll wait to hear from you Reverend," said Burgess, "We'll put on a good dinner for you."

"Our pleasure to see you, Jack," said Alice. "Don't let it be so long before you come again."

"I promise," said Jack, and he and Peter Fisher turned onto the Promenade.

The sky had lifted, and a brighter afternoon was developing. Jack and Peter Fisher walked together into the crowds. They waited until they were obscured by the people milling around. It was a school day and there were no boisterous children yet in view, just nursemaids pushing baby carriages. A good many invalids on the arms of their companions, or in bath chairs, were taking the air. It seemed the whole of Brighton had been brought out by the promise of the better weather. Despite the crush around them Jack and Peter Fisher made a concerted path through the crowds.

"Thank-you Parson, I'd have been scuppered without you," said Jack.

"That was difficult for you," said Peter Fisher, breaking their mutual reflection.

"Yes, and I hope I haven't said too much. It was more that it took a turn that was unexpacted," said Jack. Both men walked towards a more spacious area nearer the beach. Jack mused about coming clean with Peter Fisher. The two men stopped and stared down at the shoreline.

Jack said: "Inspector Hunt trusts Burgess and they worked together years ago. Burgess got too close to a case in his career and became a laughingstock in the force. It sent him into depression, and he left the police early. Inspector Hunt gave me the opposite impression to what he apparently has done himself. I thought I mustn't disclose what I'm about to do to anyone. I took a risk with yourself but on the basis that I think of you in a sort of father confessor role, as well as a trustee, I assumed you'd say nothing to anyone, and you've proved yourself golden."

"As quiet as the grave," said Peter Fisher. He smiled at Jack. "Years of small talk at church fairs has given me the skills of an inane prattler."

"Thank the Lord for that," said Jack. More seriously he added: "I still don't have permission to take anyone fully into my confidence. There was something in Burgess's tone. I can't quite put my finger on it. Something's troubling him."

"I took the opportunity to get him alone by looking at the public rooms. But breathe in the air, Jack. Let it all wash over you. Any pain now from the ribs?" asked Peter Fisher.

"A bit of discomfort, that's all. Not like it was," Jack answered. "What were you up to about a dinner?"

"A yen I have to gather friends and family around me while I'm still here and celebrate the long years God has given me. The frustrating thing with death is one doesn't get to show up at the wake. I mean to enjoy an occasion rather than let it happen when I'm dead and can't be with everyone. Burgess will give me a special price he said and send me some menus. I took the opportunity partly to put the business their way and to get it arranged before too long but also because I wanted to have a look at him on his own. You're right about something troubling him. I could hear it in the voice," said Peter Fisher.

The two men were quiet as they walked on, preoccupied with the morning they had had.

Eventually, Peter Fisher said: "It's good, you're healing. Ah, I miss the bracing air of the sea. The air on the Weald hangs heavy at times: too many trees and the oak blossom at this time of the year. I should come here more often. Today the air feels invigorating. What time are you meeting Mary?" asked Peter Fisher.

"Not until four o'clock. And only for an hour. It was all she could do to get the time away from the Royal. What are your plans now?" asked Jack.

"I shall take myself to the Aquarium for a little while, and then have a walk to find the new Library that's opened," said Peter Fisher. "Don't worry about me. I have a ready supply of Alice's sandwiches and there are plenty of places to take tea if I need to. I may make a nuisance of myself to the Vicar of St Peter's on my way back to the Curzon's."

Jack grinned, imagining the thorough questioning the new vicar would be subjected to by the Parson. He stared at the sea as it was breaking on the shore with a long grating sound. A memory came back to him. He said: "Father used to say that sound was a "rake" when the sea broke like that. I think it's a common phrase in Sussex."

"Did he? You continue to teach me, Jack. But that word rake reminds me of Shakespeare: How did that go?" Peter Fisher started to quote a passage that meant nothing to Jack:

"Let us revenge this with our pikes, ere we become like rakes; for the gods know, I speak this in hunger for bread, not in thirst for revenge." His eyes fixed on Jack's.

The Old Parson said: "Coriolanus, I think it is."

"I'll take you word for it, Parson," Jack said, and he grinned.

"Being as lean as a rake through hunger but that is not the sort of hunger Burgess has. No, not with Burgess, I fear. Be careful with him, Jack, he speaks through hunger for revenge. He has a look I've seen before of obsession with an issue."

"Understandable isn't it after it drove him out of the force," said Jack. "They were lucky, he and Alice to manage the Ship. but if you've got cast iron proof of a man's corruption it shouldn't matter what position that man holds. He should be as accountable before the law as any other."

"I agree," said Peter Fisher.

"There's more to this business though I think Parson. Inspector Hunt has hinted that there is corruption in the ranks. I think he suspects someone, or a few people, of being involved in the crime ring. It's all linked back to Burgess's time in the force, and a case I worked on two years ago. I sense it even though the Inspector hasn't been plain with me. The young thief we're after could be stealing to order. It's the type of items he's taken, rare and precious things that a collector or a person with an eye for the value they have would want." Jack stopped himself, despite there being a relief in talking to Peter Fisher. "I'm saying too much."

"A dangerous individual, Jack, by the sound of it." Well positioned perhaps and powerful. The fact the Queen has given your inspector a commission to recover items says it all to me. Care is needed and you are right to be cautious." Peter Fisher turned his eye to the horizon. "Where will it take you?"

Six

Jack arrived back at the Curzon home shortly before midday. He rooted in his pocket for the front door key that Sam had pressed into his hand almost a year ago. It had been an action of care on that fateful morning a year ago when Jack had woken and realised the nightmare of losing Harriet was a reality. It had been more than a gesture, a "just in case" token, so there was always somewhere Jack could go. The key had lain unused since that day in a dish on Jack's dresser, rather like his love. But yesterday he had used the key for the first time on his arrival with the Parson and with that action the memories had flooded back. Jack pushed the thoughts away. He called out a greeting as he opened the front door so as not to alarm anyone. A cheery, "Cooee," was the response from Grandma in the kitchen.

Jack made his way down to her and found Grandma sitting by the back door, an apron draped over her knees full of feathers from a half-plucked chicken lain in her lap. Grandma laid the bird in a baking pan at Jack's entry and rolled up the apron to contain the feathers.

"Time for a rest from this and a cup of tea. Have you had a good morning?" asked Grandma, She walked across to the stone sink and pumped water over her hands before scrubbing them with carbolic soap.

"Yes, it was an interesting one. Is Sam still at home?" asked Jack.

Grandma nodded at the window.

"He's out coaxing a bonfire at the bottom of the garden," she said. "There's a broth ready if you're hungry."

"P'raps later, I've not been short of food this morning. I'll change and join Sam," said Jack.

"Thank-you for the fish, it's on the slab ready for tonight."

"And the bird?" asked Jack.

"That's for the slow oven overnight," said Grandma.

Jack slipped up the stairs to the small box room he was occupying and changed quickly into the old labourer's clothes he had kept since his days on the farm. One never knew when they would come in handy.

Wrestling with a button on his shirt he glanced out of the window towards the end of the garden. Jack could make out a figure moving old sticks to the heap of smoking branches which were struggling to catch light but the smoke from the bonfire obscured much of his view.

"Wood's damp," he said aloud to himself. Jack pushed up the sash window and shouted: "Sam, *Sam.*"

The figure emerged through the smoke and waved at Jack.

"I'll be down to help you in a minute," Jack called.

Sam gave a thumb's up and disappeared back into the smoke. It was nearly time to finish as far as Sam was concerned but he held on until a figure came through the smoke like an apparition.

"We used to put potatoes in the ashes to bake on the farm," said Jack.

"They're in the shed if you want to try it," said Sam, pointing towards a lime washed lean-to shed. Jack went in and moments later reappeared cradling a dozen or so fair-sized potatoes. He picked up Sam's spade and moved ash away from the base of the bonfire and placed the potatoes into it. Then he raked the hot ash over them.

"You've put them in a bit deep," said Sam.

"Just spit-deep," said Jack.

"Spit-deep?" asked Sam.

"As deep as a spade goes in digging. They'll cook that way," said Jack

"Right, for tonight are you thinking?" asked Sam.

"Should do by then. I'd better mention it to Grandma. What need's doing?" asked Jack.

"Most of what I've cut is rotting down, ready for spreading later in the year. It's just the old branches burning that I've cut off to try and make some more light in the garden," explained Sam.

"Burning is optimistic, smoking more like. Look, I need to tell you about the visit to Burgess. Perhaps you can shed light on something that's been said," said Jack.

"I'm getting close to needing food," said Sam. "Grandma will be after me to eat soon. We should go in and we can chat over food."

"This needs to be private, Sam," said Jack.

Sam ran a hand across the back of his neck. A blackbird moved out of the bushes and stared at the two men before running back for cover.

"Sam, you should come and eat." Grandma was hurrying down the garden picking sweet smelling flowers from the border for the table as she went. She could make out two figures as the breeze altered, blowing the smoke back onto the men. Jack caught the full draft of it and felt it touch his throat. Coughing he moved forward out of its grip.

Grandma called: "Oh Jack, you're down here as well, come in lads and get the broth that's ready." Satisfied she had enough flowers for the table she turned back to the kitchen.

Sam thumped Jack's back and said: "Tell me quickly and then let's eat."

"I saw Burgess. He told me that Hunt had contacted him and briefed him. Field also knew that I was after someone and asked me for some way of recognising the man if he landed in Brighton. I was taken aback at the fact that Hunt had talked to Burgess but then remembered the way Burgess had left the police."

"Yes, he was ill, wasn't he?" said Sam.

Jack nodded and said: 'He and Field told me they were to be held in reserve in case there was a need for them."

"But Hunt hasn't told me this," said Sam, staring at Jack. "If I'm to liaise with Burgess I need to know. What did you say?"

"I mentioned the hair colour of the thief as a way of identifying him for Field," said Jack. "I said it was like my colour. I may have said too much. Burgess told me Hunt expected that I'd taken the Parson into my confidence and that I could be open with them."

"That could have been him fishing," said Sam. He looked at Jack. "Have you? Told the Parson, I mean."

"He worked out I'm going to Jersey from Southampton. He knows I'm tracking someone. That's it," Jack lied but he did not know if Sam had been briefed about the royal connection.

"Did Burgess mention Southampton?" asked Sam.

"No, I did. Just that the trail led there, which is true. I stopped short of telling him I would meet up with Harry and Stan. But then Burgess mentioned them, said to give them his best. I don't know whether he's been told, or he was trying to find out information." Jack hesitated at the sight of Sam's face. "Do you think I've said too much?"

"No … I don't think so, … frankly I'm not sure. It's difficult when you're on the spot. You said nothing about Jersey?" asked Sam.

"Just that I was doubling back to Southampton to get to London. Making enquiries only because of my ribs. It won't take anyone too long to find out where someone can travel to from Southampton. Most would assume France I should think. One thing I did say was what I believed about the thief," said Jack.

"Which was?" asked Sam.

"That I thought he was foreign, skilled, knew what he was about."

"Won't take much for them to work out the thief has gone abroad then. At least you kept quiet about Jersey. They'll expect France, probably. Shame about this, it's got a funny feel to it." Sam stared ahead not speaking for some moments.

"That's why I'm telling you," said Jack.

Sam said: "I suppose I should contact Inspector Hunt this afternoon, but I'm seeing him tomorrow in London anyway, so we'll know then. Harry and Stan will be at the meeting being briefed ready for Saturday." Sam paused, staring at the cloud that moved slowly from the Downs to block the sunshine. The bottom of the garden was well-shaded. Jack thought it was wasted as an area.

Jack said: "We could better use this for vegetables you know."

Sam looked surprised at the change of subject. "Haven't had time," he said.

"I can help you get this ready for next spring," said Jack.

Sam nodded, but distracted by Jack's account of the morning stared ahead and said nothing more.

"I feel guilty about not handling it better," said Jack. "I was wrong-footed given it was the two men we worked with last year."

Sam nodded again.

Jack continued: "Plus, Hunt is close to Burgess and we never know exactly what the man gets told. Of course, I forgot Burgess had been so badly affected by his investigations when he was in the police and that the case he worked on took over his life and led to him leaving. Hunt may have mentioned something quite light to try and give him encouragement that there was progress."

"We'll probably never know. At least you didn't tell them about Jersey," said Sam.

"That's about my only defence," said Jack.

"And the Parson? I suppose he will say nothing?" asked Sam.

"He views it like the confessional. Torture wouldn't get anything out of him once he knows its confidential, he handled it well and provided a bit of distraction," said Jack.

"Let's eat before Grandma gets after us." Sam frowned at his un-finished handiwork in the garden. Together the two men were silent as they walked to the kitchen.

"Ah, I was about to chase you both," said Grandma as Jack and Sam walked in. "The broth is keeping hot and there's bread and cheese in the larder. I have to get off into town to collect your brothers' boots," said Grandma.

"Is there more than a pair to carry?" asked Sam.

"There's four pairs," replied Grandma. "They all go through the soles at the same rate. I never understand why."

"If you give me ten minutes to eat something, I'll come with you. I need to get a message to London. As the cobbler is near the telegram office, I can carry the boots home for you," suggested Sam.

"Ah, work is it?" asked Grandma, knowingly. "I'll give you half an hour if you make yourself look more respectable, Samuel Curzon. I'm not going out with you in your gardening clothes. And what of you this afternoon, Jack? Do you want to come into town with us?"

"Jack has a romantic assignation, Grandma," said Sam, with a grin.

"Just meeting a friend," Jack said, kicking Sam's foot under the table.

Grandma looked from Sam to Jack. She said: "Talking of romantic assignations, I was going to take the boys out of the house when Eleanor and her mother come on Sunday. Give you free rein to walk in the garden. I assume that's why you trimmed the bushes back today? To make it tidy ready for Sunday?"

"Eleanor is it?" asked Jack, his mood lifting. "Would that be a certain young Welsh music teacher called Eleanor that I met on a train last year?"

"It would, but you'll take no credit for the acquaintance. It's taken me a year and all my considerable charm to get you out of her head," said Sam.

"And is the music teacher to change her name?" probed Jack, giving Grandma a wink.

"She might," said Sam, focusing on the bowl of soup.

"That's why I'm taking the boys off," said Grandma to Jack, her eyes wide.

Jack smiled at Sam who avoided looking at his friend. Sam maintained the relaxed, joking manner in front of his grandmother, laughing quietly while he and Jack finished their meal. Jack's mood sank again as Sam and Grandma left the table to change their clothes for town. So, Sam was to marry and soon there would be another Mrs Curzon in the house. He wondered which room the prospective Mrs Curzon would use to give piano lessons. Although pleased for Sam he felt his own ache and loneliness together with another insecurity at having said too much to Burgess. Despite the complications he knew both he and Sam had the kind of faith in Inspector Hunt that only a good chief can convey.

*

Later that afternoon freshly dressed in his Brighton clothes Jack tried to dismiss the Parson's suggestion of a new romance with Mary. On some nights his sleep had been disrupted again but Ann Black had hinted in her letter that his recent injury and the shock from it might do that. Jack accepted her good advice, but he dreaded the old dreams in which he invariably searched for Harriet. Last night's dream had woken him early, and he had sat up in bed suddenly and sworn, something he rarely did.

Jack glanced at a clock through a crowd of men standing in front of a jeweller's window while they adjusted their watches, and he knew he was early, embarrassingly so. In his mind were the Parson's words: "Friendship is an excellent way to start."

Jack turned a corner and looked up the Esplanade towards the Royal. His note to Mary had suggested a walk if she was free. Her simple response had been typical of her:

"Of course, I will come,
Your friend,
Mary."

They had written to each other, probably four or five times since last June, no more. She always responded quickly but never initiated the contact. He had been glad of a letter each time. She had answered his few brief lines letting her how he was, enquiring into her life, sending her a card at Christmas. And that had been all. She had not mentioned any suitors. There was the occasional mention of the work at the Royal, yes, but she was more interested in his life than anything else. Yet Jack could not imagine men would not try to win her.

And there she was, Mary, walking towards him in a summer dress, her brilliant eyes complimenting the blue of the sky. Smart and confident in her manner in a way Harriet had not been last time he had seen her. Much of a same height as himself Mary met his gaze whereas Harriet had to get up on her toes to kiss his cheek. Why was the memory so strong of that today?

Control your face, Jack told himself, and smile.

Mary Cunliffe laughed lightly as she saw him smiling. She returned it as she walked to him and her smile was all for him. Jack knew he would be a fool to reject it.

Aware other men were looking Jack was suddenly proud that there seemed to be pleasure in Mary's face that he was there. And now she had reached him and held out her hand. Briefly they touched fingers and then his hand dropped to his side.

"I'm glad you're here before me," Mary said, "I knew I was early but imagine the embarrassment if I got here first. Well, farm boy, what have you been doing to yourself this time to come again to Brighton?" There was the pet name which had stuck after that first meeting in the Mason's Arms on the Commercial Road, in '72.

"Only a couple of cracked ribs this time," said Jack, grinning at her.

Mary's face showed concern and she shook her head.

"I can barely feel them now," Jack fibbed. Always it was easy with her. They started walking together in the relaxed way he remembered from last year. Could life be like this?

"It seems you need to have an injury to come here," said Mary. "I thought as much. Well, we'd better make the most of it, hadn't we? I shouldn't imagine you're due back down here for a while after this."

"It will be September," said Jack. "So, Mary, how many lords are dying at your feet?" Jack asked.

Mary laughed. "There's only one way they're dying for me, and I have no intention of complying. They're here today and gone tomorrow."

Jack controlled his frown.

"Oh, I'm quite safe," said Mary, seeing Jack's concern. "The Mason's Arms was good training on how to hold male customers at bay. As you can imagine, the only men that I come into contact with are either waiters or the landed gentry and frankly, when you've picked up the latter's underwear off a floor you wouldn't be left with many illusions about them."

Jack laughed at her down to earth manner. Remembering his manners, he asked: "Would you like to sit for a while or take some tea?"

"Better to keep walking, it looks less like an assignation just in case one of the guests from the Royal sees me and reports it," said Mary.

Jack readily agreed and they started walking at a good pace. Jack felt some pain after a few minutes as his breathing increased and motioned to Mary to stop. They were about to turn into the Lanes, a series of narrow passageways densely built up. The buildings were an interesting contrast with other areas of Brighton. The shopfronts showed various wares but after a short rest Jack and Mary decided to turn for the Stein. They were comfortable together and Jack wondered if he could ever expect to feel more.

Did he need to? he asked himself.

Jack pushed his fingers through his hair. There was no spark though and it was not the same as with Harriet. It felt comfortable with Mary and as if they had always known each other. He hoped Mary was unaware how pre-occupied he was.

"You still have some pain, don't you? It shows in your face. Would you like to sit for a while?" Mary motioned towards a park bench under some trees by the road.

"No, just a pause for five minutes and then a slower pace and I think I should be alright," said Jack.

They stopped at the fountain in the middle of the Stein. A couple and their young child walked past them and there was a handful of sightseers on the other side of the railings. From there they turned towards the seafront.

Mary asked: "So, you mentioned coming back in September?"

"Yes, for my birthday, probably," said Jack. "More likely to be to Simpson to stay with the Parson."

"Simpson? Is that Selmeston? That's where your letter was from this time," said Mary.

"Yes, down to recover again," Jack grinned. He paused, an idea playing in his mind. The Parson had been encouraging him. If the Parson approved … but Mary had started speaking:

"And the Parson is the old vicar I met in the Royal recently? I served him tea and he introduced himself as a mutual friend of yours. Reverend Peter Fisher, I think. I was surprised that he knew who I was. How did that come about?"

"It was a description of you in a letter last year," Jack explained. "I'd mentioned your name and he knew you worked at the Royal. It wouldn't have taken him much to piece together who you were. He's sharp like a knife. Did you mind?"

"I took it as a coincidence, not like he had any reason to seek me out," Mary said, staring at the flower bed in front of them.

"No," said Jack, although that had been exactly what the Parson had done. Jack changed the subject: "I'll be celebrating my birthday with the Parson, in September."

Mary looked at him, waiting.

Jack felt uncomfortable. It would be better to explain. He said: "I had nothing to do with that visit of his, by the way. He took it on himself to come to the Royal."

"Is he related to you?" Mary asked.

"No, but he was a good friend to my parents and has been to me in the last year, and even as a child. I don't know what was in his mind coming to the Royal," said Jack. "I was embarrassed about it when he told me he'd been. If I'd known beforehand, I'd have tried to stop him."

Mary waited watching him and Jack felt the colour rising.

Jack glanced at her quickly. He said: "I shouldn't have said anything to him last year, but I'd had a letter from Harriet when she … I gave it to the Parson to read so that he understood why I'd cut up rough. The letter mentioned her future brother-in-law had met us at the show, that policeman on a day out. Do you remember at all? He was with Harriet's older sister and they were getting married last summer. He saw no reason not to mention he'd seen me, and her sister had been curious to see us, saw the rose and jumped to conclusions and must have told Harriet a bit of a story …"

"To see me, you mean," interrupted Mary. "That wasn't why she ended it was it? Harriet? Your young lady couldn't possibly have thought …. I wouldn't like to think …"

"No," Jack interrupted. "No, it wasn't. Harriet is … was, very young when we met and started to walk out together. She was more in love in getting on and satisfying her ambitions than with me. Although I believed she was in love with me I doubt that now. The more I've thought it over the more I believe she was egged on by the cook in the house I passed on my beat. Her letter, when it came said she'd been dismissed because she pretended to be unwell so that she could go to see one of the Sergeants and try and get a message to me while I was in Brighton. She was found out and sent packing."

"I'm sorry for her," said Mary.

"I'm telling you because that's the real reason she wrote to me and told me she couldn't marry me. It was because I got in the way of her achieving what she really wants. As I said, she's very young, but very ambitious. She wrongly thought there was something between you and I but that was down to her sister, not anything else you and I did." Jack stopped. He tried to relax the frown he knew was on his face.

"Did you get to see her and explain?" Mary asked.

"No. I didn't try. The Parson gave me good advice to be kind and to write to her a gentle letter. I wrote twice. Nothing came back. It's nearly a year now. She's alright, working again in London I hear and started at the bottom, but she'll make it eventually because that's what she wants." Jack was aware his tone had suddenly become hard. He looked at Mary and tried to smile. She returned it, gently.

Jack continued: "I only explain that, so you understand how the Parson comes to know about you and that you were at the Royal. I went to him after I had Harriet's letter, you see."

To change the subject Mary suggested: "Let's walk towards the Chain Pier shall we." Jack nodded and silence fell.

Two men on horseback passed them and the riders turned their horses to walk along the beach. On the sea-front Jack and Mary stopped and looked down on small groups of people who were sitting on the pebbles, some who had even waded out up to their knees in the sea, and nursemaids with young children playing catch. The changing huts were parked at the water's edge, their large wheels still visible ready for retreat. There was strength now in the sun and a few black umbrellas had been opened to provide some shade for those sitting. Time to move things on, thought Jack. But unsure how to he said nothing and stared at the sea.

"So, September?" Mary asked, picking up the birthday time.

"Yes," Jack smiled, grateful for her taking the initiative. "I'll be out at Simpson in September around my birthday. I've some leave to take and hope it can be then. My godparents and their children will be there and there would be a cake, if Mrs Simcock will make one and a glass or two that the Parson would put up, knowing him as I do. I thought to ask the Curzon family who live here in Brighton. Sam Curzon was in the party who were at the Royal last June when you saw Harry and I again. Sam might be married by then so that means one more if Eleanor accepts Sam, on Sunday. Who knows? Anyway, perhaps you could come? We can look at arrangements I'm sure, for you to stay somewhere overnight that's respectable. The Parson will know where you could stay, I'm sure. I'll ask him and get word to you and if you're happy I'll get him to arrange it. It would be good to be surrounded by close friends." Jack stopped his jumbled explanation as he saw the spark in Mary's eyes. She had slowly turned to face him.

"That's quite a party," Mary said.

"Yes, time I had one," said Jack, feeling pleasure at her expression.

The Parson was right, Jack thought, friendship was a good place to start.

Mary turned her head to look out to sea, gazing at it for a few moments to give Jack time for the colour in his cheeks to subside. The tide had started to roll in and a new white line of surf had begun to transform the beach as people moved back towards the top end. She was aware that Jack had joined her in gazing at the sea. It was a comfortable presence next to her.

"Well? Will you come?" asked Jack

Mary smiled at him, aware how it would look to all the others at his birthday party if she did go. It would declare her to be the future Mrs Jack Sargent.

She said: "I would love to come. Let me have the date and I'll make sure I'm not working." She let her eyes remain on his face and felt warm in the comfortable way they had together. It could be enough, she thought, if the feelings for the other girl died. Perhaps with time .....

"I'll send you a note before I go on Saturday," said Jack. "I'll check with the Parson later if there's somewhere you can stay closer than Lewes."

Mary nodded and Jack offered her his arm without thinking.

Realising that what he had done was inappropriate and could damage her position with the hotel if seen he let his arm drop to his side. Mary smiled and put her hand on his arm to reposition it, slipping her other into the crook of his. Jack accepted the declaration in her action. In silence they walked and together they reached the Chain Pier. Mary moved away, explaining: "I must go now, or I'll be late."

Jack looked surprised. "You haven't had tea. I'd intended we should go somewhere, and you be waited on for a change."

Mary gave him an honest look and said: "I think it was more important for us to understand what happened last year. I told you I would always be your friend then and so I am. I will be at Simpson, as you call it, on your birthday."

"Thank-you. Friendship is a good place to start," said Jack before he could stop himself.

Mary turned her face away from Jack to hide emotions she felt he should not see at that point. She gazed out to sea, so that all Jack could see was her profile. Mary struggled to quell a desire to cry with his acknowledgement of a beginning. Minutes went by and Jack remained silent, comfortable simply to stand with Mary.

Ensuring she had full control before she spoke again Mary watched the groups on the beach. Jack stood next to her aware of the silence but not sure what to say to break it.

Aware the time she had available was gone Mary said: "Yes you are right, Jack, friendship is what we have. That's more than many have. Dear Jack, take care of yourself in whatever you're about to do. I somehow think you're here for other reasons than cracked ribs."

'Just a good Police Surgeon that's all, who believes in getting the men he cares for out of the London air and into the country to recover. I could have done desk duty for a few weeks, but Inspector Hunt thought a visit to the Parson and some sea air while seeing Sam would speed recovery." Jack realised how easily bending the truth was becoming for him.

"When do you go back to London?" Mary asked.

"I'll do a journey in a few days," said Jack.

Accepting the avoidance of his answer Mary said: "Send me word before you leave, will you? Just so I know that you have gone and I can think of you travelling to …. I'll look forward to seeing you in September. Perhaps a gift for your birthday? Is there something you would like?"

Jack grinned and looked away to sea. He breathed in the salty air as he thought of a gift. He liked the idea of a gift from Mary. He said: "There's no need really but a book is always welcome. There's one being published at present in The Cornhill Magazine and it's to be printed as a book before the year is out. I've read a few excerpts, but I don't know the author. It's called: "Far from the Madding Crowd." I'd like it as a book if possible. I've told the Parson and he's going to get it from everyone for me as soon as he can. You could join in with that if you like. It won't be too pricey that way."

"I would like that very much. And you'll ask your Parson where I could stay?" Mary asked.

"Yes, I will. Could you give me your hand?" Jack held out his own, looking into her eyes.

Mary paused just long enough to return his gaze before she held out her hand to him. He took her hand and raised it gently to his lips as he had seen elegant gentlemen do in London, barely any contact being made. There was the desired effect of a smile playing on Mary's lips and a momentary breathlessness. It was enough to take their relationship on and Jack realised that he had played it right. He looked down at his feet suddenly embarrassed at the effect the contact had for them both.

Mary leant forward and kissed his cheek before walking back to the Royal. Jack stood and watched her go unable to think.

Seven

It was late morning on Friday, the fifteenth of May, as two men walked towards the Baptist Chapel in Princess Row just off Buckingham Palace Road. It had been a showery, windy, start to the morning and one of the men had covered his clothes with a waterproof cape. He would normally have been in uniform, but that morning Sergeant Stan Green of Shadwell was in plain clothes for the early meeting with Tom Hunt. By midday it was still cool, and he had to admit that he had been fooled by the sun into thinking it would be a warmer day.

His counterpart from Shadwell was Detective Sergeant Harry Franks and both men had been tracking Hunt from a respectable distance. However, they were now very close to needing food.

Hunt's route had gone from Great Smith Street and past Westminster Abbey until Hunt had turned into St James' Park at the Storeys Gate. Hunt had paused once in the park to check behind him causing Stan and Harry to develop a fascination for the birds kept there since 1612. Harry struck up a conversation with the Bird Keeper outside the cottage claiming to be very interested in the different types of birds he could see. Stan involved himself in examining shrubs near the cottage.

Satisfied he was being followed by his colleagues Hunt proceeded up past a lodge and cut to the left through a small walkway lined with tall hedges. At that point it would be true to say that even Stan had lost sight of him. Hunt was clear of the park.

Apologising to the Bird Keeper Harry and Stan broke into a run until they arrived at the Duke of York's Column at the start of Regent Street. They glanced quickly to the right and the left but could see nothing but the view over the park to the towers of the Abbey and the Houses of Parliament. To the left lay Carlton House Terrace and the impressive club houses. Then, light had dawned for Harry and he had laid a restraining hand on Stan's arm and said: "Marlborough House, that's where he's off to."

"How do you know that?" asked Stan.

"Well what else is up that way now? It won't be the War Office or the Oxford and Cambridge Club, that's he's going to," said Harry. "I doubt he's heading for the German chapel so that means one place. Poor man's drawn the short straw again for royal duties. Come on, Stan, my stomach says we need to eat. Where's that Chapel you know that's somewhere round here? Does it still do a good bowl of broth at midday?"

"What the Baptists? As far as I know they do," said Stan, "I haven't been up this way for some time. It's back across to Buckingham Palace Road from here. We can cut across the park to the gate if you like and then it's not too far."

The two men walked together in silence until they reached the lodge at the gate. To one side of Buckingham Gate the parade ground at the Wellington Barracks rang with the echo of troops marching. It broke the reflective mood for both policemen and Stan stopped walking. He looked at Harry.

155

Stan said: "You know what this business smacks of Harry?"

"Don't say it, Stan," said Harry.

Stan continued anyway: "We're a load of loose cannons. You know what happens to a loose cannon? It ends up overboard."

"Not before it's done some damage, though, Stan," said Harry. "That book you're thinking of had it doing quite a bit of damage to life and limb first. It didn't go overboard either. It was tethered and I've never seen a cannon badly lashed on the deck of a ship. It's the stuff of novelists, that's all. Come on, my stomach thinks my throats been cut."

They walked along the alley behind the post office and eventually past a small church near the Watney brewery. Harry grinned at Stan as he saw the Baptist Chapel. The door was closed, and Harry paused to look at how heavy it was. He asked: "Wouldn't they have that open as usual if they were doing a soup kitchen?"

"Not always, it's a matter of technique getting in," said Stan, walking forward to try the door. Inexplicable as Harry always found it that Stan's stop-off point was a chapel, he had to admit the food was edible and the people pleasant and hardworking. The chapel was a tried and tested place for Stan when up west if he was keeping his head down. Given the subject matter on the table in Hunt's office that morning this was one of those occasions. The door did not give too much resistance before Stan was able to open it with a shove.

"In you go, Harry," said Stan, standing back.

Having spent as many evenings as he could muster being fed home cooking by Rose and her mother Harry was not overly impressed with the offering before him. He moved some lumps in the soup around with his spoon, trying to see what they might be. Meat of some sort, he thought. Still, it would hold body and potentially the soul together, given the grace that had been said before they could be allowed to eat.

Stan passed Harry a plate of bread and said: "What bothers me is there doesn't seem to be anyone above Hunt now on this. Gladstone's out of it presumably. I'm getting the impression that he hasn't said anything to you about anyone contacting him?"

Harry shook his head. "Nothing," he said.

"There's no back-up, no protection for any of us if things go wrong," continued Stan. He tore bits of bread up into the bowl of soup. "And, what happens if I end up on some charge? I'm not supposed to know who Hunt was liaising with? What's your plan as you're not supposed to know anything either? Rose won't be too pleased if you disappear into the vaults somewhere while a gaoler throws away the key."

"Nah, you're being over dramatic," said Harry, shaking his head. "Anyway, you and I know what we're doing, and I don't see Hunt sidestepping responsibility if something becomes known, despite his caginess this morning. That wouldn't be like him. I think he's seen someone otherwise we wouldn't be going after a case we weren't involved in at the time. It's nearly a year ago those diamonds went missing. No, I think he's seen someone, Stan."

"I hope you're right, but my fear is still that it'll be seen that we've gone rogue. And what was all the concern about Burgess? I've not got an issue with Burgess," said Stan.

"Well, keep it under your hat about his involvement as I've yet to hear that he's been briefed by Hunt. It unnerved him, I think. We've only got Sam's word that Jack may be right on that score. If Burgess hasn't heard it from Hunt, he must have other contacts looking into things. That's the only explanation I can think of as to how he somehow got wind of the case."

Stan was quiet as he broke the bread up into his bowl. He pressed it down into the soup with the back of his spoon until the liquid was absorbed. Harry had seen him do this on many occasions. It always showed him that Stan was thinking. Once Stan was satisfied that the bread had soaked most of the liquid up, he started to eat and after two mouthfuls was ready to talk.

"Hunt can't take responsibility if he's dead, can he? There has to be a thorough record kept," said Stan, quietly.

Harry lent forward and said: "Quite right my friend and between you and me there will be reports produced. We'll lodge them with Sam. Hunt has said to send any communication to Sam."

Stan shook his head and said: "No good Harry, Sam's paid by Hunt. Even telling him what we're discussing may mean he goes straight to Hunt. It's also easier to dispose of Sam than us. We need to come up with a fool-proof way of ensuring you and I don't disappear overboard with the cannon."

Harry ran his tongue over a back tooth trying to dislodge a piece of food from another meal. His common-sense told him Stan was right, but he did not want Stan unnerved.

Harry said: "Sam has a large family, and I don't think they, or Jack for that matter, would be too quiet if something happened to Sam. What about that Parson of Jack's instead of Sam? You stayed with him last year, didn't you?"

"I did and if it wasn't for the age, I would agree with you," said Stan. "He's late eighties Harry and I've no idea what his health is like. If something happened to him and that housekeeper of his found papers … she's a good soul but who would she take them to?"

"Let's give it some thought but start with Sam as a possible safe-haven. Sam has a clerk's background and could receive if he's willing to do it. Hunt doesn't have to know what we're sending providing Sam's on board and goes along with it. We need someone to receive the papers from Sam only to be opened if any of us are in difficulties." Harry paused as Stan pushed his empty bowl across the table and got to his feet.

"Difficulties meaning incarceration or death? I've got children, remember?" Stan spat to the side, then apologised as a group of ladies from the chapel looked at him.

Harry knew the signs when Stan was under pressure. Heads in the kitchen were turning now to see what the disturbance was. A man appeared with a mop and bucket and had a quiet word with Stan. Equally quietly Stan nodded and got up. He took the mop and fulfilled his commission. Then he sat down with another nod to the ladies who started to busy themselves again.

"I wouldn't like to lose this place as an option," said Stan.

Quietly, Harry nodded and put his spoon down. Stan drained his bowl and the two men stood to leave.

Harry said: 'Alright, let's make a move and maybe something will come to us."

"Shame we didn't think of this before we left Sam," said Stan.

"We didn't have time. We had to follow Hunt. Wait a minute," said Harry. "Sam's going to Victoria to wait for his mother before they go back to Brighton, isn't he? He said he was waiting for her at the hotel by the station. We may still be in time if we get across there to catch him."

"It's close to one o'clock. He must have left by now Harry," said Stan.

"It's worth a try and it's a few blocks that's all. Come on, Stan," said Harry, starting to walk for the door, "We can nip down Allingham Street and we'll be almost opposite the station."

*

As Harry and Stan left the chapel, Sam Curzon was on the western side of Victoria. He cast an eye towards the clock on the mantelpiece inside the long brick and stone Grosvenor Hotel, with its pavilion roof and three hundred bedrooms. it was now almost one o'clock and Sam was enjoying the china on which an elegant sandwich was placed.

Sam had travelled in early from Brighton with Mrs Curzon and they had set midday as the time she would return for the train home. He should have been peaceful except that Sam was kicking himself for not being more specific about the time. His mother, he had realised, would attempt to cram in as many options as possible to pick up everything the family could need in the time that she imagined was available. Midday to her could stretch its meaning to be any time between twelve and two o'clock.

Sam had taken care with his dressing that morning and had worn the new suit tailored off Regent Street, partly as a practice run for the Sunday visit by Eleanor. He wanted to feel natural in it but had worn it because he had taken to visiting the hotel on his last few trips into London. His choice of a tailor off Regent Street had fitted another purpose. Eleanor's knowledge of music, and his lack of any, had to be addressed for Sam and off Regent Street lay St James' Hall, almost completely obscured by houses and shopfronts.

There Sam had started to build in time on his visits to London if he could see Hunt on a Monday when the Popular Concerts with the New Philharmonic Society performed. He had managed a couple in the last few months before his return train to Brighton. His education was rounded off in the Grosvenor Hotel before his return journeys, watching the rich and glamorous travellers for the Continent and dreaming of the time he and Eleanor would be on the boat train to Chatham. Over several visits Sam had taken in the luggage and the attire, the overabundance of guidebooks in some cases, and learned how to have everything convenient and secure as a passenger. It was a different world to the seething mass of London, but Sam had met the type before in his role as a clerk and had learnt to ape the accent and mannerisms of the firm's junior partner. Certainly, that morning it was enough to get him in to the lounge and once in, he only had to order tea and a sandwich.

"Excuse me, sir," said a waiter at his side, "There are two police detectives asking for a gentleman of your description. The concierge has asked them to wait at the side of the desk. A matter of a lost wallet?"

Sam recovered from the momentary shock of being addressed by a member of staff. Realising that it must be Harry and Stan as they were the only other people, apart from his mother, he had mentioned the hotel to, he stood and said: "Why yes, thank-you, do lead on."

Sam followed the young man past the arches with their medallion portraits of Queen Victoria, the Prince Consort and Palmerston amongst others, towards the reception area. There, looking uncomfortable, stood Harry and Stan.

Sam maintained the confidence and said: "Let's take this outside, shall we?" and he led the way past the staff, maintaining the illusion of the arrogant young man.

Stan gave Harry a look and said quietly: "I didn't know he could do that."

"Neither did I. He's got the walk and everything. Could be useful. I wonder if Hunt knows?" said Harry. He nodded at the concierge and he and Stan followed Sam out onto the station.

"What you doin' playing the Toff in there?" asked Stan.

"It's a thing I used to do in the office before I joined the police." Sam explained. "Everyone found it funny as I could take off one of the partners. It means I sound right in there and can learn."

"What are you learning about?" asked Harry.

"How they travel, secure and comfortable and the way their luggage is arranged. I'd like to do it one day," said Sam.

"Would you now? Hear that Stan? Well, it might come quicker than you think," said Harry.

"Mother could come back at any minute it would be better if we're quick. What's happened?" asked Sam, "Why did you come and find me?"

"We've been thinking after this morning about your clerk skills to keep records of what we do for Hunt. If he gets topped there's no back-up for us and neither Stan, nor I, want to spend our retirement locked up. The idea is we'll keep records each day and send them to you. Hunt's not to know, young Sam, do you hear?" Harry put both his hands upon Sam's shoulders and stared into his eyes. "Don't open them but you need to get them into some sort of order and pass them onto someone to hold with an instruction to open if the worst happens. Could you do that for us?"

Sam stared at Harry and Stan and then nodded. He said: "Of course I can. I'd already thought of writing down what was discussed at the meeting today and sending you a copy. Your feelings confirm its right to do that and I should probably do the same from now on about keeping any record. Did you have any ideas who should keep this information?"

"We thought of Jack's Parson but realise he's elderly and may become ill, or worse for all we know, sooner rather than later. There's no knowing what would happen to the information under those circumstances. It needs to be someone to hold the record for us who has that sort of position. Someone respected who would be listened to. You're going back today, and we wondered if you would have a chat with the Parson and see if he can suggest someone."

"Is Jack to know?" asked Sam.

"Can't see why not, can you Stan?" asked Harry.

"No, Jack probably should do the same himself," said Stan.

*

Sam's mind stayed on the same tack as Stan and Harry left him. He stared into the crowd as it surged and ebbed until his attention was caught by a woman coming towards him. Mrs Curzon weaved her way through the crowd in a way that Sam knew so well, and she was hurrying towards the hotel entrance to find him. Despite being weighed down by parcels she was clearly happy with her whole experience of shopping and triumphant in having managed to fit everything she had wanted to do into a few hours. Sam moved to relieve his mother of at least half of her burden and to stop her going into the hotel to look for him.

Sam said: "Let me take most of those, Mother. We should move towards the platform otherwise we won't get a seat."

Mrs Curzon released half of her shopping to her son and hung onto the rest of the parcels as she was jostled while following Sam through the throng of people.

Sam made the effort to mask his feelings after the morning and managed to set his face into a light-hearted expression.

"I haven't asked you about this morning. Good meeting?" asked Mrs Curzon once they had boarded the Brighton train.

"Yes, very good thanks, Mother," said Sam.

However, the opposite had been true, but Sam was not at liberty to share this with his mother. Once seated and the parcels stowed, Mrs Curzon sat back and closed her eyes, which allowed Sam to think over the morning, Hunt's poor humour and the strange request from Harry and Stan were the cause of his concern. However, there was one feature of the morning which made Sam smile.

*

The venue for that meeting with Inspector Hunt had been moved at the last minute from Camberwell Police Station to a small, free library in Great Smith Street, in a room off the entrance. Sam smiled as he reflected on the messenger who had waited for him by the ticket collector on Victoria station. He had been young and cheeky and had planted himself directly in front of Sam and asked: "Sam Curzon?"

"Yes, who wants him?" Sam asked.

"You fit the description. There's a message," the boy had said, holding out an envelope to Sam. Sam had looked at the note and read the change of venue, pocketing it. Out of charity he had tried to give the boy a penny, but the lad shook his head and stepped away.

"No thanks, Guv, I'm police too," the boy had said, with a conspiratorial air.

"What?" Sam had asked sharply, looking the boy over.

"Civilian, like you. We'll be seeing each other again." The boy had a surprising authority. Sam thought he must be about to hit his growth spurt.

"Percy's the name," the messenger continued. "Camberwell Green station, and I don't need to tell you who sent me. I do the boots. On the payroll I am. Could say I'm a trainee. You and I will be having a long association so you can't be giving me a penny every time we meet. I only tell you, so you know we're the same." Percy tapped the side of his nose with a mucky digit before he turned and disappeared into the crowd. Sam had stood watching as the wave of people folded around the boy until he had become completely lost from sight.

Sam had shown his ticket and offered the written directions to the ticket collector, asking if the man had any idea of the address.

"Out through the front there," the man explained, pointing towards the makeshift wooden huts which met travellers on their arrival at the West End Terminus. "Up Victoria Street until the Palace Hotel when you need to turn right into Dean Street.

You'll see the library opposite the bath houses after some paces."

Sam had walked through the crowds, fingering Hunt's note in his pocket. He had found Victoria Street, and then Westminster Abbey had loomed large over the area. Turning right he came to St. Margaret's and St John's Free Public Library. As the ticket collector had explained it was opposite the bathhouse and washhouses. Inside, Sam had been directed to a small room off reception used for drawing classes. Today though there were plain clothes police inside.

Tom Hunt had already arrived along with Harry Franks and Stan Green. Stan, out of uniform for the occasion, had stood at a side table and was in the process of pouring tea. He had looked enquiringly at Sam and held up a cup. Sam had nodded a greeting, recalling the last time he had seen Stan. It had been last year when Jack and Stan had come to the house and stood on the Curzon's doorstep after Jack had broken down over Harriet.

Hunt had been genuinely pleased to see Sam and asked: "How was the journey in?"

"A little slow today, an issue with a cow on the line. Mother has come in with me and gone off to do some essential shopping at the Army and Navy stores," explained Sam.

"How is your family? It seems a time since we all drank tea in the Royal," said Harry.

"All well, thanks Harry. It's almost a year since I saw you. We hadn't made the move to Brighton then. That all seems a different life now," said Sam.

"Well, you've managed to establish yourself there and support your family in quite a short time," answered Harry.

"Let's get on, shall we?" said Hunt and he had set a pace with the briefing, running through details faster than any of them had expected.

Sam had set his mind to be the piece of paper, seeing the words in his mind being written down while Hunt spoke, as if he was taking notes. Details came thick and fast and Hunt had left them all in no doubt about the tone to set with Jack about Jersey. He gave Sam the task of dealing with Burgess in Brighton. Hunt did not admit speaking to Burgess nor did he lay that conjecture to rest. Harry, however, caught the flicker of the eyes as Hunt mentioned the name and took it that it was a shock to him that Burgess knew anything.

"Right is that all clear? Jack's to identify himself only, you two are to join him at Southampton and Sam is to keep an eye on Burgess and let me know his movements," Hunt said. It had been almost curt as he pushed back his chair from the table and stood up.

None of the others stood. These had been verbal instructions only. Sam had glanced at Harry and could see the experienced detective sergeant had registered the same fact. In his mind Sam had already started to consolidate the information into categories. He found it easier to remember that way, but his thoughts had been interrupted as Stan had removed his signet ring and begun to spin it on the table in front of him. Sam had glanced at Harry and noted he looked concerned. Stan did not do well when he felt he was in a trap.

No evidence of what Hunt's told us, but there are three of us present and we've all heard it, Sam had thought. He made a mental note to ask Harry and Stan to write this point down.

His reflection had been interrupted as Stan stood suddenly which was one of the worrying signs of rebellion with him. Hunt had picked up his bag ready to leave but had looked at Stan impatiently, waiting in case the man had anything to say.

Instead, It had been Harry who spoke. He had relaxed his position in the chair deliberately showing he wasn't going anywhere soon and then asked Hunt: "In a rush?"

"Yes, I have to get back towards Victoria," Hunt had replied.

Usually, the working relationship was a little warmer than this. They all knew Hunt well and realised there was the strong focus on a timetable that day. Harry knew it could mean only one thing, but he would never voice the issue in front of Sam.

"If we're putting our necks on the line who are you working with?" had been all Stan asked.

Hunt had stared back at Stan. Seconds later his eyes had flickered across to Harry, doubt in them.

Sam interrupted Hunt's thoughts as he had asked a question: "Can I check with you, sir, that I've understood correctly that you don't want any written communication at all? Not even with me?"

"That's right," said Hunt. His eyes had remained on Harry, some suspicion that Harry had shared who Hunt worked with at times with Stan still in the gaze. However, Harry's returning stare had remained vacant.

Hunt had realised he needed to elaborate to Sam: "No notes, letters, telegrams. You will keep me informed as I've already explained."

"So, no records of this?" Stan had interrupted. He had received an irritated scrutiny from Hunt.

"Sam can make what records he likes." Hunt had snapped. "I will not, and neither will you. Nothing comes to me. You and I communicate with Sam in one direction only and he can keep whatever records his background suggests he should. They stay in Sussex with him. You communicate with Sam in whatever way you need to but never to me and certainly nothing to Camberwell New Road. Right?"

"And if I need to reach you, quickly?" This from Sam.

"You won't." Hunt had replied. "You travel in, to Victoria, twice a week as I've already explained, and we meet at an address I'll decide each time. I'll send you a message with the information as I did today, same messenger. The meeting place will alter each time and I will be there in plain clothes, understand? Nothing except a death in the team makes you change that."

"What *if* there's a death?"

Sam and Hunt had stared at each other.

"Sounds a positive note to end on," Harry threw in as an attempt to lighten the mood.

"Just making things clear." Hunt looked round at the three men.

"Then answer the man's question," Stan had said.

"It's unlikely because the man behind our thief won't attract attention to himself in that way." Hunt had his hand on the doorknob now. But his three colleagues had not moved.

"If Jack's just to identify the thief and nothing more why not let him go through the photographic records of the courts? See if the man comes up?" Sam had said.

"I doubt our thief has ever gone before a court in this country or done time here." Hunt had become irritated with Sam's persistence.

Sam had swallowed but kept on despite realising he was on dubious ground with Hunt: "But we don't know that sir."

"Oh, I think we do," said Hunt, crisply and he had left, the heavy door closing behind him.

Sam thought back to Stan's expression as he stared at the closed door in disbelief.

"So, it's off to Southampton for a sea voyage for Stan and me on Monday, Sam." Harry had said, with an effort at a jovial tone.

Sam had tried a smile but changed his mind as he looked at Stan's face.

"What will you tell your wife?" Sam had asked. Stan's eyes had widened, as he let out an expletive.

Sam had quickly said: "Your wife can get in touch with me and if anything happens with the family, I can let you know."

Stan had nodded and said: "Good of you," and he had moved across to the window.

Sam had looked at Harry and added: "And Rose."

"Don't worry about Rose," Harry had replied. "If I go quiet, she'll contact Ted. As I'm not expecting to be away for more than a few days I'll leave it with her that I'm undercover. We have an appointment with the vicar on Saturday morning, the 23rd and as it's about the wedding I'll be back for that. When is Jack due back at Leman Street?"

"That's down to Doctor Brown," Sam said. Stan had started to move to the door and Sam had looked up at him, but he had left the room within seconds.

Harry had given an apologetic shrug and said: "Good to see you again Sam. Forgive Stan's manners but his mind is on the job. We should follow Hunt, just on a "need to know" basis. Where will you be going now?"

"The Grosvenor hotel, at the west end of the Victoria terminus. I'll wait for Mother and then home," Sam had explained.

"We'll be in touch," and Harry had gone.

Sam had looked around the room to ensure nothing had been left by any of them. On his way out he had left a small donation for the library at the desk. Once outside Sam had re-traced his steps to the corner of Great Smith Street in case there was any sign of Harry and Stan. A slight movement in Great College Street had caught his eye and he could see Harry going through a wrought iron gate. Sam had followed and gone through the gate and entered a green with Westminster Abbey towering over it.

"Dean's Yard" he had read on a sign. Sam had kicked himself for being distracted at that point. He had looked around the green and felt deflated as there was no sign of Harry and Stan, but he could see there was a way out across the green at the top left of the Abbey buildings. Sam had paused, debating on whether Hunt would have gone through the Abbey with Harry and Stan in pursuit. He had decided that was unlikely and as he passed through a gate onto Victoria Street, he had accepted that he had clearly lost them and turned instead for the station.

*

While Sam and Mrs Curzon boarded the Brighton train Inspector Hunt was dressed once again in the lineage of the Prince of Wales. He stood in his usual position, by a pillar, holding an empty silver tray. For his part the Prince was irritated by his mother's views on their socialite lifestyle and ignored the man she had ordered there to protect him. If it must be that Hunt was present it amused the Prince to have Tom Hunt masquerade as a servant.

Hunt's duty was simple: protection on public occasions in which the Prince's safety may be an issue. However as this was highly unlikely to require a police presence inside Marlborough House the order had also exasperated Tom Hunt. As always, Hunt was redeployed as were many other policemen to keep order. The difference was that police were outside on the streets while he collected empty glasses. It was true that the Queen liked to keep things, "in the family," which was how she described those with long-term connections with the estate at Windsor, but given the venue, Hunt questioned the need for his presence.

It was almost one year on since the excitement of the visit of the Shah of Persia and the British establishment once again emphasised its power to another visiting head of state. The occasion this time was the lunch for the Emperor of Russia who had travelled in from Windsor that morning. It had struck the inspector as a strange marriage alliance given how diplomatic relations had been strained between Britain and Russia. Russia had rejected the Black Sea neutrality and there had been recent worries over Central Asia. Yet many felt the marriage was a deliberate attempt to ease tension. Hunt was not so sure.

Bored, Hunt reflected on his surroundings. Marlborough House, the home of the Prince and Princess of Wales, glittered that afternoon. The house had been put down for the Queen's eldest son at his coming of age, but the Prince had officially taken possession of it with his new Danish bride in 1863. From there they had established the centre of a new set that was considered fast by the Queen. On this occasion, as he glanced at some of the characters moving around the room, Hunt thought the old girl was right. Hunt accepted an empty glass from Gordon-Cumming, a friend of the Prince of Wales. Just the sort the Queen had in mind as a problem, Hunt thought. The Prince's track record in recent years had caused difficulties. Hunt's mind flicked back to the Mordaunt divorce case in 1871 where the Prince of Wales had been called as a witness. Although nothing had been proved the suggestion of adultery had left its mark on the Prince's reputation. Hunt let slip a smile as he recalled Sir Charles Mordaunt's witness statement in which he referred to warning his wife "against continuing the acquaintance with his Royal Highness because of certain circumstances connected with the Prince's character." Hunt let slip a laugh at the idea of the heir to the throne being unwelcome as a guest anywhere. And here I stand dressed as the servant, thought Hunt.

He glanced around continuing his inspection of the guests and spotted the wealthy Americans who at one time would not have got through the door. The Prince and Princess of Wales were certainly changing up who was acceptable in British society. One feat Hunt had to admit the Prince had accomplished was popularity as the most British member of a royal family whose head still insisted on describing them as German. Foolish of the woman, Hunt thought, with Prussia's activities and the unification of the German states.

Hunt's musings were interrupted by the assembly moving into dine. He took advantage of the situation and left his post. Reaching the back stairs Hunt ran down them while taking off the liveried coat.

By three o'clock Hunt emerged in the garb of a uniformed police inspector as he readied himself for the contact he wanted to see at the Emperor's reception. He was not to be disappointed as at a quarter past three, the "Grand Old Man," Gladstone, entered. Hunt thought the man still looked weary from the loss of power. He was at the reception because he got on with the Prince of Wales. Something the Queen never could understand.

Hunt knew the former Prime Minister was now very rarely in the House of Commons although he had come up to London at the same time the session began. The rumour was that the man did not miss the Commons at all.

It struck Hunt as odd as he remembered how the Queen had at one time held Gladstone in esteem. Of course, both the Queen and Mr Gladstone were different people now. He was sixty-five and no longer leading his party, and she was now Disraeli's Queen. It was clear that the Widow of Windsor had come to dislike the Grand Old Man. Hardly surprising then, thought Hunt, that his own attempts to bring Gladstone back into the investigation had irritated her.

To a certain extent Gladstone appeared to be keeping up the social side of being in London. Hunt knew Gladstone had been at Windsor for the fête at St George's Hall on March ninth and had dined at Marlborough House on March sixteenth. He knew because he had tried his hardest to get assigned to both occasions to speak to Gladstone. Both times Hunt had approached the Equerry, but his request had been ignored. The Queen had been out of sorts and not open to the suggestion for either date, dwelling on the loss of the Prince Consort and faced with the overwhelming pressure on her at having to dine in St George's Hall on the ninth of March for the first time since 1860. The only response Hunt received from the Equerry was a Queen's command for Hunt to attend his mother at Windsor on the eighth of March. And on that day, he duly complied. The expected carriage had appeared outside Mrs Hunt's cottage that afternoon with the Queen and the Duke and Duchess of Edinburgh with her. Although Tom Hunt had been allowed to take the coachman's place and drive the Queen, she never mentioned his request. Hunt had changed into the man's coat so as not to stand out too much in the role he assumed.

The coachman had whispered to Hunt: "You're to drive to the Mausoleum where they'll place wreaths, then she's going to her mother's and she'll go in with the Duke and Duchess. After that it's a visit to Frogmore house."

The Queen chattered throughout the drive only of her loss of both the Prince Consort and her dear Mama and how trying it was that she had to be the one to direct all. There was the rebuke. Hunt realised that Gladstone had washed his hands of any interest in the case and laid it firmly at the Queen's feet.

To top the Queen's sense of loss one of, "dearest Albert's" old horses, Pompey, was on his last legs and not expected to last the week. Throughout the carriage ride there was no indirect reference giving Hunt permission for his request on either date. He knew avoidance of the issue was a refusal. In fact, his request was clearly irksome as one of the dates had reminded the Queen of her own loss. Later that afternoon, when he had finished off the cake his mother had made for his visit, Hunt had left saying he would be back for the promised move in May, no matter what. As he closed the gate to his mother's front garden, he turned towards the stables to say goodbye to his old friend, Prince Albert's horse.

Hunt's attention was drawn back to Gladstone. The man was going forward to meet the Emperor. Hunt had to make a move now to be seen and he deliberately stepped out of the shadows. It was the uniform that drew the attention, just a brief flicker in the Grand Old Man's eyes, as Hunt and he looked at each other. Gladstone moved forward, the control back on the former Prime Minister's face.

Hunt hoped it was enough and quickly withdrew into a side room before he attracted interest from staff in the royal party.

Hunt and Gladstone were not friends. Their acquaintance had been a brief one and revolved around the mutual desire to prevent one man's manipulation of power and control through corruption. A year ago, Hunt had refused to confirm his suspicions when Gladstone had probed for the identity of the man he pursued. The reason for his own stubbornness Hunt had wrestled with on many occasions since but had concluded it was because he did not believe he could trust the then Prime Minister to remain silent. Going public too soon would mean the man would slip through Hunt's fingers but Gladstone's irritation at Hunt's lack of cooperation had been made clear.

Well, the irascibility was mutual. No, they were not friends.

Mutual respect might have been there, but Hunt did not experience that either. As Gladstone had withdrawn from attending the House of Commons regularly since the election result in February Hunt found even that behaviour annoying.

They were both from very different backgrounds and while Hunt was loyal to his monarch and approved of the reforms Gladstone had promoted, he also wanted to see policies go further. However, both had one trait in common. They were both men whose personalities were driven and neither suffered fools gladly. Hunt called a footman over as the man was walking past. The man took in the police uniform and then recognised Hunt and asked: "What you doin' in here?"

"Never mind that can you see Gladstone?"

"*Mr* Gladstone, yes I can see him. If you were doing what you're here for you'd be able to see him as well."

Hunt ignored the comment and asked: "What's happening now?"

"*Mr* Gladstone is talking to the Russian Emperor. Now he's withdrawing and coming this way."

Hunt stepped past the footman and remained by the door. Hunt knew that he was perfectly visible to the former Prime Minister and held his position. He readied himself to be pleasant. Gladstone's eyes were fixed on him but at the point where he was close enough to speak to Gladstone walked on. A clear message for Hunt. The inspector clenched his jaw. Something in him despised the abdication from duty as he perceived it. As far as Gladstone was concerned, he had shaken off the responsibility of the investigation and laid it squarely at the feet of the Queen.

"Poor woman," Hunt said.

"What?" asked the footman.

"Nothing," answered Hunt. Emerging from the door-way Hunt no longer cared who saw his uniform. Let them protest. He was wasting his time here. No doubt Gladstone was scurrying away to sort his papers and books at Hawarden. Controlling his face Hunt realised the footman was staring at him in surprise. Hunt controlled his black mood and said: "He's off early."

"Probably gone for a sleep before the Duchess of Sutherland's ball tonight. Him and the Emperor were complaining to each other about the late hours of the evening's entertainments. Don't you need to get out of that uniform if you're on tonight?" asked the footman.

Hunt paused, seeing another opportunity. Thinking of his wife's reaction if he did not keep his promise to be with the family tonight, he did hesitate. He would make it up to her. They'd talked of a short time away together without the children once his mother was safely off Windsor and established near their house. Tonight would clinch it and that discussion would become a promise to get away, just the two of them for the first time in years. He'd leave the choice of where they would go to her.

Hunt said: "I can be. Why, are you short? I can get a couple of my men in if you need numbers making up?"

"All hands at the pump it will be tonight." The footman said over his shoulder as he moved away from Hunt.

Hunt made his way to the Mall. A few times he did look over his shoulder in case Harry and Stan were there. But no, they had long given up on him. He made his way through St James's Park, out on to Birdcage Walk past the Wellington Barracks and walked briskly towards where he knew the post office was off Buckingham Gate. He must get a message to Morris and Phillips to come and don a servant's uniform later.

Eight

In the hope that other activities would clear his mind Sam tried not to give the day another thought until later that evening. The smell of his Grandmother's cooking helped as he and Mrs Curzon opened their front door. It should be difficult, thought Sam, to worry in the middle of the normal events of home but his mind had started to amplify potential complications with the job.

All the confidence he had displayed earlier in the day had drained away. Sam tried to focus on domestic issues, not least a host of problems, which were presented to him by his younger brothers who needed his ability with mathematics. This is just our lives and the usual preparation for the evening meal, he told himself. It should be enough in my life without the foolish belief I could work for Hunt.

Jack and Peter Fisher were sitting outside peeling potatoes, oblivious, of course, to what Sam considered from his day in London. Jack had his own issues with the kiss from Mary.

The normal things, thought Sam, focus on the ordinary, everyday issues of our lives. But Arbour Square and the poisoning, his father's death, and the responsibility he had for the family, pressed in from his past for the first time in a year and he knew the day had taken its toll.

Dinner, his brothers, and fishing tomorrow, he told himself, think of the day to come and not the past. It's different now and you've recovered fully. You will be proposing to Eleanor on Sunday ... and that brought him up short. Men with a death sentence do not have marriage in mind. All those extra cakes his mother and Grandma had made. How impossible it all seemed now. What would Eleanor expect?

By eight o'clock that evening Sam heard the chimes from the clock in the hall. He had been quiet over the family meal despite their two guests being in good spirits. The boys chattered on with Jack about cricket, his mother showed the family her purchases from London, and Peter Fisher complimented Grandma on the meal.

Jack was at last free from volunteering for dish washing, soap and suds had gone everywhere, as he had vigorously immersed his arms in the hot water. Sam wondered at how Jack could forget everything when he was surrounded by the family, but it seemed that he could as he entertained the younger Curzon's with tall tales of his arrests while the boys dried the dishes and stacked the plates on the dresser. Sam sat intensely polishing the knives and forks on a tea towel until his mother teased him that she would make sure they would shine for Eleanor on Sunday and he didn't need to wear out the cloth.

Sam only half heard her, and the rest of the family giggled at his serious face. For Sam had been wondering when Hunt might be killed for what he knew and whether they would get through the evening before a telegram would arrive. Grandma made cocoa for the younger boys and it was all a very ordinary evening.

Sam supposed the others in the kitchen could not hear his heartbeat and he tried to tell himself that the morning would come, and everything would be routine as it was tonight. From the front room Sam heard Peter Fisher's encouraging comments as Mrs Curzon showed him the material she had bought from the Army and Navy store. Sam could hear the old vicar commending her choices and the excellent value of the prices that she had paid. All very conventional, or so it seemed, and Jack carried on as if he had not a care in the world and yet the opposite must be true, thought Sam.

Spotting his chance as Jack paused between jokes with the boys Sam suggested the three men go down to the seats in the garden where they would be out of earshot of the house.

"Nice idea," said Jack.

"I'll get the Parson," said Sam, getting up.

It was still light as Peter Fisher settled into cushions on the wrought iron bench and looked towards the sky in the west. He said: "There's promise of a good day tomorrow."

Jack grinned as he glanced at his old Parson. He never heard him say anything else about a day that was to come.

By 9.30 Sam lit the candles as the evening dusk was not far off in time and then he also sat down. He had earlier laid the thin file of his notes under the cushion on his wicker chair so that the boys would not find it. He removed it and propped it against a chair leg. He was suppressing a desire to get on with voicing his fears. Instead, he made a polite enquiry to Peter Fisher: "Well, Parson, what have you both got up to while I've been in London?"

"Well, quite a bit this afternoon. It was a question of watching how much walking Jack did really so we both went to the new

183

Church Street premises of the reference library. It's been moved last year, apparently, into the modernised premises. A good place to go as there was something for us both there. I enjoyed looking into local history and Jack went into the museum and art gallery that's attached to it. We must have spent half a day in there, don't you think, Jack?"

"It was a few hours, certainly Parson," agreed Jack.

"Did you find anything of interest?" asked Sam.

"For myself, yes, the old church of St Nicholas. Although most of it was rebuilt in the '50's. However, the history, Sam, was gripping for me. It's still got the old twelfth century font from Caen, about the only thing to survive in the current building but at least it's still there."

"The art there," said Jack, taking a sip of the tea Grandma had poured for him, "was interesting as I tried to work out if it was of value financially or just kept for the sake of it. I was trying to understand what makes something precious enough to steal it for someone, especially if it's not to put food on the table or eat the item itself."

"You were thinking of our thief, were you?" asked Sam.

"Not just him," said Jack. "It's the basic idea of wanting something like a painting when you've no need to steal to sell it. You lock it away and look at it alone, that sort of thing and the fact you have it gives you pleasure. Most of the people we catch are poor aren't they and they steal to eat or they're in the pay of someone and that's why they steal. It seems more basic a driver to me if a person's starving. I can understand a hungry man, or woman, stealing. Although its wrong, Parson, and against the commandments I could put myself in the situation if I had hungry children. But, for the life of me, I can't understand the other.'

"Wealth, power, having something others don't have, I'm sure we could draw up a long list of human motives," said Peter Fisher.

"I'm sure you're right Parson. It's the motive that matters, isn't it? Hunt taught me that on this case," Jack said. I think owning something you don't need to sell must be to do with power."

"Talking of Hunt ..." said Sam, as he bent to pick up the file. He dropped it on the footrest hooked onto the front of Jack's cherry wood steamer chair. "Take a look at my summary of the day."

Jack leant forward and picked the file up. Sam had made careful notes on the train and his sharp brain had gone one step further than a simple record. He had sorted into categories all the information he had received. One never knew when it might come in handy.

Jack asked: "What's this, Sam?"

"A record of the day for future information," said Sam.

"About the trip?"

"Partly," Sam said, almost diffidently.

"And you want *me* to look at this now?" asked Jack, with a slight frown, trying to work out what Sam was doing.

The Parson as always put his finger on the issue: "Sam, I think, wants you to know of its existence, Jack."

"Alright, I know you're keeping records," said Jack. "but don't you just send any information to Hunt? The fact you're giving it to me now, on the evening you've seen Hunt, implies to me there's a problem."

Sam frowned: "You're right everything does usually get fed back to the Inspector but not for this case in a written report." Sam lowered his voice as he explained, aware the voices would carry in the still air: "I'll see Hunt to report back on what the team send me. Hunt wants nothing on paper and I'm not to hold any documents. Frankly, there could be a problem with that."

Jack read the opening page. Sam had taken information further than a record of the day and included his own hypothesis. Jack fingered the file and glanced over to Sam. Sam stared away at the spring flowers that had been left to die back naturally in the garden. From the street could still be heard carts and the clip-clopping of the horses. These were comforting to Jack as they were normal sounds. The page he had read was not the usual reading off duty. Jack wished again that he did not know who had commissioned the recovery of the diamonds. He knew his naturally open personality struggled with any form of secrecy. however, Hunt had given an order not to divulge anything and Jack had already breached that trust by telling Peter Fisher about the visit to Windsor. The Parson could be trusted, Jack knew that. To tell Sam was another issue.

Jack closed the file and slowly held it out to Sam. "I'm not sure I find this helpful to read tonight, Sam," he said.

———

"No? I wonder why that is Jack?" asked Sam and he paused, quietly staring at his friend. "Harry, Stan and I, had a chat about the implications for us all if something happens to Hunt."

Jack met his eyes without flinching. Sam weighed up the stare but there was nothing defiant in it. It was a clear, honest look, which held no fear. Unlike the other three policemen Sam had been with that day he could see that Jack held no doubts, no concern, and he had perfect confidence in what he knew. That, to Sam, meant that he knew all. So why was Hunt so edgy?

No, Jack, you don't know everything Sam thought. He finally looked away as he said: "I drew the conclusion in the meeting today that Hunt's worried himself. But frankly, Jack, what convinced me to put this file together was Harry. You know, "Hail fellow well met," Harry. At first, I was surprised because there was no sign of the hearty, confident man we know. He came across as nervy. I'd written off Stan's behaviour in the meeting as just one of his reactions and there's no doubt that he's uneasy. After I boarded the train home to Brighton, I had time to think things through. Too much time, probably. I began to think that there may be good reason for Stan being tense. Then the idea came from Harry that he and Stan send me a record and every week put a small parcel together of all papers. It didn't stop there, Jack. They thought I shouldn't hold everything myself. I'm to send it to a respectable person who would hold the records unopened unless there was a death in the team, or … an arrest. It started me thinking who might die. You need to do it as well by the way: send a record to me."

187

"I can do that if it's needed. It's just the same, I expact, as our notebooks," Jack said.

"Not really, Jack," said Sam. He regarded Peter Fisher whose impenetrable gaze was directed towards the space between Sam and Jack.

Sam turned towards the old vicar. "Parson, Harry and Stan had thought through who should hold the records and that was interesting too as they had come up with the suggestion of your good self. Don't worry," said Sam as Peter Fisher started to react. "They decided, instead, I would ask you to recommend someone respectable, someone who can't be touched. I spent a lot of time thinking this through on the journey home and the more I played with implications the more I started to realise that Hunt himself is jittery because his back-up's gone or, it can't be relied upon for support." Sam nodded then continued: "I had a nap on the train briefly. I came to with a dream of a young girl, not much more than a child, in an airless glass coffin with the file in her hand, realising she was running out of air. I woke up with her face in my mind."

"I'm always having dreams like that, Sam." said Jack. "It's Arbour Square that's done it for us both, but you especially given what you went through. You were happy this morning when you went off. Was it Hunt that triggered this?"

Sam did not answer.

"There's a good deal of paper been wasted on dreams in recent years," said Peter Fisher, cutting in. "I think it safe to say your brain was disturbed about the thoughts. Perhaps I should go and let you both talk in private."

"No need for you to go, Parson," said Sam. "I'm sure Jack has taken you into his confidence and we will need your advice shortly. Harry and Stan are disturbed about what we're all getting into."

"Why are they so disturbed about this job? Jack asked. "Nothing's changed as far as I can see with the way Hunt works."

"You weren't in the meeting, Jack," said Sam. "To answer your question, I'd say he wasn't himself. Harry suspects there's no one above him now. Jack, why would Harry think like that? Shall I tell you? Because I think Harry knew who it was. They followed him when he left.

"Followed Hunt?" Jack looked concerned.

"That's right, what does that tell you?" asked Sam, but he did not wait for Jack to answer and carried on. "To find out who he was working with. The worry is, if something happens to Hunt it will look like we're acting alone and we could end up ... well, who knows how we could end up."

"I'd keep a record anyway, of course I would, after all we would do normally as I said. I'll send it on to you as it gets it away from me just in case someone gets into my luggage. Depending on where I end up it might come in fits and starts though." Jack started to stand as he was finding the position in the steamer chair uncomfortable. As an afterthought Jack asked: "Did you find out where Hunt went?"

"No, I lost them after Dean's Yard."

"Sam, don't worry, I know who Hunt's answering to and if necessary ... if something happened to Hunt ... I'd go myself."

189

Sam stared at Jack not quite believing what he was hearing. He pulled himself back from debate about how Jack would know and said: "Now to the other issue that we need the Parson's help on." Sam twisted round to face Peter Fisher.

"Before you go into that," said Peter Fisher, "Did I hear you correctly? Did you say Dean's Yard by the Abbey? What were you doing in there?"

"I followed Harry and Stan in," explained Sam.

"My, what a team. None of you trusts each other. "A house divided, cannot stand," Sam," exclaimed Peter Fisher.

"It's not that, Parson," explained Sam. "It's not an area I would ever have been into and I acted out of concern at how jumpy Stan and Harry seemed. Hunt was just tense and irritable."

"My observation of Stan last year, mind you, was that he has had some hard times in that job of his. Out of interest where did you follow your colleagues to?" asked Peter Fisher.

"I didn't, I lost them by the time I came out on Victoria Street. I went back to wait for Mother … at the station." Sam hesitated about mentioning the hotel.

Jack avoided looking at Peter Fisher but hesitated to speak as his memory played back to the last time he had stood in front of the Abbey with Harriet and taken tea in the café at the front of the Hotel. Behind the area lay Green Park, St James's, Whitehall and number 4 Whitehall Place, home to Scotland Yard. Even Buckingham Palace, thought Jack, was not that far away but he as quickly dismissed it as the Queen was in Windsor.

"There's a police station in King Street, perhaps, he called in there," suggested Jack waiting but Sam did not speak. "Or, Scotland Yard isn't too far away," Jack added. "Perhaps he was on his way to Charing Cross to get over the river. Well, it probably doesn't matter, all part of the mystery."

Sam hesitated, dwelling on his time in the hotel, amazed now at himself for having played the charade. He started to explain: "Both Harry and Stan arrived at the hotel knowing where I'd be ... Mother was longer than I expected, you see."

"Did they say where they'd been?" asked Jack.

"I didn't ask, and they didn't tell. I was concerned mother would come back and in my own way, I was trying to be quick and keep the meeting confidential. You're right it could have been anywhere around there," said Sam.

"Sam," said Jack, looking up to the bedroom where Luke Curzon had a habit of sitting astride his open window with one leg dangling over the sill. "Our voices will carry up to that young man if we're not careful."

"Yes, he's noticeably a bright one," agreed Peter Fisher.

"Oh, ... where is he? ..." Sam looked towards the bedrooms his brothers shared in pairs and leant forward to drop his voice. Frowning at the possibility that his brother may have heard something he also knew it was unreasonable to rebuke himself.

"Parson the suggestion I pass the records to an independent party only to be opened on a death. I've since thought it should also be if any of us are arrested. Harry asked me to discuss the matter with you and to ask advice about who to approach." Sam stopped and looked at Peter Fisher.

"Why yes, it's essential by the sound of it."

"*You* think so?" asked Jack, surprised.

"Why, yes, and I have no doubts about suggesting Langton's firm hold the papers." said Peter Fisher. "He's dealing with your will, anyway, Jack. It makes complete sense to me. Sam, I can put you in touch with Langton before we go and with your permission write to him and introduce you. Have you a feel for how often information will be sent across to him?"

"I'd thought once a week. I'll collate everyone's record and include the originals, sealed, straight to him if he's happy with that. That way there's nothing on these premises to cause a problem if something happens to me."

"Or any of you," said Peter Fisher.

*

Sam and Mrs Curzon had returned to Brighton just as Inspector Hunt inveigled Sergeants Morris and Ted Phillips to join him for the Stafford House Ball.

Fitting Morris and Phillips out in footmen's uniforms was no mean feat. Hunt had given their measurements from memory and not added the inches around the waist that Morris had acquired in the last year. Hunt looked at him as Ted strained to pull tight the waist coat.

"Too much time on the duty desk," said Morris.

"Stop talking and breath in. That's it, I've got that done up now." Ted stood back and Hunt surveyed the two men. Morris he could place near the entrance but the legs on Ted's trousers were too short for him and he was left looking like they had shrunk in the wash. Plus trying to kit the two Sergeants out in a linen store, even though as such it was spacious, meant squeezing around each other.

"It's a little like I've seen all this before," said Morris.

"What?" asked Ted Phillips.

"Like something that's happened before," explained Morris.

Ted shrugged and then laughed. He said: "Well it has. It's like last year. You'd think royalty had nothing else to do, wouldn't you?"

"No, I didn't mean that. It's like they're following a formula when one of these foreign dignitaries come on a visit. 'Course it's not excited as much interest as the Shah of Persia's visit last year, but we've certainly given the Emperor a welcome," said Morris.

"We have to be cordial to him, I suppose," said Ted.

Hunt looked from one to the other. "I'm sure you're right about the formula, Morris, as it worked last year. I expect we'll see it for years to come. Apart from the rubbish the press prints about our duty to welcome visiting royalty it's an extraordinary waste of time and money to me."

Hunt stood back and looked Ted Phillips over again. Ted would not blend in at all. The stance was wrong, whereas Morris, with his many years of standing to attention looked just the ticket. That is if he didn't breathe too deeply and pop buttons.

"Look Ted, your legs are too long. If you stand behind the table and look after filling glasses no one will notice the trousers don't fit. You can keep an eye open for Gladstone, as you'll see him first and give Morris the nod, that way he can come across and get me. I'm being stationed by the Grand staircase," said Hunt.

Morris was not to be deterred by the change in subject: "Sometimes, Tom, I wonder about your loyalties with the things you say. It would be churlish to refuse the Emperor a party, and his daughter is a member of our royal family now."

"The man's an autocrat, Morris," replied Hunt.

"You have some funny ideas Tom. How long are you involved in all this?" asked Ted Phillips, attempting to head off the subject from developing between Morris and Hunt.

"On and off over the next five days," said Hunt. "The Emperor's visit to the City of London is on Monday."

"Are you riding again then?" asked Ted.

"As usual, yes. The Prince of Wales has insisted on going in the same carriage as the Emperor with the Duke and Duchess of Edinburgh. Given the number of attempts there have been on the Emperor, this smacks of being foolhardy to me. There's a group called, "the People's Will," who are reputedly hunting the Emperor. I would be happier if the Prince of Wales travelled separately." Hunt pulled the stock around Ted's neck a little too tight in his frustration. Seeing his colleague's expression, he said: "Sorry, Ted," and loosened the cloth.

"We'll be stationed at the end of the Mall before ten o'clock with our men," said Morris, trying to reassure Hunt. "There'll be three thousand officers from the Met between Buckingham Palace and Mansion House Station, posted a few paces apart. We shouldn't see too many problems as there won't be much for the crowds to see really except troop movements to the City."

"Is Paul involved at all?" asked Hunt, referring to Morris's son who worked in the City of London.

"At the Guildhall? Yes, Ed as well. They managed to get a blue ticket each as they both work nearby. They'll only be in the less distinguished crowd at the Gog and Magog end of the hall as all the dignitaries will be to the right of the throne by the righthand entrance. They were both quite excited about it."

"You don't seem too keen, sir?" said Ted.

"Tired of it, Ted. Growing up on the estate at Windsor I left deliberately to escape all this fawning. Unfortunately, it hasn't worked out like that." There was a pause as Hunt stepped back to admire the stock which he had re-tied. "That's better," he said to Ted.

Ted nodded his thanks and picked up their uniforms, stuffing them out of sight under a shelf until later.

Morris said: "You must remember your oath, Tom."

"I fully mean my oath, you know that" said Hunt, impatiently.

"Well, that's good to know. Another few days and it will be over. See it all through, it's your duty otherwise who else can the Queen rely on if not Inspector Tom Hunt?" asked Morris laughing lightly.

Hunt relaxed and placed both of his hands on Morris's shoulders and said: "She can rely on you Morris, you and Ted here and another two thousand, nine hundred and ninety-eight policemen who will line the streets, to say nothing of the troops." Hunt laughed, seeing the funny side of being able to make any difference as one man. It was the first time for days. In a moment, the atmosphere between the three men had relaxed. The relief on Morris's face was very marked.

Hunt shook his head as he continued: "I am getting to the end of my patience though."

"And probably more than a bit short on sleep," said Ted.

"Yes, no doubt that doesn't help. Does it seem right to you both that we tie up so many men looking after a handful of over-privileged people?" asked Hunt.

"An Emperor and the heir to the throne, you mean? I don't see there's any choice. But when you put it like that," said Ted, 'When we know what will happen in this huge city without the police on their beats."

"Exactly, but on a royal command from the lady I serve I will continue to dress up as a lackey, hold a tray for the evening and put up with a well-fed, pompous womaniser, who neglects his wife and despises my presence." Hunt shook his head.

Ted shrugged and said: "Careful Tom, you're not overheard. I see your point of view. When you think of what our men find going on in this city…" Ted paused. His mind played on a report he had read. He shook the memory off and continued: "That case with Constable Turton finding the murdered family in Mile End … the fact that we are tying up so many police in

196

this sort of show does sicken me when I think of cases like that."

"I know but you must both be careful what you say," said Morris. "The Prince is still the heir to the throne. This isn't the place for such talk. Knowing you as I do, you're too motivated to catch the criminal we're after to give up in this way. As Ted says, you're tired. Just a little short of sleep probably. You've set Jack up, haven't you, ready to track the man we're after?"

"Of course, Jack will be at Southampton on Monday and Harry and Stan travel down to join him after this nonsense today. Look, I know I sound unpatriotic to you, but I really feel the opposite, however, I grew up watching my father and mother bow and scrape. I came to believe it was the position and started to question why we still had it with an increasing suffrage. Oh, when I was younger, I admired the Prince Consort but when he died ... I really think all the ability died with him ... I certainly don't see it in the heir to the throne."

"Hey, enough of that," said Morris quietly.

"I doubt we can be overheard," said Hunt. "I've come to question why we still have those positions .... but then I look at other countries and see what revolutions have produced and finally understand the word. A revolution of a wheel is just a circle, and things return to be the same point, if you look at France anyway. But you haven't come here to listen to my tortured views. The Queen commands, which is why I'm here, and why you've both lost an evening off. You both know my intention tonight was to do an extra duty to access Gladstone and that's another story." Exasperated, Hunt sighed deeply.

"You're coming across as irritated on a number of fronts," said Morris.

"Gladstone's withdrawal from the fight is one of them, I admit," said Hunt.

Ted and Morris glanced at each other. Hunt saw their concern and laughed. He made the effort to shake off his black mood and said: "Don't worry, I have no intention of behaving the same way in public." Hunt looked at the doubt on both his colleague's faces and tried to reassure them again: "Seriously, I shall be the example of a dutiful policeman. Come on, it's time we took up our positions."

The three men, uncomfortable in their liveried uniforms, emerged and went to their appointed places. Hunt picked up his usual prop of a silver tray and moved to his position. Morris and Ted of course were right, Hunt thought. His own intolerance was partly due to lack of sleep but there was a mix of things playing on his mind: Two years of watching police corruption was part of the problem. The scale of the murders and manipulation of power growing stronger and no one, including himself, had come any closer to bringing the crime lord down. He was even reputed to be abroad.

Tonight, it was Gladstone, thought Hunt, that he wanted to have another crack at speaking to. True, it was Gladstone's behaviour earlier that had lost him an evening with his wife and family. That was another battle Hunt would have to fight when he got home as he had yet again broken a promise.

Still, thought Hunt, the Emperor would be back at Windsor by Sunday afternoon, and the travelling would be done more privately. Hunt knew he would at least get that time free. Which only left Monday, with the visit to the City. On Tuesday it was only from three thirty when the party would return from the review to prepare for the ball at Buckingham Palace. At least the Prince of Wales did not have far to travel from Marlborough House to Buckingham Palace. Hunt had seen the list of those who were attending. It was, in police parlance, "a very heavy list." State Balls were always difficult matters to police outside. Hunt was relieved it would fall to "A" Division. Of course, they knew he would be riding with the Prince's carriage.

Tuesday would mean another evening tying up vast numbers of police. There would be constables directing the carriages through normal traffic. Three lanes of carriages, Hunt had heard, to get them in. At least the Royal visitors would go through to the right and round to the entrance reserved for them alone. Hunt had got his way this time and had set up a decoy carriage which would look, to all intents and purposes, like an empty carriage with closed windows, which was precisely what it would be. The road would be clear, and two troopers of the Lifeguards were to ride down it. Three state carriages would also be in the retinue and they would be followed by part of a captain's escort. The hope was that the crowd would assume the Prince and Princess of Wales were in the empty carriage. After this the crowd should start to thin, allowing Hunt to get the real carriage and its precious cargo into the Palace. Hunt stared at the weather and hoped it would improve. May could be quite cold, and he spared a thought for the constables who would be on duty that night

Hunt had heard that Princess Alexandra would go to the Buckingham Palace Ball as Mary Queen of Scots. He smiled, seeing the funny side of this, as she had selected a character who had come to a sticky end. He reigned in his humour, hoping beyond hope that he had not missed something about the route in his planning, but his attention was pulled back to Morris who was pulling his ear lobe enthusiastically: Gladstone had arrived. Hunt started to move but felt a hand on his elbow.

"A great loss to the House," said the small man at Hunt's side.

Hunt looked sharply round at the man who had remained next to him. He offered Hunt his glass while raising an eyebrow.

"May I?" asked Disraeli.

"Certainly, sir," responded Hunt, straightening up and staring ahead, relying on the persona he had adopted as a footman. Disraeli placed his empty glass on the tray and into it dropped a primrose. Hunt stared at the flower, more surprised than anything that it was so commonplace. Somehow, he would have expected a more exotic bloom from the weaver of tales.

Disraeli said: "Tedious these events, Inspector. No doubt your mind, like mine, is elsewhere. Let us hope we are released to our slumbers soon. We have an acquaintance in common who has made me aware of a growing problem."

Hunt looked at the Prime Minister with disbelief, trying to control his surprise. This was unexpected and his face had momentarily shown the shock he felt. Who was it that had briefed Disraeli? Was the man referring to Gladstone when he referred to an acquaintance in common? or was it the Queen?

Hunt moved a step to the side, hoping the contact would not deter the man he hoped to speak with, but Gladstone had seen Hunt and Disraeli and had turned away. Hunt felt the sense of frustration well up.

Disraeli smiled and surveyed the room. He spoke again, softly: "A Faerie Queen we both serve has asked me to speak to you and her commands are delightful to obey. I suggest a visit to your mother's is due this Sunday afternoon. I wish you and I an early evening, Inspector Hunt."

Disraeli moved towards a circle of the politically acceptable and Hunt knew the interview was at an end for now. Gladstone was speaking to the Princess of Wales about her portrait. She was responding graciously. Hunt fished the primrose out of the glass and put the flower in his pocket. He felt like a man going under for the third time and abandoned the tray onto a side table as he walked towards Morris. His hand trembled as the thought occurred to him that he may be followed, and his home may be watched. His wife and children … he must get home.

"Come on," Hunt said to Morris, "We're done."

Hunt looked across to where Ted was dealing with a creature in the latest fashion. She was occupying all of Ted's attention as nothing she sipped satisfied her taste. Ted's face was a picture as he had started to pour a cup of punch for the American heiress who sparkled a little too much. It wouldn't be long before some English Earl was tapping into her inheritance Ted thought. He saw Hunt and Morris coming over and handed the surprised lady the silver ladle.

"Here you are, Miss, help yourself. I have to make a move," and Ted joined his colleagues.

Despite himself Hunt laughed.

Morris glanced at him and said: "Hush Tom, remember where you are."

"Are we done for tonight?" asked Ted, looking hopeful.

"In a manner of speaking. Let's change and get out of here and home to our families," said Hunt.

"Did you get to speak to Gladstone?" asked Morris, confused.

"Not quite," said Hunt, "I had a message instead, which has cleared things up. At least I know things are in hand but I've lost my Sunday off so there will be hell to play when I get home after broken promises about tonight and now Sunday as well."

"That was quite quick, Tom," said Ted, looking pleased. "I'd have preferred not to work tonight but it's still quite early. Looks like we'll get most of an evening at home after all."

"We'll go for a cab," said Hunt. "Keep your eyes open in case we're followed."

Hunt played with the primrose in his pocket. A late flower, he thought, no doubt from the woods in the Berkshire hills. Clever Disraeli, playing a chivalrous poet and borrowing from Edmund Spenser's romance in describing the short, stout monarch as a "Faerie Queen." And what could Disraeli gain? Hunt could not help himself, he had to look back. Rumour had it the man had entered politics up to his eyes in debt – but MP's could not be incarcerated for debt. What had Disraeli been like in the thirties and forties? wondered Hunt. He would no doubt benefit from playing on the Queen's loneliness and feeding her vanity. A bit like a character from one of his novels, thought Hunt.

"Come on, Tom," said Morris, pulling Hunt's arm. "We're starting to attract attention standing here."

Slipping out past the police guard at the gate they walked past soldiers whose bayonets glinted in the moonlight.

"There's the fate of those who are rebellious," said Ted, with a grin. "Watch your thoughts about overthrowing monarchy."

"I didn't say that I had any intention," snapped Hunt. Seeing the rebuff impacted Ted, he added: "Sorry, I want to see the bowing and scraping stop, and a more equal life for most of the people who we lock up." Hunt laughed as he thought that most of his views had been shaped by literature given to him by the Prince Consort to read.

"Penny for them," said Morris.

"Don't trouble yourself, I'm no revolutionary, but I am interested in moving the suffrage to include everyone and making our rulers more accountable. Why shouldn't our sons be Prime Minister?'

"Sons?" said Ted. "If you're really interested in universal suffrage Tom, you'd be thinking of that little girl of yours being Prime Minister. Oh, you two may look at me and shake your heads but it'll come … it will have to. Just a matter of time."

Nine

Part of his long journey completed Jack looked at his old friend dozing opposite him as the train drew into Southampton. A tedious journey they had had from Portsmouth as the gangs of "Perway men," held up the train's progress. Peter Fisher's head lolled to one side and he came to as the train stopped.

"We're stuck at a signal," Jack said. "I can well understand, Parson, why you only make this journey once a year."

With each change of train Jack had taken on the role of calling for porters, supervising the luggage and the hamper provided by Mrs Curzon, while assisting Peter Fisher to hurry for their reserved seats in second-class. Prolonged activity and lifting the weight of the bags had all taken its toll as Jack had had to move more quickly than Doctor Brown would have advised. His body had begun to ache and the last section of the journey with a crossing to Jersey was yet to be made. His face showed discontent, which Peter Fisher had learned in the last week or so was really pain. It had become an unspoken habit between the two men for Peter Fisher to wait until he saw Jack's face starting to relax before he spoke to him.

Neither man had mentioned the discussion to each other that they had had with Sam the night before. There was no opportunity as their carriage filled and emptied with a regular rhythm, as most passengers travelled only a few stations but had their numbers refreshed along the route. Peter Fisher had reserved window seats for them, and he and Jack had shared articles in the two newspapers collected at Brighton.

Early that Saturday morning Jack had woken as the sun's watery beams played on the coverlet of his bed. To his surprise he had slept like a baby despite the discussion the previous night. Rising and dressing before the rest of the household was awake, he had walked to shops local to the Curzon home. There he had bought a card with a design of a rose, which looked a similar colour to one he had seen exhibited at the Pavilion a year before. The other part of his purchase was a notebook.

An hour after breakfast Jack and Peter Fisher were making their goodbyes to the Curzon family, ready to start the journey to Lymington. With solemn handshakes for the three younger brothers and impromptu kisses on the cheek from Mrs Curzon and Grandma, Jack had turned to pick up his bag but not before he had seen Peter Fisher wink and slip the three youngest Curzon boys a sixpence each.

Only Luke hung back politely waiting for the guests to leave before he started his paid commission for both Jack and Peter Fisher.

"Aren't you going fishing, Luke?" Mrs Curzon asked, referring to the arranged outing that morning.

"No Ma, I'm a working man today," Luke explained.

"Yes," Peter Fisher interrupted, "I hope it is alright, for Luke to have errands from Jack and I to perform this morning?"

"Of course, Parson," said Mrs Curzon.

Jack gripped Sam's hand in a strong handshake and said: "I expact next time I see you, you'll not be a single man."

"I doubt things will change that quickly," said Sam, solemnly.

A moment's doubt came into Jack's mind as he looked at Sam and registered the worry in his friend's eyes. The life had gone out of Sam.

"What I mean is, well, time will tell." said Sam, "And it will not be that long before you and I meet again."

Jack nodded, understanding the intention. He said: "Well, strike while the iron is hot as they say. Don't have me coming back to play match maker now, will you, Sam? Remember me to Miss Davies and her mother." Jack had added as he and the Parson walked into the hall.

"That I certainly will not," called back Sam, and to Jack's relief, his friend managed a smile. "As I said before it's taken me a year to get you out of her head."

"I'm sure she soon realised it was brains not brawn that she needed," said Jack.

"You have both, Jack, but thanks for the thought," Sam said, and he waved them goodbye from his front doorstep.

Peter Fisher's night had been restless after the discussion and he had lain down after drafting a quick explanation for the solicitor Langton. However, sleep evaded him, and he had abandoned attempts sitting instead before an open window into the early hours of the morning re-drafting the letter. Several more drafts had been attempted with two finding their place in the flames in the still lit but barely glowing ashes of his bedroom fireplace. The room had grown chilly by one in the morning and the old vicar had climbed into bed having finally been satisfied with a blunt account, which told Langton as much of the truth as he knew. Secrets, thought Peter Fisher, help no one. Posting the letter was part of Luke Curzon's commission, as was delivering the card by hand from Jack to Mary.

True to his word Jack confirmed the date of his birthday supper in September to Mary. "Supper," he called the occasion as, "Party," seemed a little optimistic to a man who had grown up without any celebrations for his birthday from the age of nine. His twenty-first birthday in '73 had been quite an event in his life, not only because he benefitted under his parent's will and from the prudent care of the money provided by three trustees but also because thanks to the Parson and the Croft family, Jack had enjoyed a party. He rather fancied that he was developing a taste for celebration.

A year ago, at the Brighton Pavilion, it had been a spur of the moment decision to give Mary a rose, partly because he was generous natured and because, like him, she had no-one else to do so. There had been a meaning in selecting the card which he had bought that morning. Jack's mind had a pleasant memory of a happy occasion they had shared but she had lit a fire with her kiss yesterday.

Luke Curzon patted the pocket which held the coins Jack had given him. They were the equivalent value of the stamp Jack would have bought had he posted the card. Luke recalled Jack's words as he had looked him in the eye and told him quietly the card must not be given up to anyone except a lady called Mary. Luke had nodded, wide-eyed and solemn faced in the Curzon way at being entrusted with such a commission.

The other purchase in the shop was for a different purpose. Jack had decided to leave his current police notebook, which he had brought with him without thinking that it would be inappropriate to use it for this case. He placed it inside an envelope in a bedroom drawer at Sam's, having addressed the envelope to Sergeant Thick at Leman Street. There was nothing in it about the current case for Hunt. Sam would find it if the worst happened and Jack concluded it was for the best to separate work for Hunt from his usual notes. Jack's intention was to collect it and see Mary as a surprise on his way back to London.

Now, towards midday the vicar and the constable sat looking over the quay as the train drew to a stop outside Southampton station. Peter Fisher laid his newspaper down and Jack moved his copy onto the top of the hamper. The train was temporarily paused at a signal. Over the last few visits Jack had made to Selmeston it had become an activity between the two men to read the newspapers and share the articles. Jack had found it an excellent way to get Peter Fisher to share his wealth of knowledge.

"We've a bit of time now, Parson before we make a move again. There must be a waiting room and then I can pass you something from the basket?"

"Yes, we could eat in there. I'd like to show you the views without going too far. What fare do we have, Jack?" asked Peter Fisher.

"A fresh batch here," said Jack, lifting a corner of the cloth wrapped around a complete loaf of bread. "Mrs Curzon must have packed one for your sister. And cheese sandwiches," Jack sniffed. "Smells like Sussex Slipcote."

"Ah, "Thou crusty batch of nature, what's the news?" recited Peter Fisher.

"The Bard again?" asked Jack, raising his eyebrows. It generally was Shakespeare when Peter Fisher made a statement Jack found unintelligible.

"I only say it to show that you and Shakespeare have something in common in the roots of the language he used," explained Peter Fisher. He sniffed the sandwiches and continued: "Sussex Slipcote, now that brings back a memory of something I had meant to do with you at some point: An excursion to The Devil's Dyke. You need to be fit for it though."

Jack stifled a laugh as he contemplated the octogenarian opposite him. He swallowed his humour in respect as the wiry old vicar was no doubt fitter than himself at that point.

Jack said: "I suspect at this moment, that I would struggle with the climb. True, Parson, you'd give me a good bannicking if we were competing. Come on, what's the story? How's it linked to cheese?"

"Perhaps, I would too. At one time everyone who went to Brighton did a trip to Devil's Dyke," explained Peter Fisher. "Marvellous view of the white chalk of Beachy Head last time I went, which was back in the early sixties. And you can see the Isle of Wight if it's clear, of course. But the cheese, Jack, you should taste the cheese. There's a small inn up there whose ale and food are well known to all and sundry. I could never make out if it was the clarity of the Southdowns' air and the exercise or if the food was really that good."

"Seems fitting with that memory somehow that we should be eating freshly baked bread and cheese today then," said Jack. He glanced out of the window "There, we're moving into the platform."

*

It was as the last few stragglers completed their luncheon at the Royal that Mary first met Luke Curzon. Luke had waited all morning, refusing to give up the message he had brought. His conversation with the Hall Porter had been brief, followed by a thumb and finger around his ear lobe as he was marched to the front door and away from the hotel. But the man had at least, unobtrusively, told Mary that a lad had brought her a letter which he would only surrender to her in person.

And Luke had waited, noiselessly making his way back to the hotel entrance until he sat cross-legged, on the lawn in front of the mahogany doors. Hours had gone by it seemed. Like all growing boys Luke felt he was starving and there would be no reprieve for him for another hour until a waitress with beautiful eyes came to the door and briefly stared at him. Conversation with passers-by was fleeting for Luke, until one tried to kick him away. Unused to such treatment the man had got a couple of sharp blows in before Luke managed to dodge him. The man was rebuked by the lady who was with him, (Luke assumed it was his wife) and the couple hurried off. The doorman at the Royal had seen the attack and came out onto the top step. He managed to catch Luke's eye while the boy rubbed his leg. He called to Luke: "You alright are ya, boy?"

With an earnest expression which resembled his eldest brother Luke nodded but he decided to stand away from the doors wary of getting the same treatment again.

The doorman ran his eye over the respectable clothes and intelligent face of the young Curzon. He said: "You should get off home and get some arnica on that. What're you hanging around for here anyway?"

"I've a message to deliver," explained Luke, fishing into his pocket for the folded card. He held it up to show the doorman.

"Who is it you're after? Guest or staff?" the doorman persisted.

"Mary, on the staff," said Luke, stuffing the card back in his pocket in case the man whipped it from him.

"Well, you'll have a wait as she's serving lunch. What's the name?"

"Luke Curzon, on a private commission, I have to see her otherwise I'll have to give the money back," answered Luke.

"Been paid, have you? Lad after my own heart. What did you get?" asked the doorman.

"What the stamp would've cost. I'm not sharing, it's mine and I'll see the job through regardless of beatings, but I've never been treated like that before," said Luke, jutting out his chin. He was sure that Jack and Sam would stand their ground if it was them in his position.

The doorman chuckled and said: "That's right, that's the spirit. Alright, you get across to the bench over there and wait and I'll let her know where to find you."

Luke nodded, encouraged by the doorman's collusion. A decent sort of cove, he thought, but that other man who had kicked him was out of order. Luke was, after all, the son of a Freeman of the Thames Watermen and did not expect to get that sort of treatment. A couple of bigwigs passed him and decided the boy looked hungry. They gave him a half-penny and asked him about his mother, to which Luke, after pocketing the coin, thanked them, and said she was very well and that he was sure if mother knew they had enquired she would ask them about their health.

Shortly after two o'clock the waitress Sam had seen earlier came from the side of the hotel and beckoned to him. He crossed the road towards her, and she asked: "Tell me, who are you waiting for?"

"Mary," said Luke.

She laughed – very softly. "And why?"

"I can only tell Mary."

"And if I will tell you that I'm Mary?"

Luke felt into his pocket and brought out the enveloped card, now twisted with the attempts to get it in and out. His hunger was forgotten with the potential fulfilment of his mission, but Luke hesitated and retained the card.

"Who might have sent you this?" Luke asked as a test.

Mary did not answer at first. The doorman had given her the name of Curzon for the boy. Her bright eyes became a little pre-occupied as she recalled that tea in the Royal where she had met Sam and Harry Franks with Rose and Mrs Phillips. There! She had the similarity in the boy's earnest expression and slight build. "Are you Sam's brother?" she asked.

Luke nodded and waited, thinking that she was that close to being given the card. But although Jack's name was on the tip of his tongue, he did not dare suggest it. The woman must think of it herself before he could give up the treasure.

"Jack," said Mary, smiling. "Did Jack send you?"

"Right answer," said Luke, in triumph, putting the card firmly in her hand. Before he sped off back to Grandma and the pantry, he remembered his manners. Turning back, he bowed slightly and said: "Good day."

His coins were earned, and he sped home doing the calculations in his mind of how to spend them.

*

Lunch over while they sat in the waiting room Jack stared out of the window and considered the decision to disobey Hunt. He wanted to be sure why exactly he was writing an account and that his reasons would be clear to the reader. The direct disobeying of an order would mean dismissal if discovered.

Jack spent the greatest part of an hour thinking of how to begin. Peter Fisher read his newspaper and occasionally looked over the top at his young friend. For some reason it helped Jack to imagine Mary sitting opposite him listening to the account that ran through his mind. He started to write on

213

the second page in, leaving the first page blank. He made the point to himself that Hunt could not control everything because his men were working at a distance. If they faced a catastrophe then it would be Harry as the senior officer that would decide things. *If* Harry was still there. Stan then, if Harry had gone, wrote Jack. And if he were alone? What would he do?

It was difficult to admit what could be construed as disobeying an order as he had not witnessed this side of Sam's character before. Of course, there had been the odd glimpse of an obstinacy at times but never outright rebellion. Perhaps having faced death Sam felt he had little to lose in treading on toes. Ignoring the irritation that he could have felt at doing this task Jack noted down his own insurrection.

Jack ran the previous evening over in his mind as if he was there again. His account could not begin with yesterday. It had not started for him at the end of supper, when the younger boys had disappeared upstairs, and Grandma had re-filled everyone's cups with hot tea. Jack paused. No, he had to go further back than that. If this account was to remain sealed until his, or another team member's death, then he knew the date that he would begin his account. That would firmly fix they had not gone rogue as a team. Jack looked up and waited for Peter Fisher to turn a page of the paper. As the old vicar did so he looked up and saw Jack staring at him.

"Finished?" asked Peter Fisher.

"Not quite, I didn't expact it to take so long.

Peter Fisher glanced at him with interest but decided against asking any questions.

"Parson," Jack said. The old vicar put his paper down and looked into the earnest eyes. Jack asked: "Mr Langton won't open the letters unless there's a death, will he?"

"You can rely on Langton," said Peter Fisher.

Jack nodded and said: "In for a penny in for a pound then," and he wrote a date and location, and the people present to begin with at the top of the first page.

It read: February eighteenth, 1874.

Place: Windsor.

Those present: Inspector Hunt, H.M. Queen Victoria, Constable Jack Sargent.

*

Jack glanced through the window while the crows called to one another from the tall trees by the town on the right bank of the river Lymington. The train jerked past a salt works and it was an ominous sound. He had finished his account of events to date and would copy it later into a letter to send to Sam before Monday. There would be two copies that way and it provided an insurance against Sam going missing.

A warm welcome awaited them at Lymington, as Peter Fisher and Jack climbed down from the train. Helena and Timothy Ward, the Parson's younger sister and her husband, were waiting on the platform for the train to arrive and Jack felt his own weariness evaporating with the hospitality. As he settled into his room in their rambling country Vicarage Jack stood by the window and took in the view of the early blooms on the rose bushes. It felt he had travelled a million miles from London and started a journey towards rebellion against the status quo.

Helena Ward was Peter Fisher's half-sister as Jack discovered during the conversation in the drawing room over steaming cups of tea. She was a good thirty years his junior, but the half-brother and sister were close.

"A different marriage for our father," explained Peter Fisher. "My mother died when I was a child, much like your parents did, Jack, and to everyone's surprise my father remarried in what many would think was his dotage. He taught a young woman who kept house for him to read and write and fell in love. The result was a wedding, a new stepmother who was my junior by five years, and a delightful sister who you see before you, born when I was thirty. I was overjoyed, although it was considered scandalous for my father, as a country parson in those days, to cross the class divide. Come Timothy, pass that plate of biscuits over here, will you?"

Helena's husband Timothy was the Vicar in Lymington. His build made Jack think more of the Blacksmith at Battle than a bookish cleric. He was interesting to listen to and full of banter and got on well with his brother-in-law. After enquiring about Jack's recovery, Timothy asked questions about cases on which Jack had worked and how Leman Street police station operated. Thirty minutes had gone by as Jack and he chatted before Helena suggested: "We should have a short walk before supper and show Jack the river."

"Good idea, but do you feel up to it Jack after all the travelling?" asked Timothy.

"Thank-you, yes, it would be good to have a stretch after so long a journey," replied Jack.

Timothy nodded and said to Peter Fisher: "An old friend of yours is at the river today, Peter Berthon is here carrying out some experiments on his folding boat. We're close to the Lymington River, Jack and there's time for us to see what's going on."

"Have you heard of him, Jack?" asked Peter Fisher.

"Berthon? No, I don't recall the name." Jack answered.

"He's an inventor at heart," explained Helena, "Now the Vicar over at Romsey."

"Show Jack that photograph of Berthon's lifeboat, Timothy?" said Peter Fisher.

"It's somewhere in my study, give me a moment." Timothy said, getting up to go and look.

"I've never met him, you know," said Helena. "He should join us for supper unless he needs to get back to Romsey before dark. He'll have the services of course tomorrow, but I think we should ask him."

Timothy came back into the room holding two items. He handed a photograph to Jack of a rowing boat packed with people. Jack turned the picture over and on the back was written: "Berthon, collapsible Boat, Romsey."

Jack looked at Peter Fisher and said: "Collapsible boat? How does that work?"

"Well, best way to find out is go and see it," said Peter Fisher, smiling. "Timothy can you lead on to the river? I'm unsure of my bearings as it's a year since I was here."

"Gladly," said Timothy. "I'd like to see him as it's quite a while since our paths crossed. But before we go there is also a letter for Jack from Hastings which arrived yesterday."

Jack took the letter and the silver paper knife Helena held out to him. The letter was from Langton with the changes made to the eventuality that Jack married and produced children. A sizeable gift was made to the Croft children to be administered by Langton's firm once their parents had found a source of education. There were two copies and Jack passed one to Peter Fisher.

"Good old Langton, he's cracked on with that," said Peter Fisher. "Sign both Jack and we need two witnesses as well and then we can send one copy back. I can hang on to the other for you until you're back from your travels, if you'd like me to."

"Thanks, Parson, I would. I'd like to know a copy was off to Langton on Monday," said Jack.

"We can do that before you set sail," said Timothy offering Jack a dip pen with which to sign. "Shall Helena and I sign as witnesses?"

Jack nodded and the Wards signed. Glancing at the mantelpiece clock Timothy said: "If we get off to the river now, we should still catch Berthon."

They made their way towards the Lymington Shipyard, Timothy shaded his eyes and looked towards the right and gave a shout. Several men looked back towards him but one waved and called a greeting.

"There he is," said Peter Fisher.

"How does this collapsible bit work?" asked Jack.

"Folds up," explained Timothy. "It went on display at the Great Exhibition in 1851 and Berthon was called to demonstrate the boat for the Queen and Prince Consort at Osborne House."

"I wonder if she would remember," said Jack, almost to himself.

"Probably," said Peter Fisher, "It would have been unusual and stood out." He understood that Jack had realised he was about to have something in common with the Queen other than stolen diamonds. Picking up Timothy's point he continued: "I remember last year he started work on developing a larger model to get more people into the boats. That photograph Timothy showed you had forty people on board didn't it?"

"I didn't count them, but I would think so," said Jack.

"There's larger ones, Jack, ones which can carry seventy-five people," said Peter Fisher.

Jack looked dubious: "And you say they collapse?"

Helena laughed and said: "I know, it sounds incredible to me too."

Timothy now walked on ahead and shook hands with Berthon. He nodded towards the small group and beckoned for them to join him. As they walked over Timothy started to draw Berthon towards Peter Fisher, Helena, and Jack.

"My wife, Helena," said Timothy.

Berthon gave a small bow of his head. He said: "Mrs Ward, delighted to meet you."

"How do you do, Reverend Berthon, we hope you will dine with us."

"Thank you, but I must return to Romsey before dark. Perhaps next time I'm here I may call?"

"Of course," said Helena.

Timothy continued: "Peter you know of course. He's down for a week and has brought a young friend with him for a few days. This is Constable Jack Sargent of the Metropolitan Police, but a Sussex man, and keen on cricket I gather. He doesn't believe your boat can collapse and wants to see the evidence for himself."

"Good to meet you," said Berthon offering Jack his hand. Then he turned to Peter Fisher. "Still not retired?" Berthon asked.

"Unofficially there's still an expectation from those in the village to see me and as we've discussed before, I've no concept of retirement as a clergyman," said Peter Fisher. "Forgive us disturbing your work, but we'd seen the photograph of your experiment on the river near Romsey and Jack was curious. Congratulations on your Gold medal, by the way."

"Too kind," said Berthon.

"What was the medal for?" asked Jack.

"Oh, the boat at the International Exhibition last year. There's hope they'll be used on overseas expeditions now," said Berthon.

"I don't quite understand how a boat collapses," said Jack.

"Let me show you," said Berthon. "This is a small one though."

"Yes, I saw the photograph of the larger forty-seater at the Vicarage," said Jack.

"Did you? Stand this side and I'll talk you through how it works. Timothy, take the bottom end, will you?" asked Berthon.

Berthon started to pull out the pins, removing the seats, the struts and folded back the flooring. Timothy did the same at the other end. The boat, with Timothy's help, folded in half and an interior rib held the canvas lining. Jack stepped forward to help put it back together again and when it was done, stood back laughing at the ingenuity and the fact that it worked. He enthusiastically shook Berthon's hand and nodded.

"Brilliantly done," said Jack. "I didn't expact it to work. What is it you've put on the canvas?"

"A mix of linseed oil, soft soap and yellow ochre. It gives it a durable protection," explained Berthon.

"Well, on any future sailings I shall want to know if there's a Berthon collapsible boat on board," said Jack.

"Better still, why not try it now?" suggested Berthon.

"Here, on the river? I will gladly, and then I won't be afeard to go in one on the sea" said Jack, moving to help.

"Wait, Jack," called Peter Fisher. "Your enthusiasm is making you forget you must let your ribs heal a while longer yet."

"I'll be fine, Parson, as long as I don't fall in," said Jack.

"Well, at least stand back and let the others do the lifting," prompted Peter Fisher. "A couple of cracked ribs from making an arrest," he added to Berthon.

Berthon raised his eyebrows and nodded.

Resigned, Jack stood back while Timothy, Berthon, and his two men, got the boat into the water.

"The end of the Transatlantic cable this year was taken ashore by one of our boats from the Faraday," said Berthon as he and Timothy climbed into the boat. Jack accepted a hand down, feeling the pull in his side.

"How did you come to think of this?" Jack asked Berthon.

"It's some years ago now. I was so struck at the loss of life initially as many boats sailed with inadequate lifeboats for the number of passengers. I wanted to find a way for there always to be enough capacity."

"That's marvellous," said Jack, impressed.

"Isn't it," added Peter Fisher.

"Well, we should stop as the light will be against us and I must return to Romsey; parish duties don't you know," explained Berthon.

"I accompany my young friend back to Southampton on Monday," said Peter Fisher. "I understand that you have the restoration work under way at the Abbey. I would dearly love to see it."

"Of course, you are more than welcome. I shall be delighted to show you the work and a little more of our development of the boats," said Berthon.

On Monday Jack had called his thanks from the lane for the umpteenth time to Timothy and Helena as they waved goodbye while Peter Fisher reminded his sister that he would return before seven that evening. He would travel on to keep his promise to visit Berthon.

Always the first smells of a train when he climbed on board triggered a memory for Jack of some compartment he had travelled in as a child. He was never sure from what time in his past the memory dated, or who it was he had been with. Again, it was there, the clear memory of the colours of the company: brown and green, despite it now being 1874 and the day, the eighteenth of May. He could even recall the memory of an oval garter with a number inside it on the outside of a carriage.

Peter Fisher had insisted on travelling with Jack back to Southampton despite the early start.

The old vicar said: "I have the whole morning to fill before I can call on Berthon at the Abbey in Romsey. You wouldn't want to deprive me of your good company and conversation surely?"

"Not if you put it like that," said Jack. "Did you bring the newspapers? I didn't get much chance to look on Friday."

"Yes, I have them here," said Peter, pulling open his game bag that he generally carried. The newspapers were in the main compartment. Jack thought how incongruous it looked for Peter Fisher to wear his dog collar and carry his old game bag. But it made sense given how much the man had to put inside it. Old habits, thought Jack, die hard. He must remember to ask how long Peter Fisher had had the bag.

"How long is your crossing to the Channel Isles?" asked Peter Fisher.

"About eight hours to Guernsey," said Jack as he passed the timetable to Peter Fisher. "Then a stop and we continue on to Jersey. It will be dark before we land. Do you know the islands?"

"No, I never fancied it, more because of the time when "the Express" was wrecked off the coast of France, but that was in '59. Those old steamers never seemed reliable to me, nor did they look as though they would withstand the conditions of the crossing," said Peter Fisher, as he handed the timetable back to Jack. The return ticket was in the papers. The Parson read the destination of St Helier. "The Isle of Wight was far enough for me to go."

"I think it's a new screw steamer I'm on but I'm not sure which boat it is," said Jack. "They're supposed to be more reliable than the old paddle steamer."

"Weymouth will give the port of Southampton a run for their money if they're not careful," said Peter Fisher.

"It's a long way to go though from London, isn't it?" asked Jack.

"Well, George III made it popular and of course where the Royal Family goes the rest follow," explained Peter Fisher. "It became a watering place, Jack and was always said to have a mild climate, but I've heard Jersey's a charming place. Of course, Victor Hugo wrote of Guernsey when he said there were two kinds of men there, those who spent their lives going around in fields and those who passed their lives going around the world. I've heard you can see the sea beaches of France from high ground, stretching from the north to the south." Peter Fisher paused and looked at Jack. He ventured a question: "Of course, should you have to cross to France … but then you're not likely to, are you?"

Jack grinned and said: "I've taken it that I go hunting if I get a scent."

"What good will it do to follow this fox if you do see him?" asked Peter Fisher.

"There may be a bigger one in sight," said Jack.

"I see. You must not over-tax yourself, though, Jack. It's still early days," said Peter Fisher, in earnest. He added: "It's hard to understand when so young but injuries have a habit of coming back to haunt you when older."

"I think I have some inkling of that after the fire. The cough was troublesome last winter. But I hope Bow will mean cleaner air, which should help. What of the news, Parson?" asked Jack, to turn the attention away from himself.

"Just before you attempt to change the subject, I would hope that you and I would not have any secrets from each other if help was needed?" asked Peter Fisher as he handed Jack a paper.

Jack mouthed: "Never," and he half glanced around. His eyes crossed the carriage, but no one registered with him. He fixed his eyes on the paper. Losing interest, he turned his gaze to the countryside, but it grew less interesting the closer the train got to Southampton.

Peter Fisher had paused but was not to be deflected. He leant forward and Jack looked sharply back to him.

"What I fear is the volatile power of evil in the human heart, Jack," said Peter Fisher. "Proverbs speaks of them looking for someone to devour. You've told me enough in your casual way for me to fear for you in this hunt that you're embarking upon."

"But you surely must believe that power has to be stopped as well, Parson?" asked Jack, frowning.

"Of course I do but stopping it in my experience always brings with it a guarantee of some damage. I don't want you to be the one who receives harm."

Jack stared back at Peter Fisher, reflecting on how much he had come to trust him. The older man looked away, aware he had said too much and focussed on an article in his paper.

Several minutes went by as the Parson read a column. The subject had been dealt with, and as far as Peter Fisher was concerned, he had said all that had been needed.

"I think we might just win," the Parson exclaimed, slapping the paper down on the seat next to him. "Yes, indeed we just might."

Jack peered at the Monday morning headline and made out the name, "Shaftesbury," but that was all.

"What might we win," asked Jack.

"The factory question and the sweep's bill," said Peter Fisher. "A reduction in the hours of work every week in factories and all chimney sweeps to be registered with the police with their work being supervised. More work for you, you see Jack! Shaftesbury's been on it for years, with some small support from souls such as me. Of course, he's younger than I am, and I had hoped to see such a day come before I depart this life. Now it looks as if it might be about to happen this summer. A reduction to a fifty-four-hour week."

Jack smiled at Peter Fisher's enthusiasm, but he had other questions. He asked: "Parson, I know you're better educated than I am, but some things don't seem right. This is one thing that's been wrong. Aren't there other things that also should be changed?"

"Yes, and I believe there will be," said Peter Fisher. He looked at Jack's earnest expression and smiled at the lack of confidence. "We've come a long way in my life since children worked fifteen to sixteen hours in twenty-four."

"Yes, Parson, but there's other things I come across that don't seem right. Don't we need laws for change there as well?" asked Jack.

"Yes, of course."

"If we're trying to make sure children don't work 'til thirteen why can girls be married at twelve? That's one question but there's many. Not wishing to offend you but I find as well that it's common for women on the streets to have been … well, I don't want to offend by explaining it … you know … and at a very young age. I know there was a bill to try and do something about the age when it would be illegal, but it got rejected because girls can marry at twelve. Doesn't all that need to be sorted out as well?"

"Yes, Jack it does, and you will have your say shortly once you've bought the cottage at Turnham Green," said Peter Fisher.

"Yes, I know but why not now? It all seems so wrong that some can vote, and some can't. I see things, and you must have done, probably still do, in the line of work with the public. Our hands are tied … when we're called to a situation," Jack dropped his voice so as not to be overheard. "… because the law doesn't have a category for the crime, or it's an old law and the modern day don't fit it, Parson. And don't even get me started on why Ann Brown can't be a doctor. According to the law I should have arrested her every time I see her."

"Revolutionary talk," the Parson's whispered but his eyes twinkled with pleasure. He said: "Jack, many think the same and you're right that things seem wrong and need changing. Watch out for Disraeli and what he's doing. And as for Ann, so much progress has been made since I was young. Look at that woman Jex-Blake and the others setting up the London School of Medicine for Women this year? I'm delighted you're thinking like you do because you'll change things when I'm long gone."

"Don't talk like that. All due respect, Parson, it's been a long time since you were young, and that woman was thrown out of

Edinburgh University. Some of those other women, Ann included, already have medical degrees, as you know. Ann's is from Paris, and one of the other's, Blackwell, I think her surname is, has a degree from America." said Jack.

"I believe it will happen, Jack, and keep on about the other things you've mentioned." Peter Fisher broke off as his eyes caught sight of the station ahead. "We're coming in. It's good to know that I've passed on the mantel. What's this?" said Peter Fisher as Jack tucked an envelope in the Parson's newspaper.

"My insurance in case something happens to Sam before the post arrives. It's addressed to Langton."

"I see." Peter Fisher put the envelope in his game bag.

They stood in silence by the door of the carriage and Jack looked for Harry and Stan on the platform.

"Where did you arrange to meet your colleagues?" asked Peter Fisher.

"At the quay, but I'm earlier than expected," Jack replied. "I thought to have a look at the dock."

Peter Fisher smiled and said: "Southampton has sixteen acres of dock basin, Jack. Well, as you're early and I'm killing time, why don't we go to the High Street for a view of the bay and we can get some refreshment there."

"What time's your train, Parson?"

"To Romsey? There's another hour yet. Don't hang on for me, Jack, I'll be fine. What time are you expecting your colleagues to arrive?"

"I think they were leaving London sometime after seven o'clock. Those are beautiful views," said Jack, looking at the bay.

The Parson smiled and replied: "They are and there you have the dells of the New Forest, the castle and soon you'll see a fine street and the Old Bar Gate."

"How do you know it so well?" asked Jack.

"Oh, years of holidaying on the Isle of Wight after the Queen and Prince Albert made it fashionable. My sister had a crowded vicarage on the outskirts of Southampton, although you would not know it now as the children are older than yourself and gone some years ago. They kindly included me every summer when they took the family across the water for several weeks. That's partly what started my annual visit. Ryde was a beautiful place with good bathing. Probably it still is, but it's some years since we were last there. There was always time to kill before the boat and much to explore here."

""If you've a love of history you would want to," said Jack. "I can see that in your interest in the Sussex speech. I never asked you, how did you and Father start on that?"

"Oh, I told you he would say a few phrases on a Sunday as we shook hands at the door of the church. He awakened my ear and I started paying attention. Remember it was Bexhill in those days, not Selmeston. I've realised, Jack, areas of Sussex have rich phrases and your father did it naturally but then it became a game between us to see if I could fathom what he meant. It was the difference in the sound to how I thought it would be spelt at first. I became fascinated as some tied up with Shakespeare's phrases and you know I have a love of the Bard. After a while I really wanted to find out what roots there were and where they came from."

"And have you reached an end to it all now?" asked Jack.

"No," said Peter Fisher, chuckling. "Well, I was actually advised not to try by several of the English Dialect Society. But to say that to me was like putting a cherry bun in front of a boy and not allowing him a bite."

The two men paused, taking in the views. Jack said: "I remember the old shepherd at East Dean and Father talking together. Father used to say it was the history of the phrases that mattered not how they sounded."

"Yes, I think your father was right. I found him very helpful Jack and more than once he put me onto the right track about the geography and its influence on the speech as well as the history of the area. As an example, how do you refer to the sun, Jack?" asked Peter Fisher.

Jack pondered for a few seconds, smiled, and said: "Yes I see where you're going. I would call the sun "she", but I've stopped doing it since in London."

"Exactly my point. I assumed that you'd already started to adapt to avoid the amusement aimed at your speech. In a few years you'll have lost it completely and will stop using those phrases and descriptions, unless you're down in Sussex of course, with locals. It sounds strange outside the area, like a slang word and slang is frowned on in high society. It labels us as soon as we open our mouths."

"Does it matter, though, Parson?"

"To get on, yes, I'm afraid it does. This is a perfect example of what is happening, and such usage will be lost soon. Like all the old Sussex carols unless someone rescues them from the Downs and the Weald, bothers to document them, and carries on singing them. I hope that will happen. Had I been younger I think that would have been my next task. My small contribution to the dictionary and the work the Vicar at Selmeston is doing will ensure it won't be lost. I think the words and phrases are from the purest form of English and are like a picture book of the county's history."

"Parson, you're saying my way of speaking isn't the way to advance?" asked Jack.

"That's right. That's why with so many moving away it will be lost if we don't record it. Elements close to Anglo-Saxon, Old Dutch, Old British, and French from the Norman conquest and later the French refugees of the 14th century are traceable. Perhaps someone will read our little record in the future and it will give them some interest. You are part of that, Jack and you already know that it's not the way to advance or you would still describe the sun as She."

*

It had been seven o'clock that morning when Stan and Harry stood waiting at Waterloo Road station for the messenger from Hunt who would bring their tickets and details of the accommodation. Fortunately, the station was airy and expansive, and Harry was relieved that Stan did not display

232

any of the behaviour that crowds generally produced in him. Harry had relaxed and his thoughts went to Rose's last kiss as they said goodbye, but he could not dwell on it for long.

Stan's sharp retort as he was poked from behind in his ribs brought Harry's attention back to the present. Expecting theft Stan's first reaction was to grip the offender around the throat until he realised it was a child who was not a pickpocket but a relative.

Percival Green of Camberwell New Road Police Station made his second appearance on a railway station that week to deliver a message on behalf of Inspector Hunt. He had greeted his uncle in the manner cultivated by the man since the child had been able to reach into a pocket.

"What the ..." Stan spat out.

"Give over, Uncle Stan, I'm working," Percy spluttered.

It was not in Stan's nature to be wrong-footed for long, but he flushed and let go.

"Working at what though? I thought you were in the Grove."

"I was, but I moved on," said Percy. "I had an offer so to speak from an Inspector - no names necessary between you and me – and am in training for the police now at New Road."

"*Training,*" Stan spat out the word, "Training my eye,

"Give over Uncle Stan I'm undercover this morning. 'Course, there's a few years to fill before I join you in uniform, in the family business so to speak and I'm filling the Boot Boy position at present. Gives me opportunity to watch and learn from my mentor as it were," said Percy.

Harry exploded in laughter at the colour of Stan's face and neck. He could tell by the expression that Stan was debating whether to clip the boy round the ear or kick him up his backside. Stepping forward Harry extended a hand.

"Detective Sergeant Harry Franks, good to meet a "trainee." You're a Green, are you? What do we call you?"

"Percy to you Detective Sergeant. I knew you was a 'tec. You've got the bearing them in uniform don't get," said Percy, giving a side glance at his uncle. It was a risk.

"Is that right?" said Harry, putting a hand on Stan's arm as an expletive spat from under Stan's breath.

"Listen, you," Stan muttered into Percy's ear while he glanced to the right and left. "Don't you go mouthing off about being a relative. Does your mother know you're running errands for the Inspector?"

"'*Course not*. As I said, I'm under cover, ain't I? Like you. Anyway, as good as it is to meet the famous Harry Franks of Shadwell..."

Percy's voice went to a squeak as Stan caught hold of his nephew and enfolded him in a bearhug lifting him off his feet until they were eye to eye.

"Stop bandying names about in public," hissed Stan. "If you're under cover you learn to keep your mouth shut or you won't survive. Alert, "at all times" and remember you don't know who's watching. Got it?" Stan set the boy down and let him go.

Percy grinned, used as he was to his uncle Stan. He nodded.

"A'right, a'right, no way to carry on with a colleague, Uncle …. aha, nearly got me there. No names, right, got it."

"Right, now if you're to slip an envelope to a cove you do it quietly and quickly without announcing it, see?" said Stan. "You might as well learn now. It needs to fit in the palm of your hand. So, put your hand with the envelope into my pocket like you used to do when you were after chestnuts when you were little. Right?"

Stan turned his back on Percy and the exchange was made. Harry watched the family similarities between uncle and nephew and thought Hunt would have been interested to observe Stan's ability to train a potential pickpocket.

It was a funny thing, Stan thought, for Hunt to have taken the boy on. Hunt must have spotted something in the lad but there was no reason why the inspector should have made the connection that he was Stan's relative.

"Well done lad," said Stan, slipping Percy two pennies. "Get back quickly on the omnibus. Go fast and always change transport halfway in case you're followed. If you've any doubts cross the road to see if the person does the same. Go in somewhere busy if you think you've got a tail. Got it?"

"Thanks Uncle Stan."

"Tell your mother I'll be round to see her. Go on, get off now," said Stan.

Percy winked obviously and avoided his uncle's glare, touching his forelock to Harry.

Harry scratched his head and laughed as Percy sidled off. "Well would you believe it?" said Harry.

"No, I wouldn't, and I'll have words with my sister-in-law on this to make sure the boy's being properly paid. What's Hunt thinking of using the lad in that way? The child's always been a blabber mouth and has no idea of keeping quiet."

"He'll learn, he's a sharp one. Anyway, no one's going to take any notice of another child on the street, are they? He's got something though, and could do well," said Harry. "You should tell Hunt, Stan. Let him know that Percy's your nephew. It can only do him good in Hunt's eyes and it will come out sooner or later. Now, how about we pick up supplies in case we can't get anything until Southampton?"

"I checked and we have ten minutes at Basingstoke to get refreshments," said Stan.

"That's a long way and I won't last," said Harry. "Drowning men clutch at straws," and Harry moved to cross to an opposite platform where hot potatoes were visible. Stan looked up and down the area and having satisfied himself that the shady characters that he could see where no problem to him he followed Harry.

Money changed hands with a street vendor selling the food. Harry and Stan's presence in front of the stall discouraged a few as there was something in Stan's bearing that smacked of police. Harry knew it and quire liked the fact that Stan could clear an area by simply being there. It was a different matter for mice scuttling around, however, and as one creature never travelled alone the station must have been riddled with them. Harry worked on the fact the potatoes were steaming hot and he and Stan dug out the soft innards using their pocketknives.

Ten

A seaman called: "Nous avons passé la Corbiéthe." Jack looked at Harry who shrugged in response but a clerkish looking man sitting close by, said: "That means the worst is over."

Jack nodded and asked: "Do you live on the island, sir?"

"I do, but business takes me back to England occasionally."

"I'd not like to do that crossing in the winter," said Jack.

He and Harry had sat on deck for a good part of the journey from Southampton while Stan had remained in the second class cabin all the way emerging only now with the hope that the sea would be kind. His only companion had been a glass of brandy as the very sight of an expanse of water made him queasy. He emerged from a doorway looking quite ill.

"Reminds me of Cornwall, although I've only been once," said Harry, collecting his bag from Stan. "Around St. Ives there's a superior light that attracts painters. I'd like to take Rose one day, but the problem is, like here, it's getting to the place. Until the rail travel opens-up more it will take for ever to get there. We should look around for some transport as we get off."

"We're anigh now. I've never been to Cornwall. Southampton today is the furthest west I've got to and this island the furthest south," said Jack. "It's warmer, feels milder and the light is beautiful. There's bound to be transport on the dockside once we're off. Stan, you look ready to fall asleep."

"Stomach's off, always happens on boats. I'll be fine once I'm on firm ground again," explained Stan.

Jack leant on the rail and stared ahead at the sea as the boat lurched again. He loved the sense of freedom boats gave him. Stan groaned and closed his eyes, putting his head against the back of the bench. The boat pitched again and in unison Stan's groan went up. Jack grinned at the tough Sergeant who was defeated by the sea. Harry joined Jack by the railing to take in the first views of Jersey. Ahead were forested tops peppered with small homes and a fort. Jack pointed to it and Harry nodded.

Their clerkish fellow passenger explained: "It was built during the Napoleonic Wars."

"Funny it's still standing," said Jack.

"Oh, my dear sir, don't underestimate the need for defence on these islands to keep England safe," said the Clerk. "After all, France and the German Confederation only finished fighting three years ago and Prussian troops left France just last September when the final indemnity was paid. Some say Germany is now the leader in Europe with all its Prussian militarism. We have an unstable peace."

Jack said: "Can't see it would affect these islands, or England for that matter."

"Time will tell," said the clerk. "My business also takes me to France, and I find the French are resentful of the loss of seventeen thousand men and the annexation of Alsace and part of Lorraine. The effect on that society should not be underestimated."

"And what business are you in, sir?" asked Harry.

"Export of potatoes and other crops. My work is to help charter the boats," explained the Clerk. "And you, gentlemen, what brings you to Jersey?"

"To make sure we don't remain stationary if you don't mind me quoting Mr Thomas Cook. We're making a trip. As he would say, "Hurrah for the trip – the cheap trip." Harry said, jovially.

Jack laughed at the resurrection of the old Harry, but then hear Stan curse the sea.

"You must be doing well to be travelling," said the clerk.

"We are God-fearing workers taking advantage of the delights of a walking holiday to view the picturesque, thanks to the third-class travel the railways have offered and a goodly luggage allowance." Harry offered his hand. "Delighted to make your acquaintance, sir."

"We're coming in," said Jack, deliberately placing himself between Harry and the clerk to cause a distraction. "Not long now," he added for Stan's benefit.

"Thank God," muttered Stan.

*

The passengers disembarked from the iron Paddle Steamer at St Helier and from there the boat would resume her normal mail duties as well as the role of a pleasure ferry.

Harry moved for the walkway which was being lashed to the boat. He said as an aside: "See that carter over there? Once

239

we're off the boat ask him if he can get us to Gorey. We could do with getting a move on, Jack, as it will be dusk in an hour and I'd like to find our boarding house and eat something."

Jack was off first leaving his heavy bag with Stan, who was still at the point of making only one-word answers. Harry knew he should have realised from Stan's expression he had not yet got his land-legs and gave up the effort at conversation as they joined Jack on the quayside.

"This would be the place to make enquiries tomorrow, don't you think?" suggested Jack.

"I should think so," said Harry. "But now I need food and my bed. Stan, fish out the details from Hunt that Percy gave you and check the name of the place we're staying in, will you?"

"All we have you already know. It's a village called Gorey and we're to look for a cottage near Mont Orgueil Castle. Your hope of a boarding house is over-ambitious, Harry. Looks like we have more of a journey to do," said Stan.

Harry's face set with annoyance as he heard the carter raise the price. Jack had started to look around for other transport. All that was available to go to Gorey was the oyster cart and money changed hands. Jack beckoned to Harry and Stan and they walked over.

"He's playing his face about the lateness of the hour, but he's agreed to take us for more money. The cart has a strong fish smell, and we will stink of it, but there doesn't seem any other choice," explained Jack.

Harry nodded and Stan threw the bags into the cart. The three men climbed up to start the slow journey to Gorey. The village was close to the sea and sprawled from a harbour partly spreading up a hill. The slope rose to a castle which seemed to be on a rocky headland which jutted out above the village over the sea. The castle was displaying a flag, which was in the process of being lowered by two soldiers. Down at the shore men were involved in beaching their boats, and after more than fifty Jack gave up counting how many craft there were.

"Sunset's imminent," said Stan, casting a look over the bay.

"If you're minded to climb up to the castle you can see Normandy on a clear day," said the carter as Jack hauled the bags off the cart.

"Where can we find this place?" asked Harry showing the carter the name on the paper.

"Down by the fishermen's cottages along the lane," said the carter.

Harry's face set as he anticipated a hovel.

"Not exactly the quiet place we'd expacted," said Jack, as the cart lumbered off. "There must be nigh on two hundred boats beached on shore down there. Perhaps Hunt's put us here as it will be easy enough to pick up a boat to cross the bay."

"I suspect we've been told what we need to know and no more," said Stan.

"What name have we got?" asked Jack.

"No name, just 3ʳᵈ cottage," said Harry. He slung his bag across his back.

"By the looks of the place, Harry, there are no boarding houses here," said Stan.

"I know for whatever reason Hunt has put us in such a place there it had better be a good one. Come on, let's see what delightful accommodation we're to enjoy tonight," said Harry, as in low mood the three men walked in silence towards the cottages through the gathering dusk.

Unlike some of the roads they had seen this path was not maintained and it was unlit. For Harry and Stan who were London policemen born and bred in the city it was alarming. As the dark fell like a blanket Harry stopped and looked up at the sky, hoping for the cloud to blow over and the moon to fulfil its promise. Jack reached into his pocket and produced a box of safety matches and Harry and Stan turned as they heard him strike one against its box. The flame was enough to show this route was well trodden and the bushes had not yet become overgrown in the late spring. Far from being deserted as they expected the path had a steady traffic of figures which walked towards them as men and women finished the work at the shore. Darkness descended again as the match died and Stan asked: "How many of those have you got, Jack."

"Quite a few," said Jack, "But if I go in front, we'll use less of them as I'm more comfortable with the dark country than you both. One good thing, the dark means it will be hard to see anyone's features."

There was the odd exchange from a few people who passed by. Jack could not make out what was said, but Stan's ear worked out a type of grunted word which was given in

------

greeting. He tried to copy the sound, and this seemed to satisfy the next few curious folk.

Jack ran through in his mind what alternatives they would have if they could not find the right cottage. As the country man of the three of them he knew it would fall to him to work out an alternative for the night. Jack scanned the area along the castle wall for potential places to settle. However, he need not have worried as the clouds parted for a few moments only, but it was enough time to show them the buildings of what they took to be the third cottage.

"Here we are, I think," said Harry, as the path deviated up the hill and led to an outline of several buildings. The main cottage fronted the path but appeared to be in darkness.

"Just in time," said Jack. "More cloud is moving in. We'll not see much moon tonight."

"Let me go to the door," said Stan. "You both wait here and stand by in case we have to make a run for it. Each man should see to himself if there's a problem, agreed Harry?"

"Agreed," said Harry and he glanced at Jack knowing that he would not run far.

Jack nodded and said: "If we have to move off, I'll stay and take whatever's coming as I won't get far if I've to run. You and Harry get away and get help if you can."

Stan held out his hand and said: "Give me the message from Hunt in case they need proof of who I am."

Harry rummaged in a pocket and handed the envelope over. Jack strained his eyes in the fading moonlight to take in the country they were in. The bracken was almost six feet in height and the dead stems and fronds from the winter had developed bottomless beds preventing other plants from rooting. Jack prayed for a gust of wind so a moon would grant them time to see where they put their feet.

Stan moved forward and Harry and Jack crouched down at the foot of a steep slope where the green ferns, produced by a late spring, were still interspersed with the orangey brown from winter.

"That's a wren," said Jack as a shrill song started up.

"How do you know?" whispered Harry.

"Just do." Jack shrugged. "Where you get ferns, there's usually wrens and the other birds seem to move on. Harry listen can you hear a train?"

"Don't tell me there's a railway here," exclaimed Harry. "Why did we sit on that cart?"

"We didn't know. There must be a station in Gorey as you can tell the engine's slowing. Well at least that's convenient for moving around," said Jack.

Stan checked their positions as Jack motioned to Harry to follow him into the ferns. Jack allowed plants to enclose him, but Harry, being a true city dweller shook his head. The ferns were taller than both men and Detective Sergeant Harry Franks, had no intention of disappearing into them.

The moon's light now leant a ghostly pallor and there were no hiding places any longer. Stan gestured for Harry to get down again. It had the desired effect as Harry dropped to the ground quickly. Stan checked that Jack and Harry could not be seen from the cottage door before he knocked on it. He called out a greeting in English and hoped the person within was not going to answer in the patois spoken by the sailors and the locals they had passed.

The door opened and light flooded out into the darkening evening. A man held out a lantern towards Stan and his own face looked eerie.

"I'm looking for a bed for the night," Stan said, almost abruptly.

"Your name?" asked the man. The accent was from across the water thought Stan.

Stan hesitated. Making his decision, he said: "Green, from London."

"Wait," and the man withdrew inside closing the door. Stan could hear the man walking away inside the cottage. He turned towards his two colleagues, screwing up his face at first but then he was clearly on the alert as Stan could hear there was more than one set of footsteps coming to the door. He looked to where Harry was and held up two fingers, quickly dropping his arm as the door swung open. Harry steadied himself ready to move forward if Stan needed help. All he could see of Jack were the eyes and he made a slight hand movement for Jack to stay put.

The man with the candle was back and next to him was a soldier. Stan controlled his surprise.

"Mr Green, I need to see if you have papers," the soldier said.

Stan hesitated before he handed across the envelope Percy had brought from Hunt, but after seconds he did hand it over.

The soldier pulled out the letter and held it up to the candle.

"This is what we were expecting but we understood there were three policemen not one."

"There are," Stan turned and called: "Harry, Jack, come forward, it's alright."

Stan stepped into the doorway and was greeted by a third soldier, a sergeant this time. Jack and Harry moved slowly forward in silence as Stan disappeared with the Sergeant inside the cottage. The door remained open and as the moon deserted them again the slightly built man with the lantern stepped forward so they could see their footing. His smile put them at their ease and Jack moved first.

"You were not what we were expacting," Jack said.

"Nor you for us. We were told three policemen and were expecting uniforms. We'd written you off tonight," the man answered. "You're much later than we were told. But there's still food keeping hot on the range."

The three men shook hands and Harry's usual jocular manner, which had started to escape him with the fatigue, came to the fore.

"I wonder if you would have the usual hospitality?" asked Harry.

"I daresay we can find you a dram," answered the man.

"Are you one of the soldiers that pulled down the flag?" asked Jack.

"You were watching, were you? Yes, Private Adams is my name."

"What are soldiers doing here?" asked Jack.

"Running a flag up and down to all appearances but the cottage was requisitioned years ago during the Napoleonic wars as part of the defences of the area and someone forgot to give it back. There's me, I'm from the Army Hospital Corps, Corporal Bruce downstairs and our Sergeant, Samson."

"Jack Sargent and Harry Franks," said Jack, forgetting to add the rank.

"We expected two sergeants and a constable. You're all 'tecs are you?" asked Adams.

"There's an interesting thought," said Harry. "But you're right, we are two sergeants and a constable. I'm Detective Sergeant Harry Franks, this man is Constable second class reserve Jack Sargent and our man who you admitted first is Sergeant Stan Green, a good man to have on your side in a fight and one you should never upset. Who liaised with you about our arrival if you don't mind my asking?"

Adams shrugged: "No idea, Sergeant Samson may know."

There was a further surprise as the men entered the cottage. The entrance was into what was the upper level of the building with a lower floor dug out below. The ground floor was used as a dormitory and three camp beds had been made up for the visitors in one area of it. It was partly screened off by a sheet and Jack had a momentary thought about the snorers of the world in one room but equally as quickly dismissed it. It had been a long day, his side was aching, there was no choice and he decided tonight that he did not care.

"Clever isn't it?" A man in uniform with a Sergeant's stripes climbed up the stairs to greet them and introduced himself as

Sergeant Samson. He held out his hand and Jack and Harry shook hands with him in turn.

"The cottage was done as part of the defences in the early part of the century," Samson explained. "Purbeck limestone was put down on the lower level and it's done its job and lasted well. Come down and see. It's good down there on a cool night as it keeps the heat from the stove. Our orders are to help you in any way but first, come down and eat. We have food and drink ready for you."

Samson led the way down to the lower floor with Jack and Harry following. Behind them they heard the bolts being drawn on the door by Adams. Jack and Harry exchanged a look as it registered. They were locked in.

Samson pointed to a kitchen area where Stan was ripping apart a piece of bread. Samson said: "Your colleague is already eating as you can see. We use this floor as a living area and kitchen. There are outbuildings at the back we use as an equipment store and you're welcome to see if anything will be of use to you in the morning."

"That's very kind," said Harry. "Would you mind if we ate? It's been a long journey."

"Go ahead, plates are on the shelf and there's Jersey melon, and a mutton stew in the pot, which you're welcome to," said Samson. "How was my old town when you left?"

"You're not Jersey men then?" asked Jack.

"We're not," said Samson. "I'm a Londoner but not for some years. South of the river originally, area swallowed up into

Lewisham now. Adams is from Manchester and Bruce is border country."

"And on that subject, Sergeant, I could offer a wee dram," said Corporal Bruce, brandishing a bottle.

"A man after my own heart. That would be very welcome," said Harry, "Whereabouts in the border country do you hale from?"

"Melrose," said Bruce.

Sergeant Samson pulled out two stools at the table for Jack and Harry. Jack moved to the range and had dished up a plate as he saw them come down the stairs and he placed them at the table next to Stan, who was still tucking in.

Stan nodded at his two colleagues as they sat down with him and said: "It's good, eat up. When did you ever have melon?"

Bruce put out three glasses and a plate with more chunks of bread on it. Jack looked around for butter. He could see only cheese and cut himself a substantial piece.

"Are there usually more soldiers than just three here?" asked Jack.

"Not any more in the cottage. There's a barracks on the island," said Bruce.

"Jersey was too convenient a stopping off point for the French in the past to leave it unguarded," added Samson. "Last invasion was 1781, they fended off the French after they took St Helier. A Major Peirson lost his life. Martello towers were put up after that and fortified with gun batteries, infantry and the navy and the locals had a militia that was well-drilled. Just three of us from another place here this time and our tour of duty will end as you leave and then another team will arrive."

"Would you be able to show me the order you had about our arrival?" asked Harry.

Samson's face was first grave as he assessed Harry. However, he relaxed and said: "I don't see why not. Our orders are to assist you in any way."

"Strange that, isn't it you being soldiers?" said Jack, "I would have expected liaison with the local police."

Samson walked over to a set of shelves and pulled out papers from a leather satchel. His eyes twinkled as he looked at Jack. "We also thought it unusual but given how this island prides its independence were not surprised that the locals were not being involved." He passed the telegram to Harry and said: "There, it's short and sweet."

"It's like Jack said, I would have thought we would be liaising with police on the island if with anyone," said Harry. He searched the two lines for something to indicate a connection he would recognise. At the bottom was a single word which he did not recognise: "Ubique."

Slowly, Harry pushed the paper back to Samson, frustrated at its brevity and the muddle it created.

"Ubik?" Harry pronounced the word, "What does that mean? Is it a name or a message in its own right? That's not going to help us understand who arranged our billet with you, is it?"

"Perhaps we should accept we will never know," said Stan, holding out his hand. Harry passed the paper across the table to Stan. He looked at the brief message, shrugged and passed it to Jack, who read it over several times.

"Unusual spelling. French?" suggested Stan. "How do you pronounce that? Probably comes from one conversation between a man we know while he was holding a tray at a ball and some dignitary. Forget it, Harry. It's got Hunt's royal connection all over it. We've a bed for tonight, which at this point is all I care about and tomorrow we've got some decisions to make about this job."

"Yes, for tonight I will leave it Stan but tomorrow I want a telegram office," said Harry, irritably.

Stan shook his head. "No Harry, no communication directly, remember?"

"It does looks foreign," said Jack. "I wonder if the Parson would know?"

"You *and* me sending messages then, tomorrow," said Harry. "Where will your Parson be?"

"Still with his sister," said Jack revealing nothing.

"Write a message and I'll send it, Jack," said Harry.

Sergeant Samson sat down opposite Harry, his sharp eyes on the Detective Sergeant. "Something Stan said probably might explain how we come to be here. Mind if I pick that up with you?"

"Of course not," said Harry.

"You mentioned a royal connection," said Samson.

Harry gave Stan a look.

Stan muttered an oath and followed it with: "Sorry Harry, I dropped my guard. It's tiredness and hunger."

Harry said: "It's easily done. no secrets with friends. Our Inspector grew up at Windsor. The case we're on involves stolen diamonds from a visiting dignitary and personal embarrassment to our Queen, that's all. Easy job for you this, I would have thought. We make our enquiries and will probably be off by tomorrow night. The thief is either here or not and my money is on him being long gone to another country where we have no powers of arrest."

"So that's why we were ordered here," said Bruce. "I'd wondered what influence there was to get three of the King's Rifles here when we would be more useful elsewhere."

Sergeant Samson continued to stare at Harry, who met his gaze without blinking. Jack breathed in slowly, almost imperceptibly, keeping his expression amiable, aware that he was being observed by Bruce. Harry had told part of the truth. The question was would Samson and his men buy it as being the whole story.

Jack looked back at Bruce, grinned and said: "Bit of a waste of manpower all round, if you ask me."

"Nothing else to do, some people," added Stan.

Bruce laughed and picked up the whisky, offering it to Stan.

"Thanks, I will," said Stan, passing the tin mug over.

Samson nodded and suggested amiably: "We should then turn in as two of us will be running a flag up in the morning." He pushed his right boot off with the toes of his left foot as he said: "Good whisky, a mutton stew and a billet on a camp bed. You're remarkably affable given the circumstances and the lateness of the hour. I'll say one thing for these arrangements.

You should sleep well as you know you're safe in here. That's why you're here with us. We'll sleep better than your quarry sleeps tonight, wherever he is."

*

The dawn woke Jack after a restless night as the early sun streamed through the thin muslin at the window. Jack calculated he had had five hours sleep. Occasionally he had woken to shove Stan with his foot attempting to stop the snoring. Eventually, by four o'clock, he had fallen into a dead slumber and now Stan was shaking him.

"Come on," whispered Stan, "You can't sleep all day. There's a pump outside to wash by."

Jack took himself outside and he worked the pump until cold water splashed into his hands. Sticking his head under the flowing water he fought the cold until it had drenched the shirt which he had slept in. Pulling it off over his head he wiped the wet garment over his torso.

Harry was sitting up when Jack went back into the cottage, thumping his pillow into shape. Lifting the corner of the sheet which had divided soldiers and policemen overnight Jack could see the steady breathing of a mound that was Private Adams. Quietly, Jack descended the stairs and Samson nodded a greeting to him as he arrived in the living area.

As Jack poured tea for himself Samson said: "I won't ask you how you slept. It's an acquired way of life. The watch changed at four and Adams will sleep on."

"How long have you been here?" asked Jack.

"On the island? Three months and it's an unusual posting for the three of us together. Most of the men in the barracks are locals."

"Where were you before Jersey?" asked Jack.

"Winchester, in barracks for a while, time with the family locally," Samson explained.

"You're married?" asked Jack, surprised.

"I am and have two children aged four and one. They stay in Winchester as my wife has family near there. After this I go back for a month to the barracks," added Samson, instinctively straightening up, as he explained. "And first time I've an unusual amount of leave. Almost like I was being rewarded so I suspect I have three policemen to thank for that."

Jack nodded and sipped his tea. He said quietly: "The milk's like cream."

"Jersey breed of cow," said Samson. "We can talk quite normally down here without disturbing Adams. My orders are unusual. I'm told to protect you."

"Protect us?" Jack laughed. "Can't see why."

"Well, accept that it's the way it is. I would advise you to go about separately and try different areas, as arriving together will invite interest. You're not on holiday that's clear. I don't ask to be told anything," said Samson.

"Not much I can tell you so that's just as well but thank-you for helping us." Jack said, continuing sipping his tea.

"It's enough to be thanked. More than we usually get," said Samson. A footfall on the stairs announced Harry coming down. He looked from Jack to Samson and arrived at a decision.

"If a man is to come under fire for me and my men, he deserves to know the full story. You might have come across the man we're after. He has hair the same sort of colour as our young Jack here. Jack's the only one who's seen him close-up and all we have is a rough sketch to take about with us to try and find him. Jack and I were involved in trying to catch him during one crime and Jack saw him commit another. Shortly after that he did a third theft and all three were public and audacious."

"I would prefer to know no more," said Samson.

Harry ignored the statement. He continued: "We've other reasons why we're after him which I won't go into. There's a sketch from Jack's description and it's been checked against photographs we have on record since 1870, which are listed according to types of crime. He doesn't feature which means he's not been caught in England."

"But he's been traced to Jersey?" asked Samson.

"Apparently so, although we don't know where on the island he may be. St Helier though makes sense to start making enquiries," said Harry. He paused briefly while he accepted a mug of tea poured by Jack, then continued: "Probably on his way back through France, maybe Holland. More than possibly long gone."

"Look, I'm a soldier, and was ordered to aid three policemen from London. No questions asked. Foreigners come and go on these islands as it's easy to slip in and out on the boats. Some foreigners are more memorable than others. But to state the obvious you have no jurisdiction here as police, you know that." Samson paused and cut himself a piece of cheese. He took a bite and after he had chewed and swallowed, continued: "The working language of the law here is a form of French. It's not in my experience of education and I can't understand it. Frankly, I suspect you can't either. Adams has picked up a small amount of the local language which is called Jèrriais. It's like old French, according to Adams anyway, when you see it written down. Saying it is a different matter. Bruce can hold his own with it as well."

"Right, that's useful," said Jack. "Didn't you say your family were French at one time, Harry?"

"Back into the distant past, Jack. Huguenots, hence the surname Franks, which was their way of picking an anglicised name to get work. You had to prove you were local to get anything paid," explained Harry.

"I've heard some influences in the Sussex way of speaking," said Jack. "Just odd words, like "seine," for a mackerel net. Parson shows me from time to time when he documents a new one that he finds. He says its old French."

"That might be for different reasons it's still there in Sussex," said Harry. "My family gave themselves a name which other Huguenots would recognise but which also convinced the English they'd been born in England. No-one in my family has any idea of the language now. I've heard something spoken around Shoreditch which reminds me of a lingo my grandparents spoke but that's all."

Samson said: "As you've no jurisdiction here to make an arrest how were you to get the man back to London if you found him. The only way I know of to get a man off the island and back to England has been debt. London was able to exercise some sort of pressure to get a man removed from the island. We were called on to help as the creditors here were not over pleased the man was leaving the island."

"We're to follow, not to arrest," said Jack.

"I see. Your appearance here and disappearance eventually, with or without the man you're after, needs to attract as little attention as possible. I won't press you on your mission, but I would suggest you will be safer staying here, despite the discomfort and more welcome," said Samson.

"That's wise words, Harry," said Jack. "We should only be a few days at the most and then we'll be gone. I've never thought we were going to find the man here." Jack turned to Samson. "The assumption has always been that he's not English. If he was to leave Jersey for the continent, presumably he could pick up a boat from any small coastal village?"

"Of course," said Samson. "The fishermen are back and forth all the time between here and Normandy."

"Wouldn't that be a reason for placing us here, given there's a whole fleet of oyster catchers off this beach?" asked Jack.

"Possibly, but we'd need a lead to know where to go," said Harry.

"Who needs a lead?" Stan said, as he came down the stairs rubbing his head dry after immersing it under the pump.

"I was trying to sound hopeful. You've missed a helpful chat with the Sergeant here, Stan. We're in exactly the right place at the right time to trace our quarry," said Harry.

"There has to be a reason we've been sent here with a fleet of oyster catchers operating off the beach going back and forth between here and Normandy," interrupted Jack.

"Maybe, we should test it out," offered Stan.

"Stan," Harry barked.

"No, seriously Harry, why not test it out. We can't stay cooped up in here hiding for days. You're going back on Friday, and you've already made that clear. That's fine with me and Jack and I won't stop you regardless of how London might feel about it. So, why not get on with the investigation and take on the chin the consequences. You and I aren't given to hiding and I doubt young Jack would be." Stan sat down by the bread and started to cut a wedge for himself. "Butter would go down really well with this," he said to Samson.

"We don't run to butter but there's dripping from last night on a stone slab in the larder." Samson nodded to the storeroom.

"Even better," said Stan, and the conversation paused while he disappeared with his bread behind the curtain. He reappeared with a bunch of grapes in one hand and the bread smeared with dripping in his other hand. Stan put the grapes on the table and looked reverently at them. Jack grinned and picked one off a stem putting it quickly into his mouth before Stan could stop him.

"Guernsey grapes," said Samson. "They come in on the steamers, those that don't go to London."

"Unbelievable," said Harry, eating one.

"Grown in hot houses, I'm told. Corporal Bruce brought them back from St Helier."

Stan picked another and the taste made him smile. Harry reached forward and did the same.

"You should have these at the wedding," said Stan.

"I'm not treading on Roses' toes about the food. They are exceptional though," said Harry, taking another. "Makes for a happy Harry."

Stan resumed: "You see, all the filth and depravity in the world that we deal with, Harry, is pushed away with that taste. As I was saying, you go on Friday, Harry, which really means the night boat on Thursday for you to be back to have that meeting on Saturday morning. We're not putting your wedding off again. Today's Tuesday so we've got two days really. Let's test it. I'll go around the public houses in St Helier with that sketch of our man and Jack can go and have a chat with the towns' people."

"What do you say, Harry?" asked Jack. "We can send the telegrams from there as well. Maybe Sergeant Samson can lend us a man in his civvies for back up?"

Stan glanced across at Samson, who nodded and added: "The telegram link at Gorey pier is out of order. I don't know if St Helier is the same. Bruce and Adams are yours for the day and they'll both jump at the chance to do something other than run a flag up and down and which gets them out of uniform."

Stan chewed and stared at the three men in turn.

He said: "Something will come crawling out of the woodwork, mark my words."

*

Inactivity was never good for Stan Green. No-one knew that better than he and Harry. For a few more minutes he continued to scan the shoreline knowing his own leaning towards suspicion. Somewhere on the horizon life was going on as normal. Not for the first time did he wonder how he had managed to get sucked into Hunt's activities. It was the aroma and flavour from the grapes that had done it. The experience had reminded him there were wholesome places somewhere else than the wreckage in people's lives caused by the crimes he ended up dealing with.

Stan straightened up and took in the view of the beach. It was a hectic bay and not the remote place he had expected that morning as a variety of craft, from trading schooner and steam ship, down to small fishing boats were immediately in front of him. His peace was shattered with the realisation that it would be simple for anyone looking for them in the general mix on the sea to come ashore. Pity Jack was no good in a fight at present, Stan thought.

He passed the time of day with a man walking past and tried to engage him in conversation about the weather, but the response was a blank expression and a shrug to indicate that he did not understand what was being asked. He's no time for strangers, that's what it is, thought Stan. Something in the man's initial expression said that he understood what Stan had said although he made out that he had not. Stan thought that the people around Gorey no doubt lived in a tight community and traded through established links to France and England. What hope would a man with a Stepney accent, dressed differently and obviously not a holidaymaker, have in obtaining any in-road into information? Stan kicked himself as the very attempt would invite suspicion.

He shrugged and checked his pocket watch. "Still early, about eight," Stan muttered to himself. As he looked up, he saw Corporal Bruce walking towards him from the direction of the castle. The man must have finished his watch. He also noted that there was a wind getting up and the tide was changing.

Bruce yawned as he reached Stan.

"We're off to St Helier," explained Stan. "Sergeant Samson wants a word with you about coming with us. Was all quiet?"

Bruce looked surprised at the question but nodded. He moved towards the cottage door and called back: "Always is here. I could do with breakfast before we make a move, if that's alright as I started the watch at four."

"Get what you need. I'll follow you in," replied Stan. "I need to change my collar."

Bruce lifted the latch and went in. He was closely followed by Stan. At the stairs Stan called down, "I'll be ready shortly to get off."

Harry acknowledged the call with a wave. Stan took in the build of the young soldier who was buckling up a belt. Adams was a slightly built man and probably wasn't going to be up to much in a fist fight. Stan decided he would take the revolver that was wrapped in a shirt currently at the bottom of his bag.

"How many rounds have you got?" asked Adams as the gun was pulled out.

Stan smirked and said, "Officially? Two."

"And actually?" asked Adams.

Sam tapped the side of his nose and that was all the answer Adams received.

Harry and Samson appeared at the top of the stairs as Stan put the revolver in an inside pocket. Harry gave his colleague a look. He said: "Hunt was very specific that we were to keep our heads down, Stan. It's not your intention to attract attention with that is it?"

"You didn't bring me along because you intended to keep your head down Harry," said Stan. "You wanted me along as the last stand before someone finished you off. Instead of wasting our time hiding we should get into St Helier and make enquiries. I'm just being prepared, that's all."

Harry paused, tossing up in his mind how best to proceed before Stan created havoc. Of course, what Stan said was true. There was an innate understanding between the two police sergeants born of years of working together out of Shadwell.

Adams moved down to the kitchen area to find the pitcher of milk which had arrived earlier. Samson had arranged to have milk delivered from a farm each morning. Adams lifted it to his mouth and took greedy gulps before wiping his hand across his mouth.

"Right, I'm ready," said Adams. "Let's get off."

"About the gun, said Harry, "Stan's the only one of us that can hit anything." Harry held up his injured right hand for the young private to see. Adams nodded as he could see how stiff it was.

"To be fair, Jack's not been trained yet," said Stan.

"I could give you a try-out later," suggested Bruce quietly to Jack, as he overheard the conversation above.

Jack glanced at Harry who appeared not to have heard and nodded to Bruce. He said: "Thanks, I'd appreciate that."

"Alright, time to get off to St Helier. Separate times of leaving do you think?" asked Harry.

"Probably a good idea," said Samson. "Separate trains would be wise."

"Is There's a station near here then?" asked Harry.

"Didn't you know?" asked Samson.

"It's just that there was no detail on this place just the name of the village and we got a carter to bring us last night," explained Jack. "When we arrived at Gorey, we did hear a train but thought it must be some distance away."

"It's probably too recent for the intelligence for London. It opened August last year," said Samson. "The train will take you to Snow Hill in St Helier now and from there you can walk into the town. There are twenty-eight trains a day so no problem about when you leave but I would separate and go on different trains."

"We'll get off first, shall we?" Stan suggested to Adams, who nodded. Stan collected his coat and he and Adams let themselves out of the cottage.

Bruce nodded to Jack and said: "I'll be outside when you're ready."

"Jack, a word with you before you go," said Harry, "I heard Bruce's offer. If you carry a weapon it's without the Met's approval. You understand that? If something happened, it would go badly with you. Training requires you to hit a target with 3 rounds out of 6 before you'd be allowed to carry firearms."

"Sounds sensible," said Jack. "I thought I might as well learn from Bruce though while I'm here. If I carry arms in future at least I'll have more of an idea what to do. I hadn't intended to unless ordered though," said Jack.

"Alright, just so as you understand my good lad, that I can't give you permission until you've done the training in the force," said Harry. "Of course, if you're in a difficult situation on this job and need to defend yourself … it's not a bad idea to learn but I'm not giving you permission, understand?"

Jack grinned and said: "I understand well enough that will be how it is if there was an enquiry, but that you do think it's a good idea for me to learn to handle a handgun."

Jack joined Bruce waiting at the side of the building and they watched as Harry walked ahead. Once he was out of sight, they started down the track together and Jack took in the mild morning. The darkness the previous night had cloaked a partly ruined building at the side of the track. Now in daylight Jack wondered if anyone had hidden in it and if their arrival had been watched. What if it had? Would anyone make a move in St Helier?

Harry had followed Stan at a distance until the station came into view. As he came onto the platform, he saw Stan sat on a bench at the end lighting a clay pipe. Adams passed Stan a tobacco pouch and the two men looked as if the outing was a normal one for them. A train approached, in all its bluff and bluster and once Harry was sure that Stan and Adams were on it, he moved further up the platform, looking up the line for the next train.

An observant traveller would have seen him take a piece of notepaper from an inside pocket in his jacket and smell it. On the paper was a list of points which Rose had scribbled down for him and Harry imagined her in the scent. With it was a small photograph of Rose that he was still carrying despite knowing he should not have anything personal on him. On the back she had written a message. It was a risk, and he knew it. Hunt would take him to task about carrying the items. However, the paper remained on him despite all his years of experience.

Harry glanced at the Station Master's House and the one storey booking office. His eyes went from there to the single-track railway line and a question came to him. Seeing a man in the Eastern Jersey Railway uniform Harry called across to him:

"I understood there was a frequent service. I was told there were twenty-eight trains a day?"

"That's right, sir, you won't have too long to wait."

"If it's single track how can that be?" asked Harry.

"Oh, don't be worried, sir," called back the railwayman. "There are two passing places. It's not too busy today. The weekends and bank holidays are the busy times. Your train will be here shortly."

Jack and Bruce had arrived and deliberately moved away from Harry to the end of the platform.

"Seems a quiet place to have such a frequent service?" called Harry loudly, back to the uniformed railway worker.

"It's hoped there will be a formal connection to Gorey from France soon at Carteret. There's a small number of boats operating but once the rail link from Carentan to Carteret is done there'll be a lot of demand for the crossing with through tickets to Paris from Gorey."

"When will that happen?" asked Harry.

"They've got to extend the line first to the pier," called back the railwayman. "Personally, I think it won't be for a while, but the management is more optimistic."

"So, I could get across if I was prepared to wait at Gorey Pier?" asked Harry. He spoke more loudly than the man needed to hear. It was for Jack's benefit. Jack turned towards them and looked at the station.

"You'd pick up someone local willing to make the crossing," the man replied.

Quietly, Jack asked Bruce: "Do you know where he means in France?"

"No, but it must be the coast of Normandy as it's close. Boats go from St Helier all the time. Perhaps you'd find a willing fisherman for Brittany as well. But Normandy is not that far from Paris," said Bruce. "That's the reason for the fortifications in Jersey in the past. In the last hundred years though the island was full of middlemen for the smugglers to get contraband to England. The old men talk of it having come in at St Brelade and then up to the northern coast. They still speak of the Dog of Boulay being abroad: "Le Tchian du Bouôlay," as they say it, to encourage anyone to keep off the streets when things are going on which they don't want seen. It comes from those days of smugglers."

"How do you know this?" asked Jack.

"Just standing having a drink. Men get chatty when you buy them a drink and say things in their cups thinking I don't understand them," said Bruce.

"You should join the police," said Jack.

Bruce grinned but shook his head. He looked up the line as he heard a train whistle and said: "Where I come from in the borders, they consider us pacified and our police serve the Crown as in England, as I do now as a soldier but frankly, seeing the evictions and the famine now, there will be serious resistance soon. No, the police service is not one that I would join."

Jack frowned but his attention was drawn away from Bruce to Harry, who had walked to the platform edge as he too had heard the whistle.

"I think we can get on this one as well as Harry, rather than travel separately," suggested Jack. "There's several carriages worth of space between us."

A man walked towards them, passing close by but took his position for the train a carriage's length away. Jack turned his back on the traveller and stared up the platform in the direction of the approaching train, glancing briefly at Bruce whose eyes remained on the man. Harry remained still, giving the impression that he was oblivious.

The journey was uneventful and the train mainly empty. Once in Snow Hill Station it was a few minutes' walk before Jack and Bruce turned into Halkett Place and found a meat and fruit market. Bruce produced some money and bought chops for them all for dinner that night. Jack walked to take in the area, looking with surprise at the number of late spring visitors. Bruce caught up with him and together they found a stall cooking bacon on the edge of the market where Beresford Street began. Devouring a sandwich each as both men were so hungry Jack suggested they walk a few streets and speak to stall holders around the markets. Bruce agreed and the two men made their way past a Calvinist Chapel until they came to the fish, vegetable, and cattle markets. Despite Bruce's friendly approach while he bought supplies, no-one wanted to speak to two strangers asking questions.

"Is it because you have to come in and buy food that you've picked up the language?" asked Jack.

"Yes, it's helped me. No-one delivers here as in London except for the milk each morning. When one of us gets in we try and buy enough to last several days. It's too far to get up to the barracks every day. We never have enough for more than a few days. At least as there's two of us we can take a good stock of provisions back and try and get some answers at the same time"

"Let's try another area and see what we can find out," suggested Jack.

Bruce nodded and said: "You might as well see some views while you're here. If we turn right at the bottom of the road into Hill Street we can get to the harbour. We can ask questions there around Merchant's Quay and you could take in the view of Elizabeth Castle which is about a mile off the mainland."

"So, this is where everyone is," said Jack as they arrived at the tourist buses, each drawn by four horses.

"It's a dull place frankly, except for the bus tours, at least if you compare it to London. Only other thing to do is drink. You should see it on a Sunday, everything closes. Evenings are worse. Ministers here think it's a sinful place."

"They've never been to Stepney then," laughed Jack.

"Nor fought with battle-hardened Highlanders," said Bruce, wryly.

"Surprising there isn't a promenade like in Brighton."

"There is the castle there over to the west of the harbour, named for Queen Elizabeth and built on an old ruined abbey. It's seen some battles since good Queen Bess," said Bruce.

"Can we get out to it?" asked Jack.

"Not at high water. Once the tide has dropped there's a causeway."

The morning's walking had started to take its toll and Jack motioned to Bruce that he needed to stop as he was in discomfort. Together they perched on a wall until Jack could move again towards the harbour. There Bruce approached groups of men, using his limited Jèrriais and showed them the sketch of the man they wanted. Jack rested on a bench watching the interplay.

At last they got a response from an older man who had sat amongst a group sharing a pouch of tobacco. He stared round at Bruce and then stood to see Jack as Bruce pointed to him. The man spat and swore and launched into a tirade of angry words while Corporal Bruce backed off slightly but tried to placate the man. Jack watched while the man started to calm down a little and now it was the Corporal's turn to speak. Whatever he was explaining clearly did the trick as the man looked at Jack and nodded. Then he rubbed his fingers against his thumb in a universal language which Jack knew meant money.

Bruce carried on, placating the man until he sat down again with his friends. Once satisfied he had reached some sort of agreement Jack saw Bruce and the man shake hands and Bruce started to walk back towards Jack.

"Turn around on the bench Jack so they can't see your lips. I think we've found a lead to your man," said Bruce, taking his seat with his own back to the men.

Jack took Bruce's advice and turned away.

Bruce explained quietly: "The old man thinks we're after your brother. He sees the similarity in hair colouring and build, from what he's said. I didn't tell him you were looking for a brother but when he recognised his missing guest from the drawing you saw his response."

"Missing guest?" asked Jack, surprised.

"That's right, the man runs a guest house," explained Bruce. "From the response to the sketch I showed him you'll have gathered that he's owed money. It must be the same man you're after. He's owed a week's money in fact. I don't think there's any risk as he quietened down as soon as I reassured him that you'd pay your brother's bill. It's five shillings. If you haven't enough then I've got some coins. One thing he did say was his guest went missing three days ago and he thinks the police have traced the family and been in touch with you."

"Police?" said Jack. "They must have found a body then. We'd better not stay too long if Jersey police are involved. Our Inspector won't them starting to make enquiries about us."

Bruce laughed and said: "Don't get too worried there's only ten of them on the island and they've enough to do with all the visitors arriving. As far as I can tell the police found only a bag. I'll take the money to the man and see what else he knows. Come over with me but stand apart and let me be the one who goes in. That way they'll accept you can't understand them. Can you make a play at grief if we're right?"

Jack nodded to Bruce and pulled out coins from his pocket. He managed to look full of regret as he nodded and waved to the guesthouse keeper. The man nodded back in return but with a face like stone and he watched Bruce and Jack closely. Together they walked towards the group of men and Jack stood to one side while Bruce placed the money that was owed on the table. True to expectation it had a transformative effect. The guesthouse keeper launched into an emotional

271

explanation. Bruce concentrated, finding it hard to understand everything. The tone was suddenly different, and the man removed his hat and with a face full of feeling for Jack, crossed himself.

Bruce stared at Jack but there was an innate understanding of the man's actions. The thief was thought to be dead. Jack turned his face away in a show of grief and nodded. Bruce spoke quietly to the man and then walked over to Jack to lead him back to the seat. Jack played his part and slumped down on the bench facing away from the men while Bruce sat down next to him and placed his hand on Jack's shoulder. Bruce said: "You and I should be on the stage."

"That I'd like to see. What else did he tell you?" asked Jack.

"The police didn't find a body, but he says they wouldn't have gone down into the ravine, probably just peered over the edge. They found a bag on a branch of an overhanging tree at the cliff. There were scuff marks too, like someone had slipped. He said he'd hung on to the young man's belongings in case some member of his family came. He's accepted you're a brother and the money's sweetened his willingness to hand everything over to you. The police aren't interested and frankly I'm not surprised as they've enough to do with holiday makers arriving in ship loads on Jersey. We can get down the ravine if you want to verify if there's a body, but it won't be easy."

"No, I seriously don't think our thief is dead," said Jack. "I saw him climb a wall. No, I'm sure that he's staged a disappearance for some reason. Interesting that there was a letter and then distress. I wonder if that was the spur for him to go or he was warned we were coming?" Jack thought for a few moments: "It might be both. Look Bruce, unless our friend over there is more curious than I think he will be he'll call it a day once he's had payment for, "my brother's" belongings."

"Why are you so sure he's alive?" asked Bruce.

"I told you I saw him climb. It's almost a year ago, up the sheer face of a wall on the West India Dock offices and I watched him shin down fast, but in full control," explained Jack. "I doubt any ravine in Jersey would cause our thief problems with those skills. That same day I saw him commit another theft in public with great ease and confidence. Let's get going and see what treasure we're to get from this. Now, I will need to ask you for your coins this time.

"Gladly," said Bruce, reaching into his pocket.

"You will get it back," said Jack. "And a couple more things: ask him if he keeps a register and say we need to verify it is my brother although we've accepted his story as his reaction was so natural. Tell him I'm happy to pay for any belongings my brother left because he's been unable to let the room."

Bruce walked back to the small group of men. He kept his expression relaxed. He spoke for some time in a very soft, conciliatory, tone. A few of the other men at the table nodded at times as Bruce spoke. Jack saw Bruce smile and offer the extra five shillings and then he gave the man time. The guesthouse keeper took the money and there was a consensus amongst his cronies around the table that he had made the right decision. The money was safely in his pocket before the man began to tell Bruce quite a story. Jack turned his face into the sun and closed his eyes so as not to appear too keen but confident that he could leave any further arrangements to Bruce.

Within five minutes Bruce appeared at the bench and sat down next to Jack. Keeping his voice down Bruce started to recount the tale he had just been told: "Well, here's the thing: his guest was a climber, fit and strong and pleasant and he spent his days here exploring the hills and cliffs. That fits with your man doesn't it?"

"Could well do," said Jack.

"He didn't speak French, certainly didn't speak Jèrriais, nor English more than a few words, and his lingo wasn't German either."

"Dutch perhaps?" suggested Jack.

"No idea but the man over there tells me he served at one point alongside some Prussian troops, so he knew it wasn't German that his guest spoke. If he's been on the continent, I'd trust what he says about the language. They could only communicate between them with nods, smiles and money. He thought his guest was a nice young man because he kept his room well and didn't cause any trouble. See how he talks about the man in the past, Jack."

"Yes, so he thinks his guest is dead. I doubt that," said Jack.

"The young man went off early each morning after breaking his fast and came back late afternoon and ate in a bar. He was due to stay another week."

"Was he now. That implies he left in a hurry. Perhaps got word we were on our way. Does he know where he was going when his stay ended?" asked Jack.

"No, it never came up but the day before he disappeared your thief booked a tour on a bus to a beauty spot," Bruce explained. "There was a letter the same morning he disappeared, which he said seemed to upset his guest. He thought it must be from a woman, perhaps ending a relationship, or someone had died, the man was so distressed. The bag is back at the guest house. Look, we should go over before he gets twitchy."

"Right, what should I say," asked Jack.

"Try: Je regrette. Good, let's go over," said Bruce.

The man took leave of his friends and Jack said: "Je regretted." The guesthouse keeper patted his arm and mumbled something unintelligible. It was then the three men started to walk in silence towards La Sueur Monument.

Bruce eventually broke the silence and asked the guest house keeper's name.

"Luce," was the answer. Mr Luce led the way and together Bruce and Jack followed on a short enough walk to the guest house in Broad Street. Once there, Mr Luce shook Jack's hand, chattering on and Jack smiled and nodded and held up his hands to show he genuinely did not understand. Jack's side was aching as Bruce and Mr Luce went up to the bedrooms to bring down the articles left by the thief and he sat and waited in the hall. Bruce put everything in the bag that had been found. No form of identification had been left and there were no travel papers in the room, as there would have been, Jack thought, had it only been a genuine day trip that their quarry had left to go on. Jack took the bag and looked at it. A wooden frame was on the back and straps to go over the shoulders. He undid the flap. On the inside were written the words:

"Sekk med meis. Torg."

Jack showed the words to Bruce, but it meant nothing to the Corporal. Bruce said, quietly: "The bag is a bit like a soldier's knapsack, but I've not seen one with a frame before."

Bruce must have asked if the man had a register while they were upstairs as Mr Luce had disappeared into a back room. He emerged with a ledger and turned a few pages until he arrived at a date, which he prodded. Jack noticed the fingernails were dirty.

"Torg," Luce said, triumphantly.

Jack looked at the date at the top of the page: the ninth of May, ten days before. Jack cast his mind back to what he had been doing on the ninth of May.

"Torg's bag," said Bruce, smiling and nodding at Jack. Then to Mr Luce he said: "Pouque."

Jack flipped the top open and inside were clothes, a shaving kit, and a small box, which had been opened.

"Chocolat," said Mr Luce, screwing up his face while he shook his head.

Bruce thanked the man who almost gave a bow. Jack shook hands with Mr Luce.

Bruce said: "Mercie bian. A betôt."

"A bi," replied the man and Jack knew from the tone that it was a farewell.

"Mercie," said Jack, and he and Bruce turned to go, remaining silent until they had walked past the monument. Once sure they were out of sight of the guest house they perched on a low wall and went through the bag.

"Well, thanks to you and your Jèrriais we've got our thief's name: Torg," said Jack. "I can't believe our luck. It will come in handy for passenger registers, assuming it's the family name. If we can tie up the language and that phrase inside the bag, we'll have come a long way.

"Funny reaction about the chocolates. Maybe he'd tried one," said Bruce.

"It's a nice box though. I've only had boiled sweets in a paper bag, nothing fancy like this," said Jack. He took the box out of the bag and turned it over. "Look there's a name, Daniel, on the bottom and a number 14 and rue something, Veevey?" Jack attempted the word and held the box out to Bruce.

"It's French. Daniel may be the maker's name? Rue is the word for a street in French and in Jèrriais as well. I don't think Veevey is right as the way of saying it, but I can't be sure. V e v e y it's spelt isn't it? I've no more idea than you where that might be. Probably it's some small place in France where the chocolate came from. Maybe that's where the sender is from? Mr Luce clearly thought the chocolates were bad."

Jack started to ease the lid off the box. Inside were chocolates and a space as one was missing. Jack sniffed them and shrugged. He said: "They smell alright. Mr Luce said Torg couldn't speak French though, didn't he? Perhaps the chocolates came with the letter. Strange Torg left them but took the letter. They smell alright to me. Someone's obviously had one. Mr Luce may simply have meant he didn't like chocolate. The Parson would probably know where this Veevey place is or he'll know where to find out. There's not much my old Parson doesn't know. We should go back towards where the tourist buses are and show the sketch around in case any of the drivers remember the man. Then to the Telegram office I think, so I can get a few messages off,"

Jack picked a chocolate and bit into it, anticipating he would spit it out. Instead, he was surprised and said: "Very rich, very different to chocolate I've had. Beautiful, strange Torg left them if they were a gift. I wish we had that letter. It all seems odd to have a gift but also a letter. What upset him? You know Bruce, I think for him to go without his belongings was deliberate as it bought him time." Jack re-opened the bag and read the words again. "It's simple isn't it, just a wooden frame and a bag attached to it."

"Soldiers use a similar bag but without a frame," said Bruce.

"And this strap, what does it do?" asked Jack.

"Maybe it fastens around the wearer to stop it falling off the body?" Bruce suggested.

Jack put the bag on his back.

Bruce looked at the position and said: "The frame puts the weight on the hips. See, it keeps it off the shoulders. You could carry more of a load in it that way."

"I can feel the difference to when I had to carry sacks from the fields on my back. I'll get it off as I can feel my ribs starting again." Jack slung the bag down on to the floor and sat with it between his legs. He opened it and pulled out the rest of the contents and examined each one, first looking for labels on clothes. There were none. He said: "Home-made?"

"Nothing that he'd miss, perhaps," suggested Bruce.

"The shaving kit is a good one, isn't it? It's foreign and not cheap to us. I'd think twice about leaving that. He must have left in a hurry but where's he been since last June I wonder?" Jack mused. "Not on Jersey we know that from what Luce said. I wonder if he was on his way back to England with a new shopping list of art to steal? And I wonder where "home" is? My money is on someone getting a message to him to change his plans. Maybe it was that letter, but if so, why did it upset him? It feels like we're going around in circles. We know how he'd get to Southampton but where would he cross to France from here?"

Bruce sucked his teeth. He suggested: "Any number of places could be reached by boat if you pay enough. France is closest, but they think nothing here of going back and forward to England, and not just to Southampton. It could be to another island nearby and then a boat somewhere. Maybe he could go to Holland."

"I could do with seeing a map really," said Jack.

"We have a few back at Gorey," said Bruce.

"Stan might turn up some information around the harbour so we could go back now," suggested Jack. "If we go via the post office, I'll get a few telegrams off to England. Then I think I'll need to eat something before we go back."

"I'll see what I can pick up while you do that," said Bruce.

After talking to several drivers where the tour buses parked Jack and Bruce struck gold. A tour guide remembered the man who got off the bus at Val des Vaux because he had tried to explain to the young man that there would not be enough time to do the climb and get a bus back. Jack thanked him and they walked away.

Jack said: "Of course, he didn't care about doing the climb all he needed was to leave the bag and disappear. Alright, I'll get over to the telegram office and meet you later somewhere so we can eat."

"I'll see to the food and wait over at Fort Regent. The views are good from there, said Bruce."

*

Jack stood for some minutes re-reading the notice on the window of the telegram office as if it would magically change and conform to his will. It read:

> "The three cables uniting Jersey to Guernsey and France are broken. A repairing ship will reach Jersey next week. The cable to France is the property of the Submarine Telegraph Company."

"So, no telegram to England. Unbelievable, and the link to France has to be fixed by the company," Jack said under his breath.

Feeling his stomach roll and a sense of thirst building Jack made his way to the post office and queued to speak to a lady behind the counter. She advised him that the post would leave the island on the six o'clock boat next morning.

Jack obtained paper and envelopes and wrote a brief outline of the findings that day for Sam ready for the briefing his friend would have with Hunt. With God's grace and a fair wind, as his father would have said, the earliest Sam would get it was likely to be Friday morning. Jack was trusting that the regularity of Sam's briefings with Hunt would be the same pattern as usual. He knew his friend would wonder why there was nothing arriving sooner, but without being able to send a telegram there was nothing to be done.

His throat was dry, but Jack pressed on, kicking himself for not having eaten earlier. He spent a quarter of an hour drafting a more detailed letter and placed it in a sealed envelope, writing: "For Langton," on the front. This he folded and slipped into the envelope along with the notes for Sam.

Sam would decide what to do.

Jack coughed and started to sweat becoming aware he would not last too much longer he wrote a quick personal note and then a list of enquiries to the Parson and addressed it to the Vicarage at Lymington.

It read:

" May 20, 1874.

Parson forgive the brevity and know I hope you fare well and are enjoying your time with Helena and Timothy. I have need of your help and have a list of strange words below.

Please telegram to me at the Main Post Office, St Helier, Jersey. I will not leave the island until I hear from you. Could you address a letter to a Mr Hill?

I need to know:

Meaning of the word: Ubique;

Where this phrase is from: "Sekk med meis;"

and it's meaning if you can find it.

The country where I would find the name Torg;

Where is Vevey in France?

Do you know of a French confectioner called Daniel? A chocolate maker perhaps?

Should anything happen to me before you respond please contact Sam and Mr Langton with the answers.

I am as always, your good friend,
Jack Sargent."

And as his stomach rolled more violently this time, he bought the stamps and posted the letters ready for the mail boat the next morning. Then, mindful as always of the proprieties before ladies in the street, Jack made his way to the side of the post office where he was violently sick before he collapsed, unconscious, into the bushes.

*

Eleven

Harry Franks had missed his turning to find the Queen Street entrance to the post office. He scratched his head and looked up and down the road but was still none the wiser. Had he found it immediately he would have encountered Jack sending his letter. As fate would have it Harry was distracted as up towards the corner, he noticed a woman selling her knitwear and decided to cross over to ask for directions. He cocked his head on one side as he took in the display and wondered if Rose would like the soft knitted shawl the woman had draped across her own arms to show to him. Harry walked over to her and ran his hand over the item. Liking the feel, he nodded to the woman and asked: "Did you make this?"

With a smile the woman answered: "My daughter."

"Very nice," said Harry, "I'll take it as there's a softness to it. Wouldn't know how I get into the post office would you?"

The woman nodded to the right. Harry followed her gaze and raised his eyes to heaven as the entrance seemed obvious now he had been shown where it was.

With his parcel wrapped in brown paper Harry paid over the money the woman craved and once inside the post office he wrote to Sam as if he was sending news of a holiday to family. He asked Sam to send any answers by return to the post office in St Helier addressed to a "Mr Farmer," and hoped Sam would realise that he meant Jack. It was all he could think of as an alias on the spur of the moment.

"What time will post for England go?" Harry asked the man passing him his change.

"A mail boat leaves early in the morning," explained the man.

"Nothing later today?" Harry asked, as he realised by the time Sam had briefed Hunt and got a response Harry would be out of things in Jersey and back in London himself. A brief sense of regret at not being in on the chase struck Harry. It would be down to Jack to collect Sam's response and any further orders from Hunt. Surprised at the sudden sense of loss in leaving an enquiry Harry felt torn between work and being with Rose. Perhaps, he thought, he was too old in the tooth to change his ways. Posting his letter Harry shook the feelings off and looked up and down Queen Street. Jack and Stan would see the investigation through.

Noise from the side of the building distracted him and he briefly glanced at a crowd gathering around a man down on the ground. Best not to get involved, Harry thought, as he turned away. It would do no good to attract unwanted attention.

Deliberately, Harry followed the route back towards Snow Hill Station at the foot of Mont de la Ville. He turned in and out of the narrow streets looking for somewhere he could get a bite to eat. Nothing was open and he kicked himself for not having made use of the stalls at the market.

The old sixth sense of making sure he was not being followed made Harry hesitate at one point. Had he imagined he had heard the sound?

"No, there it is," he said, softly to himself.

It was the noise made by metal tipped boots on cobblestones. Harry ducked into a doorway and waited but no one appeared. The sound had stopped at the same time he had taken cover. He had either imagined it or someone could see him and had stopped at the same time, also secreting themselves in a doorway perhaps? Harry started off again and he went through his usual routine of crossing to the other side of the street to see if anyone appeared and followed him. But there was no sign of anyone.

Pushing down the sense of panic in not having a backup he thought through his options. Harry looked for a street sign to get his bearings and saw Regent Road at the side, registering that there were steps up to a building he had passed. He would use it as a landmark. The road looked as though it opened-up ahead and Fort Regent towered above on his right. Nothing behind him was visible but as he started to walk again Harry could hear the same boots clicking on the cobbles a street away. He knew what it meant. He had a shadow, and it was still with him.

"Wake up Harry, change your route and forget the train," he said to himself.

Harry walked on past the evidence of quarrying towards the Victoria Pier. At least, if it was he that was being tracked Jack and Stan stood a chance of being left alone and hopefully getting some answers to their enquiries.

Sounds altered slightly and Harry realised there was more than one person behind him. He ran his good hand through his hair and kicked himself for underestimating the situation he was in. He realised he had expected to find crowds as he would have done in London, not these semi-deserted streets. Visitors to the island were at landmarks and the front, of course. If it came to a scrap, he only had one good hand and a few tricks up that sleeve forged out of years on London's streets.

If he could just make it to the pier where it was likely to be more crowded and find a boat. Harry controlled the impulse to start running. There was a muffled noise somewhere behind him and the clicking on the cobbles had stopped. A stifled grunting noise echoed off the side of the buildings. He half turned but thought better of it. Whatever had happened to his tail Harry now had an opportunity and he looked ahead and started to run for the pier. Once there he slowed and walked up and down until he saw a fisherman looking for trade. Harry called to the man and waved the first coin that he pulled from his pocket.

"Gorey, if you can get me there," he shouted down to the man, brandishing the coin.

The fisherman nodded and Harry did a final turn to look behind, but no one was coming in his direction. He went down the steps, slippery with half wet weed and felt the sea wash into the only pair of boots he had as he climbed into the boat. It lurched and for a moment his mind went back to Spithead and the explosion he had been in a year before. Pulling himself together he pressed the money into the fisherman's hand and sat down on a slat of wood in the middle of the boat as the fisherman pulled the craft away. Harry had handed over half a sovereign. Of course, it was far too much money, but it had been the bait to get away quickly. From the vantage point of the sea Harry stared back at the pier looking for someone displaying too much interest. There were small groups of sightseers only and no-one apparently taking any notice of the boat he was in. If someone was on the top of the pier looking for him, they were making a very good job of disguising it. Nonetheless, despite a lack of obvious behaviour, his eyes remained fixed, almost like a compulsion, waiting and watching. The boat put more and more distance away from the shore and only when he lost sight of the people did Harry glance down and hope the water playing about his feet did not mean there was a leak. Had it not been for the hairs on the back of his neck Harry would have dismissed his senses for imagination, but he was quite sure that he had been followed and equally certain that he had heard the clicking on the cobbles of two sets of boots.

Taking advantage of the respite he sat back, turned his face into the sun and breathed deeply. He muttered: "You're safe, Harry boy."

*

A slow potential killer had visited Jack. But it had not finished him, and as he came to, he found himself in his own vomit fighting the crushing compulsion again to retch, stomach convulsions engulfing him and his head very dizzy. Faces above Jack melted into a blur until one he knew stared into his swollen eyes. Corporal Bruce, tired of waiting, had come to the post office and not finding Jack inside had followed the crowd towards the man on the ground in the alley.

"Stand back, I know this man," shouted Bruce, bending to get an arm around Jack's shoulders.

Just before he lost sight of who lifted him Jack was suddenly conscious of the state he was in and muttered: "Your clothes," but the rest was lost in more retching as the crowd moved sharply back. Jack's tongue probed his aching lips and looked at Bruce, who eventually had him firmly supported. Jack walked unsteadily, stumbling and his feet dragging at times, as Bruce trod slowly.

"Try, keep trying," was all Bruce said, as he raised a hand to a man sitting on the barge board of a cart. Together they rolled Jack into the back onto hessian sacks which the man had down. Bruce followed him in and attempted to keep Jack steady as the cart rolled and rocked. Jack's only memory later was of a profile against the sunlight and the jolting of the cart. Once back at Gorey Jack had wobbled out of the cart but Bruce caught him as he started to fall. The length of time between retching appeared to be over at last and Bruce part dragged and part supported Jack after he fell on the path outside the cottage. He was too far gone now to walk so Bruce left Jack propped against the wall as he went into the cottage in search of water. Holding a flask to Jack's lips Bruce allowed a small amount first to wet them, rationing how much Jack swallowed in case it started him off again. Then it was a case of removing the stained upper clothing and wrapping a blanket around Jack.

In the brilliant sunshine Jack looked in a bad way. Bruce moved the man into partial shade and sat down a few feet away on the grass. He said: "Well the old man said the chocolates were bad. Good job you only ate half of one."

Jack grimaced. "It's the only thing I've had that's different to you, isn't it? I wonder who ate the missing one? Perhaps our thief is dead after all if it was him."

"Rest up now. Shall I help you inside?" asked Bruce.

"No, thank-you, I'll stay in the air. My ribs feel like I've taken another kicking. We've got the rest of the chocolates, haven't we?"

Bruce nodded and said: "They're in the bag. I put it inside."

Jack spent his much-needed rest leaning against the cottage wall, occasionally sipping the water Bruce had brought him, staring out to sea as the boats came and went from the moorings. Below him the harbour and all its traffic lent interest and he felt his mood start to lift from the sense of despair at yet another problem with his health. He knew he stank of his own vomit and there would not be enough water to bathe in and momentarily wondered if he had the strength to immerse himself in the sea. But he knew he would not reach it. Perhaps in a while, thought Jack, until then he could stay outside as a kindness to those who had to live with him. Jack watched the moods of the fishermen and the women beheading fish and soon they seemed to blend with the changes of the sea as his head slumped forward on his chest. He slept, although briefly.

Jack came to suddenly, looking round for Harry but he had not yet arrived back, and Jack found himself alone in the open air in a strange place that he did not recognise at first. Then the realisation came to him that Stan and Adams must still be making enquiries in St. Helier. The initial confusion as he woke made him jerk to. He tried to get up. Had he have been at home in his own room, with Rose trying him with a little weak broth and bread, he knew he would have picked up. But he felt out in the open, as there was little comfort in a soldier's billet. Plus, there was the possibility of a journey to make. Jack had lost his sense of peace he normally felt and was starting to realise that this must be what it felt like all the time when one had a lingering illness. Another injury of sorts again turned him heartsick. What had it been to make him so ill? Ann Black would know, or Dr Brown, if he could get that remaining half of the chocolate to one of them.

What would Hunt say when he knew? Would he order Jack home? The idea of having to go home half dead made Jack think that he was not sure he could live with himself. In part he had succeeded in his commission as they knew more about the thief than before. And then if the Parson responded to his letter, they could take the case on. They had made some progress that morning, but Jack was not satisfied with a partial success. The need now was to get strong so that in a few days, when he expected to hear from the Parson, he and Stan would make a journey. And Hunt need not know what had happened until Harry had his debrief with Sam. That would not be until Monday at the earliest and by then Jack and Stan could be on their way to the place where the chocolates had been made, to France perhaps, and possibly find the thief and track the organised crime ring.

"Ah, awake now, are you," said Bruce, holding out a rifle to Jack. "Here, I think this might interest you. Take a hold of this. You said you'd shot off a gun on the farm and I thought you'd like the feel of a new rifle."

It was an attempt to distract Jack and get him thinking of something else. Jack had arranged earlier with Bruce to have some target practice but now that was out of the question, he thought. However, he recognised the tactics. Bruce said they had a new rifle called a Martini-Henry, which was being introduced into the army and this lit Jack's interest.

Jack answered Bruce's question: "Only as part of the Squire's shoot when I was eighteen," Shocked at the rasp in his own voice he continued nonetheless: "He was short of a man and they got me to fill in. They said I had a good eye because of the bowling."

"Bowling? Cricket do you mean – a boring game if you ask me. Give me a stalk across the hills any day, there's a skill, now. Do you remember what the gun was?" asked Bruce.

"Yes, it was a Purdey, a game gun," Jack replied. He followed Bruce's line of sight.

"Ah here's the Sergeant, now," said Bruce.

Sergeant Samson had emerged from the castle and started to walk back towards the cottage. Seeing Jack and Bruce sitting outside he glanced around cautiously to see what attention, if any, they were attracting. A few fishermen on shore were watching and talking amongst themselves but that was all. Samson waved a hand and the men responded in a similar way, exchanging a joke before returning to their haul. Although Samson could not understand Jèrriais he suspected by their tone that the men were discussing something about Jack.

Bruce acknowledged his Sergeant and walked up the mound to meet him. The two men stood while Bruce explained, and Samson listened.

Jack heard Samson say: "Well done," before the two men started to walk towards Jack. Samson sat on a boulder opposite Jack and Bruce went to change into his uniform.

Samson said: "You look a little green about the gills to be holding a rifle. Adams will have a look at you when he gets back. He's some experience but not much apart from bandaging wounds."

"I'm grateful for anything," said Jack, putting his head back against the wall and closing his eyes.

Samson reached over for the rifle. He asked: "May I? This is the Martini Henry. It's supposed to be an improvement but I'm finding that the cartridge frequently jams in the breach. Bruce has the eye, get him to show you when you've picked up."

Bruce came out of the cottage now dressed for going on duty. He took bullets from a bag ready to load the rifle.

"I thought I'd show you how the rifle works, and you can have a go with it in a few days. I've brought a Webley Bull Dog as well as you're more likely to use a revolver I suppose if you carry arms in the police. Here," said Bruce, passing a small pocket revolver to Jack. "You need to load it manually and it's got a firm single-handed grip. Easy to conceal it in a pocket so I thought it was ideal for a policeman to try."

Jack took the revolver quietly and looked at the fine engravings along the cylinder and receiver surfaces. Despite how he felt he was interested.

"Expensive?" asked Jack.

"Perhaps," said Bruce, "I wouldn't know. I didn't buy it. I took it off someone."

Jack stared at Bruce. The corporal had taken the gun from the Sergeant and started loading the Martini-Henry. Bruce put one cartridge in the chamber and held two cartridges in his hand. He grinned as he looked up at the searching expression on Jack's face.

"Alive or dead? Jack asked.

Bruce snorted and said: "Alive, of course, what do you take me for?" Bruce concentrated for a few moments and then added: "Three hundred yards is the limit for this one, Jack."

"Bit close, isn't it?" asked Jack.

Bruce raised the rifle and looked along the line of sight. He aimed at a point near the castle wall.

"You give the order Jack," said Bruce.

"Fire," said Jack, quietly.

Bruce gave him a sideways look and momentarily lowered the rifle. Seconds later Bruce finished his re-positioning and fired the first shot. He reloaded keeping his position and fired the second, repeating the process for the third time.

Jack was surprised at Bruce's speed.

"That's the quietest order I've ever had," laughed Bruce, lowering the gun.

"You're fast on the reloading. Loud, isn't it?" said Jack, nodding at the gun.

"When you're close. And under fire there's no time to wait with the enemy bearing down on you. Come on, let's see what you think of the rifle." Bruce handed the Martini-Henry to Jack.

"Main thing is for you to get your eye in, so when you feel like it you can take a shot with the rifle and then we can try the Bull Dog. We don't want to waste ammunition."

Jack looked along the barrel, then lowered it and gave it back to Bruce.

Jack said: "Not now, Bruce but thank you. My ribs feel like I've taken another kicking after all the sickness. Perhaps I could try the revolver?"

Bruce nodded and loaded the Bull Dog. He said: "The range is close, Jack, the sort of distance when a soldier would ask, "Friend or Foe." Fifteen yards, perhaps twenty if you need to try that distance. So, firing this on a man is going to feel personal and powerful. You need to be aware of those feelings and to deal with them before you use a gun. I've taken life as a soldier and there are things that I've had to face about myself. Things I've seen and felt. It affects us. If you're under fire, to use a gun, you know who you are and why you're doing this. Try the ferns there, that's about the right distance."

Jack nodded and held out his arm to its fullest extent, closed one eye but started to cough. He lowered the revolver and Samson and Bruce exchanged looks. The cough subsided and

Jack aimed again, looking along his line of sight. When he was ready, he fired. His sight was off, but he corrected it naturally before either soldier said anything and aimed again. The second attempt to hit a certain tall fern that he had his sights on was better. Again, he corrected his aim and fired, hitting his target less than twenty yards away. He lowered the gun exhausted and held it out to Bruce to take back. But despite his state, Jack was pleased at his own success. Bruce made no effort to take the gun back, pointing ahead instead.

"Aim for the stem," suggested Bruce.

"Harder target?" Jack asked Bruce.

Bruce nodded and Jack hit the fern again but this time the shot was closer to where the stem connected although it was still off the target he had been given. Jack lowered the gun and looked pleased.

"Better. At least you hit it. Try a different target in a minute," suggested Samson.

Bruce snorted and said: "Two out of four so, in my trade, you would be dead by now,"

"I'll try two more shots, so I've done my six," said Jack.

"Six?" asked Bruce.

"I should do six if it was police training," said Jack raising the Bull Dog to his line of sight again.

"Will it count so you can carry a gun?" asked Samson.

"It might if I can hit the target three times. There would have to be good reason to carry a firearm though. I suspect Harry will turn a blind eye here to any practice I have but it might count as far as our Inspector is concerned for the future."

Sansom thought many he had seen on battlefields had given in to far less than Jack had been through and would not have persevered.

Bruce pointed to a boat tying up in the harbour and said: "Isn't that Harry there?"

Jack lowered the gun to look and followed the line of Bruce's gaze. He strained his eyes searching for the figure of Harry Franks among the numbers moving around the harbour. Then he saw him as Harry tried to find a foothold on the ladder against the swaying of the boat. It was high tide, and the boat was far from stable. Another swell and Jack saw the boat lift. Harry had tried to climb out too soon, and his boots had received another soaking.

Sansom laughed and said: "I can imagine the oath."

Shaking the water off a foot Harry clambered up the ladder with his boots the worse the wear for the double dosing of sea water they had received that day.

"I wonder why he took a boat instead of coming back on the train?" said Jack.

Harry had paused as a local man spoke to him. It was a short conversation and then Harry went on his way towards the path.

Bruce said: "The wind's changing with the tide."

"It feels like rain coming in," said Sansom, scanning the horizon. "We should get you inside, Jack. See the squall thickening into a grey sky moving towards the shore?"

"I should go under the pump first and then get inside," said Jack.

"Have you fresh linen?" asked Sansom.

Jack nodded.

Bruce, however, was not listening. He had seen a solitary figure walking from the direction of the station. What interested him was the course the man had set himself, diverting from the path and climbing the mound towards the three men outside the cottage.

"I think we may have an interested party coming our way," said Bruce.

Jack stood slowly and grasped Bruce's hand to give himself leverage to pull against. The man was still quite a way from them and looked in a sorry way. His coat was torn at the hem, trailing on one side and a homemade bandage, which was probably a handkerchief, was wrapped around one hand. His size would normally have filled the coat which had been of good quality. The wind whipped up the coat tails and its strength appeared to make the man stagger and put him off balance. Coming closer he pulled off his hat and the gash from the forehead to the eye became visible, strands of hair matted into it.

Slowly, Jack raised the Bull Dog and aimed. "Friend or foe?" he said, hoarsely.

Bruce followed Jack's lead and picked up the Martini-Henry. He took aim and said as a quiet aside: "The man's outside your range but it's a gamble whether he knows that small detail."

"And you've fired all your bullets, remember? It's a double bluff if it works."

With an oath the man came on and as Bruce made a show of squeezing the trigger, the man stopped and said: "By God! You know the answer to that question, Jack. Tell the man who I am.'

"Maybe," said Jack, "But you stop there Mr Burgess and tell me what you're doing here."

*

Burgess had sat clumsily down on the turf despite the armed men aiming at him. Samson, who had watched the stranger's arrival, ordered Bruce to lower the rifle. Jack however ignored the order and held his position.

"I would kill for drink and then I can explain," Burgess said, in his matter-of-fact way.

Corporal Bruce filled a flask with water and handed it to Burgess. With an overcast sky and the first of the rain Harry arrived and took in first Jack's state and then the damage to Burgess.

Quietly Harry said: "You don't look like you'd be able to put up much resistance, Jack, if Burgess rushed you. Apart from which it would be a waste of a bullet when we have more dangerous characters to deal with. I'm aching to know what you've been up to given the state of you Mr Burgess and how my favourite hotelier came to be bleeding."

When Jack did not respond Harry placed himself between Burgess and Jack and changed his tone. "Constable, you are not authorised to carry a firearm, stand down."

Jack dropped his arm to his side and said: "Bruce you're right about it feeling personal and powerful. I'll return the Bull Dog to its owner, Harry, if it's all the same to you. It's out of bullets, by the way." He held the gun out to Bruce, who pocketed it.

Jack leant against the cottage wall and the rain grew heavier. He picked up the blanket which had fallen off him when he had stood and drew it closer around him.

"If that's a Scots accent, I heard I'd be grateful for any whisky you could put my way," said Burgess.

Bruce grinned at Burgess and disappeared into the cottage. He emerged with a bottle and held it out to Burgess and said: "By the way you were out of range Mr Burgess and I had already fired all my bullets."

Harry sat with Burgess and offered the man his handkerchief. He said: "So, was it you who saw off my shadow?"

"Rumour has it that it was," replied Burgess, holding Harry's handkerchief to his gash. "Although, there were two of them but one scarpered. I saw them before I could catch up with you, one stayed a way back while the first man went on without him. They followed you down four different roads before you twigged, Harry. Love is making you sloppy in your old age."

"We should go inside before the rain gets heavy," said Samson, holding out a hand to help Burgess up. "We were not told to expect a fourth man."

Bruce took Jack over to the pump and Jack endured the cold water until he could accept that the stench on himself had been dealt with. But the clothes were another story.

Sansom watched two women on their doorsteps taking in the group and called to Harry: "Before we get any answers as the wind is swinging round to the north and we are attracting too much interest, I suggest we move inside in a jovial fashion which should convince our audience on the shore that this was a training exercise. Your friend needs some attention to that cut and you Jack, should rest. We must go in now before the rain grows heavier."

Burgess swore under his breath as he struggled up. He had fallen in the struggle and was aware he was no longer a young man. He had not stayed long enough to check his quarry's injuries and had got away to Snow Hill Station before the second man returned. Burgess had hoped to find Harry there. When there was no sign of him Burgess had boarded a train for Gorey.

Harry found himself embarrassed about thanking Burgess knowing that in the next breath he should deal with the very fact that the man was in Jersey at all. But Sansom was right and Harry could see the sky was growing more threatening. There was gratitude and friendship in Harry's being and not simply because Burgess had saved his bacon today. The hotelier had provided care and accommodation for Harry and his team after the injury at Spithead the previous year. They had parted company with a depth of understanding on Harry's part.

"Does Hunt know you're here?" Harry asked, offering a hand to the burly man.

"He knows I'm an interested party," answered Burgess.

"That's not the same thing," Harry muttered.

The men moved into the cottage with a loud show of bonhomie and were inside removing their wet outer clothing in less than two minutes. Samson remained on the doorstep and scanned the shoreline until he was reassured that there was no further interest in them. The fishermen had gone back to their nets and the women had retreated inside out of the rain. With a reassuring nod to Harry, Samson went down the stairs to the room below and Bruce helped Jack to get on his fresh linen. Then he lay on his bed.

Quickly Bruce passed their finds of the bag and its contents to Harry and explained their morning and Jack's state while Harry looked at the items in the bag. He sniffed the chocolates and prodded the remaining half Jack had left but there was not a distinct smell. They were quiet as Harry took in the fact that Jack had tried one of the chocolates. Harry sat down next to Jack and the exasperation was evident in his tone.

"What possessed you to eat an exhibit?"

Jack moved on his bed and shrugged. He answered: "I didn't think there was likely anything wrong, and I'd not tasted anything like this chocolate as its fine and rich rather than the grainy pieces I've had all my life. It must be that which made me solly. It's the only thing I've had different to Bruce. The whole box should go to Ann or Doctor Brown when you go back, Harry."

Harry nodded and said: "Best be Ann Black if I can find her. Doctor Brown would go to Hunt if I saw him but with the telegraph out of action Hunt can't get a message to you anyway quickly. Look young man, don't go doing that again, do you hear? We don't know what we're dealing with. Poison's too common, alright? It's easy to see someone off. I wrote a letter to Sam as the telegram won't work. He'll reply to you, Jack, under the name of Farmer, at the post office. Make sure you go and check. Damn post won't go until tomorrow morning and under these circumstances I might as well go on the mail boat with it and get these straight to London." Harry waved the chocolate box in the air.

"I know Anne was up at the hospital in Marylebone. I wrote to the Parson, and if he's able to answer quickly that will come by Friday," said Jack. "I should be back on my feet by then. We don't know when Sam will meet Hunt again, Harry. It depends on Hunt fixing up a date."

"I'd take you back with me if it wasn't such a journey," said Harry. "You're in no fit state for it, though. I should go straight to London and find out what we're dealing with. No need to inform Sam with anything else as he can't let Hunt know anyway. Hunt was firm on the fact that he is the one who initiates. I might as well get those chocolates to Ann Black. I'll not tell Rose, Jack, in case she passes something onto Ted. There's a smell to the fact that I was followed. Burgess saved my bacon so don't go too hard on him. Someone's talked, which means it's come from inside. We know it's not you, and it's not me, and Stan has no concept of betrayal. So, Hunt's right all along to stay quiet but he must have said something that's been overheard. It's rotten at the core. No other reason for our thief to have scarpered or for them to have been following me. Someone's got a message out," Harry paused and then asked: "I wonder, did Hunt know where you and the Parson were going?"

"I can't remember," said Jack. His head was thumping now, and he needed rest, but he pressed on. "I think I said he went into Hampshire but not the place where his sister lives. You don't think Hunt ...."

"No-one's suggesting that," Harry interrupted. "We just need to be careful. Look, I know where all this work comes from. I told Stan because I had to share it with someone. Hunt told me a year ago about corruption and a group that involves someone so high up in society that they think they can't be touched. Its insidious Jack, with insiders in the police." Harry exhaled.

Jack's eyes had hardened but, as he tried to speak, he started to cough. Harry got him water and waited while he sipped it. Then Harry picked up the theme again.

He said: "Look Jack, Stan and I both know there's a royal connection with why Hunt's taken this on. You're in on it as well, aren't you?"

Jack shook his head. He said: "No I'm not in on anything I was just with Hunt when he was at Windsor. Things were said but nothing's very clear. It was as if people were talking in a code, but Hunt seemed to know what was meant."

"Which people exactly?" asked Harry.

"The Queen," said Jack, quietly.

"Damn Hunt for involving you as you'll not get free of it for the rest of your career," said Harry, sharply.

Jack said nothing but kept his eyes fixed on Harry.

Harry glanced away but continued: "Knowing you as I do, you'll be honour bound to say nothing. You see things in very black and white ways. The Queen's servant … yes that's what we all are but this connection Hunt has is different to what our oath means, lad." Harry paused and glanced back at Jack.

"Why does it matter?" asked Jack. Harry could hear how weak his voice was. He kicked himself for pushing the subject with Jack now after what had happened that day.

"Because as I said you'll never be free of it," said Harry.

"So, you're answer is to walk away? Let them win? Doesn't that make our oath meaningless?" Jack sat up with difficulty, looking drawn.

"Alright, Jack, I'll say no more. But if you need to talk to Stan or me at any time you can. Hunt told me last year what he was involved with, probably because it was all getting too much for him, and that's why, I think, he took you to Windsor that day. If something happened to him another policeman is known to be someone Hunt trusts. It means he's stacking up quite a responsibility for you in the future. The other thing you should know is that Hunt's contact last year was Gladstone. We're all on the same side. We're all fighting corruption, and, in this case, it seems to penetrate some way up the ranks in society. Anyway, perhaps I should go straight to try and see the

Parson, tomorrow. Make sure he's alright and see what he's found out, if anything, after getting your letter."

"That would be good of you, Harry. He's at the vicarage in Lymington with his sister and her husband Timothy who is the vicar there."

"Hopefully if Hunt has let his guard down, he hasn't said too much, just that you were going to Jersey. Your Parson won't get a letter back to you anyway until the mail boat leaves on Thursday and I can see him by tomorrow night. I'm banking on Burgess having caused my tail some harm mind you but whoever they were they can't get a message out quickly either."

"No, if I was in their shoes, I'd cut and run back to France," said Jack.

"Why France?" asked Harry.

"The chocolates," said Jack, "Look on the box, it says where they were made. Corporal Bruce said the address was in Rue something and that he thought it sounded French. The town is on the address on the box."

"Stan will love that," smirked Harry, "If that's where you're both off to. He hates the French. Actually, if I think about it there aren't many people Stan does like." Harry paused and sucked in a deep breath through his teeth. He put his hand on Jack's shoulder and said: "Alright, alright, if that's all we've got to go on, you and Stan had better start making plans to cross to France as soon as you get word from me. Keep Sam informed but not too quickly if you understand me. If you arrive in France before Hunt knows he can't stop you. I'll take

Burgess back with me tomorrow. It would be good to have someone with me as far as Southampton who would recognise who was on my tail, in case they try again. Then, on Friday I'll try and track down Ann Black and see what she can do for us about those chocolates. Then it's home to Rose."

"Harry, if they're poisoned, that might be what was in the letter that upset our thief," said Jack. "That might have triggered him going rather than being told we were coming. He's been within feet of me, audacious, and still carried on. I'm not sure he's afraid of us or that he would run because I was coming after him. In fact, I expact he may think we can't catch him as someone protects him. He took the letter but left the chocolates and his bag. He may have had bad news. He either deliberately left the bag and the chocolates, or he must have been very distressed to make such a blunder."

*

After a brief hesitation the previous evening Burgess had agreed to return to Brighton and to make enquiries at the major stations along the line with the sketch of the wanted man. The following morning was blustery, and the rain had persisted overnight. Jack did not envy them the journey on such an uneasy sea.

Burgess had allowed Adams to clean up his cut and sported a makeshift bandage when Jack bid him goodbye the following morning. Burgess and Harry stood on the dock as the mail for England was loaded on board and shortly after 6 o'clock on

Wednesday morning they sailed for Southampton. There was no sign of being tracked and no one paid the two men any attention. Both Harry and Burgess had long careers behind them of recognising a tail and were alert to their surroundings. Around them on the boat were the usual parties of travellers leaving for home after a happy time in Jersey. Both men waited and watched at separate positions on deck but there was nothing to create a moment's doubt about any passenger.

Jack was left with Adams in attendance overnight while Bruce did a double watch. By ten o'clock on Wednesday morning Jack was trying warmed bread and milk and Adams had helped him outside into a camp chair to take the warm air of the morning. All around him the ferns whispered in the breeze and the birdsong was drowned out by the rant of the seagulls. Down at the water men and women went about their daily work. While seated there, Jack sat and dozed until at midday Adams and Stan had bid him goodbye and set off to track the thief's travels on the island.

Stan obtained several freshly made rabbit pies from a butcher once he and Adams disembarked from the train at St. Helier. It cost Stan sorely, but he would be well rewarded with praise for his generosity by the soldiers later. Put with potatoes nothing was likely to be left-over. At first their enquiries turned up very little in St Helier. The heavens opened and they sheltered to wait out the rainstorm. After it their luck changed. Through conversations with a driver and guide of a tour bus Adams and Stan found a lead while showing the sketch and asking about the tours to Grand Val and Bouley Bay.

"It's due north from St Helier, a beautiful valley, thickly covered in trees and wonderful views from every stop. An excellent way to see the sea and the town from the top. Will that be two tickets?" asked the guide.

Stan looked at Adams, who nodded.

"Anything?" Stan asked Adams once he was sure they were out of earshot.

"Yes, the driver recognised the face," said Adams. "The man did several outings with the company, one to the Grand Val and on the other tour this bus does, to Bouley Bay. He was unusual in that he didn't speak French or English, as most visitors do, was very fair haired and the trips taken weren't close in time together. Other thing was he did a repeat tour to Bouley Bay and on that second visit didn't come back with the tour bus."

"Where is Bouley Bay?" asked Stan.

"North from St Helier and faces Normandy," said Adams. "Bouley was an old smuggling haunt with a legend of a great dog, probably made up by the smugglers to make sure everyone closed their curtains when a run was being made. It's not the only story here about black dogs."

"Most areas have tales or a myth. There would be links then, between that area and France, still?" asked Stan.

"If you mean boats going across, I should think so, but it will be small craft," said Adams.

By two o'clock a covered car was due to leave taking in Bouley Bay and the final part of the tour would be Gorey and Mount Orgueil Castle. Stan told the guide that he and Adams would walk back to St. Helier after the visit to the castle. It was not true, but Stan wanted to lay a false trail.

Rain was threatening and Stan and Adams managed to get seats under the tarpaulin cover. The pier at Bouley Bay provided shelter for about 30 oyster boats and the fishermen were out in choppy waters across the bay. Stan decided that he would prefer to cross open sea in something a little larger.

"Look at it," said Stan. "Makes me long for London."

"Why?" asked Adams.

"The sea's too restive," said Stan. "I prefer solid ground. Alright, we need to ask some locals if anyone recognises our man's picture."

"The inn over there would do. If you're free with the odd coin we'll get someone in there who will want his tongue oiled," suggested Adams.

"It will have to be quick," said Stan. "The tour will go in half an hour."

They saw a hard-looking man smoking outside the inn and Stan ambled over offering pennies for a smoke of tobacco, apologetically pulling a clay pipe from his pocket.

"Salut," said Adams, handling the Jèrriais.

The man offered his pouch for Stan's pennies and Stan helped himself to a strand of tobacco from it. While he took a seat, he filled the bowl of the pipe and said: "Mercie."

This was one of the two words in French which Stan knew. The second one was "Boisson." This Stan tried and the man nodded, half smiling. Adams took the coins from Stan's outstretched hand and disappeared into the inn. He was soon out, followed by a buxom woman carrying three frothing ales. She set them down on the table and each of the three men clinked tankards.

Stan pointed at the boats at anchor in the bay and pulled out the sketch of their quarry. Adams started to explain to their drinking companion and Stan picked up the word: "paithe," and that was all. The man stood, shook hands with Stan and nodded to Adams, drained his glass, and left.

"He looked as if he recognised our man. Anything hopeful there?" asked Stan.

"Possibly, as I told him you were the man's father. He's gone to the cottage over there, to get his brother," said Adams, nodding to a small path lined with fisherman's cottages. "He says his brother was in a crew who took a passenger across to join a boat that had left St. Sampson, Guernsey, for Saint - Malo. The man you're after is easy to remember and I said you're looking for him as the police here just think he's dead. His brother worked on a new single screw ship called "Commerce" which sailed to Jersey. She's been transferred to Guernsey now and nothing that size is going over to Saint-Malo from here."

"We need to make a move, or we'll miss the tour," said Stan.

"They're coming now," said Adams, nodding towards the cottage from which their drinking partner had emerged with two younger men, one bearded and one rough shaven. They looked curiously at Adams and Stan. The stench of fish was marked as they approached.

"Watch how much money you let on to have," Adams warned Stan.

Stan nodded and he and Adams stood up ready to speak to them as the men drew closer. Stan attempted to look welcoming.

Adams walked forward and started talking, pointing towards the tour bus. He beckoned to Stan and called: "They'll walk with us to the bus. It sounds like it was your son. I've said this is good news."

Stan tried to look happy and at the bus gave the men a handful of coins before he clambered on to take his seat. The money was more than a drink would cost.

"Tell them to have a drink on me," he said to Adams, jovially.

Adams explained and the men divided up the coins between them and responded with a mix of, "Bouan viage! Bouonne cache dés crouaîsis."

Stan waved and he and Adams took their seats.

"What was all that?" Stan asked Adams.

"Good luck, good journey, that sort of thing. I did wonder if we were going to have to run for it when I saw them."

"Not to worry," said Stan. "We've got out of there easier than we both thought we might. And we've been lucky: we've got a lead on where our man has gone."

*

Stan and Adams walked through the gateway of Mount Orgueil Castle with the rest of the tour-party. They were met by the warder who was ready to take them round. Adams turned away to avoid being recognised and motioned to Stan to hang back. Once everyone else had filed through Adams caught hold of Stan's arm and nodded to a doorway. They let themselves out and made their way into the fresh air. Climbing slowly down the castle mound they made their way to the track which would take them to the soldiers' cottage. The rain had moved in, creating puddles on the track that would soon become ponds as they spread into one another. Stan felt the water trickle down his neck as the rain grew stronger. Their progress slowed as Adams slipped and Stan grasped his arm to save him from falling. Correcting his balance Adams thanked him.

They were on the part of the track where the ferns grew tall and Stan sighted the cottage. With relief they trudged the last few paces as the wind began to increase in strength. Soaked to the skin Adams lifted the latch and he and Stan almost fell through the door.

"Here," said Stan, passing his bag with the rabbit pies into Bruce. "We've a lot to tell, haven't we Adams."

The young soldier nodded. He said: "I'd best make my report to the Sergeant."

Jack raised himself up on one elbow and asked: "What news, Stan?"

"Our man left for Saint-Malo," said Stan. "We have a confirmed sighting. Adams told them our friend was my son. Someone must have got word to him we were coming. That can only be the reason for him to have crossed to Brittany. We have it confirmed he isn't dead and he's probably heading back to this place Vevey. Get your sea legs back, lad and as soon as we hear from your Parson we're off. Now Corporal, let's be having those pies as soon as you can, and that Scotch wouldn't go amiss. Jack you should take some to get your blood moving."

"No thanks, Stan. I'll try some of the pastry on the pies later if you can save me some, but nothing more. I'll come down and get some bread and toast it. I don't want to be bysted again tomorrow. I want to be about."

"Well, I didn't understand any of that," said Stan.

"Being laying down in the daytime, ill again," said Jack.

"Right," said Stan, "How anyone understands each other in your neck of the woods is beyond me."

Jack grinned but followed slowly down the stairs. Stan saw the loaf on the side and cut a chunk roughly. He looked around for plates, but everything was dirty. There was a wooden board still drying on the drainer. Stan put the bread onto it and set it down on the table. He said: "Here y'are Jack, get stuck in now to some of this dry bread. If you keep it down, we'll get you onto bread and warm milk. I'll plate up some of the pie crust for later if you manage that." Stan dug away at some of the crust from a pie and tipped it onto a tin plate covered it over with a bowl.

Struck at how domesticated Stan suddenly seemed Jack smiled to himself as Stan walked towards the shelf over the sink. Of course, Stan had four children. Jack picked up a toasting fork and held the bread over the fire.

313

Twelve

Shortly before eight o'clock that evening Harry and Burgess docked at Southampton. There were no obvious signs on the journey that they were being watched, the passengers on the boat were in groups of four to five people and full of the joys of the holiday maker.

Harry and Burgess held back until the end of the tying up process and made their way separately off the boat. They had agreed before they left Gorey that they would meet up at the train station in Southampton as it was near the Quay, unless one of them found they had a shadow. Whoever arrived at the station first would wait for no longer than ten minutes and then board any train going in the right direction.

Harry stopped at the Custom House, a plain neat building near the pier and made some enquiries of the staff there about the man they sought. There was little information forthcoming: a fair-haired man was recalled, the name Torg, in the log, but it was an outward journey to Jersey and the date meant that it must be their man. Harry took it as confirmation that the thief had not doubled back to England. Of course, there were many places he could have come ashore in a fishing boat, but Harry drew a line under that idea. He had already decided that the team simply did not have the time to make any more enquiries.

Once ashore Burgess sent two telegrams: one to Field in Brighton to join him for breakfast on Thursday morning. It read: "Commission for us."

Burgess knew he was bending the truth, but he was sure once Hunt heard from Sam that he would want Burgess involved. On that assumption, Burgess sent a second telegram. He had assumed that Sam would be playing middle-man between the Inspector and the team and Hunt should know what had happened in Jersey. Their old working relationship had been like that. Of course, it carried the risk that Hunt may stop him from any form of involvement, but Burgess knew he must let his old colleague know what had happened.

The outcome was that Burgess's news reached Sam before the post from Jack and Harry. Sam was also invited for lunch on Thursday for a briefing. Burgess would be in pole position as the only man who could identify Harry's shadow and who had been Harry's saviour, which suited his purpose well as he knew Hunt would acknowledge how much he had been needed.

For now, there was the journey home to make and several places on the route where Burgess could put his questions. He checked the timetable. It would be midnight before he would arrive in Brighton. Alice would be surprised but relieved to see him this soon. He knew there would be recriminations for the gash on his head and the damage to his hand but as he was in fine spirits Alice would soon come around to what he had been up to. Burgess ran his mind over the staffing arrangements for the Ship Hotel for that night recalling who would cover the front desk. Rossiter, thought Burgess, yes, Rossiter would be on duty overnight. He was a reliable man who had been with them since the Burgess's had taken on the hotel. Burgess checked his watch. There was no sign of Harry. He waited as arranged but after ten minutes Harry had not arrived on the station and Burgess boarded the first train going east.

*

While Harry and Burgess had sailed back to England another interested party in the case oversaw her preparations to travel to Ballater. It was a long journey, leaving from Windsor on the evening of May 20th at eight o'clock just as Harry and Burgess queued to leave the boat in Southampton. She had travelled with little sleep and the Queen's train had arrived at nine-thirty on the twenty-first near Perth. It would likely be after two o'clock that afternoon before they reached Ballater where the carriage would be waiting at the station to take the party to Balmoral.

Before she had left Windsor there had been a few things Queen Victoria had had to do. The Prime Minister, Mr Disraeli, had to be seen and she needed to see Torrington about matters at Windsor.

Disraeli had been due after luncheon and there were titles to confer on one's children. It was always a pleasant task and making Arthur Duke of Connaught and Strathearn and Earl of Sussex, was arranged for the Queen's birthday. That had been the pleasurable part of Disraeli's visit but there was also the worrying issue of the French Administration having resigned without a new one having been formed. The Queen had wondered how long the French would take.

Sadly, as it was the 21st the Russian Emperor would start for home. The Queen had sent a short note having seen him earlier to say goodbye. But it was not this departure that pre-occupied her thoughts. She had received the sudden news before she had left Windsor that the other "Widow of Windsor," Mrs Hunt, had finally moved across the river that morning to a home prepared for her by her son, Tom. The Queen realised she would miss seeing her in her garden from the window on her return. The news had also surprisingly irritated the Queen, more because Tom Hunt had arranged the move for his mother to coincide with the Queen's departure to Scotland, knowing it could not be stopped. Surprised at how she felt Queen Victoria acknowledged to herself that it was typical of Tom's secretive nature. However, it was a trait which made him useful. A memory of how cross dear Albert had been when they both learned that the young Tom had just up and left the estate and joined the police came back to her. Such dis-loyalty it had seemed after all the effort Albert had made with the boy. Still, Torrington had said how hard the Police had worked to protect the Emperor in London and that Tom Hunt had been part of that. She would have mentioned it to Mrs Hunt had she seen her. Now it was all too late, and the woman would be gone for good and Tom's visits would stop. That is unless he was summoned.

The Queen turned her attention to the view. The country was fine and the birches green and quite forward with all the broom

317

coming out. It seemed quite odd that it was nearly the last night of her 55th year! How strange that only Beatrice out of all the nine children would be the only one with her on her birthday at Balmoral. Still Eddy and Georgy were there with her this year and the two little boys were going to recite poems for her on her birthday.

*

Harry woke on the morning of the twenty-first after a blissful night's sleep in a comfortable bed. The speed of the twenty-minute journey to Lymington had surprised him and he had arrived at the village station more quickly than he expected. Harry had jumped on the train to Lymington with seconds to spare before it pulled out while Burgess was tied up in the telegram office. Trains to Lymington were so infrequent at that time of the night that he had decided he could not wait for Burgess on the station.

The Reverend Timothy Ward had filled the doorway after opening the front door of the Vicarage to the unexpected visitor. Harry had no expectation of being given a bed for the night and half expected to spend the early hours of the morning sleeping on a bench on the station waiting for the milk train back to Southampton. However, Timothy was having none of it when Harry mentioned Jack's concern for the Parson and he had ushered him into the hall, calling Helena to come down and meet an unexpected guest as he did so.

"I'm ahead of Jack's letter," explained Harry as Helena shook his hand. "It should be here in the morning. I came to see if all was well with Jack's Parson. I'm sorry, that's how I know him and do apologise for referring to him like that. There's been a few unexpected occurrences in Jersey and Jack was concerned the Parson was alright. The telegraph cable is being repaired so he had to send a letter. The Parson doesn't know me but my colleague, Stan Green from Shadwell, stayed with the Parson last year in Simpson and I am Detective Sergeant Harry Franks of Shadwell."

"My brother is well, thank you. Do you need to see him tonight?" asked Helena, appearing at the top of the stairs.

"Yes, I do. I must be in London early and had thought to travel in on the milk train," explained Harry.

"No, no, you must stay here and have a good sleep. Then tomorrow you can go early if you must," insisted Helena. "Give me a few moments and I'll go and get my brother up. Have you eaten?"

"On the boat Mrs Ward," said Harry.

Timothy laughed: "Then you must be ravenous now," he said. "Come into the kitchen with me and we'll both go on a search in the larder."

Peter Fisher had heard the voices below and caught the name given, reference to Jack and, also Simpson being mentioned. He had already started to dress when Helena knocked on his door. It was Jack's way of saying Selmeston and a local way and it was this that convinced Peter Fisher that the visitor was genuine.

———

319

"Peter," said Helena, outside his door.

"On my way, just dressing," called back Peter Fisher. He ran through in his mind what he knew of Harry Franks. Hand injury at Spithead. Other half to Stan Green in Shadwell. Getting married shortly. Enough there, thought Peter Fisher to ascertain if he's our man.

Minutes later Peter Fisher followed Helena downstairs into the kitchen where they found Timothy and Harry dishing up cold steak and kidney pie which had been left over from the evening meal. Harry had found a cheese which he decided would go well with the pie and was in the process of cutting himself a piece when Peter Fisher walked towards him extending his hand in welcome. Harry did not offer him his right hand in response but extended his left and Peter Fisher took it as further confirmation the man was who he said he was.

"Harry Franks is a name I know well," said Peter Fisher. "You're quite a legend thanks to Stan and young Jack. How is your hand now?"

Harry spontaneously flexed his fingers, then shrugged and explained: "Better than a year ago, one lives in hope of improvement."

Timothy picked up a decanter of red wine and asked: "A glass of claret perhaps?"

Harry turned back to Timothy and nodded his thanks.

"Tuck in then, while I pour you a drink," said Timothy.

Harry sipped the rich wine and spontaneously laughed, comparing the comfort and good food to the sense of living almost a hand to mouth existence in the soldier's billet in Jersey. Then light dawned as he thought of how badly the soldiers at Gorey had been provisioned. But his mind was called back to the present by the hospitality of Timothy and Helena and he filed away his thoughts for the next day's meeting with Hunt. His good nature come to the fore and Harry said: "Stan would be spitting now if he could see me."

"Tell him you're just catching up on all the spoiling he had from my housekeeper last year," said Peter Fisher. "He likes his food, does Stan."

"Ha, you know him well," said Harry. "One thing I will say, Parson, he doesn't warm to everyone, but he did to you."

Peter Fisher gave Harry time to eat the pie and once a good half of the glass had been finished, he asked: "What has happened on Jersey to bring you on this detour?"

Harry bit into the cheese before he answered. It was soft and creamy. His face said it all, but he added: "Wonderful," in case his hosts were in any doubt.

"Yes, it's from the monthly cheese market held at Bishopstoke," explained Timothy.

"Forgive me Parson, I was not ignoring your question, but I must acknowledge the quality of the food after several nights in a soldiers base."

"In Jersey? How did that come about?" asked Peter Fisher.

Harry cut himself another piece of the cheese in case Timothy decided to remove it to the larder. He was sufficiently fed now to pause and explain.

"They were friends, I think, expecting us, but no idea who set that up, although I could jump to conclusions." Harry cut short the explanation aware the wine was loosening his tongue. "As it happened, they gave us just the help we needed, and we were safe there. Just as well, as I was followed in Jersey, but Burgess saw the man off."

"Mr Burgess was there? I didn't think Jack was expecting that involvement when we visited The Ship in Brighton," said Peter Fisher.

"Ah you've met him. I didn't know that. We'd split up to make enquiries in Jersey. They have their own lingo, so Jack had gone with one soldier who spoke it and Stan with the other man. I got a letter off and then was tracked down some deserted streets. Put the wind up me, I can tell you but thanks to Burgess I got away. There were two of them at one point and Burgess took some punishment but saw one of the men off and took on the other. What happened to them we never knew. One of our fears was that we'd be followed to Southampton, but it was clear no one was trailing us on the boat. My best bet is they scarpered off the island."

"And Jack?" asked Peter Fisher. "Why was he concerned about me?"

Harry looked into the steely eyes and knew there would not be much point lying. He cut the cheese into small squares so the experience would last longer. Timothy placed celery at his elbow and Harry smiled at the man recognising a fellow connoisseur of good food. Then he turned to the Parson and said: "Jack couldn't remember what he had told Inspector Hunt before he left London. Hunt knew Jack would travel from Southampton to Jersey, but the question was had Jack told the Inspector you were both coming to Lymington? It clearly served Hunt's purpose for Jack to accompany you but that would have been to get him to the port. As your safety was our concern we decided, Stan, Jack, and I, that I would come and see if you were safe first before I went to London."

After a pause Helena asked: "And if you were followed?"

Peter Fisher touched his sister's hand. He said: "This is Harry Franks of Shadwell, my dear. His reputation precedes him. There is no chance that he would have come here, I'm relieved to say, if there was any doubt. But it sounds as if you think Inspector Hunt may have let slip my destination if he'd known. Is that likely, that someone inside the police cannot be trusted? Jack is very impressed with Inspector Hunt. Are you thinking he isn't what he seems?"

Harry frowned at the suggestion. He shook his head and said: "No, no, Parson but things get said … overheard maybe, …" Harry waited a few moments, stemming the need to open-up.

Peter Fisher also contained himself. If there was more than he had understood from Jack about this case, then he should not leave Lymington until he heard it was solved. He said: "As far as I know Jack understood I came into Hampshire once a year. I did not tell him in the past where my sister lived but Jack had been told by Inspector Hunt that the thief had been sighted at Southampton and Jersey. I wonder who else the Inspector told?" mused Peter Fisher.

Harry registered that he must not mention to Rose where he had stayed.

"Police stations are like leaking sieves", said Harry. "One thing's for sure, Parson, if Hunt has told anyone where Jack was convalescing it won't be safe for you to go back to Simpson."

"I also was thinking the same," said Peter Fisher.

"I won't be the only one who can work out Jack will have confided in you, written for advice to you – by the way that letter will come in the morning - You are safer here for a while until we can find out where our thief has gone. I know Jack values your help and I just hope for your sake he hasn't told you too much."

Slowly Peter Fisher straightened up and to Harry's dismay he saw the same resolve in the old Parson's eyes that had taken early Christians to martyrdom. The man would die rather than disclose anything Jack had told him. And die painfully at the hands of ruthless men he might unless Harry could convince him to stay in Lymington. He had no need as Helena interrupted the two men.

"Of course, you will stay here Peter, at least until you hear everything is resolved," said Helena. "You can help Timothy around the parish just as you do at home, and there's always Reverend Berthon to visit. Would you let us know when it's all over, Harry?"

"Certainly, but you may hear before I do, once I'm back in Shadwell unless Stan and Jack can get word to me without anyone finding it," said Harry. He caught sight of himself in the mirror and in an absent-minded way he traced a finger in a grey furrow in a cheek. it was a drawn look and not flattering in a potential groom. More food was what he needed and a good night's sleep before he saw Rose. "Would you mind if I cut a slice of that cake I saw?" Harry asked.

"Please do," Timothy replied, bring it out and I'll join you."

"Good man," said Harry. "Then I'll call it a day as I should be off early in the morning," said Harry.

"The post will be here by seven," said Timothy. "There will be enough time for you to breakfast and for us to have a look at the puzzle Jack has set us and for you to be back to Southampton for the London train. That should be alright shouldn't it, Peter?"

"Yes, I would think so," said Peter Fisher. His gaze did not falter. "Look, Harry," he said, "I know there's more to this case than a random thief. He isn't the fox that you're after, is he? There wouldn't be all this concern for what I know if that was the case. I think as I'm taking refuge in my sister's home and therefore putting her and my brother-in-law at some risk that it would be good if you'd acknowledge that tracking the thief is just a means to an end. You've a greater quarry, haven't you?"

Harry let his gaze go vacant. He looked from one to the other of the three people before him and randomly shook his head. Fighting the desire to tell all and sleep well he simply said: "I couldn't honestly say. I'll call it a day if you'll forgive me being so tired."

Peter Fisher looked away in irritation.

"Of course, I'll show you upstairs," said Timothy, glancing at his brother-in-law

Harry slowly climbed up to the comfortable guest room that Helena had earlier prepared for him and despite an attack of his conscience for being obtuse fell quickly into an exhausted sleep.

But below in the kitchen the brother and sister sat together considering a change in their lives.

"I must get word to Mrs Simcock," said Peter Fisher. "She mustn't go to the cottage until I'm back. I'll write now and get it posted tomorrow."

"Well as far as we're concerned there's no need for you to leave here. Stay all summer if you like," said Helena. "Timothy will love having your help as he's still without a curate. But there must come a point when you hear from Jack, surely, about what happens."

"There comes a point when one can't hide anymore, Helena, and what's the worst anyone could do to me? Death? At my age, and with my belief, it's not something I fear."

Helena looked at her brother. Peter Fisher took her hand and asked: "What's in your mind, my dear?"

"Not just death, Peter, but the way of dying and the consequences of what someone might do or involve themselves in to prevent it."

"Jack, do you mean? No, my dear, Jack would know I'd not bend, and I believe neither would he." Peter Fisher patted his sister's hand and then gently let it go. "Come now," he said.

"Enough of this misery, I think I could eat a piece of that cake before bed, even if it keeps me up until the early hours."

*

The following morning the post had arrived when Harry looked at the clock in his bedroom. He had slept an hour longer than he had meant to. Timothy had ignored his request to wake him at six o'clock having decided the best option was sleep for Harry Franks.

Stumbling towards the washstand, Harry swilled his face and hands and put on the same clothes from the previous day. It was not how he would like to present himself to Rose but there was no choice. He was downstairs in ten minutes from waking and scanned the different rooms off the hall until he saw Peter Fisher at a mahogany dining table. An opened letter lay on the centre. Peter Fisher was alone, and he peered over his glasses, noting the unkempt look of the detective sergeant as he pointed to the sideboard and said: "There's bacon and sausage, if you'd like it."

Harry smiled despite himself and did a U-turn to look at the silver dishes. Placing a plate in front of the dishes he took in the array of chipolatas, a chubby type of sausage and the aromas of smoked bacon. He said: "I know I'm going to get back to London later than I'd hoped but I have to say it's worth it to sample a cooked country breakfast, especially after the stay of the last few days. Ah, Parson, the aroma is fit for a king."

"It certainly is. They keep a good table and are fortunate to have some land at the back of the Vicarage. It's Helena, you should thank for the livestock. The watercress is their own as well. She laid down two beds of it when they came here and has picked it and bunched it herself and sold it on to businesses in Southampton summer and winter. Timothy has disappeared into his study to check a few things Jack's letter mentions and Helena has gone to send a telegram to a friend of mine. What's all this about chocolates?" asked Peter Fisher, prodding Jack's letter.

Harry moved across to the table and picked it up.

"Oh, Jack mentioned that did he?" said Harry. "They were left by the thief with his bag. There had been a letter as well apparently according to the guesthouse keeper, but the thief had taken that with him," explained Harry.

"Yes, that's what Jack has asked me about. Do you have the chocolates?"

"Yes, I do," Harry said.

"Is that why you're going to Ann Black?" asked Peter Fisher.

Harry paused, then carried on filling his plate.

"Silence tells me something is wrong, Harry. It doesn't deter me just makes me more determined to get the truth from you. What's wrong with the chocolates?" asked Peter Fisher.

"We think they're poisoned."

"Thank-you, truth at last. Why do you think poison's involved?" barked Peter Fisher.

"Because Jack ate half of one. Fortunately, he's alright, just was violently sick. He was picking up when I left, and Stan will make sure he rests until they get your answers. The other half of that chocolate is in the box, which I'll take to Ann and ask her to tell us what it is. Then we know what we're dealing with and the sort of crime it is. One thing I'd bet my wedding on is that it's not strychnine."

"With all your experience over the years what do you think it is?" asked Peter Fisher.

"Something slow, Parson, with a build up over time. Hard to detect, that's why it's in chocolate. Apart from Jack's sweet tooth it's a gift for a woman, or from a woman, I'd bet. It's a fine box, expensive." Harry put his breakfast down and leant across the table to retrieve the letter. "It's also foreign as you'll have gathered from his letter. Do you mind if I read it properly?"

"Of course," said Peter Fisher. He waited while Harry read through the questions Jack had asked. It was slow.

Harry nodded and put the letter back in front of Peter Fisher, then sat and dug a fork into a sausage and started to cut.

"Ubique I can answer straight away," explained Peter Fisher. It's Latin for "everywhere," or if I was applying my trade, I'd say Omnipresent, but only God has that claim. It should have meant something to soldiers though because it's a motto of an Artillery regiment."

"Interesting, Jack was right that you'd know," said Harry.

"What's the context?" asked Peter Fisher.

"Sorry, Parson, I can't say. Any idea of the other words?" asked Harry, meeting Peter Fisher's gaze.

"Can't as in won't or because you don't know?"

"Just don't know. Don't know if it's a criminal motto or on the side of good."

Peter Fisher looked back at Harry and said: "Timothy is in his study digging out maps which he has. As to the other words Sekk med Meis and the name Torg we have no idea. Helena has taken a message to get off in a telegram to a friend of mine at Oxford. He studies old languages but is generally reliable at seeing roots in words. We should know by the end of the day hopefully, and I'll get a letter to Jack. He says he won't move until he hears from me. It will be Friday at the earliest before my news gets to him. You will be back in London, Harry, so you will never know the answer." The eyes had a twinkle about them as Peter Fisher picked up the letter and pocketed it and Harry knew he was in a stand-off. Harry chuckled and shook his head.

"I could say that's Queen's evidence," said Harry, "and ask you to let me have it."

A door opened off to the side and both men glanced as Timothy came in clutching a sheet of paper. Never a quiet man at the best of times Timothy allowed the door to swing back against the wall with a crash. He held up the paper and announced: "*Found it.* Vevey, here's the coordinates: 46° 27' 46.76" N and 6° 50' 36.42" E."

Peter Fisher exhaled while Harry stopped chewing trying to work out what to do.

"Is that France?" Harry asked.

"Goodness no, Vevey is in Switzerland," Timothy beamed at Harry.

"Ah so we need to get Jack and Stan to Switzerland. And that gives me an idea," said Peter Fisher. "Harry, I'm coming with you to London. There's a perfect way to get Jack and Stan to Vevey."

*

At Gorey the sea seemed to sigh after the winds as the bay was more sheltered than the port had been. Boats were pulling in on the shore after their foray for fish and many had gone out at dawn.

Jack had ventured out a little way and sat on a rock near the harbour, the castle towering above him in the morning shadow. He thought of the timings of the post arriving both for Peter Fisher in Hampshire and Sam in Brighton. Burgess would act as a forerunner with more information for Sam to filter to Hunt once the inspector arranged a meeting. Hopefully, thought Jack, answers from the Parson would come on Friday morning but if not, they would stay put until a letter arrived. Jack had complete confidence that the Parson would not let him down. Stan had done well, and they would leave for Saint-Malo as soon as responses arrived, even if they did not have explicit permission. Harry would get back to London and see Ann by midday and then, perhaps, they would know what poison was used. Perhaps when they made St Malo the telegraph would be working. There was nothing to it but to hold out until the post arrived in St Helier on Friday.

Jack suppressed the irritation he felt at the wait. The most they could do was to check how and when to get to Guernsey and pick up a boat to Saint-Malo from there, or risk crossing in a small fishing boat from Jersey.

Jack thought of the strangeness of a foreign place such as Saint-Malo. Brittany itself was a place he only associated with smuggling from the past and France a place of revolution and small groups of refugees who had influenced his Sussex speech. Some of the shopkeepers in East Sussex had started arranging exchanges with families in France for their children so they could learn a little French and master the accent. It seemed a bizarre thing to do.

Jack mused on the reasons why Torg would go to Brittany. Was it to evade arrest? Surely not, could it be that he was to receive more instructions from someone there or was it near this place Vevey? Jack could see no alternative but for Stan and himself to go to Saint-Malo if they were ever to discover who had commissioned the theft of the diamonds. It also would clarify if Hunt was on the right track.

But now he would wait and get stronger. Stan had gone off walking along the coast to keep his devils at bay and the soldiers were following their usual routine. In a way they had already been successful in tracking their quarry. Below him he watched the water glint in the sun until the warmth made him drowsy. Leaning back against a boulder he turned his face into the May sun. It was warmer here than at home.

*

By ten Harry Franks and Reverend Peter Fisher waited impatiently for Helena's return. She had stayed at the Telegraph office by Lymington station, waiting as instructed for the response from Oxford. it was now three hours since she had arrived and most of the parish who travelled to Southampton had passed Helena and respectfully raised a hat, touched a forelock, or bobbed a curtsey. A few had looked back at her and speculated on the reason why the vicar's wife was seated on a packing case. And then the telegraph had started and within minutes the clerk brought out the answer from Oxford.

Helena had burst through her front door and held the response up for all to see. She gave her brother a questioning look, seeing him dressed to travel.

"Peter? Where are you going?" she asked.

"London but I shall be back tonight," said Peter Fisher.

"And I will stay with him until he's back on the Southampton train," Harry added as reassurance.

"Come on, come on, the suspense is killing me," exclaimed Timothy, "Where's the answer?

Peter Fisher undid the telegram and read the response over several times and then laughed. Holding the telegram out to Harry he said: "Norway, the man is from Norway. Torg is a mountain there, some old legend about it. Jack said he was quite a climber. Now to find where that mountain is. Timothy, we need you to disappear back into your study with your maps."

"Right-oh, but what does the phrase mean?" asked Timothy.

Peter Fisher's eyes twinkled. "Sekk med meis just means Bag with Frame, that's all."

"So, who's in Vevey?" mused Harry.

"Someone who sent poisoned chocolates, if your theory's correct, Harry. Right, I need paper, envelope and pen and we can get the letter dealt with for tonight's boat to Jersey. Jack will have it in the morning that way."

*

In Brighton, Sam Curzon had lost his appetite over breakfast on Thursday morning after opening the post. In fact, his mother had noticed an aversion to eat since Jack had left. Of course, she knew his digestive system was never likely to be the same again after the poisoning Sam had experienced but the change since Friday had struck her as odd. In fact, he had seemed pre-occupied since they had returned from London. By Sunday Mrs Curzon was convinced something had disturbed him, particularly when it was clear he had not proposed to Eleanor.

Sam took a final sip of tea and stood up. He said: "I have to send some letters, mother, so I'll go straight out." He gathered up the post and asked: "Can I collect anything you need on the way back?"

'No, nothing I can think of right now. Is all well, Sam?" asked Mrs Curzon.

"Yes, just work. I need to forward a few things on, that's all."

"Ah, of course, but I thought you might have heard from Eleanor."

"No, there's no reason to," answered Sam. "We will meet in a couple of weeks as already arranged. I told you on Sunday we would continue as we are until we're both ready. Disappointed as I know you and Grandma are it's not time for a wedding yet."

"It's just that something seemed to change last week. You're very pre-occupied and all the happiness in you seems to have gone," said Mrs Curzon.

"Just work," said Sam, attempting a smile. "The telegram which came last night was from Mr Burgess. He's asked me to join him at the Ship Hotel for luncheon, so I won't need anything midday."

"That's nice of him," said Mrs Curzon as her eyes searched those of her son's.

Sam managed to maintain a half smile to convince her all was well, despite in his heart fearing the world outside his front door. In the small room off the hall that served as his office he sorted the letters giving a brief report for Hunt, which he would of course not send, and Burgess's telegram for himself. He read them over several times and filed them in a locked section of his bureau. He looked at the key. He would have to decide where to keep it. It had to be somewhere it would be found if something happened to him but not too obvious. Then he turned to the letters sent from Jersey to be posted on to Mr Langton. They were sealed still. Sam half wanted to know, and half knew that if he did, he would not sleep nights.

———

335

He looked at his own reflection in the mirror above the desk and said: "Come on Inspector get in touch - we need to meet." Sam had accepted Hunt knew what he was doing but found it irritating that he, Sam, could not initiate contact on this case. Jack's report, as well as Harry's and Stan's, upset the neat world Sam needed to be at peace.

For him there was a sense of nervous tension. He experienced it when he lost control of monetary balances as well. As long as he was on top of detail, Sam was at peace. Now things appeared to be getting out of control and as Sam walked to the post office nearby, he checked several times that he was not being followed. As he joined the small queue for the counter, he made a slight bow to the ladies in the shop and waited for his turn. Too much time to think never helped but that morning Sam had decided to meet his brothers out of school on a "just in case," basis and on the pretext of a treat he selected four sugar canes for them. He glanced around at the shelves to pass the time of day and noticed some rolls of fabric recently in. They were spring colours and perhaps would be a nice gesture if he bought some to be delivered for his mother. They could afford it now, Sam thought, with the work Hunt had given him and it might lift his mother's spirits to be able to make a new dress after her hopes of a wedding had been dashed. He couldn't help it and at least Eleanor agreed.

It had been soul destroying on Sunday as Sam had asked Eleanor if she might walk with him in the garden. Sam had deliberately pitched the time towards the end of the visit. He had thought that he should be honest with Eleanor and after an hour with both mothers willing him in their looks to get on with a proposal Sam had stood and invited Eleanor into the garden. He had closed the door on the expectant stares from both families and heard his brothers giggling as he and Eleanor had walked through the house to the kitchen door.

Sam had decided that there was no point in getting engaged with killers on his back. That would hardly be fair to his intended to make her and her family a target. She also needed to understand what type of work he did for Hunt then, when the current investigation was over, they could plan. Sam and Eleanor walked past Grandma's sweet peas and the struggling roses to the end of the garden where they were obscured from view by shrubs.

Sam had remained standing while she sat, and he had explained his thoughts for a full five minutes before drying up. Eleanor's response had quite surprised him. She explained:

"Oh, I couldn't think of marriage now. My music and teaching come first, for a while, anyway. I'm only just getting established in Worthing and Brighton after the move from Wales."

Sam had sat down next to her, quite shocked. It had not occurred to him that she had her own plans. Stupid as part of the reason he found her so attractive was her focus.

"And then there's where we'd live, you see, as I need to keep on the lessons, and there's no question of children for a while until the music school is quite well established. I need to fill Fridays yet. I can't marry until I've filled Fridays as there's the issue of helping mother out, you see. Oh dear, I've shocked you, but we have to be honest about such matters don't we if we're to come back to this subject at some time in the future."

"Yes, of course," Sam had said. "Is there a future?" he added.

"Of course," Eleanor had said, and she had laughed.

She had done the job for him. There had been silence between them for a while as they both stared at the area of the garden he and Jack had worked on together.

"You've made that nice," said Eleanor. She put her hand on his arm and the touch made him colour.

"Look, Sam, we can carry on as we are and meet in a few weeks, perhaps without our families around." Eleanor stood, smoothing the front of the skirt with her artistic fingers. "Go for a walk along the front, eh? Now we know what's intended on both sides. Meet on our own from now on, shall we? I mean, without the entire family with us? We should go back in now and finish tea."

"Yes," Sam had said, half getting up and then, thinking better of it, he had sat down again. He said: "No not yet. What do you mean about children? Can I understand what you mean?"

"Well, you know, …planning a family."

"I don't know even if I can have children, after the poisoning I mean. I just don't know. Would it matter to you?" asked Sam.

"It might in the long-run but not now as I don't want them," said Eleanor. "Music's my life, Sam and I want to have the school, help mother, at least until my sisters are finished being apprenticed as they'll earn more then, see. We should talk about all this on our own. You know, what happens to our work, where we live, family planning so there aren't endless children. There's five in your family, three in mine. I'm not sure I want that, all those pregnancies. I love what I do and selfish as it might sound, I don't want to stop."

"I hadn't thought about any of this, only that it would be something I'd like to be, to be married to you. But something's happened with work that may mean it's not safe right now. I don't want to frighten you, but the time isn't right," Sam had stopped suddenly and frowned. He realised he had said too much in emphasising danger. He glanced at Eleanor but if anything, she looked excited.

"Not safe to *have* a wife? For the person who *is* your wife? Is that what you mean? Because of the police work you're doing?" asked Eleanor.

Sam nodded.

"*How very exciting*," said Eleanor, her eyes wide. She looked at Sam with interest. "I had no idea you're were doing anything that important. Well, that's quite convenient really, isn't it, Sam, as we're both of the same mind at present."

Despite his worries Sam had smiled. Her reaction was so unexpected, but it had freed him.

"Can I kiss you as we're sort of promised to each other?" Sam asked.

"I should hope so," said Eleanor. It met both expectations.

"You've had a bit of practice," said Eleanor.

"Not much," Sam said.

They walked back towards the house, ignoring the scuffle of boots in the kitchen as the boys fled back to the lounge.

———

Before they had gone half-way across the lawn Sam asked: "How do we do that, what did you call it? Family planning?"

"I'll bring you a book, next time. I bought it in Bristol a few years ago, "The Fruits of Philosophy," it's called. You might have heard of it?" asked Eleanor.

"No, I haven't," said Sam.

"It's an old book but brought out again a few years ago. The publisher went to prison. I thought you might have heard of it when you were a policeman."

"No, I didn't come across it. Sit down if you like." Sam indicated the small stone bench at the side of a clematis climbing up a tree. It's not banned is it?" asked Sam.

"I don't think so, there are very few copies." Eleanor looked away.

Sam touched her fingers next to his hand on the bench. He said quietly: "And you think it would be helpful if I read it?"

Eleanor turned her head at the touch and looked down at their two hands. "Yes," she said.

It was then with her direct gaze that she reminded him of a robin that came whenever he turned the soil over in the flower beds. Her head was on one side and she was suddenly quite beautiful to Sam.

"Alright, I will," said Sam. "Now we had better go and fend off all the questions as the two mother's and Grandma are expecting a wedding."

Eleanor said: "If you're alright with this we can tell them it's on its way but that we both have things to do first."

Sam had nodded, smiled in his clerkish way, and thought how much better she made him feel.

The Davis family had left quickly after Sam and Eleanor explained together about the future as they re-joined the group in the front room. The embarrassment was evident in the group and no-one knew how to carry on normally. Sam had insisted on putting Eleanor and her family in a cab to the station rather than them walking.

The Curzon family waited on the doorstep while Sam waved to a cab travelling from the direction of St Peter's Church. Before she climbed in Eleanor had turned back and kissed Sam full on the lips. That did the trick despite appearing racy. The disappointment on both sides at there not being an engagement was knocked out of court by the kiss. It was all both mother's, two sisters and a grandma, had needed to see. Sam's brothers had made gagging noises and collapsed with laughter and while Eleanor had seated herself in the cab and glanced through the window at Sam, he had realised he was smiling broadly for the first time since Friday.

Sam had remained in the street, staring after the cab until he was joined by Luke.

"You're a cove, you are," said Luke, and he had punched Sam's arm. Sam responded by ruffling Luke's hair.

After that nothing needed to be said. At six o'clock Sam had surprised his mother by suddenly deciding to attend evensong at St. Peters. Mrs Curzon and Grandma had resigned themselves that there was no point trying to extract information from him and the only option was to await Sam's pleasure.

Thirteen

Harry and Peter Fisher started for the station as soon as Timothy could get the trap ready. The sight of the three men in the vicar's light carriage created comment from many a member of his congregation as it sped past the hedgerows. Sunday could not come quick enough for them to put their heads together and find out who was the man in the colourful waistcoat travelling with the two clergymen.

Harry waved his good hand in thanks to Helena as the trap started off. Once they had turned the corner he settled back to take in the surroundings and thought how charmingly positioned the town was on the right bank of the river. Seagulls cried overhead and Harry felt the wind on the water as he took in the men working by an engine shed. It would be hours before he and the Parson reached London.

"I will meet the train back tonight, Peter," said Timothy, firmly, as he brought the trap to a halt outside Lymington station. "Let me know which train you'll catch if you can."

"Bless you for that, I'll telegram as soon as we finish but it may not be until late," said Peter Fisher. "I must make Southampton with enough time for the mail boat to take the information to our friends."

The more he thought about what was needed Peter Fisher had realised Jack and Stan would need passports if they were to go to the Continent. He spent the journey from Lymington preoccupied until the train slowed and the two men climbed down from the train under a cloudless sky. Once settled in an empty standard class carriage and on their way to London Peter Fisher gave Harry ten minutes to doze before he tapped the detective's knee to waken him. With two early mornings and poor nights at Gorey Harry was short of sleep.

"Harry, we must go to Thomas Cook's at Ludgate Circus."

"Sorry, Parson, why's that?" asked Harry, coming to.

"I know you could argue they won't need documents but once on the Continent Jack and Stan are likely to have to establish their identity if they collect a telegram from a poste restant," explained Peter Fisher. "There's so much to do and it will cost a pretty penny to put everything in place. I must send a telegram to Langton and see if he can cover the costs out of the trust until your Inspector can reimburse it."

"I'll make sure Hunt does," said Harry, determined that once the Parson was back on the train to Southampton, he would make his own way to Camberwell New Road to see Hunt and ensure the Inspector knew what was happening. No contact to be initiated my eye, thought Harry, the whole case was in danger of getting out of hand. The Parson must be reimbursed, and Hunt must know what was going on.

"I can do the Recommendation as a Minister of Religion you see, once we're in the office," Peter Fisher continued to explain. "The only problem is getting it to the passport office and through today with enough time for me to get it to Southampton. Cook's will know what to do."

"And you think we can get them on a tour so that they have a cover?" asked Harry.

343

"We can try," said Peter Fisher. "The only problem is getting them off Jersey."

"They'll sort that out," said Harry, "There must be plenty of craft crossing to France." After that the two men settled into the journey, Harry to resume his sleep and Peter Fisher to draft two copies of a recommendation. Once done he settled to read the first novel by a new writer: Thomas Hardy, "A Pair of Blue Eyes," was the title.

By the time their train journey ended in London Harry had become impatient and edgy. He did not fear for himself, but he thought that Peter Fisher would not stand much chance if attacked. They had almost reached the cab stand when a man came walking towards them through the steam from an engine. Harry braced himself but the man walked on. Once inside the cab they made good time and shortly found themselves rattling along Fleet Street, past Serjeant's Inn, and Temple. At this point Harry put up the blind to take in their surroundings and said:

"You know Parson, I've become quite used to fresher air in the last few days than I've experienced for some time. Arriving back in London though has all the associations of home, including the stench."

Peter Fisher nodded and looked out on the scene and pondered about how long it had been since he had been in that area. He said:

"Yes, I understand what you mean although it's some years since I was here, last time I was near St Paul's must be twenty years ago. There was a cholera outbreak in the Golden

Square area that year: '54 it would have been. The physician behind the theories of germs contaminating water was a friend of mine, John Snow was his name. That outbreak killed 616 people you know. John and others tracked the problem to a faulty cesspool. Yes, that's right, I remember now. It took him years to get his idea accepted but it changed public health for ever when he did."

"Golden Square?" asked Harry. He thought of T Division and the corruption there had been at one time. "Cholera's not the only plague coming out of that area," said Harry, quietly.

Peter Fisher looked at his companion and raised his eyebrows. Harry shook his head and lapsed into silence as he dwelt on the past problems from the Great Marlborough Street Police station.

Peter Fisher peered out of the window at the dome rising above the rooftops and said:

"As grand as it is to see the dome of St Paul's I'd not change the cool air off Firle Beacon for this stench for all the wealth or position London might offer. Ah, the cabbie is slowing. We must be nearly there."

Ludgate Circus opened the route east to St Paul's, south to Blackfriars Station and the bridge across the Thames. Near the cab lay the Apothecaries' and the Stationers' Halls and the route to the Old Bailey. Peter Fisher looked up and down the roads at the changes in the area since his last visit. The older he got, he reflected, the more alone he was in his memories. Harry, Peter Fisher thought, must be forty. The detective could have little idea of the world which the old Parson remembered when he was the same age.

As he had throughout their journey from Lymington Harry nervously checked yet again that no one was showing any interest in them. He held the door open for Peter Fisher and realised that he, Harry, would not relax until he was with Rose tonight. Together the two men walked towards the relatively new Thomas Cook office. It had been there for a year and looked very smart. As he reached the door Harry realised that Peter Fisher had stopped some steps away.

"What did you mean, when you said a few moments ago, about cholera not being the only plague coming from the Golden Square area of London?" asked Peter Fisher.

"Oh, don't take any notice of what I said," said Harry, quickly adopting his genial expression. "I was just thinking about a few situations I heard about some time ago in another division round there. Police getting a little too close to some powerful people and forgetting what they're meant to be doing. A few rotten apples we might say, eh, Parson? Anyway, looks like this is the place?"

Peter Fisher caught hold of Harry's arm. The two men shared a look which communicated far more than words could. Peter Fisher understood he was with a man who believed he must stop something unacceptable from gaining control.

"Jack and I tend not to have too many secrets from each other, Harry. I should tell you that. As a result, I suspect he has told me far more than I should know. But therein lies sanity for him, you see. That's all I can give him. But you're in a different position. If you suspect that there is police corruption involved in this case, I understand why you were concerned for me. I also see why it's important to get to Inspector Hunt today for you but one thing I will tell you in case something does happen to me. I believe if Hunt dies Jack may be seen by various parties to be his successor in this work."

"Dear God, what has he told you?" exclaimed Harry.

"Enough for me to draw conclusions," said Peter Fisher. "Look your concern for me is kind but you must understand that I have lived longer than my three score years and ten. I hope to have more years but should I not I am quite resigned to seeing through a situation so that right flourishes. I am not afraid."

"I would rather not see you thrown to the lions, Parson, and I do hear you. But we grow sombre and time is of the essence as they say. Let's get this visit done and then we can move things forward. I still have two calls to make and it is already past midday." Harry swung the door to the offices wide open and extended an arm to usher the Parson in.

"Yes, you're right, I'll lead, shall I?" asked Peter Fisher.

"Please do," said Harry, stepping back.

The two men moved into the office and Peter Fisher explained the reason for the visit while he placed his two copies of the Letter of Recommendation on the counter. He had given the Vicarage at Selmeston as his address. Harry was none the wiser but, technically it was incorrect as he was not the incumbent. The Parson styled himself "Curate" to the

---

Vicar, being practically true although he doubted the Bishop would recognise him as such.

The letter required a Passport for John William Sargent to enable him to travel on the Continent, accompanied by his friend, Stanley Harold Green. An identical draft was put forward for Stan naming Jack as his friend. Although, technically, only one of the men needed a passport if together, there would be a problem if they became separated.

The clerk completed the forms, writing all Christian names in full. Harry knew Stan had another Christian name of Harold, and Peter Fisher thought things had worked well having Harry there.

"Now that will be two days before its completed for you," explained the clerk.

"No, no, we must have it today, this very afternoon in fact. Do you have someone, at a charge of course, that we can send to the Foreign office now?" asked Peter Fisher. "I must be at Southampton with them tonight."

Harry laid a hand on the old Parson's arm and produced his identity. "Police business," he said, winked and the clerk's eyes went wide.

"My goodness, of course. But to send a runner now will double the cost. The passport will be 2 shillings and 6 pence for Switzerland and 8 shillings for France. That's per person. Of course, no visas are needed but in addition there is the cost of the agency of 1 shilling and sixpence. I would recommend a case and mounting the passport and there are various styles of binding, which will all add another 3 shillings and 6 pence per Passport. It adds up, sir, I'm afraid but I've a runner here and we can get it done. Cook's never fails."

"That's fine," said the Parson placing two guineas on the counter. Harry looked concerned but Peter Fisher waived his concern away.

A runner was charged with the commission and Harry slipped the young man a shilling to be back in an hour, telling him quietly he would double the tip.

"Between you and me, lad, no need to tell Cook's," said Harry to the lad on the doorstep.

"Now the tour," said the clerk, his arms wide with possibilities.

"It must take in Paris where the friends will join the tour and then to Switzerland around the area of Vevey if possible," suggested Peter Fisher.

"I see, they're already in France?" asked the clerk, looking from Harry to Peter Fisher.

Neither confirmed nor denied.

"I see," the clerk said. "Very well, there is a little variation of time within the countries. Paris is 9 and a half hours earlier than Greenwich and Switzerland is 24 and a half hours behind."

"Struth," muttered Harry, "how complicated."

"Not to worry, you can work all that out?" asked Peter Fisher.

"Of course, that's why you've come here. Now there is a 19-day tour at present leaving Paris on Wednesday next week. They would stay in the London and New York hotel in the Place du Havre …. First or Standard class?" asked the clerk.

349

Peter Fisher paused but Harry cut in.

Harry leant on the counter and said: "Don't be funny."

Then Harry laughed at the thought of Stan in first class. He added: "Standard-class."

"Of course, your "friends" could arrive earlier in Paris and take in the sights, settle into the tour, get their bearings and so on," suggested the clerk.

"No," said Harry, "just arrange it from Wednesday and they'll get there and join the party ready for Switzerland. How long are they at Vevey?"

"Well, they'd have to get up there. There're steamers on the lake but the tour does Geneva, Lausanne …. look I'll show you on a map. They would get to Geneva on Thursday next week, then on Friday travel by train to Lausanne and their best bet for the Lake and getting up to Vevey is on Saturday as it's intended for visits to Vevey and the Castle of Chillon. They would go back that night to Ouchy. See, it's just here." The clerk prodded the map.

"That looks perfect, doesn't it?" Peter Fisher said to Harry.

Harry nodded and asked: "What happens then?"

"Well, the tour has a rest day on Sunday, which is day nine for everyone who started from London. On Monday it heads off to Berne, and Lucerne, which, from what you say is no good for your "friends." But this is the closest I can get them to the area you want."

"But you could book return passage for them from Monday morning? Via Paris to Victoria?" asked Peter Fisher.

"Oh yes, it's just a little more expensive to do it that way,"

"Of course, it is," said Harry, sighing.

"But the saving is on the accommodation so we are looking at Wednesday from Paris the 27th May leaving Switzerland on Monday 1st of June. I think we can do it. And I'll go and work out the cost."

"Thank-you," said Peter Fisher.

"Jack had better be back for the wedding," muttered Harry.

The clerk went into a back room and Peter Fisher turned to Harry. "Are they likely to have the clothes for this?"

"I very much doubt it as it wasn't expected," said Harry.

"I'll ask the clerk what we do about funds," said Peter Fisher. "He gave me a sheet about some sort of circular note exchangeable with the London Banks. Do you need to go off now to see Ann? Do give her my love."

"Yes, I do, so I'll get off now and get a cab to Marylebone to see her. I'll be back as quickly as I can. You sit tight here, alright Parson?"

*

The Cabbie who was to receive Harry as a client had fallen asleep contentedly on his box before the detective from Shadwell chose him. Cab companies, as Harry knew only too well, made little enquiry into the character of their drivers, preferring to change the horse regularly but not the Cabbie. Harry tapped the foot board and the man jerked awake.

Harry said: "There's a hospital for women up in Marylebone. Do you know It?"

351

"I do," replied the Cabbie.

"As fast as you can then," said Harry and settled into the carriage. The journey was uncomfortable and took fifteen minutes due to the pace the cabbie set for the horses. Harry was left feeling he had done another sea journey.

"Are you sure this is it?" asked Harry, staring up at the edifice towering over the road as the cab pulled up. He swung the door open and climbed gingerly down.

"Course I am, 222 Marylebone Road, Hospital for Women. You're not going in surely?" asked the Cabbie.

"That's for me to know and you to guess," Harry replied. "I'll need to go back to Ludgate. Hang on here for me, will you?"

"It wouldn't be right, you going in there. How much to wait?" asked the Cabbie.

"Sixpence extra," Harry said.

"Not worth the loss of business."

"Worth not being charged with making on the job with a lot of personal dues," said Harry.

"You talk like a 'tec. Where are you from?" asked the Cabbie, checking Harry over quickly.

"Not necessary for you to know but you're right about my profession. What's your fare?"

"I'll leave it to you under the circumstances. As one gent to another, you might say."

"Hoping for double the fare? Alright, call it two shillings extra then once I'm back in Ludgate," said Harry.

"Done, and you're a gent. 'ere what do you want in there? You wouldn't get me going in with a lot of women poking and prodding at you," said the Cabbie.

"You had a mother, didn't you? I should think she did a fair bit of poking and prodding at you," said Harry.

"My mother was a great believer in medicine and we children suffered for it. Treacle and Brimstone and a big wooden spoon kept hanging up by the range. I'd not go in that building if you paid me."

"As you're not a woman," said Harry, "It's not likely you would get the chance. As for these ladies working here, they're of well-known character and there's nothing to be said against them, do you hear me?"

The Cabbie nodded but spat before he could stop himself. Harry placed his thumbs in his waistcoat pocket and narrowed his eyes.

The Cabbie said: "Sorry, guv, I didn't think."

"I could take that personally," said Harry. "As I said bending the regulations on making on the job. I would think a Cabbie should give information to the proper quarter, so keep your eyes sharp while I'm inside and I might forget about your behaviour."

Harry ignored the stares of women queuing for help whose hard lives had left them blunted and reduced to a shell. Inside he made enquiries at a desk and was asked to wait in a side room while a message was sent to Ann Black in another part of the building. Harry had tried her alias first, used on more than one occasion by all accounts of: "Dr. George," but it was not recognised by the woman he had spoken to. He hung back a little as he followed the receptionist, sensing that he was causing some distress for a few. Then Ann arrived, looking bonny Harry thought and further on in her pregnancy than he had expected.

"Harry," Anne said, holding out her hand. "Your wedding must be very soon?"

"It is, and partly why I've deserted Jack in his hour of need as Rose and I see the Vicar on Saturday to go through the service. But I'm here for another reason," Harry produced the Vevey chocolates and placed them on the table in front of Ann. He said: "These we think are poisoned and we need to know what's in them."

"Jack's hour of need?" repeated Ann. "Jack's unwell, injured do you mean? Do you need me to come? George will accept me working here .... at present," she rested a hand on her stomach, "but not at a station. If there's a way you can get Jack to the back entrance here ..."

"He's away, on a job. These are part of some evidence and the mutt decided to sample one. As a result, he was violently sick ..." Harry explained.

Ann interrupted: "Any convulsions?"

"No," said Harry, firmly.

"Alright, leave them with me, although I shan't check them myself," said Ann. "I'll get someone to find out what's in them, although you've probably already got a good idea. Was Jack recovering alright?"

"Seemed to be, I left him yesterday morning and the sickness had stopped by the night before. Can't tell you too much, but could you let me know?"

"By message to Shadwell?" asked Ann.

"No, I'm still off duty officially. Send it to the Mason's Arms on the Commercial Road, addressed to Harry. No rank. They'll hold it for me behind the bar. I'll check each evening until I hear from you. Are you alright being here?"

"Amongst doctors and nurses do you mean?" Ann laughed, "Yes, Harry, I couldn't be anywhere better, and my mind needs to work."

"But there's a lot of sick women queuing up. Supposing you caught something. I'd be worried to death if I was George."

"And indeed he is. I'm in a back room but I can make myself useful, including getting a result for a detective from Shadwell. Don't worry I shan't do the work myself, but I'll get a message to you, hopefully tomorrow. Where is Jack if it's taken you so long to get this to me?"

Harry glanced out of the window and said: "You shouldn't know too much. I'm grateful to you for your help. I need to get back now as an old friend is waiting for me who sends his love to you. Jack's Parson is in the St Paul's area today."

"Reverend Peter Fisher? In London?" exclaimed Ann. "What are you up to? How frustrating not to be able to see him but please give him my regards." Ann paused and gave Harry a look of concern. "Why is that elderly man in London and involved with you?"

Harry sucked his teeth. She was always too sharp. He said: "The Parson provided Jack with a cover story and I needed to check he was alright. I couldn't stop him coming and as it happens his knowledge has been essential. As a result, he's making it possible for us to pursue a case." Harry stopped short realising he was making things more confused than ever.

"Is Jack alone if he's unwell?" asked Ann.

"No, another policeman is with him and a medical orderly," said Harry.

"An orderly? Hospital orderly? What is it that you are all up to? Never mind, I know you won't tell me. So, you think you're dealing with a poisoner?" asked Ann.

"Yes," said Harry.

"Male or female?" asked Ann.

"No idea, why?"

"Homes are full of poisons, most of the time they end up in food accidentally," explained Ann. "You know my aversion to the green dye in wall-paper, Harry, as much of it still contains arsenic despite the law. It can be difficult to assert there's any crime been committed at all in many cases and half the time they can go undetected. However, I'll let you go, and we'll do a chemical analysis so that you'll hear from me soon. I will try for tomorrow."

Ann held out her hand and Harry pushed away the desire to bow over it as he knew it would not be well received. Instead, he shook the hand as he would have done with any other colleague and left Mrs Ann Black to call one of the nurses to come and collect the box from the table.

Ann followed her and they both took the box into an office where a woman sat behind a simple desk. Ann quickly explained to Elizabeth Garrett Anderson.

"Something easy to disguise in the preparation perhaps?" said Elizabeth as Ann sat down.

"Could well be," said Ann.

"Maybe it's nothing more than trying to increase the profit made on the chocolates. Arsenic's been used before to eke out sugar or flour and other cooking ingredients, just look at the use of sulphate of copper." Elizabeth pulled a book from a shelf behind her desk.

"Yes, I know, and over time constant use is harmful. But it would have to be white Arsenic as generally that used in the home isn't that toxic. We need to do an analysis of the chocolates."

"It's true that white arsenic is readily available," said Elizabeth.

"Let's see what we can find and how many chocolates we might have a problem with first," said Ann.

"A woman's trade, so they say, poison. Do they think it's a woman?" asked Elizabeth.

Ann shrugged and avoided her colleague's gaze. She said: "My visitor didn't say. These chocolates are from somewhere called Vevey and there's a label on the bottom of the box. I've no idea how they travelled to England. If it's poison, then according to the newspapers it's a woman's crime. Although most murders are committed by men, or so I'm told by the police I work with, the journalists seem convinced poison is indeed a woman's weapon." Ann laughed as a thought occurred to her. "Where does that put us, given we've both qualified as chemists?"

"Top of the list I should think given the usual hysterical reaction to women," said Elizabeth. "If our husbands die under suspicious circumstances, we're for the chop. Better to keep them alive. We'll try and get this done for you by tomorrow. Is there any reason why you think it's arsenic?"

Ann thought for a few seconds before she answered. She explained: "The symptoms and the fact they subsided, no convulsions and it appeared to stop by the same evening. The person concerned ate it on the same day as they were violently sick, and it sounds as if the symptoms came on quickly afterwards. According to my visitor recovery was by evening with weakness until the following morning. There can't have been much used, although the patient may not have eaten all the chocolate. It may be in every chocolate or the person was unlucky in their choice."

Elizabeth put on white gloves and removed the box lid. "Still, it may not be deliberate as a poison. If it was mistaken for flour or sugar or even cream of tartar that might explain it. But memory says arsenic has been used as a colourant in confectionary. There are two chocolates missing?" She raised her eyebrows as she looked at Ann.

"Yes, I know," replied Ann. "Perhaps the first produced dire effects on someone else. Do you remember they were still putting plaster of Paris in sweets when we were children?"

"And the so-called burnt almonds passed off by kitchen maids when they cleared the plates of the peach and apricot stones and sold the kernels as almonds? Yes, and worse we've found in recent years haven't we. Look at the breakdown of what the sugar refiners were selling to the sweet makers. There was lime, alum, bulls' blood, charcoal, and more filthy poisonous substances." Elizabeth paused and glanced at Ann before she asked: "I take it your visitor was from the police?"

Ann met the clear gaze with her own but did not answer.

Elizabeth continued, deciding not to press any further: "I find it a funny relationship that you have, Ann. A policeman comes to you for help on a case and turns a blind eye to what you might be doing here. Ah well, at least we can get going with the School of Medicine for Women this year and the opportunities for the clinical teaching at the Royal Free. Just a matter of time now before our support increases to such an extent that society changes its attitude, and the BMA will have to admit you and the others." Elizabeth turned the box of chocolates over using a pair of long handled silver tongs. She continued: "Expensive these, I would say. You know as well as I do that people are very careless generally about how they store poison around other items. It may just be an accident. However, we still must find out what it is. Alright, leave it with me and I'll try and have something for you quickly so you can get word to your policeman."

*

359

"How much will they need a day?" asked Peter Fisher.

"About 20 shillings would cover it," answered the clerk. He thought for a few seconds and then added: "Perhaps a little more for emergencies and "service" they wish to reward. I would suggest luggage be condensed as much as possible and it is better to have something of the size which your friends can carry in a hand."

"That won't be a problem," said Peter Fisher.

"They may find they have to pay for their luggage in Switzerland unless they carry it in their hand, you see."

"As I say, that will not be a problem, they will travel light."

If anything, Peter Fisher thought, Jack and Stan will not have enough with them, neither were they likely to possess the sort of clothes they would need.

"They will need warm clothing, sir. Particularly for the mountains," said the clerk.

"But it's May," Peter Fisher looked surprised. "How do you know this?"

"There is a weather station at Geneva Cointrin. Geneva is 1300 feet above sea-level, sir, and won't get to temperatures we recognise as a summer until July. The average is about 51 degrees Fahrenheit at present. Obviously, we check with our guides on the ground before a tour goes off. I'm sorry to say this, sir, but the sort of people that go on this type of tour would naturally be prepared. There's a question of the evening as well."

"I see, you mean dressing for dinner. What are they staying in?" asked Peter Fisher.

"At Lausanne they will have three nights in the Beau Rivage hotel. It's in Ouchy but very close. It says here it has the characteristics of a palatial mansion. Oh dear, I see, you were thinking of the old reputation of Cook's. Since we opened this office we've been expanding into the type of tours where time is not limited. The sort of people going on these tours would be able to ... But they can always choose to opt out of that meal and visit the local hostelries, get a flavour of the local dishes."

"Yes, they will have to," Peter Fisher gave the clerk a wry look. "What happened to travel for all?" he asked.

"It's a new demand. Those other tours still exist. But most people who take them do so because time is limited now, A week here or there." The clerk ran his finger in between his collar and his neck. "The hotel details do say its patronised by the Swiss Tourists of every class and that the charges are as low as many inferior establishments. I can telegraph the hotel if you prefer as they have a telegram office inside. Its only 50 centimes to do so."

"How much is that?" asked Peter Fisher.

"About 5 pennies," said the clerk.

"I see, 10 centimes to a penny, is it? Alright, I think we should," said Peter Fisher. "Perhaps they can eat in a tavern, but we'd better make sure. Would you ask another question for me?"

"Of course," said the clerk.

"Ask if they can kit themselves out for the weather locally and how much it will cost? Then you and I can work out one of these circular notes you mentioned. I need then to send a telegram to Langton's solicitors in Hastings. I'll wait over here until you get an answer." Peter Fisher sat a little away from the counter, aware his body was craving rest. Determined not to give into his years and sleep he made his mind focus on Psalm 91. It was long enough to keep him awake.

"What's afoot Parson? Are we all sorted?" Harry Franks came in holding out a bag of cherries to Peter Fisher.

"Harry, you're a life saver." Peter Fisher said as he pulled out several. "I must admit to flagging a little. But to answer your questions I think we're nearly there. Just the problem of clothing for cold weather as I assume our friends will not be equipped given where they currently are. There's also the issue of an evening meal. We should have an answer shortly."

"Good, and Doctor George sends regards and wanted to come and see you. You know they're expecting? I did question what the doctor was doing at the hospital given who was queuing to be seen." Harry spat four cherry stones into his hand and threw them out of an open window. He asked: "How much has he stung you for, Parson?"

"Approximately 20 shillings a day each but there will be clothing costs, Harry, as the weather is cold until July. We should remember they may foray into the mountains. I should think, including planning in emergency costs as well we would look at 50 pounds in total."

Harry swore but apologised quickly, remembering his companion's calling. "How do you pay for this?" he asked.

"I've sent a telegram to a solicitor dealing with a trust that I know of asking for an advance to Cook's. I'm sure he'll respond and once your Inspector knows he will reimburse the fund I'm sure. Of course, it's not that our friends may spend it all, but they must have funds available. The clerk's doing circular notes for them so they can draw on money if they need to. It's a new thing. Careful now, what you say," Peter Fisher tapped Harry's elbow to caution him that the clerk was coming back.

"All arranged," announced the clerk triumphantly, waving two telegrams. "The solicitor in Hastings has given the go ahead with the funds and there's a response from the hotel that there isn't a problem as the Swiss tourists are a mixed class and many will not dress for dinner, remaining in their walking clothes. Your friends will fit in perfectly and can obtain what they need when they arrive in Geneva or Ouchy as Lausanne has excellent establishments to kit them out for the mountain walks. Always best, sir, in my experience to buy local. Now, sir, there is one leg of the journey that you and I have not planned in. I recognise I may be too cautious but have your friends arranged travel from where they are in France to Paris?"

"As I'm unclear as to their whereabouts I think we will just leave that to them. Ah, here's the boy back, hopefully, with the passports. Harry you were seeing to that I think?"

Harry nodded and gave a wink. He met the boy on the steps outside, slipped him the tip, pocketed the passports, and returned to the counter.

Peter Fisher was just finishing taking the large envelope from the clerk and said: "As you've got the guarantee from Langton the solicitor we must be on our way."

*

Harry paid a street vendor for the devilled herring roes, which had been fried in cayenne pepper, and spread on toast. At first, Peter Fisher waved the bag away, but Harry pressed him to try it. The elderly man looked white around the gills as far as Harry was concerned and he needed to have something to get the blood circulating. Harry had been determined that Peter Fisher would travel first class back to Southampton and the tired clergyman had succumbed to persuasion.

"Come on Parson," said Harry. "Jack will have my guts for garters if you go down. All's arranged and Thomas Cook has the lawyer's guarantee so all that remains is to get you safely back to your sister. Timothy said he'd meet the train and I'll let him know your arrival time?"

Peter Fisher reached for another half of the toasted food. he could tell it was doing him good. He said: "This is surprisingly tasty."

Harry smiled noticing the light was returning to the old Parson's eyes as he ate.

Harry said: "I'll see to the telegram that once you're on the train."

Harry waved at the street vendor for another portion and slapped his coins down on the makeshift counter. Once again, he turned to observe the scene before them, pushed his bowler hat to the back of his head and adopted a casual position, his elbows resting on the counter as he surveyed the hustle and bustle around them. He still feared the surprise attack. But there was no interest in either of them, or Harry had ensured the cabbie had been well paid to keep his mouth shut. There was still twenty minutes before the train would leave and as the first-class section was near the barrier there was time to get the Parson on board without a protracted walk along the platform.

"You've the package safe, Parson?" asked Harry for the umpteenth time.

"I have, and my answer is the same as it's been each time you've asked: addressed to Mr Farmer at St Helier Post Office," replied Peter Fisher.

Harry nodded and went back to his casual surveillance. He was relieved to see that the crowds on the concourse had thinned as trains had pulled out. It was time for Peter Fisher to move.

"Right, Parson," said Harry, "Let's get you on the train."

"You still expect problems, don't you Harry?" asked Peter Fisher.

"If there are shadows here, they will come in a crowd. That's thinned now and I doubt it will happen. There's only the journey for you to do. I'll wait on the platform until the train leaves and mean to have a word with the staff on the train to keep an eye you. Once the train pulls out, I'll go to the telegraph office on the station and get a message to Timothy."

The two men began to move towards the train. Harry knew any more than one man attacking them would damage their chances as he could not call on the octogenarian at his side to fight. However, the man did have a mahogany walking stick with him. Once on the train Harry and Peter Fisher spoke in low tones as the Parson seated himself. Cautiously, Harry looked round, taking in the well-dressed bald man in a corner seat, probably a company director from his manner of dress. Then it was time to shake hands and Harry allowed himself a smile as he said: "Thank-you, Parson, you have saved the day."

"Let me know the outcome, won't you?' said Peter Fisher.

"I will. As I hear so will you, but I should imagine Jack will stay in touch with you if he needs help and of course, there's always Sam in Brighton."

"And Harry," said Peter Fisher as he turned the handle of his stick to reveal a blade below. "I have a long history of other times in my past."

Harry laughed and responded: "Which I hope will remain in your past given the changes in the law these days, however I am delighted to see your steel friend and won't now worry so much about your journey."

Harry was gone, walking along the train towards the guard's van. The two railwaymen he found there were briefed to keep their eye on the elderly clergyman in first class, duly tipped sixpence each and then Harry was off the train, stumbling a little with his own fatigue. He felt drained and sorely in need of Rose's smile. But that would have to wait as Harry had one more task ahead of him.

On the platform the engine's steam and whistle provided the distraction which Harry needed to slip back past the ticket collector at the barrier. There was no one to invite his attention on the concourse and Harry walked slowly, deliberately moving from stall to stall, to give any shadow time to reveal themselves. Now the worst part of the day lay before Harry Franks of Shadwell and he pushed his bowler hat to the back of his head as he reflected on the coming interview with Inspector Tom Hunt.

The London, Chatham, and Dover Railway, known locally as the Chatham, deposited Harry at Camberwell New Road. It was a matter of a few minutes' walk to the police station opposite the Green. He knew it was a gamble as to whether Tom Hunt would even be in the station but if Harry's notion was correct there would be an advantage to arriving late in the day. The only two men with whom he reckoned Hunt was likely to have shared intelligence about Jack's whereabouts with were Sergeant's Morris and Phillips. There would be a change of shift about the time Harry calculated he would arrive at New Road and neither man would be there. It kept things straightforward that way.

In the general confusion at the front desk with staff changing Harry Franks managed to get to Hunt's door before anyone could stop him. Chances were the old hands would recognise him in which case he would not be challenged anyway. The younger cohort of new recruits were unlikely to have the gumption and would assume, correctly that the cove in the bowler hat was plain clothes.

Harry stopped in the doorway, tired and out of patience, while the man behind the desk looked up. Privately, Harry thought, Hunt was shocked at his appearance in the station, but the man was managing to control his surprise although the forehead was furrowed.

"So you're back?" Hunt waited.

Two constables came down the corridor and glanced at the man leaning against the Inspector's door frame. They hovered, catching the rare glimpse of the man behind the desk. Any chance of Harry having a private conversation with Hunt was slim.

"Have you a bit of time, Inspector?" asked Harry.

Hunt stood and said: "I can give you a little. Have you eaten?"

"I could do with a glass and to share a quick meal with a colleague," replied Harry.

Hunt said to the constables: "Time you were at the front desk, I think. The Sergeant will be on his way. I'll be back shortly."

Hunt picked up an old coat and for a while did not speak as he led Harry away. Once outside Hunt said:

"What consequences do you think this has, turning up here?"

Harry scowled. "I don't know, but I have to speak to you as there've been developments. They can't wait for you to initiate a meeting, Tom. We're walking a tightrope unless I brief you."

Hunt stood, controlling the frustration as his orders had been ignored, working through in his mind what could have happened for someone like Harry Franks to choose to show up at Camberwell. He said:

"Alright, let's share a meal. I can give you an hour. I'm on late so I need to eat anyway. When did you arrive back?"

"I got to London today," said Harry.

They walked up the street to the junction where it became the Camberwell New Road and the wind from the brewery above the Green turned the air pungent. At the William IV public house Hunt steered Harry through a side door into a private room and opened a hatch in the wall. Hunt waited until the Landlord had seen the shaft of light from the room and then held up two fingers.

Glasses clinked as the Landlord passed through two pints of beer. Harry sat and took one while Hunt put sixpence on the table. Not a beer drinker Harry generally spilt more than he consumed when undercover in the Masons Arms. He took a sip and looked at Hunt.

"It meets the regulations here," warned Hunt.

"Right, too strong to play with," said Harry, pushing the glass away.

Harry waited while Hunt and the Landlord agreed the curry would do, which to Harry meant the meat was three days old.

"Not for me," Harry said, "I'm expected elsewhere for dinner."

"Ah I can guess. Beggars can't be choosers in my case," said Hunt, as he sat down. "It's this or nothing, I'm on 'til midnight. The food is alright here, though, if you want to change your mind."

Harry shook his head and waited, aware so far that Hunt had been polite.

"Well?" said Hunt. "Tell me."

Harry inhaled and started to explain:

"The quarry had left some days before we arrived. He knew we were coming we think. From items he left we know he's Norwegian. The name is Torg, and as there's a mountain of the same name we've got the exact location of it if that's where he's from. But Jack was right that he's a climber."

"That's extraordinary good luck, but come to think of it given where I think the man that we're after is, that might fit," said Hunt. "How did you find all this out?"

"From a clever vicar. Torg staged his own death we think to disappear and left some of his belongings in the place in which he'd stayed. Local police didn't find anything, but they think he's dead in a ravine. We think he's staged it and gone. One of the items he left behind was a box of chocolates, poisoned I think deliberately, and one had been eaten. They'd arrived with a letter. He left everything except the letter. Jack being Jack ate one of the chocolates, or part of it at least and ended up unwell. He was recovering when I left yesterday morning. And the other thing that you should know is that I was tracked and hunted in the streets of St Helier."

"How many?" asked Hunt. He knew the answer, but he wanted to check out Burgess's story.

"By two men I reckon from the steps I heard. That is until Mr Burgess saw them off. Did you know he was going there?" Harry folded his arms and leant forward staring into Hunt's face.

"No, I did not," said Hunt, "but I received a telegram from Brighton yesterday telling me he was your saviour and emphasising he's the only one of you all who can identify one of the attackers."

"Sets Burgess up nicely, doesn't it, as indispensable," said Harry. "There's more you should know. But first tell me did you brief Burgess?"

"No, I did not," snapped Hunt, glaring at Harry.

"So, who did?"

"That isn't something you need to know," said Hunt. But he was on the backfoot and Harry knew it.

Harry pressed home his advantage and said: "Oh, I think it is. I owe Charles Burgess otherwise I'd be dead in the gutter in St Helier. It's time Tom. I'm sure I don't need to remind you, that you breached confidentiality last year when you chose to tell me what you're involved with. You did it again by taking Jack to Windsor in February. You've made him the heir apparent to you about all this in the Queen's eyes. That young officer will never be clear of it now if anything happens to you. I know you wouldn't have done that if you weren't convinced that your days might be numbered. Someone is briefing Burgess and they're playing two strands of opportunity to get this upper-class cove at the top. Burgess is an obvious route to go because he got close to exposing that right honourable before, despite it nearly finishing him. What we haven't got is how Burgess knew about the thief that Jack was after. My guess is he's been drip fed enough to link the pursuit of the thief with the man that destroyed his career. Question is by whom as you say it wasn't from you. Then there's the question that our arrival on Jersey was leaked, and that my friend, has to be someone close to you."

Hunt glowered at Harry, but the hatch opened, and the landlord placed Hunt's meal ready for him. It provided Hunt with enough time to consider what Harry had said and for his anger to subside. Hunt stood for a while, in silence at first, as he gathered up the plate with the fork and spoon. His face started to relax.

"I should go," said Harry, "I'm of no use in this now."

"Of great use in focusing thoughts and everything you say is right. We're pawns on a chessboard but even a pawn can threaten the King of crime if we're correctly placed. One thing about Burgess to remember: he's true. I'm going to ask him to go back," said Hunt.

"What back to Jersey? Jack and Stan won't be there for much longer. That's what I need to tell you. I went to find Jack's Parson when I landed at Southampton. I needed to check he was safe. He and his brother-in-law helped work things out like the nationality of the thief and there's a couple of other things I'll come back to which I haven't told you. This morning the Parson and I went to Thomas Cook's in London and bought a tour for Stan and Jack to get them to where the chocolates came from. It made sense for them to get to Vevey and follow that lead. The Parson got money guaranteed from a lawyer in Hastings dealing with Jack. You owe Jack about £50. But it's all set up and Jack will get all the information and the tickets by tomorrow morning. The Parson will make the mail boat with the package for Jack tonight. By Wednesday next week Jack and Stan will join a Cook's tour in Paris and leave for Switzerland. It's 6 days from then that they will travel back to London, hopefully with information, an arrest, or whatever you want. But you've got to come back in on this Tom, actively, and maintain that reputation you have of the steady pair of hands holding the reins. It's no good saying we can't initiate contact." Harry paused.

Hunt's expression was like cold steel.

Harry swallowed and pressed on:

"No good looking at me like you want to kill me. We've had no choice but to take it on because your order was not to contact you. There were developments and decisions needed and you left me in charge. Now I'm back and off the case and Stan's in charge on Jersey Gawd 'elp us."

"And the other things that you mentioned? What else have you to tell me?"

"I took the chocolates to Ann Black," explained Harry, looking away. "We'll know hopefully tomorrow what's in them. She'll get a message to me at an address I've given her. Do you want to know when I hear?"

Hunt nodded, "Of course."

———

373

"And the last thing: where did those soldiers come from at the billet in Gorey?" Harry asked.

"You know where, the regiment's headquarters outside Winchester," said Hunt.

"Who arranged that?"

"Why?" asked Hunt.

"Was it the current occupant of a nice bit of property called Hughenden by any chance?" Now Harry met Hunt's gaze.

"That doesn't matter," Hunt answered. He pushed his uneaten meal away, no longer hungry and asked: "Didn't they assist you?"

"Oh yes," said Harry, "They assisted us very well, took good care of us, including one of them being a medical orderly, which was a lucky chance wasn't it? Or was it? Bit of a coincidence having a set of skills like that with such a team. Then there's the issue of the food supplies."

Hunt controlled his sense of impatience. He asked: "What was wrong with them?"

"They were poor and smacked of a team that hadn't had time to set itself up properly before we arrived. Apart from a battlefield soldiers don't have to forage. The food, to me, said no one knew they were there. There was another issue with the soldiers as well, which Jack's old Parson shone a light on."

"Go on," said Hunt.

"Do you know our insignia? Do you know our motto?" Harry's voice had got louder.

"Gently Harry, keep your voice down, of course I do."

"... 'Course you do and so do I because we're serving police officers of the Met. And you would expect soldiers to know their regiment's famous motto, wouldn't you, even though it's in Latin? Don't worry about answering this but do you know what it is? It's a Latin word: Ubique. The old Parson knew what it meant, straight off because he's an educated gent. But those soldiers you had us billeted with didn't know it, which I find very interesting, Tom, and given the other issues I mentioned I've come to a conclusion. Those men are not who they say they are. So, come on, who set that team up to help us?"

" I can only tell you that a billet was arranged for you," said Hunt. "You were to go to Gorey and would be given accommodation with soldiers at the address I sent, near the castle."

"And who was it that provided you with that address? Was it the same office in Whitehall you emerged from last year when I met you?" asked Harry. "Who are they, Tom?"

Hunt paused as his eyes bored into Harry's. He said: "Same office, different occupant and I don't know who they are. But by God I'll find out."

Hunt shovelled some of the food into his mouth, one after the other, and swallowed. Disraeli would soon be off to Scotland. He pushed the plate with two thirds uneaten away and got up, saying: "Right, that's enough food, I think. Anymore, and I generally find I can't digest it on duty. Where will you be tomorrow if I need to get hold of you?"

"The Vicarage of All Hallows Church, Great Tower Street," said Harry. "Not 'til after we've seen the Vicar, Tom."

Fourteen

It was to be a midnight tide on Friday as Jack and Stan boarded the fishing vessel early, laying low until the darkness allowed them to move around the deck without being identified from the shore. Over the next few hours, the French fishermen made ready, calling to each other in a lingo as they went about their work: raising the mast and tending the mainsail, dealing with the cargo, and positioning the wheel. Their talk was incomprehensible to the two policemen, When it was time to leave Gorey as if by magic, the wind picked up.

Earlier, Jack had collected Peter Fisher's package from the post office in St Helier. It had been late morning and in the package that he had been handed was also a letter addressed to Stan. Jack was still weak after the sickness but had picked up sufficiently to go in by train with Stan to collect the post under his alias of "Mr Farmer."

Jack had decided to use Torg's bag as his own, partly to enter the personality but also as it was highly practical. He had slipped the package from Peter Fisher into it while in the post office. Once outside Jack had hastily torn open part of it while it was still inside the frame bag and had caught sight of the passports and bookings for Paris and Switzerland. He had parted the top of the papers, peering into the bag while doing so. He read the names on a couple of hotels and a shudder of excitement had run down his spine.

"*Paris* … Wednesday … it's a gift from the farisees! but how to get to Paris?" Jack asked himself.

———

376

Stan, on the other hand that morning, had waited for Jack by the harbour nursing a sense of being abandoned by Tom Hunt. He hated the French because his grandfather had died in the Napoleonic Wars. An impending trip across sea also added to the black cloud hovering above him. When Jack handed him Harry's letter Stan's face moved from a grimace to shock as he read it. Jack had recognised Harry's writing and turned the sealed letter over a few times wondering about its contents. He had pushed down the desire to open it anyway. Watching Stan's reaction as he read reminded Jack of a nervous dog on the farm that had been chained up for too long.

"Betrayal," said Stan, putting his head in his hands.

"What? Who by? Tell me, Stan what's happened, what does Harry say?" asked Jack.

Stan did not answer at first, sitting shaking his head, then he passed Harry's letter to Jack and said:

"Read it for yourself. Can you settle here for a while, Jack? Preserve your strength while I make enquiries. I'll walk for a while if you're alright, get my head straight. When you've read Harry's letter, write a message on it at the bottom that it's been read by us both. Go back to the post office and send it back to him at the house in Bow. You've the address, haven't you?"

"Yes, But what can I expact? Is it such bad news to affect you so? Can't you just tell me quickly?" asked Jack.

"Not now, read first. We've to use our wits, young Jack," Stan said. "We're on our own now, you and I and I need to clear my head, get a plan."

"Alright, you go on Stan, I can see you're worried," said Jack. "I'll be fine here for a while. I'll go through everything and see what's involved. I was excited we were to make the crossing at first but now I'm not so sure. Whatever's amiss we can plan our way through it can't we?"

"Pray we can, Jack if you're of a mind to. Pray we can. One thing's for sure we can't go back to Gorey today, and if I can get us a passage we'll leave as soon as the tide allows. I'll see you back here shortly," and Stan abruptly turned on his heel and was gone.

It was to be a good couple of hours before Stan returned. Jack devoured Harry's letter again and again until he could almost recite it. Harry had gone to Ann Black. Jack hoped she was well and thought, perhaps, close to her confinement. She would be able to confirm if there was poison in the chocolates, and arsenic at that. Jack felt more determined than ever to find Torg and to get to whoever was behind the thefts and understand why the Norwegian had been sent chocolates. Jack could also not forget he had a Queen's command to obey and that he was to recover the Shah's stolen diamonds.

He followed Stan's order to send Harry's letter back to him at the address in Bow and Jack signed it for Stan and himself as the evidence it had been read and understood. Part of him thought Sam should have it but Stan's order was to return it to Harry. By the time Jack got back to the post office it was busy and he pushed down the sense of irritation at having to join a queue to obtain an envelope and another queue to send the letter. At the last minute he decided to write a brief note to

Peter Fisher and send it to Lymington, so he bought writing paper as well as two envelopes. Looking around for space to write privately he moved some books to one side on a shelf and then set to, to write.

His brief letter read:

Jersey, Friday.

Parson what a wonder you are! I'm in safe receipt of your package and we are making plans now. I grow stronger.

I don't know when I shall next see you but ask you to pray for fair weather, and calm seas and safe travel. Pray for us to be safe. We leave tonight.

We need success and are unsure of so much. Please contact our friend by the Pavilion for me and let him know everything you understand. I'm under orders to contact our friend in Bow only.

Your friend: Farmer.

Just in case it's intercepted, Jack thought, as he signed himself Farmer. He would have written more but knew he was breaking confidence by even sending this short letter. But the Parson had put himself at risk and Jack felt a deep need to make contact before he left these shores with one of the only few people alive who had a link with his childhood. He hoped Sam would now hear and was sure the Parson would be faithful in discharging that request to let Sam know.

After he had left the post office Jack moved into a tavern at the top of the New Harbour and positioned himself to be able to see the spot where he and Stan had parted. A serving girl took a shine to his smile and Jack tipped her for a screened alcove by a window, ordering whatever fare the place could provide and paying well, although he had no stomach for the food. There he sat and waited, wrapping the bread and Jersey butter in a cloth the girl had placed under the plate. Jack packed it away in Torg's bag just in case it was all he and Stan had later. Then he tried the soup. soaked into the rough bread to make himself eat. He managed a few mouthfuls before he felt his stomach start to lurch. There was too much salt in it and he pushed the dish aside.

By three o'clock, Jack sighted Stan walking back along the path. Jack went to the door and put his two fingers in his mouth and gave a shrill whistle to attract Stan's attention. Stan raised a hand in acknowledgement and changed direction for the tavern.

Stan's face bore the furrows it always did when situations took an unexpected turn. He nodded to the man behind the bar and ordered whatever he could bring him placing a Jersey coin on the counter. Stan winked and the tip was implied. Standing at the bar he turned to survey the clientele. It was something he and Harry always did in the Masons Arms on the Commercial Road. Nothing remarkable there, thought Stan. After a few minutes he was satisfied and walked across to Jack to join him in the alcove. Once the food was brought to the table Stan waited until the spoon and knife was put down and the girl was on her way back to the bar, then he quietly explained: "We've a crossing and I've paid well to get it."

"Well done, when do we leave?" asked Jack.

"Tides high at midnight. I've also arranged for a false trail for the soldiers, letting them think we will sail to Carteret from Gorey. We can't take the risk of going back as we don't know who they are. You read Harry's letter?" asked Stan.

Jack nodded.

"Even Hunt doesn't know who they are. That's what worries me most. We need to disappear," said Stan.

Jack said: "But they've been more than helpful. Surely if they were going to try something, they've had more than enough opportunity to do us harm. Why teach me to shoot?"

"Get alongside you, get friendly and it opens you up. Anyway, whoever sent them is not known to Hunt. I've sent a note to the billet apologising for leaving suddenly but saying we had to spy our chance, which is true. That note will get to the billet in the morning. I'm banking on them expecting us to return as we've left our belongings. I've timed it deliberately. Instead, there's a Normandy fishing vessel leaving tonight, and the Captain will take us to the Chausey islands, closer to here than the coast of France. It's a little like the Channel Islands but French. We would need high tide to pass through the area, so we won't make it in time in the fishing vessel. There's a forty-five-foot difference between high and low tide, so we'll be collected by a dory, and taken to Grande-Île, where we'll wait until dusk tomorrow."

Stan paused again to take another mouthful of the meat pie and Ale. He'd had better but the task now was to stoke up.

"What's a dory?" asked Jack.

"Just a minute," said Stan. He smiled at the Landlord and held up more money. The girl Jack had tipped was sent over and Stan gave her a sixpence for more food. He was buying their space. He asked: "Bread? Any fruit and meat?"

She nodded and he pressed another coin into her hand.

Stan smiled at her and waited until she was out of earshot, then he leant forward again and continued: "It's a flat-bottomed boat propelled by oars, Jack, and Grand Île's the only inhabited island of the group. It's worked by about five-hundred men for the granite on it, apparently. Once there we'll camp in a barn near the Fortress of Matignon until high tide at dusk on Saturday. The dory will take us across the shelf of islands to open sea and there will be a boat to Granville where there's a railhead for Paris. The Captain's given me a rough sketch of how to find the barn and says he thinks the farmer is up on the pasture tomorrow so we shouldn't be disturbed. We get some sleep and then join up with the dory again at dusk. The boat for Granville is owned by his brother so there's been a double expense. However, I think we can trust them. The Captain thinks we're British spies and warns me that, if we're caught, we'll be shot. I did deny it, but I couldn't tell him what it was we were doing. Fortunately for us, there's no love lost between those in the Normandy area and Paris, because they believe the government mis-handled the war with Prussia. So, he's happy to help and he's been well paid. Hunt owes me."

"Right, well we can prove who we are thanks to the Parson and Harry," explained Jack. "In the package are passports for us both and we've a booking in a hotel in Paris for Wednesday night and then on to Switzerland." Jack grinned: "The places sound smart Stan. We'll need clothes but the Parson thinks we can buy local. He's found us a Cook's tour going to the place where the chocolates are made. There're time differences but we can work those out later. The tour will be a good cover for us."

"Oh, my life," said Stan. "Do you know the types that go on those tours, Jack?"

Jack shrugged and continued: "Well, we can say I've come into money, which is true. We might be a bit foreright, but we can manage that."

"What's that mean?" Stan wrinkled up his nose.

"Foreright? it means rude, plain-speaking, you know. They say in Sussex …I don't know what to do with that boy he's so foreright…"

Jack paused but Stan just stared at him.

Jack continued: "We'll be clean, fed and taken onto Vevey, which is where we need to go. There must be a link with Torg there, and if we can find him, we have a chance of getting to the man at the top. The Parson says in his letter that we need 20 shillings a day each to cover everything: that's food, bed, and travel. We'll get to Granville early Sunday morning and we're got two nights to fill once we're there; one night in Paris, and the journey to Switzerland is on Wednesday. Perhaps we can go fishing as a cover in Granville?"

Stan's face threatened thunder. Jack knew the warning signs and said: "Well perhaps I will. Once we're in Switzerland there's another six days, Stan, before we're booked on a train

---

383

back to Paris and on to a boat train for London. The Parson and Harry have worked a miracle. Harry must have collected him from his sister's house and they both went into London to Thomas Cook's. The Parson says he won't go back to Simpson until this is all over but will remain with his sister, so I know he'll be safe there. That's one less thing to worry about."

"Good, Harry's done well there, and I trust the Parson," said Stan. "Did you see in his letter Harry's gone to Hunt? Oh, to be a fly on that wall, eh?"

Jack grinned and nodded, imagining the exchange between the detective sergeant and the inspector. He put the passports and the different pieces of the paperwork on the table for Stan to see and said:

"There's some sort of banking draft fortunately and the Parson's got a guarantee for the money from Langton the solicitor, until Hunt reimburses it." Jack laughed then carried on: "So, my story is true as I could say I've paid for this. I shall enjoy it for that reason alone. Only problem we've got is that you and I have left everything in Gorey, and we will stink to high heaven by the time we make Paris, but look, here, the Parson says there's money for clothing in the banker's note and that we'll find the mountains cold, so we need to buy again once we get to Geneva."

"Right, that's what we'll do, then. Once we get to Granville, we can pick up enough to fit in and look like travellers. And find the telegraph office," said Stan. "I need to let my wife know I'm under cover." He looked at Jack who was clearly enjoying the whole prospect of the travel. "You go fishing lad, if you want to, but I feel like I need to sleep for a week after this. There'll be hell to play when I get home."

*

While Jack and Stan sat in the Tavern in St. Helier, Harry had donned his beer-stained waistcoat and assumed his tipsy persona. He leant on the bar at the Mason Arms and, as always, turned to view the clientele. That year the Commercial Road as an area had changed and the terraces had been integrated into it in a re-numbering. Everything felt out of kilter to Harry. The result was that a local feeling of pride in the place had vanished and many of the men inside the bar were no longer recognisable as locals. The road itself was no longer associated with seafaring, as it had been some years earlier and that pride and a sense of a local tradition had gone.

As expected, a sealed message was placed on the bar in front of him by Mary Cunliffe's successor. Another new girl thought Harry. No matter how attractive the stream of young women had been in the Masons Arms since Mary had left for Brighton none of them had that certain something which Mary had possessed. This one, the latest in a long line of the Landlord's young relations from the country seeking to get on in London, was quite rough around the edges. Harry did his best to remember the name: "Maisie, or was it, Daisy?" Harry shrugged and glanced down at the envelope and saw his name hoping it would be answers from Ann Black.

"On yer own?" asked the bar maid, waiting for the tip.

Harry rarely visited on his own but under the circumstances he had caught the Blackwall railway from Shadwell without his cohort of constables. The less his team knew anything the better. He nodded at the pump and the girl reached for a tankard.

"Ah, my lovely," said Harry loudly, removing his bowler hat and placing it over the letter on the bar as he leant forward towards the girl, "You and I should be picnicking in pastures green, today."

"Oh, get off with you, Harry," said the barmaid quietly, "Everyone knows you're getting married in a few weeks. Take your letter and go. And don't knock the beer over today."

"It saves drinking it but out of respect to you I won't," said Harry, placing his bowler with the letter inside back on his head. He tipped her a farthing, paid for the beer and as he usually did, kept up the tipsy charade until he was out of the Masons Arms and under the bridge. But today he was tired of it all and only the thought that he may have been followed encouraged him to maintain his performance. Outside he stopped a cab largely to get privacy inside it to read the letter. There were more changes to come to the area as Harry passed the new works which had begun to replace the bow-string bridge for a wider model. It was rumoured that the work on the new bridge would take two years to complete. Harry called up to the Cabbie as he climbed inside:

"Turn around and go down the Commercial Road towards the Arbour Square area. I'll give you directions from there."

Inside the cab he ran his finger under the seal and started to look for the signature on the letter: Ann. She'd kept her word and it had been written early morning and sent by messenger.

Harry started to read:

Dear Harry,

As you suspected from the symptoms you described we have turned up traces of arsenic in each chocolate. Whoever they were intended for may be being slowly poisoned over time. I say this as it's an exact measure in each one and therefore I would say its presence is deliberate. They certainly would have made someone very ill but not killed them if one at a time was eaten. The dose to kill would need to be stronger but if this is deliberate a build-up in the system could do it as well as causing other health problems.

There's no way I know to treat arsenic poisoning except to stop taking it. Our friend, Jack, should recover quite quickly as its only once and the amount in each chocolate was small. However, if these chocolates were intended for another person over weeks or months, together with other high levels of arsenic exposure, then that person may display complications to look for such as heart disease.

Where will this information take you, Harry? Part of me wishes to come too but I will soon start another adventure with our little one and know that this time I must leave you all to your next mystery. However, I hope you will bring your new wife to visit our family once our baby is born.

But enough of that. I must mention to you that I've discussed the levels found in the chocolates with Elizabeth and we are both in agreement that, of course, it could either be accidental, or not. However, I don't think it is accidental, as I've said.

I know nothing of the area the chocolates come from. Generally, Arsenic occurs in contaminated ground water by the way as well as being easy to obtain commercially. So many industrial processes may cause it. My advice is to look at the area, Harry.

It will always depend on the circumstances which you will no doubt uncover. Write to me at the Marylebone Road if you need more help.

I remain your friend and colleague,

Ann.

Marylebone.

There we are then, thought Harry. Jack you are an enthusiastic chump eating that chocolate, but you've focussed things nicely for us. Question is who were those chocolates really intended for and where are they now? Torg is the route to the man we want if our hunch is correct and the Norwegian must have been stealing to order. But why is our thief being sent arsenic laced chocolate? Harry reached for his notebook and flipped to the back where he had made a note of the hotels Jack and Stan would stay in. The cab was slowing as it turned into David Lane and the Cabbie pulled up outside Shadwell police station. Harry reached into his pocket for the fare. Ann's question echoed in Harry's mind: yes Ann, he thought, where will all this take us? Personally, your findings won't take me away from the arms of Rose but for Stan and Jack it's to Paris: the London and New York Hotel, Place du Havre, for Wednesday night. Harry stared out of the cab window at the old men on their way to the Sailor's Institute in Mercer Street. What would be Jack and Stan's next move now? There were five nights before the two men were due in Paris. Harry thumped the side of the cab for it to stop and said to himself: "Get going, lads, get the hell off that island."

*

Stan's breath stank of the raw onions he had consumed during the evening as he breathed rapidly with the stress of being at sea. Light was beginning in the east and Jack could make out land mass. Slowly, the dark lifted like a curtain and ahead lay a group of small, seaweed covered islands. It was low tide and Jack tried to count the small rocky outcrops but there was a myriad of small shapes in the gloom of the dawn. The men on board were setting to, harvesting the mussels. Jack walked over to where Stan was hunched against a pile of rope and sat down next to him.

"There must be hundreds of tiny islands," said Jack.

Stan nodded but his attention was drawn to the Captain who was walking over to them.

"Now you go. Look there." The man pointed towards the east and the shapes of men were visible on the horizon. Slowly they became more distinct and Jack could make out the shape of the dory as they navigated the rocky outcrops.

"These men will take you now and return tonight at dusk," the Captain explained. "I will pay them in front of you, so you know they have had the money. Be ready at dusk as they will not wait. My brother's ship is the "Marie," and he will not wait either, so please be there. Bon chance."

"Thank-you," said Jack.

The exchange was done and his boots full of water Stan perched on the flat-bottomed boat cursing. Jack's eyes peered to the back and watched as the fishing boat turned away. The light was enough now to see dwellings at the back of a beach on a larger island. Jack assumed these must be where the miners lived. From the beach other dories were setting off and picking their way, some stopping and retrieving lobster pots near the small islets before moving to the next.

"How far is it to Granville from here?" asked Jack of the men.

One of them laughed and Jack realised they could not understand English. "Granville?' Jack tried again and once more the laughter came at his pronunciation of the place.

But one man said to him: "Granville," and swallowed the double ll sound.

Jack smiled and repeated it. The man nodded encouragement at his attempt but only pointed ahead. Jack did not receive any other answer. There was a landing stage and although it was rudimentary it served its purpose. Stan and Jack were off onto the white sand from where they could see a building. Stan briefly checked the map the Captain had provided.

"The barn should be at the back of those buildings," he said. It's a farm and where there are farmers there's usually cows and chickens. Are you up for a spot of petty theft, Jack?"

"If that's an order, Stan, then needs must," said Jack. He added: "After food we should sleep. I hope the farmer is working in the fields."

"Well, you've more idea of the right end of the cow than I have. I'll look for some flat stones and try and build a fire. If you can find eggs we can try and cook them. You've still got that bread and I've some cheese."

It felt a long wait until the sun descended into the horizon. The two men had some sleep in the warmth of the day and Jack appeared with a bucket with enough fresh milk in it to keep them going. He had also been around the barn foraging for fresh eggs. Between them they drank from the pale of milk and filled it again from a trough with water. Stan built a fire, encasing it in small boulders to contain it and control the smoke. Stripping, Jack swam, more to clean himself than desiring the sea. He preferred the salt to the stench he was sure he was creating. Neither man had had fresh linen for two days and it would be another day before they would have chance to change, assuming they could purchase clothing. Little washing had been done at the soldier's billet.

The dried driftwood soon had sparks flying. If anyone saw the glow, then they would have trouble. But the fire died down with some help from Stan kicking soil over half of it and the eggs cooked in a tin mug from Stan's bag. With the bread, cheese, and the milk, they had enough until they would make Granville.

Towards the end of the evening, they had taken it in turns to sleep, while the other one kept watch. When the light had started to fade Jack's vigil at the shoreline was rewarded and he ran back to the farm and kicked Stan's boot to waken him.

"Stan, the dory's coming back. We should move."

"At least they've come, I did wonder if they would turn up for us," said Stan.

"It's a good price we've offered. And there's the fact that there's no love lost between those from Normandy and the French. If they believe we're English spies it suits them," said Jack, pointing. "I expact they won't want to hang around. Let's get down there."

It was the same men who had picked them up that morning. Once on the dory Jack tried to find out the wind direction with puffing out his cheeks and blowing: "Chausey – Granville?" he asked, mimicking the accent he had heard earlier.

The man who had helped him with the pronunciation that morning smiled and nodded. He said, "Rapide, trés fort," and did the action of clenching his fists and tensing his arm muscles.

Jack frowned then got it: "Rapide? Fast, do you mean? And strong?" Jack flexed his arm muscles and clenched his fists and the man nodded and returned the smile. The Marie loomed out of the darkness.

Once aboard the Marie, Stan fell into an exhausted sleep in a hammock below. Mumbling and dreaming of trying to find his wife and children who could not speak English when he did, he shouted out a few times. Jack stayed on deck despite the pitching of the boat, feeling better in the air and eventually, he also succumbed to sleep.

The wind drove the ship the seventeen miles to Granville and it pitched so that Stan was seasick. At last they entered the haven of the port with a sudden drop in the wind. Now the shelter of the harbour gave them the opportunity to sleep for a few hours until daybreak would give them the opportunity to go ashore.

As the dawn came across Granville there was an incongruous sight to the left as ladies and children jumped in strong waves by the beach huts. Jack watched expecting any moment for a child to be lost. But they were used to it and quite safe. It had been a strong sea that morning and the Marie had been down to one jib sail at the front of the boat as she had slipped into the harbour. Then the crew were about to go ashore, and Jack and Stan shook the Captain's hand before they joined the men to go down towards the town.

"French soil, eh," said Jack, grinning broadly.

Stan's response was to spit.

'Come on, Stan, think of the adventure. How many of our kind get to step on foreign soil?" said Jack.

"Too many in my grandfather's generation," muttered Stan. "So much loss of life. Toffs and men like us. My grandmother was pregnant with my father. She'd been a wife for six months, that's all and spent sixty years as a widow. What are you excited about? They won't understand us, and we won't understand them. Come on, you grinning idiot, there's a place over there by the landing point which looks like it's clean. It's got a fair view of the Harbour. We can maybe get our clothes washed without it being too expensive and perhaps they'll know where we can pick up some fresh clothes. I don't like the look of that sky and I would rather not have to sleep on the beach, such as it is."

"The town up there looks interesting," sad Jack. "See the church, Stan and there's boats leaving too. Where do you think they're going from here?"

"No idea, and frankly, Jack, I don't care. Come on let's get a room and food."

"Rooms, thanks Stan, I need to sleep nights without your snoring," said Jack. "I thought I'd left the snorers of the world in Camberwell New Road."

"Money to burn you have, a room each my eye."

But Jack had his way and the price for two rooms was reasonable. Dinner would normally be over by six pm they were warned and not a minute later. The owner, or Le Patron, as she called herself, was a Madame Guibon and she introduced herself with some English and accepted a hotel coupon of Cook and Son. The rooms were clean, comfortable, and modestly furnished and Stan felt the stress start to drain out of him as he lay on his bed with a body aching for rest. Within minutes he was asleep.

Jack however, had stayed below to talk to Madame Guibon in a small dining room open at the front for service to the patrons on the street. Most called in for coffee and bread, butter, and some sort of red conserve. Jack nodded to his hostess and, smiling at him she put a plate, a small glass of water and coffee before him.

"Would you have tea?" Jack asked.

"No," laughed Madame Guibon. She picked up his teaspoon and demonstrated putting sugar in his coffee. Stirring it for him she said: "Try."

He did so and persevered with the coffee between sips of the water. Surprisingly he felt his stomach settle and the energy return. Jack spread the white butter on the bread and the thick conserve and took a bite. After chewing he beamed at his hostess.

Jack had asked about the train service for Paris, and a boy had been sent out to find the times to get them to Paris on Wednesday. He had been given extra money to buy any shirts, trousers, and linen for the two men that he could find from Jack who had no idea what would come back but at least they would be clean and probably blend in more with the local men. The boy went straight to a ship's chandler by the dock and returned with the sort of garb most of the fishermen wore. It would do locally, but Paris would be another issue once they were there.

Stan pulled himself off his bed by eleven o'clock and appeared at the door. There was no sign of Jack in the place but the leftovers of a "marmite du jour" was produced from the night before and after moving it about the plate with his fork Stan tucked in. Surprised with the good flavour it, he nodded to Madame Guibon.

"Bit like a stew," he said.

"Yes, a marmite - perhaps your wife would cook in a pot on the stove all day, it is the same here."

By six o'clock that evening both men had agreed to enjoy the braised cow's cheek on the dinner menu followed by a "Tergoule," a type of rich rice pudding topped with cinnamon.

"Not much different this to home except no jam to stir into it," Jack had said, pointing to the food.

Stan had grunted as his mouth was full. He swallowed and said: "Just be grateful that you're eating well given we're in foreign parts. There's nothing wrong with the food that woman produces."

Jack's mouth dropped open. He said: "Are you actually acknowledging the fact that we're eating well?"

"Here we are, yes. Not as good as home of course, but that woman works hard to look after her guests, and she keeps a good table. Nowt wrong with anything I've had today. No, I think we've landed on our feet here. Have you seen the number of cheeses on the sideboard?"

This had to be a good sign as far as Jack was concerned. He knew he would never get Stan to pay much of a compliment, but this was positively a eulogy to Madame Guibon. Amazing what sleep and good food could do.

Stan was clearly far less nervy by dinner time than he had been all week.

They were clean at last as well, and although dressed as rough fishermen the clothes weren't stained. Over the next few days Jack and Stan could sleep, walk, and eat well before the next stage of the trip. After the stress in Jersey and the physical threat Harry had faced it was what they needed.

*

The wild wind at the coast carried on until by Tuesday there was a sudden calm. The next journey would be done so that they arrived in Paris ready to join the Cook's tour which would leave for Geneva on Wednesday.

Jack felt stronger having exercised each day regardless of the weather, slowly re-gaining energy and aware that his ribs no longer ached. Even Stan, who had been the one who was seasick, was enjoying the bracing air and a glass of local wine with the dinner. Stan had also chatted to Madame Guibon and found out that her husband had died in the final battles in 1871 with Prussia. he was struck by the animosity she expressed against the occupation of parts of France and the annexation by Prussia of areas. Stan told Jack later that the men present in the bar area had supported her claim that one day France would recover the areas.

"I tell you Jack," said Stan, "These two countries will suck us all in one day into a contest."

Stan had agreed to walk along the harbour wall that morning and to go with Jack to the railway station for the tickets for

Paris. While Jack sorted out the route and bought the tickets Stan had found the telegraph office and been able to send two telegrams: a message to his wife and one to Harry.

Slowly, Stan was aware, Jack had started to pick up bits of French to introduce them and to ask directions. He had also become quite adept at understanding what was available to eat and was greeted with a smile by the young women as he passed the same places each morning. Jack was enjoying the attention but from a distance.

The town was full of quite smart people holidaying from Paris and by Tuesday Madame Guibon had laundered their original clothes ready for the journey. She had not asked about their lack of luggage and Jack realised with gratitude to his old Parson that she had accepted the story of lost luggage overboard because Jack had booked with a Thomas Cook voucher. It had leant an air of respectability to these two men as well as being in possession of a passport.

Madame Guibon had assumed Stan was an uncle to Jack and she greeted him each morning as, "Oncle." Stan's set face at the pet name led to Jack slapping his Sergeant on the shoulder, nodding, and saying: "Oui, oncle."

"Don't push it," Stan had muttered, but he had a smile for Madame Guibon, as the woman who had made a business successful after being widowed. Out of respect for her husband who had given his life trying to defend their country Stan fixed the odd shelf and even did a bit of painting of the shutters. He would have wanted no less for his own wife.

By mid-morning on Tuesday, with the promise of a fine rain in the air, Jack and Stan left for Paris. Madame Guibon chatted to them in French without their having much understanding as they walked down the steps. It was the tone which represented friendship which invited their response. They thanked her for the rest and the good food and even Stan tried with: "Mercie."

"I fancy staying here again some time," said Jack, as they walked away.

"You're unbelievable, you are," muttered Stan. "Let's get going and the sooner we get this next bit over the faster we get home."

"What is it Stan that frits you so?" asked Jack.

Stan stopped and put his bag down. "What are you asking me?"

"You seem fraught, frightened."

"You shouldn't take wariness for fear. We have no backup, we are out of everything that's familiar to us and there's no way we can get any reinforcements," explained Stan. He looked across to the sea as the clouds were gathering. He felt irritable. and Jack's sense of excitement at things that were new had annoyed him.

"There's rain coming in," said Jack. We've got about 10 minutes before we get soaked. Might as well get going up to the station. Madame Guibon packed us luncheon,"

Both men walked in silence. Stan felt his temper cooling as he walked. By the time they climbed up onto the train he had let go of the mood. He said: "Crack open that sack of yours and let's get eating, we've a way to go."

Fifteen

"Mr Sargent, Mr Green, *delighted* to welcome you to the London and New York Hotel. Allow me to introduce myself: I am your Cook's guide, Laurence Coombs. How was your journey here?"

"Long," said Stan, ignoring the hand extended to him by Coombs. He gave him the once over.

"Yes, it was long," Jack interrupted, stepping forward. "But we've made it and next time we come we hope to travel from London with Cooks. Business made that impossible this visit," Jack shook the hand which had started to be withdrawn after Stan's rebuff.

Coombs responded enthusiastically, giving Jack his full attention. He asked: "Which way did you come?"

"Via Normandy," said Jack, "We took in the fishing on the way. Helps to get us into the fresh air after London."

Coombs looked around for the bags. Light dawned as he saw the rucksack. "Is this all?" he asked.

"Afraid so, the rest is lost," Jack said, truthfully.

Coombs jaw dropped and then his face broke into a smile of revelation. He said: "Ah, that's why your uncle has so many bags, he's brought you replacement clothing for the tour."

Jack shook his head. "No," he said, "Uncle Stan's lost everything as well. We understood we can pick up the clothing we need locally."

"Yes, you can indeed but thankfully, your Uncle Charles has obviously packed replacements for you. I wondered why he had so much. *Marvellous*. Let me get you to your rooms and then I can let him know you've arrived, then he can get you kitted out for Paris tonight."

"Uncle Charles?" asked Stan, his eyes narrowing. "We have a few Charles's in the family. Which Charles has arrived?"

"Uncle Charles Burgess, he said you'd be surprised but as it was a special birthday for you Mr Green, he pulled out all the stops to get on the tour and joined us yesterday. Let me get you to your rooms and then I can let him know you've arrived. You came into Montparnasse or Lazare? Of course, it must be across the road opposite the hotel if you came via Dieppe or Le Havre. We're well situated here on a direct line to the Madeleine, the Champs Elysée, the Tuilleries and the Louvre. Shame you've arrived so late but no doubt you can get out after dinner and take in some of the sights with your uncle. There's an English table arranged for dinner and you'll have an English breakfast in the morning. Here we are, nice comfortable airy rooms for you, a home from home. Cook's always gets preference for the rooms and you're across the corridor from each other. Your Uncle Charles is on the second floor."

"Thank-you Mr Coombs, very nice," said Jack as he leant against the door frame and stuck his head round the door to survey his room.

"Yes," said Stan, eyeing the bed longingly in the room across the corridor. He added: "What number is Uncle Charles in?"

"Can't recall from memory, but I'll pop back and let you know," said Coombs.

"No rush," said Stan.

"Good," Coombs turned his attention to Jack, who seemed the more friendly of the two men. "We always have pleasure in promoting the interest and gratification of our visitors to Paris. What business are you in Mr Sargent?"

Jack paused and then smiled: "Diamonds," he said.

"Oh, my goodness, no wonder you can afford the tour," Coombs laughed. "I did wonder at such a young gentleman booking but now I quite understand. And you Mr Green?"

"It's a family business," said Stan, winking.

"Well, marvellous, you'll fit right in with quite a few of our tour members. A few industrialists and others making their name in retail. I'll get the reception to collect the bags from your uncle and bring them to your rooms. They'll let him know you're here and no doubt he'll pop along to see you."

"I'd quite like to "pop up" and see Uncle Charles now," said Stan. "Let me have his room number, will you?"

Flustered, Coombes pulled a notebook from his pocket and thumbed through several lists. "I have it here, somewhere. You want to surprise him?"

"Something like that," said Stan.

"Alright, yes here it is. He's in 216. I will see you at breakfast to give you your train tickets. You've got the morning as your train leaves early afternoon for Geneva as I recall you're in second class. First class have all day in Paris and will be on the express train tomorrow evening."

"Amazing how you remember it all, Mr Coombs," said Jack.

"Thank-you Mr Sargent, it's the stamp of a Cook's guide. My job is to take you through Paris and get you on your journey into Switzerland. My colleague will meet you at Geneva Cornavin to take you to the Hotel Metropole there. I'll let you settle in now. A good evening to you both."

"And to you, Mr Coombs. Right, Uncle Stan, I'm going to find a bath."

Stan watched Coombs turn for the stairs at the end of the corridor before he replied. Once he was sure the guide was out of earshot Stan turned to Jack and said: "Right, I'll pay a visit to "Uncle Charles" and bring him down here. I suppose Hunt is behind this and Charles isn't acting alone?"

"Must be coming from the Inspector, Stan," said Jack. "The only other people who know where we're staying are the Parson and Harry. Harry went to see Hunt, didn't he? So, I expact Burgess has been sent by Hunt to join us. All we can do is ask him."

"And that's exactly what I intend to do. He could be useful given his understanding of the hotel trade," said Stan.

"There is that and it's a good bit of knowledge to have. Look Stan, I don't know about you but the only experience I have of staying in a hotel is last year at Brighton. While the police are open to every man regardless of the background, those we'll be mixing with are not. Burgess will be useful in his insights on how we need to behave and dress. And who knows how high we'll climb in our careers, Stan." Jack grinned at his next thought. "You could make Inspector, and I, Sergeant."

"And you should lad. If you stay, you'll advance," said Stan. "You've shown ability as an officer and it's been noted. You'll progress up the ranks on your merit as a vacancy arises. You've done your first two years nearly and had some exceptional moments but generally those first two years are not much more than getting you trained up. Harry and I only think a man's worth the notice after two years, as so many don't stay. You're young enough to make it worth your while waiting to get to those higher ranks."

"I'll stick it out Stan to do so, I've done more in the police in the last two years than in seven as a farm labourer. I could have gone for months without work if I'd stayed on the farm. I've a status now, and while its hard at times and there's been health problems, I've the chance of advancing. I've every idea of getting on and remaining in the service so hotel stays might become the normal thing for us one day, eh?" Jack laughed at his own idea.

"Well, it's a benefit I wasn't expecting at this moment. That's good to hear you've taken on board what we talked of. Right, I'll get along to room 216 and raise Burgess." said Stan.

"One other thing, Stan," said Jack." I was thinking about how Burgess got close in his career to catching the toff behind the crime group. It occurred to me who knows what links he has, and who he's been liaising with? Someone had briefed him when I saw him in Brighton and if it wasn't Hunt, who was it? Burgess was in the Met and we're the only force in the country answerable to the government, so my money is on someone high up that he still has links with. He must still be useful through what he knows. All that coverage by the newspapers and the criticism he was on the receiving end of nearly broke him. He'll want to get back at the criminals who have that kind of influence and restore his good name."

"That's as well may be, but you know the risk when an individual gets an obsession," said Stan, "They can take the whole team down with them. I'll get a telegram off to Harry this evening from the desk and find out what he knows. Harry will want to know we've arrived anyway."

All thoughts of a bath forgotten as Jack took in the life on the streets below as he stood by his bedroom window. He flung it wide open and leant on the narrow iron veranda to peer up the street. He was disturbed by a knock on his bedroom door as a porter arrived with a new travel bag for Jack and hovered hoping for a tip, but Jack did not have any French coins.

This confirmed all the porter had heard about the English.

Jack looked at the bag, a good quality leather William Bisset of Dundee, and was grateful for Hunt's attention to the detail. He left it unopened, sitting by the door, as Paris was outside his window and it did not seem right to ignore this exciting city. Then he become distracted by a crowd, which was gathering to watch a fight between two men and the shouting in French fascinated him as he registered that his brain expected English. The scene lasted for full on five minutes until soldiers arrived to break up the crowd and the fighters were pulled away by spectators.

The knock on his door called Jack back into the room. There were Burgess who beamed at him and Stan looking strained.

"Jack, my friend, Stan told me you would be bathed. I've got a suitcase full of clothes for you and you'll soon be dressed for dinner," said Burgess, larger than life and dressed smartly ready to go down to the table reserved for the tour.

"I'll see you both shortly," said Stan, "we've had a catch-up chat, Mr Burgess and I, and I need to send some telegrams. Then I'll change so I match Uncle Charles."

Jack nodded at Stan and swung the door wide for Burgess, extending his hand to the hotelier. Burgess responded enthusiastically.

Jack said: "Take a seat, Mr Burgess, and I'll be as quick as I can. Good of you to bring the luggage from England.'

"You must thank Tom Hunt for that. Harry gave him the route you were going from the Parson's planning. Must look the part you know. I'm simply here to keep an eye open for Harry's attackers assuming we'll come across them in Vevey. But, frankly Jack, I wouldn't miss this for the world."

Burgess sat on the chaise longue in the corner of the room. Jack grinned while he turned on the taps over the bath, appreciating the luxury of running water in hotel life. He called over a question: "Which way did you come Mr Burgess?"

"Better get used to calling me Uncle Charles," replied Burgess.

"Uncle Charles," Jack grinned at Burgess as he practised. Turning over the piece of soap he sniffed it: perfumed. Jack shrugged at the change from carbolic and walked back into the bedroom. He stood in front of Burgess and said: "Time to tell me who it is you're taking orders from."

"On this occasion Tom Hunt, the same as you. Here's his telegram. I've shown it to Stan." Burgess held out a paper to Jack who read:

Thursday, May 21st, 1874: 11pm.
"Join Cook's tour leaving Paris Wednesday 27th May. Tuesday 26th - Collect tickets and luggage Newhaven. Board before eight a.m. Travel – Dieppe. Rail to Paris. Stay London and New York Hotel, Place du Havre, Paris.
Tom."

"All very neat, you see, Jack. I was on the first sailing yesterday morning to Dieppe. The luggage was waiting with a young lad for me at the port. Like you I should not disclose a higher power than our Tom. But if you will, I will," said Burgess with a smile of invitation.

"That's easy. I serve the Queen, as our oath demands." said Jack.

"Yes, as do we all as her loyal subjects. Your instructions tend to come by an interesting route though in this case, mine too."

"My orders are via the Inspector and I report to Stan now as he's the senior policeman present. It's quite simple for me. But "Uncle Charles," you're a different kettle of fish."

Burgess took an immaculate handkerchief from his pocket and wiped his forehead before continuing: "Ah, well, all in good time. All I can say is the source is the same. How was your crossing? The steamer I was on left according to the tide, of course, but I arrived here very late last night. Alice was quite in a lather when I left."

"I can imagine. Look sir, I'm not trying to best you on this. You know what Inspector Hunt does from time to time and I was with him on one of those occasions. Stan and I need to know how you came to be involved to arrive in Jersey in that way. All Stan and I know is that the man behind a crime group, whose hands are dirty, is some high-ranking individual. Who is it that you are tracking and who is it that's giving you orders?" Jack turned the tap off and waited.

Burgess explained: "I had a few nights in London recently, staying with some friends. I shared a meal with an "acquaintance" we could call him. He had an interest in the case I'd pursued, believed I'd been right. The same individual I had pursued was causing a few problems and the powers that be wanted him sorted. Difficult, because when we go after someone with a position in society, it causes embarrassment to so-called good families. In that way, Jack, the law is not equal because they have protection. That's not the way it should be. We weren't set up to just police the poor and keep them in line but if we're not careful that is what the Met's in danger of becoming. All those people with birth and rank and titles hold those positions as a courtesy. In the eyes of the law, they're all commoners. As a Metropolitan policeman you decide whether you're true to your oath or if you look the other way. If you do, you're not being impartial. Some have, some have taken money, some received a favour. It's like a disease that takes over the body. It doesn't stop with just once. The smallest favour grows like a tumour."

Jack interrupted: "And is that what's happened?"

Burgess nodded. He said: "If you know the history of the case, which I fought to bring to a conclusion, then you know the family."

"Right," said Jack, "I don't. And the rank this criminal has is a cover he hides under?"

"Yes," said Burgess.

"And the affluence he has built gives him more power?" asked Jack.

Burgess nodded. "Makes him independent of royal patronage."

"And he's bought people, police?

Again, Burgess nodded. "Not just police," He added.

"But why steal the Shah's diamonds last year?" asked Jack.

"Because it was a way of getting back at the Queen for not acknowledging him in public. He'd been in her presence and pushed his way forward thinking she should speak to him. No reason why she should as others present outranked the younger son of an earl, which is what he is. Poor family but the titles remained. It was embarrassing for her when, surrounded by soldiers and police, his thief could waltz up to the Shah's horse and remove a fortune in diamonds without being caught. The Queen's a funny woman and will acknowledge who she wishes to and rely on the order of precedence when she does not. That's what she did in this case. He's unbalanced and has none of the merits and graces history tends to give to the people with a title. Or so we have been told. And the Queen is George III's Grand-daughter and has his pig-headedness. If she doesn't want to acknowledge someone she won't." Burgess checked the time on his pocket watch and started to stand. "I must let you get on. Dinner is almost over."

Jack opened the case and rummaged through the neatly folded clothes. He ran his hand over the shirts and felt a smile start. He glanced across at Burgess and asked: "Any guidance for me on what I should wear?"

"Here? Well fortunately there's no-one on the tour that considers themselves in society as far as I can see. As I am, Jack, in a jacket, necktie, would be the main things. Fortunately, there are self-made men here and their wives, risen from nothing to feel self-important as they've turned a pretty penny. Over-dressed the lot of them. I gather from Stan we're in diamonds?"

Jack nodded and said: "All true."

"Well, I hope you can hold your own on the subject as I cannot. Stan intends to present himself as security, which gives him an advantage over the rest of us as he can remain largely silent. Do you know anything about such stones?" asked Burgess.

"Only that the ones we seek are fit for a king, which is after all what the Shah is. The cut makes them I gather."

"Ha, very good. I believe there are jewellers in Geneva and some English firms have set up there. We should get through this evening then. I'll have to assign myself a role in the family business," Burgess shrugged.

"I think we could make you properties, Uncle Charles," said Jack, with a grin.

The two men laughed, and Burgess nodded. He patted Jack on the arm and said: "Good to work with you again Jack."

*

It was an uninspiring dinner largely because the three men were so late down that the tureens at the side of their table had cooled. It was English food and Jack looked with envy at the non-English guests in the dining room wishing to sample their orders. But instead, he ate what little he had the stomach for and chatted with the young lady on his left, a Miss Wheeler, the daughter of an industrialist and his wife, from Manchester. Seated at the far end of a long table of English tourists, everyone else was finishing and leaving. Coombs arrived with the train tickets for Jack's party and then also took his leave. Jack glanced at the tickets, noted they would leave at three o'clock on Wednesday afternoon, and he put them into the wallet inside his jacket.

"What business are you in, Mr Sargent?" asked Miss Wheeler.

Jack smiled as he looked into the chocolate brown eyes. He answered: "The diamond business, that's what takes us to Switzerland."

Miss Wheeler's eyes went wide: "Diamonds, you say, I should like to see some diamonds."

"Well, there I will disappoint as its to acquire them that we go to Switzerland," said Jack. "I can show you nothing right now. But I should imagine a young lady like yourself will not be without such gifts."

Stan gave Jack a look and glanced at the mother. He saw the appraising look of a matriarch who had decided Jack was a fine specimen. Her father, however seemed less than impressed.

Miss Wheeler laughed at Jack's answer and turned her attention towards Stan.

"How charming your nephew is, Mr Green," she said.

"Yes, isn't he," said Stan whose expression for Jack urged caution.

"Where do you carry out your trade?" asked the lady's father. Mr Wheeler was interested only in a potential investment.

Stan asked: "Do you know London?"

"No," said Wheeler. "This is the first time we've travelled to the south and that was to St Pancras, then across to Victoria."

Stan continued: "Well, you won't know our neck of the woods then. We're not far from Aldgate High Street."

"We're dealers, you see, not craftsmen," explained Burgess.

"Such a journey," said Mrs Wheeler, "I thought we would never get here. Still, we have to do it for Lauren's sake."

'We're thinking of getting a carriage and going to the new Louvre and the Tuilleries. Would you care to join us?" asked Miss Wheeler, changing the subject before her mother embarrassed her.

"I would very much like to," said Jack.

412

"If you'll excuse me, I'll call it a day, I think," said Stan, standing. "We have another long journey tomorrow and I'm starting to feel like I don't know where I am when I wake up each morning."

"Yes of course, we've had the advantage of resting after arriving a few days ago," said Mrs Wheeler.

"I'll join you if I may, Jack," said Burgess. "I never know if this is the only time I will be in Paris and your Aunt will expect a gift."

"Surely the diamonds are enough?" asked Miss Wheeler.

Burgess chuckled. He said: "Very sharp, Miss Wheeler, but the thing with the ladies when one's been married a while is that one must remember them from time to time with a gift, especially on a business trip."

"Have you seen much of Paris in the last few days?" Jack asked Miss Wheeler.

"Oh, parts of it each day but there's always so much more to see. There was a charity fete in the Champs Elysée today. It was beautiful and everyone was so elegant. Mother, we should be going if we are to avoid the crowds later."

Stan withdrew as the ladies stood. Lauren Wheeler and her mother went ahead, and Burgess and Jack followed with Mr Wheeler, who asked: "Have you made many connections in your business with the nobility?"

"Some," said Burgess. "And yourself?"

"We supply Lord Derby's estate, and I've contacts in Parliament."

"What business are you in, Mr Wheeler?" asked Jack.

"Textiles mainly cotton. I hope to be elevated myself shortly, but that's between you and me. The ladies mustn't know."

"How has that come about?" asked Jack.

"Wealth frankly and contributions made. I tell you this, Mr Sargent, as I sense you may take a shine to my daughter. I have to say that as much as you may be amiable and wealthy, I have other prizes for my Lauren. Marriage is the way to open the door to a title there. You understand me, no doubt."

"Completely," said Jack with a glance at Burgess, whose eyes had gone wide.

"We may see you in the Tuileries Gardens then, but I would prefer it if we did not share a carriage. Have a good evening, gentlemen."

"And a good evening to you, Mr Wheeler." Burgess called after the industrialist as he followed his wife and daughter out of the dining room.

Burgess and Jack doubled up in laughter, until they realised that they were attracting attention from the other guests.

"Well, that was to the point. That quite did me good. Do you have any coin for a cab?" asked Burgess.

Jack pulled out a handful of English coins: "Not French, perhaps they'll take English coin. I've also some sort of note upstairs which the hotel may change."

"We could try it and see what happens," suggested Burgess. "It would be a shame not to see the new boulevards by Haussmann. It's supposed to have transformed the city from a slum ridden centre."

"Well, Uncle Charles," said Jack, putting a hand on Burgess's shoulder, "Having just avoided marriage I'm game if you are."

*

Noise from the street had prevented his sleep but Jack did not care. He had sat by the open window listening to groups of friends and lovers into the early hours of Wednesday morning letting his ear attune to the sounds of the French that rose from the streets below. It was nearly two in the morning when he fell asleep in the chair and woke to Parisian sparrows as the dawn broke. Aware he was now on Paris time Jack climbed into bed and knew no more until a banging on his door disturbed him. Coombs was rounding up his tour party for breakfast. Wednesday 27th May and it was a bright day.

The morning was theirs as the train for Geneva would not leave until three o'clock. The English breakfast was soon over Jack and Stan set out to walk to the Champs Elysée. Burgess excused himself to write a letter to Alice in which he enclosed a silk scarf he had bought the night before.

"I envy him being able to be that open with his wife," said Jack.

Stan shrugged and said: "Doesn't always work Jack, my wife just wants to know I'm alive. She wants no details, just waits for the sound of the latch in the front door on my return. We don't discuss work ever."

"Wouldn't you take her a gift, though, from Paris I mean?"

"Probably, if I see something special. For the children, of course, but from me it's the gift of time that she wants, and after this that is what she'll have." Stan stared ahead.

Jack glanced at the rock-like face and tried to imagine Stan as a romantic. He asked: "Romantic old you! Have you arranged that then, time off I mean?"

"Harry knows, he'll see me right," Stan replied.

Jack's stare lasted a little too long for Stan's comfort. Stan looked away and then spat to the side. Jack grinned at the habit Stan generally had and nodded as Stan glanced over at him. That morning was the first day Jack had had little trace of discomfort since the fight at the West India Dock. He felt ready to forgive anything.

Jack said: "Shall we pick up the pace?"

In the Champs Elysée they came across a merry-go-round packed with men, women, and children of all ages. It reminded Jack of the fair at Crystal Palace.

"Come on Stan, let's have a go," Jack shouted over the din of the music as he walked towards a man taking money for the rides.

"You go ahead, not sure I feel that French," said Stan. Having spotted a stall near-by he walked over and found they were selling models of the merry-go-round.

Jack was handed a poniard like a small, slim dagger, as he climbed on a horse. Each man had been given one so they could tilt at rings hanging from a "quintain," a stand, as if they were knights in a joust. If he could be the first to gather five rings, Jack would get a free ride. Stan stood to one side having bought four small models of the merry-go-round for his children and watched his colleague's determination to get all five rings before any other man on the ride. The future stretched ahead for Stan and in an unusual moment of foresight he hoped he would still be alive to see Jack make Inspector.

*

It had seemed a tedious journey across endless agricultural lowlands of France in the hours of daylight, though good use of time had been made by Jack, Stan, and Burgess. They had a separate compartment and continued to pour over the maps provided by Cooks of the route and the surrounding area of Geneva and the Lake. When they had exhausted that they read the books they had brought with them. The three men had placed their books down at times and broke into discussion. It was towards the end of the journey that Burgess had finally chosen to reveal the name of William Gilbert as his suspect, youngest son of an earl related to the Gratton family.

"Of course, he's at the bottom of the pecking order and won't get any attention in royal circles if there's a Viscount present. That's the argument for being ignored in the royal presence. The other reason is he's obnoxious. A nursemaid went missing that worked for the family, body never found. I'm still convinced she's at the bottom of a lake he frequented for fishing. Problem was so did most of the City in the summer months. We trawled it of course but the local divers told the Coroner there were so many underwater caves that a body could be there for donkey's years and never be found. Family cut him off except for a small retainer. Anyway, he's been abroad most of his time since then. Last time he appeared in London was during the Shah's visit. Turned up at Windsor and although they let him in the royal family shunned him and the Queen wouldn't play ball and acknowledge him. Such is the ego he has that he thinks he has the right to be noticed. He's currently holidaying on an estate in Geneva."

"Convenient for you," said Stan. "You obviously keep tabs on him."

"Not me" said Burgess, "That's information I received plus a ticket to Jersey." Then he was lost in thought.

Jack waited a few minutes. Burgess continued to stare at the floor, coping with memories that disturbed him.

Jack said: "The reason to go to Jersey was to follow the thief so we could get to the man at the top. Who else believes this William Gilbert is behind a crime ring?" asked Jack.

"A man who likes Primroses and who will be picking them shortly in Scotland. Gladstone as well, his predecessor, but Disraeli seeks to curry favour with the Queen whereas Gladstone lectured her," said Burgess.

"The Prime Minister sent you?" asked Jack.

"As he has you, Jack, through Hunt," said Burgess and as he glanced over at Stan, he received a glower.

"No-one "sends" us – Hunt would make his own mind up," said Stan.

"Even Tom would bow to pressure," said Burgess, quietly.

———

418

He continued: "The corruption through the police is what causes the worry, not Gilbert's commissioning of the pinching of the Shah's diamonds. The thefts are audacious always but it's the spread of the rot through the tree especially in T Division over a number of years."

"Morris mentioned that division to me shortly after I joined. Are you telling me that this is the same man responsible for the Berringer deaths, Sam's poisoning, and the tragedy for the Doyles?" Jack sat forward, the blood pounding in his ears.

"I can't say for certain, but I wouldn't be surprised if he set in train actions committed by others. He's a notorious womaniser and Mrs Berringer had a lover, didn't she? You are going back to things I wasn't involved in there, but Matthew Doyle was my friend too," Burgess explained.

Jack brought his fist crashing onto the table by the carriage window, his face red.

"Steady, steady lad, a cool head and clear mind is what will keep you alive in this," said Stan. "Get some air, eh, in the corridor."

"I'm alright," said Jack, sitting back. "If we have evidence against him why is he still at large?"

"That's the point," said Stan, "Because we don't have evidence against him, just against those who work for him low down the ranks. We think he has a contract with those who work for him that ensures their families are looked after in the case of their arrests or deaths. No-one sings, Jack, and that ensures that the family is looked after."

"And he affords all that travel through crime? But the thing he wanted when the Shah was over was acknowledgment from the monarch, right? So, there's an ego there," said Jack.

"Now you're talking like a 'tec," said Stan.

"Find the weakness and play into it, isn't that right, Stan?" said Jack. "Gilbert's in Geneva and poisoned chocolates are from a town on the same lake. If Torg is his thief, we may find him too. If he's still alive, that is. Perhaps Torg's not playing ball with Gilbert. Maybe that was the reason for the poison in the chocolates. Perhaps he's like silly mid-off in a match?" mused Jack.

Burgess looked at Stan who wrinkled up his face. Stan said: "What?"

"Silly mid-off in cricket – it's a suicidal position too near the batsman," explained Jack. "Our Torg is named after a mountain, used to taking the sort of risks probably that you and I would walk away from. Perhaps that's why he bears the mountain's name. Might say what he does is potentially suicidal."

"We rarely know much about an offender before their incarceration. Why would a man like Torg break the law? He's a climber, isn't he? What course did he set himself to get involved with a man like Gilbert?" asked Burgess.

"Poverty, maybe, who knows," said Stan.

"But Gilbert's a criminal and even if he isn't as well off as he was born to be, he's not in the same position as many we deal with. Being a criminal clearly isn't anything to do with class If Gilbert's an example," said Jack.

"The areas we deal with, it is. And our elders and so-called betters would see a link between the poor and crime," said Stan.

"People falling on hard times, eh?" said Jack. "Like two policemen stealing milk and eggs on Chausey, you mean? Where would we be if we'd been caught. As for Torg, we know nothing about him except basic facts: He's Norwegian, looks like he's a climber, and he's sporting a name after a mountain, which invites conclusions about him, and I've seen him steal twice. And the third theft we only have a description for the thief which sounds as if it could be him. Always the crimes are audacious, full of bravado." Jack looked from Stan to Burgess.

"A little admiration there perhaps?" suggested Burgess.

"I don't deny it," said Jack. "Even his disappearance in Jersey is clever. But there's something about our discovery in Jersey which bothers me. Something untidy and out of character. He left his bag and the chocolates."

"Well, that's as well maybe," said Stan. "Chances are this is a wild goose chase, assuming Torg's gone to Vevey. He's probably back in Norway."

"He may be, but if he was stealing for Gilbert he could be in Switzerland. Perhaps Torg's gone back to Geneva to deal with Gilbert?" suggested Jack.

"In which case he could become an ally," said Burgess.

*

Dijon by nearly midnight brought the local vendors from the gingerbread factories to the train windows with warm loaves

421

and Jack bought one for the three of them to share into the early hours of the morning.

Close behind came a newly produced drink that year. Crème de Cassis was added to small stone cups of white wine and sold to passengers. Burgess bought two cups of the liquor from the woman at the window, Jack declining as his stomach would still not have taken it. After this the three men made what they could of the room in the carriage to sleep.

It was almost four in the morning when the train pulled into Macon. Jack woke to find Stan had vanished from the carriage, but Burgess was in that deep breathing stage of sleep that verges on snoring and Jack reconciled himself to staying awake until Geneva. He pulled the map out of Torg's bag and looked at Southern and Central France and then most of Switzerland. Finding the city and lake on it quickly, he looked back up the railway line on the map until he found Macon. The shape of the lake reminded him of a leaping Salmon. Lac Léman, he read, referred to by Julius Caesar as Lacus Lemanus. They had travelled about two hundred and seventy miles on the train since leaving Paris. Jack shook his head in disbelief at what they were doing.

There was still another six or seven hours of the journey to go. He made a mental note to check out the cost of first class for the journey back to get onto the express train. Folding the map in the existing creases as the squire at the farm at Battle had taught him, he realised the train was starting to slow. They were closer to Macon than Jack had thought, and he decided to go and find Stan.

Jack found the Sergeant leaning on a door with his head out of the window.

"Stan, careful," Jack called.

Stan pulled his head in and straightened up. He said: "It's not been going that fast, Jack. I'll hear if there's another train coming down."

"Had any sleep?" asked Jack.

"Some, I felt locked in so had to get my head out before I hit someone. This journey feels like we've died and gone to hell. It's never ending. How much longer have we got before Geneva?" asked Stan.

"We're due in before midday," explained Jack, "We're coming into Macon, so I'll step off and see if anyone's selling any food in the station."

Jack made his way past the engine towards a group of women standing by baskets of long thin bread and held up three fingers. Paper large enough for his hand to hold the bread was wrapped around three sticks and handed to Jack. A woman to his left tapped his forearm to draw his attention to her display of small conical shaped cheeses. Again, Jack held up three fingers and three of the cheeses were wrapped for him. Glad that he had used the Cook's note in the hotel in Paris he held out a handful of change to the women, on trust. One shook her head at him and he shrugged and grinned. The woman held up her index finger and gently took one coin. Jack had no idea what it was but felt she could be trusted.

"Fini, c'est tout," she said, and did an action with her hands to indicate the transaction for all was complete.

———

Jack nodded and tried one word which always seemed to work with a smile: "Mercie."

Stan sniffed the cheese once Jack was back on board the train and muttered: "Goat's cheese." He crumbled it and tasted and as the flavour developed in his mouth he nodded in appreciation. "Strong, but I like the taste," said Stan. "Well done, this will keep us going until we get into Geneva."

"Ah, morning Uncle Charles," said Jack, with a grin, "Just in time for breakfast."

Burgess looked a little the worse for wear after his night on the train. He scratched a leg while he peered out at the station. The train started to move again.

"Right, we're off. I had no idea where I was when I woke. Not a bad night was it? Let's have a look at what you've got there, Jack?"

Jack passed over the bread and a cheese, but Burgess shook his head: "Just the bread will be fine. Any idea how much longer we've got to go?"

"Just before midday according to Cook's timetable," said Jack. "Next stop is Culoz and then Geneva. It's getting light so we can see the area we pass through."

"The terrain is changing, we're leaving the flatness behind," said Stan as the train moved out of the station into the dawn.

A medieval town faced them. The three men stood in silence trying to take in the changes they were experiencing.

"Do you have the river name on the map there?" asked Burgess.

Jack went back into the compartment and pulled out the map. He said: "Saône, the rail line seems to wind quite a long way south of Geneva before it follows another river up country, the Rhone."

"That will be because of the terrain. The train will run along the Rhone valley," said Burgess. "We might see the mountains soon."

"Really? I'll check the map to see what they are." Jack pulled the map out yet again and spread it open on the seat next to him. "There's mention of a Mont Blanc away to the right."

"I think you'll find there's a few more than that to see," said Burgess. "It's the Alps Jack, like nothing you've ever seen. It's a different world to what we know. Switzerland is one on its own, no colonies, hard workers by all account and starting to make a name internationally with their Red Cross and the fight against international slavery. A little bird in London told me that they are influencing the laws to do with war as well."

"Same little bird who's about to gather primroses with the Queen and lay his flattery on her with a trowel?" Stan asked wryly.

"I shouldn't say," Burgess answered.

"And yet you keep on implying it don't you," Stan said, "The big man who's finally being listened to after all those years of disgrace. Got Tom Hunt over a barrel, haven't you? He's no choice but to include you in this investigation because the powers that be have decided you were right. Where are you taking this personally, Charles Burgess?"

Sixteen

Stan drew in his head surprised at the cold. The train had slowed considerably as it pulled into Geneva Cornavin. He said: "Good job that Hunt sent these sports jackets. Given its May I would not have believed it could be this cold here."

It was all he had said since his short exchange with Burgess.

"Hence the advice to buy locally," said Jack. "Eyes peeled for the Cook's guide. He goes by the name Allen."

"There's the rest of the tour already getting off the train. Mr and Mrs Wheeler and their daughter have probably been here for hours as they went First-class. Right, shift yourselves in case the train starts off again. I've got the door," said Burgess.

The train had reached Geneva just before mid-day. The three men had dozed intermittently after their early breakfast from the platform. Now they were about to board a bus provided by the Hotel de la Metropole in the largest city in Switzerland.

The tour guide, Allen, had positioned himself behind a sign announcing that he was from "Thomas Cook." Once everyone who needed to, had gathered around him he explained the hotel was in the most charming part of the town, near the English Garden, with the finest views of the lake. But the rest was lost on Jack as they filed out of the station and stood ready to board the bus. An overpowering view of mountains in sunshine, but with tops covered in glistening white snow, faced them. The whole party exclaimed but he was so lost in his own sense of wonder that he did not hear them.

Stan said; "My word, Jack boy," into his ear and Jack nodded while Burgess laughed aloud in sheer joy at the spectacle.

Allen was speaking again: "There you are, ladies and gentlemen, every day, and at different times of the day, you will all see how different the Alps can look. There you have Mont Blanc and the Aiguilles and once across the lake you will see the Jura behind the city where many families are engaged in the watch making business. The lake is next to see although we're at one end of it. Come along everyone, let's get on board as your hotel awaits you."

"So, it's down to you Jack, that we experience this," said Stan, quietly. "Whatever's to come I will never forget this view."

The rest of the party had formed a neat queue and were getting on the bus one by one. Two men had pushed a trolley piled high with everyone's luggage to the bus and were now loading it into a caged truck attached to the back.

Stan laughed and inhaled. "Smell it?" he asked.

"What?" asked Jack.

"Lack of smoke. How have they done that?" said Stan.

Allen was walking across to the three men and they shook hands with him one by one.

"You must be Messrs Green, Burgess and Sargent. One family I understand, here on business?" asked Allen, with raised eyebrows.

None of them elaborated but Jack smiled and asked: "But with such beauty we might forget commerce and try our luck in the mountains and then there's always the fishing."

"234 square miles the lake is, and I can help with hiring boats and there is salmon, trout and perch and goodness knows what else. You'll see how blue it looks in a minute." Allen paused and looked at the three men, taking in how they were dressed. "You intend to do some climbing?"

"It would be a shame not to get closer to all of that wonderful view," said Jack.

"As for the mountains don't do it unless you've an experienced guide. Many people die and if you wanted to get closer to Mont Blanc there is a dedicated tour to that area. You can look at it from the safety of a nice hotel in the village." Allen politely turned to the ladies waiting to speak to him and walked them onto the bus.

Burgess held back nodding to Jack and Stan, so they went ahead. At the bus door Burgess said quietly to Allen: "I, er, had a business transaction more than a year ago with an Englishman, a man called Gilbert. I understand he's taken a house in Geneva. Would you know of him?"

"If it's the man I think you mean yes, he's quite the milord here." Allen screwed up his face. "Renovating an old farmhouse, or rather turning it into a completely new house. You'll see the scaffolding in parkland on the other side of the lake. Apparently, he found his former house up near the cathedral a gloomy property. It was more solid than elegant. Not befitting the younger son of an Earl so the story goes. Of course, rumours abound that it was to impress his latest mistress but rather an expensive way to do it. Do you have further business with him?"

"I hope to have," said Burgess. "Manufacturing flourishes here in the jewellery and watch business I gather."

"Yes indeed, but there's a lot of competition from craftsmen in the Jura and other centres. The history I've come across is that watchmaking developed because jewellery was thought of as idolatrous under Calvinism. Hundreds of years ago, of course, nonetheless it shaped the industry. Plus, there was an influx of Huguenots who brought their skills into the Jura as they fled the persecution in France. Manufacturing tends to be home based here, and in families, you know. Now America is also having an effect in taking the trade away and the firms here appear to be concentrating at present on low-cost watches. But you may also find it helpful to know that there are English jewellers in Geneva as well if you're looking to do business. That might help avoid the language problems."

"I'm grateful," said Burgess and he climbed up onto the bus.

"Any luck?" asked Jack, as Burgess joined him.

"Considerable luck," answered Burgess, "Our man Gilbert is here."

Burgess took it logically that they would focus on Gilbert now they knew he was in Geneva. Jack could see Stan also approved of the possibilities.

But Allen was speaking to the whole group from the front of the bus: "A little bit of background for you on Geneva while we're waiting for the driver: To draw your attention to the Cathedral on the hill, called St. Peter's, historically it's the seat of Calvinism, many solid looking old buildings up there but nothing beautiful as in London. Geneva has many fine-looking quays now having cleared out a lot of the old buildings. The Duke of Brunswick who lived here in his later years in the Beau Rivage Hotel across the lake, died last year, and left his whole estate worth twenty-four million Swiss Francs to Geneva. That's close to a million pounds in our money so quite a fortune for an exiled royal. The city is now planning to build a theatre as a result and the first stone should be laid next year. They're doing other works around the city as you will see on your walks, particularly repairing paths by the side of the lake which the locals say is "kissed" by high waves from the lake."

The bus started and Allen gripped the side of a seat to steady himself. He continued: "A couple of other developments this year are that it's now law that every town have a school for infants up to forty in number. Also, compulsory secondary education since '72 and a real college for girls. One area, Satigny, has had such growth in numbers it needs five school buildings. They're ahead of us in this."

The bus crossed over the lake on one of the three bridges of the city. Allen peered solemnly through a window before he started his running commentary again.

"You'll notice the clean air," he said. "This is because they don't power factories by coal as they use water under a heavy pressure. Workshops are generally powered by electricity and the city is starting to replace horsepower in pulling the trams with steam. I could talk to you about politics, but I won't because that's not why you've come. French is spoken and they're quite proud of that because they think its cultured.

Geneva is a city of quite a few political radicals too. Ah, here's the hotel."

The driver parked outside the Metropole and Allen had a quiet word with him, slipping him a coin. The tip was not lost on Jack as he filed away in his mind that he should get some change, just in case.

"Here we are at the Hotel de la Metropole now. It's been described as superlative," exclaimed Allen. "I can recommend the Jardin d'Anglais for a stroll, or the English Garden as we would call it. Now, just some practical details for you as we are only here for one night, ladies and gentlemen. You will find your hotel is in the most favourable quarter of the town. It really has the finest view of the lake. Your rooms are most elegantly furnished. There is a reading room where you will find English, French, and German newspapers and, also, a coffee and smoking room. The evenings are still cold until July here, and therefore there will be lit stoves in each room. For your convenience, stating the obvious, Cook's coupons are accepted by the hotel. As we are only here for one evening, we have not booked rooms with lake views, choosing to save your money for Ouchy, where you will be staying for three nights. We are in time for Table d'hôte at one o'clock which, without wine, will cost four francs. Dinner, I'm afraid, is served at five o'clock .... yes, I know, but there we are. That is six francs. Breakfast is early, I'm afraid, and costs one and a half francs. Just to give you a marker on the currency rate: five francs is about four shillings. Now the views: from the other side of the lake to where we now are the views of the mountains are superb as you saw as you came out of the station, especially as the sun sets. Remember it will set earlier here than at home although its May as the sun goes down behind the mountains." Allen paused and checked a list. He continued: "I understand some guests wish to purchase local warm outerwear. Layers of linen is the favoured way here, layers of wool and a hat as the sun can be strong. Also layers of plaids if you have them are best for warmth. If you go to the mountains, then long sleeved, woollen, Jersey shirts are best. And you should obtain a walking pole if you are going to go on the snow. Don't climb without an ice axe. I would advise a blue veil or glasses as essential on the snow. The weather here can go to extremes depending on what you are doing. Again, the hotel reception can recommend where to shop but most places are on the other side of the lake." Allen paused as a man at the front asked him a question and he leant forward to hear.

"Thank-you for reminding me. Our friend here has asked about the transport tomorrow. Now, before I lose you to the sight-seeing, we will catch a steamer to Ouchy on the Simplon, the largest steamer. That will be four francs for first class and two francs for second class. I will be at lunch in case anyone needs to speak to me. All that remains for me to say now is "Welcome," ladies and gentlemen, or should I say, Bienvenu." Allen laughed at his own foray into French and began to walk down the bus.

"Mr Allen," said Jack as the Cook's guide drew level with him, "How would I go about finding a guide to do some climbing here?"

"Oh, start with the locals, without a doubt. Good guides are always well known," said Allen.

"Would you know of any?" asked Jack.

"Not personally, but I would ask at the hotel reception. We're never here long enough on this tour for me to know but I'm sure that the hotel will know the best, locally and there are likely to be men, and some women staying, who will be climbing the mountains."

"Even her Majesty, Queen Victoria, has been nearly eight thousand feet up on her visit to Switzerland. Don't you forget that she was never carried but walked, or rode her pony, up some very challenging routes," said an older lady behind Jack.

"Did she? Good for Her Majesty. How do you know that?" asked Jack, turning round.

The woman leant forward and lowered her voice: "My aunty by marriage worked at Osborne House, she was the coffee room maid to Queen Victoria when young at Buckingham Palace. She eventually went to Osborne House in the same role to her Majesty. When she retired, I stepped into the role for a few years. The Queen went all the way up to the Furka Pass and brought back a little wooden chalet which went to Osborne House. It's not just the men that do the mountains." The woman sat back, satisfied at her point.

Jack nodded, storing the fact away for the future. He wondered if he would ever get to mention her achievement to the Queen. He asked the woman: "Have you seen it, the little chalet I mean?"

She nodded and smiled at him. "I have," she said.

Stan leant across to Jack and said quietly: "You're going to ask her about it aren't you? I know that look."

Jack gave him a lop-sided smile. He said to the lady. "What was her name, your aunt?"

"Mrs Wareham."

"Thank-you, that's very interesting," said Jack. He wrote down the name in his notebook.

"Just one thing, Mr Sargent," said Allen who was back at their side: "To go into the mountains I would advise Alpine Club boots and snow gaiters. I also hear that woollen socks soaped on the outside will not blister."

"Thank-you, Mr Allen, I will take advice about a guide as you suggest," said Jack.

Again, Stan leant across and quietly asked: "You're thinking of tracking down our man Torg with a chat at reception?"

"It's worth a try." said Jack.

"It is and I'll make enquiries concerning Gilbert's property," Burgess said, "But I could do with luncheon first."

"Good idea then we're ready for anything," said Jack.

"Not quite," said Stan. "Let's remember what Gilbert is, shall we. What sort of a character does he have this aristocrat at the top of a crime group?"

Burgess narrowed his eyes and said:" Well I could tell you. He's ruthless, capable of surviving by sacrificing one goal for another. He has no perception of being limited. The area that is his is world-wide. It's an extension of the idea of an Englishman's home as his castle. In his case the world has become a small place that's his for the taking."

434

"Alright, ladies and gentlemen, the hotel is ready for us," announced Allen.

Jack and Stan stood silently, still looking at Burgess as they thought about what he had said.

Jack said: "We have to be guided by you, Mr Burgess. Let's get settled and meet in the dining room."

"Uncle Charles, Jack, Uncle Charles, and here they will call it a restaurant," said Burgess, quietly.

It was not long after checking in that Jack was the first of the three men downstairs. He glanced into the restaurant but could not see Stan or Burgess, and decided to wait for them before going in. He walked along the corridor towards the reception and waited until one of the men behind the desk became free. He heard the French spoken and kicked himself. Of course, hotel staff would speak French and he could not manage more than a couple of words. That was why people came on a tour so that the tour guide handled all the communication. Still, he made up his mind to try and as his turn came Jack walked forward with a smile and said: "Bonjour, does anyone speak English?"

A tall man said: "Of course, how can I help you?"

"I'm looking for a good mountain guide. A climber, only the best. A man in London recommended a climber called "Torg" a Norwegian. Would you have heard of him?"

"I will ask the Concierge for you. Could you write it down for me.? Are you going in to eat, m'sieur?"

"Yes," said Jack. scribbling in his notebook. He ripped out the page and handed it to the receptionist.

"Then come back after you've finished. The Concierge will be here. Bon appétit."

*

It was an hour later when Jack was directed to the Concierge. Jack welcomed standing after the lunch he had eaten, and he ignored the chair pulled out for him. The uniformed man with large whiskers approached from the corridor and introduced himself as the Concierge. He indicated for Jack to sit down.

"You are the second person looking for a man called Torg. He is obviously very good if our visitors from London and Paris have heard of him. Here is the range he climbs from Geneva; we know of no other I'm afraid although his reputation precedes him." The Concierge pushed a map of the areas around Mont Blanc and Chamoni towards Jack. The scale of the ridges and the altitudes listed shocked him, and he nodded in return.

The man continued: "You confused the clerk by describing him as Norwegian. They were part of the Swedish kingdom after 1815 – another consequence of Napoleon – just like us. That's why he directed you over here as he wasn't sure you were really a climber. There's been another man asking the same things you see. Torg is not a local, but from the far north as far as I know but I hear he's very good by all accounts." The Concierge jabbed a finger at the map. He said: "Personally if I was going up, I'd use a Swiss. Please keep it."

"You're right I'm not a climber. But my uncles and I would like to go over there at the end of this tour and hear about it from someone who knows what they're doing. Do you think someone may have hired him already?" asked Jack.

"It's possible, but he has to be found first. I wouldn't know where he is. The other guest sitting in the lounge who also asked for him has the stink of police about him."

"Why is that?" asked Jack.

"Detectives," said the Concierge, with a shrug. He looked Jack over. Jack met the gaze, wondering if he also had the "stench."

"No good?" asked Jack.

The Concierge narrowed his eyes and stared hard at Jack. He said: "Our English guests do not have any idea. There are things that came out of being occupied such as the language here being French. I know nothing of this man, but I have some understanding of his methods. You will not have this being English."

Jack's brow furrowed as he stared back at the Concierge. His mind went to the local history of the farm area he had worked in, Battle. He thought of the 1066 invasion still celebrated in mock battles, followed by drinking and dancing with pretty girls if a lad was lucky. But sense told him it was too far away in time to create any understanding of the effects of a recent occupation. The Scot, Bruce, in Jersey had implied things as well about living in an occupied Scotland which Jack just thought of as being British. He realised he had no idea how it felt.

Jack said: "My apologies, I'm not an educated man. We've made money but I know little of history outside my local area."

The Concierge shrugged again. He added: "There is a group of English climbers staying in the hotel and it's possible they may be employing this man, Torg. I can make enquiries for you with them if you like?"

"Yes, please do. I leave with the lark tomorrow though but hope to be back later in the week. The policeman – can you point him out to me?"

"Certainly," said the Concierge. He walked round his desk and ushered Jack towards the lounge opposite and nodded towards a man who was sitting in a spacious armchair by a black stove.

Jack gave the Concierge a franc, which appeared to go down well. Then Jack walked into the lounge and took a direct path towards the man. He watched the surprise on the French policeman's face, realising the man recognised the similarity between himself and Torg. In fact, although seated, his French counterpart shifted his position to be more ready to stand. Jack knew there was a momentary doubt about if he was Torg.

Jack walked right up, used his smile, and held out his hand. He had decided openness was the best option.

He said: "Bonjour, M'sieur, my name is Jack Sargent and I'm a Police Constable from London. I'm sorry I don't know any more French, and I'm a-hoping you speak English. I believe you and I are looking for the same man, a Norwegian climber called Torg."

The man stood, worn in expression and clothing, grey like the hair at his temples. He had had a long journey with little rest. He swallowed and stared into Jack's eyes for what seemed like an eternity, but Jack did not waiver, realising the importance of the open expression and the extended hand.

Eventually the Frenchman offered his own hand, and there was a firm grip on both sides. Neither dropped the stare although Jack maintained his to be more friendly. He was more powerfully built but also the younger man and his mother had taught him to respect age.

The Frenchman said: "The English never speak another language, despite their concern for commerce. There's a few of your countrymen in the hotel who can manage Latin and get on quite well with those who speak Rhaeto Romance here, but they are few." He paused and looked Jack over again, then continued: "The similarity is remarkable. You must be aware of how like the climber you are. I thought for a moment that you were him and I was in danger."

"You've seen him, Torg, then?" asked Jack.

"Yes, I have seen him. And you?"

"Yes, a couple of times. What is your interest?" asked Jack.

The Frenchman frowned at the direct question. But then a quirky smile lit up the face. He shrugged and said: "Why not? It is my interest. I have my orders and they are not something I have to share with you."

"I have no interest in Torg, other than him leading me and my colleagues to another man. There are people staying in the hotel who may know Torg as a guide or climber. The

Concierge is making some enquiries for me. We can share what we learn with you if you're still here before dinner."

"I will be. There are more than just you then? Torg has been a bad boy in England, has he? What is it that you want in exchange?"

"Background, we know very little," explained Jack. "I can say more later. You have the advantage of me as you now know my name. Join us for dinner and we can share what we know. He's of no interest to us except for where he will lead us."

The Frenchman paused, then said: "Dinner you say? Here? Alright, later, over dinner then."

"And your name?" asked Jack.

"At dinner," said the Frenchman, with a hard tone. He started to walk away but as if something had occurred to him, he stopped and turned back towards Jack.

"You know about the sister?" the Frenchman asked.

Jack shook his head. and the surprise was genuine in his eyes. "No," he muttered.

"Torg has a twin sister, a dancer … and more. But I'll save the rest for good food and wine."

The Frenchman had walked the full length of the corridor before Jack finished staring after him. Turning away he just avoided a group coming out of the restaurant and edged his way round them until he was back in the reception. The Concierge had watched Jack and the French detective and motioned for Jack to go over to him. He spoke quietly to Jack: "The only address I have for the man Torg is a gatehouse in the Parc de la Grande, as, I gather, he has stayed there. I'm going by common gossip, m'sieur rather than knowledge. He certainly has a reputation for difficult ascents, but no one seems to have heard of him for a while."

"And the sister?" asked Jack. "The Frenchman said he has a sister, a twin."

"Yes, that's right. His sister is still here of course."

"Why of course?" asked Jack.

"Because she is the Englishman's mistress," said the Concierge. "The Englishman who has bought the house in the Parc de la Grande. Did you not know?"

"No, should I have heard of her as a climber?" asked Jack.

The Concierge gave a wry smile. "Social climber only I would say, but that is gossip. She was a renowned ballet dancer in Sweden, although from Norway. There is a photograph of her somewhere dancing in Christiania, her head almost shaved, leaping so high. She was dressed in a red costume apparently although we cannot tell that in the photograph. She caught the eye, as you say, yes?'

"Yes, I would expect she did. When did she come here?"

"Some time ago, perhaps a few years now, her brother as climber perhaps, I don't know, and she, carving out a reputation for herself."

"How was that?" asked Jack.

"On a mountain partly because she dressed like a man, the head partly shaved but with a long plait at one side of her head – it invited comment, as you can imagine, but I gather it was for a part. I suspect the brother got work because of the attraction of the sister," and the Concierge raised his eyebrows.

Jack nodded. The two men understood each other.

"You rich English have nothing else to do but climb mountains. We come down them to go to work," the Concierge laughed at his own joke.

Jack smiled and said: "I'm not rich, I shall probably never come here again and like yourself, I work for my money. Keep asking around for me, will you? Use my name as well in case it gets back to Torg. Tell me how I find the Parc de la Grande."

"Your map, s'il vous plaît?" the Concierge held out his hand.

Jack passed the map across and said: "I'll write a note for my uncles, so they know where I've gone. Get this note to Charles Burgess or Stan Green, will you?"

Another franc was pushed towards the Concierge.

*

Stan almost cursed with annoyance but managed to reign himself in until the door closed. He passed Burgess the note that had been delivered to his room.

"I'll get off after 'im. The damn fool's gone off on his own."

"Hold on I'll come with you," said Burgess.

"With all due respect Mr Burgess, I don't think so. If Gilbert's around in the parkland we don't want him seeing you at present. Why don't you get word back to England that we've arrived, I'm sure your wife would like to know as well as Hunt. Jack and I will be back for dinner at five o'clock."

"Are you armed, Stan?" asked Burgess.

Stan paused unsure whether to admit that he was or not.

Burgess saw it in the eyes and laughed. He said: "Good, same here. See you at dinner."

Stan took the stairs and left by a side door. According to the very basic map Jack had drawn on his note the park was along the lake to the right. As Stan picked up pace, he turned full pelt into Miss Wheeler and her mother as they came round the corner.

"My apologies, ladies," said Stan, bending to pick up the parcels he had knocked out of Miss Wheeler's arms.

"Are you in such a rush on holiday, Mr Green?" asked Mrs Wheeler.

"I want to catch the light down by the lake before it fades. have a good afternoon," and Stan strode off.

"Quite rude," said Mrs Wheeler.

Her daughter shrugged, "They're just money mama, like us."

Stan took it for granted that social climbers like the Wheelers would naturally discount him. He lengthened his stride, walking on the road to avoid the pedestrians who were ambling along the pavements sight- seeing. But ahead of him a drama was working its way out. Stan could see a pick pocket who was getting too close to a lady. He barged into the man at the same moment the lady's companion had become aware the man was up to no good. The impact of Stan's collision sent the pickpocket sprawling across the footpath. He scrambled off seeing the look of intent on Stan's face while the lady gave a shriek. Her companion touched his hat to Stan who was already walking away: "Thank-you, sir," he called.

Stan continued walking but turned and held up a hand in acknowledgement. Reminding himself he should be friendly he stopped and asked: "Am I right for the park?"

"Half a mile" answered the Englishman.

Stan called back: "Many thanks."

"You're at the Metropole, aren't you?" called back the Englishman.

"Yes," answered Stan, stopping.

"I thought I'd seen you in the restaurant at lunch. Well-built chap and I thought, possibly military?"

Stan raised his eyebrows and shrugged.

"Perhaps you'd permit me to buy you a drink this evening as thanks for your help to my wife. Our name is Tully."

Stan nodded and allowed himself to be sociable: "Well, that's very kind of you. My name is Green. Forgive me, I have to find my nephew," Stan nodded to the lady and walked briskly on.

Ahead of him Stan could see two upright stones like those erected in prehistoric times. They were visible at the top of the parkland not far away from the ruins of a Roman villa. On the right lay a house that had to be Gilbert's. Scaffolding had been erected on one wing and there was evidence of a path being laid towards a Quay. Stan stopped and took in the building. The man was creating a kingdom for himself in a country where he could not be touched. The gardens were not English in design, though, and there was something of a style of layout they had seen in Paris. Slowly, but surely Gilbert was transforming the house and the surrounding land into a prestigious property suitable for an aristocrat.

"No plans to leave anytime soon then," muttered Stan. He looked up the hill side with its tall trees. A lone figure was walking up the valley. Recognising it was Jack Stan muttered a curse under his breath. He had an expectation that Jack was about to get himself into a situation and Stan was not to be disappointed.

Jack had explored the parkland. Staying in the valley between the hills he had climbed several hundred feet to get a better view of the lake and the Jura opposite. His side had pulled, and he had settled to stay where he was. Behind him the Alps rose majestically, and he realised that one day the new trees which were currently being planted would obscure that view. Out of the shadows of a grove Jack watched the riding party coming at a gallop, less than half a mile away from him. The afternoon sun caught the horse of the lead rider and painted it red. The other three horses had an appearance of being a chestnut, a white and another red.

Jack watched as they came closer. The woman riding the chestnut turned her horse towards him and came at a gallop. She was the better rider than the man on the red horse and he had pulled his horse up sharply allowing it to stand among the trees at the bottom of a hill. The woman slowed her horse down to a walk as she drew close to Jack and he stared into a face which he knew told him that he was looking at Torg's sister. He glanced at the man who held his horse stationary and wondered if it was Gilbert. Jack swallowed and turned his attention to the woman.

"I thought … but no matter. You are the Englishman?" the woman asked.

"I am English, yes," said Jack, surprised but also struck by how like Torg she was. Yet there was a slightness to her in comparison. He briefly wondered which Englishman she was expecting.

The woman looked pale and unwell. She was speaking: "He said you would come."

"Who did?" asked Jack wanting her to say the name.

"My brother," said the woman.

"Do you mean Torg?" asked Jack. "How did he know I would come?"

"Shh." the woman said as the man on the red burnished horse trotted towards them.

"My dear, you were mistaken but I see why, the likeness is remarkable. I would never have thought there could be two men so alike! You're in my parkland, you know."

The man had a supercilious air. Jack wondered how many people had wanted to knock him off his horse.

"My apologies, sir. Would you be Mr Gilbert?" asked Jack.

The man stopped and Jack realised he had committed a social faux pas. The eyes narrowed but then the man laughed, but with the understanding the socially privileged had about their inferiors.

"Technically it's "the Honourable," but I suppose as we're in Switzerland …. However, you're still on my land."

446

"I'm sorry, sir, I didn't know. There isn't a fence, and it all looks as if it's one," said Jack.

"Well, we won't hang you, this time. The Swiss don't bother too much with fences. However, we'll shake hands and have done with the issue," Gilbert offered his hand and Jack grasped it after a moment's hesitation. He could not be friends with this man, because they stood for different values. Neither could Jack have any respect for him but a refusal to a man who considered himself the social superior would have been an insult. Jack played along but Gilbert had already lost interest in him. He had turned back to the woman and was speaking to her: "We must tell Torg he has a double. Could be useful, under certain circumstances. I'll see you back at the house, my dear. Good-day to you, sir," and he turned his horse and trotted away.

The woman removed her hat and unwound the scarf she wore beneath it. Jack gasped as one side of her hair was shaved like a convict while the other side was long and in three plaits. She dismounted and Jack realised as she did so that she was wearing trousers under her riding habit. Her paleness and the unusual hair style gave her an ethereal presence as if she was some sort of Angel Messenger. She saw his shocked expression and smiled.

"It's for a ballet I hope to dance in soon, by Ibsen," she explained, touching her hair. The horse nuzzled her, and she responded by running her hand down the nose.

447

"Is that here? Miss er …. I'm sorry, I don't know your name, and I suspect Torg is only a name your brother goes by," Jack said.

"My name is Kari, and no, there is nowhere here to dance, yet. Perhaps in a few years. I go to Finland in a few days to the ballet there. There is no point in you knowing our family name. It will mean nothing to you if I say it. Look for the mountain whose name my brother uses, and you will find a small village at the foot. But there is no family there now, as so many have left."

"What's the meaning of you expecting me?" asked Jack.

"Let me show you," Kari led her horse while Jack walked on the other side of her. They followed a track and just above the house, she pointed down towards the wing under construction. Various members of staff were coming and going in the courtyard which ran to the edge of the garden currently being landscaped. Kari nodded in their direction and said: "There, those people come and go and do his bidding. They go through the earth as he directs."

"Gilbert's bidding?" asked Jack.

Kari tutted and said: "The Right Honourable, William Gilbert, younger son of an impoverished Earl, remember." She laughed, but it was ironic in tone. Continuing, she said: "And both I and my brother have been numbered amongst those down there, but that is ending for me, and I hope, for Torg. If you are the man Torg said would come I can be open with you. Tell me your name."

"Constable second class reserve Jack Sargent."

"Good, he said you would find him."

"How could he know?" asked Jack.

"He just does. Let me tell you quickly: I came here to be with William through love with the promise of marriage until he found I would not have his child. It would end my dancing, you see. At least not as quickly as he wanted the child. Poor Torg because he was sucked in to ensure I was safe. His climbing skills, at first, were the way William gave him work, leading parties and expeditions. But then there were veiled threats about me if he did not do those little jobs for William. Little jobs that bring police like you. Now I am not safe anyway, and I am expendable so I must go if I am to remain alive. Torg must disappear then, but for now, he waits and watches and has brought you here to finish the man. We realised recently that we cannot get away without help. This is my fault, I thought William was something he is not. By the time he revealed his true colours we were in too deep." She looked sharply at Jack and added: "Torg has stolen for him to keep me safe but even that has not been enough."

Jack moved in front of her and looked hard into Kari's eyes. He thought she looked unwell. She stared back.

Jack said: "You were expecting me?"

Her eyes gave him the answer. Jack turned away and stared towards the lake, suppressing the irritation at being played with by a thief. He said: "You rode down the hill knowing who I was, didn't you? That story about thinking I was Torg was to throw Gilbert off the scent and to get to me before he did. Where's your brother now? Can he see us?"

"Perhaps, I don't know. William doesn't know he's here. He thinks Torg has gone to lay low in Norway because he was almost arrested in Jersey. Torg is good at laying a smoke trail to put someone off and send them in the wrong direction if he wants to. He also can lay a good trail. That is how he has stayed free. Torg's story to William is that he's being pursued because of a set of diamonds apparently. William's diamonds now."

"The Shah of Persia's diamonds," corrected Jack. "And a theft that's an embarrassment to her Majesty, Queen Victoria. Can you get a message to your brother?"

Kari shook her head and said: "I won't need to he will find you tonight in your hotel."

Jack had screwed up his face in disbelief at what he was hearing. He said: "Well, you had better let him know that there's a French Policeman after him from Paris and he's staying in the same hotel as me. The man is a hunter and he's not interested in Gilbert. He wants your brother, and he knows about you. He's joining me for dinner tonight and I look forward to finding out what else your brother has been up to. Why have you stayed so long if you know Gilbert means you harm?"

"Love dies slowly. It takes a while to accept that the man you love is mad. He lives under illusions of grandeur, believes people hunt him as he is a threat to them."

"You don't have to be mad to know the police will track you down," said Jack. "He's had a good run though, some of his exploits, including murder, go back quite a few years."

Kari continued: "He changes his appearance regularly, dies his hair and moves around secretly. He has become unwelcome in his English family despite offering them the wealth they crave. They have the title still, but no wealth and they need money and being able to provide it is very important to William. Knowing he's not accepted has made him more overbearing, unconventional, and yet, to some, fascinating. I truly believe that I was selected to give him a child. Then he would have married me. But that was never in my mind at that point. Yes, I fell in love with the image he presented at first and he, with my image. Torg and I have skills which has given us a certain amount of celebrity in Norway. William liked that and the ballet I did in Sweden was avant-garde. He pursued me and I was flattered by the charm and the gifts. Yes, I admit it." She smiled wanly and continued: "We are from a poor family and our parents died when we were sixteen. Many people have left the villages in Norway now and emigrated to America. If it wasn't for the climbing skills our parents taught us, we may have gone as well or starved. Torg earned good money leading climbing parties and I went as well until he had earned enough to pay for me to be apprenticed to the Royal Swedish Ballet. They used folk dances, mainly from Sweden, but were looking for new dances. I helped take those in." Kari paused, lost in her memories before she remembered Jack's presence.

"And, you'll go back there, will you?" asked Jack, gently.

"I hope so one day, but Finland first. We did not know what William was like, you must believe me. He was charming while

451

he had obedience. My brother led parties for William from Geneva to the inn at St Martin for the views of Mont Blanc. Some would pay Torg 100 francs each a day to go to the Dôme de Goûter."

"Is that the top?" asked Jack.

"It's taken for the summit. Englishmen call it Bosses Ridge," explained Kari. A shadow of sadness crossed her face, and the voice became hard: "So between us, Torg and I provided William with a spectacle for his house parties. Then, as William became dissatisfied with me the veiled threats against my life started unless Torg performed certain "jobs" for him. My brother stole to keep me safe. Every time was supposed to be the last time. But the demands grew greater."

"I know about some of those jobs," said Jack. "I didn't know about you, though. You need to get away now if that sort of thing is going on – no point in putting up with that."

She laughed at the matter-of-fact way he said it. She said: "It took time to realise that becoming ill was down to William's deliberate attempts to harm me."

Jack frowned. He asked: "How was he doing this?"

"I think I'm being poisoned. It's clever and never done by William himself. I think it is his new woman who is from some poor Savoyard village, but she has skills. William is behind it."

Jack looked hard at her. Then he asked: "Chocolates by any chance? Did you send any to Torg with a letter?"

"You *found* them. Torg left them for you and his bag. He was right about you working it all out, and coming here," Kari said.

Kari looked into his eyes and her face was full of life for the first time since she and Jack had met.

"I see," said Jack. "Laying a deliberate trail, was he. Your brother left bait for me to follow him and then staged his own disappearance. Well, it worked didn't it. Only trouble with that was I ate one of the chocolates and it did have quite an effact."

"I am so sorry, that was not what was intended. Were you very ill? You have proved it then?" Kari gripped his arm with concern and Jack felt the sensations run through his body. She dropped her hand and glanced nervously up towards where the other horses and their riders had been in case they were observed. But there was no sign of her party.

Jack took a step back and looked away, aware he had coloured. He said: "I'll tell you this now, so you don't hang on around here. The chocolates are being tested in England. We'll know soon, but if you're right you should go. If Gilbert's behind a poisoning, then we'll prove it. We're not interested in your brother, apart from the Shah's diamonds he took which need to come back to me. If I can see him and he gets that specific property back from Gilbert, we won't touch him."

"But if I went before it was convenient for William, he would ensure Torg came to harm," said Kari.

Jack said: "Tell me where Torg is and I'll help you both get out."

"I can't yet, but soon if Torg is safe. William's new woman worships him. She's already carrying his child and he will marry her to have the heir. He's distracted by it all so I can go soon. Torg will find you. William believes Torg will end up in prison. It's William's revenge on me."

"Nice character, he sounds mad," said Jack. "I've known a few like that but with position and money it would be lethal. Look you're not the first that's been damaged by the man, but at least you're still alive. You should go now."

"I must make sure Torg is free of him, first. This policeman from Paris must be here because of the thefts there." Kari stared into the distance.

Jack wondered if she was recalling Torg's antics in that city.

"Well, I'll find out what your brother's been up to later as we're meeting the Frenchman," explained Jack.

"We? You mean there are more than just you?"

"There are two policemen, and a civilian here. We aren't going back until Torg's coughed up those diamonds, so do him a favour and let your brother know as it's clear he's about. You can. come with me now if no one's watching. We'll get you out."

Jack paused and waited but Kari shook her head.

She said: "No, Torg must be safe first, then me. You'll see him tonight. Now I must go, I've already been too long," and with that she swung herself back onto the horse and urged the animal into a trot, towards the house.

Staring after Kari Jack became aware of the shadows as the sun moved behind a range of hills. It was late afternoon, and he must return to the Metropole Hotel. Jack walked down the hill and through the parkland aware he had had a chance encounter with someone that could impact his life.

Seventeen

Stan had moved into the shadow of a thicket after he had realised it was Jack he could see in the parkland. There he had found a stump of a tree for a seat and produced the knife he always carried. He looked around for a piece of wood and, although he remained well hidden from those he observed, his view of Jack's encounter was perfectly clear. Sitting well into the shade Stan whittled off the bark and started to form a shape. From his vantage point he kept under surveillance the four horses and riders as they appeared, and he had tensed momentarily to be ready to go to Jack's aid if needed.

Stan paused his working at the wood to watch the strikingly dressed woman ride at full pelt down the hill to Jack and soon calculated that the man who followed must be Gilbert. The mannerisms and dress said the man was from a certain class and the hairs on Stan's neck stood on end as he involuntarily shivered. It was not with fear but with the memory of carrying the body of Emily Doyle from the park near Arbour Square in the case of the Faceless Woman. Somehow Gilbert's tentacles had been responsible for the deaths of three people in that case and he had ruined quite a few police careers in the trail he had left. Stan wondered how Burgess would react if he could see the man now.

Stan watched the interaction between Jack and the woman, and Jack's brief exchange with the arrogant man. He kicked himself for leaving his spyglass in his luggage thinking he would have liked to get a better look at her. She was clearly a character from what he could see of her. Not too long after she had come under Stan's scrutiny the woman had re-mounted her horse and ridden away and Jack stood alone staring after her. Stan could see the impact she had had on the young constable as Jack stood staring after her. He could smell it – the danger she posed to the young man.

By four o'clock Jack made a move and Stan tracked him at a distance in case he was intercepted, relaxing enough to close the gap in distance between them only as they neared the way out of the park. Stan quickened his pace and Jack became aware he was not alone. The footfall of the shadow told Jack it was a heavy build, capable of doing some damage. He had a hundred feet to go to the gate and there were people in the street. It would have to be a very convinced assailant, or a madman, to attack in a crowd. As the footsteps grew closer, Jack decided to turn rather than take an attack from behind. Facing him, Sergeant Stan Green grunted something incoherent before spitting on the ground.

"*Stan,*" Jack greeted him. "All alright?"

They stared at each other and then Stan leant forward and prodded Jack in the chest. He said: "It appears to be Constable."

Jack frowned and then straightened up – if that was the way Stan was playing it … "Sergeant," he said, staring straight ahead.

Stan continued: "But *you* may not have been. What's the thing you were told before you went out on your first patrol two years ago, eh?"

Jack grinned seeing where this was going. He said: "Don't go into any situation on your own, wait for back up."

Stan brushed some of the bark off his sleeve. "I'm glad you remember it. What is it between knowing that and doing it that you have a problem with?"

"It's not that, Stan ..."

"Sergeant," Stan barked out.

"Sergeant, sorry sir, I had no idea I was on Gilbert's land. They came on me suddenly ..."

"As situations tend to do," interrupted Stan. "Remember that and you'll stay alive. Alright lad, at ease. What did you learn?"

From his inside pocket Stan produced a gun. It was the Bull Dog Jack had used in Jersey. Stan said: "Put it away and have the intention that you won't use it unless threatened with a weapon and in a corner. I'm "signing" you on with a firearm."

Jack looked shocked but took the gun and put it in an inside pocket of his jacket. "Not being rude, Stan, but how did you get it?"

"I had a feel about those soldiers, as did Harry. I took it so it reduced their access to firepower in case they used it on us. I meant to return it before we left but there was no warning about how fast we'd have to leave. You can make use of it but hand it back when we get home, eh?"

"Can you make that decision? Shouldn't we check with Harry if I can carry firearms ..."

Stan interrupted: "Harry isn't here, neither is Hunt and Burgess doesn't count. I'm the superior here and it's my decision. That's it. Just don't try and kill anyone, use it if you're cornered … but only if you need to. Just get out of a situation. It's my responsibility and I think the man we're dealing with has enough of a trail of death behind him to warrant it. It looked like you spoke to him?"

They were at the gate out of the Parc de la Grande and a few people shouldered their way past them. Stan nodded to an area away from the gate and Jack duly followed his superior.

Jack picked up Stan's question: "Yes, I did, you saw the woman?"

Stan sucked air through his teeth and nodded.

Jack continued: "Torg's sister and she's officially the mistress but things are changing. Gilbert needs an heir and he's found someone to give him one."

Stan probed: "What did you make of him?"

"All the arrogance of his class and none of the manners, touchy, sarcastic … dangerous. Thinks he's a king in a tin pot little kingdom," said Jack.

Stan nodded. He said: "That makes him a threat if he thinks he's above the law."

"They usually do, don't they?"

Stan moved his next question to Kari. He asked: "And the woman? What did you make of her?"

"Former ballet dancer, tying to return to a Swedish company but going to Finland for a part by the sound of it first. Probably a good thing as it sounds like the place is the end of the world to me and she's in some danger here. She's the reason Gilbert has a hold over Torg. Her name's Kari. She said we'd never pronounce their surname. She thinks that she's being poisoned - Gilbert's order probably but there's the other woman who's carrying his heir. Kari believes it's the new mistress who's poisoning her. Those chocolates I sampled in Jersey were sent by Kari to her brother for that reason. Do you remember I told you that the old Hotel keeper in Jersey said Torg was upset by the letter which arrived with the box of chocolates? Leaving them and his bag was a deliberate set-up, Stan, to get me to follow him. He must have some faith in us if he thought we would work it out. They want out of this and Kari intends to go back to the ballet but won't leave yet until she knows Torg is safe and away. She knew it was over with Gilbert some time ago and despite having been in love with him realises the sort of man he is. She said Torg has been stealing on Gilbert's orders otherwise Kari would be hurt. Looks like their time is up now though. I told her about the policeman from Paris for that reason. Brother and sister have been trying to look after each other."

"Right then," said Stan. "When we get back to the hotel, I'll send a telegram to Harry."

"Not to Sam for Hunt?" asked Jack.

Stan shook his head. "There's only one person I trust. Hunt's let something slip to someone he's working with I think, or he's being watched by someone. It isn't you, nor is it Harry, and it sure as hell ain't me."

"Leaves the whole of P Division," said Jack.

"And more, could be someone in Scotland Yard, or even someone in the Prime Minister's office. There're too many possibilities to try and lock it down. We just go quiet and that way we're safer. I'll leave it to Harry to work out what to tell Hunt. Come on, let's get out of all this green back into the streets. It's too deserted now and it's making me nervous."

As Jack and Stan walked back towards the hotel the wind got up from the lake and they felt the chill of the day worsening into an icy wind. It seemed to reflect their mood as the world had suddenly felt unsafe. The sun was on the opposite bank to them and their route back to the Metropole was in shade. The temperature was decidedly cool out of the sun, and both men noted the need for warmer clothing. Once back at the hotel Stan paused on the front steps.

"We'd better do something about kitting ourselves out here, I'm getting tired of being cold." said Stan. "Ask at the reception, will you? See if there's anywhere likely to speak English. I'll get along to Burgess's room and fill him in with what we know."

Once they were inside the entrance hall Stan took the stairs to see Burgess. With Stan out of the way Jack's first action was to send telegrams to Sam in Brighton and one to the Parson at Lymington. Sam's was simple, and Jack hoped his friend would understand it.

The telegram read: "Weather cold and getting worse. Jack."

The messages were disobeying an order. Jack knew there would be consequences if it came out. Hunt had trusted Jack enough to take him to Windsor and despite Stan's reticence to inform Hunt Jack was loyal and trusted the Inspector. Hunt was acting on royal orders and, at some point, would be held to account. Sam would make of the telegram what he could and contact Hunt. That was all Jack wanted.

To Peter Fisher a message was sent as Jack had a need to communicate with his old Parson after all the help the man had given them. In his eyes it was coded but would let him know they had arrived in Switzerland. His message read:

"I lift up mine eyes to the hills, from where does my help come? Jack."

*

In Brighton Sam drew breath as a telegram arrived. Grandma put it on the kitchen table in front of him and the family fell silent as Sam walked into the garden to read the message.

"*What?*" They heard Sam exclaim.

Mrs Curzon held her breath and all eyes were on Sam as he came back inside. Looking around his family he quickly pocketed the message and downed the rest of his tea. He said: "Mother, I have to go out."

"Is all well, Sam? It's not something with Eleanor, is it?" asked Mrs Curzon.

Sam's eyes softened and he managed a brief smile. "No," he said. "It's not from Eleanor, it's work. I'll not be long."

Sam got as far as the front gate and realised he was not alone. Turning he saw Luke hovering at the front door.

"Do you want me to come with you?" called Luke.

Sam looked at his brother and thought that in another year Luke would be apprenticed in a trade. The child had gone and the need to be an equal was evident.

Sam walked up the front steps and put his hand on his brother's shoulder. He said: "No, not this time. You stay here and look after the family. Just in case something happens to me Luke, there are two men to contact. One in London called Hunt and the address is in the drawer in the bureau. I'll show you how when I get back. The other man is a solicitor in Hastings called Langton. Alright?"

Luke nodded solemnly, a man suddenly.

Seeing the effect of the trust Sam added: "Probably best not to tell the other boys or Mother about this. Just follow the addresses in the bureau if you need to."

"Sam, what about Grandma? Can I tell Grandma?"

"If something happened to me, yes. You can get Grandma to help. She's got a sensible head on her. It's not likely, Luke, so don't worry." Sam gave his brother a reassuring pat on his shoulder and walked away. Luke followed him to the garden gate and watched his eldest brother walk towards the main road.

In Lymington Peter Fisher received his telegram while reading in Timothy's study. His brother-in-law, Timothy, sat at his desk answering letters. Both men stopped their activities when Helena brought the telegram in.

"Go on, Peter," said his sister, "Put us out of our misery."

Peter Fisher looked at her and then ripped the telegram open. He said triumphantly: "Psalm 121 quoted. it's Jack, he's there! They've reached Switzerland."

"Oh, well done with all those arrangements, Peter," said Timothy.

"Good of Jack to let you know," Helena almost skipped with excitement. She added: "Does he say where he is?"

"No, nothing specific, but that tour was to be in Geneva today, at the Hotel de la Metropole." Peter Fisher flipped to the back of his novel and pulled out the loose sheet he had carried with him for days. He pushed it across Timothy's desk and said: "See, I have a copy of the itinerary."

"It's a rum do, all this, Peter," said Timothy, handing the paper to Helena. She read it and gave it back to her brother.

"Yes, it all seems a long way from the quiet of your wooded lanes, here," said Peter Fisher. "But we know Jack isn't alone in all this."

*

By five o'clock the English tour group travelling second class with Cook's was queuing at the door of the restaurant. Those who had travelled first class had arrived earlier that same day on the express from Paris and had spent the morning touring the old part of Geneva before returning for luncheon. In the restaurant they were seated separately from those travelling second class and had already been served their first course. The Wheeler's were over-dressed in the view of the Swiss guests who tended to stare sober faced at the finery on display. As Jack took his place in the queue next to Stan and Burgess their more reserved appearance seemed to fit in well.

A flurry of activity from the first-class group caused some comment as a couple pushed their way forward to arrive at

Stan's side. A hand was extended, and Stan looked abashed at the joviality of the young man, even doing a small bow to the lady. Burgess and Jack gave each other a look as the Sergeant was displaying an unusual level of manners and they waited to be put into the picture.

"Come now," exclaimed the young man, pumping Stan's hand up and down, "I promised I would buy you a drink before dinner, but you've evaded me. There's not enough tables and we're likely to end up with that industrialist again from Manchester. Why don't you and your party join us?"

Stan blinked and swallowed "That's very kind Mr Tully but I think as we're in the party which travelled second class, we should ... "

"Nonsense, bravery should be acknowledged," said Tully loudly. His eyes went across the group and singled out the guide. "Mr. Allen," he called, "This gentleman acted bravely this afternoon." Tully smiled at the rest of the party and explained: "Forgive me, ladies and gentlemen, but this man stopped an attack on my wife, which Mrs Tully will bear witness to. I failed to see it coming, that's right isn't it, dear."

Mrs Tully nodded and smiled at Stan. He nodded to her and thought how very young she was. She had slipped her hand into her husband's. Stan fought the memories off from his own first few months of marriage and wondered if he was right and that they were newly married.

The other guests murmured to each other and eyes were on Stan. He shrugged and glanced at Burgess and Jack, and mouthed: "pickpocket," quietly. Jack nodded and Burgess beamed and patted Stan on the shoulder.

Tully was in full flow: "Therefore I would like to invite Mr Green and his party to my table. Issues of how we are travelling should not preclude gratitude. I hope you will agree."

Tully's proposal aroused a round of applause from the Cook's party. As the clapping subsided Jack took Stan to one side and reminded him that he had to meet the French policeman.

"Look Stan, that man from Paris is going to show up and he'll give the game away as to our real occupation. What say you to my heading him off at the door and he and I can eat quietly in the lounge?"

"Good thought Jack. I'm sorry about this, it's a lot of fuss about nothing really," said Stan.

"Accept the gratitude for once," murmured Burgess, "We can go with the façade of why we're here. They're pleasant people and we can always try and excuse ourselves early."

Jack patted Stan on the arm and moved across to Allen to explain that he had a business meeting with an old contact and due to the circumstances, he would like to eat in the lounge. Allen agreed and went over to the Maitre d'hôtel to arrange it while Jack slipped out to the lounge.

The French detective was on his way to the restaurant as Jack reached the end of the corridor. The two men acknowledged each other, and Jack took him by the arm to walk him back down the corridor. Surprised at the unusual familial level of contact from an Englishman the Frenchman hid his humour.

Jack explained: "I'm returning to the lounge as my "uncle" is being proclaimed a hero over dinner for stopping a pick pocket this afternoon. I expact there's no way we'll get opportunity to talk in the restaurant, sir, so they will serve us in the lounge."

"Do not call me sir. I am called Carnot. We are the same, you, and I. We are policemen. I am happy to return to the lounge. I hear the food here is good."

"Aren't you staying here. then?" asked Jack.

The question seemed to amuse Carnot. He said: "No, I am staying in a narrow street in quartier St Gervais, full of tall, gloomy, dark houses, away from any sights. You are clearly paid much better than I am. Perhaps I should come to London and work there if you can afford such opulence as the Metropole, eh? Opposite my room there is an omnibus, that is all. The scenic has left there except for the environs, how do you say this, er, the surroundings."

They entered the lounge and saw a table by a fireplace. Jack made a concerted effort to get across the room to it.

The two men sat down, and Carnot continued: "We should order."

He half raised a hand to a waiter who responded immediately. As an aside he said to Jack: "The food will be good, because the kitchen is mainly French."

Jack looked at the menu and grinned. It was in French which meant nothing to him whereas the menu they had been given at lunchtime had been designed for the English tour group.

"I've no idea what any of this is. Whatever you choose I'll have as well," said Jack, handing his menu back to the waiter.

"Good, that shows we make progress together. There is trust there," said Carnot.

"With the food," muttered Jack.

Carnot laughed and spoke to the waiter.

"So, what have you chosen?" asked Jack.

"Don't worry, you will like it. Now the wine," said Carnot.

"Not for me, thanks," said Jack.

"You should have a little, it's good for the stomach. We can water it as if for a child if you like." Carnot was clearly amused at Jack's refusal.

"Not on duty," Jack answered.

Carnot sat back in his chair and stared at Jack. He asked: "And when, my friend, will you not be on duty?"

"When I get home," said Jack.

You are truly "le Bobby" yes? You are supposed to be the best force, the least military in the world, the most worried about liberty. Yes, you in the Metropolitan Police are studied by us Parisians. Did you know that?"

"No, I didn't," said Jack, surprised.

"We in Paris are from a time of "despotisme," also brutality and deception. We have the time of fearing the spy. I think your people do not like this and do not like you out of uniform because it seems a little like being a French policeman and spying on them."

"There is that, yes," agreed Jack. "You know a lot Mr Carnot. I don't know anything about the French force."

———

467

"Simply Carnot, please. One thing is the same – French or English there is the need for the police to be seen. And your force has become famous even though the powers of the Metropolitan Police only extend to twelve miles around Charing Cross," Carnot brought his hand down, slapped his knee and laughed. "But you know all this helps to mask the real tensions that continue to agitate your society. We both come from the lower ranks I think and know what it is to be poor. What were you before you became le Bobby?"

"I was a farm labourer," said Jack.

"Yes, it is there in the strength in your hands. I am older, that is obvious." Carnot shrugged. "I was a soldier. Why did you join?"

"I wanted to get on, saw it as an opportunity to raise myself. I didn't want to stay as a farm labourer," explained Jack. "I could make Sergeant eventually, and there's a pension now after long service. There's more respect than I knew before. Yourself?"

"There was a hole to fill after military service. Why not aim higher? Why settle for Sergeant? Ah here is the food."

"Oh, it's soup," said Jack with relief. "Chicken soup?"

"There is chicken in it," Carnot looked amused.

Conversation lapsed as the two men ate. The wine waiter came across and Carnot ordered for himself. A small carafe was brought to the table and Carnot nodded for it to be left. Carnot crumbled a little bread into his soup. Jack noted with interest the difference in social manners between the Frenchman and himself as his mother had told him it was not polite to do that in a good café. He broke a small piece of bread off and put it in his mouth as he had been taught.

Carnot said: "We are both concerned with practical matters to placate our superiors. I am sure you have spent most of your time, like me, dealing with wanderers and beggars in your work. You know what the job is, we work to keep the poor in line. It's rare we deal with someone like your English lord here."

"True, but there shouldn't be a difference if he's a criminal. Where are you based?" asked Jack, trying to steer the conversation a little.

"Prefecture of the Seine," replied Carnot.

Jack shook his head. He said: "Where would that be?"

"Greater Paris, near the Île de France. No? You don't know where I mean?"

"I've been in Paris, one night near the Tuileries, that's all," explained Jack. "Did you say Prefect?"

"Prefecture, it's in charge of the police. Did you see the river?" asked Carnot. "No? You did not go down to the river? It is the Seine and if you were near the Tuileries then you may have noticed the Louvre Museum." Carnot paused.

"Someone on the tour mentioned it. Is that near where you're based?" asked Jack.

"Yes, and I was minding my business, busy looking at child labour and underage girls employed and then Torg took a painting from the Louvre and my duties changed. It was twenty-four hours before they noticed it was missing by which time he had vanished. It's worth a fortune."

"Stealing to order," said Jack, "That's what we think he does, for the English lord, as you call him, Gilbert."

Carnot brushed a mark off his trousers, "Yes, we know this."

"How do you know it was Torg?" asked Jack.

"We have a description of a man working with a team of carpenters in the Louvre. It fits him." Carnot laughed and added; "Mon ami, it also fits you. But this Torg, he makes no effort to disguise himself, and I wonder if it is arrogance or stupidity."

"Could be, or he might just want to be caught," said Jack. A thought struck him. He asked: "Have you ever seen Torg?"

"No," Carnot replied in his clipped way. "Just a drawing made after a witness was interviewed."

"Well, there I may be able to help as I have seen him, twice, both times during a crime being committed," said Jack.

Carnot looked away in exasperation and said something Jack could not make out.

"Why did you not apprehend him?" Carnot's tone was irritated.

Jack shrugged: "The first time he was scaling down a rope and I was at an upper window in an office, he looked back at me, which I thought at the time was odd, but he was gone before I could get down there."

"You think he wanted you to see him?" asked Carnot.

"Yes, I do now. At the time I thought he was being stupid, but I've come to realise there is nothing stupid about this man. Now I believe he's trapped and wants a way out. He thinks I'm going to be the way to get it."

Carnot nodded, then continued: "You said you had seen him in two crimes?"

"Yes, and now I don't think that was an accident either. The second time I was injured and unable to move … I saw him put a rolled-up paper or cloth in his inside pocket from the display at the Alexandra Palace – It may have been a small tapestry, perhaps two. it was the day of the fire if you've heard about that?"

Carnot nodded.

Jack carried on: "There were artefacts just laying around on the grass. I couldn't move and my colleagues thought I was rambling. He was gone in seconds through the crowd."

"He must remember you as you are similar in face. What is in his mind?" Carnot asked.

Jack shrugged. "Perhaps he was asking for help."

The waiters were back carrying a tray with two plates covered by silver dome-shaped lids. Jack and Carnot turned their attention to the ceremony of unveiling the food as the waiters timed taking off the covers to be in unison. On the plates were small guinea fowl.

"Wonderful," said Jack. "But it's not the season."

"A good choice? You like game? It is from a freezer they use outside. An icehouse, I think you would say. That is what you call them?" asked Carnot.

"Yes, I think so. I've not had it since I left the farm. A very good choice, and green beans and salad … good," said Jack nodding his appreciation at Carnot.

Carnot looked pleased. "I take some thought with this choice. I think here is a young man used to the farm, perhaps the shooting. I choose well, I think. Eat, eat, and we will talk some more."

The two men cut into the roasted meat and as well as a smile from ear-to-ear Jack communicated his appreciation with noises as he took the first mouthful. Carnot laughed and dug in himself.

"You mentioned that you saw Torg scale down a wall?" asked Carnot.

Jack swallowed a mouthful and said: "Yes, he and another man but it was clear who was in charge from his manner. How did he get out of the Louvre?"

"The same, through a window and scaled down the side of the building. We found the rope, the type a climber uses in the mountains and, also, one of the carpenters noticed he was missing the afternoon before the theft was discovered." Carnot threw his serviette down in surrender. "Now, for dessert, I think. I suggest the crèpes vanille. Then coffee and you must try a liqueur."

"I've never had coffee and doubt I would enjoy liqueurs. I will, however, try the dessert, as you call it." Jack sat back and hoped his newly healed stomach would cope. He asked: "How did Torg manage to take something from a museum?"

Carnot shrugged, and said: "It's a good painting by a famous artist. Some old Italian, it matters little who. The security in the museum is what you would expect: terrible. They only informed the Paris police several days after it went missing.

Since then, a gallery in Florence has been contacted and offered the painting for a huge sum by an anonymous seller, presumably the person behind the theft. In our knowledge of Gilbert, it is unusual for him to try and sell something. Also, there was a theft in Holland last year which was similar, and Torg fits that description too. What did he take from the offices?"

"He took a very old watch meant for a museum. It was special, the first with a certain type of mechanism. Funnily enough it was made in Geneva. Perhaps Gilbert wants Torg to be caught. It seems the Englishman at the Parc de la Grande has got his hooks into him by threatening the safety of the sister and he's being made to do this," explained Jack.

"We all have choices to make. I, for example choose to put Torg out of his misery and arrest him," said Carnot with a smile. "I told you about the sister because I thought she was involved in some way."

"I saw her," said Jack.

Carnot paused in taking a sip of his wine, "When?" he asked.

"This afternoon," Jack hesitated before saying anything more. "I think she may be in danger."

Carnot shrugged. "Her taste in men is poor. But there is a matter of who her lover is in what can be done. He's related to your Queen apparently."

"No, I don't think so. It might be a story he's putting about but not everyone in the English aristocracy is related to the Queen. Anyway, that wouldn't stop us. So, what's your plan with Torg?" asked Jack.

"We must be careful here, in Geneva. They are unique in how they do things. I want Torg and am not interested in the sister or Gilbert. There is a small matter of pride involved as we in Paris don't like to be compared unequally with the London English police. You, being involved in the investigation means comparison. We naturally want to be seen to be excellent internationally. The painting went missing in Paris. If I can recover the Dutch painting as well it will earn us points. You and I will make our work known if these famous pieces are restored. There is much interest in how you do things, or should I say how "le Bobby" does things. What is it about exactly? The number of you on the ground perhaps? You have a larger number of men on the ground in London, but not in Manchester. So, we copy London and we have increased the number of agents as a result in Paris. In Lyon, like in Manchester, non!" Carnot smiled. "You divide the city up into divisions, we into arrondissements, what is the word in English? Boroughs or areas? And you are not behaving like the army, which is good because it supports social changes happening. You see you give us a "kit" of how to be good police. No old soldiers like me being recruited in London. They are like you now, young men, many I think from the country. How old were you when you joined?"

"Twenty," said Jack.

"I thirty-eight. And you are strong, and still unarmed?"

Jack did not answer. He waved at the waiter. "We should have pudding."

Carnot laughed. "No, we will have dessert. There is a difference."

Crêpes Vanille had the upper edge on Jack's potential argument about the glorious puddings he had eaten. He decided to savour the moment and realised he was smiling as he tasted the first mouthful.

"You see," said Carnot, "colleagues in arms and friends share good food and then trust comes. Have I your word that you will not stand in my way when I move to take Torg?"

"My personal word? I can't give you any assurance about my superiors. I can tell you that this duty we're on here only involves taking back certain gems that Torg stole. That's all. It's to take away international embarrassment. If he coughs up the jewels he took he's safe as far as I'm concerned, but I would rather like his help on getting to Gilbert. So, I can't promise not to get in the way of you arresting Torg too early if it prevents that."

"So, a matter of timing." Carnot put his fingertips together and stared at the ceiling.

"Yes, I expact so. Look we're away from here tomorrow with enquiries elsewhere along the lake. It's a matter of days before we return to London. There will be no one here then to get in your way with Torg. If he emerges from the shadows and will give us the assistance that we need we can help get his sister out. That's the deal we can offer him. She could leave under our protection." Jack was developing a plan on the spur of the moment without any idea if Stan would buy it.

Carnot's eyes had left Jack's face and had focused on the entrance from the corridor. He was not uneasy with what he saw. A faint smile came to his mouth. "Bien sûr, but perhaps we should ask this man?"

Stan walked quickly, making his way round the small groups raising their glasses to each other and the waiters steadying their trays. He was at Jack's side in seconds.

"Evening," said Stan quietly, looking at Carnot. "We haven't met. I'm Sergeant Stan Green but here I am "Uncle Stan" for the purposes of this trip."

Carnot stood and offered his hand. Jack followed him in standing as Stan had mentioned his rank.

"Perhaps we have a way of working Stan," Jack said. "Mr Carnot here is only interested in detaining Torg for a couple of art thefts. I've suggested he gives us the time that we're in the country before he does that to get back the property we've come for. Then Mr Carnot here, has a free rein with Torg, and we can turn our attention to Gilbert."

Stan turned to Jack, going over the suggestion in his head. His face was red, and it was unclear if it was the heat or irritation. There was silence and Carnot looked from Stan to Jack, aware that Jack had not mentioned helping Torg's sister to Stan as part of the deal.

Stan made a noise which passed for a restrained chortle. He said: "We can spare you a bit of the glory Mr Carnot. I can see Jack's worked things out with you. Alright, you lay off our man until we're gone and then do what you like. We've bigger fish to fry. I'm away to my bed, Jack. I'll see you at breakfast as we've an early start I gather from Mr Allen."

"One thing, you call me Carnot, there is no Mr. Where do you go next?" asked Carnot.

"Ouchy, on the steamer," said Jack.

"Very nice, and how many more days before you disappear?"

"We've got three more nights before we head back to a Channel port," Stan answered.

"So, time is limited for you and therefore for me. Very well, I will give it three more nights and then I will move in for the kill. I will keep an eye on the girl as you think she is in danger. She may also lead me to Torg. But I will not move to take him until another three nights has passed. Bonsoir, I will leave my money," Carnot threw some notes down on the table and with a nod, turned and made his way to the corridor.

"Quite a character," said Stan. "Did you get what rank he was?"

"No idea," said Jack. "You don't think he'll jostle us, do you?"

Stan stared at Jack. "That one of your funny words, Jack?"

"Oh, it means cheat. Do you think he'll go back on his word?"

Stan thought as he watched Carnot disappear through reception. He shook his head just as he choked back a belch.

"You alright Stan?" asked Jack.

"Yes, just indigestion," Stan swallowed another belch.

"We should try and find out who he is," said Jack. "All I know is he was a soldier before joining the Paris police. Not been in it too long by the sound of it."

Stan shook his head and said: "I've no idea how we do that."

"Hunt?" suggested Jack.

"Not too happy with that suggestion, Jack. I don't think I want to go into what we're up to frankly, not in a telegram. That's going to land on the desk of some character sitting in Whitehall, or worse still, the Sergeant's desk at Camberwell and then it will be out where we are. God only knows what sort of enquiry that will trigger. No, Jack, we'll work through this and as I said we've got bigger things ahead on this job, although I confess, Carnot's interesting. Anyway, I'm off for a walk to try and digest the food. We're up at six in the morning, according to Allen. Breakfast early here or on the boat and then onto the bus to the landing stage. I seriously don't know why people do these tours. I get more rest at Southend."

Jack grinned at the thought. He said: "But it's not why people come here. I'm going up to my room. Kari said Torg would find me tonight. I thought I'd make it easy for him."

"Best let Burgess know Jack just in case you need backup while I'm out. He's in the restaurant still. Keep your other friend I gave you close do you hear?"

"I will, I'm carrying it anyway. Look, I'll probably sit up and read, but I'll find Uncle Charles first." Jack turned to go but then faced Stan again as an idea occurred to him. "What about that day we get back to Paris? Carnot said he was based in a prefecture of the river."

"Yes, it's called the Seine, "said Stan.

"That's it, the Prefecture of the Seine, he said. How about we show up there and ask for him? It's like a division, I think."

Stan grinned but did not readily agree. He said: "I'll sleep on it for a couple of nights and see how things go. Hope you don't have to wait for Torg too long, lad."

"It's eight o'clock," said Jack. "There's only four hours left of the day and Kari said he would find me today. Is Burgess armed do you know?"

"No idea but given what Gilbert did to his career and health I wouldn't be surprised," Stan said with a shrug. "Tell you what, ask him."

Jack grinned: "Alright I will."

"And make sure you set up a signal to call him if needed," said Stan.

"I've another idea," said Jack.

"Alright but stay on guard."

Jack made his way up the main staircase to the third floor. There the three bedrooms for two policemen and a hotelier were located. Burgess, a little red in the face after the local wine with dinner, did not respond to Jack's knock at first. Jack would normally have walked away after knocking twice if it were not for the fact that he needed the reassurance of some support being available tonight. On the third attempt to raise a response from Burgess, Jack this time called: "Uncle Charles."

Burgess appeared partly screened by the door, and Jack realised the man was in a dressing gown.

"I'm sorry to disturb you, Uncle Charles," said Jack, loudly enough to be overheard if any other guest was listening.

"Not at all, Jack, I had nodded off after a good dinner that's all. Come in." Burgess opened the door wide for Jack.

Inside Jack said: "I wondered if you would do something for me and look after a friend of mine." Jack slightly opened one side of his jacket so that Burgess could see the shape of the Bull Dog in the inside pocket.

"No need, I've come equipped myself," and Burgess. He walked over to the chest of drawers and slipped his hand under the fresh shirt he had unpacked ready for the morning.

"Forgive my state of dress, I enjoyed the food too much at dinner," said Burgess. He replaced the gun and reached for his trousers, which he had draped neatly over the end of the bed. While slipping a leg inside he asked: "Where are we needed?"

"Here I think," said Jack. "It makes sense for Torg to come and find me. I may be wrong, but his sister said he would find me tonight. That's why I'm going into my room, as there's no point in making this harder. I expact to meet with him and get the diamonds back. I've made it clear to his sister we have no interest in him if the property of the Shah is returned."

"You can't be sure the man will come," said Burgess.

"I think he will because I told her it was Gilbert we wanted."

"What does Stan think?" asked Burgess.

"He agrees I wait but that I have my friend," and Jack patted his jacket where the Bull Dog was placed. "I'd like the help of another friend in case I'm wrong and I fall foul of an attack."

Burgess smiled and said: "Always delighted to help as you know." He walked across to the window and looked along the side of the building at the balconies. They were the small veranda kind, wide enough to get a narrow chair onto to take in the view across the lake, but little other space. Burgess said:

"Provided he doesn't shin up the outside I could sit on the veranda. If you leave your window open, I can hear the conversation. Are you expecting trouble from him?"

"I don't expact so, it hasn't been his style so far," said Jack. "We could be his ticket out if he believes we want to go for Gilbert. He stole the diamonds once and I doubt it will be a problem for him to take them back again. The French policeman I saw tonight will arrest Torg if he can but that's not our concern. I suspect he will disappear once his sister is safe. But I'd like the knowledge that someone else is on hand who has experience. I also could do with a witness to what I say."

Burgess walked to the sink and threw some cold water over his face and neck. He wiped his face dry, looked at Jack and said: 'You can't be sure, of course, how a man will be. If he shows up, he's some confidence he will get the help he's after. He's led you here after all." Burgess dressed for the outdoors and picked up the rug covering a chair. "I'll bring this in case we're in for a long wait. Alright, I'm with you."

The two men went to Jack's room and Burgess took up his position on the veranda, leaving one of the French windows open into the bedroom. Jack checked he was out of site of the bedroom door and nodded to Burgess that the position was a good one. Jack sat on the bed with his legs up. From there Burgess could see him clearly.

Jack said: "This business of carrying a gun, Mr Burgess, the idea doesn't sit too well with me at home. Here it feels different as we've no backup," said Jack.

"It's always been a limited use, Jack. It was something to be proud of that Peel set us up to be unarmed. I know before I left the Met there were men who were eager to carry guns, especially at night, as constables were murdered. It was restricted to dangerous beats where aid was un-likely to arrive in time despite the constable's rattle sounding.'

A knock at the door put the two men on alert. Jack called: "Yes?"

The reply was in French. Burgess shrugged and Jack climbed off the bed.

"Just a minute, er, un moment," Jack called back. He opened the door to a waiter holding a try of wine. The man was his mirror image.

Torg was dressed in the uniform of the Hotel de la Metropole and this threw Jack completely. So that was how he did things, thought Jack, get a job, probably with accommodation and blend in. The man stood a few inches taller than Jack, but he was of a leaner build and in this he resembled Kari. Jack had seen this sort of wiry build before and knew the man would have a staying power in making a run for it that Jack would not have.

Pulling himself together in case of an impending attack Jack looked down to see what Torg was carrying. The climber was holding a bottle of wine and two glasses by their stems. Another way in than Jack and Burgess had calculated for this climber of mountains. Jack wondered who was really running this encounter, him or Torg.

Eighteen

Jack swung the door wide and stepped back to let Torg walk in. There was a light in Torg's eyes at his success at finding Jack and Jack suspected that the man knew he had the advantage in the element of surprise. Undoubtedly Torg was expecting him to be alone, and of course, did not know about Burgess.

Torg took in the layout of the room and the décor and nodded at the comfort. While he did so it gave Jack the time to assess his quarry. The man looked young and strong, possibly in his mid-twenties but not too many years Jack's senior. His manner impressed Jack even though the Norwegian did not put on any show. There was a confidence born of having to assess danger in the environment and Jack suspected Torg would have a speed of reaction that Jack had yet to learn. He had no doubt if he attempted to restrain him Torg would have the greater staying power and was likely to slip through Jack's fingers.

Burgess waited, hidden from view on the veranda. In the silence he listened, waiting for Jack to speak, finding the quiet in the room disconcerting. Slowly, not making any noise he took out his own pistol and laid it on his knee. Then Burgess heard a voice: "Votre vin, M'sieur," and he relaxed. A waiter, he thought, but then neither he, nor Jack, had ordered wine.

Still Jack had not spoken but Burgess was aware of movement in the room.

Jack remained by the door but indicated to Torg to set the bottle and glasses down on a table by the window as it would be within Burgess's line of sight. Torg's back would be to Burgess but Jack prayed the hotel uniform would not put Burgess off. Burgess heard the bedroom door close just as Torg turned and saw him on the veranda. Torg's eyes dropped to the pistol on the knee, then back to the eyes of the man staring at him. Jack had miscalculated and the game was up.

Jack came into Burgess's view and said: "Come in Mr Burgess, this is Torg."

"So, you speak French, can you do English as well?" asked Burgess, as he pocketed his gun.

"A little, enough," answered Torg. He smiled and added: "Some words the same. You have to and Swedish – who learns Norwegian?"

"They thought you couldn't speak French in Jersey," Jack said.

Again, Torg smiled and shrugged. He said: "A little, but not what they speak there." He smiled across at Burgess, gestured for him to come into the room now the pistol was away.

Burgess's stare preceded him as he took up his position inside the room. Never taking his eyes off Torg he closed the French window behind him and remained standing in front of it. That left only the door into the corridor for escape.

There was nothing to indicate that Torg felt uneasy in Jack and Burgess's presence. The confidence was either because he did not at any point doubt his own ability to escape or he did not intend to. Torg sat down on the side of Jack's bed and waited. Jack knew the person in control in the room was the Norwegian and Jack needed to shift the upper hand away from him. Then Torg's eyes went to his framed bag which he had left in Jersey and which Jack had left by the wardrobe.

"Ah sekke min," said Torg, smiling.

"Your bag?" Jack's eyes never left Torg's face.

"Yes," said Torg.

"It's very useful," said Jack.

"Yes, keep," Torg smiled and extended a hand towards the bag and then across to Jack.

"Don't you need it?" asked Jack.

"I have more," Torg answered with a shrug.

"Sekk med meis," said Jack with an effort at the Norwegian, "Did you write your name in it deliberately so I would know it?" asked Jack.

Torg smiled broadly and nodded.

Burgess looked from one to the other. Somehow, he doubted Torg would have problems overcoming him, but Jack usually was a different kettle of fish. But after cracked ribs? He moved back slightly to buy more distance between himself and Torg and realised that Jack was speaking: "How long have you been working here?" Jack asked.

"En uke … one week." He added: "English I understand some, but not think good to speak."

"How did you know we would stay at this hotel?" asked Burgess.

"All English tours here," replied Torg. "Office here say."

"Cook's office? They have an office here, do they? How clever of them. Of course, Cook's will always use the Metropole in Geneva. How have you escaped Gilbert if you're working here?" asked Jack.

"Hide in people, not hard," said Torg, with a smile.

Jack looked at Burgess and said: "Clever isn't it? Hiding in plain sight by blending in with a crowd." Jack started to think aloud. He said: "You're close to keep an eye on Kari by being here. Of course, is that how you stole the Shah's diamonds at Woolwich? Did you take a job that would get you near the horses? Was it the same in Paris because you worked with the carpenters at the Louvre? Can you pass yourself off as being able to work with wood?"

"Skis, yes," said Torg.

"You make your own skis? So, you could plane some wood with the carpenters alright. And at the Alexandra Palace you blended with the crowd milling about on the grass, looking as though you were helping," said Jack.

"He must have an amazing ability to adapt and use his range of skills," said Burgess.

"You've had to survive, haven't you mate?" said Jack with some feeling. "Picked up the know-how as you went along."

Torg stared somewhere into the past but his expression quickly changed back to being alert. He asked: "The meal was good?"

"Were you there in the lounge?" asked Jack.

Torg shook his head. "In, er, korridoren."

"Is that corridor? I told your sister there was a French policeman after you. Did she tell you?" Jack asked.

Torg nodded.

So, he had seen her, thought Jack. Had he been there in the park all the time?

Jack continued: "He's called Carnot by the way, from Paris because of the Louvre theft. Did you get a look at him?"

"Ja, the Franksman I saw," said Torg.

"And you'll know him again?" Jack asked.

"Ja," said Torg and his eyes registered Jack's concern for him. The two men continued to stare at each other. Jack's meaning was not lost on Torg. Jack looked away aware that he had shown that he felt some affinity with the man. Well, it was too late to change what had been said.

Jack added: "He's good at his job, like a tracker. The Frenchman will hunt you, but I doubt he'll look for you here. You need to be careful, because it sounds as if Gilbert has got you to commit thefts that will get you caught. The Dutch painting and the Louvre thefts, I mean. The fact he's trying to sell those paintings attracts attention. Do you understand that?"

"Some. Enough," nodded Torg, standing. It was almost time to go.

But Jack had not finished. He extended a hand towards Torg and relaxed his expression. He said: "Please sit, you know that we're not after you, it's Gilbert we want and some idea of who works for him in England. There's more we need to understand."

Torg looked across to Burgess, but the stocky man continued to block the exit to the balcony. The pistol remained away and Torg had no idea how quickly Burgess could produce it if needed.

Jack indicated again with his hand for Torg to sit and he did. Jack continued: "I don't think you'd have come here tonight if you didn't want our help. You brought wine and two glasses. Shall we drink?"

"Did you bring a corkscrew?" asked Burgess, doing the actions.

Torg smiled and reached into a pocket. He brought out a simple folding knife that had a couple of implements. Torg selected what looked like a screwdriver and dug it into the cork. Jack heard Burgess exhale as the bits of cork dropped into the wine.

"Gently there," Burgess said, controlling his hotelier's instinct.

"Interesting gadget," said Jack.

Torg nodded and said: "Swiss soldiers have for cans of food and take apart rifles with this." Having dislodged enough of the cork for wine to be poured Torg filled two glasses with the red wine and handed one across to Jack and the second he offered to Burgess. Torg raised the bottle to the two men in turn and said: "Skål," and himself took a long swig of the wine.

Burgess, horrified at the wine being drunk from the bottle, froze and stared open mouthed at Torg.

Jack grinned at Burgess, said: "Cheers," to Torg and took a sip. The wine was not unpleasant, but Jack was not a drinker.

He put his glass down while Burgess in turn inhaled the bouquet, closed his eyes, and took a mouthful sucking in air as he did so.

"It's quite a light wine," said Burgess, lifting his glass up to the light.

Jack said: "I know about the watch you took in the West India Docks, that it was rare and one of the first of its kind but what was it that you stole at the Alexandra Palace fire? I saw you there and you rolled something up and put it away in your coat."

Torg shook his head and laughed. He said: "Nothing, a papir, er, paper, annonse."

"Announce? An announcement, what an advert?" Jack was incredulous. "Didn't you take something valuable?"

"No," Torg laughed. "I come for you. You see me and follow, but you did not come. Du var syk, er, hurt."

Jack leant against the chest of drawers realising he had been played. The investigation into the theft of the Shah's diamonds would never have got anywhere with this character, Jack thought unless the man wanted to be found.

Torg looked searchingly into Jack's eyes trying to weigh up if he could trust him. That was how they both stood for some moments until Jack laughed. He asked: "You deliberately let me see you? Were you trying to get me to follow you so that you could set up getting Gilbert caught and then you and Kari would be free? Did you know about the fire?"

"I follow you from the dock. It is in your eyes. Jeg tror ..."

Torg stopped and tried to think through how to say what he meant in English: "I think it finish with you."

"What finishes?" asked Jack.

"I think he means the mess they're in. He worked out you'd stop it for him and his sister," interrupted Burgess.

Torg nodded: "Ja," he said. " … er, du var syk and the man was there. The policeman, the older man, for Gilbert, he was there."

Jack sat down on the bed and now Torg's escape route to the bedroom door was no longer blocked. He gawped at Torg wondering if he had heard correctly.

"What are you saying?" Jack asked. He glanced at Burgess whose face had also registered shock. Jack had not imagined it. Burgess had heard it too and had moved closer into the room.

"There are many work for Gilbert in London's police, but I see this policeman before." Torg rubbed his cheek with the back of fingers, "The man with the … er… skjegg."

"Whiskers?" Burgess asked. He shrugged at Jack. "That's most of the men in the force."

"Do you know a name?" asked Jack.

Torg shook his head. He said: "He was by you, the older man. So, I look and take something from the ground to make him think I steal something."

Jack rose from the bed. Torg watched him.

Burgess asked: "Who were you with Jack?"

"Half the divisions in London were up there at the fire. Most of them would be older than Torg and I, so they fit the description of older men. And you're right most of them have whiskers. But near me? There were many but I was too far gone to remember. Hunt had been over. Morris and Ted were around and so was Sergeant Thick."

It was strange how suddenly something completely irrelevant came into the mind. Staring at Torg Jack briefly wondered which distant ancestor on his father's side might have come across the North Sea for it was his father's colouring Jack had inherited. Torg was so similar. As well as the impressive mass of very light-coloured hair, there was the shape of the eyes and face. Jack's mother had been a dark-haired little woman, sharp at numbers and good with the money. Older than his father she had married the young market gardener from Bexhill against her family's wishes but brought enough money with her to develop his business, buying a house and sufficient ground for his father to expand the trade to supply outlets in London. No, it was on his father's side if any that there was a link that's for sure. It was too close a likeness to be a coincidence.

But none of it was important really and Jack suspected it was his own longing for family that made the similarity between Torg and himself matter. It could have been a hundred years before and, maybe, some Norwegian fisherman had visited Hastings ….

Jack brought himself back to the present. He picked up what Torg had said: "You realised I was hurt did you? Is that what you meant? Yes, I was hurt by the smoke. I had to go away to recover. So, you followed me to the Alexandra Palace Fire and tried to get my attention by pretending to steal something in the hope I would see you and follow but also because you saw a policeman that you knew worked for Gilbert. You wanted to be caught regardless of the consequences, so all the mess you're both in would end and you could get your sister out. Did you think you could do a deal with the police? Gilbert for freedom for you and safety for your sister, Kari?"

Torg nodded. He said: "Ja, until I saw that other policeman."

"I see," Jack said and looked at Burgess. "We've been a little tardy, Mr Burgess on this one."

Jack turned back to Torg and continued: "I'd taken in so much smoke in the fire that I couldn't move, and I couldn't make my superiors understand that I'd seen the thief from the docks. The next thing you did that summer was to steal the Shah's diamonds from off his horse's bridle. The description meant we knew it was the same man as took the watch from the docks. Was that deliberate that you let yourself be identified?"

Torg said: "Ja.'

"And that was another job for Gilbert?"

Jack waited. Torg did not reply.

"You know why I'm here. I've come to take the diamonds back to my Queen. Have you got them, by the way?" Jack asked.

Torg put his hand in his pocket and thought better of it. He withdrew it and first asked Jack: "Bedr?"

"Better?" Jack repeated the sound. "Is that what you said? Am I better?"

Torg nodded.

"Yes," said Jack, "But the breathing can be bad in the winter in London."

"Gå til fjells," said Torg nodding towards the window. Jack glanced in the same direction and the lights from homes in the Jura Mountains called to him.

"It's funny we can understand. Did you say, "Go to the fells? the hills, do you mean?" asked Burgess.

Torg nodded and added: "Good air."

"A doctor sent me to the sea," explained Jack. He thought: why am I explaining this to a thief? And someone who had pointed the finger at colleagues. Among all those policemen who could be the crooked officer Torg had seen?

Jack changed tack. "And you, you've been busy in a Dutch art gallery and in Paris last year I hear. What did you take for Gilbert?"

"Paintings, liten, er, very small. In Paris, famous one, I knew the French not let it go but Kari matter first."

Jack glanced at Burgess who shrugged.

Burgess turned to Torg and said: "Never mind all that, we don't care about the paintings. That's up to the French to get those back and you need to keep your head down and get back to Norway. Jack here has a command from Her Majesty Queen Victoria about the diamonds. We don't want you, its Gilbert we want, and whoever it was you saw the day of the fire. Those diamonds that you stole go back to where they came from. Now, Jack asked you, have you got them?"

Torg put his hand into his pocket again and this time pulled out a black velvet bag. He threw it down on the bed and said: "Armbånd, For Helly, woman now for Gilbert. He marry her - two days." Torg patted his stomach. He continued: "Hun venter barn."

"Did you say bairn? My word, how hard-nosed of Glibert, one mistress still on the property and he's wedding the next who's with child," said Burgess. He recalled Torg's relationship with one of the women referred to and apologised. "Pardon me, I meant no insult."

Torg had dropped his eyes but he acknowledged the apology with a nod.

Burgess swallowed and picked up the bag. He pulled open the top and tipped out onto the bed a flash of diamonds.

"This is quite a sight," said Burgess.

"Fit for a king, or Shah. How did you get them?" asked Jack.

"Kari get for you," said Torg.

"I see, your sister took it, and did you say Gilbert's new woman is called Helly?" asked Jack.

"Ja," said Torg emphatically.

"And Mr Burgess here is right that she's having Gilbert's child?" asked Jack.

"Ja," said Torg."

Jack began to speak, haltingly to begin with: "So your sister isn't needed. Right, this is what is going to happen … Get your sister out of there … do a vanishing act *with her tonight.* Leave Gilbert to us and whoever's working for him in London. Forget this woman, Helly, who Kari thinks is responsible for poisoning her, just get out. Tomorrow we go to Ouchy and then on a trip to Vevey where the chocolates were made. You should both leave Geneva tonight and Switzerland tomorrow at the latest. Do you hear me? You've returned what we wanted, and our Government will get them back to the Shah with the British reputation restored. We won't look for you any longer but, take my advice and don't go through France and stay away from England. Tell me if you understand and will get your sister away."

"Ja, we go," Torg held out his hand to Jack. Jack glanced at Burgess whose hand had gone into the pocket holding the pistol, just in case. After a slight hesitation Jack shook hands with Torg and the climber walked slowly to the door of the room. It was slow enough for Jack to make a move had he wanted to.

As he opened the door, Torg glanced back at Burgess in case the older man had thought better of his decision about the pistol. Burgess brought his hands into full sight and Torg nodded his thanks to the older man. Burgess inclined his head slightly, in response.

Then half in the doorway Torg looked across to Jack who still sat on the bed. He smiled and said: "Tell your Queen, not all diamonds in armbånd for Shah," said Torg. "She keep the others as a thank-you."

As the door closed behind Torg Burgess said: "I think that was the kind of goodbye that meant we shall never hear of him again."

"If he's got any sense, it will be, but who knows from people who risk so much," said Jack.

"Dropped a little bombshell, hasn't he?" said Burgess.

Jack picked up the bracelet and let the lights create the sparkle in the stones. "I hope he's actually going to get out."

Jack stared at his reflection in the mirror opposite, but his mind saw back to the day of the Alexandra Palace fire and the group of policemen he trusted with his life who had clustered around him.

"Couldn't be Hunt, could it?" Jack asked Burgess.

Burgess almost spat out his response: "Don't be ridiculous, Jack. Hunt and I have worked together for the last twenty years. You said yourself, that half the divisions in London were up there."

"It might make sense, if you look at the fact that there's been an enquiry for years and it never gets resolved," said Jack.

"More likely to be Gilbert's skills in placing contacts which stops it being ended," Burgess retorted. "Hunt's honest as the day is long. I'd swear on my life that he is. He's highly respected, not just by his colleagues but there's the royal link, remember. He wouldn't last long in those circles if he was bent. The question to put your mind to is who was around you at the point Torg picked that paper up off the grass."

Jack answered: "Many people. Look Mr Burgess, Gilbert's supposed to have evaded justice so far because of his background. What if someone close to Hunt, or Hunt himself is the bent policeman?"

"A good question, Jack but discount Tom Hunt. The upper classes will only stand so much before Gilbert will feel a hand on his coat collar. We're the closest we've been."

Burgess poured himself more wine and sniffed the aroma. He sipped and then continued: "If we can link him up with this Louvre theft, we could be home and dry soon and we'll crack his network as he falls. We might even be able to do a deal with Gilbert to sing loud and clear in exchange for leniency."

Jack frowned at such an idea. "How would the public feel about that idea? Poor people who have no contacts or influence who get charged every day of the week? And, who's to say that we won't be linked in taking a bracelet with more diamonds than were stolen. Now, Mr. Burgess, any ideas what we do with this bracelet?"

"I could be tempted to give you an answer that you don't want to hear, Jack. Have you any idea how many diamonds were stolen at Woolwich?" Burgess asked.

"No, only the value and the quality. A few houses could be bought with them. All we know is they were on the horse's bridle."

Burgess gave Jack a look.

"I know," said Jack. "It doesn't sit well with me either when you think of the straights some people are in and a ruler decorates his horse with diamonds. Letbehow'twill, Gilbert's pinched other diamonds and had a bracelet made for the woman who will have his child. Kari would have taken a risk getting it."

"Well, she's done us a favour," said Burgess. "All you can do is take it and perhaps it will be accepted as if Her Majesty is being magnanimous in giving the Shah a gift. A jeweller would know the quality and perhaps the area they've come from so they can distinguish what belonged to the Shah and which ones are extra. It's not our decision. No-one may know what's been pinched if the thefts haven't been reported."

"He would have had it made up here, perhaps? Maybe we can find out what it's worth?" suggested Jack.

Burgess shook his head and said: "No point attracting attention to us. The Queen's not exactly in need of the extra stones and if anyone wants to find out the quality, I'm sure she knows a few people who can give her that information."

*

In the first light of Friday morning Stan Green was woken by Jack knocking on his bedroom door. It was too early to leave for the bus to the lakeside and Stan felt little appreciation at being woken early after his first good night's sleep since Southampton. However, he graciously let Jack in, reading the excitement in the constable's eyes.

Once he heard the story of Torg's visit Stan stared hard at Jack, swallowing the words of rebuke that had come to his tongue. He was aware that things might have gone differently with Torg. The only comfort was that Burgess had been present. But it vanished as Jack repeated Torg's disclosure about recognising the policeman at the Alexandra Palace.

"Remind me who was there?" Stan asked in a clipped manner.

Jack told him his vague memories.

"Well, Jack, good job Harry and I weren't there, or you'd be having doubts about me. Who's your money on?"

Jack stared back tossing up whether he dared say the name.

Stan said it for him: "That's Hunt, then, from your silence. Funnily enough Harry and I thought the same. Unless our climber friend is fitting our colleagues up."

"For what reason?"

"Because it could be part of Gilbert's strategy. I don't know, who do we trust?" asked Stan.

"I did trust serving police officers, now I'm not sure," Jack answered. Both men were silent, staring ahead.

"Gilbert's won either way because the effect is that it isolates any officer. The man we report to on this job could be a corrupt policeman and we have no influence to do anything about it."

"Except the one thing he's got going for him is that lady in Windsor," said Stan. "Harry and I thought the same, and because of that we followed Hunt in London and do you know where he went?'

Jack shook his head.

"All the way to Clarence House to don a footman's uniform and hold a silver tray," Stan grinned.

"So, if it's not Hunt that Torg recognised, who is it? I don't remember who was round me before I passed out. It literally could be any officer who's older and has whiskers!"

Stan busied himself in getting ready and his face was like stone. He said: "It's about power isn't it, and power corrupts. The problem is Jack, that the criminal we're after isn't one of us. We're from the working classes aren't we and providing we go after our own class that's fine. But we're dealing with a man from the upper classes who's as corrupt as Dickens's Fagin, and so far, we can't touch him. If he was one of our own class he'd be inside by now. I've no doubt he's got officers on the payroll, providing a little smokescreen here and there as the odd fire breaks out."

"Like the attack on Harriet," Jack quickly checked himself: "er Miss Fildew, while we worked on the "Faceless Woman" case. That didn't go any further did it? Gaol for the officer who attacked her, but the man never talked. What you're saying Stan, is he knew his family would be looked after if he was silent."

"Oh yes, and not just that as there'll be a job waiting for him when he gets out, providing he doesn't sing." Stan paused as a thought struck him. "Remind me which division he was from?"

Jack furrowed his brow trying to remember. He shook his head and said: "Somewhere round Golden Square. Can't recall it now. Anyway, it's how high it goes that worries me. They take Gilbert's money and, by doing so, they're giving him a licence for crime."

T division thought Stan. Golden Square was T division. He shivered involuntarily as a memory occurred to him. Instead of voicing his thoughts he asked: "How did Miss Fildew come to be involved?" asked Stan.

"We'd met up for tea in Westminster and I saw her onto the omnibus back to her employer's house. It was me that was being watched but nothing ever came out to show they knew who I was. I expected problems for a while but there was nothing, just the attack on Morris and I."

Stan said: "That's not how I remember it, Jack. Morris was injured but you were alright."

"Yes, because he pushed me out of the way," Jack explained.

"You were walking close together?" asked Stan.

"Close enough," said Jack.

Stan swallowed and looked away. He said: "No-one's looking for corruption in the police. Nor how it works. As you say that was one small fire which was quickly put out. The question is by who? All the evidence we had was small and only linked to those who were charged. Gilbert had someone in there to damp down the flames in case they spread, and it couldn't be contained."

There was a knock at the door. Stan opened it to see Allen.

"Good morning gentlemen, just making sure you're ready for the day. We'll leave by bus to the quay."

Jack left Stan's room as Allen moved down the corridor, knocking on the doors. There was enough time for a walk in the gardens for a breath of air and Jack enjoyed the contrast between the bright sun and the morning chill. Stan collected

Burgess from his room and by seven o'clock when they joined Jack for breakfast, the late spring rain had begun.

"Tell me again why we're doing the journey on a boat when we could be there by train in half the time?" Stan asked Allen as the Cook's party walked from the hotel.

"Because the Lake at this time of the year, Mr Green, looks like a garland. You won't get that effect on the train. And the station in Lausanne is a mile and a half from the lake so if you got in by train you'd have to get down to Ouchy where the Beau Rivage is. You'll have an easy stroll from the landing stage to the hotel and enjoy the vistas pf the mountains across the lake. Anyway, it's all arranged. You've just got to let me know if you're going first or second class?" Allen looked over his glasses at Stan.

Jack intervened: "First class, Mr Allen."

Stan's mouth hit his boots, but Allen's response was enthusiastic.

"Good for you, Mr Sargent," said Allen. "Breakfast is included in that price. So, you get a second breakfast Mr Green. The chef will greet you as you get on the boat and you'll be ushered into the salon where you can stay for the whole journey if you like. I have to say I did think it was a little miserable of our first-class guests as they've all decided to go second. Still no accounting for taste is there. I'll get the tickets for everyone at the lake and you can settle-up with me later." Allen moved on to the next guests.

Burgess let out a guffaw and slapped Jack on the back.

"Excellent way to do the journey. How much are you short Jack?"

"There's just your own fare, "Uncle Charles," Jack said, "The Parson planned in possibilities like this in a daily rate."

"I doubt Hunt will pay for First class," muttered Stan.

"I don't care," said Jack, staring at the lake as the bus moved off. "We shall probably never come back here, and the memory of the blue sky and the mountains will keep me going in the winter smog of Stepney."

"Well, you never know with Tom. As we've recovered what we came for, he just might send you off again," interrupted Burgess.

Jack smiled at the idea, but Stan let out a groan.

"Count me out," said Stan.

Jack pulled out the map and the three men poured over it. "Looks like there's a rail head to Bâle from Lausanne and it's a faster route then back to Calais."

"Good," said Stan. He screwed the ends of his moustache between his fingers and continued: "I was wondering what diabolical things they could do to breakfast."

"It will be wonderful," said Jack, "Because it will be different."

Stan shook his head and Burgess chuckled. The hotelier had a spring in his step since the meeting with Torg, borne out of a conviction that the tables were turning on Gilbert.

"Look," said Jack, handing the timetable across to Stan, "There's a train from Lausanne to Bâle at 1:15 on Monday afternoon, gets in that evening at 7:55. and we can get onto a night train to Paris. Then adjusting for the time difference from

Paris we can go to Calais and take a three-hour crossing to Dover. You'll be walking into your kitchen by Tuesday night next week. It keeps us out of Geneva, Stan."

"Good thought," said Stan, thinking of the surprise it would be for his wife and family.

Burgess had been peering over Jack's shoulder at the routes followed by the steamers. He jabbed the map with his finger and said: "According to the map Vevey isn't too far from Ouchy, and the steamers call in there. That's handy for tomorrow."

The bus had completed the short journey to the departure point. There was a sudden hush as Allen made an announcement: "Ladies and Gentlemen, if you would like to leave the bus as soon as possible and wait just to the left there, you will see the "Simplon" at the quay in front of you. Your luggage will be put on board and you are welcome to explore the boat before we sail. The boat will depart at eight o'clock for your wonderful journey on Lake Geneva, or Lac Léman, as they call it locally, and we will be at Ouchy by eleven o'clock. There is time before dinner tonight for you to do some shopping, explore the gardens or perhaps visit the old town. If we could start leaving the bus now, please."

"We can finally get that clothing sorted," said Stan.

"Good idea, I'll have a word with Allen once we're underway about changing our booking to go via Bâle on Monday," Jack said.

Almost exactly at eight o'clock the Simplon was on the move, and Jack, Burgess and Stan left the lower deck to negotiate their way up a staircase to a salon on the upper floor. Two men stood at the top of the stairs to greet them, one in evening dress, which was a surprise at that time of the day. It had been a good quality but now was a little worn. The other man was a chef. Jack smiled as he heard Stan groan, knowing all the Sergeant really wanted was a bacon sandwich and mug of tea. Other passengers were moving up as well but not from the Cook's party. The boat pulled away and the three men could appreciate the fine buildings along the lake as the Simplon put a distance between itself and the quay.

The sun grew stronger after a brief shower of rain and the lake became more azure and transparent as they sailed. Jack could distinguish rocks and fish as the boat progressed and he started to work out the width of Lake Geneva and was convinced it was not likely to be more than a mile to a mile and a half in width. It had become a habit over the years whenever he was on boat. It was partly his father's training when they would go fishing off Fairlight in case there came a point with a need to abandon ship. Jack knew under most circumstances that he could swim that distance if he had to but was unsure how he would get on after the injury to his ribs. He hoped he would not have to put the question to the test.

"How long is the lake, Mr Allen," Jack called over to the Cook's guide as the man arrived on the first-class deck.

"Differing opinions, Mr Sargent, say around forty-two miles," answered Allen, and he came and stood next to Jack. He followed Jack's gaze at the water below.

"Incredible colour," said Jack.

"Yes, isn't it, something to do with the sediment coming down from the glaciers. At least, that's according to a Professor Tyndall." Allen nodded to the distant peaks that had started to appear as the cloud lifted. He added: "Tyndall also thinks what we do down here changes things up there."

"Sounds clever," said Jack, following Allen's gaze. "Funny how we have no idea that those mountains are there when they're shrouded in cloud. Suddenly, it lifts, and there's such beauty."

Allen had dropped his eyes back to the lake. "Of course, if you were a couple of miles out of Geneva on the Rhone it's a different story. The murky waters which drain the Chamonix area and Mont Blanc pour into the river. Forgive me asking, Mr Sargent, but would you mind settling up for the tickets?"

"Of course, I'm sorry I assumed one of the Cook's vouchers would do it."

"No," said Allen, apologetically, "The boats are owned by a company that likes cash only. I've settled it but would appreciate it if you can let me have the twelve francs."

Jack pulled out handfuls of coins and a few bank notes. It was a good time to tell Allen they were changing their travel arrangements to return home via Bâle. Allen agreed to make the arrangements for Jack and Stan and the exchange of money was done.

Jack stayed facing the other range he had seen from the Metropole, leaning back onto the rails. He asked: "Are those tracks up there?"

"Yes," answered Allen.

"They're rare bostals,' said Jack and he could have kicked himself as he saw the enquiry in Allen's eyes at the dialect. He smiled and explained, "My family's word for a very steep path especially on a northern escarpment … We're from Sussex long ago. All families have these words, don't they?"

"They do," agreed Allen. He added: "My grandfather was a jagger – a packhorse man in the Peaks but you don't hear that word anymore." Allen paused, thought briefly and then continued: "While you're on your own do you mind me mentioning something quietly to you?"

Jack looked at Allen, wondering what was coming. He said: "Of course not."

"It's just that there is a young man on the lower deck who approached me to come and find you. Says his name is J. Croz. He'd like to have a word as he hears you're after a mountain guide. Do you know anything about it?"

"Really?" Jack controlled the surprise. "I asked at the hotel, but I didn't expact anyone to follow us on the boat."

Allen adopted a confidential air: "It's a bit irregular as he hasn't got a ticket. The purser, or whatever he is, wants to put him off at the first stop but I thought I should check with you if you'd arranged this."

"No, but it must have come via the hotel as it's the only way he'd know about us," Jack wondered if it was Torg. He continued: "Could he come up here so my uncles can get a look at him as well? If he's what he says he is it could prove useful as Uncle Stan likes to walk and, frankly, he could do with getting away for half a day. He's a bit of a bear with a sore head otherwise."

"I don't see why not. It saves finding someone at Ouchy and the advantage is your uncle can go off with the guide on his own," said Allen. "I'll send him up. He'll have to sort out his own accommodation though."

"If he's what he says he is, I can take care of the Simplon ticket," said Jack. "Maybe there's somewhere small he could stay."

"Up in the town there will be, pensions, but don't you go footing the bill," warned Allen. "He'll charge you six francs a day as a guide so he can pay his own bed and board in some small place. He probably knows somewhere anyway."

"How do you find living here Mr Allen?" asked Jack.

"I've only been here a year, but I've got used to it. I was with Cook's for years in Manchester but it's hard to imagine being back there now. This is easy in comparison to some of the places the tours are going to though. And anyway, Mr Cook senior established the first tour himself here eleven years ago so it's very easy. But Mr Mason Cook, his son, will take the company on, you wait and see."

"How do you deal with the language?" asked Jack.

"Well, you pick bits up, mainly French, enough to start a conversation and then I find I can relax into English. The Swiss keep themselves private and I find them complicated," explained Allen. "Most of the staff I deal with are not Swiss, and I don't meet many actually that are, to be frank, - even Napoleon decided they were a nuisance - and the guests we have are all English so its just liaising with the hotels and sorting any travel issues. You've probably started to pick up phrases yourself that you're hearing. The ear gets attuned to what it hears after a while."

Jack asked: "I was surprised French was spoken in this area?"

"Well, it was annexed to France. Now there's an element that are proud of speaking French and think it's cultured. You see we English are concerned about class, but not here. Language means you either belong or you don't. When we hear English spoken, we can hear class. I can tell with you and your uncles that your business is recently successful and you're late to a comfortable way of life but still the old way of hard work prevails. Likewise, you can hear it in my accent." Allen jabbed his forefinger into his own chest. He continued: "I'll work hard, Mr Sargent because I'm not going back to where I come from with its hard ways and only the Mill as an employer. You understand that don't you."

Jack nodded. He said: "More than you could know."

Allen had started speaking again: "The Swiss don't hear class you see, they hear regional differences in the dialects that give them identity and you either belong or you don't, so I gave up bothering to try and get to know the ones I met. But we do have to take them seriously and you start with their history to try and understand them because it's very complicated. Have you read Boswell's Doctor Johnson?"

"Er, no, I haven't," said Jack.

"I wondered as I saw you always have a book with you and I thought this man is like me, bettering himself by reading when he can. I mention the book as Doctor Johnson says of the Swiss ...." Allen had clearly memorised a section and Jack realised he was going to recite it no matter what. Allen stared at the lake and cleared his throat. He began: "Let those who despise the capacity of the Swiss, tell us by what wonderful policy or by what happy conciliation of interests it is brought to pass, that in a body made up of different communities and different religions, there should be no civil commotions, though the people are so warlike, that to nominate and raise an army is the same."

Jack exhaled. "That sounds very serious," he said.

"Yes, it is, but it seems as true today as in Johnson's time. They've a new constitution this year."

"I'm told they work hard," said Jack.

"They are doing well with business. You wait and see. In a few years they'll have caught Britain up and given they're such a small country that says something with all our overseas lands. There's only Britain now that's doing better than the Swiss." Allen paused for a few moments and Jack mused about what the Cook's guide had said. From the lake he could not see any industry and Geneva itself lay between the foothills of the high mountains of the Alps and the Jura, perhaps explaining why the weather seemed uncertain in late May.

"But I don't see any industry, Mr Allen," said Jack, "There's not many cattle about, some fields have been planted but I can't tell with what. Where are the businesses and the industry?"

"A lot of the work is done by putting work out. The business-men don't need money for factories to start up, they only need a small staff to put together the finished product. There will be hundreds of tiny businesses of specialists and individual craftsmen working from home or in small workshops and the man at the top of it all will pay them twice a year. Look up there in the Jura. Small towns and villages of families who will be working away in small workshops, the children working before they go to school and sometimes up to midnight after school. There will be artisans working away and they'll be educated, farming their own land as well."

"What will they be making?" asked Jack.

"They might be engraving watches of silver and gold. Family homes have machinery in the cellar. There might be embroidered and cotton goods, sometimes velvets and shawls, hats, leather goods and clocks. They've cheap power with all the fast streams as well."

"Watches, eh," said Jack, "Really now that reminds me of a theft, in London, last year. A gilt brass Verge watch signed by. G. Ferlite of Geneva, dated somewhere between 1590 to 1635."

"What a memory, Mr Sargent," commented Allen.

"Well, I'll tell you why I remember it," Jack paused as he took out his pocket watch. "Because it was the same day as the Alexandra Palace fire and in my mind, they were two momentous events. Do you have a watch like this Mr Allen?"

"I do," and Allen produced his own plain watch.

"I thought so as I've yet to meet a man in business who doesn't. The watch that was stolen dates before what we use now, before the invention of the pendulum and the balance spring. The mechanism moved the clock's hands forward at a steady rate. I remembered it when you were explaining about the watch makers in the Jura. I wonder if Ferlite worked up there?" Jack nodded towards the Jura and added: "They never found the watch after the theft, and it's assumed it's in some collection."

"That was a dreadful event, that fire. I'd only been here for a month, but it made the papers in Geneva. Could you see it from where you work in London?" asked Allen.

"Yes," answered Jack, truthfully. "Much of London saw it. Have you come across any watch collections in Geneva?"

"Watches? No, although there is an Englishman who is renovating a property in the Parc de la Grande who is reputed to have quite a collection of treasures. He's supposed to be related to the Queen. He's going to open his collection of art for limited numbers of tours apparently. Cook's is looking at incorporating it into one of our longer visits."

"Mr Gilbert, do you mean? I don't think the Queen has any relatives who would be a plain Mr. Have you met him yet?" asked Jack.

"Oh no," chuckled Allen. "It won't be for me to meet him. He'll make the offer direct to Cook's and then we'll be given dates that the property will open. Confidentially, it will be after the man's wedding, of course but I wouldn't be surprised if we only get across the threshold while he and his new wife are away on the tour."

"Has this information about the wedding, come from Cook's?" asked Jack.

Allen shook his head. He dropped his voice and in a confidential manner said: "There's a shortage of pastry chefs in Geneva and the Metropole are losing their man for the wedding reception, that's how I know. It's in a few days – before the bride is … embarrassed … if you see what I mean. Between you and me as men of the world it's out with the old mistress and in with the new one to bear the heir."

The engine noise changed, and Allen peered at the opposite bank. "Well, I should get back to the Purser and stop him putting the guide off the boat at Versoix. You must get your breakfast."

Jack went inside the salon and joined Stan and Burgess.

"Someone's shown up on the boat that says he's a guide. It might be that information reached him from the hotel, or it could be Torg. Anyway, Allen is sending him up here."

"Right," said Stan, turning his chair to face the entrance.

"We've ordered for you by the way," said Burgess.

Jack nodded and gave Burgess a brief smile. Like Stan he focussed his attention on the entrance to the Salon. Burgess, who had taken a sip of water from his crystal glass clinked it against a cup as he put it on the table and the sound broke Jack's concentration. When he looked back at the door a young man dressed for climbing stood next to the head waiter.

Nineteen

Jack shook himself like a wet bird as doubt entered his mind for the movement was too graceful. If it had not been for the dark hair which was all now tightly shaved to the head, and the slighter build it could have been Torg. Jack knew at once that the composed face of the mountain guide was a part Kari had dressed herself to play and to do so she had cut off her plaits.

Jack stood instinctively and recognised he was standing for a woman. He had some understanding of playing a role having shed many of his farm labouring ways over the last two years. That man was still there though. But Kari was the professional ballerina who had assumed a role which she saw as being required and had exchanged her elegant riding habit from yesterday into the rougher clothing of the mountain guide. She had changed in attitude as well as body since their meeting in the park and Jack could see resolve in the eyes.

"He's dyed his hair," said Burgess.

"No, it's not Torg, it's his sister, Kari. Torg is taller than me and more heavily built than Kari." said Jack. "If you do more than glance you can see she's smaller than me and more slightly built but, like you, most people at a distance could take it that it was Torg except for the hair colour. In a crowd you'd miss "him" because the hair colour is wrong."

Jack walked towards the door and smiled at the head waiter who had intercepted Kari. Jack had wrongly assumed Burgess and Stan would be willing to have Kari join their group.

"Clever," said Burgess, looking at how Kari had dressed. "Adds a complication though."

"Oh, she's clever, alright. See the effect on Jack she has," said Stan.

Jack was oblivious to his colleagues' reluctance and started to explain the guide's presence to the head waiter: "He's our mountain guide," he said, "and will join us for breakfast. I'll pay the ticket price for him."

Kari hesitated momentarily at the table under Stan's hard stare. Burgess broke the ice with an offer of coffee and breakfast and Kari gratefully nodded her thanks.

Kari said: "Just coffee is enough." The voice was deeper and Jack could hear a different accent.

"So, you made it then," Stan said, cupping his hands around the delicate cup he held, playing the role of speaking to the hired guide who was late as a waiter poured coffee for Kari.

Once the waiter walked away Burgess asked: "Where is your brother?"

"Gone now,' answered Kari.

"Why didn't you go with him?" asked Jack.

"Because I have a few reasons to stay and if he is to be completely free, I need to see the French policeman," Kari said.

Stan interrupted as Jack was about to speak: "Just a minute Jack before you answer that. How did you get away?"

Stan fixed Kari with a hard stare which she returned.

"You think I should be sitting in a salon waiting for the men to rescue me? Like most you have a mistaken view of women, I

515

am not decorative. Gilbert's staff know he has lost interest in me as well so why waste their time watching me? I climbed out before it was light, and yes, I can climb as well as my brother. I joined Torg and we walked to the omnibuses in the Place Cornavin. He took one to Fernay and he will be well over the French border now."

"Into a country where he's wanted for theft?" Jack looked incredulous.

"So? Do you seriously think that small villages in the Jura will have heard of the theft from the Louvre? Fernay is within the French frontier, about five miles from Geneva and on the road to Gex and the way to Paris. Torg will have a fine view of Mont Blanc today from Voltaire's garden. Did you know the church Voltaire built there is now used as a hayloft and that visitors to the great satirist's chateau tore the bed curtains into rags for relics? And you worry that people there will know of the painting from the Louvre? No, Torg will go over the Jura, by foot if needed. He may do some work in the mountains and will skirt around Paris. He is gone anyway."

"Gone where? Where's home?" asked Stan.

"Wherever he chooses," Kari answered.

The food arrived and created an interruption to the tense exchange which was developing. The meal was lighter than Stan had feared as it was smoked fish from the lake, and a container of cooked eggs. Burgess tasted a cordial of some sort and nodded approval to the waiter. Jack settled back into his chair and as he was always hungry he ate a second breakfast with gusto. No one spoke and the food started to take effect, buying time, relaxing the tension. Jack felt it making him drowsy and he sighed, unaware of Stan's appraising look. In the two years Stan had worked with Jack he had moved from regarding him as a risk-taking recruit to a colleague of some value.

Jack broke the silence and asked Kari: "So, if your brother's gone, why do you want to see the French policeman?"

"I want to make a deal with him. I know where the French painting is being sold. It's in Florence, and I know Gilbert is behind the sale. The money payment can be traced to Gilbert as proof he is dealing with stolen goods and the aim is to show that he bought the painting from Torg. He didn't do any exchange with my brother except to leave me alone as payment. But I have jewellery, love gifts at first but probably also stolen, that can pay the price of the painting which can be returned to the Louvre anonymously. But only if Torg is pardoned. Gilbert's stolen treasures to pay for another stolen treasure." Kari smiled sardonically, pushed back her chair, and stretched out her legs under the table as a young man would.

"How do you know what you have is enough?" asked Stan.

"I know what Gilbert is asking for the painting and he's doing it deliberately to draw attention to it," said Kari, "I know the jewellery is from pieces stolen to order, some by Torg when it became clear that I would not provide Gilbert with a child. At first bribes, then threats to my brother's freedom to get me to agree. Then he got his "whore" to gradually poison me. It's all here." Kari lifted the backpack she had worn onto the boat.

517

Stan held out his hand for it and there was a momentary pause while two pairs of eyes met. Then she handed the bag to him.

"It's all there," Kari said as Stan rummaged through the man's clothing to a package at the bottom. He spread the bag open so he could get both hands inside and tore open the sealing she had used and then the brown paper. Jack glanced at Kari and noted she had gone white.

Inside the packaging was a drawstring bag which Stan pulled open to reveal an Aladdin's cave of jewels. He tightened the bag again and handed the rucksack back to Kari. He really did not like this woman being with them, but his face had softened slightly. Jack could see it but that was because he knew the Sergeant.

"You should eat something," Stan said to her.

"It can be sold, or exchanged, some of it is probably worth more than the painting," Kari said. She reached out for a white bread roll, broke it and put a large chunk in her mouth, chewing as she continued: "Much of it is very old and very valuable. I know it's stolen, as I was only allowed to wear it on the estate. Like the diamonds in the bracelet Torg gave to you last night. Helly was only allowed to wear it around the house."

"While that might work, Stan," said Jack, "But you can't offer a policeman a load of stolen jewellery. It needs to be held somewhere and one of us tell Carnot it can cover the price."

"Take it, hold it until he agrees."

"Just a minute," said Stan, "You aren't passing that to us either. No chance, I'm not having any of us being accused of a bribe. You brought it you look after it. I'll go and see Carnot tomorrow for you. Jack you know where he is, don't you?"

Jack nodded. "The area yes, but not the actual address."

"Either I'll find him, or he'll find me," said Stan.

"I will come with you," said Kari to Stan.

"No," said Jack, before Stan could speak. "You must stay out of Geneva now. Let your brother get away. If you get into difficulty, he'll be back across the border to help you. You come with us as our guide and we'll pay you six francs a day which is the going rate and get you a room in a pension up in the old town of Lausanne. You keep your head down, it's better Gilbert thinks you've vanished with Torg. By the sound of it he's not going to be bothered."

"And you think I will sit and wait? Tell me where this Carnot is?"

"You set one foot in Geneva again," Stan said, under his breath, "And we will call the whole thing off and get ourselves back to London. If you want our help to get your brother off the hook ...."

"You misinterpret me ..."

"No, I don't," interrupted Stan. "You're a damn nuisance ..."

"There's quite the possibility that this Frenchman, Carnot, could arrest you, as a party to the crime," Burgess cut in softly. "Hold what you have there, and we will see what we can do."

Realising there would be nothing they could do to stop her Jack tried to distract her: "In the meantime, there's another issue we could do with your help on tomorrow. Come with Burgess and I to Vevey and help us identify the chocolate maker so we can get to the bottom of the poisoning. It all helps to finish Gilbert."

"And given the way you're dressed it looks as if you know something about the sort of clothing we need round here?" said Stan.

"Of course, I can get that for you in Lausanne," said Kari.

"Thank God for that," said Stan. "I haven't been warm since I left England."

Kari laughed at the obvious relief in Stan's voice. She said: "I'll get it for you all today. You are the first to help us. Thank-you."

Even Stan softened. "Alright then," he said, "I'll go and do the deal with Carnot for you tomorrow. When we get you settled, you can get yourself off to fix us up with the right clothing. Get it sent down to us at the Beau Rivage Hotel in Ouchy. Don't come with it yourself. We need to make sure you're not being followed. Once I've seen Carnot, we can meet up tomorrow. Look out, here's Allen coming in."

"Mr Allen," called Jack to the Cook's guide as the man came towards the table. "We've taken the young guide on and Uncle Stan will go off walking tomorrow while Uncle Charles and I come with the group to Vevey. Would you know of any small pension we might use for our guide in Lausanne?"

"Oh, good I'm glad that's worked out," said Allen. "Yes, I do in the Rue de Caroline, under the name P. Chevalier." He said directly to Kari: "Mention you're working with Cook's as a guide. It's very reasonable. How's the smoked trout going down Mr Green?"

'Trout? Is that what it is. It's delicious," said Stan, shovelling a piece into his mouth.

*

They reached the Port of Ouchy shortly after eleven that morning and, after disembarking, had a pleasant walk along the Grand Quay while they waited for everyone in the group to assemble. There were clear views across the lake and the weather seemed to be more temperate than the three men had experienced in Geneva. To Jack the mountains appeared to be more in reach at Ouchy than they had in Geneva.

The tour party waited around as Allen completed his supervision of the luggage as it was loaded onto trolleys ready to be taken to their next hotel. Set back from the lake Jack and Burgess took in the lavish style of the Hotel Beau Rivage with its timeless Cedar trees seeming to be standing guard.

Eventually, his duty to his guests' belongings completed, Allen motioned for his group to gather around him, but Jack walked instead to where Kari stood. Still disguised as J Croz she had hung back, not being part of the tour group. She was clearly impatient to leave. Jack offered her twenty francs meaning her to use it for where she would stay.

Kari shook her head and said: "Put your money away, you give me enough by providing the cover of needing a guide."

Jack asked: "Have you any money for a room?"

"Of course," Kari said, "You forget what I have in my bag. But seriously I have lived free for the last two years and never touched my pay from the ballet until now. It's not a great amount but will be enough while I am still here. But you will need to pay for the clothes later when they come to the hotel. I will tell the outfitter to bill you."

"Right," said Jack, continuing to offer the twenty Francs. He added: "Take it as payment for being the guide then."

"Don't be ridiculous," said Kari, looking away.

There was silence between them. Jack scratched his cheek, lost how to proceed.

Almost as a second thought Kari asked: "The one you call Stan he will save my brother?"

Jack glanced across the road running in front of the Park Haldimand. He partly turned away to hide his frown. It was a good question and he replied: "If anyone can get Carnot on side Stan will. He wouldn't go unless he thought there was a chance. He'll do his best."

An omnibus stopped just opposite the port. To change the subject Jack pointed towards it and said: "It looks as if there's some transport to the town over there."

"I will walk," said Kari, shouldering her own bag. "Too much sitting around today makes my head anxious." She walked away for a few paces, but then turned back towards him and said: "There is an outfitter I know near the Cathedral in the Old Town. I will go there and get them to send the clothes down to you at the hotel later. Tell me, tomorrow, will you go by boat or train to Vevey?"

"I don't know but I can send you word and about the time," Jack said.

"Good," Kari replied.

Jack had become aware Stan was watching them. He lifted a hand to acknowledge the concern that he saw in the Sergeant's eyes and started to walk back to join his colleagues who were standing amongst the rest of the tour party. Burgess nodded to Jack and stepped back to make room for him.

Jack glanced back, looking for Kari but she had already gone. His eyes scanned the groups and walkers across the road and could see her already blending in with the crowds walking up to the Old Town of Lausanne. He was just in time as Allen started to explain the origins of the park to the group.

Burgess inclined his head towards Jack's ear and whispered: "That woman does not need looking after."

"Her brother clearly thought that she did, given the mess he got himself into," answered Jack.

Burgess caught hold of Jack's arm and the two of them moved a few paces away from the group so as not to be overheard.

"Look Jack, there's a difference between getting her to wake up to the stupid situation she's got herself into and committing crimes to protect her. It's just misguided," Burgess said, quietly.

"But we have a good idea of how Gilbert works. How many of our colleagues in the Metropolitan police are on his list of compliant helpers?"

"The frank answer is we have never found out, but look at her, think about the way she's dressed. That should give you an idea of how used she is to the mountains and surviving.

Now Look up there," Burgess nodded towards the opposite bank of the lake before he continued: "It looks pretty exposed to me, and not the sort of area I'd choose for a quiet Sunday stroll. What does that tell you about her? Frankly, if the three of us and Kari were stranded up in the mountains overnight, she would be the one that would be alive in the morning."

Allen's voice interrupted the frank exchange as he called over: "Now you will find this interesting, Mr Sargent, as will Mr Wheeler."

Allen waved an expansive hand and continued: "An Englishman, a hard worker, and a businessman like yourselves, left the Villa and the Park Haldimand to the public. Now you may ask, how can that be? Well, let me tell you. William Haldimand was MP for Ipswich the son of a merchant and he became a wealthy man. Much of Belgrave Square in London was financed by him. He was a governor of the Bank of England, gave up his career in politics and moved to Lausanne in 1828. He gave £24,000 for a blind asylum in Lausanne, - yes, I did say that much, a fortune by today's standards, never mind years ago. He died here in 1862 and the beautiful gardens you stand in today are thanks to him. Now, ladies and gentlemen, please follow me to your delightful home for the next few nights."

The group moved off behind Allen. Jack was suddenly aware of a particular scent beside him.

"You seem to have acquired a guide, Mr Sargent?" Miss Wheeler had walked quickly away from her parents to reach Jack as the group wended their way around the first of the flower beds. From the perfume that enveloped him Jack imagined she had made good use of the perfume retailers in the new boulevards in Paris. Behind them he glimpsed Mr Wheeler who was supporting his wife.

"Miss Wheeler!" Jack said. it was the first time they had spoken since Paris. His eyes went to her mother. "Is your mother unwell? Do you need our help?"

"Thank-you, most kind of you but Mother does not do well on water. She will be better shortly now she's on firm ground. Isn't it time you called me Lauren?"

"I will if you permit me. And please, call me Jack."

"How did you obtain a guide?" Lauren Wheeler repeated her question, and this time Jack heard a hint of a tone which confirmed to him that she was used to getting her own way. Managing he would have called it in his days on the farm. Jack stared at her in the sunshine. There was barely a trace of the accent left that her parents had and no doubt, in a few years, she would have controlled any hint of the way she had once spoken completely. Like him, she would have worked at blending into whichever class she aspired to be a part of. The tone she had used would be useful with the servants then.

Jack could see his pause was irritating her. He explained: "Forgive me, it was through the hotel in Geneva, for my Uncle Stan. He's a walker and will do his own route tomorrow while we go further along the lake."

"I would love to do that. Do you think we could form a party and join him?" Lauren asked.

Jack controlled his expression imagining Stan's reaction, had he been going on a walk at all, at being joined by Miss Wheeler.

Maintaining the pretence that Kari was a man Jack said: "If your father would accompany you, I see no reason why not. It wouldn't be seemly for you to be alone with two men. Our guide is seeing to clothing and equipment for us as we came unprepared for the cooler weather. Would you need anything? I can send a message to the lad."

Lauren smiled at Jack at the suggestion her father might like to go walking. She said: "Thank-you, no, and shame on you to inflict father on a mountain! The Tullys, who had dinner with your uncles last night, would be interested in a low hill walk and I think they would be more than respectable for my parents to agree to make up a party with me. I would like to get some way up into the hills but have no desire to scale a mountain. A demanding walk for a few hours to blow the incessant journey away would be all I would need. Would your uncle mind?"

Jack could see Stan's reaction had this tale been true. He replied: "Uncle Stan is like a bear with a sore head at times and needs to wander alone really. I'm sure he'd gladly give up the guide to you for tomorrow."

"What is the guide's name?" asked Lauren.

Jack stared back into her eyes, shook his head and replied: "Didn't catch it, sorry. All I know is that he charges six francs a day I'll get a message to the pension where he's staying. I'm sure he'd like the extra work."

"Thank-you," Lauren turned her attention to the hotel as they walked. "What a sumptuous place it is. Mother is already uncomfortable at staying in such a hotel. She never adapted to the fact that Father made money."

"Tell her it doesn't matter here," said Jack. "Allen was explaining the way the Swiss see things and that they don't hear class when someone speaks like in England. It gives me confidence that hard work is respected. There won't just be wealthy English here or nobility but Swiss tourists of any background if they can afford to pay for it. It feels quite freeing."

"Yes," said Lauren, seeing how Jack had come to life. "Your business is doing well?"

"At the moment we're making good progress. Personally, I have my parents to thank for their hard work in what I have," said Jack, truthfully. "I mean to look after it and make it grow if I can."

"Very admirable, Father would commend you for that," said Lauren.

Jack stood back to allow the Wheelers to enter the Beau Rivage together and to escape further attention from Lauren. He wanted time to get his bearings in what seemed to be a palatial mansion awash with chandeliers and staff. Jack took in the other guests moving around the ground floor and gardens, confirming everything Allen had said about the hotel having nobility who cut a style but also tourists in their walking clothes. It gave him an idea for dinner.

527

Allen helped the first-class guests to check in and Jack seized the opportunity to have a word with a member of staff about the telegraph and post office in the hotel. He was directed along the main corridor past sumptuous rooms which he noted were called Salons. He paid 50 centimes postage to send a message to Kari in case she did want the work of leading what Jack assumed would be an unchallenging walk. One line only went to Sam in a telegram:

"Sam. Lausanne. Leaving in two days. Careful."

Jack walked back to the reception along endless corridors expecting to find a queue but only Stan and Burgess were left. The staff had not been willing to give the two men their rooms when they were expecting three on the booking. It was an attention to detail Stan found irritating and he was not in the mood to complete any formalities.

"I'll go into the garden," said Stan, leaving Burgess and Jack to take control of the papers and passports while Jack maintained his wonderful smile for the reception staff. Eventually it worked.

"Right, that's done," said Burgess. "We can go and collect Stan if we can find him and then go up."

"The rooms are at the side of the property so we might have some sort of a view," said Jack. Once away from reception he confided to Burgess: "I've let Sam know we're in Lausanne. There's a post office and a telegraph in the hotel if you wanted to get word to Alice," explained Jack.

"Good, I will. What did Miss Wheeler want?" asked Burgess.

"To escape from the tour, I think," replied Jack. "The couple that Stan helped yesterday are interested in getting away for a walk as well. I've sent a message up to our guide in case the work is wanted."

"Well, it will keep "our guide" out of our hair tomorrow," said Burgess. "Frankly, Jack, we could do with going to Vevey alone. We've made it this far, and that's more than I ever thought we would. We've done well, lad, but I wondered how you wanted to handle the chocolate maker tomorrow."

Jack looked at Burgess and realised that he had not given the matter any thought. "You mean do we tell the truth or make up a story?"

"Well, either way we need to get it straight between us before we go in there."

Jack nodded. He said: "We've recovered what we came for and by rights we should be on our way home. I have wondered what Inspector Hunt would say about us still looking into Gilbert's activities."

"I doubt he'd behave any differently. Ah, there's Stan," said Burgess nodding to a lower area of the garden where Stan had sat to stare at the lake. Sails cut across the view as boats plied their way on the water. Jack stared at the back of Stan's head, wondering how he would deal with the chocolate maker. He had never known the Sergeant from Shadwell to lie. He recalled an old story about a cricketer.

"I think we play it with a straight bat, like John Small did," said Jack.

"And that means?" asked Burgess.

"Well, all I know is he was a true and simple-hearted man, very important in cricket when he lived and a good example, said to be the best batsman up until W.G. Grace. Father used to say he had a sign outside his workshop in Petersfield. All it said was:

"Here lives John Small,

Makes bat and ball,

Pitches a wicket, plays at cricket,

With any man in England."

"And by that are you telling me that we go in and tell the man straight that he's selling poisoned chocolates and is being investigated?" Burgess looked aghast.

Jack nodded: "xactly," he said

It was after luncheon in an overwhelmingly large, decorous restaurant that Jack received a message from reception that parcels had arrived, with a note from J. Croz, his guide. The parcels had already been taken up to his room, but there was a bill to be settled, and he was required at the desk. Jack assumed there would only be a few items. He went to reception and gave his name. The man from the outfitter's stood cap in hand at the side of the desk and came forward as the receptionist called him. The receptionist clearly appreciated that Jack had such a guide.

"A member of the Croz family has signed for the equipment," said the receptionist, "And we have put the parcels in your room. As you have a guide from such a renowned family there will be no need to check the details.

530

The man from the outfitter needs the bill to be settled, that is all."

Jack supressed the irritation which he felt that Kari had clearly chosen an alias which carried notoriety. the last thing he wanted was for the staff to start gossiping. Jack drew breath as he scanned the list. There were a great many items supplied.

The bill was in French and he was none the wiser, except for the sheer quantity and the cost. He reminded himself that it was for three of them and, thoughtfully, looked at the total at the bottom and registered that it came to fifty francs. Jack was momentarily taken aback at trying to work out the exchange rate. It sounded a high amount, but they had given Kari a free hand and now he would have to go through with it and pay.

Jack told the receptionist: "Ask the outfitter's man to wait and then send someone to find Mr. Allen for me."

A member of staff was sent immediately to find the tour guide. Within minutes, Allen was at Jack's side. Jack explained quickly.

"Twenty francs is about sixteen shillings," Allen said, checking his notebook for the details on the exchange. "Fifty then is forty shillings and you can cover this with the hotel using one of the circular notes that you have with you and ask them to settle the cash with the outfitter." Allen looked a little concerned as he ran his eye down the list of items. He said: "Seems very high and a lot of equipment for a stroll."

"Thank-you for your help," said Jack gratefully, "It may be more than we need but we did leave it to the guide, and he does come from a family with a lot of experience judging how well known the name Croz appears to be here. It's done now anyway, so we must pay for it."

"Sounds a lot, Mr Sargent," Allen repeated quietly, "You might be able to return some of it."

Jack took out one of the circular notes from his wallet and handed it to Allen for the hotel to do the exchange with the outfitter. In a desire to close the subject Jack said: "Well, the guide thinks we obviously need it, and there are three of us. Do you have any idea who the Croz family are?"

"None at all, but we should ask as it's clearly a family of repute," suggested Allen.

Jack nodded, deciding not to ask at the desk. He wanted to know why Kari had chosen that name as an alias. A thought struck him about the amount of clothing. He said to Allen: "There's the issue of getting everything home of course, as we deliberately travelled lightly. Perhaps if I go through what's there."

"Now, getting it home is something I can help with. Just a minute while I check the cost of the registration fee from any station to London. Of course, if you are wearing some of it that will reduce the cost." Allen frowned as he flicked through the pages in his notebook until he came to the right part. He said: "Yes, here we are, from Lausanne to London, you're allowed fifty-six pounds in weight of luggage before there's a charge made on top of the registration fee of 4d per package. That's not bad. Then, if its heavier than fifty-six pounds its two shillings for every ten pound in weight extra."

"Amazing, why carry your own luggage?" said Jack.

"Exactly – of course, I shouldn't say this," said Allen dropping his voice, "but you should see the charges for the Wheelers. They're keeping the carriers in tea and cake I can tell you. Alright, Mr Sargent, I can get that organised for you for Monday when you leave. While you're here can I check with you if you had decided if you want to go by steamer to Vevey tomorrow or train?"

"Is there an advantage to either?" asked Jack.

"Not in time as you've to get into the town for the railway but there are five trains a day. The steamer leaves Ouchy in the morning at 10.45 and arrives at Vevey fifty minutes later."

"We'll do the steamer then, and enjoy the lake," said Jack.

"Excellent choice. I'm taking a group up to the Old Town later. Would you be interested?"

Jack nodded and said: "T'would be a disappointment not to see it. Yes, I'll come." He had already decided he would go and find Kari and ask her some questions. The tour would provide him with a reason to be in the Old Town.

Allen nodded and said: "I'll be leaving from the front doors at two o'clock to walk to the omnibus."

"I'll be there," Jack said.

"Excellent, I'll put you down for the tour," said Allen.

As he walked back to the terrace Jack wondered, with some amusement, how Stan would react to the parcel waiting upstairs. He avoided a small dog that shot across his path, distracted by crumbs under a chair. The sun was brilliant now on the lake and not for the first time Jack thought of his beat in

Stepney and how he would feel on his return after experiencing the beauty of Switzerland.

"Everything alright?" asked Burgess, looking up as Jack arrived at the table. Jack pulled out a chair and sat opposite his colleagues.

"Yes, we've quite a parcel upstairs from the outfitters," explained Jack. "I thought we should check it now and make sure items fit us, as it's all been done blind, and then I'm off into the old town as Allen's leading a group up there this afternoon."

"What have we got?" asked Stan.

"The list is in French," said Jack, passing it across to him.

"That's why we need to go and check everything?"

"Exactly," said Jack.

Stan paused at the price and glanced at Jack. The lad should not be paying for this, he thought. Jack nodded in return and shrugged. A cool wind through the open door reminded Stan how he would feel by evening. He stood immediately and nodded to Jack. Burgess chuckled and folded up his paper.

In Jack's room the parcel contained a note, and Jack, guessing it was the answer about leading a guided tour for Miss Wheeler and the Tully's pocketed it in case they were in the group for the Old Town. Overall, he was pleased with the clothes and quickly sized up the attention to detail which Kari had shown as he turned over the shirts, socks, and waistcoats and three containers with soap, slippers, and a sponge. He tried on one of the "Wide Awake" hats made of felt, with one side pinned to the crown, and placed a light courier bag across his torso. He stared in the mirror and appreciated the change it made to how he looked.

The three Alpenstock met with Stan's approval. He turned one over in his hands, looking at the strength of the wooden pole and the spike at the bottom.

Burgess picked up a bag and said: "The bags are large enough to take one change of clothing, but light enough not to hinder us walking."

Jack nodded as he could see they would come in handy for the journey home.

Burgess pulled out a compass, and a box stamped Casella's, Hatton Garden.

"What's this?" asked Stan as Burgess passed him the box. He read out: "Hypsometrical Apparatus and thermometer, English made, which is interesting as it's been acquired here. And a packet of tea. Any ideas?"

"Perhaps it will warm the tea?" suggested Jack.

"Good thought, there's also a tin of preserved meat, three cakes of chocolate and some biscuits," Burgess passed the items to Jack and Stan to look over.

"Useful on a journey," said Stan, "All this looks a good quality and will see us through. Pass me one of those waistcoats will you Jack. And I'll try that jacket on. It looks about my size. Wool would you say? I might as well get warm."

"Looks worth what's been spent then," said Jack. "I'll get off and meet up with the tour."

*

The fine-looking Cathedral, Jack heard Allen say, was reputed to be the best in Switzerland. They had climbed from the market to the Cathedral's terrace but from its exterior Jack wondered why they had come. He looked at the tower, which was not fully completed, and the main door which was very simple. But as he entered with the group they were met with grandeur. After seeing the thousand columns which supported the vaults Jack took in tombs of a Pope and others of Bishops, foreign Princes and Counts, plus a defender of liberty who had been beheaded by the Bernese Government in 1723. Jack noted that the Swiss had had their moments.

As Allen announced that the group would go on towards the Museum for fine paintings, Jack decided to take the opportunity to slip away. He passed the note from Kari about acting as guide to The Tully's and had a quiet word with Allen, explaining that he intended to walk and would return to the Hotel in his own time.

Jack found he was in luck as he approached a trader in the market and asked for the Rue de la Caroline. The man had what looked like a week's growth of beard. He pointed away from the Cathedral followed a with a wave of the hand towards narrow streets. Jack walked through several winding streets laid out in a haphazard fashion which reminded him of the City of London. One main difference was how spotless they appeared. Street by street he repeated his request for directions in his simple French, quite proud that he was understood and found the Pension P Chevalier part way down the Rue de la Caroline as a shower started.

The door of the Pension was open when he arrived, and he could see in the hall a woman of indistinct age sitting in the shadows with a bowl on her lap peeling vegetables. She stared at Jack and muttered something that did not sound anything like the French he had heard.

"M'sieur Croz?" Jack asked, pronouncing the name like the bird.

The woman shook her head until Jack showed her the name at the bottom of the note Kari had sent with the clothes.

"Cruser," the woman said, with a laugh. She lifted the curtain behind her and shouted. From behind the curtain a small boy appeared and stood waiting.

"Cruser," she shouted at him.

The boy ran up the stairs, and Jack could hear his steps along the floor above and then a knocking on a door. Jack thought over the best way to play his suspicions about Kari.

The woman smiled at Jack and carried on attacking the vegetables in her bowl with an old, sharp knife. He nodded to her in response and moved to the doorway to escape the smell of onion. Outside the sun had broken through the clouds and the air had developed a little warmth. But the place was a far cry from the Beau Rivage.

Then footsteps moved along the floor above and Kari followed the boy down the stairs. She was still dressed as J. Croz and she nodded to the woman, who said something unintelligible in response to her. Kari smiled and nodded and joined Jack on the doorstep.

"So," said Kari. "Are you pleased with what I ordered for you?"

Jack smiled. "We've never been so well kitted out."

"Good," said Kari.

"One gadget is a bit of a mystery, but we'll get to grips with it." Jack frowned and dropped his voice: "Are you alright here?"

"Oh yes," said Kari. "Don't worry about that woman, she's the owner's mother and never moves from her chair from early morning until they call her for dinner at five. Think of her as a watch dog if you like. The place is simple and clean, and I am fine here.'

"P. Chevalier is the owner, is he?" asked Jack.

"No," Kari smiled. Jack felt a blush begin as she looked him over.

Kari said: "The Swiss tend to call places after people who fought for their liberty from the Dukes of Savoy. Like your famous general who fought against Napolean, Waterloo."

"That's a place of battle, not a person," explained Jack. "It would be Wellington if it was the person."

"I see. Shall we risk the showers? I don't think any rain will last and it is better we talk about why you have come this afternoon away from here."

Jack glanced down the street as there was a crowd moving towards them. He scanned the faces and thought twice about moving into them. To his concern Kari stepped round him out onto the cobbles and she had moved through the first few people before Jack could try and stop her. Despite Burgess's advice that Jack did not need to look after her Jack used the bulk of his shoulders to push his way past a man sporting a cut lip. The man stumbled into a ditch and Jack moved to Kari's side. She acknowledged him with a nod as the man let out an expletive behind them. Jack kept his head down and he and Kari walked against the crowd in silence. Slowly, the numbers began to thin out, and Kari pointed ahead towards a piece of parkland.

Jack looked behind them and said: "That group could mean trouble."

Kari shook her head and explained: "They belong to the International Worker's movement. They're German speaking Swiss workers who have come in from Grutli. Wider interest in membership has largely faded in the last few years, so they pose no threat."

"How do you know that?" asked Jack.

"Two of them are staying in the Pension," answered Kari.

Jack still thought they looked dubious and he glanced towards the back of the crowd which was moving quickly away up the street. Kari followed the line of his stare.

"It's just different here," she said. "When they've had uprisings, the aftermath has been different than most places because they build communities from the bottom up out of free associations." Kari smirked and added: "They also exported most of their soldiers into foreign parts. The King of Naples made good use of them I can tell you. Maybe, if such a large number had not gone into foreign service, they would have been storming the gates here. But it did not happen. Gilbert always said the Swiss were bottom heavy and that change was slow. A joke he made after I first arrived here was that if the end of the world happened it would be two days late around Luzern."

Jack smiled at the joke.

Kari continued: "Now they will have referenda on everything after the vote this year, which will slow things down even more. Come we can get in here and sit for a while."

"But this looks like a private estate," said Jack.

"It is a very large one and we are close to the fence. Come, it will be alright." Kari slipped through and sat on a large boulder out of sight of the street. Jack looked around first before he followed her.

"How did you know about this place?" asked Jack.

"I've been to Lausanne many times," replied Kari.

"Have you met many Swiss people then?" asked Jack.

"No, only people in the shops or hotels. Gilbert only had the English guests, mainly climbers and sometimes French, the ones who would be impressed with an international ballet dancer. There isn't any ballet here, you know. But that was in the early days when he thought I would have his child."

Jack stared at her, incredulity in his eyes.

"What?" Kari asked, defiantly.

"Kari … You were building an international name in dancing! What made you sit in that man's home, accepting the kind of attentions? …." Jack stopped, suddenly embarrassed at what he wanted to say.

"And why do you think I would not? You misjudge me if you think I am the sort of woman that will sit at home and wait to marry the woodsman or the carpenter. I am not your English spinster accepting calling cards. There are reasons I can perform as I do." Kari had stood while she spoke. She continued: "We climbed with our parents as Torg and I grew up. Father made skis and taught us to use the mountains, so we were not afraid or stranded. We climbed and used the ski as do all our people. When our parents died, we carried on with normal life and Torg kept the business going. Slowly people sought him out to lead visiting groups. I went too but struggling up mountains in a skirt and hob nail boots because it was expected of me, instead of wearing trousers."

"Kari I'm sorry," Jack said.

She looked surprised at the apology: "Why? But I should remember that you are a creature of your country and have expectations of how a woman should behave. And I should not forget that you are a policeman. You ask me why I accepted Gilbert's attentions. He is capable of great charm, knows how to behave in company, and was very generous at first. To embarrass you even more there was passion on both sides, but for a while I let him run after me and kiss me without giving anything in return. And when he asked me to marry him, I accepted and thought it would happen quickly. Yes, I let him in my bed, but I was unable to get him to fulfil his promise. I would not prove I was fertile, you see." She smiled sadly.

Jack looked at her almost in disbelief that she was being so honest.

"Kari!" he said again. "You don't have to go into all this. I apologise, I was rude. It's none of my concern. My part in all this is really over and I'm not ordered to do anything other than retrieve the diamonds."

But Kari carried on: "And yet you want to find the poisoner. You want to get evidence on Gilbert. If you were only interested in obeying your orders you would have gone as soon as Torg gave you the bracelet. No, Jack, like me you want to destroy the world that Gilbert has built and take the power he has away. You see, I have spent so much time waiting, and all I had to do was to be with child. I stupidly thought he would marry me first and let me fulfil my contract for a few more years. Then we could have had the child. But as time went on, I started to realise the sort of man I was with. He was not the honourable gentleman that he portrayed. I overheard things, saw people coming and going that did not fit with the life he was hiding in. I started to with-draw but then he would be attentive and kind, but it was only to convince me to have the child. I should have run back to Stockholm. Then this year I had the offer to work with Edvard Grieg on a new work using folk music sources. You've heard of him?"

"No, I'm afraid not. I'm not very cultured," said Jack. "Could you still go and do it?"

"Perhaps, I don't know now. It was because of how we had used the Norwegian folk dances in the ballet. I've waited too long, I think. You must believe me that with Torg I did not know what Gilbert had got him to do. Torg did those jobs for Gilbert and he would be the attentive lover again for a while, but it was just manipulation. Torg was in too deep when I found out what he was doing. Because I shut Gilbert out completely when I

542

found out, he told me Torg would rot in prison. Then he took up with Helly, who was a more cooperative partner and *so* grateful for the attention." Kari's face darkened.

She looked very small suddenly to Jack. He could understand why a brother would have tried to protect her. But at the same time, he thought, what an infuriating pair the brother and sister were. Jack asked himself why on earth hadn't they cut and run a long time before now.

Jack said: "Kari ... you couldn't have known at first that there were suspicions about Gilbert, despite the family he comes from he is not welcome among them I hear." Jack paused aware that Kari was lost in thought. She moved away slightly, over to where a boulder had a hollow groove. Kari sat down in it and stared across the lake.

Jack followed her gaze and changed the subject. He asked: "Did you really climb mountains?"

"Did? I do, yes," Kari gave him an assessing look. "Many women do. The best, I think is an English woman, Lucy Walker who you may have heard of."

Jack shook his head. "No, sorry, I haven't come across her."

"No? Her success was in your magazine Punch. She climbed the Matterhorn three years ago with her father and their guide and several other mountaineers."

"I don't know about it," said Jack. "Three years ago, I was a labourer on a farm. I didn't know Punch existed then and until I came here, I had no idea that land could be so high."

"The Matterhorn is over fourteen thousand feet high. Lucy beat an American woman climber by days, determined to be the first woman, I think."

"Did she? Dressed like you are now?" asked Jack.

"No, she wore a dress and hobnail boots." Kari laughed and glanced at Jack. Still smiling she said: "She invites no criticism, unlike me. Lucy looks the immaculate English woman, nothing challenging to the men and yet she has seen so much more from a rocky crag than most men will ever know. Perhaps that is why she is accepted because she follows the social conventions and quietly gets on with climbing. When she is finished, she returns to Liverpool and plays croquet. I have already burned my boats, as you say, and don't care how I am seen anymore. It is far better not to climb in a skirt."

"Yes, I bet! But I couldn't climb that high. A nice afternoon walk, up a gentle slope on the Downs, or a sail and a spot of fishing off Fairlight and I'm happy." said Jack.

"You would not say that if you tried it," said Kari.

"It must take a lot of courage. Have you climbed that mountain, the Matterhorn?" asked Jack.

"Not yet all the way. Torg and I went up with Aloys Pöllinger a man who had been up the Matterhorn more than twenty times when we went with him. We got as far as the hut on the Swiss side and spent the night there ready for the following morning climb, but the weather was so bad we could not go on and we had to go down again. He told me I was one of a few ladies who had got that far. One day perhaps I can show you such an adventurous route near the Jungfrau." The light was back in Kari's eyes.

Jack was glad to see the change from despair. He grinned, shook his head, and said: "No, thanks, I'll stay down here and look at the mountains."

Kari caught his hand in hers. She meant it as encouragement in her excitement, trying to get across to him the wonder that she believed he would feel. "Jack, if you would only go up even a thousand feet on a well-established path … It is bliss to dangle your legs over a precipice and look down through the mist over the villages below. I am grateful I did not miss doing it, the three of us roped together, Pöllinger, Torg and I." She laughed, oblivious of the effect she was having as she held his hand. "You know the only advantage of wearing a skirt is that on the snow slopes women make a sledge of their petticoats and they get down in five minutes."

Jack joined in the laughter, seeing nothing except the animated woman before him. Jack realised he was seeing the woman she had been. Probably Gilbert had been in love with her, he thought. It would be easy to be and he half felt he was in love with her too. How lovely she was as she talked. Jack smiled back briefly, then looked away across the lake to the mountains opposite, aware that he had glimpsed the passion there could be. It disturbed him and he knew he would never be able to look at the mountains again without the memory of wondering how he and Kari would be together.

Pushing such thoughts away Jack dropped the hand which had sent a shock to his being. He hung on to the suspicions

545

that had brought him to find her that afternoon. Kari had said he was a creature of his country, with expectations of how a woman should behave. Well, so he was but he had no issue with a woman excelling. He hoped he would let a woman be an equal. He thought of Ann Black and knew he had no delusions about a woman doing intellectual work, practising as a doctor, or scaling a mountain in a pair of pants like Kari, for that matter. And then there had been Harriet with all her ambition. He had loved that about her despite her putting her dreams before him. Kari had also said that he was a policeman. And that he was, and he had no doubt that a woman, or a man, was the same when it came to cunning, deception, or murder.

Jack looked back at her and asked: "Why have you stayed instead of going back to Norway with your brother?"

"So, you think that is where he will go? Why do you think that?"

"Its home isn't it?" asked Jack.

"Its poverty," Kari answered. The mood was broken, and Jack felt regret as he watched the girl she had been die before him.

"Anyway, there is more to do yet. He will hope to get some work guiding when the English come out. Then we will see where I go," explained Kari.

"They pay the guides well, do they?" asked Jack.

"Well known guides, yes," said Kari, "especially the Englishmen.

"Is that why you've taken that name, Croz? The hotel told me it was a famous family of guides. Why is it a name the English climbers would know?"

"It is like putting up an advertisement," explained Kari. "The name would say everything about skill. M. Croz was a guide known to the Alpine Club and he was the guide on that dreadful day at Mont Cervin in '65 with Lord Douglas. J. Croz does exist but I hope people won't enquire too much. They are a large family, and many bare the name Johanne. This is the first year that women are being admitted to the Alpine Club, you know. Look, Jack I know I am good. If I and Torg can earn for a few guided climbs it will help."

So, she had lied about Torg leaving.

"Is everything you have then in that box of jewellery?" asked Jack.

The sadness descended over her face again. Kari explained: "More or less, but also to give Torg a start. I can't go back to Stockholm as I'd hoped as that will be the first place Gilbert will look. If he gets hold of me again it will be to kill me as I know too much. That danger will keep Torg here and I cannot have that."

Jack frowned. That explanation contradicted her actions in staying but Jack played along. He said: "I understand that. But the name Croz will attract some attention by the sound of it, especially from the Alpine club members who come out here. And from what you've said those toffs who belong to that club tend to stay with Gilbert when they're in Geneva. The name you're going by is going to come up, isn't it, in a casual

547

conversation over dinner. Is that the real reason you've picked it?" Jack paused, waiting for her response but Kari looked away. The silence between them went on for several minutes until Kari took a flask from an inner pocket of her jacket and sipped from it. She held it out to Jack.

She said: "This is a delicious milk."

"No thanks," said Jack.

Silence descended again. Jack waited but Kari did not engage with him at all. The resolve on her face was as immoveable as the mountains opposite. Decisively, he stood and moved in front of her line of gaze. He had to ask the question.

Kari looked up in surprise with the movement and their eyes met. Jack sat down opposite her on a fallen tree trunk but neither of them spoke. He watched the look in her eyes harden as she read his face, until she turned her head away and stared down towards the lake.

Jack swallowed and started his mind games again. He said: "So, getting away from Gilbert sounded like your main aim when I met you in the park in Geneva, and that way Torg would also leave. Now your brother's gone from Geneva, but he's remained in Switzerland hasn't he? You've changed your plan. You're both still in Switzerland aren't you? I reckon, both are disguised as members of a skilled family of guides whose reputation is known to the English Climbers. Deliberately seeking attention, it seems, and bound to attract Gilbert's attention. Why, I wonder? For which areas are you both going to make yourselves available for a climb?"

Kari's eyes flashed at him, and then she looked back to the lake. But the expression in the eyes had confirmed his suspicions. He controlled the disappointment he felt hoping that his face was impassive. Jack turned away from her and walked for a few feet to lean against one of the ancient trees. Once more he followed Kari's line of sight towards the fine views of small pieces of farmland and terraces of vines. Across the lake the slopes of the mountains were in shade at that time of the day and the greenery was dark and glowering. Several villages were scattered at various points up the slopes and Jack found himself wondering how anyone could live in such remote places.

Jack had no need of an explanation any longer having seen that look in her eyes. Kari had asked their help with Carnot to get Torg off the hook. Of course, it was important but there was a bigger picture than that keeping her in Switzerland and he now had a strong sense that there was more to why she and Torg had remained in the country. She was ready to hand over her gifts of jewellery, and the extra items that she had taken from her rival Helly to get charges dropped but Jack felt there was more to it. He glanced around as if expecting to see Torg duck behind a tree. There was no one visible but Jack believed he was near.

Stan would do his bit in the morning by seeing Carnot. If he succeeded the French police would do the deal with the art dealer and the painting would be back in the Louvre before you could blink. Gilbert would get the value of all the jewellery back as well – jewellery he had commissioned to be stolen -

but it would show him up as having received a stolen painting. The whole thing almost made Jack want to laugh. But that was not the whole picture. Behind Kari's determined eyes that stared across the lake to the mountains beyond were deeper intentions.

Jack thought further about his and Stans impending departure on Monday. There was so little time. They needed the transaction with the jewellery to be completed before they left. That way Kari had a clear field to get away, as Torg would be safe. If she did not leave, he would take it as confirmation that she had a fatal plan. Like Stan Jack had no intention of taking the hoard off Kari. No, there had to be a way of getting the jewellery valued by a bank and turned into a transaction which would give Carnot a monetary value to offer the art dealer. Then and only then, when there was a backer to change the jewels to money, would all parties be satisfied and Torg would be off the hook for the rest of his life. That could be done quite cleanly, but it did not solve his other suspicions about what Kari and Torg were up to.

Jack thought back over the conversation they had had on the boat. Kari had said Torg had gone up into the Jura from Geneva and was probably going to stay around the areas where guides would be needed before making his way across France. She had implied it would be paid work. But for all he knew Kari could have taken much more of worth in jewellery, or even money, from whatever cash or gold that Gilbert had in the house. He thought of the bag of jewellery Stan had seen. There was every reason to assume that there was more.

Jack was sure that Kari's story of Torg doing some work as a guide through the summer was a red herring. He suspected there was a time frame of a matter of days before Torg had to be in a certain place. Perhaps he would present himself as a guide there? Then a thought struck him.

Kari had carried on staring at the lake while Jack was lost in thought. He could see his questions had hit home. Well so be it, she should know he had worked out she was up to something. It all had a smell to it.

Jack said: "I gave your note to the Tully's. They're happy with the route for the walk tomorrow that you've suggested and the rate of six francs. A Miss Wheeler will be with them. We're travelling on the boat which leaves at 10.45 in the morning. It's the only one, I gather, to Vevey. We can wait for you, if you'd like us to, at Ouchy, and I can introduce you to your tour party."

Kari nodded but her eyes did not leave the water.

Jack waited, watching the face for any hint of expression but there was no further response from Kari.

"I'll bid you a good evening, then," said Jack. Again, a brief nod. Kari did not speak. The cloud had descended and hidden the sun he had witnessed earlier in more ways than one.

Quietly, Jack turned away, wondering as he walked where Kari had gone to in her head. He slipped back through the fence and looked up and down the street before he started the walk down to Ouchy. The complete and utter sense of flatness that he felt at being right had overtaken him. It was a shocking thing to realise that he was too late. Her intentions were fixed regardless of the outcome and he could not imagine that she really stood much of a chance of survival.

Jack found his own naivety disgraceful. He had missed one clear outcome and as he walked the pieces of the puzzle slipped into place.

"What is it they say about the road to hell being paved with good intentions?" he said aloud to himself. No-one else was in the street. He had walked down to an area with a sign which read: "Beausejour."

The views opened-up of the lake but it held no fascination for him any longer. He wandered into endless irregular streets, narrow and winding, but having the main thing in common: they were clean.

Finally, he had descended enough to reach the lakeside. There Jack sat on a wall and stared at the mountains opposite, distracted by the shock that he had accepted there was nothing he could do to prevent death. He just did not know whose death.

Attached to these thoughts was the certainty that Torg would never arrive in Norway and that Kati would again dance. Why else would a young and strong climber, able to turn his hand to carpentry with an already established reputation in his home territory, take all the savings and wealth his sister had accumulated? No, Jack had pushed the thought away but the more he tried the more he was convinced that Torg and Kari would travel from these mountains to a seaport.

Kari's story was a red herring.

Twenty

It was half past seven and Stan had a walk to do up to the railway station to catch the train into Geneva. Admittedly there were seven running that day which took the pressure off a little, but as he had no idea how long it was going to take to find Carnot once he arrived in Geneva Stan wanted to make an early start. Jack had remembered that the area Carnot had said he was staying in was called St Gervais. It was the beginning of a heavy day for Stan and he confessed only to himself that his mind was not at peace.

A walk with some exertion would help him fight the sense of agitation he felt, partly due to lost sleep but also because of the conversation with Jack the evening before. Alarm bells had started to sound in his head. He had reasoned through his suspicions but, try as he might, he kept coming back to the same conclusion. At the station in Lausanne Stan turned first into the telegram office. He could have used the one in the hotel, but he did not want Jack or Burgess to know he was sending two telegrams: one to Harry Franks and the other to his wife.

Harry's telegram would go to the Masons Arms on the Commercial Road. Even if someone opened it the staff would not know the names that Stan wrote down. The telegram consisted of four words. While not damaging, two names would bring the wrath of those in power down on the individuals identified. Stan hoped he was wrong but the hairs on the back of his neck could always be relied upon and they were bristling.

And our Jack, thought Stan, before he dealt with the second telegram. He was always unpredictable where a woman was concerned. Stan would back the young constable in any fight but where the young man's emotions were engaged the lad was frankly skittish.

Jack had confessed at dinner to having met Kari in the Old Town. Stan knew he had shown alarm in his eyes as Jack had caught him unawares. Jack had been apologetic for going alone. Then he had apologised for going at all when it was clear from Stan's expression that the Sergeant was not at all satisfied.

Stan had given the young man an earwigging which Jack had not bargained for and Stan was ready to acknowledge that he had been overly strong. Jack had tried to discuss things further over dinner, but each time Stan had cut him short. There was to be absolutely no possibility that Jack would repeat a visit to Kari. He would agree to not being alone with her in future. Yes, Stan had acknowledged that Jack had done well in working out what she was up to but, no, they were not going anywhere near Jack's suspicions of what that might be.

Having lost his appetite due to Jack's shenanigans Stan had pushed his half-eaten dinner away from him. There had been a stiffness evident in Jack's posture despite a compliant, "Yes Sir," and Stan had launched in sharply.

"What are our orders?" Stan had hissed, having leant forward towards the middle of the table to avoid neighbouring groups at dinner overhearing. He had fixed Jack with an unblinking stare, receiving one in return. Stan had been aware that Burgess was looking from him to Jack in surprise.

"I know what our orders are Stan," Jack had replied, equally quietly.

"Have we fulfilled our orders?" Stan had asked.

"Yes, but …." Jack had not got to finish his point before Stan butted in dropping his voice to a hushed whisper.

"There is no but. Have we fulfilled our main purpose?"

"Yes," Jack had replied under his breath.

"Yes, what?" Stan had snapped out.

Jack had coloured and his eyes went to the tables on either side of theirs to ensure no-one was listening.

"Yes, Sergeant," he whispered back to his superior officer.

"Overcoming *ridiculous* odds," Stan had almost spat the words back at Jack.

Jack had also leant forward. Anyone watching them would have thought the two men were disagreeing about confidential business, but the closeness had almost been a challenge. Stan had known that, and he reflected on it now. But Jack had been the one to sit back as they had faced each other. Yes, the constable and the sergeant had realised they could fight.

Stan mused on the situation between them last night. He would have had to see it through if Jack had not backed off. Part of him wondered who would have won had they have come to a scrap. A hint of a smile came to Stan as he was not convinced it would have been him. Even with damaged ribs Jack had fists the size of plates of meat. It would have meant the end of Jack's career in the Met, of course, and Stan would have been sorry if that happened.

There had been silence for a matter of minutes only and then Jack's tone had become more controlled as he had said: "I agree it's beyond belief where we've got to. But wouldn't we normally warn someone?"

"Who?" Burgess had asked unable to help himself, incredulity written large across his face. He had continued: "Who is it you want to warn? You can't mean ..." Burgess had just stopped himself from saying Gilbert's name. "Have you any idea of the danger you would be bringing down on our heads if that man got even an inkling of our being in the trade that we're in?"

Burgess had been angry and given his past who could blame him. Stan had turned in his chair slightly towards Burgess. The movement had had the desired effect. Burgess had glanced at Stan, held up a hand and nodded acceptance that the issue was in the Sergeant's hands.

"I repeat," Stan had continued so quietly that Jack had to concentrate to catch the words. "I repeat, we have some success, which is not going to be eclipsed by doing anything which we might regret, or which is going to put any one of us in danger. We leave in two days and we go home having carried out what we were supposed to do. There is no failure here and that counts for something. Frankly, when we started on this, I had serious doubts we'd get further than Southampton."

Stan had exhaled. It was a habit of his through partially closed lips when under pressure.

It was a warning sign well known to those Stan worked with.

There had been a natural pause while he had watched Jack.

Burgess had continued to look from Stan to Jack, waiting for one of them to commit a fatal error, but neither Sergeant Stan nor Constable Jack had moved.

In the end Stan had straightened up pressing his shoulders into the dining chair so that the arch in his back was extreme. A distraction from the anger he felt the discomfort from the chair had helped bring him through his mood.

Jack had seen this before with Stan and he had reached for the menu card on the table to try and move the situation on.

Stan too had made the effort required and had managed a relatively normal tone as he said: "Now then, young Jack, what's for pudding tonight?"

"I think here you mean dessert," Burgess had said. He and Stan had carried on talking and laughing until a waiter had arrived with the dessert trolley. Jack, however, had remained quiet and refused when offered a choice from the array of delights before them. He had felt beaten down by the exchange with Burgess and Stan over dinner and excused himself early to go to bed.

Now, as the sun streaked the sky, Stan walked to the station and knew he had gone in hard on Jack last night. Jack had still been sore at breakfast and unusually quiet for him. Stan had decided there was nothing to do but ignore it.

Overnight he had thought a great deal about Jack's whole idea of letting Gilbert know his life was in danger. He had still dwelt upon it when dawn's patterns daubed the sky.

Reflecting now on the whole operation Stan had a real sense of success in what they had accomplished and still pinched himself to check they were alive. He knew that they would not be forgotten by a grateful administration or their monarch. It would all go quiet of course but their names would be known, along with that of Tom Hunt's. It was true he did not care about the acclaim, but his cynical side also knew now was the time to apply for promotion.

But Sergeant Stan Green was not that sort of man.

The achievement was almost tangible in having travelled so far and succeeded in getting the Shah's diamonds back. But Jack's high intentions of warning Gilbert of potential foul play was almost laughable, and it filled Stan with foreboding as well. He had spent the small hours analysing his own intentions and could not get Jack's reasoning out of his head. Stan knew that, personally, he did not give a toss if someone finished Gilbert off. But there were better reasons not to follow Jack's best motives. Apart from the fact that they would not stand a chance if he and Jack presented themselves as Metropolitan Policeman to the head of a crime group there was the issue of who they were linked with in Camberwell and Stepney. Gilbert's tentacles would reach far.

Another issue was the effect on Kari's safety. Stan knew that if Gilbert got any inkling of Kari's presence still in Switzerland she would be hunted down like a dog.

As the daybreak had outlined the shadows of the tree-filled garden at the hotel Stan had reconciled himself that they were not culpable if something happened to Gilbert. They could do very little to stop it given the furrow Gilbert had ploughed in his life. Chances were, it would be somebody else if not Kari. Personally, he could not believe that slip of a woman could reap much havoc. No, the main thing was to see the tasks of the day through and leave safely on Monday. Stan had seen enough of the world in the last few weeks to last him for life and just wanted to walk through his own garden gate and gather his family into his arms.

Glancing at the station clock Stan brought his attention to bear on a second telegram which would go to his wife. He pictured her face as it arrived at the front door. She would hesitate at first, fearful of bad news and then rip it open. He deleted a few of the words to keep the cost down but said to go to her mothers with the children for a few days and he would join them once he landed at Dover on Tuesday night. Go immediately he had said. Stan knew he could report to Harry by telegram on his arrival and request that Harry let him know it was safe to come back to Stepney. He knew Harry would understand why.

With a sense of having things under control Stan boarded the train to Geneva Cornavin and once settled in a seat soon put his head back to doze.

*

Stan sat in the Café on the small square purposely having selected a table opposite a clock tower and the bridge across the Rhone. He had been there for almost an hour.

559

Now the waiter would no longer be deflected, and a menu was firmly placed before Stan. It was the area called "L'Ile," and he had asked for directions at the station.

It was true the area was built up and there was little to be seen of the lake, but Stan could think of worse areas to stay in. In front of him the Rhone was a fast-flowing river, and it provided a focus for more than just him as a patron of the café. Stan had selected his position carefully facing the bridge. It was overlooked by the tall buildings on each side and gave anyone leaving one of the buildings or crossing the bridge a clear sight. If Carnot was still in the area, he could not miss Stan. It was a gamble that the Frenchman would come out at all but without an exact address it seemed all Stan could do.

He drew a picture of the clock tower on the back of the menu, meaning to take it for a keepsake to show the children. It looked very old and different to what the children would see in London. He copied down the words on the side of the building facing him:

"Fabrique et Horlogerie
Vacheron Constantin

The dials showed three different times and Stan beckoned a waiter over and showed him his own pocket watch. Shrugging Stan held out the watch to the man pointing at the three clocks.

"Paris, Berne, Genève," the waiter said impatiently, pointing in turn to each of the three clocks.

"I see, different times then in each place?" asked Stan.

"Quoi?" said the waiter, screwing up his face.

"Not to worry, mate. I get it," said Stan.

The area seemed busy and far from being a back water as he had expected. Stan thought that he must be in the centre of Geneva as people went about their business. He realised his mission may be a complete waste of time. But why be hungry and thirsty, he thought to himself. He pointed at the menu.

"Café crème?" asked the waiter.

"I don't know," answered Stan.

"Non, Café Mélange," the waiter decided looking Stan over. He added "Complet?"

 Stan shrugged and replied: "Whatever you said," and waited to see what arrived. The waiter returned with a bowl of whipped cream, a black coffee and a plate of bread, jam, and cheese.

Stan smiled and said: "That looks about right."

The waiter gave a false smile and walked back inside. Stan decided that he would enjoy the coffee, eat what was before him, and then make some enquiries in a small Tabac nearby.

From his left a voice said: "Sergeant Green, as it is a long walk from Ouchy for you to come to this ancient crossroad, I assume that you seek assistance from the Sûreté, ou peut-être, just want the pleasure of my company."

Stan stood, delighted that his effort had paid off. He extended a hand to Carnot, which the Frenchman grasped with enthusiasm as he saw the genuine response from Stan. Carnot's eyes showed the interest he felt at the unexpected visit but before he quizzed Stan he spoke quietly to a waiter. Then he took the chair opposite Stan.

"You are a patient man, I had a little gamble with myself how long you would wait," said Carnot.

"Long enough to enjoy this food," replied Stan. "Jack told me you'd been a soldier."

Carnot nodded and said: "Bien sûr, it ended after the Prussian war … I'd had enough of the legacy Napoleon left to carry on as a soldier."

"I suppose you had little choice but to fight when the country was invaded but your politicians caused your country quite a few problems with Prussia," said Stan.

"I do not think the Prussians had clean hands in the whole thing in 1870, Sergeant. Our leaders were too stupid not to see it," said Carnot. He added: "But there is too much history from Napoleon for it not to surface. He still causes a dilemma for France despite saving the revolution. However, there were atrocities committed in the 1870 war that will not be forgotten. And you? What have you been in your life?"

Stan shook his head. "I joined the police as a young man, I've had twenty years' service now."

"And yet, you are still only a Sergeant? How does this work? You have survived. Do you have a family?" asked Carnot.

"I do. As to still being "only" a Sergeant it's more by choice," replied Stan. "It's about who I work with for me."

Carnot nodded, giving Stan a sideways look. He said: "Yes I see this. But you are le Chef of the investigation here, I think."

The waiter brought Carnot's order before Stan could reply. The man set the food in the centre placing a small black coffee by Carnot's elbow. Carnot offered both hands to Stan inviting him to share the food, but Stan held up a hand and shook his head.

"Thank-you, but no, I had breakfast and I've just had a few bites of bread and cheese. You carry on though," said Stan. He watched the Frenchman layer the cheese and meat onto his plate, then Carnot broke the bread and started to eat.

Stan continued: "As to the investigation it's true I'm the senior officer here but I'm not in charge. There's an Inspector in London we report to. The third man in our party is a former policeman, now retired but he assists us." Stan changed the subject: "The war you've just had, where did you end up?"

Carnot sniffed. "Paris, of course, being starved into submission. "Siège Cuisine" we called it as we ate anything, cats, rats and dogs and even stewed elephant trunk. People wrote recipes - That time has gone into history, but it was the poor who suffered the most. Four months we held out."

"Makes a mark on a man, that sort of experience," said Stan.

"I know, and there is chagrin."

"What do you mean?" asked Stan.

"The effect on the mind, it will take many years, for some they will never be clear of it. One thing is that it will not be forgotten," said Carnot, grimly adding: "Neither will the taking of hostages."

Stan nodded. He could see it in the eyes.

"But you have not come here to talk about the 1871 surrender of Paris," said Carnot. "Do you know where Torg is?"

"No," said Stan, truthfully. "But I do know you're wasting your time staying in Geneva. He's gone. Look, you're aware of his sister, aren't you?"

"Of course," said Carnot. "It was I who told your constable Jack about her. Anyway, she attracts the attention and is not to be missed. I hope she left as well?"

"No, she's still around and wants to make a deal with the French authorities for her brother." Stan leant forward, but Carnot frowned at the idea.

"I can be of little help," Carnot said as he realigned his fork with the knife. "I do not hold the cards to make deals."

Stan watched the accuracy of the movement before he continued: "Hear me out before you dismiss the idea. I think it makes sense from your angle, otherwise I wouldn't have come. Torg's sister Kari has come up with an idea to provide the French authorities with enough funds to buy the painting from the art dealer in Florence. Then the idea is to return it to the Louvre and implicate Gilbert as he received stolen property in the first place and is the one selling it."

"Que diable?" Carnot said softly. "What do you say? What funds are these?"

Stan saw the interest in the eyes. He explained: "She's got a bag of jewellery, some given to her during the relationship, and the rest she's swiped before she left. Most of it has probably been stolen and reset in pieces for Gilbert to dispose of as he pleases. Obviously, she's in hiding but Gilbert will think she's gone with her brother. Any man would think that under normal circumstances, but she's quite a different sort of female."

Carnot sat back in his chair and stared at Stan. Then he laughed. He said: "You know she has this jewellery?"

"Yes, I've seen it as she tried to give it to me for safe keeping. I wasn't having that." Stan stopped as the waiter had appeared at his side for payment.

Carnot nodded and continued to stare at Stan. Then he held up a hand to stop the waiter and asked Stan: "Cognac?"

Stan looked dubious at first but realised this suggestion could mean Carnot was coming round to his idea. After a slight hesitation as he glanced at the clock, Stan nodded and said: "Bit early, but if it seals your agreement, I'm game."

"Of course, we have no idea if she has enough to buy the painting from the dealer," said Carnot.

"I suspect she already knows what Gilbert wants for the painting and has made sure she has enough. She's no fool. What are the dealers asking?"

"All I know is the seller, how do you say this, "a baissé" his price." Carnot pushed down with a hand.

"Lowered," said Stan. "Wants a quick sale and to get Torg arrested, so he's asking a low price. It's not the painting that's the objective. Things haven't worked out for Gilbert with the woman and his angle seems to have been that Torg would be punished if she didn't play along. All to do with getting an heir by the sound of it, but the girl wouldn't play ball without marriage. And from what Jack tells me, she wanted to carry on dancing. No, Gilbert wants to attract a lot of attention from buyers but the more respectable will smell a rat and walk away. Can you find out what price the dealer has been told to get from your superiors?"

"Bien sûr, with a telegram. I need also to know it if we are to play this game and to get permission from my superiors. What is your plan?"

"You're on board then if the answer is yes from Paris?"

"If it works, yes," said Carnot.

"I think it will," Stan continued. "Look we three are here under the guise of diamond dealers. We could represent ourselves as having something to sell and needing a valuation. Perhaps get a bank with links in Italy to agree to come to our hotel this evening and value the jewellery."

"But the girl has the jewellery." Carnot shrugged, while he looked at Stan the waiter reappeared with a tray on which were two glasses and a bottle of Cognac. Carnot inspected the bottle and nodded for the waiter to pour.

"It's a good French one," Carnot said to Stan. "We don't want the Swiss kirsch brandy."

Stan said: "You don't like the Swiss too much, do you?"

Carnot shrugged. He asked: "Do you like the French?"

Stan motioned with upturned hands, and said: "What is there to like?"

Carnot smirked. "Cognac," he said.

Stan laughed which was an unusual occurrence for him and waited until the Cognac was poured. He sensed Carnot was on the hook, but Stan still had to make the deal so that the

French would call off the dogs and wipe the slate clean for Torg. But this French policeman he could trust.

Carnot lifted his glass and said: "Respect if not friendship."

Stan gambled that Carnot was sufficiently ambitious to return to Paris with an outcome and that the French wanted that painting back badly. After a slight hesitation he too raised his glass and said: "Respect *and* friendship."

They drank and shook hands. Stan could never be friends with a Frenchman, but he could with another policeman and come to a common agreement.

The toast over, Stan continued: "What is the painting of and who did it?"

"I have no idea, it is small and valuable and all I know it is by some old Italian," said Carnot.

"Not French then?" Stan asked, with a grin.

"Nor English," Carnot laughed.

Stan took another sip of his cognac. It was not to his taste but, he would join with Carnot to get him on side.

Stan said: "We could get Kari to bring the pieces of jewellery to our hotel tonight if we can get hold of the right sort of bankers."

"That's not hard in Geneva," said Carnot, tersely.

"If you get permission for a swap of money for the painting and get it back to the Louvre the bank could underwrite the value of the price in exchange for the jewellery. Once the underwriting is done your superiors in Paris can get word to the dealer in Florence. But the price is that Torg goes free for life."

" I like the first part of your idea, but the second …" Carnot shook his head. "Peut-être, d'une manière ou d'une autre …," Carnot paused. "Forgive me as I cannot agree without getting authority. But I am inclined to agree that it is worth the risk of being sacked to suggest it. And I can always go back to being a soldier. But one thing, you have forgotten: how to get the painting to the Louvre?"

"Nice little trip for you to Florence, perhaps?" suggested Stan.

"Yes, that would be enjoyable," said Carnot.

"I'm surprised," said Stan, "Aren't the French still thought of as the enemy?"

"No, not in my experience. We're heroes because the French army ended the Austrian tyranny in Italy. I have been in cafés in the north near Milan where I have been applauded for being French."

Carnot threw some coins on the table and raised a hand for the waiter. "L'addition, s'il vous plait," he called.

"I need to settle my bill," said Stan.

"Please, you are about to win me promotion," Carnot smiled.

"And you're probably going to get me the sack," said Stan.

The two men laughed, and each took a final sip of their cognac. Stan stood as Carnot settled the bill. He listened as Carnot and the waiter exchanged a volley of French and then Stan walked a few steps away from the table. The waiter and Carnot shook hands and Carnot joined Stan.

The two policemen strolled for a few minutes to the edge of the area, until they could see the opposite side of the Rhone.

The sun's light caught the windows of the solid looking buildings facing them as if in a stand-off.

Carnot waved an expansive hand and looked at Stan. He said: "Across there – some of the banks."

For a few seconds the two men stood in silence as Stan gazed across the river to the robust, plain fronted buildings, comparing them to the picture he had in his mind of the grand stately edifices in the City of London.

"Don't look much do they," said Stan. "You'd pass them by in London."

Carnot said: "And in Paris but here the wealth is in the vault which is why the Swiss almost match your country now and have overtaken mine." He looked at Stan, who shrugged. Carnot continued: "You have dressed well, I think, looking like a Swiss. Not too young, a little lined on the face and grey in parts but there is an air of authority. It could work. Yes, voilà, you will do. Choose the bank."

"No idea," said Stan. "Never heard of any of them. What we don't want is a failure."

"Well, no, there is one which is also in Paris and I think in Italy, which might place it well for us. There was something a few years before the war with Prussia about them having small capital. But they were able to inspire confidence so that those interested in them forgot this fact and were captivated. The key is for a banker to become a courtier."

"Yes we've a few of those in London. Load of conmen, in other words," muttered Stan.

Carnot shrugged and said: "That is one view but the rich and successful perhaps do not feel they can do without them. It obviously works to get on the side of the rich, and those in power. Look at the buildings they do business in. From here, business was done on reputation and the network they built up in Milan before 1870."

"Did you investigate them or something?" Stan suddenly asked.

"You might say there was a little, "pushing the game too far," in Paris in the way situations were explained when lending money to governments. But you know, statesmen only play along with bankers if it means they keep a grip on power so, who is the crook?"

"Good point," said Stan. "We might as well go with the one you know about, then," said Stan. "If they've an eye for a deal in the way you say they probably won't ask too many questions. In fact, they sound ideal!"

"Good, we can arrest them tomorrow but today we do business," said Carnot.

Stan chuckled and pulled his jacket to, buttoning it against the chill off the Rhone.

"Let's get into the sun, shall we? Will you join me, Carnot?" asked Stan.

Carnot gave him a look and asked: "Do you speak French?"

Stan shrugged and said: "A little, I can manage "oui" and "non." At the best … that's all."

Carnot winced. "Do you really suppose that means you can speak French?" He pointed a finger at his own chest and said: "If we are to see success, I, Carnot, am speaking but not you."

*

The morning had brightened by the time to leave for Vevey. Jack had woken with the sun in a cloudless sky. By the time he and Burgess were on the quayside there was a fresh breeze and they waited, listening to the alternating high and low sound which the wind made as it moved through the cedars. The Tullys had killed time with them for a while in case the guide came early but Lauren Wheeler had decided to go on board with her parents. At five minutes before departure there was still no sign of Kari in her guise of J Croz, and the crew was readying the boat to leave.

The guide Allen had whipped around the breakfast tables earlier that morning ensuring that those who were going to Vevey and Montreux would be in reception ready to leave just as the very exact Swiss clock struck the quarter of the hour after ten. A back way through the gardens had brought the group out onto the edge of the park and from there they had walked at a good pace for the boat.

Now Allen leant over the side from the top deck, calling: "Mr Sargent, Mr Burgess, Mr and Mrs Tully, I can't hold the boat! Please get on board as they will leave on time."

Then Jack saw Kari, running at a steady pace towards them. Whether it was the effect of exercise or a good sleep, she called cheerfully to Jack and Burgess as she came up alongside the gangway. She had a similar bag to the one which Torg had left in Jersey and which Jack now owned as his own. Today it had been slung over Jack's shoulder before he left the hotel. As he looked at her animated face and eyes that were full of life the shadow cast by the previous day's meeting may never have happened. He beckoned to her to hurry and as she passed them Jack and the others moved quickly towards the boat.

Jack said once on board: "May I introduce the guide Mr Croz." He extended a hand towards the Tullys and continued: "This is Mr and Mrs Tully. You made it just in time. The crew are about to pull up the walkway."

The Tully's quickly made their greeting as Kari presented herself as their guide: "I say, good of Stan to step aside for us to use your skills today? How do you do. Mr Croz is it?" Tully extended his hand.

Kari gave a firm handshake but as the group were then ushered out of the way by an irritated crewman whose eye was on the clock at the Ouchy Port buildings.

"There," said Tully, looking at his pocket watch, "Ten seconds late, that's why the man is annoyed. We'll go up and find the others."

Mr and Mrs Tully turned to the stairs leading up to a half empty first class.

The rest of the group were ushered into a small, veneered salon to get them out of the way of the leaving process by the gangway. But Kari hung back and motioned to Jack to remain as well.

"Stan has gone?" Kari asked once the door was closed.

"He was away early for the train and should be with Carnot by now," Jack answered. He nodded at Kari's backpack and said: "Sekk med meis."

Kari smiled at his attempt at the Norwegian.

"We should introduce Mr Croz to Miss Wheeler," interrupted Burgess, glancing at the boat's clock. He added: "There's only forty-five minutes before the steamer will be at Vevey and I'm sure you must want to discuss your route."

Jack explained: "He means we'll come up with you. They may not expect you in First Class, so you need to be ready for that."

"I am a skilled specialist," said Kari. She knew the look to adopt. She continued: "Where you travel, I will travel. I am not going to be treated as a servant. I know what the English are like, remember. They will rely on me to keep them safe so I will be treated with respect. If not, I will leave them at the top and they can find their own way down."

Jack laughed and said: "Alright, I think I know how we can handle that one. I'll see to your ticket. Burgess and I will come in First Class with you and I'll introduce you to Miss Wheeler who is the other person in your party. It's J Croz still isn't it?"

Kari nodded.

Burgess gave Jack a look at the idea of taking Kari into First Class. But he went along with it and led Kari up the stairs. Jack saw to the tickets, grinning as he bought three for First Class.

———

It might not work in England, he thought, to put the hired hand in with the toffs but this was Switzerland.

Tully was first on his feet at the sight of Jack with the guide. Kari looked the part again, thought Jack as he glanced at her and waited to see how the effusive welcome had gone down. She looked pleased and slightly amused.

"Do come and join us, we're aching to know where you're going to take us." Tully led their guide over to the table.

Jack caught her words as she sat down, hearing her lower the tone of the voice to a more guttural sound. He registered that this was just another part for Kari to play.

Kari said: "We will disembark at Vevey and keep to the foothills. I will show you on the map. How are your boots?"

Lauren and Mrs Tully bent forward slightly, and they must have lifted skirts to display their footwear for their guide. Tully stuck his foot out and Kari nodded with approval. She then turned to Lauren and Mrs Tully.

"Good, good, these will do for today. Have you eaten well this morning?"

Jack could not hear the responses, but he could see that Kari was pleased with them. She was asking another question:

"Ladies have you climbed before?"

"A little in North Wales with my brother and we live not far from the Pennines," said Lauren.

Mrs Tully looked surprised. She asked: "What exactly do you mean by climbing here? Surely you're not intending to take us up the side of one of these mountains?"

"I ask to know what to expect," said Kari. "Your answer is all I need to know. We will take a gentle incline." She produced a map from her bag and spread it out on the table in the middle of them all. "Here is Vevey, here is the Jorat. Look here on the map," Kari said.

Jack strained to hear Kari's next words as she jabbed at an area with her finger.

"We can leave the path and follow the water courses but stay out of the woods because of the snakes. As its early summer we might see the white narcissus," Kari explained.

"How lovely," said Mrs Tully.

Kari smiled and became more expansive: "That is why I need to know about your boots. We do some walking towards the Jorat. The town is built on the south slope and we finish with a small visit to the Chateau de Blonay which has belonged to the same family for centuries. They are clients of mine and will have some refreshment for you. A little soup, some eggs and wine. Many of the first vines in the canton were planted around here and we may be able to see Chatelan Castle above Vevey among the vines. Here there is a small waterfall, very beautiful and a small stream. We will cross by the stepping-stones to a stone bridge. You will like it."

"It sounds charming," said Lauren.

"Yes, and here, we will get the fresh milk for you to drink and some cooked cheese, so that you try it. After this a carriage to the train for Lausanne. I will escort you back to your hotel as I need to see the Englishman Stan for tomorrow. The views are good, you will enjoy."

Jack said to Burgess: "She's a radical."

Burgess drily agreed: "A good actress! Look they've bought into it. So, Stan is getting a visitation tonight, lucky him!"

"If she's coming back to the hotel with them I expact she'll want to find out if Stan's been successful with a bank. It will all turn on what Carnot agrees to though," said Jack. He peered through the window to the opposite side of the lake. A cutter with a double mainsail tacked away from the steamboat.

Jack continued: "It seems that we're almost at the end of the lake. I'm going up on deck to take in the views. Looks like the mountains are higher here than at Geneva." Jack turned to go.

Burgess nodded dourly. "I'll join you," he said. "We need to be off sharpish anyway to find that street. What was it again?"

"Rue des Bosquets," said Jack. He was unlikely to forget the address of a chocolate maker whose goods they suspected had poisoned him.

The two men left the salon, Burgess preoccupied with the task ahead of finding the chocolate maker, Jack with another question in his mind. It was almost a quarter past eleven and as the boat did not make a stop between Ouchy and Vevey the time had gone quickly. Jack had wanted to catch Allen before they disembarked with a query. He spotted the Cook's guide on the top deck towards the stern and Allen acknowledged Jack and Burgess eagerly as they walked towards him.

Jack nodded in return to the guide and asked: "Mr Allen, I was meaning to check with you if you knew which particular area of the mountains the English climbers would visit from Geneva?"

There was a pause while Allen thought. Burgess peered over the side of the boat, giving an air of disinterest while straining his neck to see the armchair shaped end to the lake.

Allen said: "Well, I think the principal route would be the high Alps called The Aiguilles Rouges and the Valley of Chamoni. Its where the best guides are if you're a climber and want an arduous experience such as Mont Blanc and the Aiguilles. Mont Blanc is thought to be the highest mountain in Europe although there's discussion between the French and Italians as to the actual height. The guides who take climbers up are expensive so it must be a challenging place to climb and many come out to do just that. We run a few tours that take in Chamoni if you're interested and Cooks only uses the best hotels. But climbers tend to go under their own steam."

"I would be interested, but for another time," Jack said. "You say the guides are expensive? My Uncle Stan's guide is only charging six francs today."

"Here, yes, but if you're going to climb Mont Blanc from Chamoni it takes seventeen hours up and six to come down."

Jack raised his eyebrows.

Allen continued: "Each person doing that needs a guide, and those guides charge one hundred francs each to get you to the top. You see if a guide was going up Mont Blanc he'd only look after one person in the party. That's what would be needed, you see because a climber needs the expertise of the guide. If you put a foot wrong, you're gone! You've heard about Lord Hastings back in the 1860's?"

Jack nodded. He asked: "Was that the man who climbed with M. Croz? Our guide mentioned that it was a relative involved in that tragedy," said Jack. "I can see that its big money."

"It certainly is, but they work for it,' said Allen. "Your guide's having a rest doing this sort of terrain. But it's good advertising, you see, because our friends who will walk with Mr Croz today will go home and recommend him to others. Then they come out and look for him to take them up the more difficult routes. That's how it's done."

Allen pulled out his copy of the Cook's continental handbook and found the page he was looking for. Then he passed it to Jack without a word. From another pocket Allen produced a route map which he opened as if performing a ceremony.

"Here we are," said Allen. "This is how you would go. It seems to me the route that our tours are built around has the reputation of being a bit of a hard journey for the short time you would be there. You see on the tour you would go by an old French coach called a Diligence, in stages." Allen dropped his voice before continuing: "Frankly, the journey looks arduous enough I can tell you without doing any climbing. Imagine being in an old French coach, rattling round those narrow roads. I haven't done it myself yet, but I will later in the summer and from what my colleagues tell me there are points along the journey where you get enough of a view of Mont Blanc without climbing it. The other thing to mention is it's two thousand and forty feet higher than Lake Geneva. So, you can imagine the temperatures even in the summer. Here's the best place to stay, by all accounts, at the inn in St Martin but to be honest, Mr Sargent, I'd go somewhere else."

Jack grinned at Allen's frankness. He nodded towards the town at the foot of the mountains and the views on all sides of the boat reflected in the deep blue waters of the lake. He asked: "Is that Vevey?"

"No, Montreux … very nice," Allen replied. "We're about five minutes away from Vevey which is smaller than Montreux. The Romans called it Vibiscum, according to the history books."

"Vevey does look quite a small place," said Jack. "But the mountains above Montreux look magnificent."

"Yes, Montreux has a lovely position. Vevey has a reputation for being a lively town though and is very popular," explained Allen. "Try the chocolate while you're here, it's made differently and there's quite some experimentation going on in using milk by a chocolatier called Daniel Peters."

"I should say there is," muttered Jack.

"If you'll excuse me, Mr Sargent," said Allen. "I need to round up our party that are getting off at Vevey, but while you're here there are lots of paths that intersect the valleys and hills."

"Are you going on to Montreux, Mr Allen?" asked Jack.

"Yes, I have to as we've a tour to the ancient Château de Chillon close to Montreux," said Allen.

"Oh, can you point it out from here?" asked Jack.

"Not really, but as you're a reading man, you should look for the poem by Byron called the Prisoner of Chillon." Allen cleared his throat, raised a hand, and launched into a recitation: "My hair is grey, but not with years,

———
579

Nor grew it white

In a single night,

As men's have grown from sudden fears:" Allen stopped and said: "It'd not a cheerful recitation but I do dine out on it when back in England." He continued:

"My limbs are bow'd, though not with toil,

But rusted with a vile repose,

For they have been a dungeon's spoil,

And mine has been the fate of those

To whom the goodly earth and air

Are bann'd, and barr'd – forbidden fare;

But this was for my father's faith

I suffer'd chains and courted death;"

Allen stopped as quickly as he had begun.

Jack applauded and shouted: "*Well done*, Mr Allen."

"Good grief," muttered Burgess, "How depressing."

Allen looked pleased at Jack's response but modestly held up a hand to stop the clapping. He said: "That's as much as I've managed to learn. There're 392 lines of it all about a Genevois monk called François Bonivard who Byron sees as a martyr. Of course, the facts are a bit different, but I thought a little drama in the confines of the Chateau would lend some atmosphere."

"And, so it will," said Jack.

Allen continued to warm to his theme. He said: "The chateau was used as a prison in 800 but was conquered by the Duke of Savoy sometime in the thirteenth century. Right lot they were, shutting people up in it. There's a hotel named after Byron in Montreux, you know. We don't use it, but it's got a very good reputation. Why did you choose to get off at Vevey, Mr Sargent?"

"Work," said Jack.

"I didn't think there were any high-class jewellers in Vevey, but I could be wrong," said Allen.

"We've got to correct something that was faulty," said Jack.

"Oh, I see. One of the wealthy families I take it?" Allen asked.

Jack glanced away as he replied: "It certainly involves a wealthy individual. We're coming in, Mr Allen."

Allen excused himself and Jack joined Burgess to descend to the lower level. The gangway was pushed to the quay almost in symmetry as a member of the crew jumped from the boat onto the quayside. In the noise around the staircase Jack noticed the familiar figure of J Croz at the doorway listening to Lauren Wheeler. Jack beckoned to Burgess to follow and slid through the clusters of people to join the party of four.

Kari nodded to Jack, before she turned back to Lauren. He heard her say: "Come, let's go now."

*

It was midday by the time they reached the chocolatier's premises. Jack wondered if he was imagining the more temperate climate in Vevey. The mountains perhaps, he wondered, sheltering the town. It had clearly rained earlier, and the scent of the foliage mixed with the aromas from the damp soil raked up the deep memories Jack had of the farm near Battle. It was a fine place on the lake and not surprising that the town was popular.

Jack and Burgess walked past many fine public buildings: a palais with pleasant gardens, the Hotel de Ville which, to Jack's surprise, was not providing accommodation but was the town hall. He laughed at himself for his mistake. There was also a hospital. Burgess beckoned Jack over to where new quays were being constructed and they found a map carved in stone on a stand down by the lake, which identified the mountains as the Jorat to their rear, and a dramatic Dent d'Oche towering over a town on the opposite side of the lake called Evian.

"The river's called the Vevayse, apparently," said Burgess.

"Here's the street that the chocolatier is in," said Jack tracing it on the map. "Shall we get on with it, Mr Burgess, seeing as it's why we've come?" Jack asked.

Burgess nodded and said: "We should, although I'm unclear what good it will do."

"We must try Mr Burgess."

"Have you been to St James's around the area the chocolate sellers are in?" asked Burgess as a memory came back to him as they walked.

"Once a few years ago but it wasn't as pleasant an area as this man's workshop, and mostly sold in the market but there's nothing there like the texture of those chocolates I ate in Jersey," said Jack.

Burgess pointed to the sign which read: "Gala Chocolat."

"I wonder what that means?" he said.

They were shown into a room by a woman dressed in blue, who spoke only what Jack took to be a local dialect, perhaps the Swiss German he had heard about. It was so different to the French that he had heard in Geneva.

He and Burgess were not the only customers and it was quite a crowd at the counter. Jack moved among the displays and the woman smiled and invited him to taste a sample on a plate on the counter. He declined, more from his last experience than a real unwillingness, but Burgess stepped round him and chose some chocolates which were quickly boxed. As he paid for them Burgess asked for Mr Peters.

The woman smiled and gave quite a long explanation shaking her head, which Burgess took to mean that the proprietor was out. The woman turned away to deal with one of the other customers in the shop.

To buy them time Jack picked up a small box and waited his turn to select a few chocolates. As he was helped with his selection, he played a longshot purely on instinct.

Smiling Jack asked: "Is Helly here?"

The woman shook her head. Smiling in return she made a gesture towards the outside while she gave an answer neither man could understand.

"Gone?" said Jack copying her action.

The woman shook her head, but her face was animated, and she beckoned to him to come to the window continuing to offer an explanation that Jack could not understand.

Burgess and Jack looked across to a simply decorated church. Everything about the woman's face was excited and happy. Then she held up her hand for them to wait and produced a box from under the counter. The lid had a picture of a bride and groom on it.

"Good grief," said Burgess. "She's telling us Helly is getting married."

Jack pointed to the groom and shrugged.

The woman laughed and pointed at Jack. She said "Englischer Herr wie du."

"English?" said Burgess picking up the word the woman had said. "She's telling us the groom is the Englishman."

"Gilbert?" asked Jack, smiling at the woman.

The woman knew the name. She nodded enthusiastically.

"Good grief, he doesn't waste any time, does he. Out with the old, in with the new. He must know the dancer has gone," said Burgess, under his breath.

Jack held out the box he had chosen to the woman and said:

"For Helly, please choose." Jack waved an expansive hand across the chocolate display while the woman made the final selection from some memory that she clearly had of Helly's penchant for the chocolates.

"Preferably without the arsenic," muttered Burgess.

But the woman heard the word, dropped the empty box and put both hands up to her face and blurted out: "Arsen?"

The rest they could not understand but she was at pains to reassure them, her expressions and actions being suppliant.

"So, she certainly knows about it. Someone must have challenged them." Burgess nodded at her, his own expression gentle and reassuring. He pointed to a shelf with tall storage jars and asked: "Was it the Cocoa?"

"Nein, nein, es war Wasser …" the woman was quite beside herself, carrying on a long explanation pointing to the ground and lifting her hand up and down.

"Something out of the ground?" asked Jack.

"Wasser, wasser," she repeated over and over.

Jack shook his head. "I'm sorry I don't understand."

The woman went to a counter and picked up a jug and a glass. Into it she poured water and held the glass out to Jack.

"Wasser," she said.

"In the water," Jack reiterated.

The woman nodded forcefully.

Jack asked: "Helly?"

The woman carried on nodding, raising her eyes and hands to heaven. She continued to make more explanations which neither Burgess nor Jack could understand.

Jack paid six francs and turned to leave. The woman turned the chocolate box over and showed a space for a message.

Jack recalled a phrase one of the sailors had said at the end of the journey from Jersey as he and Stan disembarked in France. It would do nicely given the man Helly had just married. He said: "Bon chance."

Outside Burgess and Jack stood in silence, fixated on the church. There was no one around it and the ceremony had clearly taken place earlier. Around the portal was a homely decoration of local flowers.

"A quiet wedding," said Burgess. "The head of a crime organisation marries a poisoner by implication. What a couple! A member of a titled family but shunned by the Queen. I'd love to see the guest list for this one."

"Yes, 'xactly," answered Jack. "Not the sort of wedding a toff would have, is it? It must give you some satisfaction, Mr Burgess, that you've been right about him all along."

"In some ways, yes, I do feel vindicated," said Burgess. "But it's all gone on too long, Jack. The damage Gilbert's done has been allowed to get too great. That's what continues to give me grief."

Jack mused: "How did she do it I wonder? Someone would have noticed Arsenic being brought in surely. The woman kept pointing to the ground didn't she, I wonder if it was in water Helly brought in? Is that how she did it? Bring it in from home."

"And did Gilbert know? Did he encourage it? Make her promises if Kari was out of the way. Is she local I wonder or from another area? Do you remember, Mr Burgess, seeing the white stuff at the side of the smelting works? Father used to tell me the work done there made arsenic and to keep away from it. He said there were places not to drink the water around the works."

Jack picked up a few fine pebbles and ran his thumb and index finger over the smooth surfaces. He continued: "The bride has proved to the groom that she can conceive a child and although the groom needs a legitimate heir it's still a quiet wedding. But she needed to move Kari out or face disgrace. Perhaps she thought Kari would go, that she would suspect Gilbert and run away. Instead, she stayed and probably Helly had to keep giving her bigger doses to make her very ill."

"Makes sense," and Burgess then paused. "Well, I think we've established who put the poison in the chocolates and that they were intended for Kari. What was it made you suspect Helly had a connection here?" asked Burgess.

Jack shrugged then grinned wryly: "Just a thought while we were in the shop. I could feel it in my gut if you pardon the bad joke. It's too fashionable a shop for it to be a mistake that Peters would make. Gilbert must have come here at some point to buy chocolate and perhaps that's how he found his new mistus Helly." Jack paused but added cynically: "She must have been very obliging in ways Kari wasn't. Somehow, he dropped the hint that he'd marry the woman who would give him an heir, and once that was done perhaps Helly had further encouragement to get rid of her rival."

"I wonder at what point he moved her into the same house as Kari?" mused Burgess.

"It would be easy enough eventually, I've seen it done in the big houses in Sussex when I was working on the farm, a young girl the owner fancied given a position in the house," Jack explained. "Helly would have had skills with the chocolate, and perhaps she went to work in the kitchen first. I shouldn't think anyone working for Gilbert is under any illusions about him and even if they didn't think much of his activities what could they do about it? I wonder if Kari knows about the wedding?"

"I doubt it. There's a touch of irony that she's leading a walk here today. Must be a reason it's here in a small church and not in Geneva, don't you think?"

Jack nodded and he and Burgess stood for a while as the sun moved from behind a mountain peak across the lake. The green slopes lit up in the sunshine and the view changed from the sombre dark green that it had been. The two men watched the children playing in the graveyard in front of the church and Jack threw a couple of the pebbles onto a path some way ahead as he had no further use for them. There was nothing else to keep them in Vevey and the two men started the walk to the railway station.

After a silence as they reflected on the situation Jack shrugged and said: "Of course we don't actually know it was arsenic. The thing about those chocolates was they didn't have a bad taste. It was fortunate I only bit a piece off and didn't fill my mouth with a whole one. But then I had such an intense thirst that I could have emptied a basin of water in one gulp. If it was Helly using water with arsenic in it, she must have known what she was doing to spread her intentions over a long period of time and make Kari ill rather than kill her straight off."

"There was certainly malice there, but perhaps Helly did want Kari to go instead of killing her?" suggested Burgess.

"I expect it's possible. Wouldn't you have to know what you were doing with measurements of a poison though to do that?" asked Jack.

The two men looked at each other as the penny dropped.

Jack said: "We've been making assumptions about this woman Helly, haven't we? We know nothing about her as a woman, but we've assumed she's ignorant. Why have we have done that?"

"Good point. Probably, because she assumed a domestic role in Gilbert's house. It doesn't mean that's all she could do. Perhaps to get this job with the chocolate maker she'd had training somewhere. It's possible," replied Burgess. He stopped and looked at Jack as a thought occurred to him. "How would she have got it into a particular batch of chocolates though and not others?"

Jack said: "She may have made a batch of them, but she knew what she was doing alright. How does a chef prepare a special meal? You know, the sort you and I don't eat usually. As good as your hotel is, Mr Burgess, it's not high cuisine is it? What about a chemist? Maybe she's trained in a chemist's? Where did Kari say Helly was from? Somewhere over the border into France wasn't it?"

"That's not a conversation I was privy to. Ask her when we get back," said Burgess. "Come on Jack, we should go. I've suddenly developed a distaste for this place. Let's get back to Ouchy before we waste any more time. I've a fancy for a kip and you've got a telegram to send."

"Have I?" asked Jack in surprise.

"Yes, I think its time we found out if Harry ever got those chocolates to Ann Black. We might find a telegram office at the railway station instead of waiting until we get back to the hotel. That way we stand a chance of getting an answer today. How long will it take to get back on the train?" asked Burgess.

"Got to be quicker than the boat. I could send a message from the station p'rhaps. Get one off to the hospital in case Ann's there. Avoids complications with George if I send it there," said Jack.

"What sort of complications?" asked Burgess.

"George had been a little odd about the working relationship between Ann and I in the last year ever since the case at Fairlight."

"Wife gets on well with young constable," mused Burgess, 'As a possible motive for murder I mean."

"I wouldn't go that far about George," said Jack, shocked.

"Well, there's been cases hasn't there with jealousy as a factor and there's enough in literature and the press about such a bad passion. Stands to reason it exists given the number of men committed to Broadmoor during my career," said Burgess.

"But doesn't that mean there's more outrage against it now? Anything I've read makes the man out to be likely to be insane or heading for death," said Jack.

"Not in France though," said Burgess. "The woman ends up dead in a brutal murder at the hands of the husband. A crime of passion, young Jack. So watch your step."

Twenty-one

Precisely at five o'clock that evening Jack collected the telegram off the silver tray as it was presented to him, a hint of his last discussion with Burgess at the back of his mind.

Ann Black's response to his questions made him smile to himself because of the speed and the very miles between them and the facts of the modern engineering which had achieved this miracle. He had given up trying to work out what the time was in London, but Ann had still been at the hospital when his questions had reached her. Ever the faithful colleague he could always rely on, thought Jack.

Burgess had gone straight up to his room to make the most of a comfortable bed when they arrived back from Vevey. But Jack had first walked along a lonely path set in the small orchard of fruit trees near the hotel grounds. He had reflected on the friendship with Charles Burgess which had developed over the past year. They had much in common despite the difference in age, both being un-questioning when dealing with a man like Hunt. Equally they were both capable of absolute dissension once doubt was planted and both were ready to risk all to make the arrest. But in Burgess's case, thought Jack, he had damaged his health and career in his pursuit of Gilbert.

Now Jack was seated overlooking his favourite view from one of the Hotel's grand lounges. He was quite alone in that section of the lounge. The great settees closer to the windows were largely empty except for two ladies. One a rosy faced matron in extravagant dress for that time of the day who sat reading to an older woman dressed entirely in black except for her jewelled hands. They were not English, and Jack did not think they were French. He listened in awe to the marvellous musical sound of whatever language the woman who read spoke. It sounded so full of passion and made him feel happy to listen to it.

There was only one time he had heard anything to compare with it in English and that had been the summer when he was eighteen. A group of travelling actors appeared at the sheep fair performing a play said to be by William Shakespeare. Jack had watched spell bound as the actors appeared in a play which was described as a tragedy about a Scottish King. He had confessed later to the Squire that he had not understood most of it but what had struck him was the way the words were used. The performance had felt thick with grief.

Jack eased himself forward to avoid the sharp pain he stlll occasionally had in the ribs. Since stopping his beat his body had felt stiff most days. Of course, he had walked since Jersey, but Jack was used to pounding his beat for eight hours, day after day. He turned over Ann's response again and again letting the minutes go by as he moved his feet up and down to relieve the feeling of tautness in the calves. It had been a longer walk that morning than he had done since he had left Southampton.

Jack had almost relished the suspense as he opened the telegram. Ann's answer started with a quote:

"All things are poison. Nothing is without poison. Only the dose permits something not to be poisonous."

It continued: "A in each. Exact amount equals knowledge. Ann."

Jack had read it over three times. Each chocolate had a poison, Ann called it A and the same amount, that must be what she meant. Ann said: "A in each," and the woman in the shop had said Arsen and wasser. It mut be arsenic.

His mind played on the time in the shop and he realised he and Burgess had missed a trick and should have asked how Peters and his staff had found out that they had sold chocolates which had been poisoned. But for now, he needed help with the language the woman had used.

Jack pressed the bell to call the waiter. A different man, burly in build appeared at his side in seconds and Jack realised that the man had been standing by the door ready to respond to the needs of guests.

Jack asked: "Could someone help me with two words? I think they may be Swiss?"

"I will try sir," said the man.

"Arsen and vazer," Jack said, trying to get as close as he could in his memory to the way the woman had pronounced the words.

At first there was silence as the man looked surprised, then he coughed and said: "Sounds German, perhaps Swiss German. Were you discussing poisons, sir?"

"Chemicals, yes, I'm in the jewellery business." The half-truth made Jack uncomfortable, but he could hardly say he was a policeman.

"Ah, then it could be arsenic and water. Is that helpful, sir?"

"Very, thank-you, your English is better than mine," said Jack with a grin.

"I have worked in London for twenty years, sir, at Brown's in Mayfair, starting in the kitchen and ending in the restaurant." The man smiled as he added: "The view is better here."

"I should say so," replied Jack. "What would I call you?"

"Johanne, sir, but I was John in England."

"Like me," said Jack.

He tipped Johanne five Swiss francs, which won him respect and a partial bow before the man turned to leave the lounge. But he thought better of it and hesitated. Jack glanced at him as Johanne turned back.

"Have you thought of something else?" Jack asked.

"Excuse me, sir, but are you interested in the people who build up an immunity to Arsenic in a particular area?"

Jack stared at him. It was as if it was Christmas and his birthday all in one. He asked: "In Switzerland is that? It sounds very interesting."

"There's a professor, a Swiss, who has been studying them for the last ten years after a big poisoning case. The police weren't sure after a man died if he'd been poisening himself or if he was the victim of a poisoner. Tschudi's the professor's name. It's an area around Mont Blanc that he's looking at and where there's a smelting works, and the run-off got into the water over many years."

"Does the professor live around here?" asked Jack.

"I wouldn't know where you'd find him, sir, but he did publish a book in the 1860's about his findings. He did a great deal of studies about the villagers. There was a lot of publicity too about his findings and the medical profession were very interested in it. That book might be in the guest's library here if you're interested."

"Could you come with me? In case there's a language problem," asked Jack, standing. Another five francs changed hands.

"Delighted, sir," said Johanne.

Jack thought about how over time the build-up in Kari's system of arsenic would have taken its toll. Who knew how many other such boxes of tainted chocolate she had enjoyed before her suspicions made her seek Torg's help. If Helly was one of those villagers who self-dosed perhaps she had encouraged Kari by eating the chocolates herself as if there was absolutely nothing wrong with them. He needed to establish where Helly was from though.

A small room by the standards of the Beau Rivage formed the guest's library with shelves of books from floor to ceiling. Johanne spoke to a member of staff seated by the door who shook her head, but she disappeared into a back room and some minutes later brought out a book which she placed in front of Jack. He looked at the title and did a rough translation.

"Try this one," suggested Johanne. "Everything on the shelves is fiction. But there are some serious books in the back. This is "Affaires Criminelles," and if it was a famous case it may be mentioned in this."

Jack flicked through the chapters in case there was anything in English. He shook his head and handed the book back.

"I can help if you permit?' suggested Johanne.

Jack nodded and said: "Please, I'd be grateful. Perhaps there might be a list of authors of the articles at the back. How do you spell the professor's name?"

Johanne wrote the name down for Jack who turned to the back to look in the references. He said: "Here, there are several pages where he's mentioned."

It was in French and Johanne read through a paragraph. He translated it for Jack: "According to Tschudi during a trial the question was raised if the murdered man was a toxicophagus. That's what he called the group I told you about who take it deliberately. It was unknown to the medical profession at the time. These people bought preparations from pedlars made with the deposits from the water after smelting arsenic rich minerals. The professor found communities had been eating these preparations as long ago as the sixteenth century. That is all it says but I have heard of this before."

"What happened in the case?" asked Jack.

"It doesn't say," answered Johanne. "Just that his research was important because it showed some people can build up a resistance over time and the medical profession did not know this. I'm sorry, sir, that is all there is, but I have known areas where the locals do this in the Alps."

"No, that's very interesting and helpful," said Jack.

Jack glanced at the clock on the ornate mantlepiece. They had spent thirty minutes in there and it was time for Burgess to join Jack in the gardens after his rest. Jack wrote down the title and the names involved, nodded his thanks to Johanne and stood to leave. Then a thought occurred to him.

"Are you French or Swiss?" Jack asked.

"French, sir," Johanne waited.

Jack asked: "Where was it that you heard of people doing this strange activity?"

"In a few areas but I was working in the Mont Blanc area most recently."

"Was there industry there?" Jack asked thinking about his father's advice to him.

"Some, yes and Arsenic in the water of certain rivers, and near where sprays were used on some crops."

Thank-you Johanne," said Jack.

"Is there anything else I can assist you with, sir?" asked Johanne.

"No, excuse me, I have to send a telegram."

It seemed an age and Jack was aware that he was keeping Burgess waiting. Would he be in time to get an answer from Ann?

Jack hung around room acting as a post office in the Beau Rivage waiting for his answer. Thirty minutes, then one hour and finally an answer came through.

Ann said it was favoured in some treatments like syphilis, and experiments being done on treating some cancers - a chemist would be likely to know what they were doing, she said. Jack was more than ever sure of Helly's background and kicked himself for the way they had underestimated her.

———

In Geneva Stan suffered greatly through the interview with the bank. Most of the time he had no idea what Carnot was saying or what the bank was agreeing to do but Carnot's briefing had been to tell him to maintain an expression of understanding. This he hoped he had managed to do when towards the end of the interview a banker had bestowed a benevolent smile upon Stan and the hand shaking had begun. It was a new atmosphere in the room and suddenly, Stan was everyone's best friend.

Once out on the uncrowded street Stan dropped the charade and asked Carnot: "Well? What have we just agreed to?"

"My dear Sergeant, I have called the shot," Carnot replied.

"Shots," corrected Stan.

"Exactement," said Carnot. "They are like the fish on the line and will come tonight to the hotel, with a jeweller who does work for them. He will look at the jewels."

"Sounds dodgy, bankers having a tame jeweller."

"Pas de tour c'est indispensable. Some of the debt they buy is not all cash," explained Carnot. "They will come after dinner. We have time to see the woman, get her to bring the jewels of value and most important of all, eat and digest. I will join you in your hotel. *Splendeur*, the food is good, right?"

"For foreign food it is. Right then, you'll come back with me," said Stan, stiffly.

Stan followed the direction of Carnot's gaze. Across the lake the clouds had lifted to reveal the snow-covered peaks of the Mont Blanc range. He was thankful to see it again before he left and paused to ensure he would always remember the sight. Both men stood in silence with the same intent.

Carnot broke the mood and started to walk back towards the bridge over the Rhone. Stan caught him up and they walked together, but in silence pausing just once at the middle of the bridge to stare up the lake as the panorama opened out ahead of them.

Once across the two policemen completed the walk to the telegraph office used earlier that day and Carnot went in alone. It mattered little to Carnot what was the answer from the Sûreté but Stan did not know that. Stan stood alone and glanced up at the clock with its three time zones. He thought about his wife and children who he hoped were now in Kent. Time had moved on in those three cities represented on the clock and the world was being changed by people like those bankers. Of course, there was hope that Carnot's superiors would give their permission and tonight's operation would have some sort of paper trail if Carnot had managed to convince the chain of command. After ten minutes of waiting for Carnot to reappear Stan managed his disgruntled mood and took a table at the same café that he had patronised that morning. He ordered and waited.

Carnot returned looking up and down the square with the air of a man who did not care about the outcome. He located Stan and smiled as he saw him seated at the café. He spoke to the same waiter from earlier and placed an order after the usual social chat. However, once with Stan he slapped him on the shoulder and showed no concern at all.

Cognac appeared yet again on a tray at his side and this time Stan knew that he needed it. He felt rattled and Carnot sensed it as they sat together.

"Come, my friend, what troubles you?" asked Carnot.

Stan said: "The whole thing feels dishonest, but I should thank-you for setting that meeting up. It's true I wouldn't have got anywhere without speaking the French but one thing I don't understand is why the bankers were so friendly towards the end? I watched them and there was a distinct change in their posture, and they started smiling. That's what is bothering me. Up to that point they'd looked like they were on a trip to Clacton on a wet Sunday."

Carnot paused: "I do not know what that means," He shrugged and continued: "Of course, they were pleased to meet an English diamond merchant. There is likely to be a good commission."

"From the French, you mean. There's a commission from your lot?"

"Pas de moi!" Carnot said loudly as he held up his hands. He continued: "Mais, bien sûr … from the jeweller. A little from the woman with the jewellery if she values the service to set her brother free, but of course, not from le Bobby et le Gendarme. Rien!"

The body language was sufficient for Stan to know that there would not be a backhander from the French police.

"No money changes hands from us, that's not how we do business," Stan barked back, stiffly.

Carnot exhaled. "My friend, that is what I say. But from the jeweller and the bank, and the woman. Perhaps it is a diamond, a ruby, a little emerald, something a little special that the woman who values her brother's life has spare. She *will* have something spare, my friend, they always do."

"Alright then, that's up to Kari. I don't have your experience of such women. But we're not having anything to do with it," said Stan.

"That is what I say. Why do you repeat all the time? You comprehend it is an arrangement fee for their services. It is not a bribe." Carnot gave Stan a sideways look and said: "You are a non-conformiste, eh? How do you say this, a … maverick?" asked Carnot. He shook his head and laughed as it was contrary to his nature to be irritated for long.

Stan looked away clearly put out by the laughter.

But Carnot slapped him on the shoulder and added: "Look, we have done the deal, the painting will be back in the Louvre once I collect it in a few days, and the climber will go free for the rest of his life. And le Bobby has evidence that Gilbert is a crook. Now, we should go and wait for the answer from the Sûreté."

"We will be in a right mess if the answer's no," said Stan.

"Well, if the answer is no, perhaps the telegram never arrived?" said Carnot.

"You'd disobey the order?" asked Stan.

"I disobey nothing if it does not come," replied Carnot.

"So, we're on for tonight then, regardless," said Stan. He added to make sure: "Are you serious about that?"

"Serious? Quoi, je ne comprends pas." Carnot looked away.

Stan was quiet for a few minutes until Carnot left some coins on the table. It was time to leave and together the two policemen walked towards the Gare Cornavin.

The walking as usual helped Stan's humour and as they boarded the train for Lausanne, he managed a smile.

*

Jack had seen the stiff-back of the man but not his face as he and the waiter, Johanne, came out of the reading room. Immaculately dressed like a prince as if for a ball he was the centre of attention, surrounded by men and women all expressing their appreciation at his presence. He would not have been out of place at Windsor, thought Jack, as the people smiled and laughed as he held court. Then the Master of Ceremonies made an announcement which Jack did not understand, and the guests followed their leader like a herd, as the prince-like god moved slowly towards a ballroom. It seemed a grand affair and Jack could see the garlands of flowers that decorated the doors.

As the crowd cleared the mirrored corridor Jack saw the man Johanne, who had helped him in the library. He half caught Johanne's explanation as he moved past him: "A wedding breakfast for the English lord."

Jack looked around for the bride, but she was nowhere to be seen. He stared and his eyes took in the mix of guests, the jewellery on some, and the idle social chatter as people filed into the ball room to take their places.

Like a moth to a flame Jack followed and peered through the open doors. Burgess had a taste for architecture and Jack thought to bring him later when the room was empty. His eyes went across the tables to the one at their head.

Seated as the English lord walked towards her was a fair woman. The groom still had his back to Jack, but he was more and more convinced that he was witnessing the wedding breakfast of Gilbert and his new wife, Helly. Again, he asked himself why he had dismissed her as a peasant when he would have been classed as one himself? Her smile would have got her noticed anywhere and she was dressed in flawless silver rather than white. Jack suspected that the jewellery announced her groom's pride in the child she was carrying. There was more of value to the man than just his bride as he had secured a succession to a title in a childless family.

The rest of the party at the top table had all the arrogance of the English upper class. Jack's eyes went across the room assessing the wealth and he noted the grace and refinement of those taking their seats while engaging in casual talk. This was an event some had not wanted to miss.

As silently as he had appeared Jack slipped away from the gathering and found the door into the garden. He scanned the area to the right and left until he saw Burgess who had found the plans for an ornate structure that was to be built as an extension to the hotel.

"Uncle Charles," Jack called, for the sake of appearances.

"Ah, there you are, Jack, I was starting to wonder if I should come and find you."

Jack walked across the grass to Burgess. He explained quietly: "I've found what I think is Gilbert's wedding celebration. I didn't manage to see his face but I'm certain its him and his new wife, Helly."

"What, here?" exclaimed Burgess, "What are the chances of that. This I must see."

"And it would undo everything if *you* were seen. I've more to tell you about Arsenic poisoning and I've the response in my pocket." Jack pulled out the telegram and handed it to Burgess. Jack waited while he read it through.

"So, another offence chalked up to Gilbert as it will be at his encouragement that the woman Helly will have done this," said Burgess.

"She comes from the area researched by a Professor Tschudi. See, its mentioned in a book here. The area's near Mont Blanc, which I'm sure I recall was where Kari said Helly came from. There's a group known as arsenic eaters there and Tschudi did some research into them as they built up an immunity. We've so little time now," said Jack. He added: "I'm more and more convinced that she would have persuaded Kari at the start that the chocolates were normal by eating one herself. if we're right and she has a chemist's background she would have the knowledge. I'd like to go to the area."

"That's just a theory you have. At the back of it there's Gilbert. Whatever Helly has done would have been at his persuasion. You have my word on that as I followed his antics for years. You must leave Jack, for you've fulfilled your orders. There's no way Stan will let you go over there looking for evidence. But I could go," said Burgess, firmly.

Jack said impatiently: "If I could see what you could achieve by staying, I'd agree. But you'd be alone, there's no back-up you can call on and worse of all, you're known to Gilbert."

"I'll stay a week more as my time is my own and there's good reason why Tom Hunt asked me to come," Burgess said.

"But he didn't ask you did he, Uncle Charles. You got your way somehow with the Inspector. Hunt would never have sent you after Gilbert given what you'd been through." Jack had voiced it finally.

Burgess replied: "If I go leave here with you and Stan, I'd feel I hadn't fulfilled my charge. I'd like to keep an eye open on Kari's movements as well in case something sparks with her and her former lover. Her presence here still doesn't fit too well to me. I'll get myself across to Mont Blanc if Kari makes a move to go there. Having come this far I promise I'll see it through."

*

When Stan and Carnot arrived at the Beau Rivage there was already a long queue to be seated for dinner. The two men went through the entrance hall and joined the procession of mixed travel groups.

Carnot murmured a greeting here and there, oozing charm as he bent over an extended hand or two while he enjoyed the blush on the plump cheeks of several ladies. Stan paid little attention to Carnot's antics as he had seen Jack and Burgess ahead. Completely the opposite to the Frenchman he moved quickly, wending his way through the small groups waiting to be seated, ignoring the babble of those talking nineteen to the dozen about their day.

Burgess acknowledged Carnot and tapped Jack's arm as a member of staff beckoned to the three men for the table. Burgess stopped him from placing them in the middle of the room. He also mentioned a fourth gentleman would be joining their group.

Carnot continued to progress slowly and at the sight of Lauren Wheeler opened his eyes wide. Of course, they had seen each other before in Geneva at the Metropole but on this occasion, Lauren was decked out in French lace and wearing perfume. She nodded to Carnot in return, aware of a conquest. Carnot played along and Jack watched the interplay as he took his place next to Burgess, deciding he could learn quite a bit of how to treat the ladies from the Frenchman.

Stan made a brief introduction as Carnot arrived at their table. The first name he could think of was from the number of French workers in the City of London he had come across: "Our colleague, Le Blanc, from the Paris workshop,"

They shook hands in turn with Carnot as he played along.

"I should take advice on your skills with the ladies," said Jack.

Carnot laughed. "Look, your English ladies are proud, but only a little different from French women in their response to attention. Their indifference is the fault of the English man. When you have a garden of beautiful flowers you must stop to admire them, drink in the scent, and if possible, pluck one. Come with me after dinner, and I will show you how."

Jack laughed but Stan's face was a picture. He fixed Jack with a hard stare and hissed: "As you're on duty you'll behave with respect."

Carnot winked at Jack and said: "Peut-être, your Sergeant cannot stay awake all night."

Burgess pushed the wine list towards the Frenchman, "Your choice," he said in an attempt to change the subject.

A waiter interrupted the mood as he bent towards Carnot and spoke.

"Le telegram, m'sieur,'

"Mais oui," replied Carnot and excused himself.

"My choice, then" said Burgess, as he scoured the wine list.

Carnot reappeared with a look of triumph. He slapped Stan on the shoulder and explained: "I have a little rail journey to do to Mestre, mon brave, and then onto a gallery in Florence. It will be a good 10,000 that will be paid and do you know they tell me that is a bargain for an old Italian!"

"All I ask is that we eat before we spoil the evening with work," said Burgess

"D'accord" replied Carnot. "There's time enough before we have to be serious."

"We have until eight o'clock. The bankers and their advisor arrive at eight," said Stan.

"More than enough time then," said Burgess. "We've a lot to tell you as well, but that can wait until after the bankers have been and gone. Try and put that sense of duty on one side for an hour Stan and enjoy your dinner."

And what a dinner they supped on. Carnot's excellent knowledge took them from a quick stab at the menu to a group of men playing gourmets. Jack felt the colour rise with the alcohol as he tried a different wine with each course. The men shut out their task ahead until the dessert plates were cleared and Carnot ordered liqueurs as a digestif.

Jack abstained and excused himself to get out into the fresh air. Never a drinker he was aware the alcohol had nonetheless built confidence and his gaze was a little more interested in Lauren Wheeler. He walked away towards the salon overlooking the gardens and occupied himself with trying to understand the valuation from the gallery. It sounded a ridiculous figure for the painting. How many houses would that buy? The price was beyond belief as far as Jack was concerned. But there was more to it than that as he could not believe that Kari would have any jewellery that could possibly pay the price asked.

Carnot had presented them with the telegram he had collected from his superiors. The actual value of the Italian renaissance painting was held to be the equivalent of £13,000. But the seller would take £10,000. A sheer fortune by anyone's standards.

The Bankers and their jewellery expert were due at eight o'clock and Carnot had advised they should be put in a small salon at the back of the hotel. Somewhere with a working air about it, nothing opulent but a setting which would put such men of business at their ease. Kari had agreed to come at seven and Jack had offered her dinner, but she had shaken her head at the idea, almost laughing at his naivety that their guide should dine there. In the end Burgess had offered his own room for her to wait in and primed the reception with a tip to put the guide in there.

By eight o'clock the two very anonymous looking bankers arrived. They were followed into the reception by a man dressed entirely in black. Stan was summoned to reception, but he and Carnot went together. All three visitors were safely and very privately received into the Beau Rivage. The jeweller spoke English so it was decided that Burgess would take him straight to his room where Kari in her disguise, waited. For the purposes of that evening she was introduced as a member of the domestic staff of a wealthy woman. Still dressed in her Croz outfit she represented herself as the go-between for her "mistress," who wished to remain anonymous.

The jeweller showed disinterest in who presented the stones. He had an amazing mastery of the quality before him. A silence descended on the room as he worked his way through the pieces of jewellery losing his air of pessimism as he came to a particular diamond necklace which could form different pieces such as a broach and bracelet. He looked into the colour and the cut and as he spoke his tone carried just a trace of a tremor. He asked: "Where did your mistress get these stones?"

Kari shrugged and turned away. Burgess glanced at her and was convinced that she knew the origin of the pieces. He wondered if Torg had been involved.

The jeweller stared at the guide's back. He turned to Burgess and held the necklace up to the light and said: "This alone would raise a good amount. I need to be sure of the carat of each one."

Burgess nodded. It was a cheerless task in his opinion, and he sat feeling the need to stifle a yawn while the jeweller carried on setting himself up, reaching into the bag at his side and producing a set of weights and a measure for each stone.

"I need to break the necklace up," the man said. "Here, it subdivides into a brooch, and this section would fit into the centre piece of a tiara if we had the sides that go with it."

Burgess first glanced at Kari, but she did not engage so he nodded, and a tedious procedure began until the sections were free and various stones measured in size. Finally, after he had worked through the process and itemised each one the jeweller indicated that he was ready.

"We should bring these alone," said the jeweller. He waved a hand of blessing like a priest over the sections which had once formed the necklace.

Kari glanced down at him in surprise.

"Just those?" she asked keeping in character in her gruff voice.

The jeweller nodded. He explained: "I think, they're South African from the Orange River area. There are a few such stones coming through which I have seen but to see so many in a necklace implies the maker has links to the area. Each of these stones I think are more than twenty-one carats putting the value at £500 each. Twenty stones will provide the value for the transaction that I understand is being done between a dealer in Florence and the bank?"

Burgess nodded and then said to Kari: "Excellent, and your mistress gets to keep the rest of course. Does she have any idea of the value?"

Kari shook her head and Burgess realised that she was shocked at the value. As an aside he said quietly to her: "There must have been a great deal riding on him producing the heir to be this generous. Was that a gift to you?"

Again, Kari shook her head. She had turned quite pale. So, she had taken them from Helly's room, thought Burgess. He turned to the jeweller blocking his view of Kari to give her time to pull herself together. Burgess asked: "Could you give an estimation of the value of the remaining pieces for the manservant here to take to the lady? There's the issue of the fee, of course and your own expenses."

The jeweller nodded separating out a ruby and sapphire.

"Yes ... perhaps ... let me look at the sapphire," he said. "If it is an Oriental, it will more than cover anything further as far as the bank is concerned. A lapidary in Amsterdam bought one recently for the equivalent of £2,600."

"You know your business, sir," said Burgess, "But forgive me I didn't catch your name when you arrived."

"You only need to know me as the jeweller. The bank employs me, because I do know my business, and for me this evening has been worth my time as the stones are a good quality. I will be well paid. Usually there is little time to spend on a negotiation and business is business. Yes, this will do." He looked up at Kari and held the sapphire between his finger and thumb. "You can return the rest of these to your mistress."

"Very well," said Burgess, "'But before we go the lady to whom these jewels were given has not been treated particularly well. If you could glance over a few of the pieces, her man here can give her your opinion of the value. It will be helpful for her future life if you understand my meaning. Then you and I can re-join our colleagues."

The jeweller looked irritated.

Burgess added: "I'm sure the servant's mistress would be happy to make you a small gift for your opinion. Johanne, what would your mistress say?"

Kari nodded.

The jeweller complied as his appetite was wetted for his own benefit. He held up the ruby and looked at Kari. She again nodded and the stone disappeared into his inner pocket.

The jeweller turned to the other items and said: "The stones in the bracelet here are also from the Orange River, I am sure of it. I'm surprised that she doesn't know the quality of these stones. Not as good as the necklace but the quality is good, you see. They're meant to be worn as a set. She should get them valued. If I had more time I could do it properly but I would hazard a value of the equivalent of £5,000… but I am leaving tonight and must go now."

"Travelling so late?" asked Burgess, as he ushered the jeweller to the door. Kari gripped the table with emotion.

"Yes, once the business is completed," said the jeweller.

"Going far?" Burgess asked as he followed the man out of the room. He closed the door after glancing across at Kari. She was lost in thought.

"Yes," said the jeweller.

"Then you are not Swiss?" asked Burgess.

"No, I am not a Swiss."

"Business must be good to bring you a long way," said Burgess.

The man inclined his head but that was the only answer Burgess received. The two men had reached the main staircase and walked down together, Burgess keeping his pace to equal that of the other man. Composed, they walked as one along the corridor to the room where the bankers and the policemen in their guise as diamond merchants were waiting.

The vivacity in the room as the jeweller passed the jewellery to the bankers and whispered to one what Burgess presumed was the value was typical between men made rich by such deals as this. And from his own colleagues there was a sense of euphoria with the smell of the chase reaching its conclusion. Yet at the back of his mind Burgess thought of the distress of the woman he had left upstairs still in her disguise but now rich in her own right. He was conscious of how she and her brother had been exploited and fallen so low. It was the distress of a world in which love did not conquer all.

Burgess shook off his mood and joined in the handshakes having ascertained one of the bankers called Hegner had recently bought a restaurant. He invited the man to look him up if he came to England but from Hegner's expression Burgess knew the man would not wander far from his mountains.

The room finally emptied of businessmen, jovial for Swiss bankers at the success of the evening. Stan undid his tie and removed his stiff collar and said: "That's over at last, what a bunch they are." He glanced across at Carnot who was in a light-hearted mood and asked: "When will you leave?"

Carnot had made the agreement that he would oversee the return of the painting and a bank employee would deposit the monetary value once the detective arrived in Florence.

He said: "I will go tomorrow, that way I can take in Milan and enjoy being feted."

Jack said: "Interesting to hear there's big pickings in South Africa. P'raps I should change profession and go there instead of back to London."

"We know nothing about the problems out there. It's the Orange River area apparently. But you should think on it Jack. You're young enough and have no ties here. That's where we should be heading if we were single men. There's enough in a bag upstairs to set that young woman up for life, anyway," said Burgess.

Carnot licked his lips: "Celebration of this evening mes amies before we return to police work. Are we to think there are more cases to be solved represented in that bag upstairs?"

"Leave it alone," said Stan, frowning.

"But my friend I only think it is necessary to move fast, before she disappears," Carnot said. "And if Gilbert has interests in diamonds, we should ask some questions."

"Not us," Stan said. "We return to London next week, satisfied that we've done the necessary work we were sent to do. Given who we're dealing with we're lucky to still be alive."

"Unfortunately, I cannot say the same," said Carnot. "There is the hope of more gloire for me as an old soldier. I do not have years ahead like the young bobby here and I leave for Milan tomorrow with the banker's man, then to Mestre and so to Florence. Where is the girl now?"

"Why don't you just leave it?" asked Jack. "She's not the one who stole, if indeed the pieces she's taken from Gilbert were stolen in the first place. Without her having that jewellery we wouldn't be on the way to getting your painting back."

"Peut-etre, there is a reward if any of the pieces are stolen or if their gems can be identified?" Carnot took a deep breath. It was not in his nature to look for a fight, preferring to work with these men. But he would stand his ground if a fight started. He sensed there was a physical attraction to the girl for this young "bobby." Carnot continued: "She starts again, with a reward and without the problem of turning jewellery into cash."

The Frenchman paused, glancing from one to the other.

"It is better for her, yes? I think I make enquiries of my superiors. But I sense that you do not agree my young friend. What does your Sergeant think?"

Before Stan could answer Jack blurted out: "Haven't you ever been poor?"

Carnot paused while he glanced at Stan. Stan looked irritated at Jack's outburst. Carnot wondered how much control he would exert over his young colleague. Stan's expression hardened further, and Carnot was not disappointed. He had no need to answer as Stan stepped forward and blocked Jack.

Stan said: "Everyone takes a step back. Think of what I said this morning, our job is done here."

But Carnot picked up Jack's question and said: "No, I will answer. I have not been poor in the way you mean. I have fallen on hard times because of war, but I always had something to sell. A pistol, a book, but you know a different poverty than that, don't you my young friend and you feel what she endures. Does it make her attractive to you?"

Jack frowned and moved towards Carnot, but Stan barred his way turning a shoulder into Jack's chest. The blow registered more because of the injury to his ribs than because Stan had exerted much force. Stan saw it and registered Jack would still not be able to give him any back up in a fight. His eyes went down to Jack's fist and saw it clench. It was a reflex action and Stan followed it up by gripping Jack's arm.

Looking him in the eyes, Stan said: "Whatever you feel she is no prize. Whatever you hope for your life to be she will not settle to it. How long do you think it would last between you? A year? Six months? There'd come a day when you'd finish your shift and come home and find her gone. *Let it go.* Let's finish this with the success it is without you taking a swing at men who are your superior officers. Don't go back to your division in disgrace, which will be something you'll never recover from."

Burgess effortlessly interrupted by placing a hand on Jack's shoulder as he had seen a figure standing in the doorway. He looked from one to the other of the two men and said: "Look."

Kari stood, watching and her expression showed she had heard Stan's words. Her marvellous blue eyes met Jack's and he realised they were cold. Her expression changed to one of understanding only.

Kari said: "He is right, you should listen. Kind as you are you are not for me and I am not for you. We both have things to do to finish this."

Jack pushed past Stan and stood in front of her. it was Kari's smile which convinced him that the Sergeant was right. Sympathy was not something he wanted.

"If we are done, I will go," said Kari.

"Go where?" asked Carnot.

"To the mountains," Kari said.

Jack looked intently at her realising he was making a fool of himself. But before he could speak a waiter with a large tray slipped into the open doorway of their room to avoid a prattling group in impeccable dress coming along the corridor.

The Bride and Groom were leaving.

Kari had seen something and murmured a name. In less than a moment she had moved into the chain of people proceeding past the room. Jack had heard it and followed but at the door he turned and said to the other men: "She's seen Gilbert."

"Better stop her," called back Stan.

Burgess moved through the crowd in his smoothest manner, now the hotelier again, excusing himself graciously. Stan, slower than Burgess and uncomfortable in crowds, followed, aware that his manner of dress was inviting more attention. None of them had a suit fit for the occasion they now were witnessing. He made no effort to be polite and several women steadied a tiara as Stan pushed past. Carnot held back, following at the rear. Aware he had almost provoked a confrontation with the young constable he decided he would wait and watch until he was needed. He had no doubt that the three Englishmen must need him soon. As Carnot reached the reception, he moved towards the front of the crowded guests by staying near the wall. It allowed him time to take in the tiara and necklace which glittered on the Bride's skin. She had seen more sun than was considered fashionable in Paris and London. The bride was no lady then, thought Carnot.

Jack had caught up with Kari and blocked her progress. He dragged her into the doorway of an empty salon. She was like a lost child.

Jack said: "Come, what good will it do for you to confront him?"

"Have you not seen the sky tonight? The sky is purple like my pillow when spotted with vomit. I can still smell the rancid odour as it filled the air of my room and taste the scum it left on my lips. And although it was by her hand it was him who put the idea in her head that she could have everything if I was gone."

"You're not in your right mind," said Jack. "Come away. The man thinks you gone. You've succeeded against him by getting out and Torg will be free for ever. By all accounts you've enough in that bag of jewellery to set yourself up for life. Get yourself away and join that man Grieg you mentioned, dance and be happy."

But Kari was like someone intoxicated: "No, she will not make her mixes against me. Do you see the necklace and the tiara? For the bride who refused me water when I begged for it? The bride who he found mixing the chocolate maker's recipes. She who was so willing to make a small adaptation to the recipe to remove me."

"Do you know how she did it?" asked Jack.

"No idea but she ate one without any effect."

"So, she is one of those people, then," muttered Jack, "An arsenic eater." Jack stopped as Kari stared at him. "

"There was a case that's how I know about it," Jack explained.

Kari said: "When I challenged them in the shop about the chocolates making me ill, they knew it was her. But, of course, she was already supplanting me."

Before Kari could respond Gilbert looked their way. Instinctively Jack moved in front of Kari, smiled, and made a slight bow, realising he had been recognised from the other day in the park. Stan arrived behind Jack and took Kari's arm and she allowed herself to be led away.

Gilbert murmured to Helly. She nodded and looked in Jack's direction. It was the similarity again to Torg that would draw him, Jack knew that. From the expression on her face Helly could see it too. Gilbert started to come across through the guests towards Jack. They were a well-dressed group, obviously English from their manner and dress, and they showered him with congratulations.

"Easy does it, young lady," said Stan tightening his grip as he felt some resistance, "Don't go putting yourself or us at risk. Come away now and let Jack head him off."

"Un moment," Carnot had got through the crowd as Kari tried to free her arm from Stan's grip. "A little something to distract the man, perhaps? From your bag? Diamond merchants should make a gift to the bride, don't you think, and it will be a nice little bid for future business."

"Agreed, Jack did you hear?" asked Stan.

"I did," Jack responded quietly maintaining his position.

Kari was angry. "*Never,*" she spat the word out.

"Come ma petite, what can you do?" said Carnot. He shrugged as he added: "He has married the woman and she has his child in her womb. Be free, start your life, and you and I both know that most of what you have in that bag of yours he had already given to her. Give something back and go, join your brother."

"Perhaps this," Kari produced a small, jewelled vase.

"Where's Burgess? Make sure he stays out of sight," said Jack, as he took the vase.

"He went to the side and joined a large group," said Carnot.

Jack stood his ground, controlling his expression, and waited.

"Right Gilbert's coming and we're going. Come on, give Jack a stone as well." Stan took the bag, prised the flap open and pulled out a single stone. He gave it to Carnot. "Here you go, stay with Jack, will you? Tell Gilbert we go on Monday and try and make an appointment with him for tomorrow, so he might do some diamond business with us," said Stan.

Jack half turned and said: "What?"

"Don't turn, do what I say, give him the stone and the vase, tell him its old, that's an order. We're going," said Stan.

"I curse him," said Kari as if she was in a trance.

"I have no idea what that means from your country. Now, if you were Italian that would be different. But go!" said Carnot.

Stan turned Kari round and woodenly she let him lead her through the crowd. Carnot stepped to Jack's side and the two men waited.

"Allons y," said Carnot. As Jack glanced at him, he translated: "Let's go"

"Thanks," Jack said quietly, and they waited until Gilbert detached himself from his well-wishers.

"We meet again," said Gilbert, assessing Jack.

Jack worked at his smile, making sure he met Gilbert's gaze in as open and friendly way as he could manage.

"We do indeed, sir," Jack said.

———

"Ah what a great coincidence, this being your wedding day and we, meeting for business here. Allow me to introduce myself. I am an associate from Paris, Monsieur le Blanc." Carnot raised an eyebrow but made a small bow as he said: "Felicitations, monsieur, et madame."

Gilbert inclined his head in thanks.

"And if we may," Jack carried on, "a small gift of our esteem for your lovely wife."

The emerald between his fingers glinted in the lights.

"Peut-etre mounted in a ring?" suggested Carnot.

"You are a jeweller?" asked Gilbert.

"I have some skills," Carnot waved a hand to show it was not an issue before continuing: "Take the stone, m'sieur for your bonne femme."

Gilbert took it as a matter of course, holding the stone up.

"It looks perfect, but sometimes a flaw ..." he said.

Jack was aware of movement coming towards them as people stepped aside. A rustling of fabric as dress and train swept along the floor and then a fan patted Gilbert on the shoulder. He coloured but turned his head towards his bride who would secure his title and Jack saw the greed in the eyes as he considered her. She took the vase.

"My love, how delightful, and see these gentlemen bring another gift for you." Gilbert pressed the emerald into her hand and while she lifted the jewel to the light he continued: "This gentleman has suggested a ring."

"And I thought it was business," said Helly.

The accent was French and confirmed how wrong they had been for the English Helly spoke was easy. Jack sought for something to say remembering his manners as he coloured, but Carnot bowed, and the French came fast as he spoke softly to the young woman. It was direct and she clearly understood and exchanged a look with Carnot to show she had accepted whatever compliment he had paid her. It clearly was not disagreeable to her.

But Gilbert had not caught everything Carnot had said, however he was aware that his new wife had not found it distasteful.

"Are your ladies with you tonight?" Gilbert asked.

"They were to have come but there was too much business involved in this trip," Jack said quickly before Carnot could reply.

"I would have asked you to join us had they been with you, but I think gentlemen alone may cause a little difficulty with the arrangements. Where did you say you came by the Emerald?" asked Gilbert.

"I didn't, but we have interests in the Orange River area," replied Jack. He met the responding flash in Gilbert's eyes with interest.

"I see you're familiar with the area, sir," Jack said.

"I have some interests. Tonight, it's not the occasion but while you are both here, perhaps next week when we return from our visit to Mont Blanc…" Gilbert turned again to Helly, and it was said as a statement, not a seeking of her agreement: "My love, before we leave …"

"D'accord," Helly said with a glance at Carnot. His eyes left hers as he bowed.

"Next Wednesday then, at the Parc de la Grande, you know my house, I think," and Gilbert swept Helly away.

Jack bowed his head and nervously dropped his eyes, fingering the cuff on his left sleeve. When he looked up Carnot was in conversation with a man on his right and the exchange was frank. Then the man excused himself and Jack and Carnot were alone for a few moments.

"I have no secrets from you, that man is my constable. He will travel with me to Italy." explained Carnot.

"Has he been with you all the time?" asked Jack.

"No, no, he arrived today, when I sent for him Paris dispatched him here. He will keep an eye on Kari, tonight."

"I could do with some air," said Jack, watching the excitement of the guests ahead.

"Yes, I noticed a stench in here as well, which is stronger than sweat. The man is unpalatable I think you say?"

"That's a polite way of saying it," said Jack.

"And the music is growing loud, trés forte, and too much to think, but here is your Burgess," Carnot said.

Burgess came with great ease, past the waiters balancing trays and waitresses who avoided the wrong attention.

"Did you see?" asked Jack.

"Everything," Burgess nodded.

"We should move in case you're seen," Jack looked towards the door that Gilbert and Helly had gone through.

"We should certainly move," said Burgess.

Carnot quietly drew Jack and Burgess to one side, and they were standing in the front entrance of the hotel before they knew it. The last guests had gone through into a ballroom where the music was beginning.

"Shall we walk?" asked Jack. Once outside he asked Carnot: "What did you say to Helly?"

Carnot shrugged: "I said things that a bride should hear on her wedding night – even such a bride as she. I think she will not be told such things by this man she has married. It is too much of a business contract."

"But what did you say?" asked Jack

"Ah, le Bobby desires a lesson from the great Carnot in how to make love to the woman?"

Jack looked uncomfortable. He said: "I wouldn't go that far, but you clearly have a way with the ladies."

"I talked of the moon, the stars, love … it will lose its meaning if I try and tell you in English. But know one thing, if I was the groom, I would watch my step with that woman. She will have his children, but she may do the job on her groom of the executioner for you. Son problème avec l'arsenic – trop facile d'ajouter de la soupe."

"Arsenic I got there, and soup? If you're saying he needs to watch his soup I would agree. She clearly knows what she's doing with doses as I learnt to my cost. Am I right that the French she speaks sounds educated to you?"

"Mais oui," Carnot nodded, "She has been to a good school."

Twenty-two

Jack and Stan arrived at Dover early on the Monday morning after quite a departure and journey. Stan had taken the decision not to wait until Sunday to leave as they had originally intended. As the senior officer he gave Jack an order that they should get out fast. They would simply disappear, and Burgess would explain to Mr. Allen that they had been called away on business.

For his own part in all this Burgess decided to stay around for another week and had confided to Stan that he would keep Kari in his sights. As a cover Burgess arranged to stay for a few more nights at the Beau Rivage in Ouchy but was ready to carry out his mission of tracking Kari at a moment's notice so sure was he that she would go after Gilbert. He had waited years to arrive at this stage with Gilbert and would seize the opportunity if it meant getting more evidence on his long-time quarry. A week could do it, he told himself, although it was all the time that he could spare for he must then return to Brighton, to the normality of a busy season, and to his Alice.

Two nights of lost sleep Stan and Jack endured. They took whatever seats they could with time spent on making endless changes via Bâle, Paris, and Calais. There had only been one argument between the two men. It had been heated and both had expected it as inevitable. It was, of course about Kari and Jack had refused to back down. Stan had however stood his ground working on his own inclination to give Jack a clout but he had managed to keep his voice quiet and stand with sufficient distance from Jack to be out of hitting distance. They had the row, and no one came to blows but Jack came close. Insubordination Stan knew it was, but he chose to let it vent and never had he worked so hard on his own reactions. It had caused them to miss the faster ship to Dover from Calais.

Stan had said: "I won't risk the mission to help her further. What is done is done. Look to the future now. The mission is a success. Forget her."

"That I can't do," said Jack.

"Then bear it, pour yourself into your work is my advice," said Stan. "You go back after a successful mission and time will help all you feel now. Will you shake hands with me, Jack? As colleagues, not as Sergeant and Constable but as two men who have worked together on a difficult mission and won."

Jack had stared back, more stunned at Stan's approach as it was so out of character. Part of him felt foolish but it was a question of loss of face and Stan had given him a way out. Never one to harbour a resentment he had held out his hand ready to shake Stan's.

it was a quiet crossing after that and Jack sat alone on deck as Stan occupied a bench below. As the ferry from Calais approached the white cliffs of Dover Jack took in the work going on at Granville dock. The intention of the work seemed to be to deepen it and enlarge the quay space. It looked enormous, probably several acres in size, Jack reckoned.

As the ship started to slow down to enter the harbour Stan joined Jack on deck, and the two men stood together in silence, their recent exchange making casual talk difficult.

Scanning the scene Stan pointed to where the clock tower was in the process of being built. Jack nodded, but no words were exchanged. It was a healing of sorts as they both engaged about the building work they could see. It was enough for Jack to re-establish respect for his older superior.

"Are those screw steamers?" Jack asked, nodding towards where the Calais and Chatham vessels were docked.

"Looks like it, goods only," said Stan. "We'd better be getting in the queue to get off."

They picked up their bags not having been able to send the luggage on ahead as all the forward planning had collapsed with their early departure. As the ship docked and they disembarked Stan's first act on shore was to send a telegram to his mother-in-law's home.

Jack waited for the Sergeant to finish at the telegram office, kicking a stone a few inches ahead and pulling it back towards him with the toe of his boot. The anger that he had expressed earlier had now dissipated with the reality of the working relationship. But unlike Stan he had no-one waiting for him.

Stan emerged and walked over to Jack. He simply said: "You are off duty until three pm Wednesday. I don't care where you go or who you see but you and I are not in England. Got it?"

Stan started to walk away, and Jack called after him: "Stan, where on Wednesday?"

"Camberwell, unless you hear otherwise," Stan called back. "Present yourself at three pm, no earlier, see. Don't come in uniform. Be prepared for trouble but come just as you are now."

Jack nodded accepting that would be the meeting with Hunt. He now had the issue of where to go until Wednesday morning when he must make the journey to London. Wherever it was he had to make sure he could be standing before Tom Hunt at the assigned hour. Jack thought of Burgess and wondered if Kari had indeed followed Gilbert and Helly. If that was the case where would Burgess be now? Pulling out his pocket watch he checked the time and compensating for the differences thought he was right that Carnot would be leaving Mestre on his way to Florence.

Stan had told Jack very little about his own movements on Saturday night. After avoiding a stand-off between Gilbert and Kari Stan had walked her back to the guest house and left her on the doorstep. He had checked the exits and stayed in the shadows for hours, watching in case she left. By midnight Stan made the decision that he had taken enough precautions to avoid Gilbert's murder at the hand of his former mistress.

At least on that night.

It was as he left his watch that Stan decided that Jack and he would leave immediately and avoid any blood-stained encounter Kari might initiate with her former lover and his new wife. What she did once the two policemen had gone was none of their business. Once back at the hotel Stan tapped repeatedly on Jack's door until it was opened.

"Stan? Is everything alright?" Jack was still dressed.

Stan nodded indicating to Jack to keep his voice down. Jack stood back to let his Sergeant into the room and once the door was closed Stan explained where he had been.

"Gilbert's such an unsavoury character that I don't give a toss about the man's future chances. If Kari does polish him off, she'll be doing us all a favour. Look, get your things together and we go now."

And go they did.

Now in Dover Jack had been left to his own devices and continued as he had been since early morning, staring at the sea while he considered where to go. He thought of a couple of nights at Sam's and finally declaring himself to Mary. Stan had encouraged him to settle down and forget Kari and even Harriet. It had rankled with Jack despite there being wisdom in the advice. He played the last few days over and over in his mind like a child turning the pages of a picture book. The story however was without an ending.

And Mary? What were his true feelings about her?

He thought she would accept him but in the last few weeks Jack had barely thought of her and now felt false if he followed Stan's advice. To go to her without warning because he could not have either of the women that he really wanted seemed dishonest. It had been a sudden thought of his to consider proposing to Mary and then Jack had been shocked by his feelings for Kari. They were physically overpowering and different to those even that he had for Harriet. It had been more than a year since he had received Harriet's letter ending their relationship. There had been nothing more from her and he never expected to see her again. With Harriet there had been a tenderness, a protective instinct. But not so with Kari.

But Stan was right in the long term if Jack was to avoid the overwhelming loneliness in his life. Better to make a good faithful match with a partner who would work alongside him. They were comfortable together, he and Mary and perhaps, in time, he would feel an overwhelming love for her. There would be passion, he had no doubt of that as she was desirable, but it would be a taking of it, a function of desire.

Jack turned his back on the sea and stared at the dock buildings. No, there was no long-term hope in that kind of relationship. To marry he knew he had to feel there was no-one else. But if they were blessed with children? Of course, they could find love through them.

But there again was the picture of Kari with her eyes alight as she talked of the mountains and of her passion for the climb which translated into laying in his arms. But it would not be, and he knew that he must push the thoughts down forever.

It would be better to remain as he was. Many did remain single in his line of work and many were successful. Anyway, Jack thought, there was time to let the bittersweet memories fade and Mary would not expect to see him until September and perhaps by then he would feel differently. With that decision Jack dismissed the idea of making a sudden appearance at Sam's home. His arrival there could alert Hunt to the fact he and Stan were back in England if Sam felt duty bound to contact the Inspector. But there was one man he could go to without Hunt's knowledge and that was the Parson. The more he thought of it the more convinced Jack was that getting across to Lymington was the better thing for him to do.

Time under the Parson's counsel he was sure would be helpful.

*

The other two protagonists Carnot and Burgess had a very different start to Sunday. For his part Carnot enjoyed a good night's sleep as little was likely to disturb the French detective. That Sunday morning, he would start the journey to retrieve the painting for the Louvre. His star was in the ascendancy, the food was good, and he had enjoyed the time with "le Bobby." He also had several days ahead of being feted by the Italians on his way to Florence and once back in Paris with the old painting he would be the toast of the Sûreté. He slept like a baby and on Sunday morning met up with his constable at the Lausanne station, after making his farewells with Burgess.

Much to his surprise Burgess received the suggestion of a visit to England from Carnot and agreed to play host in Brighton on condition that a few bottles of wine accompanied the Frenchman. Burgess realised that this French Detective had an instinct for surviving politically, which Burgess wished he had had in his career. But they also shared a love of food and drink and had an intense loyal nature in friendships. Burgess had no doubt that such an alliance would lead to advantages for Carnot in his career and that he, Burgess, would be the means to a link with Hunt for the Frenchman and possibly even higher. Burgess determined to mention the role Carnot had played to Tom Hunt for, who knew what potential there was in having a visit to Paris? Alice would like that, he thought.

So by daybreak on Monday Burgess had taken the risk and endured a sleepless night in an uncomfortable coach. Some of the equipment Kari had bought for them in Lausanne had come in useful in a long and tedious coach ride. There was just one other traveller and apart from a nod neither man had introduced themselves, but both man's demeanour had been friendly enough. Burgess gave a brief thought to Stan and Jack and wondered if they had made the fast ship from Calais to Dover.

*

By Monday evening Jack reached Lymington.

No-one at the Vicarage was expecting him as he had not had time to send word before running for a train to start the tedious journey across from Dover. Then, hours later, there he was suddenly in the Vicarage garden as Timothy looked up from his papers.

He was only half-concentrating on the task on his desk as Timothy saw the young man, grinning broadly with his face showing evidence of having seen the sun and waving a hand at the startled Vicar.

"*Jack,*" Timothy exclaimed and was round to the front door, helping to take the travel bag while Jack dropped the rusk sack he still wore onto the step.

"Helena, Peter," Timothy called, as he pumped Jack's hand up and down. "There is a friend here you will want to see."

"I'm sorry for not giving you notice I was a coming, I know I'm not expacted. We only landed at Dover this morning and I had to run for the train," said Jack, and the greetings continued as Peter Fisher appeared. Despite the unexpected nature of his arrival the welcome was all the warmer.

"My boy! What a treat that you've come back to us here," said Peter Fisher.

Jack and the old Parson embraced and added in a handshake in an enthusiastic reunion. The old Parson noted quietly how Jack's face looked worn. He was grubby too from soot and travel.

Helena followed close on her brother's heels and then stopped as she remembered the propriety of the situation as an older woman, a mother with grown children of Jack's age and the wife of the local Vicar. But Jack kissed her quickly on the cheek and dispelled any fears of impropriety.

"We have followed your journey as well as we could," said Helena.

"I'd have been earlier if I'd worked out the train times. It was a last-minute decision to leave on Saturday night and Stan and I made it to Dover this morning."

"When must you return to London?" asked Timothy.

"In two days, they don't know we're back yet."

For a few moments Peter Fisher was silent, working out that Jack and Stan had fled. He asked: "And Stan? Where is he now?"

"Gone to join his missus and the family at her mother's in Kent," explained Jack.

"Not London? Anyone on your trail?" asked Peter Fisher.

"No … no, I'm sure there isn't," said Jack. He added: "Stan didn't take any chances that's why we left two days early."

"But you didn't want to go to London?" asked Timothy.

"Not yet," Jack looked from one to the other. He added: "You see Stan hasn't let the Inspector know we're back this quick." He paused avoiding the real reason Stan had not let Hunt know: "We, er, got out before things developed so we're not expected until Wednesday. Time for a catch up with family for him and to come and see good friends for me."

"Well, you're in time for supper, but there will be a price to pay. We want to hear about all the places you've been to," said Helena.

"I'd expact nothing less for bed and board," said Jack, grinning.

"But first you must wash," said Helena, taking his jacket. "And I'll see this jacket is given a freshen up tomorrow."

Conversation across the table made Jack realise how tired he was as a sense of normality took hold of him. Then as the plates were cleared Timothy disappeared into his study, returning with a map, which he placed in front of Jack. It was a section of Europe which showed the south of England with the main ports marked, France and across to the borders of Italy, taking in Switzerland as well.

"Ready when you are," said Timothy expectantly, as he

635

settled back in his chair and raised his eyebrows for Jack to begin.

Jack smiled at first as the three faces before him each had an expectant look. But then he grew serious. He started with: "You both being of the priesthood as it were, this will have to be like it was the confessional."

Peter Fisher glanced at Timothy who nodded. Helena, disappointed with the signal that what Jack had to share was for the two clergymen only, realised that she would hear the travels on another occasion and started to withdraw, But Jack caught hold of her elbow and said: "Now there's no taking the remains of the sponge pudding back to the kitchen. I'm in need of your counsel as much as the two reverends here."

And so Helena sat while Jack began his account. For the next twenty minutes Jack did most of the talking while the three friends listened only intersecting his silences with a carefully phrased question to prompt him to continue. Jack used Timothy's map to show them the routes he, Stan, and Burgess, had travelled. Of course, they knew which hotels Jack had been staying in from Peter Fisher's visit to the Cook's office with Harry. But Jack put flesh on the bones about the scenery, the journey, the people, and the food they had enjoyed.

But Jack talked then about how they had solved the case and his audience remained silent until he saw the exchange of glances between Timothy and Peter Fisher. Jack realised that he was sharing information about Kari, the poisoning he had experienced and his own illness. In a need to talk to confidantes Jack spoke of the influence Gilbert had had over the young climber Torg. Peter Fisher's expression called Jack out of his monologue as he glanced into the old Parson's eyes. Jack froze, horrified that he had disclosed so much. Not only that but it was information which could place his friends at risk. He had also let his reserve about the woman slip and Jack had shown his feelings for Kari. The empathy was there in Helena's eyes. But worse of all he sensed he had mentioned Gilbert's full name and position.

The name wasn't familiar to Timothy and Helena but it was to Peter Fisher. Jack could see it and realised he had rambled on, partly because of the state he was in but also because he had done exactly what Hunt had once advised him not to do: relax.

"Did I say his name?" asked Jack.

"Yes," Peter Fisher answered.

"You know of him?" Timothy asked his brother-in-law.

"The family, yes, long ago," said Peter Fisher, "But I remember the succession problem they have to a title and wealth. It created a competitive drive in the younger generation as they were growing up. I vaguely remember the man you referred to as a small child. He must be mid-thirties now?"

"Could be," said Jack.

"And what of the woman that you mentioned?" asked Timothy.

Jack shook his head, unable to answer.

The two men registered the danger present in the information they had acquired, but it was the fleeting expression of pain Jack had allowed himself to show that took Helena's attention. Jack saw their concern, especially in the old Pastor's eyes as Timothy quietly quoted:

"Grief melts away

Like snow in May,

As if there were no such cold thing."

"The Bard again is it?" asked Jack, feeling exhausted now.

"No actually, it's a clergyman called Herbert, which I copied out when I was studying theology. I've got them still if you want to have a look. He was born during Shakespeare's life, but it's a devotion through faith he writes about, not the other kind of love," explained Timothy.

"But surelye snow can linger, and I've now seen a part of the world where it doesn't melt," Jack said, no longer masking his emotion. "It's a poem written by someone who's not seen that, not seen the harshness that the mountains can have. A Swiss or a Norse wouldn't have written that. They'd understand the long dark, cold winter that does linger."

Peter Fisher glanced at Timothy and tried to lighten the tone: "Good point, I would have liked to be in a tutorial where that was raised. That's what travel does for you. Timothy, have you any of that brandy left that you produced at Christmas? If you have, I think four glasses wouldn't go amiss and Helena … cake I think."

Both obligingly left, returning with a tray, decanter and glasses, fruit cake and a golden liquid.

Jack took a glass and sipped, managing not to pull a face as he swallowed. He put his glass down and apologised:

"I've been rude, I'm sorry. I've been a fool and got involved. I know that now and it coloured how I saw the truth. Stan was right to give me an earwigging about it. There were things that should have been unspoken, though and I can see I've disclosed too much by the look in your eyes. Mother used to talk of life being like profit and loss in the books when we did the numbers together. I can see what she meant now. Sometimes gain and other times loss."

They waited for Jack to say more but he remained quiet. There was a clear sense that the young man had more he could tell them but now had resolved to keep his own counsel.

Eventually Peter Fisher said: "I hope this sadness will pass, for I cannot see what future there would be in such a relationship for you, Jack. But nothing matters now in that case you've told us about except that you are returned and it is solved. Timothy, Helena, and I will forget what we have heard tonight, as we have on so many occasions in our calling. Come, let's walk our meal off before the evening falls and enjoy the air."

Jack offered Helena his arm, talking of the food he had eaten in grand surroundings. It was his deliberate attempt to lighten his mood.

"You will go home and attend to your beat again? And see your regulars in the shops and houses?" asked Helena.

"A different home shortly," said Jack. "I'm following a bride to her new home in Bow soon as she becomes Mrs Franks and suspect my bed in her old home has already been moved. I shall be begging a floor from the groom."

"I'm sure you will not be forgotten," said Helena.

Jack laughed as there was a certain amount of truth in her statement. He changed the subject: "How is the watercress business?"

"Doing well, the month of May is the best time now. I've only half an acre, which is just as well given the clean running water needed but there's such a demand from London. It gives the local women work too, and the carter to get it up to the station."

"Perhaps I could help tomorrow?" asked Jack.

Surprised, Helena stood back and looked at him.

"You will be the only man there apart from the carter."

"Being surrounded by women was never a problem," Jack said and grinned at the thought. He added: "And I expact it will probably do me good to paddle about. Anyway, I've eaten too well and sat about too much in the last week. Some hard work will help my thoughts."

"Alright, thank-you, I'll not refuse an extra pair of hands. But take care you don't leave yourself open to situations tomorrow. I would save you from a widening of involvement with one or two of the girls. Let me leave it at that." Helena looked away, then added: "I'd say the same to my own sons."

"They would be very safe with me," said Jack.

"It's not the women I'm worried about," said Helena. She had stopped walking and returned Jack's gaze with a frank look.

Feeling out-gunned Jack flushed and felt the colour in his neck. They had reached the right bank of the river and the sound of the blackbird singing before dusk brought the group to a stop to listen. The bird was in a tree quite close by and the group heard his song answered some distance away. Dusk in the west was gathering and it would soon descend like a blanket being folded across a bed. Jack found it extraordinary that he was standing again on the banks of the Lymington river staring at the harbour. He thought back to a few weeks ago when he had helped with the boat demonstration.

Timothy turned to lead them back up Quay Hill over the cobbles while Jack looked into the distance adjusting his expectation of what he would see. The mountains across the lake in Geneva were still vivid in his memory and a sense of loneliness hit him as it was not a memory that he could share with his current companions.

*

Burgess had forgotten what it was like to have the jarring in the legs, every muscle twisting, as the coach negotiated narrow roads, hitting the holes still waiting to be filled. Now he could have kicked himself for his obsession about Gilbert. He should have left well alone and not gone up to the Pension to see if Kari was alright. Leading a climb the proprietor had said Mr Croz had left to do. Mont Blanc was the destination.

The coach, or "diligence" as the driver had called it, had made Cluse and then onto Maglan and so through the valley to

St Martin. Burgess had paid 30 francs and been assured that a good hotel, the Hotel du Mont Blanc, awaited him – First class it was he had been told. It would have to be after this thought Burgess. He had also been assured that the road was fit for coaches. To go onto Chamouni from there would be another 15 francs. And why, he asked himself, was he enduring this torture?

It was because the woman Kari had disappeared and because he felt he owed it to Jack to see she was alright. No, he told himself. That was not all of it. Part of him wanted to see what was going to happen to Gilbert. His waters told him something was afoot and that the ballet dancer had started a final performance.

On Sunday morning Burgess had gone to the small Pension and asked for J Croz only to be told that "monsieur" had left the night before to lead a tour to Mont Blanc. Kari had probably twelve hours lead on him. The rational man inside him told Burgess to forget it. But the obsessive reflector was struggling to take hold and without Jack and Stan to reason him through Burgess had started to sink again into the dominating tendency that had made him ill.

But that was not all.

A dark suspicion in his mind Burgess got himself back as quickly as he could to the Beau Rivage and packed. Carnot had already left, as had the Cook's tour, and there was no one to inform about his impending departure except the reception. Earlier he had decided to stay for another week and had made a fresh reservation. Before Jack and Stan had left Ouchy, he had wanted time to allow observations about Gilbert to unfold. But now there was no time for that. Burgess informed the receptionist that his plans had changed but there was no issue about cancelling the rest of his stay. The hotel was busy, and Burgess had no doubt that they would let his room. He sent two telegrams: one to Alice and the other to Hunt's home. Someone should know where he was going in case he disappeared.

Gilbert and his new wife had stayed in the hotel for one night after their sumptuous reception and left the following morning. Certainly, he could understand a visit to the area to celebrate with her parents and relatives. Gilbert would tolerate that, once, thought Burgess. Helly's family clearly had not been among the glamorous wealthy set he had witnessed at the reception. The daughter of provincial French would see a different lifestyle to the one she was used to once she had produced the heir so longed for.

It all fitted together.

Kari had headed to Mont Blanc to lead a tour dressed in her disguise as J Croz. She was the dancer who was used to hard physical regimes in her parts and a mistress of disguise, thought Burgess. Jack had told him about the mountain climbing as well. The stories of dangling her legs over a precipice, in particular. There was strength there certainly. Surely there would be the odd nuance in the voice or the occasional mannerism that would give her away. Burgess thought of his Alice and was sure that no matter how she presented herself he would know it was her.

Burgess steadied himself as the coach lumbered over some obstruction on the road. He and his fellow passenger glanced at each other, bound together in an interminable discomfort. Then the exchange was over, and Burgess put his head back, attempting to stop the jarring to his neck. He closed his eyes to fight the nausea and set his mind to focus on Kari.

There was only one reason Burgess could see why she would have embarked on her masquerade. Like himself whatever dark plan had formed in her mind Burgess could understand the compulsion to finish Gilbert. He had felt that himself but, in his case, he had been a servant of the Crown, a policeman, and had ignored orders to drop his obsessive pursuit. Kari had no such authority. Perhaps, in her mind, she had a greater authority. A calling almost, to hold herself out as a renowned climber to Gilbert and risk recognition so to remove his infection of the world. Yes, in his more unbalanced moments Burgess could understand that mission.

Burgess was brought out of his reflection as they were passing a waterfall, and his fellow Englishman held up a map for him to see. Reading it would have made Burgess feel ill with the swaying and he nodded his thanks but shook his head.

"Can't see small print," Burgess said.

"Nant d'Orli," said the fellow traveller anyway, "A fine waterfall but further up there's one called Nant d'Arpena, eight hundred feet high, like the Staubbach near Lauterbrunnen. Do you know it?"

"Sadly no, this is my first time in the Alps." Burgess smiled, amused at the thought of coming regularly to this world.

"I didn't think you were a climber." The traveller leant forward and offered his hand to shake Burgess's. He continued: "I come each year, but so far the top of Mont Blanc has eluded me, but the exercise and scenery are good generally. Don't tell me you're putting yourself through the journey for the views alone?"

Burgess noted there still had not been an introduction but shook the man's hand and said: "Some friends of mine just left a day ago and I was due to meet up with them. They clearly thought I wasn't coming so I made haste to get the first coach I could. I must say I think the journey alone requires stamina. I shan't go back this way." Burgess gripped the window frame as the coach hit another hole.

"Where do you go back to?" asked his companion.

"I'll make for Calais," said Burgess.

"Get to Culoz and you can pick up several services a day to Paris. Saves doing this again to get back to Geneva. I do it so I can see friends. You'll find the views from St Martin are good enough of the mountain and you should see a fine sunset which will turn Mont Blanc red. Where are your friends staying?" asked the passenger.

Burgess answered: "If they're still there at the Hotel Mont Blanc. If not, I'll go on to Chamouni tomorrow and try and find them."

"Sounds as if they like fine places. Probably try the dear ones then: there's the Royal de l'Union, the Londres, or the

Angleterre – you'll see why the hotels have names referring to England when you get there. It will be packed all season with English."

The traveller settled back into his exploration of the map. Burgess murmured his thanks and returned to reflecting on Kari's intent. He thought of the wealth that she had stored in jewellery. His mind went to her brother and not for the first time Burgess wondered where the man had gone. If the woman had any sense, she would join him, but sense was usually deficient in matters where revenge had become paramount. He knew that too well.

"Is it dangerous to go up Mont Blanc?" asked Burgess.

"You need a guide who knows what he's doing. They're a bit pricey now, 100 francs a time per guide and most parties take four of them." The traveller jabbed the map again with his finger and Burgess glanced briefly down before putting his head back again to control the nausea.

The man continued: "It depends on the route. Serious climbing would have each person with one guide, and you'd be roped together and go up at midnight, walking eighteen hours. Some routes take eighteen hours over the snow and over complex parts of the glaciers. People have died on the Col du Géant you know, coming down on the Italian side. It was a few years ago, the guide as well. A lack of care of course and shouldn't have happened."

"You sound very experienced,' commented Burgess.

"Well, it becomes a challenge after a while to do as much as one can of the area, year after year. I shall finish at the baths at St Gervais near Chamouni before I return to London. And yourself, where do you hale from?"

"I'll return to London," Burgess answered, thinking of Hunt.

"Well, if it's to go up to the point you can see from Chamouni which is taken for the summit called the Dome de Gouté, go from the Pavilion de Bellevue and you can get up and down in a day." The man added: "It's a popular excursion and there's little danger."

"Thank-you, if I survive this journey and find my friends, I can see I shall be looking at the mountain from the safety of a hotel terrace," said Burgess managing a smile.

His fellow traveller laughed and glanced out of the window. Minutes passed and Burgess felt the coach steady and slow.

His companion lowered the window blind and stuck his head out. Burgess thought the man must have a cast iron gut to move. The man said: "Ah, we're close to the inn at St Martin. This is the best view in my opinion."

Burgess changed sides as the coach had started to slow, and there was a splendid view of Mont Blanc, with a church in the village framed against the mountain at an angle. When the coach finally stopped the two passengers got out and the chill was like a knife. The stop was a brief one and they were back in the coach, over a bridge and onto the hotel Mont Blanc for Burgess's overnight stay. Collecting his bags and the one holdall with the equipment he bade his fellow traveller farewell and wondered if the man would get any sleep that night or if he would start his climb at midnight.

Inside the hotel reception Burgess tentatively made enquiries for his "friends," explaining that they may have been part of a larger party and have a guide called J Croz with them. They were a couple recently married, he said and explained he was a relative who was visiting from England.

The receptionist shook her head and seeing that he was getting nowhere with his enquiries Burgess tried Gilbert's name. But he was without luck and the couple were not staying in the hotel. Burgess saw little point in trailing around the village as he could not imagine Gilbert staying in anything but the best. He ordered a carriage for the morning and resigned himself to a good dinner that night, a beautiful view, and a warm bed before the next journey.

However, the following morning was bright, and Burgess took his exercise once the sun lit up the street in front of the hotel. He had woken at various points of the night, once falling over his bags which he had dropped in the middle of the room, so fatigued was he. Still sensing the motion of the coach just as a sailor would who had spent a long time at sea Burgess passed a woman with a basket of bread and bought a loaf in the shape of a ring. He tore chunks off it and ate as he walked enjoying the newly baked fresh smell.

A one-horse carriage collected him at eight o'clock and he began another journey, this time to Chamouni, preparing his mind to accept the time it was all taking but resolved not to return home via the same route to Geneva. He had spent years waiting to get Gilbert and this was just one more day in his life. He settled back to enjoy the fine views and wrapped a rug around his knees. Despite the sun the air held a chill and Burgess realised that there was an art in the way to dress in these hazardous mountains.

The carriage entered a long valley and Burgess looked out on alpine plants and green pastures, towered over by mountains the driver said were called: "The Aiguilles," and he told Burgess a story of two ladies on a col who had been buried in an avalanche.

"English ladies, and their guides, in such a wild place," the driver said.

Burgess nodded but turned his head away. Surprised by the number of people he could see enjoying the area he understood what his fellow passenger from last night had meant by the reason the hotels had names with an English connection. The area clearly was a popular destination for his fellow countrymen and women.

"Will you go up, Monsieur?" asked the driver.

"Perhaps if I could ride up," said Burgess.

"You don't have to go so high to have a good view. You can ride a mule to Planpras, three hours, and then sleep there. Ask at your hotel."

"Would I need a guide?" asked Burgess.

"There are parties for ordinary excursions about the valley. The one to Mont Anvert stops at a pavilion with night quarters. It comes down across the glacier. It is like a sea, the Mer de Glacé. It's the most popular unless you are a climber. The Mont Anvert has many rhododendrons, and you can explore it without a guide. Be careful of the danger of avalanche though."

"Like the ladies? Did the ladies really go?" asked Burgess.

The driver laughed: "There is little danger, perhaps fatigue and the climb from the Chimeneé is steep but you have English lady climbers I think?"

"Do we? You know more than I. My friends are recently married, the lady with child, but I think she is a local woman, and the man is English. Would she be able to manage?"

The man thought: "If she is a local then she will know the mountains. I would think they would go to the Mer de Glacé, but if you go up you will need more clothes," he said.

"That's most kind advice," said Burgess. To go would be a gamble he thought plus it may be a wild goose chase, but it was the only local information he had. He added: "I think I have what is needed in my luggage. A guide helped me in Lausanne. You may have heard of him, name of J Croz." Burgess waited.

"Croz, did you say? Of course, well-known here as a family of guides. One of the younger ones perhaps?"

Burgess did not answer the question but told the man to stop at the most expensive hotel in the valley. Resigned that he may have to sit on a mule for the next few hours if he was to follow Kari Burgess set his face to join the crowd in the most patronized spot in the High Alps.

"How long now?" asked Burgess.

"Here, the Royale," said the driver bringing the carriage to a stop. "The best is expensive. You will pay three to four francs a day and more for breakfast."

"Well, what-must-be-will-be," said Burgess as he climbed down from the carriage. A man came immediately from the hotel and took his bags. Burgess followed him in.

"I'm here for the wedding group by the name of Gilbert." Burgess was all bonhomie despite how he really felt.

"They are out, Monsieur, left a few hours ago to meet their guide. Are you to join them today?" asked the receptionist.

"That was the plan, I'm a relative from London," explained Burgess. "The guide was J Croz?"

"I believe so, he came with them and went to stay with family in the town."

Burgess leant forward: "I'd be interested in taking one of them up with me. Have you the address?"

"They're expensive, but you can go with a tour on the donkeys. No need to pay a hundred francs for a Croz," explained the receptionist. "Anyway, it's unlikely any are free."

"Can I get up there with a tour and join them before the end of the day?" asked Burgess.

"It is possible, and they will stay at Planpras tonight. Should I get a man to take you to the next group going up?"

"Yes and, er, keep the luggage will you as I'll return here tonight rather than Planpras. I'll just get a few more appropriate things out." Burgess pulled some coins from his pocket and laid them on the counter. It was meant as payment for the room, but he knew he had put down too much and would not see any change.

Opening his bag, Burgess set about the extra clothing that Kari had bought for them. He chose the flannel shirt and wool layer, pulling them over the one he was wearing and tucking the plaid wrap under his arm. Burgess had already put on the second layer of woollen socks that morning as they were more than two thousand feet higher than Geneva, but he had not had chance to soap the inside to prevent them from blistering. If he was going to be on a mule he should not need to do so. Anyway, he thought, there's no time now.

"It is good you are so early, or you would miss the day." the receptionist clicked his fingers and a young boy of about ten or eleven walked quickly over.

The receptionist gave the boy instructions but as they were in French Burgess felt he had to ask that he would be taken to the right tour party.

"Excuse me, is he taking me to the tour for the Mer de Glacé?" Burgess asked.

The receptionist said: "Yes, the boy will take you to the tour, but you must hurry as it will leave soon."

And hurry they did.

When the sun was at its peak Burgess and the party he had joined dismounted at a rocky ridge. From their vantage point they were overlooking the Mer de Glacé which seemed to go on for miles. Burgess could see an icy grotto which was closed off. He pointed to it, but the tour leader shook his head.

"Is it safe to go over to the cave?" Burgess asked.

The man shrugged: "Le grotto? Non, il y a des gens sages et des gens qui prennent des risques," the man said.

Burgess heard the word "risques" and nodded sagely in response to the guide as if he had understood everything the man had said. But, as he glanced around, he could see a party of three people roped together making their way towards the icy grotto. Burgess felt the chill as he watched and realised that it was not the altitude having that effect but the hazardous route that the guide was taking. Moreover, he believed that he recognised the dark-haired guide as J Croz. If so, it was Kari. Slowly he reached into his bag to find the small opera glasses which Jack had left with him before leaving Lausanne.

"You never know, they might come in handy," Burgess could hear Jack saying and had barely put them to his eyes before the three people started across a highly fractured and complex part of the glacier. Unable to stop himself Burgess waved and shouted to get their attention. He resorted to shouting Gilbert's name. Nothing would deter him despite the tour leader's warnings of avalanche. While the right honourable Gilbert looked up having heard his name echo around the valley the rope linking him, J Croz, and the new Mrs Gilbert to the rest of the party some metres further back, snapped. The party further back toppled, but the three leaders disappeared down a crevasse that had been covered with a slight layer of frozen snow. Their screams echoed around the mountain, but they were seen no more. The chill and the silence that followed were profound. The last face Gilbert had seen was that of the burly ex-detective Burgess who had pursued him for so many years.

And as for Burgess never had he witnessed such a murder.

*

After an hour, Burgess had almost passed out with fatigue and cold. He had remained below a peak towering on the right with other on-lookers from the tour. Although it was May the snow from the crags blew in flurries around them. The onlookers watched as the local rescuers crawled back and forth across the ramshackle slats of wood which they had put over the crevasse. Several were lowered down, and Burgess concluded there must be ledges below the surface onto which a body may have fallen. It was a military style operation and one of the men was clearly hurt as he emerged. There had been no sign of those three who were lost, and it was declared to be an impossible rescue.

Burgess refused to return with his tour, declaring to a few men in Gilbert's party that he had come out from London to see the new couple. He was included therefore in the general grief and shock of that group as someone close to Gilbert. It was true. He had been and he affirmed that truth. But the reality was Gilbert had always slipped away from him as he just had yet again. From this disappearance the man would never return.

Time seemed to have stood still and now Burgess was being offered extra wraps against the cold and creamy milk to drink which turned his stomach. A local added liquor from a flask which smelt like brandy and indicated Burgess should drink. He nodded his thanks and found it more palatable.

Two sounds punctuated the silence. Away in a valley somewhere he could hear the cow bells ringing. Such a bizarre sound it seemed, so normal in some ways in that setting but out of place in this tragedy, for such it was despite his feelings about Gilbert. The second was a sudden crescendo of grief as a woman, about Alice's age sobbed inconsolably. She was enfolded in arms and a cloak wrapped around her and Burgess was told it was the bride's mother.

That Kari could have sacrificed herself and an innocent unborn child made Burgess retch. He thought that even Gilbert's child deserved a chance and for Kari, he grieved at the loss of one so young and talented although tainted by what she had known of her lover's antics. And for the brother Torg, criminalised in acts committed out of love for a sister, Burgess felt a distress as the man was not likely to know of his sister's fate.

For Helly and Gilbert he had no remorse.

A Frenchman offered him an old waterproof cloak and a woollen shawl for his head. Burgess nodded his thanks, realising that Gilbert's party and his own group were going. Burgess was being offered transport back down. He nodded his thanks and accepted the offer of transport in a respectable looking coach.

The same man who had given him the cloak held out a chunk of toasted bread covered with melted cheese. Burgess realised he must look rough as there was concern in the Frenchman's eyes and Burgess accepted the food gratefully. It was being cooked on a griddle over a brazier at the side of the glacier and locals were eating it in the hand. Burgess nodded his thanks and made the required noises of appreciation. As he lifted the food to his mouth he realised that his hands were shaking, and instinct told him that Alice needed him to keep trying.

"Bon, mercie," said Burgess and the Frenchman nodded in return.

The food eaten Burgess followed the others down a rough narrow path towards the carriages and realised that the light was going. It was still only mid-afternoon, but the mountains blocked the sun, and it would not be long before the light was too poor to be out there. The group went step by step ahead of him and he realised that the surviving guides who had accompanied Gilbert's party had one aim: to get the group off the mountain before the light went and before clouds drew the day to a close and the weather changed.

Burgess had not realised how the time had gone and as the carriages started off he saw the shadow of the mountain spread across the few buildings as the sun dipped below the peak. It had been now two hours since the tragedy on the glacier and those who were lost were no longer the priority: It was the living that mattered. Burgess told himself he must leave and get to Hunt in London. He could not trust the telegram because of who might receive it at Camberwell. If Stan was right in his suspicions then he, Burgess, must be cautious. Any communication must go to Hunt's home.

Back at the hotel his instinct led him to the dining room and Burgess paid over the odds for a parcel of food for a journey. He reached Annecy by midnight, surviving another rickety route while he fell into an exhausted sleep once he had paid for a quiet room near the station. By six o'clock on Tuesday morning he was on a train for the two-hour journey to Culoz praying they would not be late as once there he would have only ten minutes to make the train for Paris. His train arrived with five minutes to spare and at 7.49 am to the second Burgess was seated on the train as it slowly pulled out for Paris.

So far so good, thought Burgess but he knew making the Calais train would be tight. They were due in at Paris at 3.30pm with a tight change-over and the train for Calais would leave at 4pm.

Burgess made the decision to travel first class this time as he felt he had earned it, and to send the necessary telegram from Dover to Tom Hunt's home. He hoped that Tom would wait for him on Wednesday and find the time for Burgess once he knew about Gilbert. Burgess told himself that the affairs that could be set in train from Gilbert's death were too pressing to wait. He pulled out the last message from Stan and read the name again, hoping Stan had moved his family and that Stan's suspicions might be wrong.

*

In Lyndhurst it was a brilliant morning of sunny weather and the old Parson donned his straw hat and walked towards the water cress beds in the shallow pools. He passed Helena at the point where she unbent and straightened up from the digging in her lavender and peppermint plots. She hailed him

657

and Peter Fisher waved to his sister reflecting on the proverb of the wife of noble character, as he did so. He concluded that his sister certainly fitted the bill: rising early and providing food for her family, considering a field, and buying it, setting about her work vigorously.

His mind went back to some of the women that he had known in his eighty odd years who had run businesses, raised children, some had been mistresses of vast estates, and yet he truly believed that women would be in for a fight to get the vote.

Helena had started to walk towards him, and Peter Fisher called over: "I'm off to help Jack."

Helena nodded vigorously and smiled: "Have you breakfasted Peter? You're out early," she called.

"A habit in recent years. I find I wake early and snooze more in the evenings," Peter Fisher explained. "But yes, breakfast as always was excellent. Will you be long here?"

"Probably another hour," said Helena. "Enjoy your walk."

Peter Fisher walked on brooding a little on whether it was a favourable time to bring up the issue of Mary with Jack. Nor did he know if he did so what position Jack would take on the matter. There were some months before Jack's birthday and he quietly resolved to write to the girl and send her a firm invitation for Jack's birthday. Better to let the issue alone with Jack until September and hope that time would allow the young man to reflect on his infatuation for the dancer, Kari.

As Peter Fisher came up on the area set in a square, he could hear the laughter and Jack's singing. It was a popular song:

"If ever I cease to love,
If ever I cease to love,
May the moon be turned into green cheese,
If ever I cease to love."

George Leybourne wasn't it, the Parson asked himself, written a few years ago. There was Jack, holding court in front of two comely girls both standing knee-deep in the watercress pools, their skirts hooked up on either side into their belts. Jack stopped and grinned as the Parson approached and the girls moved respectfully away, although one glanced back at Jack a few times.

Jack dipped his hand in the clear water and wiped the back across his forehead removing a muddy smear. He walked over to Peter Fisher and said: "You'll need some pattens on if you come down here. Father used to call them pig's pettitoes."

"Yes, I've heard him say it," answered Peter Fisher. The impact of a mutual memory produced a smile from Jack.

Peter Fisher carried on: "I came to see if you'd had enough yet and would join me in a walk. You look better this morning than you did last night. The work has done you good. You looked peaky."

"The travel I dare say. We'd not slept much, Stan and I," said Jack.

"Not that I want to take you away from your new companions," said Peter Fisher, sardonically.

The two men stood looking in the direction of the two girls who were smiling back at Jack.

"Letbehowt'will," said Jack, waving farewell to the women. "I'm not looking for such complications. I'm not too clean to accompany you, Parson."

"I don't mind, it's a country walk." Peter Fisher poked with his stick at a small heap of muddy soil left by an earthworm. It was always a good sign with Jack when he went into Sussex dialect. Part of a test Jack set for the Parson but it also showed a re-emergence of the young man's good humour. An indomitable spirit thought the elderly man, and one which augured well for the rest of Jack's life as he would recover with sleep and good food. The two men walked away and climbed over the stile to join the footpath. Jack tried to help the Parson but Peter Fisher waved the strong hand away. Instead he asked: "The name you mentioned yesterday, Gilbert. What will happen to him?"

"I don't know, nothing probably," said Jack.

"How come?"

Jack shrugged and said: "Well Parson, he's out of reach of justice in Geneva and living like the Lord he wishes to be. Stan said we'd done our job, and it wasn't anything for us to be concerned about. I'm not sure Mr Burgess agreed. He stayed out there. I hope it's not to be paying off an old score."

"Revenge you mean?" asked Peter Fisher sharply.

Jack nodded.

"I don't see Mr Burgess succumbing to that, surely. Ensuring justice is done I could see but not taking matters into his hands, Jack."

"I don't know, Parson," said Jack, "Gilbert destroyed his career, made him ill. It can't be easy seeing the man prospering in a beautiful part of the world, away from the reaches of the police."

"What would you do, Jack?"

"It's not my call," Jack answered. "I'm not to have any part in bringing the man down, that's clear. If he stays out of England none can touch him."

Laughter floated across from the watercress beds. It brought both men out of their reflection.

Jack continued: "Gilbert has to live with himself, all the shameful things he's done. If he crosses my path in the future, I'll deal with it. We may have stopped his death this time. That won't always be the case, and ultimately he faces mortality as do we all."

The Parson was not so easily deflected. He said: "Did you ever speak to him, Jack?"

"A couple of times," Jack grinned as he recalled their audacity on that last evening.

"In what capacity?" asked Peter Fisher.

"He thought I was a diamond merchant."

"Then he'll remember you," said Peter Fisher, with some sadness. "And that raises my concern."

"Not too likely he'll come across a constable in Stepney," said Jack, grinning. He added: "He'd be hard-pushed to get back to England."

Peter Fisher frowned and said: "That may well be true now but in twenty years who knows what or where you will be. And I will not be here to keep an eye on you. As flippant as you are being, I recall that you did not want to leave me at Selmeston over the summer because of the reach the man has here …"

"Quite right, Parson," Jack interrupted. He perched on a wall and watched as the Parson knocked some weeds down with his stick. Jack continued: "It's true there's more than just him here. I'm not in the know of how many but I believe Stan has a feel. He was too twitchy on the journey home and anxious enough to get his family away from London until he was back. Anyway, I've said enough, perhaps too much, and none of this you needed to know. Best to let sleeping dogs lie."

"But they don't, Jack," said Peter Fisher. "In all my years situations which people think are best left alone have a habit of re-surfacing later in life and with worse consequences. No, issues should be dealt with firmly at the time and I am inclined to think Mr Burgess is right to track the man."

"It's wisdom you speak, Parson. But I fear the guns are pointing in our direction rather than at Gilbert."

"We must fight as best we can Jack and take a stand."

They walked on but Peter Fisher had not finished with Jack yet and he said: "And I don't think for one minute that you truly believe that leaving a situation alone is the best way. I doubt

Gilbert would have become so audacious if his own family had dealt with his behaviour earlier."

Jack shrugged but said: "I've no doubt you're right and there comes a point where we all have to decide where to draw the line. The deaths I've seen have convince me of why I should stay in the Met."

The two men continued their walk and were joined at one point by a duck and her seven ducklings. The antics of the birds acted as a distraction from the sombre mood the discussion had created. They continued past the water pump where children were drawing water for the family and two matrons part curtseyed at the sight of the Parson. He was known to all after years of visiting Helena and Timothy. Peter Fisher stopped several times on the walk to acknowledge and enquire after the health of locals.

Jack stood silently to one side and remembered the smells from the animals on the adjacent farms. His stomach turned as he thought of the havoc Gilbert could reap in a life and with sadness, he remembered a girl who had dangled her legs from a crag in Switzerland. He thought of Stan's advice and once the Parson resumed their walk decided to see what Peter Fisher thought of seeking advancement.

"Stan has been talking to me of trying for Sergeant," Jack said.

"That's good, you'd do well, I think," said Peter Fisher.

Twenty-three

On Wednesday morning Tom Hunt delivered his young daughter Daisy to the gate of the school at the top of the road. It was a rare treat for Daisy to have her father take her and, as that area was still on the edge of the countryside, the air smelt clean and damp with dew on that late May morning.

Usually, the children went all together in a group, but that day Daisy Hunt had proudly walked hand in hand with the man she adored, for he was not on duty until that afternoon.

Or so the family had thought.

From the school gate Tom Hunt watched his little girl join the other children in a line-up while the teacher who had rung the school bell waited for them all to fall silent. Hunt half glanced around to see who was about. Well, it was still a good area, he thought, considering the joys and fears of parenthood, and weighing them against the sheer delight he felt in his children. As Daisy disappeared into the school building Hunt turned and started to walk back home.

He reflected on Burgess's telegram which had arrived at six o'clock that morning. The messenger's banging on the front door had been a shock to Mrs Amelia Hunt given Tom's usual division between home and work. It had always been that way since they had the children and allowed her Tom to keep his sanity while protecting his family from knowledge of his cases.

Burgess had kept it brief:

"Arrived Dover. Gilbert dead. Witnessed it. Meet in London. Will wait at Dover for your decision."

So, it had happened – Tom Hunt had known that at some point there was likely to either be a victim that would remove Gilbert, or one of his followers would become ambitious. He thought, quickly running a few names through his mind, of characters that he had suspected for some time would likely be potential successors. As usual proof was lacking.

The last thing Hunt wanted was Burgess showing himself in Camberwell New Road. Or Around Victoria Station for that matter. Hunt was too well known in the area from Victoria, St James's and up to Whitehall to meet Burgess, in case it started tongues wagging. They must meet half-way between Dover and London or perhaps between Brighton and London if Burgess could get across to that line quickly enough from Dover.

Hunt had scribbled a response, paid, and included a tip for the telegraph boy. The boy touched his forelock and Hunt was closing his door when he had second thoughts and chased after the lad. Hunt added another message to be sent to a man in his home at Hughenden. Although Disraeli was officially on holiday as the House was not meeting it was a long shot that the Prime Minister would still be in Buckinghamshire. The man could have left for Balmoral for all Tom Hunt knew and be picking primroses with his sovereign in the Linn of Muich.

Reflecting on how the telegram had affected him Hunt pushed the anger that was brewing away before he reached his garden gate. He took in the scent from the few early roses already blooming. These Amelia had successfully protected through the wet few years since they had moved there in '72.

All very normal but Hunt's world had changed with Burgess's news.

Hunt pondered again if he should have accepted staying on at Windsor and stepping into his father's role. There would have been no disturbing news by telegram at their garden gate, but the house would have gone with the job, to be kept or removed at the vagaries of a monarch. Tom Hunt thought with a slight shudder of the Queen's death and the Prince of Wales and the dislike he had for Hunt. Well, no one would take this house away as Hunt had bought and paid for it. Yes, the flowers might have been the same in Windsor with Amelia's green fingers and the school would have been a few minutes from home as it was here. But it would have been the Windsor estate school for Daisy, and their two boys Michael and Horrie. Their sons would have followed their father into the Queen's service, and as for Daisy … no service job for her. All three were as bright as buttons and he hoped his boys could be something better than someone's servant, even if that someone was a monarch. Daisy must have her chance as well … something more than learning how to sew and cook … no he and Amelia had been right to leave Windsor. Hunt thought that he was still really ruled by the Queen's comings and goings and the cycles of court life. But at least their front door was their own.

Now if Burgess was right and Gilbert was dead an organisation which had been dominated by one man could even split into a multi-headed monster. "The King was dead, long live the King," was the standard response when a monarch died– but who would become king of Gilbert's organisation?

Better the devil you know, thought Hunt.

He closed the garden gate behind him and looked back towards the school. In hoping the world would be kind to his family and the young friends of his children he experienced turmoil. Given what his team were dealing with fear plagued him as if someone walked over his grave.

He should have had a clear day until three o'clock when his duty was due to start. The meeting with Stan and Jack must now be off-site and not at Camberwell as originally intended, for which he would use the Boot boy Percy again to head them off. The lad was showing a real talent for undercover work. There was no way he could contact them as he believed them in the middle of a journey from Switzerland. And neither Jack nor Stan had been in touch anyway to dissuade him of this.

Harry had said he would try and get across the river but was officially on duty at Shadwell. It was not lost on Hunt that Stan had probably been communicating only with Harry. There had been a colleague named according to Harry and a promise to disclose it to Hunt later. All very cloak and dagger but suspicion was like that. It made one take unusual steps to protect those one loved. Hunt felt weary of such issues but was resigned to Stan's need to protect his family. After all he would take such action himself in similar circumstances.

Meeting up with Harry at Victoria would be fine and Hunt made a mental note to get a message to Harry to meet at Victoria.

Tom Hunt looked at the sky, and thought that Amelia was right about the weather, it was going to break and there would be rain by midday. Before then he would have met Burgess, listened to him, and decided on the best course of action. Jump the wrong way and a man's reputation could be damaged by being accused of being a crook, possibly even a murderer, but dressed as a serving policeman. There was also the risk that the wrong man would have been warned off, maybe even to disappear, taking his stock of information with him.

Yes, it was a seminal day – the status quo was about to change and he, Inspector Tom Hunt, was about to roll the ball down the hill to knock out the skittles. He thought again of who it would be that he, Hunt, would be arresting tonight? He had a choice of two or three men. Two he had counted as trusted friends. The third was a stickler for the rule book and could never be Hunt's friend. One of the three had betrayed his oath. But not just that. Betrayal was a disease and every colleague had been more at risk because a policeman had chosen to take a thief's shilling. The duplicity had led to the perpetuation of a criminal group and provided certain individuals with untold wealth.

His thoughts turned to the success of the operation. They had the diamonds, according to Harry. There were more than had been stolen and Harry had hinted as much according to Stan's information sent to him. Harry had said the Shah's diamonds were indistinguishable from others in a bracelet. The Queen would get the lot. She would be pleased about that and would enjoy being seen to be magnanimous by giving an opulent gift of the whole bracelet to the Shah. But the thief had gone free. Would anyone care? Probably not, thought Hunt, it had always been about saving a royal face.

Hunt wondered what Disraeli's reaction had been to his telegram. Hunt could not know that the unexpected outcome of the team having met Gilbert in Geneva and one member having witnessed his death would rocket Hunt's name to the top. Disraeli had received the news even before Hunt's telegram arrived while seated at his desk overlooking the Hughenden Valley that morning.

*

It had taken Amelia Hunt all of two minutes to realise that a morning with her Tom was not going to happen. Irritated at first her matter-of-fact nature soon took over and the sense of duty long cultivated from her childhood at Windsor, reinforced by being a policeman's wife, led to acceptance of the situation. Amelia was under no illusions about why Tom was often at Windsor. Of course, his mother had been part of the reason until she had moved but the summons came regularly from another matriarch. Amelia and Tom may have left the estate, or "run-off," as her father had described their actions, but they were never really out-of-service once Tom joined the police. Amelia's brilliant eyes looked at her husband knowingly as he opened the kitchen door. But she smiled to his relief, and as if it was the first time, he experienced the marvel in a belief that they would always be alright just so long as Amelia gave him that smile.

"What time are you off?" she asked.

"As soon as I get a response from Charles if I'm to meet him part way," said Hunt. "I suggested in my message to him that we meet on the Brighton line. He's got quite a convoluted journey to get across to it, but it will be better for him on his journey home and no one will be looking for me on that line."

Amelia nodded. She was too aware that Tom should not tell her so much. But they had worked together so many times from when he had become a Sergeant and had moved into a station house. Amelia had been drafted in to attend to female prisoners in the absence of any other female present, and she had cooked and cleaned for the two constables that had lodged with them. She knew this was not unusual. It was the same for so many wives of policemen. That was how it was, and she had accepted it, despite the prisoners in the lock up stinking of urine and gin.

"You've still not told me why there's all this secrecy between you and your men, or why you're meeting Charles Burgess on the pretext of still having a half day's leave," Amelia said.

"Well, the half day was not a pretext it was a real attempt to try and get some time with you," said Hunt. "Circumstances are now such that I must hear first-hand what Charles has to say, before I meet my men at three o'clock. Then I have an arrest to make but, I'm having an argument with myself as to which man is the crook."

"Doesn't Harry know?" asked Amelia.

Tom Hunt laughed: "He thought it was me," he said, and went to his favourite seat by the window, the one which overlooked the garden. He decided he had said enough.

Amelia was not to be distracted. She said: "Is it that difficult?"

Tom Hunt nodded: "It has been, and even two weeks ago I had no idea but there was that one evening I was at Clarence House and I let slip some information. It was acted on by one of the two policemen I was with. Yes, that helps talking to you. That knocks the third possibility out. The activity in Jersey means it could only be one of two men. Now Burgess says the head of a crime group is dead. That might flush someone out."

"And if you get the wrong one?"

"I suspect the right one will disappear. Or I will have to. No, my love, I'm sorry, my humour is a little twisted these days." Hunt moved quickly to his wife's side as she had reacted to the impending danger. He carried on trying to reassure her: "I shan't be in danger and neither will you and the children. I won't be alone tonight when I make the arrest and I promise you that no action will be taken until I am sure."

Her stomach had rolled, and Amelia steadied herself with her hands on the table. Remembering to breath while her Tom held her, she kissed him in return.

*

"You're taking a risk, Tom," said Harry Franks.

He looked across at Hunt, distracted by the fact it was the first time since they worked together that he had seen the Inspector in civvies. It did not bode well, thought Harry.

671

The simple reason was Tom Hunt had not had time to change. There had been a delay in getting back after his meeting with Burgess and he had abandoned the idea of getting his uniform.

But what struck Harry was how monochrome Hunt's clothes were, without even a hint of colour. He glanced down at his own waistcoat which some would have described as brash - Stan for instance – but not Harry. He put it down to his French blood, this desire to cut a dash and it had become his calling card in recent years. Harry looked out of the window at the bustle over on the station and then across to where he could see an engine on a turning circle.

Hunt had chosen to meet at a part of the station where the engine works were carried out because there was always a high turnover of men. As a result, the only other customers were engine drivers and the maintenance crews. He and Harry were seated at the only trestle table, tin mugs of well-stewed tea before them. Harry shovelled in extra sugar to drown the strong taste.

"Midland Railways are abolishing second-class apparently." It was Harry's attempt to make conversation with a "PerWay" man standing next to him.

The man responded and reached for the sugar. He said: "I heard that, not surprising given the number of people moving around now. They'll use the second-class carriages though.'

"Is that right?" said Harry. "Better journey then for the likes of us."

"Should be. But there's more who'll pay a third-class fare so it stands to reason. You in the booking hall?" The man had glanced at Harry's waistcoat.

"Mostly," Harry answered. "You?"

"Fettler on the lines."

The conversation, such as it had been, had come to a natural end and Harry's eyes flickered across to a woman with a baby who was begging. Hunt had been watching her too. He exhaled audibly with the weariness he felt of such situations and the fact that they, as policemen, should stop her. She saw his look and came over, holding out a hand first towards Harry, who pulled out tuppence and beckoned for her to come closer. Pressing the coins into her hand Harry said: "Be careful who you ask for money."

Hunt watched the exchange. Reaching into his own pocket he added a threepenny bit.

"The butcher round the corner will give you the mutton bones for a farthing," said Hunt. "Boil them up and give the broth to the child."

The woman nodded, took the money, and blended into the crowd.

"I used to think we'd see an end to that sort of thing," said Hunt.

Harry looked up from his tea and raised his eyebrows. "Did you, why?"

"I don't know, books the Prince used to get us to read when he came to the school. Perhaps if he had lived things might have changed. The Queen was certainly more aware of things because of his influence."

"What sort of stuff was that then you read?" asked Harry.

"Ideas called "Socialism," the satisfaction of human needs, law of value – he wanted us to know it was there. That and music by Schubert," Hunt laughed, more at Harry's expression than his memories.

"Sounds like dangerous talk from such as you," said Harry.

"I don't think Schubert would be considered as dangerous," said Hunt.

"Funny man, all that though, you being the child of servants, and all. Not like he was into opening the flood gates and sharing what he and his lady wife had, was he? Bit of a risk putting stuff like that into a child's head. Probably the reason why you left." Harry sniffed as the steam from his tea made his nose run.

"He'd have respected the decision to leave. To answer your point, we all take risks every-day; that doesn't stop you or I from leaving the house. Changing the subject how's the new one in Bow?" asked Hunt.

"The house? It will be fine once the furniture's in, it's piled high with tea-chests at present, all from Rose's," said Harry. "It will be better still when she is there. Not long now 'til the happiest day of my life. Goodness knows how she'll react to all this tonight when I tell her. Are you sure you're right?"

"Well, yes," said Hunt, then he added: "No, frankly I'm not, but it will all blow apart this evening. I'd rather not do it at the house out of respect for the family. I plan to get him across to the station before his shift starts. It will depend how quickly others connected with the dead man will move."

"And if he's heard about the death and doesn't show for work?" Harry deliberately did not refer to Camberwell New Road.

Hunt had made a decision on that possibility: "If he doesn't, we have no choice but to go and get him at home."

"And Stan and Jack?" asked Harry.

"I'll get a message to them to meet me at a pub," said Hunt, standing as it was time to leave. "I don't want them anywhere near work."

"Usual messenger?" asked Harry.

"Yes, why?" Hunt asked.

"You know Percy's Stan's nephew?" asked Harry, cautiously.

"I didn't … no. Of course, Percival Green," Hunt smiled at the coincidence, paused and sat down again. He thought the revelation through while Harry waited. "Related to Stan, eh…" Hunt let the thought register and decided he liked the idea. He added: "I think the lad is my man, though and he's got ambition, you know."

Harry shuffled on his chair. "Who's going to be your heavy, tonight?"

"Stan's the obvious choice. Jack shouldn't take the risk after the kicking he had. If it wasn't for your hand …"

"Yes, I know," said Harry. "You'll get word to me when it's done?"

"It would be a help if you were in the background," said Hunt.

Harry looked intently at Hunt. He asked: "Are you going to be carrying?"

Hunt nodded. "If it comes to an argument, given the number who've died … if there was a way of avoiding it, I'd take it …"

"Do a deal then, why don't you?" suggested Harry, earnestly. "Get details from him– he could write them down. I'd be the witness. That way you'd clear the lot out."

"What? And let him go? We can't do that. He's had benefit over the years. Look at the house they live in. People have died, been hurt or damaged. No I can't do that."

"I know Tom, but if he turned, the family could all go somewhere else together, and he'd get his pension in the future. Start again, change the name … think on it."

Hunt glanced around as the detail was becoming too specific. He stood again and motioned to Harry to move away from the hatch. They stared at the hustle and bustle on the station and both were silent.

Finally Hunt shook his head and said: "No, he won't turn informer, at least not in the way you mean. For him to do that would mean the family knowing and I doubt he will want that."

"They'll know anyway once he's arrested," said Harry.

"I've no authority to offer a deal. But if he does give me a list, I'll turn a blind eye for thirty minutes, give him enough time to leave and see his wife and then it's every man for himself. I'll leave what they have alone providing it's a good list. This mess is not of his family's making and the man has saved my life on occasion. I owe him that much."

He thought how his critics would bay for his head, including the new Chief Inspector Arnold in H Division, if the prospect of making a deal ever got out. Well, thought Hunt, the new Chief Inspector had a reputation for treating everyone the same. Rich and poor, he would lock anyone up so why would he protest at breaking Gilbert's organisation? Perhaps Harry had a point - a comprehensive list on Gilbert's group could go a long way to persuading Hunt to do a deal.

One fact did worry Hunt though. Harry, Jack, and Stan were based in H division and he, Hunt, and Arnold, differed so radically in their methods. What lay ahead for Hunt's men in Stepney, he could not say but he could imagine. If Arnold got wind of their connection with Hunt, there would be trouble. Arnold outranked Hunt and would mean there could be delays if he blocked Hunt drafting in those men again. There was only one solution as … politics must come into play. It was a manoeuvre that Hunt despised but which he acknowledged was going to be necessary. Disraeli owed him a favour after this job as the Queen would be very happy with the prestige that the recovery of the diamonds had given and would no doubt be open to persuasion by her Prime Minister.

But how to carry on and preserve the team?

One way was to get Harry moved to Bow, as there was an Inspector's post going. It was time for Sergeant Harry Franks to move up the ranks.

Stan would be in line for promotion after this too, but the question was where? Hunt needed a senior officer in Stepney.

677

And Jack? Still too soon for a Sergeant's position for him, although Hunt knew that their antics that evening would create a Sergeant's vacancy in Camberwell. No, the only movement in Jack's grade at this point could be Constable First Class but any whiff of Jack being Hunt's man would invite unpleasant attention from the new Chief Inspector in Stepney.

Then there was Ann Black. Hunt did not want to lose Ann's input no matter how informal it was but had heard that she was resigning from her post as Doctor Brown's nurse at Leman Street. That needed tidying up as well. It was the husband that was the problem apparently. Not that Hunt blamed the man. He would have felt the same during his own wife's pregnancies, but he gathered there was concern that the association with Jack might put Ann at risk. Well, that could be handled.

An idea that had been brewing was to ask Doctor Brown to go and see Elizabeth Garrett-Anderson at Marylebone and clarify if some position could still be carved out for Ann? She'd need help with the baby of course. It was whether husband George would wash the idea? Doctor Brown had said George was being inflexible since Ann had become pregnant. Perhaps Doctor Brown could see George to emphasise the research side, a nice little office in the house with nursemaids on hand to help Ann look after the baby? Perhaps even the Prime Minister could intervene? A letter commending Ann's work perhaps. Hunt was not beyond asking the Queen to help. He had a sense that she would understand the need for work given her own determination in the early years of marriage not to disappear behind her husband.

Hunt's team faced doom and disaster unless he could get some influential help. The progress in policing that he and the team had made and the likely reward in all their fortunes would come to an end. It was not in Hunt's nature to call in a favour but perhaps now was the time to do so.

Harry moved to go and Hunt knew the unpleasant truth. Harry must go to Bow, Stan into Harry's old role at Shadwell, which would look like a step up although the pay would be the same, and Stan would be plain clothes and able to indulge more that ability to interfere that he had. And he would still be near home.

Hunt, himself was also ripe for promotion, something he had resisted as the Inspector's role kept him close to the ground. It could not last though, and the recovery of the diamonds and Gilbert's demise would show that he had managed the team to glory – a complete fiction, he knew, as they had not even consulted him.

He would resist a move for as long as he could as it was the last thing he wanted at present for his family. But Jack? The writing was on the wall if he stayed where he was with Arnold coming in. Give Jack six months under Arnold's regime and he would be off. There was nowhere else to put him at present. Nothing for it, thought Hunt, Jack must take an order from Hunt to stay in Stepney at Leman Street and endure Arnold, for a few months anyway. Hunt would get him his First-Class status. Why not? The lad deserved it and a few more years and he would make Sergeant. There was no-one Hunt could trust more to follow through. After all there was a precedent with talk that Constable James Garrow in Lancashire would move quickly from second class constable to first class in less than a year. Hunt had heard there was to be a development of adding a briefing role to a first-class constable's position in the Met. It was to liaise with the flurry of crime journalists who had become increasingly common in the last four years. It was hoped, high up, that some inroads might be possible to head off the media induced scares in the public mind and focus attention onto actual criminals rather than encouraging accusations against the poor and ignorant.

Yes, Hunt could make a case to Disraeli, and even the Queen if he had to, that Jack was worth retaining and deserved 'Constable First Class."

*

While Hunt and Harry chewed the cud, Stan had arrived at Camberwell New Road railway station. He was not the only member of the Green family present. It was unexpected, but Percy was there as well. The lad was not quite as cocksure as usual, and he blundered into his uncle in the booking hall. Firing questions at his uncle he watched as Stan's face turned a red colour. Stan gripped the lad's collar and frog-marched him out and away to the back of the brewery. There he pressed him up against the back wall and hissed: "Right, young Percy, you fool, stop right there."

"'Ere let go, Uncle Stan, what's up with ya?"

"I spent the last few weeks undercover and you, in less than a minute, blow it for me. What's afoot?" Stan let go of the ear.

Percy straightened up and put some distance between his uncle and himself. He replied: "You're not to go to the police station, the Inspector's not there. Head into London and look for him at Blackfriars Station. Where's the other one? He said there'd be two of you."

Stan cursed and spat.

"None of your concern, we got separated that's all. Stay at the railway station and head Constable Sargent off. Like me he'll be in civvies. Once you've delivered your message get yourself home and stay there, d'you hear? Don't go into work. Got it?"

"Cor blimey, something's going on, eh?"

Percy got a thick ear from his uncle for his question. Stan peered into the lad's eyes and said: "Stop asking questions. Yes, something's on, that's why the Inspector has gone. If you're going to be a constable one day, you should shut up, and do as you've been told. You'll live longer that way. Here take this."

Stan pressed a shilling into Percy's hand and walked back towards the platform.

"Thanks, you're the Guv'nor" called Percy.

Stan kept walking, resolved to put as much distance between himself and his nephew as he could.

*

Twenty-four

For Jack, after a long journey from Southampton, he decided to ride on an omnibus from Waterloo Junction. There was still the struggle about Kari as he reflected on the last few days, but now he was back in the familiar territory of London there was an element of comfort and protection in doing so.

Jack took in the preparations underway for the expansion of the station to bring it closer to Westminster Bridge Road. It was still not a convenient place to arrive for those working in the City and Jack, distracted for the first time since he had boarded the train at Lymington, wondered why an underground line had not yet been built. As he looked at the teeming mass of people moving around England's capital city it felt chaotic after Switzerland. But then he knew the real reason why he had preferred those mountain views. Cleaner air and uncrowded streets were not really part of it. He had left a woman of spirit there and he kicked himself for not having declared himself to her.

And the fact was that Jack was tired, not just physically but emotionally.

He thought back to how he had let Kari go. No doubt she would have laughed at him and Stan was undoubtedly right that he, Jack, could have been used as an escape route for her to come to England. But he would have married her and there would have been a passion, despite the inevitability of her leaving eventually.

The crowds on the pavement swam before him. He knew he was not at his best after this last leg of the journey from Southampton. It had felt tedious and he had spent the journey penning a letter to the lawyer to let him know that he had returned to London. He doubted that Hunt knew yet that he and Stan had returned early. But they had a good reason and Stan would no doubt explain they had fled the possibility of attracting unwanted attention from Gilbert.

It was not in his nature to feel discontented for long but the prospect of making a report to Inspector Hunt, in a small room at Camberwell New Road, put Jack into low spirits. The omnibus was at the stop close to St Georges Circus and he decided to get off and take a walk up the Borough Road, partly so that he could pick up a train to Camberwell. Jack also thought that the exercise would lift his spirits and perhaps help him to exult in the success of the mission. Jack tried to think himself into a positive state of mind, and instead found himself staring at the quantity of traffic circling the first purpose-built roundabout in London. He had asked for a ticket to the obelisk and received a funny look from the conductor. But the penny had finally dropped, and Jack had been treated to a grin.

The conductor said: "Oh, you mean the *obliss,* guv. That's tuppence."

Jumping off the omnibus, he caught sight of the Asylum for the Blind and all the different religious chapels and churches bordering the Borough Road which competed for God's attention.

Jack had tried to look to the future, but his mind had focussed for most of the journey on the places and people he had met since setting sail for Jersey. Not for the first time he wondered exactly who the soldiers at the castle at Gorey really were.

His mind went over the names and the backgrounds of all the people he had met and whether he would ever run into the Cook's tour guides again as the men had been particularly helpful.

Carnot of the Sûreté, particularly raised a grin, and Jack wondered whether the man had arrived in Florence by now. A soldier turned policeman. HIs reflections moved to himself and he acknowledged how different his life had become from two years ago when he had been a farm labourer.

The bus was at the obelisk quickly and Jack found himself distracted by four lamps on it which seemed an incongruous place to have put them. He shrugged, accepting the need for lighting with all the traffic going around it, and also noticed distances had been put on the base. They read:

"London Bridge one mile, 40 feet.

Palace Yard one mile.

Fleet Street one mile, 350 feet."

His eyes moved to the area and Jack noted it was grubby with too much industry, noise, and smoke from the London to Chatham and Dover Railway. The muck had driven out the toffs that had lived around there. However, Jack could see there were still some buildings with the original concave fronts around St Georges Circus and they stretched along the

Borough Road. He found himself wondering if the Parson as a young man had seen the area after it had first been built.

And that thought brought into his mind how he and the Parson had made their goodbyes in the Vicarage in Lymington. Helena, and Timothy too, had been sad to see Jack go. Plus, there had been a scare in the night as the Parson had fallen getting out of bed. It was only to be expected, Helena had said, but at the Parson's age it had focussed Jack's mind on how much he valued the man, and how much he would miss him when that inevitable day would come.

"Long life to you Parson," Jack muttered to himself as he glanced back at the chapels and churches. Perhaps it would do as a prayer? It had been a long time since he had been in a church. Christmas 1872 wasn't it? Jack asked himself. Before Emily Doyle's suicide. Somehow, he found it hard these days to accept the phrase: "God's in His heaven and all's right with the world."

Jack's friendship with the Parson, although recently found again, had been a very positive one. Jack could not forget the picture he had in his mind of the clergyman who had ruffled his hair as a small boy of nine. He could almost see himself as if he was a bird looking down on the scene of where he had stood at his parent's funeral in Bexhill, as he had held the hand of a woman that he did not know who had turned out to be his aunt. She had abandoned and forgotten him, but the Parson had not. The upsurge in Jack's fortunes in the last year were largely due to the Parson's sheer determination that justice would be done for that nine-year old boy, now a man.

Jack had taken his leave early that morning of his friends in Lymington but before six o'clock he had slipped into Peter Fisher's room to check the man's breathing. As he had approached the bed the Old Parson had opened one eye, and then followed it by opening the other.

Jack had smiled with the fact he had been caught out.

"Mornin' Parson," he had said.

Peter Fisher had replied: "I heard you come in, are you off now?"

"I am, yes Parson." And Jack had re-arranged the pillows and helped his old friend sit up.

Peter Fisher had sunk into the cloud of white cotton stuffed with down. It was too soft, and Jack slipped a bolster in behind the man.

"A lot of fuss, this," Peter Fisher had said.

"Well Helena loves looking after you so indulge her for a day, eh?"

Jack had been struck by how small the man had looked in the bed. He added: "Stay put for a bit here in case anyone traces me to you. I'd like for to know you're not on your own at Simpson."

"Timothy has quite a list of things for me to do for the rest of the summer here," Peter Fisher had replied. "I think it's exaggerating the risks involved from your work, but I'll do what you ask for a few weeks more. Perhaps you'll let me know the outcome as soon as you can? The garden will need tending

———

686

and the Vicar at home could do with me back. Write and let me know how you get on."

"I will, Parson. I'm grateful for your help."

And then time had been against them.

They had carefully shaken hands, taking time to do so as both men were aware that it would be September before they met again. The level of the Parson's faith Jack could accept. He realised the Parson was not afraid to die.

Once he was downstairs in the hall, Jack had kissed Helena on the cheek and received a hug in return, in which he lingered a little longer than usual for that motherly embrace.

"Come again soon if you can." Helena had said.

Jack had nodded and walked out to where Timothy was waiting for him in the trap. He had swung his bags in and climbed up and with a flick of the wrist Timothy had urged the horse forward. Jack had turned and watched until the Vicarage was out of sight. They had been at the station in no time.

"Write, won't you? The more amusing it is the better," Timothy had said.

"I will, and I trust the Parson will pick up soon," Jack had held out his hand to shake Timothy's. It had been a firm grip on both sides.

"He will, Helena will see to that, and I'll keep him here as long as I can, but do me a favour," said Timothy.

"Of course, what is it?"

"Keep it light and amusing, Peter will worry about you."

The awkward silence that comes when friends want to say more to each other than convention allows had fallen on the two men. Jack had nodded and then he pulled his luggage down onto the road and looked at Timothy who had so eagerly engaged in the travelling he had done notwithstanding being at a distance. Another friend in his life thanks to the Parson.

Jack later recalled saying: "Thank-you, I'm not without some understanding of the way you have helped."

Timothy had chuckled and replied: "My pleasure, and it added some excitement to the routine of parish life. Any time you want an accomplice in a clerical collar get in touch. I'll be there like a shot."

Jack smiled to himself at the picture that came to mind. He noted the willingness though and filed the idea away for the future.

He had stood and watched as Timothy turned the trap round and urged the horse on. Jack had raised his hand in a wave, Timothy also raised his hat in response and then had gone along the lane lined with hedges.

And now Jack snapped out of the reflection having climbed aboard the train for Camberwell New Road, just one stop down the line. He did not feel he had much appetite for starting duties again but there was no alternative, and he prepared his mind for work. He knew he was in good time and decided once he was at New Road he would walk to the Green and smell its freshness.

The platform was damp after the midday rain and quite empty. Certainly, there was no sign of Stan at all. Jack had half thought they might meet but he looked at the boy who was walking towards him with some purpose, not yet old enough to have started that growth spurt. The feet were large though and implied he would pass Jack by in height once he started to shoot up.

For his own part Percy had deliberately adopted a different method after receiving a thick ear from his uncle although the shilling had gone a long way to assuage his irritation. He looked at Jack with a blank stare which feigned innocence and slipped a note to him as he passed. Jack stopped and watched the boy disappear into the booking hall and then slipped the folded paper into his pocket. He had noticed the boy was clean, but the clothes looked like they were hand-me-downs which did not quite fit. He was no street urchin though.

Jack reached the booking hall and walked about as he took in who was there. Nothing appeared to offer threat. Four men were in a corner, one of them leaning against a pillar. However, they showed little interest in Jack.

He walked out onto New Road and read the note, interrupted only by a stray dog coming too close. The dog returned Jack's attempts to shoo it away with a whine until it resorted to barking at the pigeons. Jack read Hunt's note several times and muttered an oath under his breath. He turned back into the station to look for the next train to get him to Blackfriars. He would now be late. Jack threw the note into a brazier, pausing to ensure it started to burn. He walked around the woman sitting there warming herself. She extended a hand too late to get his attention.

At Blackfriars, which was only a few minutes' walk away from St. George's Circus, Jack muttered a curse as he had wasted time. There was no sign of Stan as he glanced around the station, so he stepped out onto the Blackfriars Road. Jack deliberately made himself visible in case Hunt or Stan were about. He walked to the junction with Stamford Street and scanned the crowds for faces that he knew. Jack looked across to Christ Church and saw that there was a police station near the church green on Collingwood Street. One of Hunt's stopping off points, perhaps? But though he waited Jack saw no-one that he knew.

And then he felt a tug at his sleeve.

Jack turned and there was the same boy who had given him Hunt's message at Camberwell.

"How did you get back here so fast?" asked Jack.

"Caught the same train as you, didn't I? Just you didn't see me. I've been following you down from the bridge. Thought I'd better stop you now and give you the rest of the message. You're to go to the "Dog in the Pot," on the corner of Charlotte Street near Nelson Square."

"Who are you?" asked Jack.

"Boot boy at Camberwell, Stan's my uncle. Inspector Hunt's seein' to my trainin' like."

"Is he?" said Jack, amazed. "And you say you're Stan's nephew? I expect that's why the Inspector's taken you on then. I hope you do well, lad."

Percy bowed and as quickly as he had appeared moved into the crowd, but Jack's words of encouragement had gone home. He watched Jack leave the junction and Percy moved quickly to track his new compatriot.

690

Jack cut along Southwark Street past Hopton's Alms-house until he found a street stall selling hot potatoes. He bought one, together with a cup of watery soup and stood chatting to the street vendor while he dipped the potato into the steaming liquid. It was always the best way to get directions to part with a few pennies and help someone make a living. Who knew when Jack would be back this way again but he may need information in the area and the man might remember him in the future if there was a good tip? In response to Jack's request for Charlotte Street the man pointed towards a junction off on the right and said:

"Down Gravel Lane, you'll come to Charlotte Street in a couple of minutes."

Jack nodded his thanks and set off passing the Dyers buildings and Swan Company, logging them away in his memory for his route back. He found Charlotte Street and strode onto the door mat of the Dog in the Pot, leaving the door slightly ajar while he allowed his eyes to grow accustomed to the dim light inside. It was full of men at the end of a shift drinking their day's pay away.

He couldn't see Inspector Hunt or Stan but walked to the bar and stood at one end deliberately positioning himself to be visible. He ordered a beer, which he would not drink, and spilt some of it intentionally. He lifted it to his lips while he stared across the rim into the gloom but the only face that he saw which he recognised was the cheeky face of the Boot Boy Percy who grinned at him from the doorway. So, the lad had followed him, thought Jack. Well, so be it, Percy was at least an ally.

Percy touched his forelock to Jack before he disappeared outside. He would remain on watch by a lamp post until Jack re-appeared. For some reason known only to Percy Jack's word of encouragement had been more appreciated than a coin.

Inside the public house Jack called the Landlord over and asked him for information: "I'm looking for two men I was to meet here on business. One's about my height and the other would fill the doorway in size. Might you have a back room they could be using?"

"Your name?" asked the Landlord.

"Sargent," replied Jack.

The Landlord turned to the shelf behind the bar and moved a bottle. Underneath it was a note which he handed to Jack.

"They left suddenly but asked me to give this to a young man answering to the name of Sargent. Called away I think."

"Did someone come?" asked Jack.

"I wouldn't know, we're busy, see." The Landlord pointed to his customers and turned back to serving the next group of men.

There were more than forty men in the bar, and one jostled Jack. He found it difficult at first to control his irritation. It was an accident, it was nothing, but the strength of feeling it produced would start a fight. Instead, Jack saw sense and turned for the door. Outside he read the one word on the paper and a letter. It was a name known well to him and the letter was a T.

"Train, Thames, what does that mean?" Jack said. Had it been a G he would have guessed it was Gilbert, but a T?

Was it linked? Were there developments regarding Gilbert? He spotted Percy and beckoned him over. In silence Jack led the boy until the two of them were positioned at the best vantage point on Nelson Square. Where to go from there though? It was unlikely Stan and Hunt had returned to Camberwell and more likely they had gone to help the Sergeant named on the paper.

Jack waited and watched, and he and Percy stayed put for twenty minutes. For a lad that was so conversational Percy managed to stay silent, taking his lead from Jack. From their position on Nelson Square, they could observe the routes to the Blackfriars Road, down to Surrey Row and over towards Gravel Lane. Whatever it was that had cut short the Inspector's time and made Stan and Hunt leave the public house might still be underway. If necessary, Jack could stay in the square for hours, but there was the issue of the lad with him. The owner of the name scribbled on the paper must be in trouble or Hunt and Stan would never have left.

A couple of workmen cut through Nelson Square and, once they had disappeared several ladies, who were quite well dressed, came out of a house on the corner opposite Jack and Percy. It was the time of the afternoon to take the air. Most of the people moving around appeared to be reasonably well-to-do which struck Jack as funny as the rest of the area was poor. The hedges were high though and it was not too clever a place to wait. Still in his travelling clothes Jack realised that he would stand out as would Percy. He should get rid of the lad in case they attracted unwelcome attention.

"Alright Percy, you get back to Camberwell. I don't know where your uncle and Inspector Hunt have gone but my money would back that they are not at the station. I think they may have a call to make on Sergeant Morris at home."

"He's on duty this afternoon," said Percy, "I saw the rota."

"How come?" asked Jack.

"For the boots," explained Percy. "They have to be done."

"Well, he might be, but I suspect something's happened to him, that's why Inspector Hunt and your uncle have gone."

"Is it to do with the job you've been on, Uncle Stan and you?" asked Percy.

"Could be," Jack answered.

"Uncle Stan says I shouldn't ask questions."

"He has a point, but you won't learn anything that way. Here," Jack slipped Percy tuppence and pointed to Gravel Lane. "Go back up Southwark Street and you'll find a street seller with hot potatoes. Buy one for yourself and be polite so he remembers you for the next time you're in this area. Who knows when you'll need a friendly face, eh? Then get back to the station and do your job."

"Then what?" asked Percy.

"Go home," said Jack.

They stood in silence until Percy said: "Sergeant Morris was nice to me."

"He was to me as well," said Jack. "I expact he might be alright but I'm working on the fact that as Inspector Hunt wanted to see me and your uncle away from the station that Sergeant Morris isn't there. He might be at home. That's where I should go first in case I'm needed. Let's hope there's no need for prayers-going."

"We won't refer to this again, will we?" asked Percy.

"Why do you ask that?"

"That seems to be the way the Inspector works," said Percy. "There's a nod, or he asks how I am, but no one talks about what happened last week, or yesterday. But everyone knows what's gone on and officers understand things."

"Next time we meet we'll behave as colleagues do," said Jack.

Percy held out his hand. "Colleagues," he said. Jack and the boy shook hands and then the Percy was gone.

He should not delay, thought Jack. With the whole day having been spent travelling he set his mind to getting across to Morris's home. To do so would mean yet another train journey and he hoped he would be in time for whatever Inspector Hunt had in mind.

*

In Herne Hill Sergeant Morris and his wife, Violet, were standing opposite each other in their front room. They had sat at first on the over patterned settee, something they rarely did as the room was not a place he liked to be and for her it was a show room. But that was now all over.

"We'll be slighted when it all comes out. How could you?" asked Violet, her voice higher with the emotion.

"For you," said Morris.

She looked shocked and moved away from him.

"I wanted everything for you," Morris continued, "That's how it started, then I was in too deep and they had too much on me."

The look on Violet's face was fear and shock.

"The boys ...." she said, "They'll lose their jobs. Oh my God, how can you sit there and say it was me who caused this? How dare you do this to us. It's disloyal to me and your sons, what you've done. You stood for something once."

"I couldn't fix it," said Morris. "I tried and that's why I went to Camberwell and moved us out here. It was to end it, but it was all too big. It was small stuff at first with quite paltry amounts, looking the other way, getting a tip of half a crown every week but they wanted more and more. Then it was Information about investigations and putting false leads in to distract the teams. It wasn't just me. T Division was rife with it. It didn't matter where I worked, they had too much on me and I'd had too much from *them*. Now Gilbert's dead and there will be a struggle for the top and by the looks of it there will be some nasty stuff kick off. Before I had no choice, I had to give them information."

"There's always a choice," said Violet.

Morris shook his head: "You don't understand, it's gradual like a seeping wound that grows until you can't stem the blood. Now it's different and the cost to you and the boys is too great. It's what paid for this house. All the things in it that you wanted."

"Which we'll lose of course. Why would you think I'd want it on those terms?"

"I won't let you lose the house," said Morris. He felt the envelope in his pocket as if seeking reassurance that it was still there. He pulled it out and laid it on the occasional table at his side then he said: "Tom Hunt will come shortly as I haven't turned in for my shift."

"Here? Come here to arrest you?" Violet was horror-stricken. "And everyone in the street will see. Oh, the shame of it. What do you mean that you won't let me lose the house? You'll be in *prison,*" shouted Violet.

The inclination to hit him was there in her. Instead she got up and walked to the door. Turning Violet stemmed the tears that she had been crying for the last thirty minutes. Her anger and fear had grown cold now and she said: "What did you think would happen? How was it going to end in this world in which you've been playing a double role?"

Standing in front of the man of whom she had been proud, had loved, born children for, she looked down at the envelope he was now holding out to her. She shook her head and wouldn't take it.

Morris stood and Violet took a few steps away, unsure she knew him anymore and afraid of what he might do to her.

But there was no violence in his mind. Morris was tired and wanted the charade to end. He said quietly: "I'm going shortly, Hunt won't find me here and he knows enough not to make a scene for you. Give him this envelope when he comes, will you, and tell him I've been like a rat in a trap trying to break free but it's all too big. This," Morris waved the envelope. "This will ensure you don't lose the house."

"No," Violet shouted. "No, I'll not join in your dealings no matter what it costs us." She left the room, slamming the door behind her.

Morris stood staring at the door until the realisation dawned that he would not see his wife again. He put the envelope against the clock on the mantle-piece and looked at the darkening room as the sun's position moved its rays across the wallpaper. From habit he walked to the sash window and pushed the bottom up a little. The air that entered the room had a calming effect. He stared at the closed door of the room and heard his eldest son Paul let himself into the house after a day working in the City. Paul was whistling as he always did and Morris prayed: "please God he will never know the truth."

Quashing the desire to see his son Morris did not move as he waited for Paul to finish in the hall. Nothing should be allowed to undo the positions his Paul and Eddie had. He heard Paul's heavy footfall on the stairs and then the click of the bedroom door as Paul closed it. An instant resolution for right and an inevitable choice for the sake of his family had overcome him. The sea-change that Morris had dreaded had come with the leadership of the crime group changing as the news of Gilbert's death came through a few days ago. Morris had gambled on how quickly Hunt would hear, even prepared for Ted Phillips to take the blame if it bought him time. Poor Ted, if ever he knew that he had been one of the suspects.

Now Morris worked out that he had no more than a few minutes before Hunt and his men would arrive and wondered which of his old colleagues would come. They'd have got word from Phillips that Morris hadn't turned in for his duty today. That would have clarified things for Hunt nicely. He wondered when Hunt had worked out which one of them had betrayed the team over Jersey. Morris had also gambled that he would get away with it and so he would have done if those soldiers hadn't been sent to the castle. He had staked everything on Jack and Harry going alone. Had that been the case, especially as they were both injured, things would have turned out well for Morris. They'd have taken a beating and would have limped back to London. But Morris had not supposed Stan would be there, nor those three soldiers. Not for the first time he wondered who had sent those 3 men to Gorey and who they really were? He had nothing against any of his colleagues, liked them even, had trained Jack initially, but the chips were down, and it was his family, reputation, and the final fight for survival that had made him provide the information to Gilbert's group about the trail of the young thief leading Hunt's team to Jersey.

Now the fight for survival which had made him as he was, was over. It was his family that mattered now, and he was no longer the rat in a cage. Yes, he would give a good account of himself when the time came and would take away with him any shadows that he might have as they tracked him. But it would be in a place of his own choosing that he would confront them.

Gilbert had been greedy, and arrogant. Part of Morris despised the man and his background despite having taken his money. How stupidly arrogant Gilbert was. Fancy wanting diamonds from the Shah's horse. The man should have left well alone as regards the Queen's reputation internationally. If he had just left it small scale that young Norwegian would have gone, but no Gilbert had grown more and more greedy and it had become a power game not just with the English establishment but also with that dancer Gilbert had. Morris remembered how on that day in '73 at the Alexander Palace fire he had frozen when he had seen the young thief there. Of course, the young man had recognised Morris. Thank God Jack had been too badly injured to register what the young thief was up to as the man had stood and stared. Jack had seen the thief but thankfully was too far gone to get up and follow him.

Yes, Jack's injury had bought Morris time.

And Gilbert? No-one had foreseen Gilbert's death either. An accident apparently and his line would die with the incident. Well, so be it. At least it would have been quick for them. He hoped his own demise was likely to be as quick.

Morris knew that he was leaving Violet a lifetime of sorrow from the choices he had made. Well, she could be sorrowful comfortably at least. Again, he fingered the envelope he was leaving for her to give to Tom Hunt. It would make good reading for Tom as it contained the list of names that Morris knew of policemen who had taken payment from Gilbert and those who had actively worked to foil investigations. It was a gamble because it was an incomplete picture. That was how Gilbert had worked but someone on that list might turn and give more information. Morris believed Hunt would let his family alone in return for it.

And now it was time as there was one final twist he had to engineer to ensure his Violet and sons Paul and Eddie would retain a reputation, a home, and a pension.

Silently, Morris picked up his helmet and truncheon and positioned them perfectly while he looked at his reflection. Habit took his fingers to his fine moustache. He straightened his jacket and turned along the corridor to the back door of the fine little house his lapse had paid for.

Once on the street Morris scanned up and down but could see no one that was unfamiliar. He saluted the woman across the road in her front garden for the final time, she would be the witness he had left. He was certain that he was being watched by Gilbert's people.

He closed the front gate quietly so as not to alert the family that he had gone out. Eddie had not yet returned from work and Paul would think he was off to Camberwell New Road and take no notice. But what of Violet?

If she cared any more for him that is, thought Morris. Momentarily he glanced up at their bedroom window. No-one appeared to wave him off.

Twenty-five

Morris walked on at a good pace, smart, upright, to all appearances a man the people could trust. But for Morris this was his final mission. At the end of the road Morris half-turned his head and saw all he needed to know. He had a shadow who would no doubt stay with him until he reached some remote area. Where there was one shadow there were always others.

Lead them away, don't look round again, Morris told himself, and get to an area where colleagues he had trusted, and who had regarded him as a rock, would eventually find him.

Jack arrived at Herne Hill minutes after Morris had boarded a train out. Something he always did was to read the advertisements on the platform. Today was no exception and because of the sort of day it would become he would always remember the details:

Fifth anniversary of the Iron Chapel.
Tickets a halfpenny each.

Sermons to be preached by the Rev. A Jones.

Another read:

Sale by Auction of 11 Lennington Road, Herne Hill.
Fitch and Fitch, Solicitor.
24th May 1874.

———

Jack walked out onto the street and saw Stan and Inspector Hunt. He paused briefly as it was the first time that he had ever seen Tom Hunt out of uniform, and he needed to make sure it was him. It was a fine cloth the Inspector was wearing but all black except for the white shirt. These were his recollections later. Not a hint of bright colour present anywhere. It struck Jack that it was as if Hunt was making up a funeral party.

For his part Stan's attire out of uniform never changed. He looked the same as he had when they had landed at Dover and Jack wondered if the man had bothered to change.

Stan nodded in Jack's direction and the young man, from habit, started to salute.

"Damn me, not now," Hunt hissed.

Jack said: "Sorry, sir, have you found Sergeant Morris?"

Stan snorted. "Would we be standing on a platform if we had?"

"He's alright then," said Jack, relieved. "At least for now. Perhaps something happened at home to delay him?"

"You think he's the victim, do you?" hissed Stan. "Needing our protection? Is that what brought you hot foot here after you got our message at the pub?"

Jack looked at Stan and then across at Hunt. Reality dawned in his eyes until it moved to sadness. Gilbert's man at Camberwell New Road was Morris. The sad sentiment did not last long and was quickly replaced by anger.

Jack understood Stan's behaviour at last and for want of something to say to fill the silence Jack added: "I met the boot boy, your young Percy."

Stan muttered an expletive and spat to the side. "Young idiot will get himself into trouble hanging around."

But Hunt moved the subject back to Morris and said: "It's touch and go whether we find Morris, but home is the obvious choice. Prepare your mind for trouble. He's our man I believe. Stan thinks so too. Let's get going."

They walked at a brisk pace. Jack was shocked but followed behind his superiors while the implications dawned on him.

Morris was a traitor.

Morris had nearly got him killed.

Morris had been behind the attack on Harriet.

As the three men reached Morris's front door Hunt paused and called across to the only neighbour he could see. It was the woman in her garden.

"Would you have seen Sergeant Morris this morning?"

"You've not long missed him." The woman called back, nodding her head towards the end of the road. "Just going on duty by the looks of things."

Hunt smiled and nodded to her. So, Morris was in uniform.

The three men stood together in front of the neat little garden which denied any wrong could possibly have been contained within its home. As if he had to be the first to break the reflective silence Stan confessed to never having liked Morris.

"Too perfect by half," he said. They had trained at a similar time and there were situations Stan had caught a glimpse of at that time which he had dismissed as being his imagination. Morris had always covered up of course with a good reason.

"Easy to say that now," said Hunt but added: "Easy for all of us. Let's get on with it."

Stan grunted and rocked back and forth on his heels.

"We're never going in, are we?" Jack asked.

"'Course we are," Stan barked back.

"But … the family could be in there now. They've been kind to me, and I expact Mrs Morris doesn't know," Jack stood back.

"I strongly expect she *does now*," Hunt said. He turned towards the house and used the door knocker in a way that left no doubt that he meant business. Stan was a pace behind the Inspector and Jack wondered if he was armed. Hunt as well for all he knew. Hunt stepped back to leave a distance between him and the door.

Stan nodded his head at the neat garden and said: "Nice isn't it, all paid for by Gilbert. If you've got problems with this Constable Sargent, ask yourself who's responsible for those men who followed Harry on Jersey? Who would have had the beating of you and him if it hadn't been for those soldiers and me going with you to Jersey at the last minute, eh? Been kind to you have they? Maybe Mrs Morris is genuine, maybe she's not. But Morris's treachery would have seen you in the graveyard if he'd had to make the choice. And if you feel so sympathetic to them let me tell you something. Paul Morris is stepping out with Miss Fildew."

Jack looked sharply at Stan.

"Yes, that's right. Not so sympathetic now eh? All that fine education that makes him such a good catch while you were labouring on a farm, eh? So, Constable Jack Sargent, second class reserve and a man the Sergeant and the Inspector present can usually trust, which way are you jumping today?"

"No need to ask is there?" Jack said resentfully.

"Good to know all the same," answered Stan. 'You position yourself in the hall in case someone in the family is in on it and tries to do a runner."

The front door opened as Stan finished and Paul Morris took in the three men in their civvies on the doorstep.

"Policeman's outing?" he asked before he laughed at his own joke, but the humour was not shared. "Father's gone on duty I think, was he supposed to be joining you?"

Hunt ignored the question and said: "Could I have a word with your mother, Paul? I think your father may have left a message for me."

"Come in won't you, and go into the parlour. I'll spare you the birds on the wallpaper in the front room eh, Jack? How are you by the way? Father said you'd had some misfortune recently."

"Misfortune?" Jack's eyes narrowed.

"Taken a beating," Paul elaborated.

"Goes with the job," said Jack. "I can give as good as I get - heard you're walking out with Miss Fildew?"

Paul had stepped aside to let Inspector Hunt in and there was a hint of colour at Jack's question.

Stan interrupted before anything developed: "Constable, you stay in the hall. Lead on Paul will you."

The tone was an order not a suggestion and meant to head off a potential fracas.

Jack stood to attention, but he did not stop staring at Paul as the younger Morris led Hunt down the corridor. Stan however planted himself in front of Jack, his bulky frame moved to block the view.

Stan said quietly: "Keep your mind on the situation in hand, and in case they're involved, and he does a runner this way you floor him, right? I'll take care of the way out through the back."

Jack nodded but as Stan walked down the hall a movement from the top of the stairs made him look up. Violet Morris started to come down. She thought better of it and stopped on the second step from the top. Before she moved back into the shadows Jack saw enough of her face to register it was swollen from crying and although she was immaculately dressed as always there was a look in the eyes that told Jack that she knew. By the level of distress that she must have had he knew Morris had only recently told her.

"Jack, I thought I heard Tom Hunt. You're not alone, are you?" Violet asked.

"No, Mrs Morris, the Inspector and Sergeant Green have gone into the back with Paul," answered Jack.

"And you're guarding the door? I see, so you know. You've probably known longer than I have. But he's gone, in uniform Jack and he left by the back door. I heard him go. Gone for good now."

"I've only just been told." Jack bit his lip aware he should say nothing more, but there was a longing to give the woman comfort. Instead he asked: "Any idea where he's gone?"

Violet shook her head. Silently she went into the front room and returned with an envelope which she held out to Jack. It was addressed to Inspector Hunt. Jack gently took it from her.

 as she said: "Give this to the Inspector, will you. I think my husband said it would help us and that's all I'm interested in now. He's not the man I thought he was. It's all been a sham for years. He's gone, but he was in uniform, which seems a contradiction. The boys, like me, know nothing of what he's done or who with. You do believe me, don't you? I was never aware … never entangled in it. I would never …"

Jack looked at the small woman. A great pity overwhelmed him for her at all the trouble she must endure, and a gratitude was there for the way she had cared for him a year ago.

Jack said: "I know that … You go and rest up. I'll take this letter through to the Inspector. We'll try and find him. He might have gone to try and put some of it right. The fact he's stayed in uniform makes me think he might be going to try and make an arrest …"

Jack stopped as another thought had come to him. No that wasn't Morris's intention and arrest was not the reason Morris was in uniform. They were wasting time here. But where would Sergeant Morris have gone?

Jack watched Violet Morris walk slowly back up the stairs and then he knocked on the parlour door and stuck his head round it without permission being given for him to enter.

———

708

He explained: "Mrs Morris has just popped downstairs and given me this from Sergeant Morris for you, sir." He looked at Paul and continued: "Your mother could do with a cup of tea as she's a bit off-colour."

"Alright, you get on with that Paul," said Tom Hunt.

Concerned Paul hurried out of the room and Jack remained in the open doorway, still able to see the front door. Hunt opened the envelope and removed a handwritten sheet, which his eyes scanned quickly. As he finished Hunt looked up at his two colleagues and folded the paper. He put it in his wallet and tucked it away in an inside pocket.

Stan said: "Well? Any surprises?"

Silently Hunt stood and said unemotionally: "Yes, quite a few. We've enough and the family will be taken care of."

On impulse Jack said: "He's gone to die hasn't he, sir, in uniform - make sure the family get the pension. Question is where's he gone?"

"I doubt he's alone wherever it is. He'll have a shadow I would think. It could be anywhere that he's gone but I agree with you Jack. He would want his body found so there's no question that he died on the job," said Stan. "If it was me, I'd lead them away from my home and family and head for the Thames."

A thought had occurred to Hunt. He said: "Jack, have a look in that bureau will you and see if you can find paper and envelopes." Hunt pulled his wallet out as if he had had second thoughts. "One thing we must do is get copies of this message made and sent this afternoon," Hunt said. "Call Paul down, Jack."

"Paul, sir? Paul Morris?"

"Yes," Hunt stared at the list. He smoothed it out and laid it almost reverently on the table. "By all accounts Paul is doing well and may make money – legitimately. Full of ideas, from the enquires I made. Let's give the family chance to redeem themselves from the sins of the father eh?"

Jack handed sheets of notepaper and envelopes to Hunt. The Inspector pushed a sheet at Stan and set the original list between them. Stan glanced down the list and inhaled. He met Hunt's eyes and if he had been outside, he would have spat.

Hunt licked the lead of his pencil and started to write out a copy of the list. Stan watched him as the seconds went by and then started to do the same.

"I gave you an order, Jack," said Hunt, quietly and Jack moved to obey it.

Jack found Paul Morris sitting on the end of his mother's bed, holding her hand as she cried softly. He had knocked on the door which was ajar but remained on the landing until Paul came out and closed the door softly behind him.

Paul said: "I don't know what ails her, she was fine this morning."

Jack had pushed the anger he felt about Paul and Harriet down deep inside. His heartache had surfaced that afternoon and it had shocked him that the control was so insubstantial. He was also unsure if part of the anger was mixed up in the way he felt about Kari. Despite feeling shocked at Hunt's summary about Paul he realised that the fragile cap which he had put on his emotions would not take much to split open. Standing beside the young man who was doing well and may make money and who Hunt was prepared to give a chance to sickened him. But Jack focused on the task in hand. He eyed Paul over as the prospective husband for Harriet Fildew. There were four people in the house who knew the truth about Morris. None of them would share it with this young man standing by his side and Jack would let Paul go on believing that his father had been a fine policeman.

So be it, thought Jack, it was Hunt's call. He concentrated on the matter in hand and said: "Inspector Hunt would like your help with the delivery of some important messages. Your father is involved in them and if you would come down, he'll explain."

Paul looked at Jack, struggling to ask the reason why. He said: "Is father in danger?"

"Yes," said Jack. "I expact that he is."

"Does mother know?"

"Yes," said Jack and he walked towards the stairs. It was enough. Seconds later he heard an urgent footstep following him down.

"Why are you asking me?" Paul called after him.

"I'm not, the Inspector is," replied Jack as he opened the front door and went out. Trying not to look like a policeman as he stood in the front garden he bent and uprooted a few weeds. Before long Hunt and Stan appeared at the front door and behind them Jack could see Paul Morris reaching for a jacket on a peg.

The four men walked in silence taking the direction of the railway. Outside the station Paul moved off without a word to the other three and climbed into a cab.

"Where's he off to?" Jack asked.

Hunt explained: "He's two letters to deliver, one for the Prime Minister, wherever he is at the moment, so to Downing Street he will go and the other letter goes to Scotland Yard."

"S'truth," said Jack.

"'Xactly," said Stan.

"What does he know?" Jack persisted.

"What he knows is a legend – that his father has been involved in blowing the cover of policemen who are corrupt and will no doubt pay for it with his life. Well, that much is true. Paul's carrying the two copies of the original list which is in my pocket. He knows the pension is safe for his mother if his father dies in service, which is likely if we don't stop talking and get going. As to whether we catch him and arrest him will depend how fast we can pick up a trail. Whether we should rush I am uncertain about. Dying somehow seems the honourable thing for Morris to do and he places his family in a better secure position than they will be in if we find him alive. I don't have the answer I'm afraid but You take the porter over there, Jack and see if he knows Morris by sight. Ask him if he saw him catch a train about an hour ago. Stan, go to the booking office and do the same. I'll go and send a telegram now to Disraeli and then I'll have a word with the cabbies over there in case any of them noticed Morris. He's well known so if he's taken a train someone is likely to remember. If we can find the direction that he's left by, we can muster forces from there."

The porter had a poor memory until he saw a flash of silver between Jack's thumb and finger. Then he recalled seeing Sergeant Morris board a train going into London.

"Anyone with him?" Jack asked.

"Hard to say," the porter suffered from memory loss again until another sixpence was produced. "Not with him exactly, a few coves got in the same carriage as the Sergeant. Third class it was."

Jack nodded to the man and walked over to Stan who had come out of the booking office.

"Anything?" Jack called over.

Stan gave him a look which showed irritation. Jack kicked himself for shouting.

Stan waited to respond until Jack was next to him and said, quietly: "He bought a ticket but asked an odd question, which the booking clerk remembered because he thought it was a strange thing for Morris to ask. He also thought it was unusual Morris was buying a ticket in uniform as he generally just boarded a train if he was after someone."

"Laying a trail?" asked Jack.

Stan nodded, then said: "Wait a mo for Hunt and then I can fill you both in."

Hunt was walking back towards them. He raised his eyebrows in enquiry as he drew close.

"Find anything?" Hunt asked.

"Yes, sir," said Jack before Stan could speak. "He was here just over an hour ago, caught a train towards London. The porter remembers other men getting into the same 3rd class carriage but not exactly as if they were with Morris."

"He's bought a ticket," Stan interjected, "Which he never did when in uniform, but he's asked questions about the direction of the train, the route through to the docks, mentioning the Blackwall line, and, if the ticket was valid. He's gone to Shadwell division I reckon. I need to get hold of Harry."

"I wonder why he'd go there. Harry's on stand-by anyway, as I saw him earlier. Get a message through to him to pick men and get them over to the basins, and the docks."

"What about the port police, sir," asked Jack.

"Any contacts?" asked Hunt.

Jack said: "A couple of officers around the West India Docks, they helped me when I took a kicking. There's a fighter as well came to my aid, an artist by profession but really fights to earn enough to eat. A Mr Boyes. I know his address, it's anigh of the dock. Good man, powerfully built, could do with the work probably and I'd value him at my back at this moment."

"Right," said Hunt. "Get the messages off, and I'll get the tickets, as we, unlike Morris, are not in uniform. Meet up on the platform."

Jack notified the London and Docks police by telegram while Stan sent a message to Harry. The other message was a chance that Mr Boyes would be at home and inclined to help.

Neither Stan nor Jack had asked who it was in Disraeli's office that Hunt had contacted. Neither spoke of it.

Although initially they had no exact idea where Morris would go there was comfort in the fact that the Docks police would cover a wide area. Jack had given Morris's police number as information for the search just in case they were too late.

Across London's railway network they traced Morris's route. He had laid a trail for them by making enquiries in such a way to make himself memorable at each point where he had a change of direction. It was tedious and time consuming but at every junction the three men asked their questions. There was no doubt that Morris wanted to be found.

From Herne Hill they travelled separately to Loughborough Road Junction on the London Chatham line keeping alert in case of shadows. After that it was north via Champion Hill station until at Peckham Rye they climbed down onto the platform and bought pies and strong tea. It was now close to half past five.

Here a dilemma faced the men as there were multiple lines, and it was a choice to go west to Bermondsey and work their way back across the river towards Shadwell and the docks further east, or north to Deptford to make their way across the river. The final choice was simply to opt to go east towards the railway timber yards by the Surrey Canal.

Hunt made a decision and said: "We'll split up. Stan you take the west side and if there's nothing get across to the police station on the Bermondsey road and somehow link up with Harry. He's making his way across to the floating police station

715

at Waterloo Pier. Get across the river and pick up the start of the Blackwall line. I'll go north to Deptford. Jack, take the east side. We shouldn't go into anything alone. And regardless of what you know or don't know we should meet by seven o'clock. If one of us isn't there we'll know the direction to go in."

"Mason's Arms on the Commercial Road?" suggested Stan.

"Perfect," said Jack and Hunt nodded. Stan and Harry would cover the east side of the Blackwall line that way.

For Jack his route would bring him close to the Rotherhithe Tunnel station. He could get across Shadwell Basin with a brisk walk and reach Stepney station and the Commercial Road before seven o'clock. There would be time for him to get across to muster forces and see if Planterose Boyes fancied some extra work.

*

The following hour after leaving his home in Herne Hill would become an absurdity but there was a role Morris was resolved to play. He was aware that he had not been alone on his journey and Morris had deliberately chosen busy carriages to discourage his pursuers from acting too quickly. That and engaging railway staff at each point where he changed trains was to build a trail. It was part of his plan to ensure the death in service status for the good of the family.

It had taken an hour to get to the West India Docks and his shadows were close. He knew there were three of them now and hoped it would be men from Shadwell police station, or Leman Street, who would be called out when his body was found.

People who knew him as they did would do it right.

Harry, Jack, or Stan would see to things for the family once the police were called by the workmen that inevitably would see his body in the dock. Hunt would honour the information Morris had left for him of that he was sure. It was a good ending and for the first time in years Morris had a sense of lightness. As he heard the footsteps draw closer, Morris decided to turn and give his pursuers a welcome. He had been right, there were the three men whose faces he had noted on the journey.

Morris had his old truncheon with him that day, the highly decorated one he had been allocated as he started training. It had seemed fitting to him to select that one as it was linked to a time when he had believed in honour. No doubt it would be found if his body was not and the decorations on it would be recognised by Hunt. They went back far enough to know things about each other.

Morris gripped the ring turned handle, his hand covering the V.R. monogram. He hoped the Queen would forgive him once she got those diamonds. Something inside wanted her to know.

The first blow knocked him face down and then they were on him and from the difference in the blows Morris knew all three of them would finish him. He was face down in dirt his Violet would have wept about.

717

It did not matter who they were, or what they shouted at him, this was the cleanest way out. He hated leaving his Vi, hated not being able to take care of them but his family's future was worth dying for and the pension would be safe now that he would die in service.

Just before he lost consciousness, Morris heard the distant sound of a policeman's rattle before he hit the dark water of the dock. It enfolded him as a brief fight ensued in his body before he suffocated in the water.

*

The story will continue in the 4th Jack Sargent mystery:

A String of Deaths

Appendix

The next pages are references to research sources used and notes to accompany chapters in the book which the author's hope will be of interest.

Chapter One

Roberts, Martin (2001) Britain: 1846-1964: The Challenge of Change, Oxford University Press.

Little, Tony: Liberalhistory.org.uk: A torrent of gin and beer: the election defeat in 1874.

Queen Victoria's Journals, the months of January and February, to Wednesday 25th February 1874.

Affie and Marie: The Duke and Duchess of Edinburgh.

Lost Railways of Berkshire: www.thamesweb.co.uk

Daily Telegraph and Courier (London) 5/5/1874:
https://britishnewspaperarchives

Icc-cricket.com
theguardian.com Death of Dr W.G. Grace Monday October 1915.

A Dictionary of the Sussex Dialect and Collection of Provincialisms in use in the County of Sussex. William Douglas Parish, 1875.

Queen Victoria's relations, p 115, Buchanon.

Understanding the Royal Name Plantagenet, by Dr S. Plant

Jeffery Green: Historian: Black London 1874-1875 0.56:
Several accounts are recorded of black men assisting the
police during this time. One such in Chelsea was Plantagenet
Green, who described himself as an artist but whose real
occupation seems to be that of a pugilist.

 Green was the first to go to the rescue of a PC Townsend in
Chelsea and prevented two men kicking the constable while
he was down on the floor. This incident in chapter one has
blended in the above story and one of John Joseph, a ship's
steward, of the West India Road, robbed by Ann Cain and
Emma Lavis, pick pockets. Witnesses described Joseph as a
black man. The women were caught and sentenced to 12
months in prison.

The two dock policemen mentioned were from:
Port of Tilbury London Police and the former constituent forces
of East and West India Docks Police, London, and India Docks
Police: Both are mentioned in the Roll of Honour:

PC John William Smith: Died 6/5/1877, aged 28 as a result of
a violent assault attempting to arrest a suspect,
And:
Sergeant Michael Flynn, died 23/8/1896 aged 46, found
drowned in the docks after being bludgeoned about the head.
Both are mentioned lest we forget.
British-history.ac.uk Victoria county History: Middlesex.

Chapter Two.

Ncbi.nlm.nih.gov "Investigating the body in the Victorian Asylum

Stamford's Library Map of London and its Suburbs 1872.

Journal of British Studies: Gladstone's Resignation of the Liberal Leadership 1874-5, by Matthew R Temmel vol. 16. No 1 (Autumn) 1976, pp 153-177.

A brief history of the Metropolitan Police in Brentford and Chiswick. By PC John Collins: Chiswick W4.com.

Chapter Three

Map of Selmeston surveyed 1791-1874. Francis Frith.

Historical overview: Selmeston.

British history online: Agriculture since 1870.

Eastbourne Gazetter April 29, 1874.

Sussexarch.org.uk.

Fraser's Magazine: editors James A Froude, J Tulloch 1844: "Regina's Regina."

Recollections of a Sussex Parson 1815-1906: Rector of Berwick.

Reference to John Ellman of Glynde: A farmer of repute between 1780-1832, tenant of Place Farm. Reputedly the developer of the Southdown Sheep breed. Journal article: Sue Farrant: John Ellman of Glynde in Sussex. The Agricultural History Review, Vol 26. No 2 (1978) pp 77-88. British Agricultural History Society.

Peasants, Servants and Labourers: The Marginal Workforce in British Agriculture, c1870-1914. Alun Howkins: The Agricultural History Review Vol 42, No 1 (1994) pp 49-62.

"Serving Victoria: Life in the Royal household," Kate Hubbard, Harper Collins Publishers, 2012.

Chapter Four

Brighton and Hove Historic Character Assessment Report. Sussex Extensive Urban Survey: Roland B Harris.

Britishmuseum.org Collection online: Hog boats near the Battery, Brighton.

Coriolanus: Play by William Shakespeare: A tragedy.

Chapter Five

Photography: A Means of Surveillance? Judicial Photography, 1850 to 1900. Jens Jäger. Crime Histoire & Sociétés, vol 5, no 1, 2001.

The Flintshire Observer, Friday May 22nd, 1874.

Matthew H.C.G. "Edward VII (1841-1910)." Oxford Dictionary of National Biography. Online edition 2006.

The Guardian: Bertie: A life of Edward VII by Jane Ridley, review. Bernard Porter 14/9/12.

A Curious Royal Romance: The Queen's Son and the Tsar's Daughter: Merritt Abrash, The Slavonic and East European Review, Vol 47, No 109 (Jul 1969).

The Queen and Mr Gladstone by Philip Guedalla, 1934.

The People's Will: in Russia reputedly the first terrorist organisation: Lucy Wordsley, Empire of the Tsar's: Romanov Russia.

Gog and Magog: mythical figures associated with being guardians of the City of London. Current figure are made of lime wood by sculptor David Elms in 1953 and are nine feet tall.

Reference to the Czar's visit to London is taken from the Aberdare Times, May 23, 1874, as is the case mentioning the action of Constable Turton re the murder of a woman and four children by the husband and father.

Royal collection Trust.

The Flintshire Observer Friday May 22, 1874.

Disraeli's Flowery History, Tom Crewe. History.blog.gov.uk Queen Victoria sent a wreath of primroses to Disraeli's funeral with the message: "His favourite flowers." The Primrose League formed after his death and had over a million members by 1891. Primrose Day was the anniversary of his death in 1882.

Edmund Spenser, The Faerie Queene, first published in 1590. Poem as a tribute to Elizabeth 1st.

Chapter Six

Far from the Madding Crowd was printed in the Cornhill Magazine in 1974 anonymously. It was by Thomas Hardy.

Chapter Seven

The book referring to a loose cannon was by Victor Hugo, Les Travaileurs de la Mer.

Victoria Railway Station and the Former London, Chatham and Dover Railway Station including Train Shed: Built 1860-1862 by the Victoria Station and Pimlico Railway Company. The London to Brighton side opened in 1860. The Brighton side train shed and the screen wall along Buckingham Palace Road were rebuilt and replaced by office blocks in the 1980's. Britishlistedbuildings.co.uk

british-history.ac.uk: Regent Street and Piccadilly.

Chapter Eight

Westsussex.gov.uk: Brighton and Hove Historic Character Report. Sussex Extensive Urban Survey, Roland B. Harris.

New psychologists, philosophers and clergy wrote dream literature from 1860-1910 which was reflected in popular magazines of the day.

Disraeli: Kit Kowol, University of Oxford.

Chapter Nine

Bradshaw's Handbook, 1863.

Perway Men: Permanent Way – railway lines maintained by gangs of workers.

Sussex Slipcote: fresh ewe's cheese produced still in West Sussex. Slipcote is an old English word that means a little (slip) piece of cottage cheese. Slipcote describes the tendency for the cheese to slip out of its rind. Made in England since the Middle Ages.

Berthon.co.uk: Berthon History. Berthon Collapsible lifeboat. Research by Jim Hazel, ex Berthon Drawing Office Staff member 1947-61. The Berthon Boat Co. concentrates now on high class yachts but collapsible boats carried on being supplied until the outbreak of World War II.

LB&SCR Liveries pre-1870.

Sophia Jex-Blake, The University of Edinburgh, retrieved 30/4/2019: fought a court case against the university for not allowing her to do a medical degree on the grounds of gender.

Proverbs 28.

Lord Shaftesbury: Anthony Ashley-Cooper, 7th Earl of Shaftesbury KG. https://www.britannica.com
Effective social reformer in the 19th century. With Rev. George Bull and John Wood he took up a bill to restrict hours of child

labour to a maximum of 10 a day in 1833. He was chairman of the Ragged Schools Union for over forty years.

In 1840 he helped set up the Children's Employment Commission, piloted the Coal Mines Act in 1842, and backed research by William Dodd on the treatment of children in Textile Factories in 1842.

In 1863 Shaftesbury published a report on children aged four and five working from 6am-10pm in some Textile factories. The Chimney Sweeper's Act came in in 1875. Shaftesbury died in 1885.

The dancing medieval folk tunes heard in Derbyshire and Sussex were documented by Cecil Sharp and Ralph Vaughan Williams in the early 20th century before they disappeared.

Chapter Ten

"Hurrah for the trip -the cheap trip:" Thomas Cook 1854.

"Simplon" – The Passenger Ship website: Services from Southampton.

Three Men and a Bradshaw: An original Victorian Travel Journal, John George Freeman, edited by Ronnie Scott.

The Army Hospital Corps was formed in 1857.

Corbière lighthouse was completed in 1873, the first in the British Isles to be built of concrete rather than stone.

Dictionnaire Jèrriais-Francais, Le Maistre, Jersey 1966.

Jerseyheritage.org.

Birdsontheedge.org

Photography: A means of surveillance? Judicial photography 1850-1900. Jens Jäger: Crime, History and Societies, pp 27-51

Chapter Eleven

Les Grandes Affaires Criminelles de Suisse Romande, by Jacques Rouzet.

Disused stations: St Helier (Green Street) Station; Gorey Station source: Nick Catford.

Torg: short for Torghatten which rises 258 metres vertically from the sea at Brønnøysunde . It plays a heroic role in the Nordland fairy tale of trolls that froze to stone and became the mountains along the Nordland coast.

19th century sugar prices dropped in Britain as beet sugar developed cheaply instead of cane sugar being used. In 1874 the tax on sugar imports lifted helping the poor access sugar over the next few decades as part of their staple diet in the form of jam, boiled sweets, and condensed milk. After 1870 milk chocolate came onto the market.
BBC 2017: "The Sweet Makers."

By 1874 the chocolate maker Daniel Peter would have been close to his recipe of Milk chocolate in Vevey at 14 rue des Bosquets, Vevey. He teamed up with Nestlé shortly after who used evaporated milk instead of fresh, which stopped chocolate going mouldy. By 1879 Lindt developed a conch machine which mixed chocolate to be smooth instead of gritty.

Jersey folklore and superstitions Volume one: Comparative study, by G. J. C. Bois.

Gosset's plan of the town of St.Helier.

www.gov.je Conservation statement, Fort Regent.

The Vintage Gun Journal 6/12/2019, "Hammer Guns Appreciated."

Chapter Twelve

J.P. Dodd: Hampshire Agriculture in the mid-nineteenth century. From Hants. Field Club Archeol. Soc. 35 1979 239-60.

Historytoday.com Musing on the sea off Brittany, Natalie Aubert, Volume 67 Issue 5 May 2017.

The "Torrington" that is referred to is Viscount Torrington 1812-1884, formerly Prince Albert's permanent Lord in Waiting from 1853-1859 and for Queen Victoria from 1859-1884. Known as well for his harsh suppression of the 1848 civil uprising in Ceylon. A caricature of him appeared in Vanity Fair in1876.

"The Fruits of Philosophy" was re-printed several times and in 1870 the Bristol publisher was sentenced to hard labour. It became the subject of a test case in 1877 as it dealt with reproductive physiology and birth control.

Chapter Thirteen

Thomas Hardy published his previous two novels anonymously.

John Snow: Cholera outbreak August 1854: he showed that the Southwark Vauxhall waterworks was taking water from a sewage-polluted section of the Thames and delivering it to homes. Regarded as the founding event of epidemiology.

"Opposite a Cabstand" from:
" London Characters and the Humorous Side of London Life,"
Anonymous.

The hospital referred to is now the site of the Landmark Hotel opposite Marylebone Station.

Elizabeth Garrett Anderson was the first woman to train and qualify as a Doctor in England. She was admitted to the BMA in 1873 and the door was then closed to other women for some years. Our character Ann Brown studied medicine in Paris.

Data re Swiss weather taken from: the meteoswiss.admin.ch records for May 1874.

Chapter Fifteen

A Work Life History of Policemen in Victorian and Edwardian England. Haia Shpayer-Makov, University of Haifa Israel.

The company of William Bissett was an English leather portmanteau maker around 1870. The bags had painted initials.

Toff: mid 19th century: perhaps an alteration of tuft, used to denote a gold tassel worn on the cap by titled undergraduates at Oxford and Cambridge.

Merry-go round: from an article in the Graphic, page 116 August 1874.

Conservatives and the Struggle for the Abolition of Slavery at the end of the Nineteenth Century: David Thomas, Schaufelbuehl, Janick Marina, 2010: Political Science.

Chapter Sixteen

Bradshaw's Pedestrian route book for Switzerland, Chamouni, and the Italian Lakes, ed: by J.R. Morell, published by Scholar Select.

Cook's Continental Time-Tables and Tourist Handbook. March 1873 and reproduced by Cook's 2013.

République et Canton de Genève: ge.ch

Corsier: "Destin Helvétique d'une Commune Savoyarde, 1791-1918." Bernard Cuénod.

"Satigny de Jardis a naguère," by René Feuardent and André Pozzi.

The Bird Tree: Geneology of the Bird and Musgrove Families.

Chapter Seventeen

Police Detectives in History 1750 - to 1950. Clive Emsley.

Nordics.info Aarhus University.

Bradshaw's Pedestrian Route-book for Switzerland, Chamouni, and the Italian Lakes.

The Policeman as a Worker: A Comparative Survey c.1800-1940, Clive Emsley. International review of Social History Vol. 45 No 1 April 2000.

Capital Policières: Londres, Paris et Berlin. Quentin Deluermoz **https://www.jstor.org/stable/24753281**

Schweizerische Meteorologische Beobachtungen Prof. Rudolf Wolfe 1874. Available from Meteoswiss.admin.ch

Chapter Eighteen

Beau Rivage Palace from 1857 in Ouchy. Opened in 1861 and the annex was built in 1867. Historic Hotels of the World.

CGN: The Simplon 1860-1874: the company hired the Simplon for one year in 1873. After 1874 the steamer was out of use until 1879 when the company bought it and converted it into a pontoon in the Jardin Anglais in Geneva until 1935.

How did the British Conquer Switzerland? The Journal of Transport History 1850 –1914. Tissot. March 1995.

There is a memorial stone to John Tyndall at Belalp, Valais, Switzerland. He wrote: " … the aqueous vapour of the atmosphere must act powerfully in intercepting terrestrial radiation; its changes in quantity would produce corresponding changes of climate. Subsequent researches must decide whether this vera causa is competent to account for the climatal changes which geologic researches reveal." John Tyndall, Proceedings of the Royal Society of London, 1860-1862, 11, pp 100-104.

Boswell: "Life of Johnson," (1970, Oxford) page 112. Edited by R.W. Chapman.

R.A.G. Miller: "The Watchmakers of the Swiss Jura, 1848-1900."

"Why Switzerland? third edition." Jonathan Steinberg.

Chapter Nineteen

Sevenoaks History.org.uk

"A straight bat" takes us to John Small, an 18th century cricketer who made the first straight cricket bats and was reputed to be the first to score the 136 in 1775 for Hampshire against Surrey. Reputed to be the best batsman until W.G. Grace. John Woodcock 1997 article in the Times: "100 Greatest Cricketers of All Times."

Abraham Stanyan, "An Account of Switzerland," (London 1714), p. 144.

Lucy Walker lived in Liverpool and in 1865 climbed the Matterhorn with a group which included her father and a guide. Clare Roche is a British mountaineering historian, and she has written about Lucy Walker. The Alpine Club Photo Library has a picture of Lucy Walker with family and friends and Swiss guides dated 1870.

Emily Hornby started climbing within a few years of Lucy Walker's Matterhorn ascent. Extracts from letters and notebooks by Emily Hornby were put together in 1907.

Edvard Grieg, (Norwegian composer) started to collaborate with Ibsen on the fairy tale Peer Gynt from 1874-76. It was written in Danish which was the common language of Denmark and Norway in Ibsen's time. The music was composed by Grieg and it was first performed in Christiania (now Oslo) in 1876.

Siege of Paris French History 1870-1871: John Swift, Senior lecturer in History, University of Cumbria.

Chapter Twenty

The Origins of Swiss Wealth Management? Genevan Private Banking 1800-1840. Stefano Ugolini, 2017. HAL archives-overtes.

The Prisoner of Chillon: François Bonivard, the hero of Byron's poem, was really locked in the dungeon underground from 1532 until release in 1536 as he opposed the Duke of Savoy to protect Geneva's civil liberties. He became a Protestant and received a pension from Geneva and married four times.

Les Grandes Affaires Criminelles de Suisse Romande by Jacques Rouzet.

Popular Science Monthly/ Volume 4/ February 1874/Corundum

Chapter Twenty-One

Astrologer Paracelsus: (1493–1541)—who is widely regarded as the father of toxicology.

John Parascandola. "Pharmacology and Folklore: The Arsenic Eaters of Styria." Pharmacy in History, vol. 57, no. 1-2, 2015, pp. 3–16. JSTOR, www.jstor.org/stable/10.26506/pharmhist.57.1-2.0003. Accessed 4 June 2021.

Chapter Twenty-Two

Journal of the Royal Society of Arts vol 58 no.2995 April 15, 1910 pp 526-538. Arthur T Walmsley: "The Port of Dover."

Poetry Foundation.org: George Herbert poet and Church of England Clergyman.

The Mer de Glacé: Chamonix.net. It's claimed the Mer de Glace as it is described today is the largest glacier in France being 7 km long and 200m deep. Today you can take the train of the Montenvers from Chamonix centre. This started operating in 1908. There is a café and a restaurant, and you can overlook the Mer de Glace and see spectacular peaks.

Chapter Twenty-Three

Proverbs 31. The wife of noble character – also called the good wife.

George Leybourne: English music hall and song writer: "If ever I cease to love," 1870. Also wrote "the man on the flying trapeze." If ever I cease to love is still used in the Mardi Gras.

Marx and Engels collaborated on a body of ideas and wrote the Communist Manifesto in 1848.

Criminal and Constable: The Impact of Policing Reform on Crime in Nineteenth Century London. By Gregory J Durstun, L.S.E. Ph.D. 2001.

Anstey: In 1874, A policeman called Arnold went back to H Division as a Chief Inspector and would become part of the team working on the Jack the Ripper murders as did the character called Sergeant William Thick.

The obelisk: was returned to St. George's Circus in 1998 but without the oil lamps. The obelisk has been Grade II listed since 1950 when it was situated at Geraldine Mary Harmsworth Park, in front of the Imperial War Museum. National Heritage List entry 1285642 historicengland.org.uk

Chapters Twenty-Four and Twenty-five

Nelson Square: although relatively middle class in 1874, slums existed nearby.

The actual site where the Dog and Pot had been as a shop was at 196 Blackfriars Road.
by Juha Repo, nelsonsquare.wordpress.com

Appignanesi, Lisa, History of Crimes of Passion.

Sussex Dialect in order of appearance in the book

I am a-going: going as soon as I can.

Awhile: for a time.

Expact: expect. The "e" becomes an "a."
Also, in excapt, neglact.

Bout: A day's work.

The Old Father: the man giving away the bride, not the bride's father.

Radical: a risk taker

Snicker: to sneer or laugh inwards.

Rough: passionate or angry.

What the Rabbits! An exclamation.

Yoe: a corruption of Ewe.

Surelye: added at the end of a sentence to give emphasis.

Solly: a tottering or unstable condition.

Chokly: dry, parched.

Simpson: Selmeston.

Spit-deep: as deep as a spade goes in digging.

Seine, or sean: a very large net for catching mackerel or herrings.

Rake: a long dragging sound of the sea on pebbles.

Anigh: near.

Batch: A quantity of bread baked at the same time. The quote is found in Troilus and Cressida Act v scene 1.

Bannicking: a good beating.

Best: to get the better of anyone.

Jostle: to cheat someone.

Letbehow'twill: let the consequences be what they may.

Bostals; a steep path especially on a northern escarpment of the Downs.

Masterful: overbearing.

Farisees: fairies.

Paddle: to trample about in the wet and dirt.

Pig's pettitoes: patterns – foot wear.

Peert: Lively.

Prayers-going: Service in church

*

Jersey and Jerriais

Corbière is the extreme southwestern point of Jersey and the phrase, "Nous avons passé la Corbiéthe" is used to mean the worst is over.

La Tchien du Bouôlay: The Dog of Bouley.

A betôt: Goodbye.

A bi: a response to goodbye.

Mercie bein des fais: thank-you.

Fraithe: brother.

Paithe: father.

Bouan viage! Good Journey.

Bouonne cache dés crouaîsis: good luck, fingers crossed.

Mistus: mistress

*

Also by J Ewins L Telfer

Other Jack Sargent crime novels:

The Faceless Woman, Jack Sargent's first murder.

Set in 1872 Jack Sargent joins the Metropolitan Police and encounters crime, murder, and love.

Cords of the Grave.

Starting in the docks in 1873 where Jack and Detective Sergeant Harry Franks begin the pursuit of a thief to the ruins caused by the Alexander Palace Fire. Jack copes with injury and the tentacles of organised crime while the visit of a foreign potentate launches policing onto a completely different scale.

Set in London, the fashionable area of Brighton and on to the mysteries of Pett Level.

Other books by J. Ewins L.Telfer

Archdeacon Goes Live.

(Full of Bright Ideas and only 46!)

A hilarious story starring A.D. the Archdeacon with his outstandingly funny team of long-suffering assistants. This is the first of the amusing exploits of A.D. as he prefers to be known by those who love him, (and he believes there are many.)

In his side-splitting way A.D. thrives on life, love, and God's faithfulness. Full of humour but at times a tender struggle the story tracks changing times in this lovable, entertaining story.

Married to Louise, a Finance Director and father to three daughters, A.D. sets his mind to which one of his assistants would be the right partner for his two eldest girls, Eve and Charis.

A.D. is determined to take the church "out" of the building and answers the call from the B.B.C. From London to the beaches of North Devon's surf scene journey with him, and meet Storm, Chris, Ellie and Mike.

Children's stories:

Ma and Me: Walk.
Age 0-3.

Ermie and Azar and the Vortex.
Age 5-8.

Also Writing under pen names;

M.D.Wigg and Jay Heyes:

Monologues for performance/reading:

1.Following in the Way of the Cross (for Easter)

2. To the Ends of the Earth.

3. The Dawning.

Printed in Great Britain
by Amazon

79295346R00428